Schultz

Cash McCall

· · · · ·

books by Cameron Hawley

Executive Suite
Cash McCall

Cash McCall

a novel by

Cameron Hawley

HOUGHTON MIFFLIN COMPANY · BOSTON
THE RIVERSIDE PRESS · CAMBRIDGE

1955

as always

to Elaine

. . . . .

One

:
:
:

ON THE TWENTY-FOURTH DAY of March, which fell this year on a Tuesday, a party of ninety-three men met at a breakfast sales meeting in the Fontainebleau Room of the Hotel Ivanhoe. Sixty-one were salesmen for wholesale firms engaged in the distribution of Andscott television receivers. The others were executives, major and minor, of the Andscott Instrument Corporation, augmented by a few quietly anonymous clerks from the Andscott offices who had been brought in to swell the crowd.

Fortunately, the presence of this latter group had proved unnecessary. No comparable event in Andscott's merchandising history had ever been so well attended. But the normally lethargic personnel of Andscott's wholesale distributors had not been attracted, as the corporation's officials wished to believe, by a resurgence of zeal, nor even by a resurrected hope that the Andscott line would soon begin to sell in real volume, but rather by the prospect of eating in what was widely reputed to be one of the ten most expensive restaurants in the United States. Not one of these wholesale salesmen had ever before set foot in the Fontainebleau Room, none having expense accounts large enough to permit the entertainment of customers on such a fabulous scale.

Although the Fontainebleau Room is advertised as *The Mecca of the Gourmet,* its successful existence is less an index to the culinary prowess of its famous *chef de cuisine,* Max Nicollet, than to the phenomenon of the unlimited expense account, and the tolerance of the Bureau of Internal Revenue in the auditing of accounts chargeable as ENTERTAINMENT. The Fontainebleau Room grew to its present eminence during the days when corporation executives first made the discovery that a ninety per cent excess profits tax made it possible to buy an eight-dollar lunch at a net cost to the company of only eighty cents. Even the most conservative comptroller could not argue that eighty cents was too much to spend in order to give a valued customer a good lunch, plus the experience of having eaten in one of the most expensive restaurants in the world.

The uninitiated are frequently surprised that a restaurant of the Fontainebleau Room's character exists in Philadelphia, a city characterized in most minds by the frugal and unostentatious members of the Society of Friends. In truth, the Fontainebleau Room is rarely patronized by Philadelphians except when eating on an expense account, a circumstance that affects normality as profoundly in the City of Brotherly Love as anywhere else.

The real explanation of the Fontainebleau Room being in Philadelphia is found through acquaintance with a woman whose name is Maude Kennard. There would never have been a restaurant of this character in the Hotel Ivanhoe had it not been for Mrs. Kennard's canny appreciation of the opportunities inherent in a situation where eight dollars could be collected for a lunch that would cost the payee only eighty cents, as well as her talent for teaching that simple arithmetic to men possessing expense accounts large enough to qualify them for gourmet status.

Many of the regular patrons of the Fontainebleau Room are under the misapprehension that Maude Kennard is the general manager of the Hotel Ivanhoe. They are unaware that she is, by title, only the Assistant Manager. Few know that there is a General Manager. This is understandable, for Everett Pierce is seldom seen in the lobby, and on those rare cases when he does put in an appearance, no one would suspect that he holds the position he does. His appearance and personality do not conform to the accepted standards for hotel managers. He is not gregarious, his handshake is limp, and his spare figure and gray skin coloring leave the impression that he has never eaten a hearty meal in his life. One of the bellboys, exercising his occupational skill in pigeonholing strangers, once wisecracked that Mr. Pierce looked like a certified public accountant on a skim milk diet— and accountancy was, in truth, the profession that he had followed during the early years of his business life. Becoming a hotel manager had been a genealogical accident. Will Atherson, president of the bank that had taken over the Hotel Ivanhoe during the depression, was a distant relative. He had given young Everett a job untangling the bankrupt hotel's snarled accounts, kept him on to install a cost record system, and then elevated him to the managership. Everett Pierce had gratefully accepted the position but not without the fear that he might prove inadequately qualified. It was a fear from which, even after twenty years, he had not completely recovered.

As is so often true of the perpetually frightened, Everett Pierce was a ritualist. By doing everything in the way that he had done it before, he guarded himself against the commission of error. When larger matters were concerned, that course was consciously pursued. In smaller matters, it was unconscious but so thoroughly ingrained in his character that it was apparent even in the manner of his opening the door of his two-room suite and in the way he stooped to pick up his morning newspaper.

On this morning of the twenty-fourth of March, he retrieved his newspaper at eight forty-two, only a minute or two off the schedule that governed his timetabled life. Without opening the paper, he went into the living room of the suite and placed it on the small breakfast table that, the night before, had been moved to its designated position in the curve of the bay window that overlooked Rittenhouse Square. Only one place was laid. Everett Pierce is a bachelor.

With the newspaper ritual completed, he crossed the room again and went into the kitchenette where, in the otherwise empty refrigerator, he found three roses lying on a bed of crumpled wax paper. This morning the roses were yellow instead of his preferred pink but he accepted them tolerantly. His morning roses were salvaged from night-before banquet tables and the fact that the roses were yellow instead of pink meant only that Maude Kennard had gotten a better buy on yellows. Under his tutelage, she had become a very clever buyer—unusual for a woman but Mrs. Kennard was a very unusual woman. He had, of course, taught her everything she knew, but she still deserved a certain amount of credit, if only for being teachable. So many women were not.

Gently cupping the roses in his thin-fingered hands, he carried them to the table and placed them in the slender vase that was always there, carefully arranging the blooms so that he would be looking into the hearts of the flowers after he sat down. Then, and only then, did he look out of the window, finally facing the every-morning unpleasantness of realizing that he was now on the fourth floor.

A year ago, prodded by a suggestion from Will Atherson, the president of the Freeholders Bank & Trust Company, Everett Pierce had moved out of his tenth-floor suite and allowed it to be rented to a guest whose name was Cash McCall. It was true, as Mr. Atherson had pointed out, that the fourth-floor suite was, although substantially smaller, completely adequate. It also was true that a guest who was willing to pay a thousand dollars a month, plus the entire cost of completely redecorating and refurnishing the suite, could hardly be turned from the door. Nevertheless, Everett Pierce felt himself irretrievably demeaned. Even though McCall eventually moved out and allowed him to recapture his old suite, it would never again be the same. The remodeling and decorating had destroyed the character of his twenty-year habitat and he was a man to whom change was abhorrent. In that tenth-floor suite, familiarity had been his antidote for loneliness. Here on the fourth floor, loneliness and disappointment had been stewed into a deep-seated hatred of the man who had dispossessed him, not Will Atherson but Cash McCall.

Looking out of the window, he noticed for the first time that it was raining. Clear weather had been forecast in last evening's newspaper. Automatically, his mind began to tick off the check-list of annoying adjustments that would have to be made to compensate for this failure on the part of the Weather Bureau, but he had gotten no farther than cocoa matting for the lobby when the intrusion of recalled experience assured him that Mrs. Kennard would already have taken care of everything that needed to be done.

It was eight-fifty and Andrew still hadn't arrived with his breakfast. He was on the point of calling the kitchen when the old waiter finally appeared, his drawn face evidencing the intensity of his effort to keep the silver warming covers from chattering with the trembling of his palsied hands.

"You're late this morning, Andrew," Everett Pierce said.

"Mr. McCall ordered for the same time, sir, and I couldn't take care of both of you at once."

"Wasn't there anyone else who could serve Mr. McCall?"

"He always asks for me, sir," Andrew said, as if that were all the explanation that was necessary.

The manager sat in rigid silence, so immobilized by anger that his shirred egg was cold long before he started to eat it. Then, discouraged by the congealed butter that now framed the egg, he pushed the dish away and contented himself with a half piece of dry toast. He was considering a second half when the telephone rang. The voice on the other end of the line was that of Nathan, the chief room clerk.

"Sorry to disturb you, Mr. Pierce," Nathan said in a tone that made his regret seem something less than genuine. "There's a gentleman here to see you."

"I'll be down right away," Pierce said, finding it impossible to with-

10

hold a guilty glance at his watch. It was three minutes after nine.

"He says that it's a personal matter." Nathan's voice dropped to a guarded whisper. "I think he's an income tax investigator."

Everett Pierce was instantly struck by terror but, having spent his whole life in the suppression of other unreasonable fears, his experience came to his aid and he said quite calmly, "Send him up, please."

The man who came to the door a few minutes later confirmed Nathan's prediction with an identification folder verifying the fact that Irving J. Teller was a duly authorized Special Agent of the Bureau of Internal Revenue.

"I believe you have a permanent resident in your hotel named McCall," Teller said, withdrawing a sheet of notes from the file folder he had taken from his briefcase. "Cash McCall?"

"Yes, that's right," Pierce said quickly, brushing aside the temptation to debate that word *permanent,* urged on by this confirmation of his own opinion that it was about time some law-enforcing agency caught up with a man who spent a thousand dollars a month for a suite that he occupied less than half of the time.

"I'd like to ask you a few questions about Mr. McCall," Teller said, and then went on as if reciting from something memorized. "In doing so, I'm sure you understand that there's nothing unusual about this procedure, nor should you interpret it as reflecting upon the subject of our investigation. This is quite normal procedure and a part of our regular routine."

"I understand," Everett Pierce affirmed. But he was in no way fooled. Teller was clever. All of these income tax investigators were.

The special agent looked at his notes. "I understand that Mr. McCall uses his apartment for business as well as residential purposes. Is that true?"

"I wouldn't know," Pierce said, attempting to convey the meaning that he knew nothing whatsoever about Cash McCall's suspiciously secret business affairs.

"At least you don't know of any other office that he maintains?"

"No."

"And he does have men come to see him here?"

"Well—yes," Pierce said somewhat more reluctantly, disappointed that Teller seemed more interested in whitewashing Cash McCall than in really digging for the truth.

"And he has business calls that are handled through your switchboard?" Teller asked, checking off another note, then suddenly looking up. "But I don't suppose you'd know whether his calls were business or personal, would you?"

11

Pierce saw his chance. "We don't handle his calls at all. He has his own direct wire—and it's an unlisted number."

Teller didn't seem to get the point. "He does some entertaining, I presume—dinner parties and that sort of thing?"

"Yes."

"Tell me, Mr. Pierce, what sort of people come to see him? Would they strike you as being substantial citizens—businessmen?"

Everett groped for some special memory to the contrary. The wasted moment lost him his chance.

"Oh, skip that," Teller said hurriedly. "Rather a pointless question, anyway. The total rental on Mr. McCall's suite is one thousand dollars a month. Is that correct?"

"Yes, that's right."

"In addition to that, how much would you estimate that he spends with you on other things—these parties he has and the entertaining he does?"

"Well, I could get the figure for you easily enough."

"Oh, that won't be necessary. Would you say that it would average more than two hundred dollars a month?"

"Two hundred? Oh, yes, more than that."

Teller studied his notes through a moment of silence, and Everett Pierce had the hopeful premonition that Teller was finally ready to get down to business. Instead, startlingly, he stood up and extended his hand. "Thank you very much, Mr. Pierce. Sorry I had to bother you, but it's my job, you know."

Everett Pierce's first reaction after the door closed behind Irving J. Teller was that he again had encountered an object lesson in the incompetency of governmental employees. As he thought about it, however, the very innocuousness of the questions became a cause for suspicion. Teller must be more clever than he had seemed. If he were not, it was hardly credible that he would be a Special Agent for the Bureau of Internal Revenue. Wasn't it possible that the income tax people might be out to trap Cash McCall in the same way that they had helped the police break up that dope-peddling gang last fall, by proving that the ringleaders had falsified their tax returns to make it look as if they were in the real estate business?

Again, fear speeded the beat of Everett Pierce's heart. It was not difficult to imagine what Will Atherson's reaction would be if the good name of the Hotel Ivanhoe were smeared all over the newspapers as the habitat of some gangster! This time his fear did not subside. It was sustained by a reasonableness that seemed difficult to refute.

Picking up his telephone, he asked to be connected with Mrs.

Kennard. Waiting for her to answer, he found himself taut-nerved with anticipation. Relying upon Maude Kennard had become increasingly distasteful of late, but there was no one else to whom he could talk.

••••• 2

Standing in the center of the Hotel Ivanhoe's small lobby, Maude Kennard heard the telephone ring in her mezzanine office, but acknowledged it with only the briefest of upward-flashing glances. Nothing, at the moment, could be allowed to detract from the rapt attention she was giving the bulbous little man who stood in front of her. He was Park Cady, Vice-president for Merchandising of the Andscott Instrument Corporation, and whether or not there were to be more of these weekly breakfast-time sales meetings was entirely in Mr. Cady's hands.

The check she had given him—which he still held, unsigned—was substantially larger than the Hotel Ivanhoe's total breakfast receipts had ever been before. If the Fontainebleau Room could be made to earn a breakfast profit it would be a miracle of hotelkeeping, another accomplishment to add to her record, and she was a woman driven by a passionate need for superior accomplishment.

"Yes sir, Mrs. Kennard, you sure did things up brown for us," Park Cady said with belt-bouncing enthusiasm. "Yes sir, wonderful breakfast! Say, tell me, Mrs. Kennard—you know those buns, sort of cinnamony?"

She picked up the cue without a lost beat. "Would you permit me to have a pan of them sent to your home, Mr. Cady?"

"Hey, would you do that? Say, that would be swell! Sure would like to have the wife try those buns."

"It's as good as done, Mr. Cady. By the way, we have another very interesting specialty that we plan to serve next week if—but you haven't decided about next week, have you?"

Her eyes, trained by experience to observe simultaneously every detail of a guest's behavior, saw his pudgy pink fingers tighten, bending the pale green cardboard of the check. Her instinct, as well trained as her eyes, told her that he was about to suggest a reduction in price.

"Or perhaps," she countered with adroitly hidden haste, "since you've gotten off to such a fine start here at the Ivanhoe, you may be

13

able to drop back now to one of the more commercial hotels. Of course the atmosphere would be different but you could save a few dollars by going to—"

"Heh, what are you trying to do, get rid of us?" Park Cady demanded in a fat-throated gurgle. "Can't do that, Mrs. Kennard. No sir, you can't back out now. You just reserve that room for Andscott every Tuesday morning. No, wait! Next week it will have to be Wednesday."

"Consider it reserved," she said, noting with satisfaction that he had reached for the gold pencil in his vest pocket.

He scrawled a hasty signature on the check and handed it to her. "I'm a man that likes breakfast. Always say that breakfast is the best meal of the day. What's that you were saying about what we'd have to eat next week?"

She raised a forefinger, smiling. "I'll bet I know something else about you, Mr. Cady."

"What's that?"

"Unless I'm mistaken, you're the kind of man who likes to be surprised."

His eyes opened wide behind his horn-rimmed glasses and there was that belt-bouncing chuckle again. "Say, you're all right, Mrs. Kennard. Yes sir, you're all right." He took a single backward step to confirm his estimate by seeing all of her at once, rolling his round head as if it were a ball precariously balanced on his shoulders. "See you next Wednesday, Mrs. Kennard."

"Until Wednesday," she said softly.

He started a turn to the door and stopped. "Say, if you should see Mr. McCall, will you just tell him everything worked out fine? I guess you know him, huh? I mean he lives here, doesn't he?"

"Is Mr. McCall a friend of yours, Mr. Cady?"

"Knew him when I was with Padua Furniture. Just happened to run into him on the street the other day. He gave us the idea of trying this out—so you just tell Mr. McCall that everything was fine."

"Thank you, Mr. Cady."

The gratitude in her voice was feigned. Knowing that someone else had a lien on her accomplishment destroyed the satisfaction that had been so warmly felt a moment before. The skirt of her black gabardine suit snapped as she walked quickly across the lobby toward the grilled opening through which she could see the telephone operator.

"What was that call, Mrs. Adams?"

"Mr. Pierce. Shall I get him for you? He's in his office now."

She hesitated. "No, that can wait. I want to check the kitchen first."

14

Crossing the lobby again, she was aware that the two bellboys on duty were watching her intently and she chose to believe that it was at least partially because of her physical self. It was a thought unusual enough to make her conscious of its rarity. Perhaps that twelve dollars hadn't been a waste after all. Actually, she didn't need a girdle, and there weren't many women of thirty-nine who could honestly say that, but it did give her a pleasantly slim-hipped feeling, close-held and competent.

"Where's Frank?" she asked the first boy, suddenly recalling that there was a change to be made on the bulletin board.

"Frank? He's doing something for McCall on ten. Anything I can do to help, Mrs. Kennard?"

"No."

This second intrusion of Cash McCall's name was a compounding of irritation and it was only after she had crossed the Fontainebleau Room that her annoyance lost itself in her overriding consciousness of the dank dishwatery odor that hung in the passageway to the kitchen. She felt again the nausea of frustration that the back of the house always incited. The original kitchen had been hopelessly small and the only solution had been to break through the walls into the semi-basement of an adjoining building. Despite the installation of modern equipment and as much remodeling as was physically possible, the kitchen was still a badly arranged assortment of odd rooms, an echoing bedlam of dish-rattling confusion, poorly ventilated, and so damp that there was an eternal scabbing of paint from the walls.

The extra waiters who had helped to serve the Andscott breakfast stood in a ragged cluster around the time clock, their poise and dignity stripped off with the green and gold jackets that now hung on the uniform rack in the locker room.

"Good work, boys," she said crisply. "Fine job this morning. Same thing next week. You'll get a call."

They nodded to acknowledge her favor and Louis, the headwaiter of the Fontainebleau Room, began tearing pink pay slips off the pad in his hand, but stopped suddenly as she passed him.

"Madame?"

"Yes?"

"This dinner party tonight. For me it is the evening off, but if you should wish—"

"What dinner party?"

"You do not know? But Max tells me last night that Mr. McCall is having—"

She strode off without waiting for an explanation, knowing well enough what it would be. Cash McCall had gone directly to Max again! Who the hell did this character McCall think he was? Just because he was paying a thousand a month for a suite didn't give him a right to act as if he owned the place!

Max Nicollet, only now reporting for duty, was standing with Julius, the second cook, who had supervised the breakfast. Normally, Maude Kennard would have approached with caution—the *chef de cuisine* was a man of cyclonic temper—but now, goaded by anger, she bore down on him with unflinching purpose. "Max, what's this I hear about you talking to Mr. McCall?"

The chef took a deep breath, inflating the enormous balloon of his body to even more startling proportions. "So what is it I do?" he asked, his voice oddly accented by the half dozen languages that he had attempted to learn during his lifetime.

"You know very well, Max. There's a standing rule that no special orders are to be accepted from any guest without the approval of my office."

"Ahah!" Max shouted, a battle cry announcing that he was fully ready for the fray, his black eyes blazing, the waxed points of his mustache bristling fiercely. "So now I am good only to slave in this rat hole of a kitchen. To the guests I must not speak. That is what you are saying?"

She saw that all work had stopped in the kitchen, that she was encircled by watching eyes. "Now, Max—"

"One man in this garbage can of a hotel who knows what he eats—for the rest it could be slops for hogs—but to this one man I must not speak!" His gigantic arm swept up, snatching his tall white cap from his head and hurling it to the floor. "Madame, I do not take the insult!"

"We'll talk about it later," she said, her face blanched as she turned back toward the Fontainebleau Room, struggling for self-control. Max was excusable. Good chefs were always a little crazy, the better the crazier, but it was high time that something was done about Cash McCall!

She crossed the lobby, remembering when she was halfway up the stairs to the mezzanine that Everett Pierce wanted to see her. Their offices were side by side, marked by glass signs glowing green in the rainy-morning gloom. She went past her own office and opened the door of his.

He was holding the telephone as she entered and exhaled his relief as he saw her. "Oh, there you are. I've been trying everywhere to find you."

She knew immediately that he was frightened, that in a moment he would be begging her to tell him not to worry, asking for her promise that she would take care of whatever it was that was wrong.

"The income tax people are after McCall," he blurted out. "They had a special agent in to see me this morning."

She looked at him without expression, consciously withholding the opiate of assurance that his eyes were begging her to administer.

"What do you think of it?" he asked, his lips puckered with anxiety.

"They're after most people these days, aren't they?"

"I have a feeling this is different."

"Why?" she asked, knowing the reason but forcing him to acknowledge it.

"I know what Mr. Atherson's reaction would be if—well, it wouldn't help the hotel any, being mixed up with some sort of gangster."

Pierce's voice had dropped off with his last words, suggesting that his suspicion had been weakened by exposure to the light of day. She moved quickly to restore it, but so circuitously that her motive could not possibly be discerned. "I don't see how Mr. Atherson could hold you responsible. He was the one who sent him here. Anyway, it might not affect the hotel too much. Remember the Kefauver investigations—Costello having his hair cut at the Waldorf-Astoria?"

"Costello?" Pierce said, looking up at her with the startled expression of a little gray rabbit.

"The Waldorf managed to survive," she smiled.

"Yes, that's true," Everett Pierce said, but his blank stare remained unbroken and she knew that the seed had been planted. All she had to do now was let it grow.

The pleasure that Maude Kennard had once found in the ease with which Everett Pierce could be handled was difficult to resurrect. It had been a dulled sensation since that day when she had discovered, only partly by accident, that his salary was almost double her own. That, on top of the fact that he had the whole tenth-floor suite while she was still living in a single room on six established an injustice that would have been impossible to stomach had not her experience already taught her that the spectacle of a totally incompetent man holding down a good job at a high salary was not a rarity. She had come to know many such men in her years at the Ivanhoe, stupid oafs like Park Cady who could be bribed with a pan of cinnamon buns. At least Everett Pierce was no worse than the rest. He had the sense—most of the time—to stay out of the way and not make a nuisance of himself.

"I tied up the Andscott breakfasts," she said, making it neither a report nor a request for approval, only a prod to test the depth of Everett Pierce's preoccupation with Cash McCall.

Apparently he was awakened only by the sound of her voice, un-

17

aware of what she had said. "You must admit he's a strange character. His bill with us last month was over fifteen hundred dollars. That's a lot of money. And he's only here half the time, not even that. His own plane. Flies all over the country. It takes money to live like that. I'd say he spends at least fifty thousand a year, just on his own living expenses."

"Yes, that's a lot of money," she agreed, prodding him on.

"You know as well as I do, Mrs. Kennard, that no one makes that kind of money these days—not legitimately—not with taxes what they are. It's impossible."

"What are you thinking?"

"Where does all the money come from? Do you know anything about his business? Has he ever told you? Why does he have a private line that doesn't go through our hotel board?"

"It does sound a little suspicious, doesn't it," she said encouragingly.

"If you ask me, Mrs. Kennard, *more* than a little. It wouldn't surprise me one bit to wake up some morning and find ourselves spread across the newspapers. That would be a nice state of affairs, wouldn't it? How could we get up on the witness stand, you and I, and swear that we didn't know something mighty queer was going on?"

She modulated her voice, letting it plant another seed casually, knowing that there was nothing in the world Everett Pierce wanted more than to be restored to his tenth-floor suite. "What are you planning to do—get him out of the hotel?"

Everett Pierce fidgeted. "Well, if it were my decision—*yes!*"

"But isn't he a friend of Mr. Atherson's?"

He nodded a nervous affirmative. "I'm afraid so. At least it was Mr. Atherson who sent him here—and approved all that waste of money for redecorating."

That was not strictly true, Cash McCall had paid for the remodeling, but this was no time to split hairs.

She gave him another nudge. "Perhaps Mr. Atherson doesn't know as much about him as he should."

He rose to the bait. "That's exactly what *I've* been thinking. If I only had some *facts*—"

"Why can't you get some facts?"

"How could I?"

"Get a report on him."

He sighed and shook his head. "I've already had a report. There's nothing in it—just that he has a high rating and is prompt in his payments."

"What kind of a report did you get?"

"Dun and Bradstreet."

"There are other kinds."

He twined his fingers. "Yes, I suppose there are."

"You could get a Lockwood," she said, pausing, sensing his reluctance to admit that he didn't know what she was talking about. "A Lockwood report would give you more of a personal record on the man himself."

"I—well, I wasn't thinking of having him shadowed or anything like that."

She noted with satisfaction that he had already made the idea his own. "I know you weren't, Mr. Pierce."

"I suppose something like that would probably be expensive, wouldn't it?"

"Not necessarily. Lockwood might have a file on him already. They often do. Wouldn't it be worth something just to protect the hotel?"

"Yes—yes, I suppose it would."

"If you want me to, I'll take care of it," she went on with quiet assurance. "I know a source that could handle it without anyone ever being aware that the hotel was involved."

"Who's that?"

"Judge Torrant. You remember him—he handled the legal work when we bought the property next door?"

"Oh."

"He's an old family friend."

His eyes were anxious, as they always were when he found himself about to be committed to a decision. "Well, if it doesn't run into too much money—"

"I'll see him this morning on the way to the bank."

"You'll have to watch your step, Mrs. Kennard, not get us involved —but I'm sure you realize that."

"I'm no fool," she said—and meant it. Cash McCall would find that out. No one could make a fool of her and get away with it! McCall knew as well as Max did that all private party dinner orders had to be cleared with her.

Two

. . . . .

LOOKING DOWN upon Suffolk, Pennsylvania, from Grant Austen's home on Orchard Ridge, the city may be seen—as his daughter Lory once pointed out to him—to bear some resemblance to the cross section of a giant tree trunk. It has the same circular shape, the same rough-barked outline, and it is not too difficult to imagine the curving streets and avenues as the annual rings of an old tree.

In much the same way that a tree's history can be read from the variations in its lines of growth, the development of Suffolk can be traced in the changing character of residential architecture as, street by street and avenue by avenue, the growing town spawned its new cell structure of tree-edged blocks and hedge-bordered lots.

Jefferson Street marks the edge of the heartwood, the red brick homes of colonial days. State Street is the outer limit of the "Philadelphia rows" that were built to house the influx of immigrant millworkers during the years immediately preceding the Civil War. Jackson Avenue was the north limit of the town at the end of the nineteenth century and, during the Gay Nineties, iron deer on the lawns of the town's newest mansions stared sightlessly across that avenue into open fields. Now, a half century later, those gingerbread old houses are buried deep in the city's hardwood and the cambium layer is the scarcely broken circle of real estate developments that all but ring the city. Even in mid-March the cell spawning goes on with mad prolificacy. Far up the slope of Orchard Ridge, now well beyond Boulevard Drive, there is the constant sound of a hammer and

20

saw and the air is ever pungent with the new-building odors of saw-dust and plaster and asphalt.

It is only to the west, in the wedge between the radial lines of the state highway and Conomissing Creek, that the residential cell pattern of Suffolk is disturbed. There, as if by some accident of nature, the cells are of a radically different character. The cell walls are not shrub hedges but wire fences, high and barb-topped, and the odors are not fresh and clean but odd and foul—the rotten-egg stench from the Marble Chemical Works, the fetid smell spewed out by the Hermann Adhesives Company, the sharp carbolic tang of the Suffolk Moulding Company, a half hundred other strange assailments of the nostrils.

Subconsciously, as he made the turn into Mill Street, Grant Austen's nostrils anticipated the characteristic odor of his factory. The first whiff of phenol was a part of the pattern of his life. This morning he missed it. The windows of his blue Cadillac were closed against the cold March mist that fogged the city. The weather report in last night's paper had predicted a clear day and the defeat of anticipation seemed a plausible excuse for his depression of spirit. Hopefully, he told himself that he would feel better once the winter was finally over. It had been a long time since he had driven to the plant with that effervescence of spirit that had often made him the first to arrive. This morning it was almost nine-thirty.

Piloting his way down the stone-paved street, cautiously aware that the age-worn cobbles were slippery with rain, he turned in at the plant gate, parked in the factory garage, and started across the black-topped yard toward the Administration Building. Halfway, he felt the insistent nudge of instinct and, reluctant but submissive, turned back toward the tool shop.

What he saw as he stepped through the door confirmed the suspicion that his instinct had aroused. The most important job in the shop—a set of experimental injection dies for the control panel on Andscott's new line of television cabinets—was stopped on dead center. The machines and work benches were deserted. All of the men were in the back of the shop clustered around Ed Berger who, with the base of the hobbing press as a soapbox, was venting his highly profane spleen at "the stupidities of them goddam blueprinting engineers."

Grant Austen silently dispersed the men, studied the blueprints for a scant minute, saw that Berger's idea for the relocation of a pinpoint vent might be a slight improvement over the original design—at least it would do no harm—and traded his approval of the change for a promise that the Andscott molds would be finished on schedule.

The whole incident took less than five minutes but it brought down upon Grant Austen's shoulders the full weight of his weary resignation to what his life had now become. There had been a time when the refereeing of another episode in the running feud between Ed Berger and Jake Crown would have been a duty discharged with bland tolerance, almost with pleasure. In those days, the Hatfield-McCoy relationship between the foreman of the tool shop and the head of the engineering department had served a purpose. Their rivalry had been responsible for many of the improvements in molding technique that had helped to build the firm's reputation. Now, after all these years, Grant Austen was unhappily aware that the quarreling wasn't worth the strain that it imposed upon him. New developments weren't so important any more. All that mattered now was keeping the Andscott production schedule. That's what the molding business had become—mass production.

Starting back toward the office building, he found himself trapped by George Thorson, the foreman of the pressroom, who had seen him enter the tool shop and waited where he couldn't be avoided. His escape blocked, Grant Austen followed the foreman to his little office on the far side of the pressroom and sat down to listen to Thorson's recital of his accumulated troubles. He was tempted, as usual, to comment that Thorson's taste in wall calendars was hardly in keeping with the dignity of his position as General Foreman, but caught himself before any damage was done. Thorson was the man who kept the Andscott cabinets moving out on schedule. Calendars could be overlooked, the schedule couldn't.

During the next twenty minutes, he agreed to an increase in the backlog stock of the special phenolic resin that was used for Andscott television cabinets, approved the renewing of runners and sprues on two sets of dies, turned down a request for the purchase of six new inspection tables, and ordered the payment of a month's dismissal wages to an unfortunate young girl in the packing department whom Thorson was being forced to discharge because her illegitimate pregnancy had progressed to the point where it was now causing lost time through a constant succession of sympathy meetings in the women's rest room.

Finally escaping, walking out through the pressroom, he felt the deadening weight of fatigue. He was more tired at ten o'clock in the morning than he should have been at the end of the day, but that was not an unusual situation and he accepted his debility in the same spirit with which the chronically ill bow to the inevitability of pain.

He had gone through the Johns Hopkins clinic in October. The doctors had found nothing wrong. He had known they wouldn't. No doctor could diagnose the atrophy of hope, nor understand what it meant to face what he faced—thirty years of building a company and now only this dead end of hopelessness.

Outside the pressroom, standing on the edge of the shipping platform, he looked past the tool shop and saw the vacant lot beyond, the rough scraggle of dead weeds that ran all the way down to the creek bank. That was where he would have built his big factory if he could have carried out all the plans that had been bound between the black morocco covers of A POST-WAR PROGRAM FOR THE EXPANSION OF THE SUFFOLK MOULDING COMPANY. The government had wrecked all that—Truman and Korea and taxes and controls.

The mist had become rain and the March wind swirled it through the yard, the chill penetrating to his body as he made his careful way down the wet steps of the shipping platform. Little pin jabs of protesting pain flickered across his shoulders and down the long muscles of his back. His body joints were stiff, gritty in their sockets.

Picking his way around the shallow puddles that dotted the pavement, he made the conscious attempt to lift his spirits by contemplating the Administration Building that, only three years ago, had seemed his one best promise of a pleasanter life. There was no lift. There never had been. It hadn't worked. Air-conditioning and fluorescent lighting were poor substitutes for lost hopes. His new private office, even though guarded by double doors and a forced passage through his secretary's office, had done nothing to protect him. There were no fewer annoyances heaped on his desk, no fewer people pushing in to demand that he resolve, over and over again, the same problems that he had been solving for a quarter of a century.

Suddenly, startlingly, Grant Austen was struck with the strange fantasy that it was not he who was moving toward the building but that it was the building that was moving toward him, a window-eyed monster crushing down upon him, threatening to swallow him up in the black mouth of the tongue-flapping doorway.

He blinked away the mental aberration, restoring his sense of controlled movement even before his stride was broken, but he could not banish the hallucination of impending engulfment. Nor could he easily accept the strangeness of the tricks that his mind had been playing of late. This was not the first time that he had been victimized by one of these frightening moments of lost orientation.

He was tired. But the convention was only ten days away. That would give him a break. Maybe he'd take a few extra days. But you always had to come back. The longer you were gone, the more things got fouled up. There was no one to carry on when he wasn't there. That would have been the big difference if he could have gone through with the POST-WAR PROGRAM. By now there would have been sales volume enough to support a real executive staff ... the five vice-presidents that the organization chart called for ... big men, all of them ... big enough to lift the whole management load from his shoulders ... not little men who only added to his burden by their failure to take responsibility. That was the trouble with a business like Suffolk Moulding ... everything on your own shoulders ... too much for one man, not enough to justify the salaries you had to pay to hire top men with real background. The idea of getting young fellows out of college and training them yourself didn't work. If they turned out to be any good, some big company outbid you and you lost them ... Packer ... Dinsmore ... that boy from Penn. If they were flops, you were saddled with them ... Brown and Wellett ... and now Paul Bronson.

There was no excuse for Bronson. Didn't he have a master's degree from Harvard Business? Hadn't he spent two years with General Electric and over a year with Finch & Slade in New York? With that kind of a background, shouldn't Bronson be making a real contribution by now? But what had he done? Oh, he was clever enough with figures ... give the boy his due, he had gotten the office paper work in fair shape. But you couldn't run a company like Suffolk with figures and paper work. Could Bronson have handled Ed Berger this morning? No. The boy didn't have what it took ... no mechanical sense at all ... been around for over two years now and he still didn't know that you had to go to dielectric preheating when you were working with a preform that was more than an inch thick. That had come out yesterday when they had been discussing the bid on that Gridlux job.

Deep in Grant Austen's mind, bleeding the weak caustic of another lost hope, were the ashes of the very secret dream that he had sheltered during those first months after he had hired Paul Bronson. Paul had started dating Lory and for a while it had seemed that something might come of it. But nothing ever had. Now nothing ever would. Of course it was a good thing that it wouldn't. Paul didn't have the *breadth*. It would take a dozen Bronsons to manage the Suffolk Moulding Company. Lory knew that. She'd gotten the boy's number in a hurry. Of course she'd never mentioned it ... one of those things that she couldn't talk to him about ... but Lory *knew*. There was one smart youngster ... a lot more in that little head of hers than anyone else realized. People underrated Lory ... thought because she was an artist that she didn't understand business. They were wrong. When he had a problem to thrash out and needed someone to talk to, Lory made more sense than anyone else.

As always, the thought of his daughter warmed Grant Austen's mind but it was not, at this moment, a warmth that could be sustained against the chill of a truth that was as inescapable as the cold wind that swept along the back side of the office building. The recognition that his daughter was so often the only person with whom he could talk forced the conscious acceptance of what, usually, he managed to keep deeply buried in his subconscious mind—that his whole life had become pointless.

He was headed for a dead end. He knew it. There was no one to carry on. Everything would be different if he had a son ... or even the right kind of son-in-law coming along. He didn't. Yes, he should have recognized that before ... even the POST-WAR PROGRAM couldn't have given him a son. But there had always been that blind hope that somehow it would work out. It hadn't. Now it never would. Lory would marry some day ... she was only twenty-six ... but it wouldn't be the kind of man who could take over the Suffolk Moulding Company. There weren't any men like that around any more. They were all like Paul Bronson, narrow and single-talented, trained to do one job and nothing else. Jay Bross had summed it up at lunch the other day. "What a lot of people don't appreciate, Grant, is that men like you and me are running seven-ring circuses and we have to be in all seven rings at the same time. I'd like to see one of those big business hot-shots take over my desk for just one day! Brother, he'd find out something—what it's like to have it all on your own shoulders, no legal department to check contracts, no market research department to tell you where to go to get some business, no research department figuring out new things to make. Yes sir, I've said it before and I'll say it again—the smaller the business, the bigger the man on top has to be."

He was but a stride away from the back entrance of the office building, reaching for the door when it suddenly burst open, the handle snatched from his fingers. Only a reflexed backstep avoided a collision with one of the youngsters from the engineering department who came rushing out with an armload of blueprints.

He brushed aside the boy's embarrassed apology and stepped in through the door, hesitating on the landing at the bottom of the staircase. The violent interruption had given him the detachment of full realization and he was angrily self-critical for having done again what he had promised himself so many times he would not do. Why

25

did he let himself start worrying? Why couldn't he control his mind any more? He had to learn to *relax*. Nothing would change. This was what he was going to be up against for the rest of his life.

He raised his head and squared his shoulders, rejecting the support of the rail as he started up the stairs. A man didn't dare give in to weakness. When you did you lost control. You couldn't fool anyone. They'd see it in your face.

His secretary, Amelia Berk, greeted him with reassuring normality and he knew that he hadn't betrayed himself. If he had, her expression would have reflected it. He greeted her pleasantly and went into his office, firm-carriaged, poised, grasping for the saving realization that he was the President of his own company. At least he wasn't in a spot like Jay Bross, trying to please a dozen big stockholders.

He hung his gray topcoat in his private washroom, carefully straightening the shoulders on the hanger, washed his hands to remove the oil smudge that he had picked up in the tool shop, combed and palm-flattened his graying hair, adjusted his blue polka-dotted necktie, and came out to his desk.

He felt a little better now, not quite so tired, but the relief was only momentary. The basket of incoming mail was stacked high. It would take at least two hours to get through it. The President of a company ought to have a secretary who could handle most of his mail without his ever seeing it. Miss Berk couldn't. She had tried and failed. Her self-written letters were always too short, too cold, only what had to be said and never a word more. But there was nothing he could do about it. Miss Berk had an invalid mother to support. In a big corporation you could hire and fire whenever you wanted to. It was different in a company like Suffolk Moulding. You couldn't toss off a secretary any more than you could discard a cousin or disown an uncle.

Settling into his chair, he fanned letters until Miss Berk, having satisfied her modesty by waiting until he was certainly out of the washroom, entered the room and emitted the sigh of recurrent despair that was the vocalization of her personality.

"Awful lot of people want to see you this morning," she said.

He nodded, accepting the inevitable. "We'll get at this mail first. Bring in your book."

She sniffed, sitting, showing him that she already had her notebook. But she didn't open it. First there were the messages that had been left for him, so hastily shorthanded on odd bits of paper that he was, as always, forced to sit through the painful process of her sorting and deciphering. His annoyance impaired his hearing and he heard only part sentences and broken phrases.

26

"—check for the Republican County Committee before tomorrow so he can report it at the meeting—Jake Crown is ready to show you some drawings that you wanted to see—with Mr. Bronson and said he'd be ready whenever you had time to—"

"Who was that?" he asked, something missed.

"Mr. Clark from Corporation Associates. He said that he had—let's see, it's something about a report on—"

"I know," he said, again letting her voice drone past his ears, the mention of Gil Clark suggesting the question of whether or not he ought to retain Corporation Associates for another year. The contract for management counseling service had an automatic renewal clause. If he wanted to cancel he would have to give notice by the first of the month ... five thousand a year was a lot of money ... most of the things Gil Clark came up with only confirmed what he already knew ... but it helped sometimes to have someone to talk to, someone besides Lory ... and Gil Clark was a good boy. It was too bad that Lory couldn't have found some boy who ...

He was interrupted by the consciousness of silence. Miss Berk had finished the recital of her messages and sat waiting. He began to dictate, driving through the burdensome triviality of his correspondence. But what could he do? When people wrote to the Suffolk Moulding Company they wrote to him. He *was* the company. In a big corporation it was different ... the president was protected ... vice-presidents to take care of the details ...

"I beg your pardon," Miss Berk sniffed, her accent critical.

"Read me that last paragraph," he said.

She read what he had dictated and his words came back, remembered not as he had said them a moment before, automatically, but as the memory of all the other times he had submitted to the minor blackmail of a page of advertising in the high school annual. He began to dictate again, time-worn words, phrases so often spoken that now they spoke themselves without effort or volition, and the sound of the words became a part of the jangling sound-flow of the day, of his telephone ringing, of the door opening and closing, of the paper rustle of orders and schedules to be initialed, of the parchment crackle of blueprints to be approved or changed, of the cacophony of voices and voices and voices, begging, wheedling, cajoling, demanding. Miss Berk in and out of his office, in and out, in and out ... damn it, how did she expect a man to work if she was constantly interrupting him!

"I'm sorry, Mr. Austen," she was saying, "but Mr. Bronson has to see you right away. He's just had a call from Andscott."

"All right," he said wearily.

27

Bronson entered almost immediately, his forced smile more ominous than a scowl. "Hate to break in on you like this, Mr. Austen, but—"

"Andscott?" Grant Austen asked, hoping to short-circuit one of Bronson's typically long-winded preambles. That was the trouble with these youngsters, they couldn't get to the point.

Bronson nodded. "Joe Keening called me a few minutes ago about this new television cabinet. I know you said last night that we weren't interested unless they were willing to—"

"We still aren't interested," Grant Austen snapped back. "Nobody would be crazy enough to go ahead on their kind of deal—a quarter of a million investment and no guarantee of volume."

"I'm afraid, sir, that someone *is* interested."

Grant Austen felt the choke of shock. "Who?"

"Heckledorf in Newark."

There was the tightening constriction of apprehension in Grant Austen's throat. "All right, let him have it. We've got enough Andscott business as it is, enough eggs in one basket."

"Afraid it isn't quite that simple, sir," Bronson said. "Heckledorf's made them a rough proposition. He'll go ahead and do what they want—put in that 2500-ton press and give them their new cabinet—but for a pay-off he wants all of the rest of their business."

"All of their—that's crazy. They can't."

"I'm sorry, sir, but that's the way it is. I double-checked Joe to be certain."

A plunging knife seemed to have cut through the control nerves of Grant Austen's body. He sat in mute paralysis, conscious that his face was betraying his weakness, yet momentarily unable even to tighten the slackness of his lips. More than half of the plant's capacity was now taken up by Andscott production. To lose all of that volume in one fell swoop would rip the very backbone out of the business. There was no place to turn for substitute orders that would come anywhere near making up the loss.

"Puts us in a difficult position, no doubt about that," Bronson said glumly.

"They're bluffing!" Grant Austen slashed in.

Bronson shook his head. "I'm afraid not, sir."

"But they can't pull those jobs," he fought back. "They're our molds."

"Andscott owns the molds, Mr. Austen. They can do anything they want to do."

"But they're built for our presses. They'll have trouble. You know

28

that as well as I do. Damn it, Bronson, why didn't you point that out to them?"

"They know they'll have trouble," Bronson said with quiet patience. "Joe remembers the headaches we had when we tried to use those tools they took over from Randall."

"Well then?"

"There's nothing Joe can do about it, sir. He's got his orders from the top. General Danvers has made up his mind they're going to get that new cabinet molded and that's all there is to it. If we won't do it, then they'll sign with Heckledorf."

Grant Austen sat, silent, trying to brush off the prickle of annoyance that had been raised by Bronson's patronizing patience. He knew what was coming ... Bronson would ask him to change his mind ... and what else could he do? He didn't dare lose the Andscott business, even if it meant doing the thing that he had sworn he would never do again. It would cost at least a quarter of a million dollars to buy a 2500-ton press and get set up to produce Andscott's new console cabinet. An investment of that size couldn't possibly be financed out of surplus. He'd have to arrange a big loan and that meant going back to the beginning, to all those years when he had lived under the black cloud of mortgages and bank loans. He'd thought he'd won when he'd finally gotten out from under. But you *never* won. You *couldn't* win in a little company. The cards were stacked against you.

"—know how you feel about bringing any new capital into the business," Bronson was saying, "but I don't see what the alternative is, sir. If we don't—"

"How long do we have?" Austen demanded.

"Joe wanted an answer by Friday night but I told him we'd have to have more time than that. I finally got him to give us until the first of the month. That's a week from tomorrow."

"I'll let you know," the president said, his voice crisp with dismissal.

Bronson rose reluctantly. "Well, if there's anything I can do—"

"I'll call you."

"I have the specifications on this new cabinet," Bronson said, exhibiting the file folder he carried.

"Leave it on the desk," Grant Austen said impatiently, rising, driven to the need for physical outlet, walking to the window, waiting out the fading carpet-muffled sound of Bronson's departing footsteps.

With the click of the door latch he wheeled back to his desk, pressed the buzzer and told Miss Berk to put in a call for Will Atherson, president of the Freeholders Bank & Trust Company in Philadelphia. He was trapped . . . there was only one thing to do, get it over with . . . the sooner the better!

Waiting, he tried to concentrate but his brain refused the discipline, short-circuited by the flinch of pain. There was a tearing claw inside the cage of his ribs, an iron fist closing over his heart. He breathed deeply, open-mouthed . . . *relax . . . relax . . .* "We've found nothing organically wrong, Mr. Austen . . . distress that you experience on certain occasions is probably psychosomatic . . . induced by nervous tension . . . have to learn to relax, Mr. Austen . . . when a man passes fifty . . ."

Voices cross-faded and he turned to see Miss Berk standing in the open door. "Mr. Atherson is out of his office now. He'll call back within an hour."

He nodded and the door closed. Then, tricking him, it reopened. "Shall I send in Mr. Clark now? He's been waiting a long time."

"In a few minutes."

He faced down her look of disapproving inquiry, tight-lipped until the door had closed again.

Relax . . . relax . . . relax . . . try to think. There was some talk about a new Washington ruling on speeding up depreciation . . . that might give him a chance . . . maybe something about it in the paper this morning . . .

The newspaper was on his side table. He scanned the front page, found nothing pertinent and turned to the financial section. The first thing he saw was the headline of a small advertisement.

WHY NOT SELL
YOUR COMPANY?

He read the short paragraph . . . *unusual opportunity for owner of business to cash in and avoid problems created by today's heavy taxes on operating profits.* Probably some kind of racket. There were a lot of gyp outfits looking for suckers.

His eyes wandered over the two pages, reading headlines . . . MULTI-MILLION EXPANSION FOR OIL COMPANY . . . CHEMICAL FIRM TO BUILD NEW PLANT . . . CORPORATE FINANCING ON UP GRADE. All big companies. They were the only ones that had a chance these days.

Suddenly, happening so swiftly that there was no consciousness of the moment of transition, the claw grip in his chest was gone. His mind had cleared. A single thought hung suspended, as attention-compelling as the sun in a cloudless sky and, like the sun, it was without support or tie, a thought seemingly virgin-born, spurning the ancestry of association or memory, and so it became an idea miraculously created, totally his own.

He would sell the company.

He waited for the backlash of reflexed resistance that had always before been generated by any suggestion that he might ever sell the Suffolk Moulding Company. Back during the war someone had asked Will Atherson to sound him out on whether or not he was interested in selling. He had answered then with immediate rejection, almost in anger, not even bothering to find out how much the unnamed buyer might be willing to pay. Now nothing happened. His mind remained clear. The situation had changed in these last ten years. Now, obviously, the thing to do was get out—and in a hurry, before the Andscott business was lost! That only gave him a week. Could it possibly be done? It might. He had to see Will Atherson at once. Will had the connections and would know how to go about doing it.

He went to the door and flung it open. "Miss Berk, hasn't that call from Mr. Atherson come through yet?"

"Not yet, Mr. Austen. Shall I try again?"

He shook his head.

"Are you ready for Mr. Clark?"

He hesitated, abruptly aware of the need to talk. "All right, send him in."

Gil Clark entered with an easy smile, rejecting apology for having been kept waiting. "That's all right, sir. Those things happen." He was opening his portfolio, taking out a thin folder in the gold cover that Corporation Associates used on all of its client reports. "This is on that tax business, sir. I went over it with Patterson. He doesn't think there's much hope of it being allowed. He says there are certain situations where you can adjust your base but he doubts if—"

"Let that go for a minute," Grant Austen said, suppressing his growing excitement. "Something else I want to talk over with you." He studied the younger man's face, speculating on what his reaction would be when he told him what he had in mind. "This is confidential."

"Of course, sir."

"Nothing definite about it, just an idea that I'd like to get your slant on."

"I understand."

The question that dominated Grant Austen's mind squirmed restlessly behind his lips, demanding to be voiced, yet there was the restraining realization that even the asking would be a partial commitment. "What would you say if I were to tell you that I was thinking of selling the company?"

Nothing registered on Gil Clark's face except the alertness of interest. For a moment, Grant Austen was surprised, almost disappointed. He had expected an expression of something close to shock. Then, slowly, came the realization that Gil's matter-of-fact acceptance was a confirmation of the soundness of the whole idea. Encouraged, he pressed the question. "Well, what's your reaction?"

"I'd say it was a possibility that was very much worth considering."

"You would?"

"Definitely."

Grant Austen leaned forward, easing the tension of his stiff-necked pose, amazed now at how easy it was to accept a possibility that, until a few minutes ago, he could never have forced himself to even consider.

"Of course," Gil Clark went on, "it would depend on the kind of deal you could make—not only the price you could get but the tax situation that would be created."

"Naturally. That's what I—well, what I wanted to talk to you about," Grant Austen said, not entirely truthfully. He had not anticipated that the conversation would go this far. Now, expectation outdistanced, he wasn't sure of what he did want to talk about. "I wouldn't sell, of course, if I couldn't get the right kind of deal. Maybe I couldn't, I don't know."

"If you decide to go ahead, we might be able to help you," Gil Clark said casually. "Mr. Glenn has been involved in the sale of several of our client companies. I know that he'd be more than willing to step in and do anything he could."

"Well, I might call on you folks," Grant Austen said cautiously. "I don't know yet how things are going to develop but—"

The buzzer of the intercommunicating system sounded and he depressed the listening key. Miss Berk's voice said, "Mr. Atherson's on the line. Do you want to talk to him now or shall I have him call back?"

"I'll talk to him."

He felt the necessity of rejecting Gil Clark's gestured offer to leave the room but, picking up the receiver, he was conscious of the restraint that his presence demanded. Hesitating momentarily, he thought of his original reason for calling the banker and decided that there was no need to tell Atherson the whole story over the phone. All he would do was make an appointment to see him tomorrow.

He leaned back, uptilting the receiver. "Will? Grant Austen. I was

32

wondering what your schedule was like for tomorrow. There's a new development in the Andscott situation that I'm anxious to talk over with you. How would you be fixed if I were to drive down tomorrow forenoon—get in about noon?"

They made a luncheon date and he hung up, pleasantly aware of Gil's courtesy in having gotten up and walked to the window.

He cleared his throat and Gil turned, talking as he came back to the desk. "I've been thinking, Mr. Austen—of course, I wouldn't do this without your permission—but if it's agreeable to you, I'd like to mention to Mr. Glenn that you're thinking of selling. Even if you do have a deal of your own brewing, there'd be no harm in bringing another buyer or two into the picture. Selling a company is no different from selling anything else—it takes more than one bidder to get the price up. Mr. Glenn has a lot of contacts with investors—people who want to buy industrial properties and companies that are looking for expansion possibilities—so it's just possible that he might be able to put you in touch with something interesting. Suppose I have a preliminary talk with him. He may not have anything to suggest. I don't know that he will, but if he doesn't, there's no harm done. If he does, it's all to the good."

Grant Austen gripped the arms of his chair, reacting to the feeling of being hurtled toward the edge of a precipice. If he agreed, it was almost a final decision. He hadn't had time enough to think it through yet. He needed to talk about it, thrash it out ...

His eyes, subconsciously guided, turned to the north window and found, across the smoke-plumed gray roofs of the city, the spot on the slope of Orchard Ridge that marked the site of his home. His eyes saw only the blue haze of distance but his mind saw the big studio window in the second floor of the carriage house ... tonight he'd talk it over with Lory ... Lory would understand ... know that it wasn't weakness ... that he wasn't running away. Lory would understand that he was being smart ... that now was the time to get out ... before Andscott ...

Gil Clark said, "Did you have any price in mind, sir?"

"Price? Well, not exactly."

"I just thought it might help if I could give Mr. Glenn some rough idea."

He hesitated, facing another commitment. "You know the business, Gil. What do you think I could get for it?"

"Oh, that's hard to say, sir. All depends on what someone would be willing to pay for it." He opened his briefcase and took out a notebook, fanning it until he found what Grant Austen saw was a copy of the company's last balance sheet. Gil sat for what seemed an eternity, noting figures on the edge of the sheet. "This is only a stab in the dark—but I'd say you might get somewhere between a million six and a million eight—maybe two million, I don't know. Of course, you'd have income tax to pay, but it would only be capital gain. Even if you only got a million five or six—well, you'd still have a million clear for yourself."

Grant Austen stared incredulously at the gray blur of figures on the balance sheet. Strangely, he had never thought of them before as representing personal wealth, only as symbols in an equation that had to be kept balanced. It had never occurred to him that he was actually within reach of becoming a *millionaire*.

"All right, Gil," he said with as much composure as he could manage. "I'll call you when I'm in Philadelphia tomorrow."

Gil Clark rose.

"Sit down a minute," Grant Austen said. "How much would I have to get—gross—to have a million left after tax?"

• • • • • 2

Lory Austen pushed back the end panel of the folding screen that partitioned the corner where she worked from the rest of the cavernous studio. The light over her drawing board was no longer the coldly bright sun of her little cloistered world. Now it was only a feeble glow in the pervading grayness.

She wrapped her arms across her breasts, her body tight-held, sheltering a small warmth, feeling again the bleak frustration that her father had imposed upon her. She had wanted only a small workshop, intimate and secure, but he had commissioned a Philadelphia architect to plan the remodeling of the old carriage house, ordering the creation of a "studio." The result had been this enormous barnlike room, more appropriate to a sculptor of monuments than to an illustrator of children's books.

She had tried to stop him but, as always, there had been no way to do it without making it seem a denial of affection. Defeated, she had tried to make the best of a bad situation and, for a while, the screen around her drawing board had partially achieved the intimacy of atmosphere that her creative mind seemed to demand. But of late the screen had lost its efficacy. Since early morning she had been struggling to find a starting point for the key drawings in the new book that she had been commissioned to illustrate, but every time an idea had seemed about to flow from her fingertips, the gray gloom of the day had filtered in past the screen and congealed her imagination. The wastebasket was piled high with the crumbled tissue of discarded sketches. Nothing that she had drawn was usable. Even worse, there was not even the filmy tendril of a vague idea that might, later, grow into something more substantial.

She walked toward the huge studio window, facing the up-rising slope of Orchard Ridge, her eyes subconsciously skipping what they did not want to see—the parallel gashes of the new streets and the low-roofed houses that lined them—lifting to the gray-violet of the distant woods, blued by the cold mist that even the rising wind had failed to clear. Searching, she found not the faintest hint of a green overcast on the leafless trees, no sure promise of the coming spring that would, she hoped, break the clutch of depression that the winter had fastened upon her. She had thought that a new book might do it. It hadn't.

She watched the ragged clouds that the March wind was driving in over the comb-edged crest of Orchard Ridge. They were the colorless color of the dirty brush washings of India ink, the cold smoke of a flameless fire, dropping burnt embers that were crows searching the dead earth, loose-winged and graceless, awkwardly fighting the cold wind. When spring came, the crows would be gone. They were still here in uncountable thousands.

Her gaze moved slowly across the high face of the hill, finding the ravine where the virgin white oaks still stood, the great trees that she had sketched for the forest scene in *The Knight of the Hawk*, the first book she had illustrated. The big oaks were lost in the smudge of distance, as lost as the heart-pounding drive of creative urgency that she had felt on that day when she had climbed the hill to make her sketches. That was a long time ago now ... four years ... four years and more ... four years last fall ...

She had come home from Maine that summer after she had graduated from art school, blindly running away from terror, needing escape as she had never needed it before, and the commission to illustrate her first book had been a saving miracle. There had been nothing in all of her life as consciously needed, no story so desirable as one of Marybelle Hudson's romantic fairy tales, no publisher so much wanted as Clark-Dudley.

There had been an unmatched thrill in that first letter from Jefferson Clark, asking her to come to Philadelphia to discuss the possibility of illustrating Marybelle Hudson's new book, *The Knight of the Hawk*. Somehow she had lived through those six days of waiting until the appointed forenoon, and then through the hours and minutes and seconds until, at the stroke of ten, she had opened the door of the Clark-Dudley reception lobby. The frumpy old lady behind the bronze wicket had told her that Mr. Clark was busy, he would see her when he could, and Lory had sat for over an hour in the torture chamber of that musty little hall, tying and retying the black strings of her portfolio.

She had been called in at last, standing because she had not been invited to sit, watching Jefferson Clark's aristocratically noncommittal face as he leafed hastily through her portfolio, seeming to miss all of the samples that she most wanted him to see. She had met him twice before, once when he had lectured at art school and again at his cocktail party in Maine, but he offered no sign of recognition and she, quaking, had said nothing to recall the occasions.

Finally sitting at his gruff command, she had been subjected to a half-hour dissertation on the impending demise of the whole book publishing industry, a situation that he seemed to charge to negligent booksellers, the nefarious plotting of eccentric writers, and upstart young females who imagined themselves to be artists. She gained the impression that Jefferson Clark strangely envisioned the idyllic state of a publishing house as one in which books would be unwritten, unillustrated, and unsold.

He had, in the end, commissioned her to illustrate *The Knight of the Hawk,* but the joy that it should have given her was dimmed by his making it seem an act of paternalistic charity taken against his judgment. But even that had not mattered then. All she wanted was a chance to prove herself and he had given her that. No Prather graduate had done better—a major commission in her first year out of school—and from Clark-Dudley!

There may have been purpose in Jefferson Clark's method. Later, she thought perhaps there had been. Calculated or not, his manner had incited a desperate fear of failure and it was that fear that had driven her to superlative effort during the three short weeks that he had given her to complete the twelve drawings he had told her to make.

An extension of that fear, more terrifying because there was no predictable end point, hung over her during the days after she had delivered the drawings and was waiting for some word of approval. It never came. When, finally desperate with anxiety, she had called Jefferson Clark, his tone of voice made her feel that she had annoyed him unnecessarily. The drawings, he said, were "quite all right" and the book was on the press.

She had waited for publication day with the anticipation that, in some not quite realized way, the whole color and substance of her life would change. It didn't. The day came and went without event. Her complimentary copies, badly packed and battered in the mailing, did not arrive until several days later. Her name was not on the jacket, only in small type on the title page. Five of her twelve drawings had not been used.

The only person who asked for her autograph was Mamie Breckenridge, who had taught her high school class in "Art," and Mamie had dictated an inscription that made the volume a tribute to her own genius as a teacher.

Her father, of course, had praised the book but what pleasure she might have found in his approval was destroyed when he had said, after she had answered his question about how much money she had received, that she had been cheated. He told her that he had paid more than twice that amount to a New York artist for the design of a molded plastic housing for an electric hair dryer.

There were reviews in the special children's book issues of the *New York Times* and the *Herald-Tribune,* both praising her drawings, but even that reward was short-lived. A few days later she received a curt reply to a letter that she had written to thank Marybelle Hudson for having interceded in her behalf with Jefferson Clark. Miss Hudson coldly denied having had anything to do with the selection of an illustrator, the tone of her short note making it only too obvious that she was greatly disturbed that the illustrations had been more favorably reviewed than the text. Lory knew that she would illustrate no more books by Marybelle Hudson. As the weeks dragged by, she began to doubt if she would ever illustrate another book by anyone. There was no word of any kind from Clark-Dudley.

It was a full year later when she received a note signed *T. Martell.* As she probably knew, he wrote, Clark-Dudley had been sold. Jefferson Clark was gone. The firm had a new policy. It was now publishing only low-priced children's books for mass distribution through supermarkets and chain grocery stores, probably not the kind of thing she would be interested in illustrating, but if she happened to be in Philadelphia some day and wanted to waste a half hour he would be glad to talk to her.

She had driven down that next morning. The Clark-Dudley offices were still in the same building but their atmosphere had changed. A platinum-blonde receptionist was the key motif of the new order. The lobby was now paneled in tube-lighted corrugated glass, broken with niches in which pyramided stacks of books were displayed like soap flakes, or canned soup, or the latest precooked baby food.

Tony Martell's littered cubbyhole at the end of a long corridor, safely beyond the boundary that supermarket merchandise managers were allowed to pass, was as incongruous to the scene as Tony himself. The artistic sensibility which his eyes admitted was denied by his manner. From the beginning—although not without continuing question—Lory sensed that Tony Martell wore the cloak of hard-boiled cynicism in the same way that the fearful so often hide behind bravado.

"This is strictly a junk operation," Tony had said, sipping coffee out of a wilted cardboard container. "We're geared to a fourth-grade mentality and working like hell to make sure that nobody ever gets promoted to the fifth. We can't use stuff like that *Hawk* book of yours any more, Lory. Too dangerous. Might destroy the little brats' taste for comic strips. That's our shining goal—prepare the youth of America for their destiny as readers of the comic strips. Now what are you doing around here, anyway? You're no cartoonist. You're an artist. What would you be doing illustrating this tripe about a space ship to Jupiter where there's some queer element in the atmosphere that makes all of the visitors from earth act like intelligent human beings? Fantastic idea, isn't it? Crazy as imagining that you might want to do this book. You don't, do you?"

Through that early spring she had done the illustrations for *Space Ship to Jupiter,* preserving the demanded format of the comic-strip panel yet striving to make her drawings as artistically sound as if they had been destined for a museum's wall.

There had been one flashed moment of reward—Tony Martell's appreciative astonishment when she had unwrapped the package and handed him her first drawings. "Beautiful," he had whispered. But then he had snapped down the curtain of his cynicism. "Afraid you're counting on too much imagination, Lory. Kids have imagination—granted—but kids don't buy books. Mama is the literary purchasing agent and she lost her imagination with her virginity. And you've made Jupiter much too beautiful—no monsters with sparks shooting out of their ears. Mama won't like that. She wants something to scare the hell out of her little brats by telling them the next time they set fire to the davenport that some jughead goblin from Jupiter is going to shoot their little behinds full of astral buckshot. But we'll take a swing at it and see what happens."

Her check, when it came that next week, was for five hundred dollars instead of the four hundred that Tony had originally promised her. She had made the mistake of telling her father. Grant Austen said that he had recently paid an industrial design firm a thousand dollars for the design of the molded cover for a bathroom scales.

There were no reviews of *Space Ship to Jupiter.* Beyond an occasional word of regret for the down-grading of "a fine old publishing house" the reviewers now paid no attention to Clark-Dudley and its outpouring of cheaply printed books. There was no supermarket in Suffolk that handled the Clark-Dudley books. But Lory felt no regret that her friends wouldn't see *Space Ship to Jupiter*. Her drawings were reproduced on paper as gray as newsprint, the color crudely raw, all subtlety lost. Heartsick, she told herself that at least there would be no more like it.

But six months later Tony had asked her to come to Philadelphia. "Quite a hot number, aren't you, gal?" he had said with his lip-twisting grin, surprised when he discovered that she didn't know that her book had sold almost a million copies. "You're the Mickey Spillane of the kid book racket and the front office is panting to sign you into permanent white slavery. How about a contract to do two more at a thousand bucks a throw?"

Tony had laughed away her objection and taken her down the glass-paneled hall into the great glittering office where she was introduced to the president, a little pot-bellied man with a set smile that made him look frighteningly like her father. Tony and the president had taken her to lunch at the Fontainebleau Room in the Hotel Ivanhoe, toasting "more million-copy sockeroos" with their third Martinis, to which she could respond only with an empty sherry glass and flaming embarrassment.

In the end she had signed the contract, feeling no exultation, motivated only by the pressing need to fill the empty hours of the days ahead and the vague hope that the signed contract might give her the courage to tell her father that she could no longer go on living in Suffolk. But of course she hadn't—as she had known she wouldn't—and somehow she had managed to exist through the repetitious monotony of *Space Ship to Venus* and *Space Ship to Saturn*.

During the long days in her studio, introspection sharpened by loneliness, Lory began to suspect that her desire to be an artist had been largely self-deception, motivated by a recognition that she had always been someone apart from the crowd, never the center of admiring friends, never one of those most envied girls who could pick and choose among a half dozen clamoring beaus, always handicapped by the fact that she looked like "such a dear, sweet child." No one ever believed that she was as old as she really was. Even at art school, the instructors had treated her as if she were a child prodigy. Ray Cummings, the one boy she had dated in Philadelphia, had admitted that one of his friends who had seen them together had kidded him for being a "cradle snatcher."

She was old enough now so that the mistake was no longer made but, looking back, her impelling desire to be accepted as an adult seemed a logical explanation for the urge to gain recognition as an artist. She had reached that goal now but it had, if anything, set her even more apart than she had ever been before. There was often the feeling that people around Suffolk experienced a certain embarrassment in her presence, acting as if she lived in a world quite different from their own. An "artist" didn't quite fit in with "the crowd." When she was invited out to dinner and a hostess was forced to provide an extra man, it usually turned out to be either Dale Withers, who taught English at the high school and once had a sonnet published in a poetry magazine, or Somerset Hart who was the "decorator" at the Home Store. Both of them were what Suffolk called "artistic," the generally accepted meaning of the word being not entirely complimentary.

In December, when she had taken down the last of the drawings for *Space Ship to Saturn*, hurriedly revised to fit a sudden change in format, she had protested another assignment in the same series and Tony, surprisingly, had said, "I was wondering how long you could take it. I'll see if I can't dig up something a little less corny. There's a pretty good chance of it now—we're making so damn much money around here that the front office is about due for a sudden attack of artistic integrity. Sit tight and I'll deal you in."

Tony had made good on his promise. The manuscript had finally arrived, a translation from the French of a completely charming tale about a teen-age romance, alive with illustrative possibilities, and the roughly penciled dummy that Tony had given her was an encouragement to freedom rather than the confining dictation that his layouts for the other books had been. She saw at once that it was a chance to go on from where she had stopped with *The Knight of the Hawk* but, terrifyingly, there had been no responding rise of creative imagination. She felt only the dead emptiness of her mind, a lethargy of spirit that she could no longer blame on Tony and Clark-Dudley. Nor could she blame her father. That, too, had been self-deception. She was an adult. She was twenty-six years old ... old enough to live her own life ... to have her own home ...

Involuntarily, her eyes dropped from the top of Orchard Ridge and her mind, as if freed from the suggestion of the endless milling of the hovering crows, settled into a simpler pattern. Looking down from second-story height across the high hemlock hedge, she saw the row of little houses that now crowded in against the back line of the estate. Her eyes came to rest on a kitchen window of one of the houses. The light that had been turned on against the grayness of the day was as yellow as liquid honey. A young woman in an organdy-frilled red apron was lifting a baby into a high chair ... a woman no older than herself ...

Lory backed a step from the studio window, conscious of the embarrassment of invading a denied privacy, yet unable to break the grip of the scene's fascination. She saw with an artist's eye—"Madonna and the Child"—but her senses were the senses of the woman in the kitchen, hearing the gurgling laughter in a baby's throat, feeling the aliveness of that little wriggling body, smelling the milky aroma of its warm breath, knowing that ...

There was the sound of an opening door on the floor below. She tensed, listening. There were footsteps coming up the stairs and she recognized them as her mother's. Quickly, she crossed back to her drawing board, reaching it as the door at the head of the staircase opened.

Her mother stood in the doorway, silhouetted by the light from below. "I didn't want to disturb you, dear, but Paul called and asked me to tell you that he'd pick you up about six tonight."

Delivering the message from Paul was a transparent excuse. There was nothing urgent about it. It could easily have waited until lunchtime. Her mother had something else on her mind. But she was still standing in the doorway, respecting their understood but never mentioned agreement that the studio was not to be entered without invitation.

"You're not disturbing me," Lory said. "Come in."

Lory Austen's relationship with her mother had never been as she had wanted it to be, and she was sure that her mother was no less dissatisfied, yet they had rarely been able to break down, for more than a passing moment, the indefinable but oddly impenetrable wall between them. Lory had come to accept the situation, not with the bitterness that she might have held if there had been any doubt of love, but with genuine sympathy for her mother's inability to conquer the reserve that made it so difficult for her to express affection, or to create the atmosphere in which affection could be easily offered.

There was no lack of respect in Lory Austen's appraisal of her mother. Humanly, she admired most those qualities that she herself did not possess—stature, poise, strength of mind as well as body, the whole city's recognition of her long service as an effective leader of civic and charitable organizations. Miriam Austen wasted no time on nitwit diversions, concentrating her full energy on such solidly tangible accomplishments as the establishment of the city's first day nursery, the addition of a children's wing to the hospital, and the financial solidification of the county's welfare program, a task that had previously baffled a half dozen supposedly better qualified males.

Lory suspected—never with verification—that some of the channeling of her mother's energy into public service had resulted from her failure to find an adequate outlet in marriage, a feeling that grew out of thinking of her parents as living through a quietly unhappy relationship. She had never heard either of them raise a voice against the other, but neither had she observed any evidence of that warm-hearted sharing that she thought of as the essence of marriage. The blame, Lory thought, was largely her father's. Her own experience had taught her that he accepted expressed love as an invitation to domination. The slightest display of even sympathetic understanding seemed to encourage him to become a difficult and demanding person, selfish and self-centered. When she had come back to Suffolk that fall after she had graduated from art school, her father had seemed a worn and tired man, enervated by the constant frustration of his plans to build his company into the great corporation that he envisioned. Out of sympathy she had let him talk to her—even, in the beginning, encouraged it—not realizing that she was being trapped into displacing her mother as her father's closest confidante. Night after night, using one subterfuge after another, he would call her into the library to discuss his business problems, turning silent if her mother entered the room, seemingly most pleased when he heard his wife's footsteps on the staircase as she finally went upstairs to bed.

Although her mother had never evidenced resentment, it was difficult for Lory to believe that some such feeling did not exist. They were mother and daughter, but they were also woman and woman, and Lory's imagination left no doubt as to how she would feel in a reversal of roles. It was that awareness, almost as much as an understanding of her mother's natural reserve, that had made it so difficult for her to make any move toward the fulfillment of her earnest desire for a warmer relationship. But there was still hope, aroused again now by the evident eagerness with which her mother had accepted her invitation to come into the studio.

Lory cleared a chair, avoiding the embarrassing incongruity of a formal invitation to sit down, then stripped off her smock and began a quick rinse of her hands in the little brush sink behind her drawing board.

When Lory turned back, Miriam Austen was sitting watching her. "Paul told me you are going down to the Elberths' farm tonight?"

"Yes," Lory said, flinching at the realization that she had thoughtlessly failed to share her plans, a little thing that she could have done so easily, and it would have meant something to her mother. "Yes,

Grace is having a dinner party for some friends of Gene's from Baltimore. The man is an artist. I suppose that's why she invited me."

"It's the first time you've seen Paul for a long while, isn't it?"

"Ages," Lory said lightly, flipping a hand towel. "Grace asked him to bring me and there was no way the poor man could get out of it."

"You know that isn't true," Miriam Austen said, earnestly sober. "Paul has called you for dates, time after time."

There was a reaching quality in her mother's voice, a tentative bid for intimacy, and Lory accepted it, pulling over the stool from behind her drawing board, quickly perching herself on it, a teasing smile on her face. "Would you really like to have Paul Bronson for a son-in-law?"

"Don't be silly, dear."

"I might be able to manage it," Lory said, mocking seriousness. "Of course, Dad would have to give Paul control of the company for a dowry but that shouldn't be too high a price to pay to get rid of an old-maid daughter."

"Oh, Lory, you're not!" Miriam Austen said, the words escaping, revealing embarrassment.

Lory reached out for her mother's hands. Their damp warmth evoked a strangely distant memory, something stored from childhood, unremembered since. "Don't worry about me, Mother. I'm all right."

Their eyes met and, astonished, Lory saw the warning mist of waiting tears and the fleeting passage of a tremor across pale lips. She knew then that her mother's concern was not what she imagined it to be. It was something more serious than that.

"What's the matter, Mother?"

There was silence during that moment of moments when the barrier between them was being challenged—and then it yielded to the soft impact of Miriam Austen's low voice. "Lory, what's wrong at the plant?"

"Wrong?"

"Something is. I know it. I'm terribly worried about Grant."

They had broken into new ground now. Lory could not remember her mother ever before, talking to her, calling her father by his given name.

"I don't know what you mean."

"Something's wrong, but I don't know what it is," Miriam Austen said tremulously. "He doesn't talk to me. You know that. He never has. That's the way it started and that's the way it's always been. But he talks to you. I know he does. I've heard you at night—down in the library—"

Her voice broke with strain and Lory, in transposition, could feel the ripping tear that the confession must have cost her mother.

Instantly, they were in each other's arms, the reserve completely down, the only time it had happened since that night when Lory had come home from Maine—and because that was true, the meaning of the moment was heightened to a crescendo of emotion, too high-pitched to sustain and they parted, slowly. But the parting was only physical.

Words whirled through Lory's mind, all tested and discarded. It was impossible to deny that her father talked to her. Even a white lie would be a violation of the moment and the barrier would rise again. "I know that he's been tired lately," she said cautiously. "There are a lot of little things that are worrying him at the plant, but I don't think there's anything serious. I'm sure there isn't."

"There must be, Lory. He's been so—I don't know what it is, but I can always tell when something is really wrong. And he worked so late last night."

Lory tried to lighten her voice. "They were figuring a rush esti-mate—getting in a bid."

"Maybe that's all it is," Miriam Austen said uncertainly, her face showing the inner struggle to regain her poise.

"Honestly, Mother, I don't think it's anything to worry about."

"Perhaps not. I suppose I'm just being foolish. It's such a gloomy day." She turned toward the window.

"It's put a hex on me, too. I haven't accomplished a thing."

Miriam Austen seemed not to have heard. "If anything should ever happen to the company, I don't know what Grant would do. It's been his whole life—everything."

"Nothing's going to happen."

"I hope not."

Miriam Austen stood and the barrier rose with her. "Are your clothes ready for tonight? Is there anything I can do to help?"

"No. I asked Anna to press my dress."

There was only the barest flicker of an expression on Miriam Austen's face as Lory watched her walk toward the stairs, but she could not suppress the lingering thought that her mother had somehow been hurt. Was it possible that so little a thing as asking the cook to press her dress ... no, that didn't make sense. But so many of the crazy things that went on in people's minds didn't make sense ... even in her own ... most of all in her own.

Conscience-stricken, she hurried after her mother, stopping her at the head of the stairs. "Mother, don't worry about him. You'll be go-ing down to the convention in a few days now and you're sure to

44

have a wonderful time, both of you. You know how much good the convention always does him. It will do you good, too."

"You haven't changed your mind?" Miriam Austen asked guardedly.

"Two's company, three's a crowd," she said lightly, without thinking, and hearing herself say it inspired her to go on. "It's about time you two had a vacation without me underfoot."

The tight-held line of Miriam Austen's lips was more of a shock than sudden tears would have been. Lory watched her all the way down the stairs, sensing that she would not glance back. She didn't.

Three

. . . .

THERE ARE THOSE along the Main Line who look upon Will
Atherson as a violator of his inheritance, an opinion that is largely
accounted for by the building that he had caused to be erected to
house the Freeholders Bank & Trust Company of which, by right
of primogeniture as well as ability, he was president.

On a street where every door looks as if it might open at any moment to disgorge some bewigged and gaitered contemporary of Old
Ben himself, the Freeholders Building is indeed incongruous to the
scene. Designed by a disciple of Frank Lloyd Wright, it was judged
by one of the architectural magazines to be an outstanding example
of "the best in unfettered contemporary design, free of any taint of
traditionalism, radical in concept, daring in execution." That, in 1940,
it most certainly was. The later influx of countless chain shops and
supermarkets, all designed in the apparent belief that glass is the
only proper building material, has made the Freeholders Building
seem less unfettered, daring and radical, but it still raises doubts in
certain quarters about Will Atherson.

The more generous Old Philadelphians excuse the building as one
of the lapses of which even a gentleman may be guilty—there was a
"folly" of one sort or another in most of their families—but the other
school of thought holds that a gentleman's folly must, like an affair
with a woman, be carried on in privacy and with discretion. Will
Atherson's folly was unpleasantly public. Although none of his old
customers went so far as to stop doing business with the bank, most

of them still cringed at the necessity of transacting their financial affairs with no more privacy than a fish in a bowl. That sort of thing was accepted in New York, of course, but this was Philadelphia.

Will Atherson had made no attempt to explain what he had done —he wouldn't, he was that kind of man—and, fortunately, his indiscretion was limited to the bank building. He was guilty of no other denials of his heritage. He continued to affect the tweedy dress of a Main Liner—or a British country squire, the two being almost indistinguishable—and smoke a stubby briar pipe which, because of his taciturnity, he was seldom forced to remove from his mouth. He still lived at "Starwood," the old family estate near Devon, occasionally rode with the Hunt, raised dahlias which he exhibited with restrained pride at small local flower shows but never at the big commercialized affairs at Convention Hall, bred hunting spaniels over which he never hunted, and more or less regularly attended the meetings and banquets at which his presence was called for by heredity, tradition, or a good sense of business. In short, there was nothing about Will Atherson or his actions, before or after, that helped even his most ardent supporters to explain away the Freeholders Building.

Standing in his balcony office, looking down through the glass wall at the banking floor, his face was a purposeful enigma. No one who might glance up, either employee or customer, could have known what was on his mind.

Maude Kennard did not glance up. She was at one of the teller's wickets along the north wall, depositing the day-before receipts of the Hotel Ivanhoe. Even from the high angle of his vantage point, she looked unusually smart and trim this morning, not that he hadn't always thought her well dressed and perfectly groomed, but she was particularly attractive today. That red cast in her hair was probably not entirely natural—living in the same house with a wife and three daughters had taught him numerous facts of life—yet, he recalled, her hair had been of a reddish sort even back on that day when he had discovered her. That, most definitely, had been a fortunate coincidence. He'd lunched at The Wharf that day and old Judge Torrant had happened to overhear him say that he was looking for a young woman of good family, but with an interest in business, to take over the catering department at the Ivanhoe. Torrant had suggested Maude Kennard. Everett Pierce, of course, hadn't wanted to hire her. Everett had never been much of a judge of people ... conservatives seldom were ... but they had their place, men like Pierce. He was a balance wheel and they were a good team, Everett Pierce and Maude Kennard. Between them they had developed the Hotel Ivanhoe into an excellent property.

47

She still hadn't glanced up and he stepped out on the balcony and started down the aluminum spiral of the open staircase. Halfway, she saw him and he met her eyes with a temperatureless recognition, allowing his face to be neither warm nor cold. He waited, patiently, liking the way that she was finishing her business with the teller before she turned to talk to him.

Then he asked, "Good day yesterday?"

She smiled. "Not too bad."

There didn't seem to be anything else to say and he was surprised when she asked, "Did Mr. Pierce call you?"

"About what?"

"Our visit this morning from the F.B.I.—or whoever it was."

He shook his head.

"It seems they're checking up on Mr. McCall. Something about his income tax."

He permitted himself a small smile. "That happens to all of us these days."

"Oh, I know," she said lightly. "But, of course, I've had all sorts of fun teasing Mr. Pierce about it. I think I have him half believing that you're liable to come over at any moment and close us down as a disgrace to our fair city—harboring unsavory characters."

"Is that the kind of ogre you make me out to be?"

"Now don't you start teasing him, too, Mr. Atherson, or you'll have the poor man beside himself."

Her forefinger tapped his hand in mock admonishment and he felt the lingering sensation of her touch. She was quite a woman ... irrepressible ... yes, definitely irrepressible ... and clever. Perhaps a little too clever.

"You must be avoiding me," she said as if it were a stored grievance. "You haven't been over for lunch in almost a week—and the last time you swept by me as if I were a jardiniere."

"That would have been quite impossible," he said with grave gallantry. "And I'll be there tomorrow—lunching at The Wharf. I have a guest coming."

"Who?"

"Old friend of yours."

"Really?"

"Grant Austen."

"I'll roll out the carpet," she said with a flashed smile, not as if she remembered Austen as anyone worthy of the flattery of her special attention, but as if she were a willing partner in a pleasant conspiracy.

"You always do," he said in guarded compliment.

48

Her smile flashed off. "Oh, by the way, Mr. Atherson—speaking of Mr. McCall—I know that he's a friend of yours. I've been wondering how *good* a friend."

He hesitated, searching her face for some hint of what she had in her mind. "Why do you ask, Mrs. Kennard?"

"It's purely a management problem and I don't want to bother you with it. It's something that I can handle quite easily myself, but I do want to know whether there was any special background I should have. Is he a *close* personal friend of yours?"

"What seems to be the trouble, Mrs. Kennard?"

Her laughter was a thin veil. "I'm afraid that Mr. McCall is occasionally under the delusion that he owns the hotel."

Will Atherson found himself caught off guard, an unusual occurrence and not a pleasant one. He puffed his briar, hoping that he hadn't betrayed himself by letting his face reflect his shock. He couldn't be sure. Was this only a fishing expedition? Or did she really know?

"I can see how that might be," he said slowly. "At the price you're charging him for his suite it's quite understandable that he might imagine that he was buying the hotel on the installment plan."

It was an unaccustomed attempt at lightness and he was pleased to find that it had been worth the effort.

Maude Kennard laughed, her face free of suspicion. "Perhaps that is the reason. Well, I'll see you tomorrow, Mr. Atherson."

He watched her as she went out, her slim figure slipping lithely in and out of the revolving glass vanes of the door. Yes, she was clever ... but she hadn't gotten away with it this time. He wasn't exactly a fool himself.

He ascended the stairs, satisfaction giving way to concern as his thoughts returned to Cash McCall. Maude Kennard wasn't the only person who had come snooping around for information. Apparently she knew little or nothing about him but there were beginning to be others who did—and the first thing that everyone seemed to discover was that he was in some way tied up with the Freeholders Bank & Trust Company.

In the beginning, when the stories of Cash McCall's financial exploits had started getting around the town, Will Atherson had found a certain satisfaction in having the name of the bank linked with Cash McCall. It did no harm, he thought, to let the word spread that someone backed by Freeholders had turned a nice profit. Of late, however, Cash's deals had become more and more spectacular and the gossip, outdoing truth, had begun to take on a lurid cast. That was *not* good for the bank. It was bad business, particularly for the

49

Trust Department, to let the impression get abroad that the Free-holders Bank & Trust Company had abandoned the tenets of conservative banking practice.

Lately, even the directors of the bank—who had little actual power but a great deal of nuisance value—had begun to ask questions that pried into the details of Cash McCall's activities. He had been able to tell them enough to justify the sizable loans that Cash was being given, but not enough to satisfy their curiosity, nor to counteract completely old man Peregrine's cracked-voice warning that a man that tried to keep secrets from his banker was a man that would bear a lot of watching.

Will Atherson was forced to admit that Cash McCall never told him any more than was patently necessary for the granting of a loan or the handling of some detail of a transaction. What he could not admit—because it was something not fully recognized—was that the very secrecy of Cash's enterprises was one of the reasons why he found his own association with them so intriguing. Attempting to outguess Cash McCall had become a game that, more effectively than anything else, relieved the stolid monotony to which the banking profession had been largely reduced by the endless restrictions of governmental regulation.

Once, a few months ago, he had felt himself duty bound to tell Cash what was being said about him by men like Peregrine, warning him that there were those who interpreted his secrecy as a cloak for shady dealing. It had been a difficult thing to say, even more difficult to sustain against argument, the more so because he so greatly admired Cash McCall's integrity and also because Cash had so quickly countered with a statement that completely expressed his own inner feelings. "I have never felt," Cash had said, "that a man's soul is any cleaner because he launders it in the public square."

All thought of Cash McCall was banished from Will Atherson's mind as he entered his office. His secretary was holding his telephone, her hand over the mouthpiece. "It's General Danvers," she said.

Major General Andrew C. Danvers, U.S.A.F., Ret., was President of the Andscott Instrument Corporation, and Andscott stock was the principal asset of one of the largest estates administered by the Trust Department of the Freeholders Bank & Trust Company. It was a circumstance that always incited Will Atherson's regret that war heroes were not retired with large enough pensions so that it was unnecessary for them to become square pegs in the round-holed upper levels of industry. General Danvers, for all his military genius, had made some bad tactical errors in the management of Andscott Instrument, not the least of them an entry into the home receiver television business, an ill-fated venture that was piling up serious losses and badly depressing the value of Andscott stock.

"How are you, General?" Atherson greeted him, his tone flat, hiding the hope that whatever Danvers had on his mind might indicate a turn for the better.

"Fine, sir! And you?" General Danvers boomed back, evidencing a belief that he had picked up from somewhere that a heartily jovial personality was a necessary attribute of the successful corporation president. "Will, I've just been briefed on a situation that has me a bit concerned. Like to have your slant on it, old man."

"Glad to be of any possible help, General."

"Suffolk Moulding. You're rather closely connected there, aren't you?"

"Yes, I'd say so."

"My boys in Purchasing tell me that we're considering the placing of a new cabinet order with those folks, but that the president—Austen, I believe his name is—"

"That's right—Grant Austen."

"Well, my lads seem to feel that Austen is getting a little shaky financially. Naturally we wouldn't want to foul up our line of supply by extending our relationship where there might be any difficulty of that sort."

"I don't believe I'd be too much concerned on that score, General."

"You wouldn't? Well, as I get the story, this new cabinet is going to require a little capital investment on Austen's part—nothing important, couple hundred thousand—and Austen seems reluctant to go ahead. Concerns us, of course. Can't afford to launch an attack if we don't have strength in our reserves. But you'd say that there was nothing to be concerned about?"

Atherson hesitated. "I would say this, General—an expansion of that size would, of course, be one of considerably more moment to Suffolk Moulding than to a corporation of your size."

"Obviously. But he *could* finance it? Or couldn't he?"

"I'd see no reason why he couldn't. Providing, of course, that he felt it desirable to make the move."

"Of course. Thanks, Will. Just wanted to have your slant. Good to talk to you."

Will Atherson hung up, his mind transposing suspicions. He had suspected earlier that Grant Austen's coming to Philadelphia was no more than so many of his other calls had been, simply an excuse to be invited to lunch at The Wharf. Austen had done that more and more frequently of late, actually making something of a nuisance

51

of himself, but it was clear now that there was point and purpose to his coming tomorrow. If Andscott was high-pressuring him into a two hundred thousand dollar expansion, Grant would be in need of some financing.

The banker relighted his pipe. There was a serious question as to whether or not it would be a sound move for Grant Austen to base an expansion upon the present prospects of Andscott Instrument. On the other hand, if he advised Austen against going ahead, it might further deteriorate Andscott's situation. A new cabinet could mean cost savings and savings were badly needed if Andscott was ever to get its television operation in the black.

He pressed his buzzer. "Bring me the folders on Suffolk Moulding and Andscott Instrument," he said when his secretary appeared. "And be sure the last operating statements are in them."

With the spirit of a man about to sit down at a chessboard, Will Atherson waited for the arrival of the files.

●●●●● 2

Maude Kennard walked briskly toward Broad Street, unmindful of the thin spatter of snow-rain that the wind was whipping out of the gray clouds. She was vibrant with high-keyed speculation, intensely alive to the startling probability that Cash McCall owned the Hotel Ivanhoe.

Intuition argued in the affirmative but she knew that her instinct was not always a reliable informant. But this was more than intuition. She had seen that instant of revelation on Atherson's face, too fleeting to be really studied, too quickly gone to be analyzed, yet it was obvious that something she had said had tripped him up.

"... under the delusion that he *owns* the hotel" ... yes, that was the sentence that had caught him ... the sentence and the word ... *owns.*

She turned the corner and her breath was momentarily snatched away by the wind. Pivoting, she walked backward for two steps and then, recovered, went on. Suppose it were true ... it might not be but suppose it were ... if Cash McCall *did* own the Ivanhoe ...

Park Cady had told her this morning that Cash McCall had suggested bringing the Andscott breakfasts to the Ivanhoe. Would he have bothered to do that unless it meant something to him?

Her mind began a frantic juggle to adjust itself to a new set of circumstances. A moment before she had been proud of her adroit handling of Atherson, the way she had watched him in the mirror reflection in the glass of the teller's cage, not looking up at his balcony office as he had expected her to do, forcing him to come to the banking floor to see her. Now all that was meaningless trickery. Atherson didn't count any more.

And the time she'd spent with Everett Pierce this morning had been wasted effort, too. Or had it? If Cash McCall *were* the owner of the hotel ... and Pierce should make the mistake of trying to throw him out ... yes, that would cook his little apples and good!

Maude Kennard, *General Manager* ... no, *Managing Director* was better. And why not? She *was* the manager of the hotel ... the *real* manager ... everyone knew it ...

Everyone?

A grimace of regret twisted her lips. It had been a mistake to let Pierce handle so many of the arrangements with McCall. But the little fool had been so upset about losing his suite ... and there were so few things that he could do. No, she had to face facts ... letting McCall slip out of her fingers had been an inexcusable error. She hadn't talked to him more than half a dozen times since he had moved in. That had been a bad mistake, but it wasn't too late to correct it.

She was at the corner of Chestnut Street now and remembered that she had promised Everett Pierce that she would see Judge Torrant. Was that still the thing to do? Yes, now more than ever. Torrant had handled the legal work when they had bought the building next door in order to get extra space for the kitchen. Surely he would know who really owned the hotel. But what excuse could she have for asking him?

Did she need an excuse?

A passing man gave her a strangely puzzled look and she realized that he must have misinterpreted her smile.

• • • • • *3*

Clay B. Torrant, Esq., was the fourth generation of his family to hold membership in the Philadelphia bar, a fact that largely accounted for what little legal practice he had. He was usually called "Judge" but that, too, was more a tribute to his heredity than himself. He was by no means an incompetent attorney, particularly in those phases of the law that had once been the backbone of the profession,

53

but he had little aptitude in the skills of the accountant and a hearty contempt—slightly flavored, perhaps, with the taste of sour grapes —for his fellow members of the bar who were following up their lucrative discovery that the best rewards of the "legal" profession fell to those who most successfully searched out ways by which clients could reduce their income tax payments.

Since he was never a busy man, Clay Torrant had ample time to pursue his two diversions. One was his place on the House Committee of his club, The Wharf. The other was the composition of what he called his "papers." He had written a great many of these essays which, although masked as humorous puncturings of the foibles of the legal profession, were penned with an acid bite, never more so than when they were directed at the "Bureau boys," Torrant's appellation for lawyers who went in for tax practice. Some of what he wrote found publication in the *Quarterly* and that gave him much pleasure, all the more because there had been so little happiness in his life.

The message that his secretary had just given him was a sharp reminder of the unhappiest period he had known. Maude Kennard was outside, waiting to see him.

Miss Fitch seemed to share his disturbance. "I told her that you were very busy and I didn't know whether you'd be able to see her or not."

Clay Torrant nodded, accepting the white lie that he was busy but wishing that the subterfuge was unnecessary. He should be capable of simply telling Maude Kennard that he didn't want to see her— but that, he knew, was something he could not bring himself to do. He had never been able to tell Maude Kennard anything that he had wanted to tell her, whether to come or to go, nor to resist any demand that she had ever made upon him—except the one demand that she had never known she had made, nor known that it had imposed upon him the most severe test of character to which he had ever been subjected.

"You are going to House Committee meeting, aren't you?" Miss Fitch asked.

That was a ridiculous question. She knew that he never missed Tuesday at The Wharf, occasionally a Wednesday luncheon when the place was jammed with visitors but never the committee meeting on Tuesday. She must have something else on her mind. "Yes, Miss Fitch. Why do you ask?"

She blushed—which he considered rather silly for a woman of fifty-two, but explainable on the ground of her being a spinster and undoubtedly still a virgin—and he guessed that her concern about his taking a long lunch hour meant that she had an appointment with the doctor who was treating her to alleviate the effects of menopause.

During these last few months, Miss Fitch's flush-faced nervousness had often incited his sympathy and he frequently wished that there was something he could do to ease her burden, but the subject was unmentionable and it seemed that the only kindness he dared show her was to disregard her distress and overlook an occasional error in typing of which, before, she would never have been guilty.

"I have an appointment," she said, flat-voiced. "I could cancel it."

"No need for that, Miss Fitch. And don't worry about getting back. I won't need you until at least two-thirty. Give me about two minutes to clear my desk and then send in Mrs. Kennard."

Miss Fitch went out, stiff and straight-backed, and he could feel the loneliness that she took with her and the loneliness that she left behind. He was glad that it was Tuesday and that he had the committee meeting to attend.

But first he had to see Maude Kennard. In a way the two things were connected—if Maude's father hadn't been a member of The Wharf it would never have started in the first place.

The Wharf—its full and proper name is The Company of the Free Wharfholders—is one of the half dozen clubs that stand at the top of a long list of organizations dedicated to the preservation of a Philadelphian aristocracy. The members, all of whom are fair-minded gentlemen, concede that the Fish House is older, having been founded in 1732 in the reign of George II, but they make no further concessions of superiority on any score.

The exact date of the founding of The Wharf cannot be authenticated because the nature of the original enterprise was such as to demand secrecy and an absence of written records, but it is known to have been functioning prior to 1754. In the beginning it was an organization of merchants whose prosperity depended upon the importation of goods. Thinking themselves penalized by a monopolistic alliance of those who owned the wharfs and controlled the waterfront, the merchants established The Company of the Free Wharfholders. The purchase of a stretch of waterfront was enough of a threat to force the old wharf owners into line, but the organization continued to hold the land as a safeguard.

The land was rented and, according to legend, when the members were unable to agree as to how the rent money should be distributed among the shareholders, a compromise was reached by deciding to use the fund to pay for free meals to be served at noon on all Wednesdays, except those falling during the month of August, in a small waterfront building on the land that the organization had acquired.

As the rental money increased with the growth of the port, the noon luncheons grew to banquet scale. The building being small, there was not room enough to accommodate all the members at tables. The service was from mahogany hunting boards and the meals were stand-up affairs, the origin of a still maintained tradition.

The land was sold to a shipbuilder during the War of 1812—an act forced by patriotism—but the organization persisted. Enough of the profit from the sale of the land was withheld to acquire an uptown residence which was converted into a clubhouse. Long before the Civil War the privilege of membership had been solidly established on the basis of inheritance. There was no more highly prized legacy of a well-born son than a Wednesday noon place at the hunting board of The Wharf, nor no censure so severe as having his silver plate withdrawn from the rack and delivered to his home, that being The Wharf's way of dropping a member who had been judged not to have fulfilled the promise of his blood. The power of dismissal was not only held but exercised and high position was no guarantee of grace. The hopes of one man who might have been governor of Pennsylvania had been blighted one cold morning after a dark night, when he found his silver plate from The Wharf lying on his door-step.

Although most of the members were comfortably well-to-do, wealth was no prerequisite. If it had been, Maude Kennard's father could not have belonged. John Bardon had no more than his salary as a clerk at City Hall, but he had been accepted on Wednesdays as a gentle-man and accorded a special respect for the fact that he kept his desk through all changes in city administration. Bardon had been in a position to do an occasional small favor for Judge Torrant around City Hall and it was in that way that a minor friendship had grown, never to the point where their at-home social life was mingled, yet warm enough so that when John Bardon had come to his law office that hot morning in mid-June of 1932, Clay Torrant had been able to ac-cept the visit as a quest for personal advice rather than legal counsel. There was, in fact, no legal action that could be taken. The runaway marriage of Bardon's daughter, Maude, to young Wilfred Kennard was an accomplished fact. Neither was there much that Clay Torrant could offer by way of personal advice, except to counsel patience and forgiveness. He told John that young Kennard might not turn out to be such a bad sort after all and that there were worse places for his daughter to live than Chicago.

Privately, Judge Torrant had no faith whatsoever in the Kennard boy—his family had been a harum-scarum lot ever since Wilfred's grandfather had married into that Pittsburgh blood—and subsequent events confirmed his stand. Two years later, Maude came back to Philadelphia. Kennard had deserted her. John Bardon died that summer and, whatever the doctors may have said about the cause, everyone knew that it was a broken heart.

Even in those days, Clay Torrant's wife, Margaret, had been an invalid and it had seemed to be in his family's best interest, as well as a humane gesture to the daughter of a member of The Wharf, to offer Maude Kennard a chance to make a home for herself as a combination practical nurse and housekeeper. It was the bottom of the depression, there was no other employment available, and desertion had left her penniless. There had been no other motive in what he had done—he could swear to that on his honor as a gentleman, and subsequently did, after Margaret's neurotic jealousy finally reached the point where he had no choice but to accede to Maude's suggestion that perhaps it would be better if she left.

There had been absolutely no physical basis for Margaret's jealousy. Yet Clay Torrant could not bring himself, then or afterwards, to blame his wife for her imaginings. No matter how fantastic they were, his own had been even more so. In the horrifying dream world of his nighttime mind, he was guilty of adultery. During the aloneness of a hundred nights, Maude's image had invaded the darkness and, together, they had committed erotic sins that were completely beyond daytime belief. Morning after morning he would awaken with a sense of terrible guilt that he could not entirely banish with the sure knowledge that it had all been a nightmare. Night after night he would go to sleep with a silently sworn resolution never again to permit such fantastic dreams, but what happened after his eyes were closed was as uncontrollable as it was unexplainable. Nothing about the whole thing made sense. He was quite certain that he had no suppressed desires, he loved his wife and willingly bore the loss of sexual relationship that her invalidism demanded, and he was sure that he felt no special affection for Maude Kennard. She was twenty years too young to offer comfortable companionship and too sharply shrewd to be appealing as a woman.

Yet he could not escape that secret sense of inner guilt and, through a perversion of that same feeling, he felt that he had somehow wronged her. When he helped her, financially, to start her catering business in Ardmore—done in a way that could never come to light —he did so with the not quite defined feeling of fulfilling a gentlemanly obligation. At least, after that, his dreams were less disturbed.

He had resolved then never to see her again. Unfortunately, Maude could not be told of his resolution and when the building in which she had her catering business burned, it was only natural that she should come to him for help in collecting the insurance.

His finding her a job at the Hotel Ivanhoe had been pure coincidence. Will Atherson had mentioned one Wednesday at The Wharf that he was looking for a bright young woman with a good social background to take over the Hotel Ivanhoe's catering department. John Bardon's daughter, who if she had been a son would herself have been eligible for membership in The Wharf, was obviously qualified.

After that, Maude had come to him occasionally about small legal matters—which he always handled without charge—and he had, of course, seen her several times when the Hotel Ivanhoe was buying a small property from an estate he represented. Then, too, she had come to him frequently during the period when she was campaigning to move The Wharf, after its old clubhouse had been condemned to razing, to the ninth floor of the Hotel Ivanhoe. He had been against the plan at first but, as Maude had done so many times before, she had somehow defeated him and in the end he had found himself supporting her. Admittedly, the move to the Ivanhoe had been a success and he had no reason to look back upon it with regret, any more than he had a sustainable reason for his reluctance to see Maude Kennard this morning. In his submission he accepted the inevitability of punishment, a truth that was seldom admitted in the philosophy of law but often proved by the lives of men.

"Mrs. Kennard," Miss Fitch announced.

He looked up, surprised at the hard edge of his secretary's voice, then not surprised as he remembered that all women acted a little strange when they were going through menopause.

Maude Kennard entered smiling, offering her hand as if it were a gift, and when his fingers closed over it, feeling the warmth and softness, it was like a gift—but a gift that frightened him as he would have been frightened by the offer of a bribe.

There was a sharp clicking sound as Miss Fitch closed the door, a sound like the cocking of a gun.

"How nice of you to see me," Maude said.

"How are you, Maude? Sit down."

She sat quickly, not in the chair across the desk as he had planned but close to him in the chair that Miss Fitch used when she took his dictation, and when Maude Kennard crossed her legs the curve of her left ankle was so close to his leg that he was forced to sit with stiff caution.

"How are the girls?" she asked.

He answered that question and then others, all pointless and delaying, small talk that only heightened his perturbation.

"You look tired," she said.

"No, I'm fine," he said, incongruously wishing that he hadn't worked so late last night on his paper for the *Quarterly*.

"Well, I know you're busy—" she finally said.

"I am a little, this morning," he admitted.

She leaned forward, fingertips to her chin in a too-well remembered pose. "I need some help and you're the only person I can count on—the only person I've *ever* been able to count on."

His reaction was one of on-guard caution, too quick-rising to be kept from showing on his face, and he felt the constraint of embarrassment when he saw from her expression that she was aware of his feeling.

"Please don't worry," she laughed. "All I want is a little advice, personal and not financial—*very* personal."

He picked up his letter opener and sightlessly examined the intricately carved handle of yellowed ivory.

"I do hope you aren't going to think I'm asking something unethical," she went on, the words still overlaid with teasing laughter. "But don't they say that all's fair in love and war? And I've heard you yourself say that one has to be practical to get along in this hard, cruel world."

He attempted a smile, not too successfully. What was she suggesting—that there was a man, that she had fallen in love? Or that some man had fallen in love with her? That would be more like it.

He rolled the letter opener between his thumb and forefinger, thinking, his mind impelled by the professional habit of tracing fact to consequence. If she were to marry, he would be rid of her, once and for all. Then she would stop coming in to see him.

"I want some information about a man," she said.

Hope confirmed, he hurried her by asking, "Who is he? Anyone I know?"

"I think so."

"What's his name?"

"Cash McCall."

The point of the ivory blade dug into the flesh of his palm. Was it possible that she had trapped Cash McCall, as clever as he was? Yes, possible. Men like McCall weren't always as smart about women as they were about money.

"Is he a client of yours?" she asked anxiously.

"No, indeed."

She seemed relieved. "Then there's no reason why you can't tell me all you know about him?"

"I know very little, Maude."

59

"Tell me what you *do* know."

"It's mostly hearsay. Nothing but gossip."

"I want to know that, too."

The prize of release dangled before the eye of his mind. Obviously, the thing to do was to make McCall seem like a very desirable catch. But that, he realized, would be a difficult task, forcing him to submerge all the attitudes and opinions to which he had committed himself with his contributions to the *Quarterly*. In fact, the essay on which he had been working last night was an attack on just such holier-than-thou lawyers as Winston Conway who, despite all his stuffed-shirt pomposity about professional ethics, kept himself in champagne and Cadillacs with the juicy fees that he must be extracting from Cash McCall who was about as sharp an operator as ever took a capital gain.

Still toying with the letter opener, protected from the necessity of an immediate reply to Maude Kennard's question by the pretense of difficult recollection, he decided that it might be possible to tell her the absolute truth, thus not compromising his own honesty—and yet in no way detract from McCall's luster as far as Maude was concerned. Her standards were not his own.

Experience suggested the one thing about McCall that would most impress Maude Kennard. "I suppose you know that he's a very wealthy man?"

"How wealthy?"

"I'd have no way of knowing."

"*Very* wealthy?"

"I'd suspect so—from what I've heard. The gossip has it that he's piled up a fortune of several million dollars in the last seven or eight years."

"Is that possible?"

"Possible? Of course."

"I didn't think anyone could make that kind of money these days."

"Why not?"

"I mean that he couldn't have kept it. Wouldn't income tax have taken most of it?"

He was surprised that she was so naïve. It was out of character for Maude Kennard. Or was she trying to trick him? Perhaps. But then it might be true that she didn't know. There were a great many people who didn't. "That's a rather commonly accepted myth, Maude —that no one can pile up a lot of money these days. The truth is that some enormous fortunes are being made."

"Legally?"

"Yes, legally."

"I know that it can be done in oil—that there's some kind of special tax deal on an oil well."

"Yes, there's a depletion allowance on natural resources. It's very beneficial where it's applicable, but you can still get rich these days without an oil well."

"By greasing the right palms in Washington?"

"Yes, that's happened in a few instances, but it's not the common case. Most of this new crop of big-money men go out of their way to stay within the law. Your Mr. McCall, for example. I happen to know that he's represented by Jamison, Conway & Slythe and Winston Conway isn't the kind of lawyer to miss a loophole. No, Maude, it's quite possible to get to be a millionaire these days and still stay within the law. Goodness knows there are enough of them around to prove it. You should know that."

"I?"

"No man without a millionaire's income could afford to eat in that restaurant of yours."

"They aren't millionaires," she laughed. "They're on expense accounts. It's the expense account business that keeps the Fontainebleau Room alive."

He shook his head. "Not all of them. I noticed the Wilger boys in line last week. Harry and his brother Ed."

"Wilger?" she puzzled. "I don't believe I know them."

"Quite so—and that's typical. These new millionaires make a point of not being known. It's quite different from what it used to be. I recall the *nouveau riche* crop that came out of the first World War. We had one of them move in near our place—vulgar, loud-mouthed, ostentatious, a horrible sort of creature. Bought the old Kinsbury mansion—lovely old house—but he had it painted bright yellow with red shutters. Put an electric sign with his name on it in the front yard. Poor Father couldn't raise a curtain of his bedroom without seeing it. Didn't get a decent night's sleep for five years."

"I can imagine."

"This new generation are a different stripe," he went on, talking more easily now that he had worked the conversation around to one of the points that he had made in what he had been writing last night. "Our new crop of millionaires have their big houses, but not out on the main road. They get away somewhere—a gentleman's farm —but with a screen of trees to hide the mansion house. Of course, that's only one variety—the white-fence crowd—but if you get around the country enough you realize how many of them there are. Been out in Bucks County lately?"

"No."

"Virginia, Maryland, Kentucky, the Eastern Shore—oh, it's everywhere. Over in Jersey, up in Connecticut, around every big city—millions of miles of white fence and behind every mile of it you can be reasonably certain that there's some man who's found a way to make money and keep it. Your Cash McCall, of course, is a different brand—the city type—a big suite in a hotel or in some fancy apartment house. I was involved with one such establishment out on the Main Line. You probably haven't even heard of it—the Carwick Arms?"

"I don't think so."

"Not very many people have. The promoters planned it that way. No advertising—back in the woods on a dead-end drive—gatehouse with a watchman. Do you know what the minimum rental is?"

"I have no idea."

"Eighteen thousand a year. Twenty-four apartments and every one of them rented before the roof was even on the building."

"Makes me sound like a piker," she laughed. "I'm only charging Mr. McCall a thousand a month."

"I'd guess he could pay five times that and still stay solvent."

"But how does he do it? I still don't see how anyone can make that kind of money. I suppose I'm a little stupid, but you make me feel like a babe in the woods. Apparently I haven't known what's going on in the world."

Her earnestness was obviously genuine now and he found his mind warmed by her pleasant recognition of his superior knowledge. He spent a long pause attempting to phrase the principles of the methods by which men like Cash McCall were making their fortunes and then, discouraged by complexity, began to search his mind for a pertinent example. Association suggested the Padua Furniture case ... but that had been McCall himself ... better to keep it anonymous. But why? It was common knowledge all around town, openly discussed at The Wharf. There was no reason why he shouldn't use it as a case in point. "Have you heard of the Padua Furniture Company?" he asked.

"No."

"It was an old furniture company, family owned, factory out in Ardmore. I was involved in a very minor way because a client of mine had acquired a little block of stock through marriage into the family. As is so often the case with those family companies, Padua had been quite successful as long as the old gentleman was alive. After the sons took over, it was a different story. They managed to do well enough during the war but when the demand for furniture slacked off they started going downhill. The company was offered for sale—on the market for some time as a matter of fact—and was finally purchased by Mr. McCall for about a half million dollars. He reorganized it, converted the plant to the manufacture of cabinets for television sets, and then sold out to Andscott Instrument for—well, this is purely rumor but it seems to be fairly well substantiated—something over a million dollars. Of course, he may have put in a little money to convert the plant, but the story has it that he made close to a half million for himself."

"But wouldn't income tax take most of his profit? If he was up in the half million bracket—"

"That's the point, Maude. That half million he made—if he did—wasn't earned income. It was a capital gain. Consequently, the most he had to pay was a top rate of twenty-six per cent. That's one of the easiest ways to make money and keep it these days—work things to get a capital gain."

"But why would those people sell out for only a half million if their company was worth so much more—or were they just fools?"

"No indeed. Actually, that was a good price from their point of view. It was far more than they could ever have hoped to make out of earnings. And they had some tax hurdles, too—a potentially bad situation as far as estate tax was concerned. The deal was made in a way that cleared up that situation."

"But if half a million was a fair price, why was Andscott willing to pay a million?"

"Two reasons. First, McCall had increased the value of the company by getting it into the production of cabinets. Second—this is conjecture, but a likely possibility—the merger helped Andscott's tax situation. There was probably a big loss carry-over to reduce the tax on their own earnings. Then, too, the purchase may have favorably affected their excess profits base. There are many cases, Maude, where one company has bought another company and got the full purchase price back out of tax savings in a very few years. I suppose all that is a little difficult to understand but—"

"Not at all," she said crisply. "It's all a matter of juggling tax situations."

"That's what most business is today."

"Apparently you can make more money by buying and selling a company than you can by operating it?"

"That's often true under today's tax laws."

"And it's all legal?" she persisted.

"Yes. The law provides certain alternatives and the taxpayer has the right to select the most favorable."

63

Her quick laugh was unexpected. "Sounds like nice work, if you're clever enough to pull it off—and apparently Cash is."

He nodded, not missing the fact that she had called McCall by his given name.

Her laughter persisted as an amused smile. "His nickname seems quite appropriate, doesn't it?"

"Nickname?"

"Isn't it?"

"Perhaps so. I'd taken for granted that it was a family name. Had a client by that name once—old Philadelphia family—the Hamilton Cashes."

Her voice picked up the easily casual quality of his own. "What do you know about Cash McCall's family?"

"Family? Not much, I'm afraid."

"He seems very much of a gentleman."

"I'd guess that to be an acquired characteristic. Goes with the type. When you start digging in, you usually find that these new-money men have much the same background—poor family, no opportunities, none of the advantages. That's what gives them the drive to do the things they do, the desperate desire to get ahead and have all of the things they never had as children. It's that desperation that gives them such an advantage over—" Clay Torrant cut himself off, suddenly aware that he had absent-mindedly slipped into something dangerously close to criticism. "Of course, I don't know that that's the case with McCall. As I said before, I know very little about the man, almost nothing."

"I want to know *more* about him," she said, crisply demanding.

"But I don't know any more, Maude."

"There are ways to find out more, aren't there?"

"I'm afraid I wouldn't know how to—"

"Remember that report you showed me on Winkless?"

"Winkless?"

"The man who was threatening to hold up the deal when we were buying the place next door."

"Oh, yes. We got a Lockwood on him, didn't we?"

There was the quick feint of a smile, then the thrust of her voice. "That's what I want you to get me on Cash McCall—a Lockwood report—*complete*—everything they can possibly find out about him."

A protest rose to his lips, but she cut him off. "I'm no fool, Judge. I want to know the score. You can't blame me for that, can you?"

"No, of course not. I—"

"Then you will handle it for me? Good. You can understand why I don't want to be involved myself."

64

"Maude, there may be—"

"I want it as fast as possible. Bill it to the hotel—attention Mr. Pierce. He's authorized it. But no detail on your bill. Just mark it legal services."

Her fingers had wrapped her bag as if she were preparing to leave and he felt the hopelessness of protest, the onrush of the same defeat to which she had always subjected him.

"You're such a dear person," she said, rising. "The one real friend that I've always been able to count on."

He stood, managing a weak smile. Maybe it was the thing to do ... help her all he could ... if she married Cash McCall he would be free ... then she could get her claws into Winston Conway.

"Oh, one last question," she said. "On this capital gains business, you have to hold a property for a certain length of time, don't you? I mean, with a business you'd have to operate it for a while before you sold out?"

It took him a moment to make the abrupt change of thought. "Yes, six months."

"Only six months?"

"That's the required holding period to establish a long-term capital gain."

"Then why do you suppose that Cash has held on to the hotel as long as he has?"

"Hotel?"

She gave him a sharp glance of surprise. "Oh, didn't you know that he owned the Ivanhoe? I thought that you would—from handling the real estate transfer when we bought that place next door. Didn't you represent the owners?"

For a moment his mind was blank. Then he remembered how Atherson had made such a point of not telling him who was back of either the Ivanhoe Corporation or the Frontage Holding Company. So it had been McCall. He should have suspected something like that.

"I had no contact with anyone except Will Atherson," he said and then, feeling a need to explain, added, "As a matter of fact I've never met Mr. McCall."

"You haven't?" Her eyes were charged with pleasure. "I'll have to arrange that sometime." She backed a step, a prelude to departure. "Thanks so much for helping me, Judge. There are so many things that Cash never has the time to explain and I do hate being a silly little ninny who doesn't understand things. That's why I'm so grateful to you for helping me."

"I'm afraid I didn't help you very much."

And then she was gone and he was aware that she had kissed

65

him on the cheek. He waited, wondering why it meant so little. Almost nothing. It was the same kind of kiss that his daughter had given him the night she came to tell him that she was marrying Charles.

Slowly, feeling the weight of age, he walked to the window and watched the rain-wet street until he saw Maude Kennard come out of the revolving door, waiting until she disappeared around the corner. Back at his desk he felt a vague sense of loss, too ephemeral to be crystallized into regret, yet momentarily mind-filling enough to keep him from realizing that Miss Fitch was watching him through the open door.

• • • • • 4

Walking briskly down Broad Street, Maude Kennard felt herself buoyed by the self-satisfaction of a skilled performance. She had all the confirmation she needed that Cash McCall owned the Ivanhoe. There was still much to be learned but she knew enough already to make her realize what had to be done . . . and *quickly*. It took only six months to establish a capital gain. Cash might make up his mind to sell the hotel at any minute. There was no time to lose.

She glanced at the white card that she had taken from her purse and checked the address. Sansom Street. At the corner she saw it— *Laurette* in a flowing script across a small shop window. It had been three months since the card inviting her to attend the dress shop's opening had turned up in her morning mail. Three months was about the right time to wait. There would still be good things in stock but hope would have dwindled to its lowest ebb. By now Rose Bahm would be starting to worry whether the opening of her own shop was as good an idea as it had seemed when she had quit her job at Wanamakers.

Maude Kennard saw that Miss Bahm was alone in the shop—they usually were by the third month—and she noted, too, the hungry eagerness in the little woman's eyes as she came forward to greet her.

"Why, it's Mrs. Kennard," Rose Bahm said revealingly, too eagerly, as if she had accidentally said aloud what she had intended to say only in the aloneness of her mind.

"How nice to see you," Maude said with contrasting reserve.

"This is just wonderful, Mrs. Kennard. You know what I was saying to myself the other day? I was to the Ivanhoe for lunch with this gentleman that's the representative of a very good house—lovely things in his line. Maybe you saw us? He goes to Paris himself every year. Italy, too. Well, this is his very first trip to Philly. You know, like a tourist they all got to see the Liberty Bell and eat at the Ivanhoe? Well, I was saying to myself when I saw you there in the Fontainebleau Room—now wouldn't it be nice if some day Mrs. Kennard would drop in for a minute, just so I could show her the lovely things I got. You know what I mean?"

Her eagerness was a little pathetic. It always was along about the end of the third month. But you didn't dare let it get you.

"I guess it was maybe a couple of months ago," Rose Bahm said as if afraid that her story of lunching at the Ivanhoe hadn't been believed.

"I had intended to come before," Maude said. "Guests do ask about shops, you know, and I never feel right about recommending a place until I've gone there myself."

"I'm glad you could come," Rose Bahm said, her voice finally under control, less the frightened shopgirl now, more the proprietor of the exclusive little shop where every customer received the personal attention of Laurette herself. "Won't you sit down, Mrs. Kennard. I'll show you some of my things."

"Oh, please don't bother, Miss Bahm. I happened to be going by the door and stopped in, that's all."

Desperately quick, Rose Bahm opened a sliding door on a rack of dresses. "It would be a twelve, wouldn't it? Of course it would—that lovely figure of yours."

"I'm sorry," Maude Kennard said, clearly begging forgiveness for having been guilty of an error of impression. "Your things are much too fine for my purse, Miss Bahm. After all, I'm a working girl, too. Fortunately, I do have a good many connections—friends in the business, you know. That does help."

She saw the quick side glance of Rose Bahm's black eyes as she lifted a glass-green taffeta frock from the rack, the moment of hesitation before she turned. This wasn't going to be difficult at all. Rose Bahm was smart. They usually were, girls like that. They'd been around long enough to know that business was business.

Rose Bahm gave her full attention to the dress, spreading the skirt, letting the light ripple and glint on the glassy surface. "Of course, anything you'd want for yourself, Mrs. Kennard, I'd be glad to give you a special discount—twenty per cent."

Maude Kennard resisted the temptation to thank her. That was always a mistake, letting anyone think that they had done you a favor, and could some day ask for a favor in return.

67

She walked to the rack, fanning the fabrics with her fingertips, professionally flipping a cuff to examine the needlework. "Yes, your things are nice, Miss Bahm, very nice indeed. Thank you so much for showing me around." She tucked her purse under her arm in a gesture of departure.

The green taffeta was still in Rose Bahm's hands.

"Just a minute, Mrs. Kennard, please." There was a quality of special pleading in Rose Bahm's voice, a note beyond fear, the cherishing of a vitally important hope. She tossed the green dress and disappeared through the curtain into the back room, returning almost instantly with another dress in her hands. The openness of pleading was gone from her black eyes. They were bright now with something beyond an asking for trade, or favor, or even approval. They were the eyes of the zealot connoisseur, of the near-artist, and what there was in her eyes seemed to flow through her whole body, out of her fingertips and into the dress as she held it against herself, making it come alive with a beauty that was something beyond style.

Involuntarily, Maude Kennard's hand reached out, knowing that she was betraying more interest than was wise, yet unable to restrain herself.

"It's an original Velucci from Milan," Rose Bahm said in a low tone. "I couldn't keep from buying it, even if I don't ever sell it."

"How much?" Maude Kennard asked, keeping her voice flat and matter-of-fact.

Rose Bahm hesitated. "A hundred and sixty is the price I should get—that's low for what it is—but I know you're in a place you can help me, Mrs. Kennard."

Maude Kennard stood purposefully silent. There was only the sound of the traffic outside, the dull rumble of a passing truck and the insistent bleating of even more distant car horns.

"All right, Mrs. Kennard—a hundred dollars to you."

"I'll try it on."

She hardly needed a mirror. It was *right*. She had sensed that the minute her hands had touched the fabric, known it for certain as it slipped over her shoulders.

"It's wonderful for you, Mrs. Kennard, just wonderful."

"Yes, I might be able to use it. Let's see—a hundred dollars with my twenty per cent discount would make it eighty, wouldn't it?"

Rose Bahm looked startled. "But I meant—"

Maude Kennard was already unfolding the bills that she had taken from her purse. Cash was always the clincher. By the end of the third month they always needed cash. "And you'll have it sent over to the hotel right away, won't you? I may wear it tonight."

68

There was a long moment of silence as she counted the bills into Rose Bahm's hand.

••••• 5

Max Nicollet, *chef de cuisine* of the Hotel Ivanhoe, was not what a psychiatrist would call a normal and well-adjusted person. Indeed, had anyone in Max's presence ever argued the point in his favor, he would have screamed them down with denial. The normal and well adjusted he knew only too well. They were the sons and daughters of imbecile pigs whose pocketbooks bought them the privilege of ruining his masterpieces—salting his perfectly seasoned *Caneton Rouennais,* slopping catsup over his *Châteaubriand,* insisting on making his *Tartelettes à l'Aurore* an idiot's delight by ordering it "à la mode."

The colossal wrath that such desecrations generated within the ample vessel of Max's enormous body would, in a more normal man, have been a sure precursor of apoplexy. Max was a man of a different sort. He cherished no myth that peace of mind was an idyllic state. He relished rage. Life was only worth living when he could feel his veins bursting with a fresh supercharge of adrenalin.

There were those among his circle of perpetually frightened assistants—anyone incapable of instantaneously registering fright soon left the circle—who attempted to excuse his more violent outbursts as the result of his "French" temperament. This, unfortunately, Max dared not deny. His professional rating would have dropped like a cold soufflé if he had ever admitted that his father had been a Greek, his mother a Turk, and that he had blithely snitched his present name from the avenue in Minneapolis on which he had acquired most of what he called his "Continental" experience. After all, who could say that North America was not a continent?

That Max Nicollet had become one of the great chefs—and he was —could only be explained by the efficacy of rage as a stimulant to superlative effort. After one of his more volcanic outbursts of distilled venom, anything less than a triumph would have been unthinkable since it would have destroyed his license for a repeat performance. His *Sauce Nicollet,* now famous on more than the North American continent, had been created as the back thrust of his colossal anger at being told that his *Sauce Marguery* was "almost as good" as some money-bagged pig claimed he had eaten at *Coq D'Or* in Paris.

This particular day in Max's turbulent life had started in astoundingly good fashion. Until now, Mrs. Kennard had been of little value to him. She had never before inspired anything beyond the antipathy that he felt toward all employers, slightly enhanced by the fact that she was a woman. But today she had surpassed herself and inspired a first-class rage. Even now, recalling it, his eyes still blazed like a fat-spattered fire. Outstretched in his enormous left hand he held the plump carcass of a faintly blue-tinged guinea hen which he had originally intended as two servings of *Faisan à la Normande*. The carving knife in his right hand cut a whistling arc. A fry cook scrambled for his life. That woman had dared to tell the great Max Nicollet that there was a guest to whom he could not speak! He would show his defiance in a magnificent way. He would create a new dish! He would call it ...

His anger burned into a blue brandy-flame of pure inspiration. There was only one possible name—*Faisan à la McCall!*

With a howl of demoniacal glee he tossed the dead fowl high in the air, bounced it off the low ceiling, caught it, clutched it to his breast like a fierce beast defending its new-born young, glaring back at the frightened faces of his cowering associates.

Mr. McCall was his friend, his very good friend, but even if he had never been his friend before, he would be his friend now.

Max Nicollet threw back his head and howled with the rage of great happiness.

• • • • • 6

Frank, the bell captain, saw her as she came into the lobby and Maude Kennard acknowledged his signal, waiting for him at the bottom of the stairs to the mezzanine.

"You want me, Mrs. Kennard?" he asked anxiously. "I hear you was looking for me, huh? I guess that must have been when I was up unpacking them boxes for Mr. McCall."

"Boxes? What sort of boxes?"

"Books, ma'am. I figured I'd better lend a hand."

She held her smile until the end so there was a moment when he was tricked into thinking that she disapproved. "All right, Frank."

He grinned his relief. "Sorry I wasn't around."

She remembered now what she had wanted. "There's a change to be made on the bulletin board."

70

"You mean shifting that luncheon to the Velvet Room? I got that. Louis gave it to me."

"Oh, good. Is Louis still here?"

"Louis? Yah, sure. Saw him in the Fontainebleau Room not more'n a couple minutes ago. Want me to get him for you?"

"No, give him a message. Tell him not to worry about Mr. McCall's dinner tonight. I'll handle it myself."

Frank repeated, "He's not to worry about Mr. McCall's dinner, you'll handle it yourself."

"That's right."

Everett Pierce was waiting for her, stepping out of his office as she reached the top of the staircase.

"How did it go?" he asked anxiously.

"How did what go?"

"The report on—" He substituted an upward-pointing gesture for Cash McCall's name.

"All right."

"You got it started?"

"Yes."

"How—how long will it be before we get something?"

"Quite a while," she said, deciding that the report, when it came, would serve her own purpose best if Everett Pierce didn't see it too soon ... maybe not at all.

She started for her office, stopping as she glanced over the mezzanine rail, and saw a small woman in a black coat step through the front door and into the lobby. There was a box in her hands. It was Rose Bahm. She was delivering the dress herself.

●●●●● 7

Impatiently, Gil Clark waited in front of the occupied telephone booth in the lobby of the Hotel Conomissing. There was no alternative to waiting. He had to catch Harrison Glenn before he went out to lunch, yet he dared not talk from an open phone. This was the only closed booth that he could remember having seen in Suffolk. Of course this whole business might not mean a thing. It was four years since the president of Corporation Associates had ordered that he was to be immediately informed, without the slightest delay, if Grant Austen ever gave any indication that he might be willing to sell Suffolk Moulding. Four years was a long time. Harrison Glenn's special interest in Suffolk Moulding, whatever it had been then, had probably faded long since. But that assumption involved a risk that was too great to take. It was never safe to assume that you knew what was happening behind the granite mask of that great stone face.

The man who had been in the booth backed out and Gil shoved in past him, put in the call, wincing as the bell clang of the dropping coins deadened his ears, finally hearing the familiar chant of the Corporation Associates' operator, then the cautiously suspicious voice of Harrison Glenn's secretary.

"Is he in?" he asked. "This is Gil Clark and it's important."

The president's voice was wordless, sounding like the rumble of a rock slide.

"Sorry to bother you, sir," Gil said, fighting the unexplainable breathing trouble that he always had when he was talking to Harrison Glenn. "I remember you saying once, sir, that you wanted to know immediately if Suffolk Moulding ever came up for sale." He paused but there was no response. "I don't know whether it means anything now—whether you're still interested or not—" There was still no sound in the receiver clamped to his ear. "Well, anyway it is. I dug it out this morning. Austen is all set to sell—I think to Andscott Instrument. He's coming down there tomorrow to talk it over with Will Atherson of the Freeholders Bank."

Harrison Glenn finally broke his silence. "Where are you?"

"I'm still in Suffolk, sir. I just left Grant Austen and I—"

"Get down here as soon as you can," Glenn ordered, the receiver choked with the power of his voice, suddenly cut off as the connection was broken.

Gil Clark hung up, feeling out of breath, leaning for a moment against the booth wall. Released now from the urgent first-things-first task of getting word to Harrison Glenn, he began to think through all the implications of the situation. His initial reaction to the possibility that Suffolk Moulding might be sold had been one of great relief, but he had been thinking then only of the hope that a new management might relieve the frustration that he had endured because of Grant Austen's pompous fumbling and do-nothing attitude. Now, embarrassingly, he was conscious that he had missed a key point. A new ownership of Suffolk Moulding might well mean that Corporation Associates would lose the account. It would be almost a certainty if Austen let himself be squeezed into selling to Andscott Instrument. It was entirely possible that Harrison Glenn's silence, and then the barked order to come into the office, had been occasioned by that realization. The president might even blame him for having let

Grant Austen get too many eggs in one basket. But how could he have done anything with Grant Austen? Hadn't he tried? Time after time! The file was full of plans and recommendations that Austen had approved and then done nothing about. The guy was solid dry rot from the neck up. And it was a damn shame . . . Suffolk Moulding was a sweet little company . . . all it needed was the right management.

73

Four

.
.
.
.

IS THIS WHAT you want, Mr. Austen?" Miss Berk asked. She held a large blank book, its cracked leather binding proclaiming its antiquity.

"Yes, thank you."

She placed the book in front of him, sniffing at the sight of her smudged fingers, holding her hands away from her body as if the dust of the record room were some lethal poison to which she had been dangerously exposed. "If you won't need anything else, I'll go to lunch now."

"All right," he said, anxious to be alone.

After the door had closed, he took a dust cloth from the bottom drawer of his desk and wiped the binding of the book, careful not to dislodge the label. It was already loose, edge-curled where the old adhesive had lost its bond. The words were lettered in Fred Gunsmann's heavy Teutonic hand, the once-black ink faded to a watery brown. This was the old ledger in which first Fred, and later he himself, had recorded the early stock sales and transfers. From it, Grant Austen hoped to find the answers to some of the questions Gil had asked about what the tax situation would be, particularly on the stock given to Alvin T. Manson and later transferred to Lory.

He opened the record book and the turning cover wiped across his mind like a scene shift in a motion picture. On the marbled end-paper, Fred Gunsmann's hand had repeated the title on the back-bone label, the protected ink blacker here, the memories that it

74

incited as clearly seen as if they had happened yesterday; in truth, even more sharply focused because what had actually happened yesterday, or on any of the days of these last few years, was already dimly vague by contrast with his detailed recollection of those first days, now thirty years past.

He found the first entry bearing his own name; *10/14/22—100 shrs. —value recvd—G. Austen.* That was the stock Fred had given him for working that summer of 1922, putting the electric wiring into the old mill building. Everyone around Suffolk had told him he wouldn't be paid. Fred, they said, was a no-good. There was Pennsylvania Dutch blood in most Suffolk veins and no standard of judgment was more rigidly applied than a man's credit. Fred's wasn't worth a dime. Even worse, he was said to be "slippery." He hadn't paid Henry Diffle for the SUFFOLK MOULDING COMPANY sign, maintaining that Henry should not have put a "U" in MOULDING, but everyone could see that Fred had gone ahead and hung the sign on the old gristmill building down on Conomissing Creek, trying to fool people who didn't know him into believing that he amounted to something. No one was fooled. Everyone knew that SUFFOLK MOULDING COMPANY was just crazy old Fred Gunsmann.

Admittedly, Grant had been disappointed when Fred had paid him off with stock instead of cash, but it hadn't mattered too much. He had graduated from Penn State that spring and was just hanging around, anyway, hoping that General Electric would be taking on some more student engineers in September. Wiring the mill was good practical experience.

September came and went, and there was still no offer from G.E., so he stayed on with Fred, helping to rebuild and install the hydraulic press that Fred had somehow managed to hornswoggle out of a Philadelphia junkyard. He hadn't been much concerned with what Fred was trying to do—at that point it was only the "engineering" that really interested him—until one October afternoon when they made the first trial pressing. The mold was placed in the press, a carbolic-smelling powder spooned into the cavity, and the hot platens brought together. When the press opened, a miracle had taken place. The powder had miraculously become the socket for an electric light bulb.

In the enthusiasm of accomplishment, Fred took some sample sockets to Philadelphia and came back with an order for ten thousand. He forgot until he returned home that he had no money to build the production mold upon which he had based his selling price. Every cent that he could beg or borrow had already been spent. It was then that Grant Austen made the decision that set the whole course of his life. He agreed to talk to Alvin T. Manson and attempt to get a loan. That was the beginning of everything.

Alvin T. Manson was the president of the Suffolk National Bank but, by a life-shaping coincidence, he was also president of the Conomissing Valley Electric Company. The power company was interested in employing a bright young electrical engineer with a burning zeal to talk Suffolk residences into using more light bulbs and electrical appliances. Mr. Manson had been adamant in his refusal to lend money to a proved bad risk like Fred Gunsmann but he was willing, after Grant Austen had agreed to take the job with the power company, to make him a personal loan of two hundred dollars. It was to be repaid, with interest at seven per cent, by the deduction of twenty-five dollars a month from his salary.

But that was not all that had happened on that day. A girl came into Mr. Manson's office. He introduced her as his daughter Miriam. Less than three years later, on the fourth day of June, Miriam Manson became Mrs. Grant Austen. Everyone in Suffolk agreed that the wedding was as nice as anything you'd ever see in Philadelphia and that Miriam had looked surprisingly pretty in her wedding gown. It was whispered about that she was twenty-seven, two years older than her husband, but in the general buzz of excitement, that fact was relatively unimportant to anyone but the town's worst gossips. It was the first time in the history of Suffolk that anyone had staged a lawn party for a wedding reception. For the special guests who followed Alvin T. Manson's whispered instructions to inspect the second-floor sun porch, there was French champagne that was said to be right off the boat and a waiter in a white coat to serve it.

As wedding presents, Alvin T. Manson gave the couple a small house out on the pike beyond the edge of town, a membership in the country club, a maroon Essex sedan, and promoted Grant to assistant manager of the electric company with a substantial raise in salary. The generosity was well timed. Financially, Grant Austen was poorly prepared to undertake matrimony, a fact that he could not conceal from his father-in-law since his bank account was in the Suffolk National. Actually, he made no attempt at concealment. When, later, Mr. Manson asked him if he had ever gotten back the two hundred dollars he had loaned to Fred Gunsmann, he said that it was "settled," simply not mentioning the fact that he had taken stock for the money as well as the wages that Fred owed him.

In the same way, Grant did not tell his bride that he almost invariably stopped at the old stone mill on his way home from work, that his Saturday and Sunday afternoons were more often spent with Fred than at the country club, and that the drawings he worked on at night were ideas for molded parts that Fred might sell to the manufacturers of electrical appliances. No evasion was necessary to keep Miriam from knowing what he was doing. She never asked. She had become pregnant in the third month of their marriage and was interested in little else than her own distress at what she made him feel was a catastrophe for which he was solely responsible. As the weeks went by, she spent more and more of her time at her parental home, often staying overnight. She was there for several weeks before Lory was born and for most of the month that followed.

Grant's mother, with whom he once reluctantly discussed the situation, said that Miriam had been "spoiled by her rich parents" and that she would probably "settle down" after the baby was born. Afterwards, he could not deny that his mother had been right, but he could never completely erase from his mind the feeling that Lory was more his than Miriam's because it was he who had wanted her when his wife had not.

Everything that happened from then on was dated from Lory's birthdays. She was a month past her second when Conomissing Valley Electric Company was scooped up in the gigantic merger that formed the Mar-Penn utilities combine. Alvin T. Manson became one of its eighteen vice-presidents and Grant was offered an engineering job in the Philadelphia main office. Instead, he decided to throw in his lot with Fred Gunsmann at the Suffolk Moulding Company.

Looking back, he always thought of that decision as a courageous act but, admittedly, it was also the product of desperation. His father had died a few months before and his mother had received two thousand dollars from the insurance company. On the strength of a contract that Fred had gotten for the molding of radio dials, Grant had induced his mother to lend him the money to buy a new press. No sooner had the press been installed than Fred began to show symptoms of restlessness. He was an inventor at heart, bored with the repetitive routine of molding the same thing over and over again. Grant saw the danger that Fred might, at any moment, decide to pull up stakes and depart for a more adventurous enterprise. The only way he could protect his own and his mother's investment was to get into the business himself.

Before Lory's third birthday, Fred Gunsmann was gone. One Sunday morning—Grant was on the back porch painting a doll house that he had built for Lory—Fred came hurrying up the alley. He said that he wanted to go to Hollywood and work on an idea he had for three-dimensional motion pictures. He needed money. His half-ownership of the company was for sale.

Something happened then for which Grant was totally unprepared.

77

Miriam had been in the kitchen and overheard the conversation on the back porch. Almost frantically, she had begged him to allow her to give him the money he needed, apparently imagining some resistance that did not exist. Her father, she said, had five thousand dollars that belonged to her and she left the house immediately to get it. She returned empty-handed, explaining that her father had put her money in some investment that couldn't be quickly converted into cash. She was terribly upset—it was the first time Grant had ever seen her cry—and, although disappointed at not getting the money he needed, he was pleased at Miriam's implied approval of his buying out Fred and taking over the company. He made himself believe that it was an evidence of love, and it became one of the too-small store of incidents that seemed to indicate a secret affection for him that Miriam was never quite able to express, either vocally or physically.

That next morning he went to Philadelphia to find some place to borrow money. With no knowledge of Philadelphia banks other than the memory of the name that appeared on the checks he was receiving in payment for radio parts, he walked into the Freeholders Bank & Trust Company. There he met Will Atherson and that had been the beginning of his since unbroken connection and an equally unmarred friendship. Will was young, scarcely older than he was, and they had spent a pleasant forenoon studying the account books that Grant had brought along. Will Atherson had said, after a noontime consultation with his father, that the bank judged the Suffolk Moulding Company to be worth at least twenty thousand dollars. They would be willing to loan six which would cover the five that Gunsmann wanted, plus an extra thousand for working capital. Grant Austen bought a doll carriage for Lory and went home.

Fred was satisfied with four thousand. He said that it gave him as much as he needed to work out his new invention and he was anxious to get going. It was all Grant could do to get him to wait long enough to sign the necessary papers.

Less than a month later, the Suffolk Moulding Company was threatened with a suit for the violation of patents on a molded radio-tube base that had become an important part of the plant's volume. Grant never knew whether or not Fred had been aware of the pending suit—he was inclined to think him innocent—but his suspicions taught him a lesson in the dangers of partnership and, although the threatened suit was amicably settled by a license agreement, he lived through some terrifying weeks, culminating in the October break of the stock market and the almost simultaneous collapse of the Mar-Penn utilities combine. Alvin T. Manson, who had taken Mar-Penn

78

stock for all of his holdings in the old Conomissing Valley Electric Company, crashed into bankruptcy and he carried the Suffolk National Bank with him. Most of Suffolk Moulding Company's working capital was in the closed bank. Grant would have been bankrupt, too, if Will Atherson had not come to his rescue with another loan.

For most businesses, the depression was a hurricane of calamity but for the Suffolk Moulding Company it was a strong fair wind and Grant Austen was in a perfect position to ride with it. Circumstance and temperament were fortuitously timed. He was still in the first flush of the excitement of being in business for himself, thrilling to the adventure that he had never suspected there was in business management. His confidence in himself was at a high point, buoyed by the fact that he had proved he could run the business without Fred. The money he owed was a goad to superhuman effort and both his body and mind had the sustained capacity to respond. He had never thought of himself as anything but an engineer, and it came as something of a surprise to find that he was a good salesman, but as no more of a surprise than the discovery that he could do almost anything else that was required of him. He unraveled in short order—as the owner of a small business must always do in order to be successful—the mysteries of dozens of specialized tasks that the big corporation president can delegate to his vice-presidents. Grant Austen became a whole executive staff rolled into one man. He hired young engineers to help him develop his ideas but delegated little responsibility. The important decisions were all his own. New orders came in as fast as he could expand the plant. More machinery was constantly being installed, much of it bought at bankruptcy prices and set up in a new building that was erected at depression cost levels.

On Lory's tenth birthday he gave her what she said she wanted more than anything else in the world—"a studio like Miss Tassman's." Eloise Tassman was a commercial artist who lived at Chester Springs. Grant had employed her to model some designs for watch boxes and, on one of his trips to inspect the work in progress, he had taken his daughter along for the ride. After that, Lory always insisted on accompanying him, entranced by the little studio that Miss Tassman had created by remodeling an old smokehouse on the farm where she lived.

Miriam had said that building a "studio" for Lory seemed rather silly—a ten-year-old child couldn't even know what the word meant —but he had gone ahead and built her a little playhouse in the back yard. If Lory wanted to call it a "studio" what harm was done? Anyway, he could afford it. Suffolk Moulding was beginning to make

79

enough money so he didn't have to worry about small extravagances.

He took gambles during those early years but more paid off than failed. His percentage was good and that was all that success required. His only serious mistake was taking in Alvin T. Manson as Secretary and Treasurer. He did it because he thought Miriam would appreciate it as a gesture of kindness to her father who, since his bankruptcy, had been living on the few dollars that he could weasel away from the referee—plus, Grant Austen suspected, a portion of the too-generous allowance that he gave Miriam to cover her personal and household expenses.

The announcement that he had given her father a job had brought no response from Miriam except an expression of cold shock. He had hoped that what he had done would somehow draw him closer to his wife but it appeared to have produced the opposite effect and, since she offered no explanation, the only conclusion he could draw was that he had committed what was, to her, the unpardonable sin of forcing her adored father into a position of demeaning subservience.

Two years later, after another in a series of his father-in-law's pompous fumbles had cost the company an important customer, Grant Austen finally accepted Will Atherson's suggestion that the old man be "retired." To ease the blow, he gave him a block of stock in the Suffolk Moulding Company, the dividends from which would keep him comfortably for the rest of his life. The gift of the stock was not a part of Will Atherson's suggestion but Grant Austen made it with the hope that Miriam would be pleased. If she was, she never gave him the satisfaction of telling him so.

It was then, for the first time—and he remembered it as if it were an event, even recalling where he had been when the thought first came into his mind—that Grant Austen asked himself whether he had ever really loved his wife. He could not be sure. If it were true that his marriage was not happy, it was equally true that it was not actively unhappy. He had none of the petty complaints against his wife that he heard voiced by other husbands. With the same stubborn tenacity with which he pursued the never-defined ideas upon which his business was being built, he clung to the hope that eventually something would happen to bring about the fulfillment of his vague dream of what a happy marriage would be. He tried to do things to please Miriam but was handicapped because she so seldom expressed a desire for anything.

When, to his surprise, she suggested a European trip with Lory in the summer of 1939 he agreed at once, even though it meant having his daughter away from him for six weeks. It was impossible to take the trip himself—that was the summer they were getting started with extrusion molding—but Lory's letters were the next best thing to actually having her with him. She wrote a letter every day. Miriam sent an occasional postcard.

When they came home he had a surprise for them. He had already broken ground for a new press building. Lory laid the cornerstone on August 24, 1939. He had a photographer come up from Philadelphia. On the night of the day that the prints were delivered, he heard the sound of weeping and discovered Lory in tears, a torn print of her picture crumpled at her feet. After long minutes of gentle prodding he finally wormed out her adolescent consciousness that she was not a pretty girl. He tried his best to make her think differently but was aware that he accomplished little. He didn't know the right words to use and, even more seriously, there was the handicap of possible truth. He knew that he couldn't judge—to him she was a beautiful child—but his fact-loving mind recalled how many people had remarked on her resemblance to him and so he accepted the blame for her unhappiness. If, as Miriam afterwards implied, he was from then on even more extravagant in the things he did for his daughter, there was a secret reason. Again, he could afford it.

In February of 1940 he bought out two small competitors, dismantled their plants and moved the machinery to Suffolk. The expansion was well timed. War clouds were gathering and orders soon began to rain down. Earnings leaped to a level where he could have paid himself an annual salary of $100,000—the hallmark of a *Big Business* president—but Grant Austen knew from his increased contact with the world of Washington, New York and Detroit that the Suffolk Moulding Company was a painfully small example of what was referred to as *Small Business*. His standing in the world of industry was the sociological equivalent of an underprivileged sharecropper. At industry banquets, which he had not before had the inclination to attend, he found himself a lost soul at the pre-dinner cocktail parties, and was invariably seated at a table behind one of the balcony posts. His name was never read off when committee appointments were made. When he went to Washington he could no longer get a reservation at one of the best hotels. From overheard lobby conversations he deduced that he was an "outsider" without "connections." He didn't know a single Congressman, bureau-topping official or White House satellite well enough to be called by his first name. He didn't even have a "Washington representative." None of his shortcomings in any way stopped the flow of business that kept his factory flooded with orders, but Grant Austen was nevertheless disconcerted.

In June of 1942 something serious happened. The Chadwick

School rejected Lory's application to enter in September. They wrote a trying-hard-to-be-nice-about-it letter, saying that they were sorry that prior applications precluded the possibility of accommodating his daughter. Grant Austen knew better. There were other men whose daughters had applied afterward and been accepted. There was only one possible conclusion—he wasn't a big enough man to count. The Chadwick School was like so many of the men he met in Pullman club cars—they had never heard of the Suffolk Moulding Company. Being president of a small company didn't mean a thing. There were thousands of little one-man outfits like Suffolk Moulding and every one of them had a president. He saw himself then in a new perspective and it was a sharp-roweled spur to his ambition.

Lory insisted that Chadwick didn't matter, that she would prefer to stay on at Suffolk High, but he didn't believe her. Again, as when she had seen her pictures, he blamed himself. She seemed a perpetually lonely child and it was easy to imagine that quality of character as something inherited from him. Since his mind was so constituted that it could not contentedly accept the unexplainable, he evolved an explanation for Lory's tendency to spend too much time alone and her failure to make friends. It was, he reasoned, because she was so small for her age. That made sense. In his own high school days he hadn't been able to make the football team because of his lack of weight. But he had stuck it out and in his senior year had won his letter. Lory didn't seem to understand that loneliness was something that had to be licked. She was always running away, hiding herself in that little studio, spending her time making drawings instead of out making friends. That was why he had been so anxious to get her into Chadwick. Something had to be done to break the child out of her shell. He shrank from the prospect of separation but was willing to trade his own loneliness for the curing of hers.

Although Chadwick was unattainable, he finally managed to enroll her in Mount Oak, thanks to Bruce Martinson whom he had been lucky enough to talk into accepting the Suffolk Moulding Company as one of the firms he served as Washington representative—most of Bruce Martinson's other clients were much larger companies—and after the way Bruce handled the Mount Oak affair with a single telephone call there was no doubt that he had the right connections. Mount Oak was every bit as good as Chadwick, in some ways even better. There were the daughters of a lot of big men at Mount Oak.

Except for the black-market Buick—Miriam had said Lory was too young for her own car—his wife had seemed to approve of sending their daughter to Mount Oak. At least, during the weeks after Lory left and the two of them were alone in the house for the first time in sixteen years, their life together changed for the better. He took her along when he went to New York in December for the N.A.M. convention and it was the best week of their married life. They had a theater party every evening—except the night of the big banquet —and Miriam did a surprisingly good job of handling herself as the wife of a corporation president. Their guests were other presidential couples, all of whom outranked them in corporate net worth, but Miriam held her own. She was pleasant and friendly without sacrificing either dignity or poise. During the days while he was attending convention sessions, she managed to get acquainted with two women whose husbands were both officers of companies that had their securities listed on the New York Stock Exchange.

On one of those days, Grant Austen made a secret shopping expedition during the noon recess and bought a diamond clip. It had taken a certain amount of courage to enter Tiffany's—he was not sure that they would ever have heard of the Suffolk Moulding Company —but he was treated with respect and his check was accepted without question.

He had intended to keep the clip for Miriam's Christmas present but they were so happy together that he decided, on their last day in New York, to give it to her so that she could wear it at the banquet. They were sitting that night at the table of the Regional Vice-president who, just before noon, had asked Grant to serve on a committee charged with drafting a program for *Post-War Planning for a Greater Small-Business America.*

Several weeks later the committee had its initial meeting. It was the concensus of opinion, duly recorded in a unanimously adopted resolution, that there was no essential difference between post-war planning for *Small Business* and post-war planning for *Big Business.* The committee decided, therefore, that there was no need to hold more meetings. That was all right with Grant Austen. It was not his post-war plan to go on being *Small Business.* But the meeting was not a waste of time. He had learned that "contacts" were important and he made some good ones.

The only flaw in the day was that the committee meeting reminded him of that week in New York and he couldn't help wondering why Miriam was so different back in Suffolk. He resolved to try to find an open weekend when he could again take her to New York—some week when he didn't have to go down to Washington— but that was hard to do. Washington took a lot of his time that spring. Mount Oak was only seventy miles away and Lory usually drove in and had dinner with him. Every time she came, there were more recognized faces to point out to her. In one evening they saw Jesse

Jones, John L. Lewis, Harold Ickes, Henry Wallace and a lot of top men from big corporations. One of the vice-presidents of General Electric stopped by their table in the main dining room of the Carleton and Grant recounted how close he had come to being a G.E. man himself—how only a quirk of fate had intervened—and the G.E. vice-president had said that what had been Suffolk's gain had been General Electric's loss. Lory got a great kick out of that.

She never said anything any more about not being pretty and he was grateful that she was beginning to show signs of maturity, the realization that there were more important things in the world than a pretty face. Lory was smart. She was getting straight A's at Mount Oak. He was disturbed by her talk about going to some art school after she finished—he secretly hoped that she would go to Wharton Business at Penn—but when he found out that she was planning to study Industrial Design he stopped worrying. There was a big need for that in the plastics industry and Lory would be a real help to him when Suffolk moved into consumer goods after the war.

That spring, before Lory came home to spend her vacation, he bought Orchard Hill, the town-touching estate of the Cathart family, the once wealthy owners of the now defunct paper mill. The big old house demanded considerable remodeling and refurbishing but, despite wartime restrictions, it was rapidly accomplished and in a manner discreet enough not to arouse any unnecessary talk around Suffolk. Even the swimming pool slipped into the back lawn with almost no one aware of what was happening.

Miriam approved of the house—at least she said nothing against it—and it was obviously an advantage to her to have a nice place to hold all of her meetings. She had become more and more immersed in community activities—Chairman of Home Service for the Red Cross, Vice-President of the Community Chest, a director of the hospital, and active in the Planned Parenthood League. His contributions grew to substantial proportions but he wasn't too much concerned. As was frequently pointed out at N.A.M. meetings, every industrialist had a social responsibility—and CONTRIBUTIONS TO CHARITY was, of course, a deductible item.

When there were weekend guests at their home—and they became more and more frequent as he broadened the circle of his influential acquaintances—Miriam was a pleasant hostess, vaguely recalling that week they had spent together in New York, but it became increasingly apparent that she lacked a talent possessed by the wives of other corporation presidents to whose Detroit, Wilmington and Long Island homes he had been invited. Miriam never seemed to be able to spend money without worrying about it, and she had an unfortunate tendency to fuss over unimportant little details like meat-rationing coupons and whether she should order a three-rib or a four-rib roast. She couldn't seem to accustom herself to the fact that, at the scale of living to which they had risen, an extra rib had no significance whatsoever.

Lory worked at the office that summer, drawing charts for Ralph Andrews, the L. & E. Whitford man who was working on a projection of the company's post-war expansion. L. & E. Whitford Company was one of the top firms of management engineers and Lyman Whitford himself was supervising the Suffolk account, which was a good indication of how the firm sized up the future of the Suffolk Moulding Company.

Eventually, the locked bottom-right drawer of Grant Austen's desk was reserved for a top-secret notebook. Its scarlet label proclaimed it the POST-WAR PROGRAM FOR THE EXPANSION OF THE SUFFOLK MOULDING COMPANY. At first he had held back from having his hopes committed to paper but, afterwards, he had been glad that he had let Lyman Whitford talk him into it. The neatly typed words gave his dreams the pleasant substance of reality. The language was a little fancy for his taste—he didn't want to sound like a New Deal economist—but still and all it was a good idea to know where you were going. And Lory thought it was wonderful. Her eyes sparkled with excitement when, coming into his office in the evening after everyone else had gone, he would read paragraphs out of the POST-WAR PROGRAM and explain what they meant. After the war they would move into proprietaries—nationally advertised consumer goods—dishes, appliances, housewares. There was no future in being only a custom molder of plastic parts for other manufacturers. As the POST-WAR PROGRAM said, "The future of the Suffolk Moulding Company lies in its manifest destiny as a major supplier of many articles of high utility to the American Buying Public."

Before Lory went back to Mount Oak in September he told her that he was increasing her allowance but she said she didn't need it. She still had over four hundred dollars left from last year and all of her salary from the summer was untouched. So, very formally and both of them having the time of their lives, he sold her a block of stock in the Suffolk Moulding Company, the stock to be paid for out of her increased allowance.

There was a legend on the flyleaf of the POST-WAR PROGRAM that read, "To be Activated on the Day of Victory," a phrase that conjured the sound of whistles and bells signaling the beginning of a return to good old American Free Enterprise—*freedom* from controls, *freedom* from raw material restrictions, *freedom* from government interference—what Lyman Whitford so aptly called, "the freedom of self-determination."

It didn't happen that way. V-J Day was an anticlimax, dulled by the anxious but certain anticipation that had begun with V-E Day in May. When the officially proclaimed Day of Victory finally came, the bells were dutifully rung and the whistles blown but everyone knew that it didn't mean anything. There was more fear than exultation.

The POST-WAR PROGRAM FOR THE SUFFOLK MOULDING COMPANY stayed in the unopened drawer of Grant Austen's desk. Cancellations had cut back the plant to where most of the presses stood idle. Men who had been foremen dropped back to press operators and were happy to have even that much of a job. For the first time since the start of the war, Grant Austen made some customer calls himself—high level, of course, president to president—and found that his salesmen were right. Profit had to be cut almost to the vanishing point to get an order. There was excess capacity all over the plastics industry. This was no time to expand. All he could do was to wait until things settled down and got squared away.

Lory had started at Prather Institute of Art the September before, but not until after he'd had a good straight talk with Harley Cunningham, the executive director, and assured himself that Mr. Cunningham was a fine man. After measuring Mr. Cunningham's caliber, he accepted an invitation to serve on the Institute's Advisory Council, an appointment that Mr. Cunningham assured him would take very little of his valuable time since the Council seldom if ever held a meeting.

Some of the drawings that Lory brought home from Prather disturbed him. He knew that art schools had classes where the students drew from nude models, but he couldn't see the point of exposing an innocent young girl like Lory to that sort of thing, particularly when it had nothing in the world to do with Industrial Design. There were several other times when he was tempted to drop a note to Harley Cunningham, but the only time he ever did was after his discovery that Lory had been made to spend several weeks working on illustrations for some book about one of those heathen religions they had over in India or somewhere. He had assumed, he wrote, that Prather was a good Christian institution and hoped that there'd be no repetition of anything like that. Harley Cunningham had replied that the whole thing had been a mistake and that the responsible instructor had been severely reprimanded.

With Lory in Philadelphia, Grant Austen saw Will Atherson more frequently, often dropping in on Wednesday so that he could have lunch with Will at his club, The Wharf, whose clubrooms had recently been moved to the ninth floor of the Hotel Ivanhoe. The members of The Wharf were big men in Philadelphia—it was an honor even to be invited as a luncheon guest—and, looking around the room, Will told him that half of the men were in exactly the same spot he was, ready to go ahead and expand as soon as that mess in Washington started to clear up. Grant thought that the situation might improve after the election in November. If the Republicans got control of Congress things would be different.

The Republicans did get control, both the House and the Senate, and when Lory came home for the holidays, Grant Austen showed her the preliminary sketches for the new plant addition to handle melamines and butyrates. The architect was going ahead with the detailed plans and contractors were working on tentative bids. Ground would be broken as soon as there was something definite from Washington on a tax cut.

It was a year after that next April when the Senate finally passed the tax bill, but no ground was broken for a new Suffolk building. The final bids were almost fifty per cent higher than the preliminary estimate made two years before. Obviously, a period of inflated costs was no time to build. And it was becoming clearer every day that a depression was overdue.

Fortunately, things weren't too bad at the factory. It was beginning to look as if the Andscott business might turn into something really big. Of course, it was all custom molding, not the nationally advertised consumer goods that the POST-WAR PROGRAM called for, but now that taxes had been cut there was a little money to be made—not enough but every little bit helped—and piling up a good husky surplus wasn't a bad idea. Lyman Whitford argued that he was taking too much Andscott business, getting too many eggs in one basket, but Whitford was always inclined to take the theoretical instead of the practical approach, and Grant Austen reasoned that if he had the cash it would be easy enough to move ahead when the time was ripe. Then, after the expansion, the Andscott business could be brought back into balance again.

Lory graduated from Prather Institute in June and the Athersons gave her a big party at their Main Line country home near Devon. Although Grant Austen had always considered Will Atherson one of his closest friends he had never been invited to his home nor, until the evening of the party, had he ever met Helen Atherson. He had, however, not considered that strange since he had always accepted Main Line society as something remote from the orbit of his own life and generally unattainable. To his surprise he found himself

87

treated with pleasant equality, his pleasure diluted only by the revelation that Lory, without telling him about it, had already been at the Athersons' twice before with some of her classmates from Prather, one of whom was a niece of Mrs. Atherson's. Lory had also made some other friends among old Main Line families, again without ever having told him, thus creating a little world for herself of which —unthinkingly, of course—she had not made him a part.

There were other revelations that night. As he watched his daughter, Grant Austen became aware that Lory had changed. She was no longer the sum total of all of the superimposed images of her childhood that he had stored away in his mind. As a child she had seemed, despite her small stature, to be surprisingly mature, older than her years. Now, almost as if there had been some unnoticed period of arrested growth, the years seemed to have overleaped her development. There were flashed moments that night when she seemed astoundingly young, her laughter rippling and her eyes shining like a child's. Of course some of her friends from the art school acted like kids, too—that was to be expected of them, but not of Lory. A number of people remarked about it. Even Will Atherson had said, "Grant, that little girl of yours is a mighty sweet youngster." He had made no reply—there was nothing that could be said—but it disturbed him that Lory was making that sort of impression. She had always been so solid before, feet on the ground, and he wished that he hadn't been so backward about advancing his suggestion that she go to Wharton Business. Allowing her to go to Prather had probably been a mistake.

Miriam was no help at all that night. When Lory had come to them, all excited about a chance to spend the summer at some art colony in Maine, Miriam raised no objection. It was probably true, as Lory said, that some of that fine arts stuff would help her with her Industrial Design, but he couldn't understand why she had to go off to Maine to do it. There was as pretty scenery right around Suffolk as you'd find anywhere.

He had tried to talk to Miriam about it but she hadn't seen what he had seen—the way Lory had changed. Miriam couldn't seem to understand how important it was to get Lory home and in the right atmosphere as soon as possible. He went as far as he could. Lory would have blamed him if he had tried to keep her from going after her mother had offered no objection.

It was a bad summer, hot and muggy, and the day after Lory left for Maine, Dewey was nominated instead of Taft. From then on everything went wrong. U.S. Steel caved in for the third round wage increase and there wasn't anything he could do but ride along—a straight nine per cent right through the plant. The C.I.O. Rubber &

Plastic Workers already had an organizer in town. The television business was boomed by the conventions and Andscott boosted its orders, but they had no sooner stepped up the schedule than Congress passed a fool law that gave the Federal Reserve Board the power to clamp down on installment sales. The only bright spot was in the future—the communist investigation was licking Truman. After that "red herring" business, Dewey was as good as in the White House. But even that prospect wasn't enough to dispel the strangely ominous feeling of impending disaster that haunted Grant Austen. There were many days, more and more as the summer wore on, when there was no letter from Lory.

It was the last week in August when his premonition of disaster crashed down upon him with the terrifying confirmation that his fears had not been unfounded. He had been in Washington that day with Park Cady, Andscott's Vice-president for Merchandising, trying to get to the right people in F.R.B. about the installment selling regulation. It had been almost midnight when he had gotten home. Miriam had met him at the door, blocking the way, her voice a voice he had never heard before. "Lory is home, Grant, and I don't want you to talk to her."

He pushed past his wife as she attempted to block the staircase, frightened when Lory didn't answer the knock on her bedroom door, then crushed by the blow of realized tragedy when Miriam had finally told him, "She's had a love affair, Grant. If you hound her about it—if you ever even mention it to her—I'll leave you!"

It was an empty threat, not because Miriam didn't mean it—her eyes vowed that she did—but because there was no spirit within him that was left to be killed. He had failed Lory. When she had needed him most he hadn't been there. That in itself was a kind of dying.

But as the days went by, in the warmth of Lory's unspoken forgiveness, there was a new relationship with his daughter. She had changed, mature now in a way that she had never been mature before. It took a long time before he could block his mind to the gagging realization of why she had changed, but by then they were closer together than ever, drawn by the bonds of a mutually survived tragedy.

When she finally asked to have the second floor of the old stable remodeled into a studio he knew that everything was all right again. He hired the best architect in Philadelphia and he really made a job of it. Lory was as pleased as Punch. A publishing house in Philadelphia commissioned her to do some illustrations—it didn't really amount to anything, just some kids' book, only a couple hundred dollars—but Lory was as happy about it as if it had really been something big. Lory's happiness was all that mattered. Money wasn't important. The older you got, the more you realized that. He had recently obtained a new Andscott contract that would gross close to a million—and it didn't mean a thing, particularly with the way that Truman, unbearably cocky after his victory over Dewey, was demanding six billion dollars in new taxes. It was a time for caution. All anyone had to do to know that was to read *Dillingham's Washington Letter* every Monday morning.

L. & E. Whitford Company wasn't showing up too well—Lyman Whitford was getting a little too big for his breeches, seldom coming to Suffolk himself any more, not even mentioning Suffolk Moulding in a speech he made at the Congress of Commerce. Fortunately, about that time Harrison Glenn happened to drop in. Glenn was one of the really big men in management counseling, the kind of man who didn't say much but what he did say carried a lot of weight. A month later, Suffolk Moulding signed up with Corporation Associates and Harrison Glenn, as he had promised, put one of his best men on the account, young Gil Clark. It was a good move. Harrison Glenn had a lot of contacts. Suffolk Moulding hadn't been a Corporation Associates client for more than a month when Grant Austen was named as Chairman of the Inter-Industry Committee of the Congress of Commerce.

He dusted off the plans for the new factory, telling Gil that he wanted to be ready to move when the price break was deep enough. The smart time to build was in a depression. Wasn't that when he had built Suffolk Moulding? He had hired bricklayers for eighty cents an hour—and bricklayers who really laid bricks, not these slow-motion holdup artists that got two-eighty an hour and had a union that would let them lay only so many bricks a day. This was no time to build factories.

Even going ahead with the new Administration Building had made a deep hole in surplus—but Gil agreed, and Harrison Glenn backed him up, that the office building couldn't wait. It was bad business to give customers the impression of the Suffolk Moulding Company that they were getting from his old office in the mill building.

That year at the annual meeting, Grant Austen was elected Fourth Vice-president of the American Association of Plastic Molders. The next year he was Third Vice-president, working his way up the ladder to the Presidency—and it would have happened if Heckledorf hadn't been chairman of the nominating committee that year. There was a lot more underhanded politics in the Association than most people realized. Heckledorf had his gang and they thought they *were* the Association. But there were plenty of members who knew what was going on and realized that Grant Austen should have been

Second Vice-president. If that hadn't been true, they wouldn't have given him that testimonial dinner and presented him with a scroll honoring his *Quarter Century of Outstanding Service to the Plastics Industry*. Andscott had taken a whole table at the dinner and, as Harrison Glenn had said, it was indeed a tribute when a man's customers paid twenty dollars a plate for the privilege of honoring him.

Disillusioningly, it was less than a week later that Andscott had started getting new bids on the T21 moldings and he'd been forced to shave the unit price another six cents in order to hold the business. Cost savings would have justified the price cut if he had seen his way clear to spend sixty thousand dollars on the kind of press that the competitive bidder planned to use, but how could anyone have known then that business was going to hold up the way it had?

Grant Austen looked up at the plaque on his wall. A quarter century was a long time. Actually, it was more than that now—thirty years if you counted back to those first days with old Fred.

It was a long time since he had heard from Fred, longer than he realized until he stopped to think about it, no word since that letter some time just after the war started. Fred had been in Tulsa then, fooling around with some new invention. Grant Austen had replied to his hard-luck letter with a check for five hundred dollars. The check had been cashed but he'd never heard again from Fred. It didn't matter. The five hundred had long since been charged off as a "bad debt." After tax it didn't mean a thing. And he could afford it. Fred was probably dead. He never had been much of a business-man—four thousand dollars for a half interest in the Suffolk Moulding Company. If he'd had sense enough to hang on, he could have been a millionaire, too.

••••• 2

Gil Clark had been waiting for twenty minutes in the anteroom of Harrison Glenn's office, rankled by the delay, thinking how pointless it was that he had not broken his speed run from Suffolk with a stop for a sandwich. He was beginning to feel the dull throb of a head-ache, more acceptably chargeable to hunger than to the nervous tension that he always felt while waiting to enter the president's office. Acceptance of the alternate explanation would have been an admission of a fear that he was certain did not exist. He was not afraid of Harrison Glenn—there was no reason why he should be—but there was, invariably, this belly-tightening mixture of tense anticipation.

There was one explaining association. It was the same way he had always felt when, as a boy, he had been called into the library to face his grandfather, often as not to be offered some kindness, rarely for censure, but always feeling something that was vaguely associated with his Sunday School confusion at the frightening duality of a deity that was said to be the fountainhead of man's love for man, yet was reputed to be capable of surpassingly cruel punishments for minor transgressions.

His grandfather was one of the few men for whom Gil Clark had felt almost total admiration. Harrison Glenn was another. Although they were unlike physically, both had been men whom it was impossible to imagine as ever being guilty of any act that would breach a gentleman's code of honor. It was Harrison Glenn's reputation for unflinching integrity that had brought Gil Clark to Corporation Associates. After two years with George Farrar and Nick Peters at Simonds, Farrar & Peters had all but destroyed his faith in personal honor, Harrison Glenn had restored it.

A buzzer sounded and Miss Neal said, "You may go in now, Mr. Clark."

He stood up, straightening his tie, feeling as if the breath in his lungs was unexpellable, tentatively reaching out to the doorknob. The door swung to the touch of his hand and he saw Harrison Glenn sitting at his desk, the giant body inhumanly motionless, making him seem more than ever an unyielding monolith rough-hewn out of some coarse-grained stone, a monument to the endurance of man's belief that silent immobility was somehow a demonstration of wisdom. Gil had never made up his mind whether or not Harrison Glenn was as wise as he seemed, but he knew that there were clients of Corporation Associates who paid large fees to have him sit at their conference tables and considered themselves well compensated by his presence, even though he often sat through a whole afternoon without uttering a word. In any event, surpassing wisdom was not, by Gil Clark's standards, a prime requisite for an admirable man.

"Sit down, Clark," Harrison Glenn said.

Gil sat.

"What happened?"

"Not much more than I told you over the telephone, sir."

Harrison Glenn's giant hand went up to touch the roughly folded edge-seam of his ear. "You think Austen will really sell?"

"Yes sir, he—definitely, sir."

"Did he say so?"

"Say so? Of course."

"He said that he was ready to sell?"

"Yes, he—well, we spent a half hour or so talking about what his tax position would be. He wouldn't have gone that far if he hadn't made up his mind."

"Why?"

"Why, sir? You mean—?"

"Why does he want to sell?"

"Well, for one thing, Andscott has him pretty much over a barrel. You see—well, I've been hammering at him for two or three years not to keep on taking more and more Andscott business—you've seen my recommendations—but he's just followed the path of least resistance. Andscott business has been the easiest to get so he's just gone on taking more and more of it. He's at the point now where it's fifty-five to sixty per cent of his total volume. Well, yesterday Andscott turned on the heat. They want some trick new television cabinet—takes an enormous press to do it, a lot of other equipment, too. Austen figures that it would mean an investment of somewhere around a quarter of a million."

"And he doesn't want to make it?"

"The point is this, sir—I didn't get this from Austen himself, but Paul Bronson told me—Andscott won't give him any guarantee of volume. On top of that, they're even asking Suffolk to finance the construction of the molds—and if Austen doesn't do what they want, they're threatening to pull *all* of their business. You can see what that would do to Suffolk Moulding, more than half their volume lost."

"Sounds like a squeeze play to force Austen into selling."

"That's my conclusion, too. Don't see how it can be anything else."

"Didn't think General Danvers would stoop to that sort of thing. Are you sure of your facts, Clark?"

Gil hesitated, warned to caution by the tone of the president's voice. "Well, Paul Bronson gave me the story and there'd be no reason for him not to tell me the truth."

The president's giant fist unfolded into an enormous hand that he wiped slowly across the glassed surface of his desk. "Has Andscott actually made a move toward buying him out?"

"I can't say about that, sir," Gil replied. "But I did overhear a telephone conversation while I was in Austen's office. He called Atherson of the Freeholders Bank and told him that there had been 'a new development in the Andscott situation.' Then he made an appointment to come down here to see Atherson tomorrow noon."

"Do you think Andscott has actually made a definite offer?"

"Possibly—but I doubt it. I don't think it's gotten that far. You see, after he talked to Atherson, Austen asked me what I thought he could get for the company. From the way he talked—well, this is more of a hunch than anything he actually said—no, I don't think he's had a definite offer yet."

"Then isn't it possible that his seeing Atherson tomorrow may be nothing but an attempt to borrow the money to go ahead with this new press setup?"

Gil shook his head. "Yes, that's possible, sir, but I don't think that's it. Austen wouldn't be so worried if it were that. He could get the money easily enough if he wanted to. The company is in good shape —no debts, not even a current bank loan. He'd have no trouble raising two or three hundred thousand."

A scowl came to Harrison Glenn's face, the change of expression so slowly accomplished that the movement of his features was almost imperceptible. "Then I fail to see why he feels himself squeezed into selling."

"Because—" Gil stopped, aware of the difficulty of expression that so often plagued him in the president's presence. "The truth is— well, actually, I don't think this Andscott business is the real *reason* he's selling, it's only the precipitating incident."

Harrison Glenn's scowling stare was a demand for explanation.

"What I mean," Gil went on, "is that—well, I've sort of sensed this coming. He's been making a mess of managing the company and I think it's finally beginning to penetrate. He's just smart enough to see that he'd better get out while the getting is good."

"You don't have much respect for him, do you, Gil?"

Gil recognized the danger of an honest reply, but faced it squarely. "No sir, I don't."

The president's voice rumbled, "Grant Austen started from noth- ing and built the Suffolk Moulding Company into a fine business. No man who can do that is a fool—nor is he stupid."

"Of course," Gil said in demanded agreement. "I realize that he must have had a lot on the ball at one time. He couldn't have done what he did if he hadn't. The point is, sir—well, the way it looks to me, he's just run out of gas."

There was the encouragement of Harrison Glenn's mumbling, "Yes, that happens sometimes," and Gil went on. "He's been running the same company for twenty-five years—actually, it's thirty if you go clear back to the beginning—and maybe he's gotten bored with it, I don't know. Or maybe he's just getting old. At least—"

Too late, Gil realized that his tongue had tripped him into a trap. Harrison Glenn was deep in his sixties, a good ten years older than Grant Austen. "*Mentally* old, I mean," he said in hurried correction. "Some men go to seed and some don't. Anyway, with Grant Austen the drive just isn't there any more. And it's a darn shame, too—Suffolk Moulding is a fine little business—or at least it could be with the right kind of management."

He cut himself off, aware that nervousness was making him talk too much. He watched Harrison Glenn's face, wondering whether the president was still annoyed because of that slip of the tongue that had labeled Grant Austen as an old man.

But as had happened so often before, the stone mask of Harrison Glenn's face had effectively hidden what he was really thinking. Unexpectedly, there was the dull explosion of his voice saying, "Dangerous attitude, Clark."

"What's that, sir?" Gil asked after a moment of blind groping.

"You like that company, don't you?"

"Like it? Well, I—"

"Always a mistake to let yourself get too fond of any company," the president rumbled. "Like a doctor falling in love with a patient. Destroys your perspective."

Gil was still groping. "That hasn't happened to me, sir."

"Sure?"

"I don't think I've lost my perspective."

"Be honest, Clark," Harrison Glenn demanded. "You want to hang on to Suffolk Moulding, don't you?"

"Of course. It's a good account."

"I don't mean as a client. You'd like to run that company yourself, wouldn't you? Isn't that what you're hoping—that someone might buy it and put you in there to manage it?"

Gil laughed an automatic denial. "I'm not crazy enough to imagine that anything like that could happen!"

Or was he? Could it be that his mind had been sheltering a subconscious hope so fantastic that he hadn't dared acknowledge it? Was that why he had experienced that choke of excitement when Grant Austen had said that he might sell, the wrench of fear that had twisted inside of him at the prospect that Suffolk Moulding might fall into Andscott's hands?

"Tell me this," the president said. "If that were your company—if you were Grant Austen—would you sell out?"

Gil waited out a moment of blankness, attempting to force a saving smile. "I guess the point is, sir, that I'm not Grant Austen."

"You wouldn't sell, would you?" Harrison Glenn broke in, defying denial.

"No sir, I—of course not."

"Then why did you advise Austen to sell?"

Gil felt himself reeling as if the words had struck him a blow. For a moment he couldn't believe that he had heard correctly.

Harrison Glenn repeated the question.

"But I didn't, sir."

"Sure of that? Be careful now, Gil. This is no idle question. Did you, or did you not, suggest to Grant Austen that he sell the Suffolk Moulding Company?"

"Absolutely not, sir."

"How did the matter come up? I want the whole story, step by step."

Gil waited through a thought-collecting moment. "Well, I'd brought down a report on a readjustment of their depreciation policy —one of Austen's brainstorms but I had to go through the motions of giving him an answer. I'd just started to show it to him when he asked me to hold up, said that he had something else he wanted to discuss with me. He told me then that he was thinking about selling the company and wanted to know what I thought about it."

"*He* opened the subject?"

"Yes."

"What did *you* say?"

"I said that I thought it was an idea worth considering."

Harrison Glenn held him with unblinking eyes. "Did you tell him that he might make a lot more money—come out better in the long run by selling out rather than continuing to operate his business?"

"No, sir. It was Austen who said that."

"*Austen* said it?"

"Yes."

"What was your reply?"

"I said that I thought it was possible that he might—depending on how much he could get for the company and the tax situation that would be created by the sale."

"You did not—at any time—advise Grant Austen to sell his company?"

Gil Clark choked back the rising gorge of resentment at the president's pounding inquisition. "I did not *advise* him to sell. I did *agree* that it was an idea worth considering." He had made his words sharply precise, emphasizing the difference between advice and agreement.

There was no hint of understanding in the stone face but, surprisingly, the barely moving lips said, "Don't get your back up, Gil. There's a point to this. I must be absolutely certain that Austen himself initiated the idea."

"He did."

96

"And you think he has a deal on to sell to Andscott?"

"Yes sir. I—well, there's one thing I didn't mention before. Atherson of Freeholders has a lot of interest in Andscott Instrument. I know that from my days over at S.F.&P. And he's been Grant Austen's banker since the beginning of the company. Wouldn't he be the logical man to act as an intermediary?"

The great paws of Glenn's fists slid slowly across the desk. "That's a little thin, Clark—possible, of course, but—"

"But there's this, too—after Austen told me that he was planning to sell, I said that even though he had *one* deal boiling, he shouldn't jump too fast. The point is that he did not deny that he *did* have one deal on the fire."

"What did you mean—that he shouldn't jump too fast?"

"Well, I told him that selling a company was like selling anything else—the more possible buyers he could line up, the better price he could probably expect. I may have gone a little too far in suggesting it, but I told him there was a possibility that we might—that *you* might—be able to put him in touch with someone interested in buying his company."

There was an astounding break in the mask of Harrison Glenn's face, almost a smile. "The hell you did!"

"I hope that I didn't—well, I thought that if someone other than Andscott bought Suffolk, at least there might be a chance of our holding the account. I knew there'd be no chance at all if Andscott moved in."

Harrison Glenn seemed not to have heard, turning slowly in his chair. Then, surprisingly, the giant body started to unfold and he stood, moving toward the window with a shoulder-weaving shuffle. Gil felt the tightening tension of the unexpected. This was out of character, the seated statue rising and walking away from its pedestal. Harrison Glenn rarely rose from his desk chair.

The president stood at the window, his enormous shoulders almost spanning its width, his voice booming back from the reflecting glass. "Good work, Gil. Glad you got your oar in."

Gil rose, welcoming not only approval but also relief from the constraint of sitting. "Do you mean, sir, that you know someone who might be interested?"

"Was at one time," the president said in a gruff grumble. "Don't know whether he still is or not. Haven't been able to get in touch with him yet."

"Who's that, sir?" Gil asked, not conscious that the question was an impropriety until Harrison Glenn pointedly evaded an answer.

"Stay close enough to your office so that I can reach you in a hurry," the president ordered. "He may want to talk to you."

Accepting the dismissal, Gil Clark turned to the door. As he glanced back he saw that Glenn was still looking out of the window and, even with allowance for his natural immobility, his stare seemed too fixed to be pointless. Gil's impression was too unsure to be given the weight of certainty but it seemed that the object of Harrison Glenn's attention was the distant top floor of the Hotel Ivanhoe.

●●●●● 3

Luncheon was almost over in the Fontainebleau Room. There were only two tables still occupied, a party of four women at one of the alcove banquettes and a love-sick couple mooning over a deuce. Maude Kennard decided that it was safe to leave her post at the door. She told Louis, the headwaiter, that she was leaving and looked across the lobby. Frank, the bell captain, jumped at the signal of her raised hand.

"Frank, get a couple of housemen to help you and go to the second-floor storeroom. There are some barrels there—a Royal Doulton china service that I bought last month at the Dietz estate auction. I want to use it for a dinner that Mr. McCall is giving tonight. Bring them down to the kitchen, have them washed, and then take them up to the service pantry of Mr. McCall's suite."

She pivoted away, not waiting for his reply, picking up the house phone. "This is Mrs. Kennard. Get me the florist."

"You want all them barrels?" Frank asked.

It occurred to her then that Max hadn't given her the menu and a table setting couldn't be planned until she knew what was to be served. Signaling Frank into silence, she gave a crisply detailed order to the florist and then, anger-driven, strode toward the kitchen. Frank followed her but she didn't answer his question until she was across the Fontainebleau Room, almost at the kitchen door. "Yes, bring up everything. I'll pick what I want afterwards. Oh, one thing more—get hold of the housekeeper and tell her to meet me on ten in five minutes."

The clattering after-lunch din of the kitchen had subsided into a distant rumbling thunder of the dishwashing machines. The order counter and the steam tables were deserted. Only one cook was in

98

sight, mopping his face with the tag end of a once-white towel that he had tied around his neck for a kerchief.

"Where's Max?" she demanded.

"He go his office," the cook said.

Maude Kennard broke her stride as she debated having Max called out, but her impatience quickly overrode her distaste and she walked on toward the chef's office, the too-well remembered evidence of one of her unpleasant defeats by Max Nicollet. When the kitchens were remodeled, her plan had put the chef's office in its logical location —near the storeroom record clerk's, across from the door where the kitchen personnel checked in, conveniently accessible to everyone who might have business with the chef, herself included. Max had rebelled, demanding that his office be created by remodeling an old coal bin that he had discovered down at the end of one of the rabbit-warren tunnels that connected the scattered rooms of the old cellar. It was a ridiculously inefficient location, and the change in plan had caused a sixteen-hundred dollar budget over-run that had to be balanced by an unwise cutback on the cold-storage installation, but in the end she had been forced to give Max everything he wanted, even approving the payment of the invoice for a shower cabinet that he had ordered without authorization, helpless against his defense that he had saved money by buying a cheap shower and not insisting on a tiled bathroom. There was no question about the cabinet being cheap—it was a flimsy sheet-metal affair that crackled metallically whenever it was touched—and, as the ultimate defiance, Max had insisted on having it installed beside his desk where, when the mood moved him, he could use his giant fists to pound out a thundering tin-drum obbligato to his roaring baritone.

As she approached the last turn in the tunnel, Maude Kennard heard a blast of sound that warned her that Max was actually using the shower—which she had hitherto doubted—and since he was singing in Greek and not French, imagined himself to be completely alone. She stopped, mentally gagged by the revolting expectancy of Max's unclothed bulk, and peeked cautiously around the edge of his office door.

Max was facing the back of the shower cabinet and the white duck curtain, although bulging like a wind-blown tent, was a reasonably safe covering. She stepped into the room and screamed his name over the roar of song and water. The sound stopped as if blasted by sudden shock. Tin crackled and the cabinet rocked precariously as the too-tight fit of Max's turning body threatened disaster.

"Get out!" he screamed, his voice breaking into a frightened falsetto. "I take the bath! Get out, get out, get out!" His big hands showed at the edge of the curtain as he clutched it drum-head tight against the great bulge of his belly.

Maude Kennard saw that the chef's embarrassment gave her a clear-cut advantage and she made her voice chillingly cold. "Where is the menu for the McCall dinner?"

"The desk, the desk," Max screamed. "On the desk! Get out, get out!"

She advanced toward the desk as Max glowered over the top of the curtain rod, a furious elephant trapped in a tin coffin.

The menu, handwritten but legible, was lying on the green blotter pad and she read it quickly.

"What," she demanded, "is *Faisan à la McCall?*" ready to recite the standing order that no dish was ever to be added to an Ivanhoe menu without her specific approval, then suddenly smiling at the realization that Max, unwittingly, had played into her hands. Cash McCall couldn't help but be pleased that she had had a dish created expressly for him.

She closed her ears to Max's scream-cracked falsetto and hurried back toward the kitchen, driven by a strange sense of excitement that, finally recognized, proved disturbing. She was so seldom affected by any emotion that she could not immediately trace to its source, that she felt herself oddly disabled in not being able to do so now. Could it be that crazy idea that old Judge Torrant had put into her head ... that she and Cash McCall were in love?

Crazy?

Why?

The impact of thought was physical, blocking, stopping her at the door of the Fontainebleau Room. It had been years since she had considered the possibility that she might ever again marry. There had been no man with enough to offer. But this was different. Cash McCall owned the Ivanhoe. If she married him, she would be in complete control. There would be no more Everett Pierce, no more bowing and scraping to Will Atherson. No one would dare stand in her way ... no, not even Max! She would be rich ... no more skimping and scraping, no more discount chiselling at grubby little dress shops ... no more worrying about getting old and ...

Old?

In another year she would be forty.

It was the first time Maude Kennard had allowed that realization to be more than a passing shadow across the face of her mind. Now, permitted to linger, it became the last weight on the scale. Her decision was made and, once accepted, it seemed in no way strange or unusual, but so completely sensible and logical that it was difficult to imagine why she had never thought of it before.

Calmly, smiling pleasantly at a pimply-faced bus boy who was punching out at the time clock, she took the service elevator to the tenth floor.

••••• 4

The strain that Gil Clark had felt during the twenty minutes that he had spent waiting to see Harrison Glenn was as nothing compared with the tension that had built up during this hour and a half that he had sat in his own office, waiting for the president's call. What he had then thought of as a headache had, by now, built itself into a brain-pounding torture that was exploding pain bombs with every beat of his heart.

He heard the door behind him open and spun around in his chair. Harrison Glenn's enormous frame all but filled the doorway.

"Talked to him," the president said. "You're to have lunch with him tomorrow noon. His suite at the Ivanhoe."

Gil Clark's throat seemed to have been dried by a blast of flame. His lips moved but no words came.

"What were you about to say?" Harrison Glenn asked after a long pause.

"Would you mind telling me who he is, Mr. Glenn? I mean—if I'm going to have to talk to him—" He stopped, tortured by silence as he waited for the reply.

"I thought you knew," Glenn finally said.

"No."

"His name is Cash McCall."

The name came like a sneak punch, slipping past the guard of his self-control, striking without the warning consciousness of its impact, awareness coming only after he felt the weakening peristaltic wave of reflexed revulsion.

"Do you know him?" Glenn asked.

Gil shook his head, knowing that an explanation was impossible. The quickly debated attempt had confronted him with the recognition that his total impression of this man named Cash McCall was based upon nothing more substantial than washroom gossip. Yet even that recognition did not alter his instinctive judgment. The stories he had heard about Cash McCall, no matter how heavily discounted, still made him the cleverest of all the jackals and vultures that preyed upon the laggard members of the business pack. Even the gossip-mongers made the man seem more legendary than real, but he had known enough other *operators* to shape the pattern in his mind—the quick-money boys he had been forced to work with during those two years when he had been with Simonds, Farrar & Peters, beasts of prey who were forever lurking in the background, waiting to ambush some unsuspecting company through a loophole in the tax laws. There had been Nathan Rosset who had pounced on the Shag Knitting Corporation and liquidated it with a million-dollar profit for himself, Evans who had trapped Rainer Brothers in an estate-tax squeeze, Eiseman who made a fortune out of his nefariously legal juggling of canning companies—the worst of the lot, Harry Guizinger. It was Guizinger who had finally made him give up and leave S.F.& P.

"You've never met McCall?" Harrison Glenn asked.

"No."

"You've heard of him?"

"Yes."

"What?"

"Not much," Gil Clark said evasively. "But enough so that—well, I'd hate to see him get his hands on Suffolk Moulding."

"Why?"

"I've seen it happen to too many good companies. They're never the same after some fast-buck operator puts them through the wringer."

There was the break of a long silence before Harrison Glenn said, "That's not like you, Clark—making up your mind before you have the facts. You've admitted you don't know him. Wait until you do."

Gil Clark nodded grimly, recognizing the criticism as justified but finding it no less hard to take.

Harrison Glenn went on. "But let's get one thing straight so there's no possibility of a misunderstanding later on. Grant Austen is a client of ours. If he wants to sell his company, we have a professional obligation to help him get the best possible price."

"Of course."

"We can't keep anyone from bidding on the property."

"I know that."

"If Cash McCall is willing to outbid Andscott and Grant Austen decides to accept his offer, that's no affair of ours. It's Austen's company. He owns it."

"Yes sir."

The door closed and Gil was alone. The draining away of resistance left dregs—the almost incredible suspicion that there might be an undercover alliance between Cash McCall and the president of Corporation Associates. If there weren't, why hadn't Harrison Glenn tried to save the Suffolk account by fighting back against Grant Austen's plan to sell the company? Why was Glenn so willing to let the company be sold? Why had he been so anxious to get in touch with McCall?

There was a background for suspicion. The partners at Simonds, Farrar & Peters had more than once nudged a client into selling a company and then cut themselves in for a secret profit on the deal. But was it possible that a man like Harrison Glenn would stoop low enough to share a vulture's carrion?

No, it couldn't be true! Harrison Glenn was an honorable man. That's why he had been so anxious to make certain that selling was Grant Austen's own idea, to make sure that nothing had been done to encourage him. And Corporation Associates *did* have a professional obligation to help Grant Austen get the best price he could! Harrison Glenn had been right, too, when he had said that there was no reason why anyone shouldn't be given a chance to bid. If Cash McCall was the high bidder ...

A single thought floated upward, detached, freed from the turmoil that raged in Gil Clark's mind. No matter who bought Suffolk Moulding, someone would manage it. With Grant Austen gone, there would have to be a new president.

Five

. . . .

FOR THE LAST HOUR there had been the bustle of comings and
goings in and out of the pantry door of Cash McCall's suite as Maude
Kennard had kept a half dozen employees scurrying about the hotel searching for the hundred and one things out of which, only now,
a finished table setting was beginning to emerge.

Twice, with the table almost set, she had ordered everything re-
moved and a fresh start made. The pantry shelves were loaded with
the silver and china that she had first ordered and then discarded as,
with the metamorphosis of her attitude, her objective had been
changed. In the beginning she had been guided by a hotelkeeper's
standards, but the longer she had worked the more clearly she had
seen herself in the role of Cash McCall's wife, and the table as one
over which she would preside as the hostess in her own home.

Maude Kennard's mind was no lazy loom spinning the gossamer
stuff of daydreams. It was a machine, precisely geared to the reali-
ties, seldom deceived by false hopes, set in motion only when she
was certain that her desire was an achievable possibility. In two hours
of weighing and testing the idea of marrying Cash McCall she had
discovered only one reason for caution—the prospect was, if anything, too totally appealing.

Experience had taught her to be suspicious of any proposition that
seemed to be too much in her own favor. The too-perfect prospect
usually meant that there was some deep-hidden fault. Yet, try as she
would, probing the idea from every angle, she had found no hint of

flaw. It was a good deal, two-sided as a good deal always had to be. He would give her the Ivanhoe and she would give him a home, a *real* home, not the emptiness of a lonely hotel suite but the kind of home where he could live as a rich man had a right to live, dinner parties where she would entertain for him as . . .

The housekeeper stood before her with a pair of heavy brass vases in her hands, outstretched for inspection.

"No, I'm sorry, Mrs. Schilling, those won't do at all." The vases were from the Fontainebleau Room, too obviously *hotel*, not the sort of thing she would ever have in her own home. "Here's what I want you to do. Go down to the Wharf rooms. Get the key from Frank. There's a pair of low silver bowls on the sideboard under that big ship model."

Mrs. Schilling's gray eyes voiced her silent shock at being asked to violate the order that never, under any circumstances, was anything to be borrowed from the ninth floor.

"Get them," Maude Kennard ordered. "You can return them the first thing in the morning."

The housekeeper went out and Maude Kennard followed her to the pantry door, closing it and turning back to give the table a final inspection, circling it slowly, touching a knife to move it a fraction of an inch, centering a service plate and then shifting a wineglass, finally reaching the head of the table, standing with her hands on the back of the chair where Cash McCall would sit, lifting her eyes to follow the thin blade of light at the edge of the door to the living room, an opening that she had purposefully gauged to be invisible from the living-room side but wide enough to let through the sound of a voice. An hour ago she had heard Cash McCall tell someone over the telephone he would pay four hundred thousand dollars for some company, tossing out the offer as casually as if he were flipping a coin on a check girl's tray. What she had heard had been complete confirmation of everything Judge Torrant had told her.

She was suddenly conscious of the feel of cold metal in the palm of her right hand and, looking down, saw that she had, without volition, crossed the dining room and reached out to touch the polished brass knob of the living-room door.

The door, unlatched, yielded to the weight of her hand. The living room was deserted, but Cash McCall must be somewhere in the suite. She hadn't heard him go out. She hesitated, inventing the protective excuse of asking him to approve the table setting, and took three soft-footed steps into the living room. She stopped, listening. Silence. Three more steps and she was clear of the turn of the wall, looking through the arch into the foyer. The door of his bedroom stood ajar. Through the opening she saw a corner of his dressing table, an emerald glass bottle and a leatherbacked brush, a thin slice of the mirror that hung over the table.

A white-brown image flashed across the mirror and, an instant later, she heard the sound of a turning faucet and the whish of the shower. She realized then what she had seen but her reflexed movement had been faster than thought. Without volition, she found herself back in the dining room again, the door solidly closed behind her. Her reaction was not immediately explainable and she stood rigid, frightened as always when she caught herself doing anything that had not been purposefully willed. Then came the slow fading in of critical understanding.

Now she saw the flaw in the too-perfect prospect. She had been a fool to imagine that she could win with no more than an exhibition of her talent as a hostess. That wouldn't be enough to satisfy him. He was a man. There was only one thing that ever satisfied a man.

Again there was the consciousness of an uncontrolled reflex, a shudder that was an unwilled attempt to loosen the grip of taut muscles. It was impossible to explain away the feeling that had come over her, this ridiculous importance that her subconscious mind had given to something that wasn't important at all. What a man wanted of a woman was such a simple thing ... a lot of fuss about nothing. But it had been such a long time.

Admittedly, some of what she felt was the trepidation of an actress facing the necessity of re-creating a long-forgotten role ... Ted Sprague in that awful Wilmington hotel room ... Jimmy in the greenhouse ... what-ever-his-name-was from Princeton in that basement room where the dance decorations were stored, the tinsel starting that rash on her thigh that had frightened her so terribly until the doctor had assured her that it was only an allergy. But it wouldn't be like that now ... Cash was no hundred-handed young fool in the back seat of a jalopy ... no sex-mad maniac like ...

Revelation flashed, not fully seen but clear enough to be recognized as a memory that could never be completely examined ... that awful night in Chicago, the night that had been the end of her marriage, opening the door and seeing her husband with that little bitch! Yes, that was when it had happened. Something had snapped inside her mind ... the horror of it, the ugly nastiness, not even another woman, just a little high school girl that had come in to help with ...

The pantry door squeaked and she wheeled to face the housekeeper who stood with the two silver bowls from The Wharf.

"These the ones you want?"

"Yes, thank you." She hesitated and then made her decision. "There's no reason why you can't take over now, Mrs. Schilling."

"Me? You mean I'm to finish up?"

"Yes," she said, hurriedly explaining what remained to be done. "I've really given too much time to this already. I should have been downstairs a half hour ago."

Outside, waiting for the elevator, she assured herself that it was not weakness that was forcing her to escape. She had been too impatient, tried to move too fast. You couldn't force things. It took time. Tomorrow would be soon enough ... tomorrow or the next day.

●●●●● 2

Leaving downtown Suffolk and swinging into Boulevard Drive, Paul Bronson tramped the accelerator and the convertible hurled itself against the demand of the sharply rising hill. At the hairpin turn around the end of the reservoir, he shot a glance back down the road, apprehensive that Grant Austen's car might be following him. The old man had still been in his office at five-thirty but he might have left by now, he might even be home.

He pressed the accelerator to the floor, hopeful that he could get Lory out of the house without being forced to see her father. It was bad enough to be tricked into dating her again. Another dose of old man Austen would be more than he could take. He'd had enough for one day ... *enough for a hell of a lot of days!*

Damn it, didn't Austen have any sense of organization at all? Jake Crown had blown his top over the way that he'd let Berger mess up that mold design, and you couldn't blame him. How could any department head do a decent job if the ground was being cut out from under him all the time?

And giving Thorson authority to build up raw-material stocks! A week ago it was Austen himself who was screaming his head off about the capital that was tied up in inventory. How crazy could a man get?

A stone retaining wall reared ahead of him and he twisted the wheel with only a split second to spare, gritting his teeth through the screaming protest of tires clawing the wet pavement. Angrily, as if suddenly discovering the false dusk of the gray-clouded evening, he flipped on the headlights and momentarily let the car coast out its momentum, feeling the ache of unclenched jaw muscles, then easing his foot down and down on the accelerator.

Austen hadn't even had the common decency to call him in for that session with Gil Clark on revision of the depreciation schedule. Probably trying to pass it off as his own idea. Hell of a lot of good that would do ... Gil knew where the idea had come from. Gil was no fool. He had the old man's number. Everyone did. But what difference did it make? What could you do about it? Nothing! That was the hell of it in a little one-man company. One man was everything. No one else mattered. He did what he wanted to do and, crazy or not, there was nothing anyone could do to stop him.

All the gang around Finch & Slade had told him how smart he was to get out of the New York rat race and into a sweet little outfit like Suffolk Moulding ... all that crap about the opportunities in a small business ... *all right, he'd been a fool and fallen for it!* So what? He was admitting it, wasn't he? He'd been a green kid, fed up with New York, and Austen had come along and played him for a sucker with all that talk about expansion plans. *Expansion!* The only thing that would ever expand around Suffolk Moulding was the old man's hat size. That happened every time somebody made him chairman of another damn fool committee. He wouldn't spend a few hundred bucks for those inspection tables that would pay for themselves in six weeks, but he'd hand out a month's pay to that little tramp in Shipping. Sure, he loved that ... Grant Austen the great humanitarian! Wasn't that a fine precedent to set? From now on, every dumb dame that got herself rolled in the bushes would be coming around with her hands out, wanting a month's pay for a bonus.

A red light glowered and he brought the car to a lunging stop, his hands clenched into hard fists on the thin circle of the steering wheel. The old man would never have the guts to put in that new press they had to have to hold the Andscott business. This was the beginning of the end. The plug would come out when they started losing the Andscott volume. But what the hell was he worrying about? Let the old man wreck the company if he wanted to. He wouldn't be there to see it happen. Tomorrow morning he'd be in Philadelphia following up that lead he'd gotten from Jack Hildreth at the employment agency. Lucky coincidence, that letter from Hildreth-Paris happening to turn up just when it had. If this Andscott thing worked out ... of course it might not, but at least Andscott had been really interested when they knew who he was ... Jack had set up a date with General Danvers himself, none of this Personnel Department business. Andscott Instrument might not be the hottest outfit in the world ... last statement looked pretty bad ... but that was when a comptroller had a chance to make a showing. Anyway, it was a real company, none of that sweet-little-outfit crap ... big enough to have some *organization*. Imagine General Danvers pulling some of the stuff that old Austen pulled ... that was a laugh!

The light changed and he drove on, tire-screeching the road bends. He should have been quicker on the trigger when Grace Elberth had invited him. He ought to have known that she'd rope him in to picking up Lory. But he'd already accepted and there'd been nothing he could do. He couldn't say, "Listen, Grace, I've sworn off little Miss Lory Austen," the way you'd say that you'd sworn off cigarettes. He'd go through with it ... take it easy ... not let Lory know what she did to him. It was that cold act that always got him ... *knowing* that it was an act. But if you could ever crack that shell ... find the combination ... touch the right button ... *no, to hell with it!*

The black bulk of the crenellated castle that was the Austen home loomed ahead and he slowed for the turn, glancing right as he coasted up the drive, his eyes caught by the side-seen flit of a figure across the lighted window.

The terrace door burst open as he stepped out of the car and Lory, tiptoed and waving, signaled that she was coming. He stood immobile, staring at her retained after-image against the blankness of the closed door, tricked into an unsummoned resurgence of the feeling she had incited the first time he had ever seen her and, repeatedly, had re-incited during those months until he had been smart enough to figure out the score.

No girl that he had ever known, even that kid from Bryn Mawr that he'd taken to New York that weekend, had ever so bedeviled his mind with the erotic challenge of innocence unknowingly pleading for conquest. For a while Lory had driven him almost off his rocker ... like trying to work out a puzzle where you couldn't figure the first move ... but that was lucky. It might easily have gone too fast. The way it had been, he'd had time to think it through. If he'd let himself fall in love with her ... and there'd been times when, alone at night after he had left her, he couldn't be sure that he hadn't ... he would have wound up marrying her. She was the kind you married. The first was the last. But he wouldn't have been marrying Lory ... no, that was the hell of it ... he would have been marrying Grant Austen's daughter. The price was too high for the pay-off.

Coldly—and now he could admit the coldness of his calculation—even the promised inheritance of the Suffolk Moulding Company wasn't enough to compensate for what he'd have to go through while he waited for the old man to get out of the way. Anyway, at the rate Grant Austen was going, there'd be nothing left that was worth waiting for. The handwriting was on the wall. That was one rule of business management that you could always tie to ... you went either forward or backward. You couldn't stand still ... and with Grant Austen's kind of gutless fumbling you went backward in a hurry. Be different if there were any hope of the old man giving up and retiring ... his kind never did. In big corporations they had a way of cleaning out the dry rot ... forced retirement at sixty or sixty-five ... but Grant Austen owned the place and made his own rules. He would be messing things up until he was ninety. Those wiry little guys lived forever.

The terrace door opened again, the path of light scissoring out across the flagstone, and he steeled himself against quickening excitement. Lory was talking to her mother, standing with her back to him, but even in black silhouette there was the insweep of her tiny waist, the outcurve of her hips, and in the flashed instant of her turn, the momentarily seen upthrust of her breasts.

She came to him running, lightfooted and flying, borne by the rush of March wind.

"Hi," he said, the iron-banded constriction of his throat choking off anything else that might have been said.

"Nice of you to pick me up," she said—and that was all she said.

Damn it, there wasn't anything else to be said ... only that it had been a long time since he had seen her ... and there was no point in saying that.

She was curled against the door, sitting as far away from him as she could.

Damn her, damn her, damn her! But it was only for tonight. He could stand it that long.

• • • • • *3*

The same oddly perverse disruption of normality that made Max Nicollet find inspiration in rage caused him to approach his climactic creative moments with gay abandon. Executing a light-footed dance step that made him seem Gargantua imitating a bouncing balloon, humming a snatch of song in a piccolo falsetto, he poised a knife above the first guinea hen, freshly lifted from its perch above the steaming herb broth by the trembling hand of Carlos, his *saucier.*

Twice the knife flashed and the breast of guinea hen, severed with a surgeon's skill, fell into the nest of parchment in Max's left hand.

His right hand traded the knife for the spoon that Carlos offered and he dipped it into the sauce with which he tenderly anointed the savory morsel. Carlos retrieved the spoon and Max, squealing a high note in the melody of his unbroken song, twisted the parchment into a tight packet which he delivered to the roasting oven with the flourish of a dueling thrust.

Twelve times the wordless pantomime was re-enacted, varied only by improvisations on the theme of the accompanying song. Only then, with the last serving consigned to the oven, did the *chef de cuisine* sufficiently relax the rigidity of his concentration to become aware that Maude Kennard was watching him.

The needle points of his mustache quivered.

"Is everything all right?" she asked.

Max's body seemed to swell as if, like an enormous pufftoad, he possessed some inner organ of inflation. "And why would it not be all right?"

"I'm sure it is," she said.

Since rage was an emotion that Max Nicollet reserved for a special purpose, he saw no point in wasting it on Maude Kennard's uncalled-for intrusion. She was obviously an unworthy adversary, too easily defeated, already walking back toward the door of the Fontainebleau Room. His breath whistled out through his pursed lips but it did not disturb his smile, the smile of an enormous cupid upon whose apple-cheeked face some mischievous child had crayoned a black mustache.

• • • • • 4

In much the same way that some men are inspired to reverence by the crossing of a church's threshold, Will Atherson rarely approached Starwood, his Main Line estate, without conscious awareness of love for his wife. His feeling was usually expressed in a needless reminder to himself that he was an unusually lucky man. After more than a quarter century of married life, he still came home from the bank every workday evening with a warmth of anticipation little dimmed by the passage of time. Actually, in many ways, he loved his wife more now than he had in the first years of their marriage. The only aspect of their relationship in which there had been a deterioration was no longer of great importance and, even there, the loss was considerably less than he had been led to expect by the satiric humor of his friends at The Wharf.

A part of Will Atherson's affection for his wife came from a sustained consciousness of its existence, love growing out of the awareness of love. Another part—and it was a considerable one—resulted from the fact that Helen had, in all particulars, vastly exceeded every expectation that had been in his mind when he had asked her to marry him. In truth, love had been far more a product of marriage than of courtship.

He had proposed to her because he had given up waiting to be struck by a grand passion, because Starwood needed a mistress—his mother had died two years before—and because he could think of no soundly logical reason why Helen wouldn't make a competent manager of his household, a pleasant and reasonably intelligent companion, and a good mother of his children. She had enough social standing to make her acceptable to his friends, yet not enough to force him into riding the dinner-jacketed treadmill. She had been raised in a family of reasonable substance, yet there was no danger that Starwood and all the other material things that he could offer her would not be received with gratitude and appreciation.

On the debit side of the balance sheet—and he had not been blinded by love—she was a large girl with a quite obvious tendency to take on weight, a face that suggested the adjective *wholesome* rather than *pretty*. When he had taken her on a tour of Starwood—a calculated preliminary to proposal—she had proved to be more interested in the kitchen than any other room of the mansion, according the master bedroom no more attention than a nod of apparently unconcerned acceptance.

It had been a startling surprise to discover on their honeymoon that his careful planning of the groom's reticently tender approach to the frightened bride was totally unnecessary. He was, in fact, overwhelmed before he even had a chance to give the plan a fair trial. He discovered then that there was, at the core of her being, an essential earthiness that came through freely and boldly, far more appealing in its uninhibited honesty than would have been any practiced feminine wiles.

As the years had gone by, Will Atherson had observed that the wives of his friends developed in one of two directions, coming eventually to a state where they either coarsened themselves by too frank remarks about matters of sex, or went to the opposite extreme of middle-aged prudery. Helen was wonderful. Outwardly, she was as conventional as his mother had been, the proper mistress of Starwood, yet she could—and always, it seemed, at exactly the right

112

private moment—break through with a good bawdy remark that brought a sensation like the recapture of youth. She was his perpetual antidote against the proprieties forced upon him by the double handicap of his position as the head of the Atherson family and the president of the Freeholders Bank & Trust Company. She never allowed him to become aware that he was getting to be an old man. That, perhaps, was the most important reason of all for the way he felt about her.

She met him in the front hall tonight, wearing a dinner dress, her arm encircling his waist, walking a few steps with him before she hesitated for the kiss that she always found some way to take out of the pattern of expectancy. Reaching behind his back, she produced a just-mixed scotch and soda from its hiding place behind an arrangement of red carnations on the hall table.

He drank his highball a bit too hurriedly, recited his cliché insistence that she had not told him they were going out to dinner, accepted another scotch and soda as an affectionate peace offering, and went upstairs to change his clothes.

Helen came in as he was finishing dressing, sitting on the edge of their double bed to watch him as he tied a careful bow and shrugged into his dinner jacket. He suspected that she had something on her mind and asked an opening question.

"I'm coming in to town tomorrow forenoon," she said, "and thought that I might be clever enough to trick you into taking me to lunch."

"Darling, I'm terribly sorry but—"

"Tied up?" she asked, disappointed. "I was afraid that you might be."

"I'll cancel it."

"You'll do nothing of the kind."

"But it isn't important."

"Neither is this."

"Darling, it's only Grant Austen."

She laughed. "Tomorrow must be Wednesday."

"I'll call him and—"

"Of course you won't. You know how he dotes on The Wharf. What you should do, Will dear, is to get the poor man a membership of his own."

"Well, he does have an excuse this time," Will Atherson admitted in Austen's defense. "He needs some financing. But there's no reason why I can't cancel out on lunch. He can see me after—"

"You'd break his heart."

"But I'd much rather—"

"Will, honestly it was only a silly notion. We'll have lunch together next week."

"Sure you don't have something else on your mind?"

"Nothing, dear."

"Positive?"

"I just like having lunch with you."

"Damn it," he said tenderly, kissing her cheek, then making the pretense of pushing her back on the bed.

She escaped the pinning arch of his arms, laughing. "You're much too easily seduced, no resistance at all. A girl doesn't even dare tell you that she likes having lunch with you."

"Depends on the girl."

"Time to change the subject," she said over a trickle of gay laughter. "Why does Grant Austen need a loan?"

He hesitated, not sure that her question was seriously asked.

She added, "He isn't having trouble, is he?"

"Trouble? No, I don't think so. As a matter of fact—well, I'm only putting two and two together. Had a call from Danvers at Andscott and he told me that they were after Austen to expand—put in some new presses—so I'm imagining that's what he wants to see me about."

"Of course you'll make the loan?"

"Yes, I suppose so," he said, searching out a cigarette case and beginning to fill it, scowling at the prospect of an evening without his pipe, then seeing that his expression had brought concern to her face.

"You don't like him as well as you used to, do you, Will?" she asked.

He started to protest her misinterpretation but, instead, let his thought stream flow into the channel cut by her question. "It's never been exactly a matter of my *liking* him," he said, hesitating over the slightly emphasized word as if not satisfied with its accuracy. "At one time I had considerable respect for him. He really did accomplish a great deal."

"I haven't seen him for several years," she said. "Not since that party we gave when his daughter graduated from art school, but he struck me then as being on the verge of turning into a stuffed shirt."

"I'm afraid now that he's beyond the verge," he said with genuine regret. "He's like so many self-made men—they always come to a point in their lives when they run out of material. Hadn't we better be leaving?"

"What's happened to his daughter?" she asked, going to the closet for her wrap.

"Still illustrating children's books, so far as I know."

"Not married yet?"

"No."

114

"Strange—such an attractive child, too," she puzzled. "Why do you suppose she's never married?"

"Now, now," he said, a smiled warning against another outbreak of her perpetual interest in matchmaking, recalling a rather silly conversation after the party they'd given for Lory five years ago.

There must have been mental telepathy—he often suspected its existence—because Helen said, "I still think I'm right about her."

"If I were twenty years younger," he began, repeating the words from memory, "I might be able to speak with more authority."

She paid him the same pleasantly erotic compliment that she had five years ago and he followed her out of the door, again feeling himself an astoundingly fortunate man.

Six

.
.
.
.

As HE OPENED the library door and stepped out on the terrace, Grant Austen heard the sound of wild geese from the midnight sky and, looking up, saw the half-moon racing through the wind-torn clouds. It was a March night, dramatic with the turmoil of the changing seasons. The wind had veered after the sun had gone down and now it came from the south, warm with the promise of an on-rushing spring but still riotously tempestuous. He breathed deeply, filling his lungs, his eyes slowly adjusting to the focus of infinity. For one fleeting moment he saw the breaks in the clouds as cracks in the shell of the universe and his mind was caught up by the enormity of the irresistible forces that were loose in the night.

Suddenly, the moon seemed to cease its motion and then it was the earth that was moving, tilting under his feet, and he felt himself dizzy and losing his balance. Quickly, instinct demanding self-control, he looked down to orient himself with the familiar rectangle of the swimming pool in the center of the wide-spreading lawn. The pool became an island solidly anchored in the black sea of the night. The earth stood still again and the moon took up its race through the ragged clouds.

There was no physical betrayal of inner turmoil. Grant Austen had long since taught himself the necessity of concealing his emotions and the veneer had become an inseparable part of his character. It did not fall away even when he was alone in the darkness of a March night. He stood very straight, almost artificially so, the exaggerated uprightness of carriage that is often affected by men of less than average height. But his posture was also the result of his subconscious belief that fear could be dissipated by containment.

Looking down through the bare branches of the leafless trees he saw, in the valley below him, the grid of lights that marked the streets of the city of Suffolk. Habit-guided, his eyes found the fluttering red neon of the downtown section and then traced King Street to the bridge where it crossed Conomissing Creek.

For an instant he felt the panic of strange alarm. There was only empty blackness where he should have seen the bead-strung lights of the Suffolk Moulding Company. Then he recalled that most of them were blocked from his vision by the new Lee-Bross warehouse. He identified the distant pinpoint of light that marked the watchman's shack and then, moving west, found the triple window in the end of the power house. Memory easily filled in the black void.

He saw the old mill building where the business had been started —once it had housed everything, now it was only a warehouse for carton storage—and with the quick strides of imagined walking he was in the tool shop, incongruously bright with sunshine through the sawtooth roof, pungent with the musk of hot oil, alive with the nerve-tingling sound of steel cutting steel. He walked on into the tool storage shed, seeing the molds stored behind the wire-fenced walls, the whole history of the business written in those chalked numbers on the oak-plank shelves, dates that went as far back as 1923, the male and female steel that had given birth to radio tube bases and bottle caps and switch assemblies and drill housings and rouge boxes and tool handles and watch cases and a thousand other things molded out of plastics, some remembered, more forgotten.

He was in the big general pressroom now, brown-dusted and carbolic-odored, hearing the steam-hissing suck of the opening presses, feeling the jarring thump of the hydraulic rams, following the conveyor line through the firewall door into the sharply contrasting quiet and cleanliness of the warehouse and the shipping room, out into the yard, past the high-stacked powerhouse, up the back steps into the Administration Building.

Fluorescent lights flickered hesitantly at his touch, then leaped into triumphant brightness, sparkling on glass and chromium, softly reflected from the light green walls of the corridors, even more softly from the wax-rubbed paneling of his private office. He sat at his desk in the quiet that his gruff command demanded ... *no telephone calls, Miss Berk ... something I have to think through ... important decision to make ...*

He was not one man now but two—the man on the terrace and the man at the desk—experiencing the strange duality of two minds, independent yet linked by a common consciousness; two pairs of eyes, one pair to watch with the clarity of distance what the other saw too close to be sharply focused; two voices, one emboldened by separation to say what the other had not yet dared to word ... *all this is yours, Grant Austen, the Suffolk Moulding Company. You built it ... all of it ... from nothing to this. If you sell the company, will you ever be able to fill the empty hole that it will leave in your life?*

The man on the terrace walked across the lawn toward the garden wall. His hand brushed a boxwood and he heard the unseen flight of small birds startled from their hiding place, the sound quickly snuffed out by the wind. He was alone now, the man at the desk suddenly gone, his disappearance a baffling trickery, and Grant Austen felt the pointlessness of having walked out into the empty night.

Had he been a more discerning self-analyst, and more experienced in the vagaries of the various forms of affection, he might have recognized his impulse to draw physically closer to the factory as a last gesture at recapture before the final abandonment of a lost love. It was very like that last attempt at reconciliation that his conscience would have forced upon him if he had been contemplating the divorce of his wife. What he had once felt toward the Suffolk Moulding Company had truly been a form of love, and the fading of affection had not differed greatly from the way that the flame of man's love for a woman is sometimes dimmed to a flicker so faint that it becomes only a memory to inspire the restless hope for a new way of life. That was all that was left—except, as always for every lost love, the puzzling question of how what was now so obviously unworthy could ever have so completely claimed his affection.

An airplane passed overhead and its sound, drawn out by the wind, was a high wail of loneliness. He turned to the road that came up the hill, watching for headlights. Of all the nights that Lory might have deserted him, why did it have to be tonight?

He glanced upward at the second story of the big house. The windows of the master bedroom were dark. His wife had gone up to bed at eleven. He had wanted to talk to her ... once tonight he had even called to her ... but she hadn't heard him ... working on the pledge cards for the hospital drive. Probably just as well ... always hard to talk to Miriam ... and, anyway, she was asleep by now. He was alone ... alone ... alone ...

But Lory would be home in a few minutes. Then he *could* talk. That's what he had to do ... talk it out. He needed someone to understand ... Lory ... Lory would understand ... she always did.

The March wind still carried the sound of the plane.

Lory Austen saw the traffic light at the corner blink from green to red and, waiting as Paul Bronson slowed the convertible, told herself that she knew what he would say as he stopped the car.

As always he proved predictable. His right hand fell away from the steering wheel and she knew that, in the pretense of accident, it would touch her thigh where her coat was parted, where there would be only thin silk between his hand and her flesh.

There was the lost heartbeat of waiting and then she felt it—only the hard brush of his knuckles, instantaneous and then gone, no more than that. No tremor flashed inward from the touched nerve ends. There was no response from her brain, no lingering of sensation, now not even the persistence of memory.

It was another confirmation of the fear that had come to haunt her —that some weird atrophy of desire had dulled her nerves and deadened the lobe of her brain that made her a woman. Would she never again respond to the touch of a man's hand? Was that something that would happen only once in her life and, having happened once, could never happen again? No, that was impossible ... crazy ... neurotic! But how could she know that it wasn't true?

"It isn't so late, Lory, only a few minutes after midnight. How about stopping by the apartment for a nightcap? I told Jim and Anne that we might."

"Not tonight, Paul."

Not tonight ... not any night ... he was only playing out the sham of their man-and-woman masquerade. Oh, he would be willing enough to marry her. But not for herself ... because she was Grant Austen's daughter ... because a marriage certificate would be exchanged for a stock certificate that would someday give him control of the Suffolk Moulding Company.

His body swayed toward her as the car started into the turn and she shrank away, purposefully evasive. She didn't need him ... no, not Paul Bronson nor any other man. It was archaic nonsense that a woman had to have a man in order to be happy. She could live alone and make her own life. And it would be a *good* life! Hundreds of women had proved that it could be done. Thousands! What was so wonderful about marriage? Dull routine ... boredom ... bickering ... divorce. No, this was better ... an artist's life ... and she *was* an artist. No one could deny that. Four books illustrated and a fifth ...

Through the thin screen of the bare-branched trees she had caught a glimpse of her home, identified by the multi-colored glow of light through the leaded glass windows of the library. Her father was still up ... waiting for her ... another of those horrible middle-of-the-night talks ...

"Sure you won't change your mind, Lory?"

She hesitated, tempted. If she went to Paul's apartment it would be possible to lose an hour. By then her father might have given up and gone to bed, pardoning her from the torturous pretense of attempting to understand the things he always wanted to talk to her about ... phenol-formaldehyde extrusion of the melamine ratio of standard costs to the excess profits of the pressure per square inch on the net profit of the year-end polystyrene ...

"I'm sorry, Paul. Not tonight."

They drove on until stopped by another red light.

This time his hand did not fall from the steering wheel. That, too, was expected. She had somehow known that it wouldn't happen again.

The car was moving and, between two houses, she caught another glimpse of the library windows. A black silhouette moved across one of them. Her father was out on the terrace, waiting for her.

"Go up the back drive, Paul."

He would stop the car at the library terrace and, seeing her father, would not attempt to kiss her.

••••• *3*

There was the fanning sweep of the headlights as the car turned up the drive and Grant Austen stepped back into the moon-cast shadow of the giant columnar yew at the corner of the terrace.

Waiting, he heard the wind-muffled sound of Lory's voice, a car door opening and closing, and then he saw her running up the path toward him, her coat whipped back, her dress molded against her body by the March wind. In that moment of first seeing she was a moon-sculptured nymph suddenly sprung to life out of the mysterious wonder of the night.

Her voice was a startling return to the earthy reality of flesh and blood. "Fine thing," she said, terrier-shaking his hand in mock admonishment. "You'll never get rid of your old-maid daughter if you do a thing like that."

120

"Now what have I done?"

"Frightening away the only man in the world just as he might have been about to propose."

Her voice was an invitation to laughter and he tried to accept it. "Time a child of your age was in bed."

Instantly, he felt the fear that he had hurt her, that being called a child might be an unpleasant reminder of what he knew troubled her most—that she was twenty-six and unmarried.

But there was no break in the soft ruffle of her laughter. "What about a child of your age? What are you doing up so late?"

"Waiting for you."

She looped her arm through his. "No, you weren't."

He made a show of looking at his watch, subconsciously restrained from admission. "I'll have to speak to that young whipper-snapper. No good at the office if he's up all night running around with the boss's daughter."

"But it's very nice for the boss's daughter."

Her words were gaily tossed and he felt a cold shiver of fear. Was it possible that she had meant what she had said about Paul Bronson proposing? He set his lips on guard before he spoke, carefully filtering his concern from his voice. "Have a good time?"

Her throat made a wordless sound, liquidly pleasant.

"Nice dinner?" he asked.

"Very."

They stood silent and again there was the wild-geese sound from the sky.

"Spring's coming," he said. "Wind's changed. It's warmer now than it was this afternoon."

She threw back her head and her face was blue ivory in the moonlight. "It's March. There couldn't be a night like this in any other month but March."

The car was turning at the end of the drive and they were caught for a moment in a blazing glare of its headlights. He waited until the black night came back. "I didn't really break up anything, did I, Lory?"

"Of course you did. Two minutes more and I would have been one of the world's two greatest experts on the amortization of tool costs."

He chuckled, consciously showing his appreciation. She was a wonderful girl. There was no one like Lory, no one in all the world!

"And," Lory added, "you needn't worry about my distracting Mr. Bronson from his job. He's undistractable."

"Even by the boss's daughter?"

"Particularly by the boss's daughter."

There was a sense of guilt in his feeling of relief and he tried to ease his conscience. "Paul's a good boy, Lory. He's all right."

"Are you really so anxious to get rid of me?"

He flipped his open-fingered hand. "You know better than that."

They went through the door together, Lory wrinkling her nose at the foul still-smoke-filled air of the library, glancing accusingly at the heaped ashtray and the paper litter on the top of his desk. She swung sharply to face him, her hands on his shoulders. "What's wrong, Dad?"

Instinct counseled evasion but his caution was overwashed by gratitude for the quickness of her perception. His wife had not known but his daughter did. It was always like that, always Lory who knew when something was wrong. Miriam had been in the house all evening and the only thing that she had said was, "I think I'll go up to bed now, dear. Don't work too late or you'll have one of your headaches in the morning."

"Something's wrong," Lory said, reiterating her awareness.

"Afraid I am up against a tough one," he admitted.

"Shall I make some coffee?"

That was her idiomatic way of asking if he would talk to her about it. She often made coffee for their middle-of-the-night talks. Strangely, Lory's coffee never kept him awake as other coffee usually did.

"I'd rather have a highball tonight, Lory."

He savored her surprise. It was the first night he had ever asked for whiskey instead of coffee. Her hesitation was clear evidence of her concern for him.

"Scotch?" she asked.

He nodded, watching her as she crossed the room and went into the pine-paneled bar, finding an odd pleasure in the way that her hurried anxiety made her fumble at the unaccustomed task.

There were two glasses in her hand when she came back into the library and he smiled inwardly as he noticed that the water in her glass was almost crystal clear.

He sipped, tasting. "There's more than a jigger in this, young lady."

"You looked as if you needed it."

He felt the warm flush of his gratitude ... Miriam would probably have said, "Do you really want a drink this late at night, dear?"

Lory curled into the big red leather chair beside his desk, kicking off her shoes, and he was reminded again that she was only a girl, only twenty-six ... twenty-six was so much younger than you realized when you were twenty-six.

"All right, tell me what's wrong, Dad." It was a soft command, smile-tempered. "The truth, the whole truth, and nothing but the truth."

He hesitated, facing the barrier of beginning, the difficulty of finding the first words. Now that Lory was here he couldn't quite recapture the mood of wavering uncertainty that had hung over him before she had come.

"I'm up against a rough problem, Lory." He shuffled the stacked papers on his desk as evidence.

She had leaned back and her face had fallen into shadow as it moved out of the cone of light that fell from the desk lamp. "Oh, you've been up against rough problems before."

He was stopped by alarm. There had been the sound of a yawn in Lory's voice. Something was wrong. She didn't understand. Hadn't she heard what he had said? Could it be ... yes, she had glanced toward the window ... Paul Bronson ... she was still thinking about Bronson.

"This is serious, Lory," he said sharply, driven by the urgency of recapture. "It looks like I've come to the end of the line."

Shockingly, her voice was still lightly unconcerned. "You can't make me believe that."

What was the matter with Lory tonight? Always before he had been able to count on her. Tonight she didn't understand. He felt the spreading nettle prick of terror, shuffling the litter of papers in front of him, silent, finally realizing that he couldn't expect Lory to understand what he hadn't told her.

"Andscott is forcing us into producing a new television cabinet that's too big to turn out on any of our presses," he said carefully. "If we don't do it, they'll take all of the rest of their business out of our plant. If we go ahead, it means plowing back a lot of money—at least a quarter of a million dollars, maybe more."

"Couldn't Mr. Atherson help you?"

She still didn't understand!

"But, Lory, can't you see—" He stopped, waiting for the draining away of annoyance. "I'm going down to see him tomorrow. But I know what the answer will be. There's only one way I can get a quarter of a million dollars."

"How?"

"Let someone else into the company—sell someone a block of stock."

"Could you do that?"

"Of course, but—Lory, can't you see what that would mean? If I had to sell a part of the company—well, I might as well sell all of it!"

He had raised the pitch of his expectancy to the breaking point, the now-or-never moment when Lory *had* to understand.

Suddenly, miraculously, as the ultimate justification of faith is always a miracle, he heard her say, "Well, why don't you? Why don't you get out and let someone else take all the grief?"

A tremor ran through his body at the release of tension and he felt a welling warmth of rightness that erased any doubts of Lory's understanding. "Well, maybe you're right. I know this—we can make a lot more money by selling out now than by going on operating the company. Here, let me show you."

He shuffled hurriedly through the papers, finding the long tabular sheet where he had summarized his calculations. Lory had gotten up and was standing behind him, her hand on his shoulder, and words came more easily now. "Here are some figures that I've worked up tonight. This is a projection of what our total net profit might be for the next ten years. That's the best I could hope for. I've even allowed for some cut in taxes. But look—here's what I'd have to plow back into the factory just to replace worn-out equipment and do the things we'll have to do to keep up with our competitors. You can see for yourself what it means. I'll have to put back more than we can possibly earn. There's just no point in going on, Lory, no point at all."

"Then why do it?" She pivoted quickly, half-sitting now on the edge of the desk, looking down at him.

"That's what I wanted to talk to you about."

"You've had so many years of it, worked so hard, taken so much out of yourself. Why go on?"

"You want me to sell?"

"Dad, it isn't a question of what I want. The only thing that—"

"No, Lory, it *does* matter what you want." He stopped, lost, and then out of nowhere came a suddenly touched memory. "After all, I couldn't sell the company without your agreement. You're the second largest stockholder."

"I'm what?"

"You own almost five thousand shares. Don't you remember our deal when you left for Mount Oak? I sold you a block of stock. I've been paying for it out of your allowance ever since—plowing back your dividends—and then there's your grandfather's stock. He left that to you in his will. Whether you realize it or not, Lory, you're quite a wealthy young woman. If I could sell the company for two million, your share would be something like—well, close to two hundred thousand."

She stared at him, wide-eyed with astonishment.

"There'd be tax, of course," he went on. "But it would be only capital gains—maximum of twenty six per cent."

"But could you get two million for the company?"

"Well, I had a talk with Gil Clark this morning and he thought I *might* get that much. Depends, of course, on finding the right buyer. Might not be able to quite hit two million. I'll get a better idea tomorrow. I'm going down to have lunch with Will Atherson."

She was looking at him intently, studying his face. "Dad, you're really serious, aren't you?"

He tried to soften her face with a little joke that he hoped would make her smile. "Of course I'd have to have your agreement—second largest stockholder."

"You aren't worrying about me?"

"Not now."

No, not now ... Lory understood ... she knew that he wasn't giving up, that he wasn't running away, that the smart thing to do was to get out before the Andscott business blew up.

"Dad, could you be happy without the company?"

"Happy? Why not?"

"I was just wondering."

"Don't worry about me being happy, Lory, not me."

"Would you sell for what you said—two million?"

"Would I!" Uncontrollably, there was the sound of exultation in his voice. "Just let someone offer me two million and he'll own the Suffolk Moulding Company so fast it'll make his head swim."

He reached out to take her hand, feeling the wonderful warmth of her agreement. The touching of their hands was a pact, a pledge, the promise of a happiness beyond anything there had ever been before. He'd been a fool to wait as long as he had, imagining that the final break would be hard to make. It had been so simple, so easy.

●●●●● 4

Miriam Austen lay in the darkness, her lips parted to quiet her breathing, courting the hope that absolute silence might permit her to pick words out of the distantly faint buzz of conversation that drifted up from the library on the floor below. Occasionally a word-sound did rise tantalizingly close to the threshold of recognition, only to lose itself in the whistling moan of the wind outside.

What her ears did not hear, her imagination supplied. Her body, responding to her mind, was warm-damp with the vapor of burnt-out anger and the still-burning small fire of jealousy. Her nightgown felt sticky and clinging and she turned restlessly, trying to free its sodden grasp. Then, death-still again, her ears took up their word-hungry search.

She told herself that after all these years she should be able to accept, without recourse to hope, the plain fact that she could never be as close to Grant as Lory was. She *should* ... but she couldn't, not completely.

Her despair was not rooted in resentment. What had happened was not Lory's fault ... or Grant's either. It was her own punishment for having made such an abysmal failure of her marriage. The most frightening prospect was that Lory might make the same mistake that she had made. The circumstances were alarmingly similar. She, too, had worshiped her father. She had married Grant Austen without love ... yes, that was a sin in itself, but a small one ... and there might have been love if, in that first year of her marriage, she had been able to break her bondage to her father. Her life would have been different if she had only realized that Alvin T. Manson had not been the superlative creature that she thought him to be, that Grant Austen was so much more worthy of her love and respect.

Actually, there had been love ... at least moments of love. On that night when her mother had whispered the horrifying confidence that Alvin T. Manson was guilty of fraud, that he had appropriated funds that were not his and hidden his guilt in the closing of the bank, hadn't her first impulse been to tell her husband? Didn't that prove that she really loved him? But there was already that high wall between them that could not be broken down with words ... afraid that Grant would not be able to understand that her love, declared then, was something more than a rebound rejection of her loyalty to her father.

She had hated those after years when she had been forced to sneak money, Grant's money, out of her household allowance and give it to her father. A thousand times she had wanted to tell her husband and seek the absolution of confession ... just as she had wanted so desperately to warn Grant that her father shouldn't be taken into the company and made its treasurer. Even after he had finally left the company, there had been that lingering terror because she had never known what had really happened. Grant had told her nothing, only that her father would be taken care of for the rest of his life.

At least there was that difference ... Lory could always be proud of her father ... but all the rest was an alarming parallel. She, too, like Lory, had been an only child in a marriage that hadn't worked. In her daughter's case there was an excuse. In her own, there had been none. Grant was honest and fine and good. The fault was her

126

own. It was she who, out of fear and delusion and weakness, had failed her husband and driven him to turn to Lory.

It was only in these last few years that Miriam Austen had been able to face that terrible self-accusation. But, finally accepted, it brought the partially compensating recognition of what was really happening between Lory and Grant. Before she had come to that truth, Miriam Austen's desperate loneliness had driven her far beyond the bounds of reason, goading her into the suspicion that there was something revoltingly abnormal in the relationship between her husband and their daughter. Now, long since, she had conquered that insane nightmare. It was all normal, perfectly explainable, and the endpoint was plain. Lory *must* fall in love, not merely to marry as she had married Grant, not because she had thought it was something her father wanted her to do, but to fall in love so wildly and passionately, so totally and completely, that affection for her father would fade to such a dim thing by comparison that it could never cast a shadow over her marriage.

A faintly bitter-sweet smile crossed Miriam Austen's face as she recalled what she had seen a half hour before. She had heard the car in the drive and had gone to the window to look down, safely unseen in the darkness. Lory had gotten out of the car almost as soon as it stopped. There had been no moment of lingering as there would certainly have been if there were the slightest danger that Lory might be considering a loveless marriage to Paul Bronson. That would be no solution. But Lory knew it. Lory knew what it meant to be in love ... that man in Maine, whoever he had been. If you were really in love once you could never be fooled again.

Miriam Austen's lips moved in the darkness, almost voicing the words that she had said silently so many times before ... *why couldn't it have been that man in Maine ... why, why, why?* No matter who he was, no matter what had happened between them, that would have been the answer to everything. But that was over ... done ... years ago. Lory had to fall in love *again* ... she *had* to!

Miriam Austen's mind, saving itself, spun the pink floss of a dream. Lory would meet a man this summer ... fall in love ... run away ... marry ... live in London ... Paris ... San Francisco ... any place that was far away. Then she and Grant would be together again, alone, the way they had been alone together that week in New York ... the diamond clip and his boy-bashful voice saying, "You've been wonderful this week, Miriam, just wonderful and I want you to have this." He had kissed her then as he had never kissed her before or since ... but he would again ... when Lory was gone ... when they were alone ...

Footsteps were coming up the stairs . . . Grant . . . Lory . . .

"Goodnight, Lory."

"Goodnight, Dad."

In the instant before the door opened, an unconquerable impulse made Miriam Austen close her eyes. For a moment, the hall light glowed dull red through her lowered eyelids. It snapped off. Grant tiptoed across the room. She tried desperately to force a word through her lips that would tell him she was awake, but her voice froze in her throat as it had so many times before. Defeated, she lay in the too-still stillness of feigned sleep.

There was the latch click of the bathroom door closing and she opened her eyes. Moonlight marbled the wall with the writhing veins of racing cloud shadows and she was struck with the hallucination that she was staring into the organic depths of her own brain.

●●●●● 5

Lory threw open the south window of her bedroom and the curtains whipsnapped in the March wind. Her hands caught them back and she stood in the darkness with her arms spread, feeling the wind against her body.

The clouds were unbroken now, the moonlight gone. A sparse spangle of lights marked the town in the valley below and she imagined the deep sleep of all the people who were lying in their beds under those black roofs. It was a purposeful thought, consciously provoked as an attempt to incite sleep, but she knew there would be no result. She was hopelessly awake. This would be another of those sleepless nights.

Would her father really sell the company, or was it only another of his midnight ideas that would be gone and forgotten by morning? Probably. She'd been a fool for a minute or two, letting herself be tricked, accepting hope as fact . . . her old trouble, the same mistake she had made too many times before.

There was a distant moving light, an automobile circling the reservoir, its headlights drawing a self-erasing chalk line on the blackboard of the night. Paul? No, he'd be in bed by now, asleep, dreaming his cost accountant dreams . . . "You see, Lory, what your father doesn't seem to comprehend is that bringing in new capital would favorably affect our whole tax base. Our carrying charges would be offset by a tax saving so that . . ."

Her forced smile twisted into a scowl of inquiry. Had Paul been trying to tell her that her father was incompetent, slipping, losing his hold ...?

She felt the angry counterthrust of filial loyalty. It wasn't his fault! It was this crazy world and what it was doing to good men ... battering down their courage ... weakening them ... destroying their initiative. The world wanted weaklings now, cringing little men whose bible was the income tax manual, hunting for salvation in the fine print that promised absolution from the hellfire and damnation of the Bureau of Internal Revenue, little men like Paul Bronson who priced himself so cheaply that he could be bought for a marriage certificate ... if there was enough common stock attached.

Paul had said it himself ... "There isn't much chance to build a business out of earnings these days." No, you didn't *build* it, you *married* it! That was his shoddy little plan, the petty conniving of his dollar-sharp mind, the insult of imagining that she could be tricked into responding to him as a woman was supposed to respond to a man she loved.

I hate him and everyone like him!

She shouted the silent words and then waited for the confirmation of anger. It did not come. It was as if one part of her brain was set against the other, a guardian segment that weighed and measured every thought, passing only the true and rejecting all that was false.

She accepted the rejection, realizing now that anger was a false emotion, untenable, another attempt to make herself believe what she wanted to believe, that her inability to respond to Paul Bronson's invitation of affection was chargeable to him and not to this terrifying inadequacy within herself. It wasn't only Paul Bronson, it was *any* man, *all* men ... even her father ...

Her father?

No, that was different. The affection of a daughter for a father was not the same thing at all as the love of a woman for a man. Or was it? Even with her father she had never been able to respond as she should have responded. Was there something wrong there, too?

The oscillating pendulum of her wildly fluctuating mood swung wide, touching sensitive contact points that had never before been joined. Was it possible that there was a connection between the way she felt about her father and this atrophy of desire that had grown within her woman's body, this deadening that had destroyed the thing that made her a woman?

It was a terrifying thought, pushing her toward the depths of what seemed an unexplored cavern. Yet, as she approached the blackness, there was the vague suggestion of familiarity, as if in a dream, or in another life, or in her early childhood, before reality had become something separable from instinct, she had walked into this same unlighted cave.

Lory Austen had known, seemingly always, that she had not been what her father had wanted her to be. She had been a disappointment. He had wanted a son. She could see now that he had, relentlessly, in a thousand little ways, with a patience more terrifying than force, tried to remold her into the image of what his son might have been.

She was closer now than she had ever been before to an understanding of the instinctive resistance she had always had to conquer before she could do the things he wanted her to do. She could remember the horror of his taking her through the molding plant when she was a little girl, so small then that he had carried her from the car to the door on his shoulder, but forcing her to walk when they entered the man's world of the factory. When she had cried with fright, he had said, "Look at the men, they aren't afraid." That was how he had first let her know that he wanted her to be as a man would be, as his son would have been if he had had a son, and that was the same day when, to her speechless embarrassment, he had taken her to the *men's* toilet.

She remembered the doll he had brought her from California, a boy doll instead of a girl doll, and the bicycle that was a boy's instead of a girl's, and he said that he had "forgotten" when her mother had pointed out the error and made him correct it. She remembered, too, the time he had wanted to give her a Shetland pony because they had seen a little boy riding a pony. By then she must have known, even if subconsciously, because she had protested that she didn't want a pony—which had not been true before but had become true with the offer—and it was then that she had asked him to build her a studio like Eloise Tassman's.

A part of her decision to become an artist had been based upon her childhood belief that artists were always *women*—like Eloise Tassman—and that a studio was something inviolately feminine, a haven of escape from the world that was trying to make little girls into little boys.

Her later memories were more positive evidence ... those weekends when her father made her come to Washington from Mount Oak to meet his businessmen friends ... forcing her to spend that summer working in his office ... wanting her to go to Wharton Business instead of art school. She had fought against Wharton but her victory had been no victory at all. It had ended in the compromise of Prather and the promise that she would study industrial designing.

Always, he had talked to her about her plans for the future—when she would join him in the factory—as if he were continually forgetting that she was not his son.

There had been a hundred nights like tonight when he had drawn her into the library and forced her to take a man's role, asking her for a man's advice and a man's counsel. She had always played the part as best she could, pretending an interest that she had never felt, but now there was the terrifying suspicion that, like an actor too long identified with a single role, she had lost herself in the part she had played, that her father had finally won, that despite her resistance he had imposed a maleness upon her that now could never be escaped, that something had been killed within her and could never again be brought to life.

No, no, no ... that wasn't true ... she was a woman! It was only because it was Paul ... there was nothing wrong with her ... it had happened once ...

She flung herself on the bed and, with the same abandoned submission that overwhelms an alcoholic no longer able to sustain a vow of temperance, she did what she had promised herself a thousand times that she would never do again. Purposefully, she opened the floodgates of her mind and let herself be overwhelmed with the one memory that proved what now so desperately needed to be proved.

Her memory, drawn from an artist's sharp observation, brought back the undeniable reality of that evening in Maine when she had seen him for the first time. She denied herself the quick memory of the climax, lingering over all the little preliminaries, tracing the chain of linked circumstances that had made it happen—the preamble of the drunkard sipping his first drink of the night, the narcotic addict's slow ceremony of the preparation.

It had started with Barbara Hough. It was Barbara who had invited her to come to Maine and talked her into taking that lithograph class under Eric Linksman. It was Eric who had shown her two lithographs to Marybelle Hudson, who wrote children's books, and it was Miss Hudson who had been responsible for her being invited to a cocktail party at the Maine summer home of Jefferson Clark, the Philadelphia publisher.

The crush of the crowd at Jefferson Clark's party had been so great that she had been swept away from her host after his first blank greeting. All evening she had waited for Marybelle Hudson to fulfill her promise to arrange a talk. Finally, with the special loneliness of accepted disappointment, she had let the swirling tide of the crowd carry her aimlessly toward the quiet backwater of the porch. Then, alone, she walked down the path toward the shore.

Now, forcing hesitation, delaying, she lingered over the last of those preliminary memories, sketch notes caught with the needle-sharp focus of her artist's eyes ... the cerulean and lemon-chrome greenness of iris leaves beside the path ... the black-blueness of a delphinium spike palette-knifed against the blue-blackness of the night sky ... the overpainted wraith of the insect swirl around the bare lamp bulb at the end of the wharf ... the viridian-edged waves that were breaking in the pool of light.

She had been watching the waves when she heard footsteps on the wharf and had turned to see him walking toward her, materializing out of the night, tall and dark, loose shouldered but tight-hipped, moving with the easy grace of a powerful animal and, when he spoke, his voice carried that same suggestion of enormous suppressed strength. But she remembered neither what he had said nor what she had answered. Her memory was an artist's memory, of the eye and not of the ear, and what had been preserved in her mind was a page from an infinitely detailed sketchbook, recording every line and plane of his face.

Front-seen, it was square-cut and block-jawed, strong-boned, the face of a young Highland warrior in an old portrait. In profile, however, his features were an odd denial, not roughly chiseled as the front view suggested but drawn with a clean, dry-point line. It was a face of contradictions—stubborn strength set against sensitivity, reasoned intelligence against unreasoned instinct, courage against shrewdness. Seeing him there on the wharf she had been momentarily torn between approval and caution, but more attracted than repelled even in the beginning, and after the beginning there had been only attraction.

"I've been watching you," he said and she knew that it was true, as true as all of the other things that she had imagined into reality.

They found the little sloop moored to the wharf and the night wind carried them soundlessly out into the dark water and around the headland that shut away the lights of the house and the sound of the dance music.

There were a hundred memories of that hour on the water, sub-consciously recorded then to be sharply recalled later, but none so vividly remembered afterwards as what he had said when the moon came up. They had joked about it looking like a chromo postcard—the defense of bathos—and then he had said roughly, "Damn it, I wish I were ten years younger."

The power behind his voice had suggested that he could make any wish come true, even that one, but it was then that he flattened the mainsail to the backwind of the headland and, silently, they sailed around the point and back to the lights and the music and the crowd.

He disappeared as he had come, into the night. There was no chance then to ask him his name nor, since he could not be pointed out, any way to ask anyone else who he was.

Five days later, back at the art colony, bending over her sketchboard, she had sensed a presence and looked up to see him watching her. There had seemed no need to ask how he had found her, only to accept the fact that he was there. Without command or decision she had closed her sketchbook and they had walked away together, lingering in the pine-smelling coolness of the woods when the sun was still high, then wandering the shore after it was shadowed by the mountain, coming finally to the Inn where he had told her he was staying for the night.

They had eaten together in the dining room but there was no memory of food, only the blur of racing time, and then walking down the road toward the terrifying inevitability of reaching the door of the house where she was living. The terror had become reality and he had left her and she was standing alone in the darkness of the front hall. He had not kissed her, only reached out to touch her hand, but as it had fallen away it had accidentally brushed her thigh.

Now, lying on the bed, her hands clenching the coverlet, what she remembered was not so much a true memory as the recollection of an incredible fantasy. The touch of his hand had been the plunging needle of a hypodermic syringe, flooding her arteries with a stimulant so overpowering that she had lost all semblance of self-control. Her body had become a self-thinking entity, cut free from her brain, and without the direction of volition she had followed him to the Inn.

That was what *must* have happened because she had no conscious knowledge, then or afterward, of how she came to his room at the Inn, only that there had been a time when he was kissing her and crushing her to him and her child's flesh had become a woman's flesh, suddenly ripened by the narcotic of desire to a tremulous anticipation that hovered between ecstasy and terror.

It was terror that triumphed. His arms were steel bars that held her away from him ... "Lory, it can't be—no, no, no—you don't know what you're doing!"

And then she had been caught up in a spasm of trembling that must have shaken loose the knotted ends of every nerve in her body for, even when she was in the car and driving alone through the night, there was a sense of disembodiment. Before, there had been only her flesh and afterwards only her brain, her body disowned by the disgrace of its animal passion.

But afterwards, long before now, there had been a fading away of the stain of convicted vulgarity that her body had smudged across her child's mind, replaced by the all-important knowledge that once she had been a woman ... *once* ... and that what had once been would sometime be again. It couldn't have been destroyed that night ... *no, no, no ... it was something too powerful ever to be destroyed!*

Her clenched fingers opened in another outpouring of her endless night-after-night confession of what a fool she had been, running away like the child that he had thought she was, not waiting to prove that she was the woman he had made her become ... not knowing who he was, nor where he had come from, nor where she could ever find him again, only that one tiny barest scrap of knowledge about him. Walking the shore that afternoon, she had asked him to tell her his name and he said that his name was Cash McCall.

Seven

:
:
:
:

IN THE KITCHEN of the Hotel Ivanhoe, it was the calm before the storm. Wednesday was the big day, the Wharf luncheon on top of everything else. All morning long there had been a gradually up-building swirl of activity. Now it was that moment of almost suspended animation while the cooks and their helpers stood by, watching the swinging doors to the Fontainebleau Room, waiting for the first rush of orders.

Max Nicollet, impersonating an avenging god on an inflated self-contained throne, darted his black eyes about the scene searching for a worthy object upon which to practice a warm-up rage. Finding none, he did the best he could and bore down on the shining cart that a waiter was cautiously moving toward the service elevator. Snatching off the enormous silver cover of the tureen—in itself no mean feat of strength—he bent over and dilated his nostrils to catch the savory odor steaming up from the *Crab Ivanhoe* that was destined for the luncheon in the Velvet Room.

Clapping back the cover with the crash of a giant cymbal, he threatened to impale the waiter with his bristling mustache and demanded, "What is wrong? You tell me! What is wrong?"

The waiter quavered.

"You are not proud to serve this?" Max challenged.

The waiter did his best to execute the demanded assignment of simultaneously registering both pride and fright.

Max was not satisfied. His big hands carried out the orders that his

135

voice barked. "Push in the stomach! Straighten the back! Square the shoulders! Now you are better. No more do you look like the man who carries slops to the pigs."

With a well-placed slap of his bear-paw hand on the waiter's bony behind, Max propelled him toward the elevator. Then, dusting his hands with satisfaction, he rolled back toward the stoves, a behemoth threatening to crush everything in its path.

• • • • • 2

Easing her foot from the throttle, Lory Austen let the Cadillac glide toward the changing light, caught the flash of green, glanced right and made the left turn onto Lancaster Avenue, heading for downtown Philadelphia.

She had seen her father's face when she had looked to the right and his expression had again confirmed what she still found it so hard to believe—that his determination to sell the company had actually survived the night—and, even more miraculously, that it had so quickly changed him into such a very different person. She could not remember ever having seen him so happily carefree as he was this morning. The remarkable change had been evident at the breakfast table and the fear that it might be a transient thing, easily lost, had caused her to invent the excuse that she wanted to see her publishers and prompted the suggestion that she drive him to Philadelphia. He had accepted with an enthusiasm only slightly dimmed by the two hours that he had spent at the office. Even that loss had been quickly recouped after she had picked him up and they were on their way.

The night flying horrors of her imagination had been so completely banished that there remained only the filmiest wisp of daylight doubt that the sale of the company would completely break the hold of her father's domination. She could see now, measured by his relief, the terrible weight that the company had put upon him. That was why he had clung to her—to satisfy the simple human need of having someone to whom he could talk. When the company was sold, the son-wish would die. There would no longer be need for the outlet of those midnight talks. He would be free of the fears and worries that had made him cling to her and she, in turn, would be free of the trammeling ties that had bound her to him and to Suffolk.

But there was still that restraining final need for clinching confirmation—that when the company was sold he would willingly set her completely free—and she asked, "Do you know what I think you should do?"

"What?"

"Take Mother and go on some kind of wonderful trip—maybe around the world."

"What about you?"

"I think it's something you should do by yourselves, just the two of you."

She waited, breath-held and tense, and then she heard him say, as wonderfully casual as if there had been no real decision involved, "Might not be a bad idea at that. Something I've always had in mind doing. Never had the time before."

"And, Dad, it would mean so much to Mother. You can't imagine how much."

"Yes, I suppose it would," he said in soft speculation. "We've never had time to do very many things together, your mother and I. Always been too tied down with the company."

"You'll be free now," she said—but the echo of her words was distorted to the exultant shout that it was she who would be really free.

A memory thrust itself forward as if it had been waiting for this moment, the recollection of a brief item in last month's *Art News* noting that Eric Linksman, with whom she had studied that summer in Maine, had established his studio at Fiascherino on the Ligurian Coast of Italy and was accepting a limited number of advanced students.

That was it! She would go to Italy. Eric would snap her out of this slump she was in ... Eric and the kind of people he always gathered around him. That was what she needed, the inspiration of companionship with her own kind, those wonderful sessions they used to have under the trees in Maine ... nights around Eric's fireplace ... her brain exploding fireworks and the sparks coming right out of her fingertips when she sat down at the drawing board. Of course she would go! Why not? She could do what she wanted now ... her own money ... there was nothing to stop her.

She turned to her father, ready to confide her plan, but found herself interrupted by the strangeness of having thought of Maine but not, until this afterthought, of Cash McCall. It had never happened before and, exultantly, she realized that now he, too, was something of which she was free. All that cancerous memory that had grown like some terribly abnormal thing in the soft tissue of her mind had been ripped out and thrown away.

"Lory, I've been thinking," her father said.

She voiced a wordless sound of inquiry.

"You know, last night I was talking about getting two million for the company?"

"Yes."

"Maybe that's a little high. Might get it, of course—know more after I talk to Will Atherson—but I'm not going to hold out for it. As long as I can get a fair price—maybe a million seven or a million eight—I'm going to sell. Confound it, now that I've made up my mind to do it I feel like getting it over with. What do you think?"

"As a minority stockholder, I vote *yea.*"

He answered with a low chuckle. "You're wonderful, Lory, wonderful. No president could ask for a better minority stockholder. All right, it's decided. Passed unanimously."

"Unanimously," she said, and the lift of her voice was the sound of freedom confirmed.

• • • • • 3

Gil Clark came to the edge of the Square and, looking across, saw the Hotel Ivanhoe through the bias-weave veiling of a sudden shower. He was arriving too early for his twelve-thirty luncheon appointment with Cash McCall, but the impulse that made him hesitate and then step back under a sheltering doorway was something more deeply rooted than an awareness of time.

His mind had been in a state of bubbling ferment ever since his meeting yesterday with Harrison Glenn, but the turbid distillate would not come clear no matter how many times he ran it through the hot still of his brain. Over and over again, he had reminded himself of what Harrison Glenn had said—that Corporation Associates had a professional obligation to help Grant Austen get the best possible price for the Suffolk Moulding Company—yet he could not conquer his aversion to allowing the company to fall into the hands of someone like Cash McCall.

Harrison Glenn had been right, of course, in his warning against a prejudgment of McCall ... *but damn it, the man even lived at the Hotel Ivanhoe!* That alone was enough to brand him for what he was. The Ivanhoe was the vulture's roost, the jackal's lair, the hangout for the quick-money crowd. That's where you saw them ... the chiselers and gougers, the sharpies and the tax-money boys, the *operators.* They'd all be there this noon ... five-dollar lunches in

138

the Fontainebleau Room ... folding-money tips. Expense didn't matter to them ... what the hell, it was deductible, wasn't it?

Resolutely, he tried to damper the rise of his revulsion by admitting to himself that he was prejudiced against the Ivanhoe. How could he help it? That was where you really saw it, had it rubbed under your nose, crammed down your throat. It didn't matter any more who you were or what you stood for ... honor, ethics, standards of conduct. The only thing that mattered now was the color of your money ... the table you had in the Fontainebleau Room.

He stepped out from under the balcony and let himself be carried along by the flow of the crowd that spilled across the Square, feeling the familiarity of place and direction but oblivious to dated time. He had walked this same pavement as a boy when, home for the holidays, his father had taken him to the old Ivanhoe where, as a tradition of long standing, the prep school sons of respected patrons were served without charge on Saturdays, always black bean soup on Saturday noons, and the day that Alonzo, the old headwaiter, handed you the sherry cruet was the day you became a man and started paying for your own lunch ... a dollar bill ... eighty cents on the check and you left the change for a tip.

Even in '40, when Barbara came out, a dance in the old Ivanhoe ballroom was still considered an appropriate and sensibly economical way of introducing a group of Main Line debutantes to society. The war, of course, had changed that. By the time he had married Barbara, on his furlough in '43, the Ivanhoe had taken on a new character. The old ballroom had become the Fontainebleau Room and there was a Continental chef and a billboard menu with prices calculated to drive away the penny pinchers who would bother to look at them. The war-contract crowd did not. They were all on cost-plus.

Once, sentimentally, in that week before they were married, he had insisted on taking Barbara back to the Ivanhoe for lunch. She had warned him what would happen, but he couldn't believe that they wouldn't be able to get a table, certain that Alonzo would remember him. But Alonzo had disappeared with the rest of the old Ivanhoe. There was a type-cast headwaiter with a French accent, and a velvet-wrapped steel rope to hold back the commoners while the cost-plus aristocracy went their unimpeded double-breasted way. "It's the war," Barbara had said. "We'll find another place for lunch."

But the end of the war had not brought back the old Ivanhoe. The velvet rope stayed up and the passport requirements of the Fontainebleau Room remained unchanged. You had to be in the big money to make it ... one of the fast-buck boys, an operator ... a Harry Guizinger.

Gil Clark's mind gagged on the memories of that week he had been forced to spend with Harry Guizinger. It had been one of his last assignments at S.F.&P., working on the organization plan for Tronic Wire & Coil, lunching every day in the Fontainebleau Room with Guizinger, sitting across the table looking at that boar's head face, those greedy little pig eyes, his fat lips licking at the prospect of all the money he was going to make by liquidating the old Harris Wire Company and swallowing up all the profit in a tax-free transfer to Tronic Wire & Coil ... "Six lawyers I had already and not one says I ain't absolutely legal!"

Cash McCall would be another Guizinger ... what else could he be?

Coming full circle, Gil Clark's mind began to retrace the rut of tortured questioning that he had worn so deep in the last twenty-four hours. Was this the inevitable end of every small manufacturing business ... to fall into the hands of some operator, to be liquidated with nothing left but a dry pulp to discard? Or, as the only alternative, be tossed into the maw of some big corporation, digested and assimilated, lost in nameless anonymity?

He found it difficult to accept the limit of those two alternatives. Acceptance impinged upon an attitude fundamental to the hope and belief upon which he had built his life. Unlike most of his University classmates, Gil Clark had not drifted into the College of Business Administration because of any inability to make up his mind about what he wanted to do after graduation. His goal was set long before matriculation—to go into business and become a key man in some manufacturing enterprise.

In the same way that the boys in the College of Medicine had somehow become dedicated to the ideal of ministering to the ills of man, Gil Clark had been captivated by the prospect of "improving the human lot through the making of better and better products to aid in the fulfillment of richer lives." He had once written those words in a term paper that, unexpectedly, he had been called upon to read aloud. Spoken, it sounded like a pompous commercial on an institutional radio program, but the words expressed what he meant so he hadn't been too bothered by the tongue-in-cheek grins of some of his classmates.

The intricacies of the functioning human anatomy, which so excited the medical students, were paralleled for Gil Clark by the fascinating involvements of the modern manufacturing corporation. Industrial organizations were—again as he had written in his paper

140

—the "key structures of an industrial civilization, and it follows as a necessary corollary that the men who manage them are citizens of a high order."

To his astonishment, he had eventually discovered that the dean of the College of Business Administration, Dr. Willis Lee Cottrell, held no such views. The dean's senior seminar on *The Modern Corporation* revealed an attitude that black-marked industrialists as heartless and greedy enemies of the people. Cottrell saw the large corporation as a cancer on the body of society that must be excoriated at any cost. He preached the legitimacy of "small business" but what he regarded as *small* was impossibly so. Few manufacturing establishments, even the smallest, could qualify under his definition.

Cottrell's teaching purpose, apparently, was to evangelize his students into government bureaus. He was notably successful. Many of the members of the Class of '41—those whose physical unfitness saved them from service in the armed forces, as well as a number for whom occupational deferments were wangled—eventually landed in Washington.

Even if Gil Clark had not joined the Navy, he could never have belonged to the group that came to be called "the Cottrell boys." He saw the dean as a despicable character, as traitorous to the College of Business Administration as Dr. Weeker of the College of Medicine would have been had he set out upon the unthinkable mission of destroying the medical profession.

Actually, Gil had been mystified that the Board of Regents, two of whose members were heads of large corporations, hadn't booted Cottrell out of the University. Instead, both of their companies had paid Dr. Willis Lee Cottrell large fees for his services as a "management consultant."

The day after Gil Clark had been mustered out of service, he had gone to work for Clark-Dudley, the family-owned publishing house, and immediately undertook an analysis of its tottering affairs. One thing the study revealed was that the firm offered no opportunity for the early fulfillment of his own ambitions. Blocked, he took what he hoped would be a short cut to his war-postponed destiny by finding a place on the staff of Simonds, Farrar & Peters, a newly organized firm of business consultants and management counselors, hoping that he would be given a hand in directing the affairs of those clients who would now be turning to the manufacture of the wonderful new post-war products. Instead, he found himself one of a roomful of assistants to Nick Peters who, as the firm's income tax expert, was the busiest man on the staff.

It was while he was working with Nick Peters that Gil had learned about the jackals and the vultures. Around the S.F.&P. office they were known by the group name of *operators*. There was, it was true, enough similarity to justify the group naming but they were, nevertheless, rigidly individualistic men. They worked alone, in secrecy and without confidants, their steely eyes forever alert as they stalked companies that might be turned to their highly profitable purpose.

There was never a shortage of victims. There are always businesses on the down-cycle of success and, in those days, the number was swelled by factories staggering under the problems of reconversion, others drained to weakness by high taxes, still more that were family owned companies facing estate settling problems. Nor was there a shortage of potential buyers. All that had to be done was to locate another company that, through a combination of merged asset and earning figures, could effect a favorable change in its base for the calculation of taxes. Sometimes there were "loss carry-overs" to sweeten the deal, or a profit-dripping disparity between actual and book values. The "special situations" were almost endless, limited only by the ingenuity of the operators at finding companies that could be fitted to some fine-print crack that they had discovered in the tax regulations.

Most profitable of all—although it took a special skill to pull them off successfully—were the "liquidations" in which a company was sentenced to a slow death, gradually dismembered, and then sold piecemeal as a "distribution of assets." The end result was usually an empty factory building, often in a small community prostrated by the loss of the company payroll, but the *operators* didn't worry too much about that. By then they had collected their profit and stored it away, safe from the ravages of the tax collector. Everything they did was meticulously checked for legality by the best lawyers that money could retain.

Gil Clark disliked all of the *operators* but he reserved a special antipathy for the *liquidators*, despising them in much the same way that he had detested Dr. Willis Lee Cottrell, and for the same reason —they were *destroyers*.

The main impetus behind Gil Clark's shift to Corporation Associates had been his desire to escape the profit-mad scheming that pervaded the whole atmosphere at S.F.&P. By contrast, Corporation Associates' clients were mostly long established firms, solid and substantial, and as Jack Hildreth at the employment agency had pointed out, Harrison Glenn was a man no one could fail to respect.

For a moment, yesterday afternoon, that high estimate of Harrison Glenn had been threatened for the first time. Glenn's willingness to allow Suffolk Moulding to fall into the hands of an operator like Cash McCall had seemed a serious indictment of the president's character. Afterwards, however, Gil had convinced himself that Harrison Glenn was right—Corporation Associates had an undeniable obligation to help Grant Austen sell his company to the best advantage—and it was Austen, not Corporation Associates, who would make the choice of a buyer. The black mark that Gil Clark had momentarily placed against Harrison Glenn's name had been completely erased, but he had not been able to completely wipe away the accusation that Glenn had lodged against him—that his own interest in Suffolk Moulding was not as coldly dispassionate as it should have been.

Overnight, forced by Harrison Glenn's perceptive probing, he had come to acknowledge the truth that he could never be completely happy as a business analyst. What he needed was intimate identification with his own company and the more tangible sense of accomplishment that such an association would offer. Suffolk Moulding could give him what he wanted but, after that moment of unreasoned hope when the idea had first occurred to him, he had discarded the possibility. If Cash McCall bought Suffolk Moulding, there would be no opportunity to build it into the kind of company that good management could make it.

He was across the Square now, standing at the curb, waiting for a break in traffic that would let him cross the street to the Hotel Ivanhoe. The light on the corner changed and he ran, darting behind a taxi, cutting in front of a blue Cadillac that was gliding to a stop under the marquee, hurrying on toward the revolving door.

●●●●● 4

"That was Gil Clark," Lory Austen said. "I'm sure it was. He just went in the hotel."

"Could be," Grant Austen said. "Almost everybody eats here—not all of them up in The Wharf, of course."

The doorman hovered. "Park your car, miss?"

"Sure, that's the thing to do, Lory," Grant Austen agreed. "Leave the car here and take a taxi wherever it is that you're going."

She slipped across the wide seat, looking back to be sure that she had left the keys.

Her father waited for her. "I don't know what time I'll be through, Lory, but suppose you come back—well, make it three o'clock here in the lobby. If I'm not ready by then, I'll leave a message for you at the desk."

"Good luck," she said.

His eyes lighted. "Maybe I'll have some news for you."

He waited, not moving toward the revolving door.

The doorman's whistle had brought a cab and he asked, "Where to, miss?"

She bridged the moment of hesitation and then gave the address of the building where Clark-Dudley had its offices. The travel agency was only a block or two away.

"You'll get yourself some lunch, won't you?" her father asked anxiously as she was getting into the cab.

"Don't worry, Dad. I can take care of myself."

She closed the door, smiling.

He returned the smile.

••••• 5

Gil Clark bought a pack of cigarettes at the newsstand and, as he was pocketing the change, caught a glimpse of Grant Austen standing in the middle of the lobby. His first impulse was to step forward to tell Austen to be certain to call him after lunch but, seeing Maude Kennard approaching Austen, he waited and watched, half hidden by the newspaper rack.

He had once discussed Maude Kennard with Ken Sullivan, who had made a Corporation Associates study of the Hotel Ivanhoe last year. Ken had said that she was "smarter than a she-fox" and Gil's own observation of her during the time that Guizinger had been in town, and on scattered occasions since, had fully confirmed that judgment. Despite his distaste for what she had done to the old Ivanhoe, he found himself forced to admiration. The hotel business was a rough game, particularly with an old house that couldn't make a profit on the rental of its too-large rooms, and Ken had told him what Maude Kennard had accomplished. It had been her concept—Ken had given no credit at all to Pierce, the manager of the hotel—that the only way to make big money was to concentrate on the restaurant end and attract the expense-account trade. She had knowingly driven away the patronage of Main Line society, business that any other hotel manager in Philadelphia would have crawled on his knees to hold, explaining to Ken that there was no profit in selling

144

tea and chicken salad sandwiches to old dowagers who insisted that a luncheon check gave them the privilege of cluttering up the hotel with a bridge game afterward.

Now, watching Maude Kennard in action with Grant Austen, Gil Clark could believe what Ken had told him about the way that she could loosen up a thick bankroll ... "She's a dame that really missed her calling—could have been the greatest madame in the world."

Maude Kennard's voice was lost in the lobby sounds but pantomime and facial expression were enough to verify the fact that she was giving old Grant the full treatment—and was he falling for it!

A group of men came boiling in through the revolving door and Maude Kennard shifted her attention.

Gil stepped out and crossed to Grant Austen, surprised at the warmth of the greeting he received, deciding that Maude Kennard had had an uplifting effect on Austen's spirits.

"On that matter that we were talking about yesterday," Gil whispered, "I believe we have something that will interest you."

"Fine, fine," Austen bubbled. "Where can I get in touch with you after lunch?"

"I think I'll be back at the office. If I'm not there yet, talk to Mr. Glenn."

"What do you have in mind?"

"I can't tell you anything definite at the moment but if I were you I wouldn't decide anything until—"

Will Atherson was approaching and Austen whispered, "I'll call you."

Gil had met the banker on a previous occasion but it had been some time ago and he acknowledged the introduction. Then, excusing himself, he walked quickly toward the desk.

A hand reached out to grab his arm and he turned to see a face, at first strange, then dimly recalled. Fortunately, the recollection carried the memory of a matching name. It was Dale Turner who had spent a few months at S.F.&P. as one of the rotating complement of crew-cut assistants in Nick Peters' tax section.

They traded old-grad greetings, pointlessly hearty, and Turner asked, "Still in the same rat race?"

"I'm with Corporation Associates now. Have been for several years."

"Yeh, I'd heard about that," Turner said. "Thought maybe you'd gotten wise to yourself by now. Ought to get in my racket. Guess you know, huh—full partner with Wemberley & Fields, tax consultants? I'm manager of the Washington office."

"That's fine," Gil said flatly, remembering that Guizinger had been a Wemberley & Fields client.

"It's a living," Turner said with a lip-twisting smile. His clothes testified to his modesty—you didn't buy a suit like that out of a Corporation Associates paycheck, even if you were budget-stretching to impress a new client.

"Good to see you," Gil said, glancing at the wall clock. The minute hand was racing now, only two minutes until twelve-thirty.

Turner had taken out his card case. "Give you a name to remember, Gil, just in case any of your righteous clients ever have a fire break out in the Bureau of Internal Revenue. Just sound the alarm and we'll be on the job. We're quick on our feet when it comes to a fast hosing job."

"Sure, Dale, sure," Gil said nervously, glancing at the clock again. "Sorry. Got a date upstairs."

"Got one myself," Turner grinned sardonically. "Relieving one of our public servants of some of his inhibitions."

The clerk at the desk greeted Gil with a look of supercilious inquiry suggesting that his presence in the Hotel Ivanhoe might well be a mistake.

"What's Mr. McCall's room number?"

The clerk was insolently hesitant. "May I have your name?"

"Gilmore Clark."

The clerk lifted the telephone instrument as if it were a teacup, carefully avoiding the brush of his arm against the maroon carnation in the lapel of his morning coat. "Mr. McCall? This is Mr. Nathan at the desk. Sorry to bother you, sir, but there's a Mr. Clark to see you."

What he heard seemed to disappoint him. He replaced the receiver in its cradle. "You may go up. Tenth floor."

"What room number?"

"Mr. McCall's suite occupies the entire floor," the clerk said, turning wearily away as if the whole affair had driven him beyond the limit of his condescension.

Gil Clark started for the elevator.

Inside, looking out, he saw Dale Turner greeting two men, a gray-faced old warhorse with the stamp of a ward-heeler on him, and a great porcine slob who, with just a little more greed in his pig eyes, might have been mistaken for Harry Guizinger's younger brother.

••••• 6

Grant Austen waited while Will Atherson inscribed his name on the guest register and then, with a sigh of expectant satisfaction, entered the first of the four rooms that constituted The Wharf's present quarters, a room so skillfully reconstructed that it did not vary by as much as a single sliver of walnut paneling from the entrance hall of the old clubhouse.

Against the wall opposite the entrance were the mahogany racks that held the engraved silver plates of the members, flanked by a small teak table with a low stack of plain plates to accommodate the strictly limited admission of guests. In front of the plate rack stood old Willis—himself as much of a fixture as any piece of furniture—holding a tray of crystal goblets half filled with wine. No liquor was ever served before lunch in The Wharf and the wine, a special vintage supposedly imported from the island of Madeira, was always offered in goblets that were exact replicas of the crystalware that had arrived from England on the barque *Morning Light* which had docked in Philadelphia on October 29, 1752, after a passage from Liverpool, Lisbon and Funchal. There was a picture of the *Morning Light* above the center hunt table.

By tradition, luncheon was not served until one o'clock and, today, there was no early gathering crowd. Except for the waiters who were in the next room arranging silver bowls and tureens, they were alone and Grant Austen, as he took the goblet that Will Atherson handed to him, debated the propriety of immediately broaching the subject of selling his company. The atmosphere of The Wharf seemed to argue against it. He knew, as Will Atherson had more than once suggested, that a lot of big deals were pulled off right here at these Wednesday noon lunches, but he mistrusted his own ability to bring up the matter in precisely the right way. There was too much danger that he might miss, even if by the narrowest of margins, the achievement of that perfection of conduct that he had come to admire so much as a demanded attribute of a member—or potential member—of The Wharf.

It was, in fact, the very narrowness of the margin by which he so often failed to be exactly the man that he wanted to be that always plagued Grant Austen on these days when he was a guest at The Wharf. He had schooled himself in the amenities of gracious living until he had no concern about committing a grossly ungentlemanly blunder. It was the little things that bothered him now, those tiny margins of error by which he betrayed himself as not quite belonging to the world of The Wharf.

He had his suits made by the same tailor that Will Atherson and many other Main Liners patronized, yet there was always a difference in the finished result, too subtle to be recognized and pointed out at the last fitting, yet it must be there. He felt it every time he came here. He knew that it wasn't his figure—which wasn't at all bad for a man of his age—nor did he suspect his tailor of short-changing him because he wasn't a second- or third-generation Main Line customer. It was something about himself, exactly what he didn't know, his perception hovering in that no man's land between knowing that something was wrong and yet not knowing quite what it was. The unfortunate result, as he fully recognized, was that he was always a little on edge when he went to lunch with Will Atherson, inclined to say just a word or two too many, laugh just the faintest shade of a tone too stridently. Yet there were no occasions that he found more pleasantly stimulating than these guest visits to The Wharf.

He raised the goblet to his lips and tasted. "Great wine you have here. This some of the special stuff you were telling me about?"

Will Atherson nodded, silent.

Grant Austen noticed the way the banker's fingers held the glass and rearranged his own.

Three members had entered the room and one of them bore down on Will Atherson. His suit was of a fabric that Grant Austen recalled having seen at his tailor's, his appearance craggily distinguished.

"Judge," Atherson greeted him. "Want you to meet my guest— Grant Austen, president of Suffolk Moulding—Judge Torrant."

They exchanged greetings, shook hands, and Torrant turned to Atherson, craning forward, bringing his lips as close as he could to the banker's ear. "One quick question, Will—something a client of mine asked me yesterday."

"Yes?"

"There hasn't been any change in the ownership of this hotel, has there, Will?"

Will Atherson fingered his pipe. "There's been no recent change in ownership."

"Thanks, Will, thanks. Didn't think so, just wanted to confirm it. Glad to have met you, Mr. Austen."

Judge Torrant moved away, swallowed up in the crowd that was now pouring in from the hall.

148

"Judge Torrant?" Grant Austen asked, using the technique that he always employed to establish the rating of a newly made acquaintance. "Haven't I heard that name before?"

"Possibly," Atherson said, preoccupied. Then, catching himself as if he had missed a cue, he added, "Yes, he's one of our attorneys." He hesitated and then, with a show of intimacy that warmed Grant Austen's heart, whispered, "Good enough lawyer, but something of a bore. Never sees you but what he has some silly question to ask."

Grant Austen nodded knowingly. Then, as carefully as he might have made a written note, he filed Judge Torrant's name away in his memory. You never could tell when a contact like that might come in handy.

●●●●● 7

Facing the door that fronted on the tenth-floor foyer, touching the push button for the second time, Gil Clark was doing his best to keep his promise to Harrison Glenn that he would meet Cash McCall with an open mind. Perversely, the harder he tried to curb his imagination the more persistently it exhumed the matching memory of the morning he had gone to Harry Guizinger's suite in this same hotel ... the door opening on that hog-snout face, those hairy hands clawing his perpetually slipping trousers back to the high bulge of his enormous belly ...

The door opened.

The man who faced him ... *no, it couldn't be Cash McCall.* This man was too young ... no older than himself ... someone else ... an assistant ...

"I'm Cash McCall," the man said, extending his hand.

Dry-mouthed, Gilmore Clark heard himself speak his own name and then they were walking together into the big living room. In the instant of first seeing, the room seemed a startling fulfillment of Gil Clark's oldest adult dream. It was, in almost precise duplication, the room that had been his haven of imaginary escape on those endless nights of tortured waiting on the carrier, the same room that he had again dreamed into being during those fever-burned weeks before he had awakened to discover the antiseptic reality of a hospital ward. Now fantasy had become truth. It was all here, the miracle of a dream come true ... those same deep-set windows, the packed bookcases, the waiting chairs and the soft spillage of dimmed light, the narrow-framed prints on the cork-covered walls ... a Frost watercolor over the mantel, Bishop etchings, a painting of a dart of pintails coming in over the decoys ...

His moving eyes froze their attention. There, facing him, was a drawing of a hawk held high on an armored falconer's wrist ... no, he couldn't be wrong! It was Lory Austen's original drawing for the frontispiece of *Knight of the Hawk*. How had Cash McCall managed to ... ?

"How about a drink, Mr. Clark?"

The words had a shocking quality, not in themselves but because they brought the startling realization that, in his preoccupation, first with the room and then with the Lory Austen drawing, he had hardly looked at his host. He studied him now, seeing him as perhaps a little older than he had guessed after that first glance at the door ... late thirties, possibly forty ... English doeskin slacks and cashmere jacket ... more like a professional athlete than a businessman. There was a Western look about him ... Texas or California. Millionaire playboy? No, he wasn't the type ... eyes too sharp, as sharp as his mind must be ... seeing everything, missing nothing ...

Gil remembered that he had expected the counterpart of Guizinger and then, instantly, there was the more urgent memory that Cash McCall had asked him if he wanted a drink. Did he? Yes ... but careful now ... easy to make the wrong impression. "I'm not much of a noon drinker," he compromised, "but I'll be glad to join you."

Cash McCall stood over a low table in the center of the room, his hands spread fanwise over a bristle of decanters. "Martini? Or do you prefer whiskey?"

"Martini'd be fine."

Gil Clark watched his host as he mixed the cocktails, noticing his hands, quick and deft yet with the suggestion of enormous strength, as if with the closing of his fingers the crystal mixing urn would have shattered. There was that same suggestion of latent power in the movement of his body when he went to the sidetable for glasses, the deceptively soft-muscled grace of a lion.

The cocktail was excellent and Gil was tempted to a compliment, but when he tried the words in silent rehearsal they seemed pointless. A perfect cocktail was a part of the scene. It was impossible to imagine Cash McCall mixing a cocktail that would not have been perfect.

"Glad you could lunch with me," McCall said. "Hope it wasn't too inconvenient?"

"No, not at all."

"Good. Most people talk more easily over food. Hope you're one of them. I want you to do some talking." He lounged back on the giant couch, a bedlike affair upholstered in green glove-leather.

Gil Clark wished that he hadn't chosen a straight-backed chair. He felt stiff and uncomfortable, wordless.

Cash McCall fixed him with a narrow-eyed smile that suggested clairvoyance and his words brought a confirmation of the power. "No need to get your guard up, Mr. Clark. If I ask questions that you don't care to answer—don't." The smile softened. "That's a privilege I claim for myself every now and then."

"I'll tell you anything I can, Mr. McCall."

"Mind starting now? Or would you prefer to eat first?"

"The sooner the better," he said, wishing after the words were out that he hadn't spoken so quickly, betraying his bewilderment at finding himself in a situation so completely different from what he had anticipated.

"What do they call you—*Gil?*"

"That's right."

"Mind if I do?"

"No indeed."

"My first name is Cash. If you've heard rumors to the contrary, it's not a nickname. Cash was my mother's family name."

Gil Clark shifted uneasily. There it was again ... McCall had read his mind, knowing that he had thought *Cash* was a nickname.

"I hope you won't resent my inviting you here under a false pretense," Cash McCall said.

Gil stared his lack of comprehension.

"I may be interested in buying Suffolk Moulding," McCall said casually. "I don't know. I was several years ago but I'd more or less forgotten about it until yesterday. At the moment I'm interested in you."

"In me?"

Cash McCall was looking at him across the rim of his raised glass. "I'm thinking of offering you a job. I hope you're open-minded enough to consider the possibility."

Gil could not breach the silencing grip of surprise.

"How much do you know about me, Gil?"

"Not much," he said, forcing the words.

"I'm what you might call a dealer in secondhand companies," Cash McCall said. "I buy them and sell them."

"I know that much," Gil Clark said, attempting to match the smile that crow-footed Cash McCall's eyes.

"When I buy a company, I usually put in someone to operate it for a time—long enough to give it a general overhauling, refurbish it, attempt to make it a more valuable property than it was when I bought it. Then I sell it at a profit. Or at least that's the objective. For example, if I were to buy Suffolk Moulding—"

Cash McCall paused and Gil Clark knew that the quick rise of his desire had already shown on his face.

"Then you *are* interested?"

It was too late for denial and he nodded.

"Harrison Glenn thought that you might be," Cash McCall went on.

"Mr. Glenn?"

"I've discussed you with him on several occasions," Cash McCall said, letting a grin break and then adding, "As I presume he's discussed me with you."

"No, sir. That is—well, not discussed you."

"He's never told you about my relationship to Corporation Associates?"

"No."

"I own Corporation Associates."

Gil Clark felt a quick-knotting constriction that choked back exclamation.

"Had you guessed?"

"No, I—I hadn't."

Or had he? Was this another case of knowing without knowing, of his subconscious mind having realized what he had failed to acknowledge, a confirmation of his suspicion last night that there was something more between Harrison Glenn and Cash McCall than the president of Corporation Associates had admitted.

"At least now you're certain," Cash McCall said. "Your worst suspicions are confirmed."

"I wouldn't say that," Gil Clark said, and then wondered why he had.

"But my position does strike you as—perhaps slightly unethical?"

"Well, I am surprised—naturally."

Cash McCall crossed his long legs. "That's something we can discuss later, after we're better acquainted. Until then, how about giving me the benefit of the doubt and telling me something about yourself? Suppose you start with a quick rundown on your life—vital statistics, family, education, business experience, so on. I know that's putting you on a spot but at least it's a way to make you start talking."

His voice had been easy, intending reassurance, but the effect on Gil Clark was the opposite. His host's manner only emphasized, by contrast, his own disturbing lack of poise. His thoughts spun themselves into a tightly wound ball and he could find no loose thread to pick up for a beginning.

"You're Main Line, aren't you?" McCall prompted.

"Yes, for several generations back."

"Both sides?"

"Yes. My grandfathers were Phares T. Dudley and Gerard Clark. They founded Clark-Dudley & Company, the publishing house. It was carried on until a few years ago by my uncle, Jefferson Clark."

"Your father didn't go into the family business?"

"No, he spent most of his life in public service."

"For example?"

"Well, various charitable organizations. At one time he was general chairman of the Special Services Foundation. He didn't have much interest in making money."

"In other words, he lived largely off your grandfather's estate?"

Gil sipped his cocktail, consciously delaying an answer. Cash Mc-Call's question had probed a sensitive realization. It was true that his father had lived off the estate, used it up to the last penny.

A quizzical grin formed slowly on Cash McCall's face. "Gil, why do you feel the necessity to defend your father?"

"I don't. I—" His voice caught and the break was an admission that, once made, allowed no turning back. "I suppose by some standards he did live a rather useless life."

"By *your* standards?"

Gil Clark wasn't sure what his inquisitor meant, nor toward what blind corner he was being led, and he felt the need for a side-stepping escape. He attempted a laugh and it came off better than he expected. "If you're asking me if I have any objections to making money —personally—the answer is no, none whatsoever."

There was something like approval in the way that McCall chuckled. "There are people, you know, who do feel that making money is rather ungentlemanly, something that isn't done in the better circles."

"Perhaps that's because they're having so much difficulty doing it these days," Gil said, pleased after he heard his voice that he had managed to say it as well as he had.

There was a clipped laugh as Cash McCall put down the urn. "In case there's any doubt in your mind, Gil, I don't belong to the better circles. I'm a thoroughly vulgar character—I enjoy making money."

Gil felt himself stiffen, oddly shocked, and them impelled to rebuttal, his eyes involuntarily sweeping the room. "I'd hardly say that you—"

McCall cut him off. "Don't let the trimmings fool you. I'm no gentleman. I don't fit the prescription. A gentleman spends all day beating his brains out to make money—and then goes out to the country

153

club at night and tries his best to convince everyone else that he's a very high class character who would never stoop so low as the pursuit of a fast buck."

"That isn't far from true," Gil said, smiling in spite of the warning in McCall's eyes that he was not indulging in aimless chatter, that everything he said was pointed toward a purposeful end.

"We have a peculiar national attitude toward money-making," McCall went on. "We maintain that the very foundation of our way of life is what we call free enterprise—the profit system. We're so serious about it that we'll fight to preserve it—literally go to war—but when one of our citizens shows enough free enterprise to pile up a little of that profit, we do our best to make him feel that he ought to be ashamed of himself."

Gil Clark smiled automatically, his mind occupied with the oddly effortless way that McCall's voice ranged from the easy colloquialism of street speech to something closely approaching a tone of polished culture.

"Of course it could be argued that there's nothing really current about that attitude," Cash McCall went on. "Oddly enough it's always been one of our Christian precepts that poverty is somehow associated with virtue, but it still strikes me as something of an anomaly that here, living under the profit system—fighting and dying to defend it—we've come now to regard the accumulation of profit as a crime against society. It's gotten to the point now where the only way a millionaire can expiate his sin is to endow a charity or a cancer research foundation."

Gil Clark thought of Guizinger and the half million he'd paid to have his name chiseled in granite on a hospital wing. "I guess it's the monument urge," he said.

McCall nodded appreciatively. "Granted—particularly now that they can buy monuments with tax money and let the government pay most of the bill. But I think my point still stands—that money-making is generally regarded as something essentially vulgar, a secret vice indulged in by all but never mentioned in the best society."

There had been, up to this time, a hazy suspicion that Cash McCall was somehow, perhaps subconsciously, searching for self-justification, but his manner was such a complete denial of that possibility that Gil Clark found himself retreating to his earlier judgment that everything the man had said was a purposeful part of a sharply pointed inquisition. He wanted to give McCall what he seemed to be asking for—a denial that he was a Main Line snob—but he could think of no way to say it without making a fool of himself.

154

With gratitude he heard McCall say, "You said before that you had no objection to making money—personally."

"I'm all for it—personally or otherwise."

"Would you have any moral compunctions about being associated with a low character who happened to think it was a more interesting game than golf—providing, of course, that you did a little money-making yourself in the process?"

Gil Clark was becoming conscious that he was, almost against his judgment, being forced to like Cash McCall. "I've never cared much for golf," he laughed, thinking humor a way to avoid commitment.

McCall bent his head to his glass. "Well, let's get off the sidetrack, Gil, and back to the vital statistics. What about college—liberal arts?"

"No. Business."

"Then you weren't planning to go into the publishing house?"

"Yes, but on the business end."

"Why?"

"I didn't feel myself qualified—temperamentally—for editorial work. As for the business end—well, I didn't agree with my uncle that there was anything wrong with making a profit in the publishing business."

McCall got the point and smiled. "Your uncle, I take it, believed that art shouldn't be tainted with the sordid stain of profit."

"Something like that," Gil agreed. "But my grandfather had made money in the publishing business and I didn't see why it couldn't still be done."

"In other words, you felt yourself more in sympathy with your grandfather than your uncle?"

Gil looked at him, puzzled by the point of the question.

"I'm not badgering you," McCall explained quickly, making Gil realize again that his face must have betrayed him. "I'm simply trying to find out what sort of person you are. You did go to work for the publishing house—for Jefferson Clark?"

"Yes. For about a year after I got out of the service."

"What service?"

"Navy. I was a pilot."

"Do any flying now?"

"No sir."

"Get enough of it?"

"No chance, that's all."

Cash McCall looked at him speculatively. "Maybe you could give me a hand now and then. Ever fly a B-26?"

"No, I had all my time in—" He found his voice blocked by the all but incredible implication that Cash McCall owned a B-26 and was using it as a private airplane.

"Picked one up as surplus," McCall explained. "Had an outfit out in California rebuild it. After they got through there wasn't much left but the old airframe. Made a good job of it though. Put in a couple of new Pratt and Whitney twenty-four hundreds with reversing props. Gives me around three hundred an hour. Range of about two thousand. Makes a nice airplane."

"I should think so," Gil replied with purposeful blankness, attempting to conceal his speculation as to what the plane had cost. Harry Guizinger had spent over a hundred thousand on his DC-3. To rebuild a B-26 as McCall had described must have meant the outlay of at least twice that much.

"I know," Cash McCall said in another disconcerting exhibition of mind reading. "It's a lot of airplane. But it's what I need. Gets me there in a hurry. I don't like sitting around waiting for things to happen." Then, as if in incongruous denial, perhaps even as an act of intentionally subtle humor, he lounged back and asked, "What happened after you came back to the publishing house? Why did you leave?"

Gil hesitated as he reached back to pick up the thread of the conversation. "My uncle and I couldn't quite agree on where the firm was going. Actually, it was two businesses in one—a publishing house and a printing plant. I made a study of the situation and wrote a long report on what I thought should be done. I'll admit I was pretty much of a cub then—and I suppose it was a rather amateurish attempt at business analysis—"

"What did you recommend?"

"That we sell the printing plant to get the capital that was needed to keep the publishing house going, drop a lot of unprofitable kinds of books and concentrate on the juvenile field. It was my idea to merchandise children's books through the chain grocery stores. That's fairly common now but in those days it was a rather new approach."

"What happened?"

"My uncle didn't agree. I couldn't see any future the way he was headed, so I decided to get out."

"And the publishing company—what happened to it?"

"A few years ago my uncle got into a rather tight financial situation and sold out."

"Squeezed out?"

"No, I wouldn't say so. From what I heard he got his asking price."

"To whom did he sell?"

"A New York corporation—Paper Enterprises."

"Who was behind it? Who owned it?"

"I don't know. I was out of the company myself so I wasn't too much concerned."

"What did Paper Enterprises do with the publishing house?"

"They sold the printing plant—I understand for about the same price that they paid for the whole business—and then started chain-store distribution of children's books. They were one of the first to get into it in a big way and it worked out pretty well."

"In other words, they followed your recommendations?"

"Yes, substantially," Gil said, feeling the restraint of modesty. "At least that's what I've heard."

Cash McCall tapped the edge of his glass with his thumbnail and there was a bell sound in the moment of silence. "Paper Enterprises still own the publishing business?"

"No, after they got it going they sold out."

"Probably at a nice profit?"

"So I understand."

"And you still don't know who was behind Paper Enterprises?"

"No. As I said, I—"

His voice cut off as he saw the leatherette cover on the volume that Cash McCall, reaching back, had lifted from a table beside the couch. *It was the report he had written on Clark-Dudley!* How had Cash McCall gotten hold of it . . . could it be that he was the man behind Paper Enterprises?

"I'm your man, Gil. Found this in the files after I bought Clark-Dudley. I'm very grateful to you for the ideas. And you're quite right about my making a nice profit out of it. That's one reason I asked you to come here today."

Gil Clark felt himself speechless, his mind dulled with the opiate of shock.

"Let's go on," Cash McCall said. "You went from the publishing house to Corporation Associates?"

"No. I was with Simonds, Farrar & Peters for about two years."

"Happy there?"

Gil hesitated, feeling that his answer involved an important decision. "No sir—not particularly."

"Why not?"

"I didn't like their type of clientele."

Cash McCall studied his face, his expression suggesting that he was going to pursue the subject, but he didn't.

"Then you went with Corporation Associates?"

"Yes."

"How did you get that job—through what means?"

"Means? An employment agency."

"Do you recall the name?"

"Yes. Hildreth-Paris."

"You approach them—or did they come to you?"

"As I recall, they wrote me a letter. Then I went in to see them."

Cash McCall sipped the last drop in his glass. "Just to keep the record straight, Gil, the agency approached you because I asked them to. I owned Hildreth-Paris. I still do."

Gil Clark felt himself groggy, unable to think, but he had to say something. "I don't get the connection—Hildreth-Paris, I mean."

"I've found an employment agency an extremely valuable adjunct to my operations." He reached back again, and Gil saw that now he had picked up a copy of the last Corporation Associates report on Suffolk Moulding Company. "This is a good job, Gil, excellently done, but I know quite a few things about Suffolk that you weren't able to dig out."

"Through the employment agency?"

Cash McCall nodded.

"Someone from Suffolk looking for a job?"

"Yes."

"Who?"

"Paul Bronson."

"No!"

"Surprise you?"

"Well, I—yes, it does."

Cash McCall laughed. "I must say, Gil, that's the one thing about you that doesn't quite measure up."

"What's that?"

"You're too easily surprised."

"After today I doubt if anything will surprise me," he said, trying to say it lightly but it didn't come out that way.

Cash McCall shot him a quick glance and then said crisply, rising, "Lunch is on the table. Ready to eat?"

A door had opened silently behind them and, in the next room, a table had been set for the two of them, crystal and silver sparkling against white napery and black-red mahogany.

As he approached the door, Gil's eyes fell on the Lory Austen illustration that he had noticed when he had come in. Filling a moment of silence, he said, "I suppose you picked that up when you owned the publishing company?"

He was unprepared for the odd expression that flashed on Cash McCall's mobile face, revealing something that he had not seen before—nor now, seeing, could understand.

"You know the book?" Cash McCall asked, the words sounding suspiciously like a blind to cover others unspoken. "Clark-Dudley published it—but I think it was after you left."

"Yes, but of course I've gotten to know Lory since. You do know that she's Grant Austen's daughter?"

Cash nodded. The last evidence of whatever had momentarily disturbed McCall had now vanished. "I hope you like oysters."

"Very much."

"Good."

They sat and began to eat in a silence that Gil Clark, for no reason that he could understand, felt disinclined to break. Far back in his mind there was the vapor of an odd suspicion—that the face of the man in the Lory Austen drawing, the face of the knight with the falcon on his wrist, was the face of Cash McCall. He could not be sure, perhaps he was wrong, but his curiosity was aroused.

• • • • • 8

Lory Austen had waited no longer than the gear shifting to change her instructions to the taxi driver, telling him not to stop at the building where Clark-Dudley had its offices but to turn into the side street where she remembered having seen a travel agency. This minor deception of her father, slight though it was, added the rare-flavored spice of adventure and she curled back into the corner of the seat, relishing her aloneness as a prediction of the freedom that would be completely hers as soon as her father actually sold the company.

This was not the first time she had sheltered the hope of escape— once she had even gone so far as to inspect apartments in New York— but, always before, her desire had been a nebulous thing, courted but not accepted, a fantasy that she knew would never survive translation to reality. This time it was different. Hope had been given the substance of truth and it was made more tangible with every passing moment, anticipation heightened by every ratchet click of the taximeter.

The streets were blocked with rain-snarled traffic and the cab's progress was annoyingly slow, but she found that her determination could not be weakened, even by the attrition of delay. The consciousness of freedom was self-strengthening and she was, almost for the first time in her life, vibrantly aware of the wonder of the free spirit.

The cross-street corner was choked with a dense massing of noon-hour pedestrians and, facing a delay that could not be brooked, she got out of the cab, overtipping the driver because she could not wait for change, and pushed her way through the phalanx of umbrellas that jammed the street. She found the travel agency halfway up the block, exactly where she had remembered it to be, and the man who came to her when she stepped up to the counter was exactly the man he should have been, the look of far places in his gentle old eyes, the faint overtones of a foreign tongue in his words.

"Fiascherino?" he asked after her question. "You have been there before?"

"No."

"Then you are to be envied. It is a most wonderful thing to see the Ligurian Coast for the first time—and you will be there in the spring when there is no more lovely place on earth." He paused to smile. "Perhaps now you do not believe me but when you are there you will know that I do not exaggerate."

"You've been there?" she asked, hesitating, suspicious for a delaying instant that he might be a clever salesman, then knowing that his almost reverent enthusiasm was something beyond that.

"When I was a very young man," he explained, his voice low and warmed with memory. "It was but one spring after D. H. Lawrence had lived in his villa on the Lerici road—and there was a very old man at San Terenzo who claimed that he could remember Shelley's days at Casa Magni. It is the bay of the poets, you know—Petrarch and Dante and Byron. You, too, perhaps are a poet?"

"No, I—I'm an illustrator."

"Ah yes, an artist!" he said with a self-deprecating gesture indicating that he should have known without being told. "How is it that you wish to go—by the boat or will you fly?"

"I really don't know. Is it difficult to get there?"

"Difficult?" he asked, syllabizing the word as if it were foreign. "You mean, perhaps, is it expensive?"

"No. That doesn't matter. It's—" She caught herself, stopped by the fear of ostentation. "It *does* matter but—"

"I understand," he said quickly, skirting embarrassment with courtly deference. "No, it is not difficult to reach Fiascherino. You ask for my advice?"

"Of course."

"Then you will go by the sea to Genoa. It is the proper approach—the Mediterranean."

She nodded agreement, listening as his voice quickened with enthusiasm, his expressive hands modeling the images of his words—the ship and the sea, the landing at Genoa, the road along the coast, the little studio apartment that would be ready and waiting for her in the villa that was now a hotel run by an Englishwoman who was herself a watercolorist.

"All of that, everything, I will arrange for you," he said. "There is but one thing you must do—tell me when you will sail. Next week? Or perhaps that is too soon?"

"I'm afraid it couldn't be next week."

"Then the sailing after that—three weeks from Saturday?"

She hesitated, tempted. It was so easy, so simple. All that was needed was a nod and the decision would be made. "I—I think I can let you know in a day or two. Will that be all right?"

His eyes cooled with disappointment. "For me—yes, of course, it is all right. For you—perhaps it is best not to delay."

"You mean that space might not be available?"

"You will permit me to advise you?"

She nodded.

"You are very young," he said softly. "When you are young it is best to let the heart decide. When one is young, there should be no fear of the impulse. There will be enough years to come when that cannot be done."

She broke the magnetic pull of his eyes and her glance, escaping, caught a clinging eyehold on a poster that hung on the wall behind him. It pictured a Maine headland bold against the sky, the sea breaking at its base, the black-green of pines, the incised whiteness of a boat's sail ... *"Lory, it can't be ... you don't know what you're doing ..."*

"I did not mean to give offense," the old man said anxiously, sharply concerned, and she realized then that she had let the anger of defiance flush her face.

"I'm sorry," she said, and then automatically defensive, "I'm not as young as you think."

His smile was young-old, the smile of an old man whose eyes had lost less of youth than he imagined. "There is a line of verse—my translation is perhaps clumsy—'It is only the very young who will protest their youth, the older claim it when it is not their due.'"

She tried to make her smile hide her disappointment with herself for having allowed the breaking of her promise that she would never again think of Cash McCall. But more had been broken than her promise. The fragile shell of the enticing moment had cracked, letting in the gray rain-fog of Philadelphia to snuff out the imagined sunlight of Fiascherino.

"Three weeks from Saturday?" he asked again.

"Yes," she said, suddenly decisive.

The old man voiced the soft sound of pleased relief and then there was a printed form in front of her, and she was signing her name, and there was the low buzz of question and answer between ear and lip, scarcely heard because the mind-words of exultation were so much more strongly voiced. She had won the last skirmish. This was the end of the battle. Defiantly, she looked at the wall. The poster was only ink on paper.

"Before I leave," she said, "would you give me some literature on trips around the world?"

"After Fiascherino?"

"For my mother and father."

Again there was the murmur of his pleasure and the soft glow of approval in his eyes.

• • • • • 9

Cash McCall put his napkin beside his empty dessert plate. "Yes, the food here is good. Max is an excellent chef. More coffee?"

"No, thank you."

Gil preceded him into the living room, hoping that now at last there would be a return to the subject that had been so pointedly avoided all during the luncheon. Their conversation, guided by McCall's rather astounding scope of interest, had ranged all the way from trout fishing to the philosophy of Santayana, from Al Capp to Hemingway, from Purdey shotguns to springer spaniels, but not once had there been a mention of either the Suffolk Moulding Company or the job that Cash McCall had in mind for him.

The gray clouds outside had thinned and the soft glow of mist-screened sunlight came in through the small-paned windows.

"Well, what do you think?" McCall asked, his back to the windows, the expression on his face hidden by concealing shadows.

"About what?"

"Going to work for me."

Gil Clark's smile came freely, not forced against caution as it would have been an hour ago. "As far as I can see, I *have* been working for you for some time now."

"This wouldn't be quite the same. You'd leave Corporation Associates."

"I'm afraid I'm a little vague about what my job would be."

"I'm a little vague myself," McCall admitted, dropping to the edge of the couch, sprawling his long legs out across the floor. "It would depend on developments. I told you before that I was a dealer in secondhand companies."

"Yes."

McCall leaned back like a lazily stretching animal, his extended hand picking a thick packet of papers from a shelf behind the couch. "Here's this week's crop of reports on companies that can be bought. One of your jobs would be to screen them. When you found one that appeared to offer interesting possibilities, you'd dig in and make a preliminary survey."

"I see," Gil said, disappointed that what McCall had in mind seemed to offer nothing that might lead toward a continued association with the Suffolk Moulding Company.

"Apparently that doesn't interest you," McCall said.

"I wouldn't say that it doesn't interest me," he said, feeling again that transparency of thought that had bothered him before lunch, McCall's apparent ability to read anything that was in his mind.

"It wouldn't be too different from your present work, would it?" McCall asked. "I am right, that's what you do now, isn't it—go into a company and try to find out what's wrong with it?"

"Yes, that's usually the starting point."

"That would be the starting point for us, too. When a company is for sale, there's always a reason, always something wrong. The first order of business is to find out what that something is."

"I can see that."

"Sometimes it's a situation that has nothing to do with the company itself—some special circumstance that makes the owner want to sell. These days, it's usually taxes. If that's the case, we explore the owner's tax situation and work out some kind of deal that will solve his problem."

"I understand."

Cash McCall snapped a light to a cigarette. "Sometimes the company is in trouble. Then we have to decide now much overhauling it would take to put the property in salable condition. Often there's nothing more needed than a thorough housecleaning—sweep out the dry rot, wash the windows, polish the door handle and invite the right buyer to come over and have a look."

"You make it sound easy," Gil said, violating his resolution to make no further comment but feeling himself forced to break the silence of McCall's expectant pause.

A veil of cigarette smoke floated lazily upward from Cash McCall's lips. "That's the whole trouble, Gil. In a good many cases it's *too* easy. All you wind up with is a chunk of money."

163

"I can think of worse things to wind up with," Gil smiled.

"But it's like trout fishing, Gil. It's easy enough to make money—like catching trout with worms—but once you've graduated to dry flies you lose your taste for worm fishing."

"I suppose that's right," Gil said uncertainly, unable to believe that Cash McCall had intended the simile to be taken seriously.

"Does that make me sound like a conceited ass—saying that money is easy to make?"

Denial threatened to make him sound naïve. "Well, I wouldn't say that there'd be too many people who'd agree with you."

"That's exactly what makes it so easy—there's so little competition. Most people have been raised to believe in the old copybook maxims about hard work and frugality. They've had it dinned into them since childhood that money's something that has to be grubbed out, a penny at a time."

"I guess I'm one of those people that were raised on the maxims. I've known there were ways to make big money but—"

"But you never realized how easy it was?" McCall supposed.

"If you're smart enough to do it."

"You don't even have to be very smart."

"I'd argue about that."

"No, Gil, it's easy. The tax structure these days sets things up like pins in a bowling alley. Look—" He sat up and leaned forward, elbows on his knees "—the only way the owner of a small company can cash in these days is to sell out. Isn't that Austen's situation?"

"Of course," Gil agreed, suddenly realizing that he had momentarily forgotten Grant Austen and the Suffolk Moulding Company.

"And because of the tax situation the country is full of Austens," McCall went on, gesturing toward the pile of letters and reports. "There are hundreds of companies for sale, thousands of them."

"I know."

"And the same tax setup that makes it advantageous for the small company to sell out makes it equally desirable for a big corporation to buy—especially if the companies can be merged to improve the tax base."

For an instant, Gil's mind reverted to the train of thought it had followed on the way to the hotel.

McCall smiled, mind reading again. "I don't make the rules, Gil. I only play the game. I never thought much of the kick-for-point after touchdown, either, but as long as it's in the rule book, that's the way the game is played."

"I suppose so," Gil said. "But the situation is sure to change. There'll be a revision of the tax laws one of these days."

McCall agreed readily. "Yes, there'll be some new rules, but it'll still be essentially the same game. It's gone on from time immemorial. There's never been a period in our history, even at the bottom of the depression, when there weren't men who were making money by the very simple process of buying a company in which someone had lost faith and selling it to someone else who could be made to have faith in it. That's my business, Gil—and I get a wallop out of it. I think you would, too. That's why I've called you in. I'd like to tackle something bigger than anything I've done up to now. If I do, I'll need some help—an extra pair of hands, someone to feed me ideas, follow through on detail, pick up the ball when I fumble, warn me if I'm about to commit a foul."

"That sounds like quite an assignment," Gil heard himself say, his brain occupied with the thought that what Cash McCall had in mind eliminated all hope that he might work his way into the management of the Suffolk Moulding Company. Disappointment impelled him to ask, somewhat incongruously, "Is that what you have in mind for Suffolk Moulding—to buy it and then sell it?"

An oddly unreadable expression came to McCall's face. "I'm not certain that I have anything in mind for Suffolk Moulding."

"But I thought from what Mr. Glenn said that you were interested in buying it—at least that you were at one time."

"Yes, at one time. But it was never anything more than a hunch. It just happened that I—"

Gil had momentarily looked away, but the abrupt break in McCall's easily flowing voice made him turn back to sense, more than actually see, what seemed to have been a glance toward Lory Austen's drawing on the wall.

"What's your size-up of Suffolk?" McCall asked abruptly.

Gil was caught off balance. "Well, I—I think it's a fine company. There *are* some things about it that—but there's nothing wrong with Suffolk Moulding that couldn't be corrected with the right kind of management."

"Suppose you were managing it," McCall bored in. "What would your approach be?"

He averted his eyes, anxious not to betray the resurrection of his hope.

"I thought you might have some ideas," McCall pressed.

The challenge was unmistakable and Gil rose to it. "I do. Basically what needs to be done is—I don't know how familiar you are with the molding business but—"

"Assume that I know nothing," Cash McCall cut in, lounging back on the couch again. "Go ahead and give me the story."

He hesitated, hurriedly collecting usable sentences and phrases out of all the reports. "Well, as you probably know, Suffolk Moulding is one of the oldest molding plants in the country. All of the business is what we call *custom* molding—making molded plastic parts that are used by manufacturers of finished products."

"Like the cabinets for Andscott television sets," McCall supplied.

"Yes. As a matter of fact, that's—well, that's the whole issue right now."

"How so?"

"Well—"

"I'm sorry. Don't let me throw you off the track. Go ahead and give me the background."

"Well, there is some background. You see, in the old days Suffolk got most of its business on difficult jobs that required a lot of development work—the kind of molding problems that no one else would tackle. One of the big electric companies, for example, might have its own molding plant, but if they'd run into something that was way off the beaten track, they'd turn it over to Suffolk. A good many times it would mean working out some entirely new production technique or inventing a new kind of a mold. It might even involve building a special press."

"Suffolk built those molds and presses itself?"

"Built the molds and did the development work on the presses. The special presses were usually built by Hartzell-Bauer, but Suffolk did all the engineering."

"By Suffolk you mean Grant Austen?"

"Yes, I suppose so," Gil said, aware that he had made his words sound like a too-reluctant admission. "That was before my time, of course—I can't speak from personal experience—but, yes, I'd say that Austen was the sparkplug. Apparently he was a good engineer and a clever development man. I know, for example—well, Christiansen of Cavalier Chemical told me one time that some years ago they used the Suffolk Moulding plant almost as if it were their own laboratory—trying new materials, working out the processing bugs, setting production standards, that sort of thing."

"And it was Austen who made the place tick?"

"But there were a lot of other good men around the place, too. Still are, especially in the tool shop."

"But the nature of the business itself has changed?"

"Yes, pretty much. You see, all through the war Suffolk ran chockablock with straight production orders, long runs that racked up a lot of profit without much effort or worry."

166

"And after the war was over, Austen couldn't get back in the old groove," McCall supplied. "Or at least he didn't want to."

"That's about it," Gil agreed. "By the time I got on the account in '48, he'd already taken a big Andscott contract at far too low a price. Of course, he excused himself by saying that it absorbed overhead. I've battled that until I'm blue in the face. That's been his excuse for taking all this Andscott business—absorbing overhead."

"And now he's gotten himself in a spot where Andscott is about to absorb the business."

"Exactly." Gil let his thoughts race ahead of his words, preparing an explanation of the Andscott threat that would be honestly factual, yet not too discouraging, and he was caught unaware when Cash McCall suddenly asked, "Does this man Bronson know that Austen is planning to sell?"

"Paul Bronson? Well, no I don't think—at least I'm almost certain that he didn't know when I talked to him yesterday morning."

Cash McCall seemed amused. "He's down here today talking to Andscott about a job."

Surprised, Gil said, "Then maybe he does know."

"At least it seems to confirm your theory that there's a deal on," McCall said. "Might even be wrapped up by now."

"Oh, I'm sure it isn't. I talked to Grant Austen just before I came up here and he gave me a definite promise that he wouldn't do anything until he talked to me. But it may mean—" He stopped, recognizing the danger of appearing to high-pressure Cash McCall into a fast move, and finished weakly, "I met him downstairs. He's here in the hotel having lunch with Atherson of the Freeholders Bank."

"I may have to move fast if I'm interested, is that it?"

Gil nodded, impressed again with Cash McCall's clairvoyance.

"*If* I'm interested," McCall said, suddenly standing. "Frankly, I don't know whether I am or not." He walked the length of the room. "You think it's a good property, don't you?"

"Well, that would depend on what you'd have to pay for it," Gil said, weighing words. "If it could be bought at the right price—and if you could get the right kind of management—well, I'm sure it could be operated at a very handsome profit."

McCall swung around sharply. "I thought you understood. I don't buy companies to operate. I buy them to sell. I'll let someone else do the operating."

A protest leaped to Gil Clark's lips but Cash McCall's voice blocked it. "Look, Gil—you like that company and you think Austen has made a mess of it. You think you could take over and square it away. You probably could. But what would you have when you got through?

167

No more than Austen had ten years ago—a nice little company that can get about so big and no bigger."

"But it *could* be built into—"

"That's what Austen thought," Cash McCall snapped. "That's what the owner of every little one-man business thinks—that he can go on building and building and building. More often than not, he doesn't *think*. He just goes on hoping and dreaming, believing in the American legend. Once in a while someone makes it, but not often any more. Successful companies come in two sizes these days—small and large. It's the medium-sized ones that have the tough go—too big to be handled with one-man management, not big enough to support a real organization. You have to find some way to jump that middle period, Gil, and it's getting tougher to make the jump all the time. Austen sees that. That's what's taken the steam out of him. And it's no unusual situation. I know a hundred Grant Austens. The country is full of them."

Gil Clark found it difficult to accept that too-simple excusing of Grant Austen's fumbling mismanagement of the Suffolk Moulding Company.

"I know what you've been up against with him," Cash McCall went on. "It's a frustrating experience to try to work with a man like that. Makes you want to shove over on the seat and take the wheel out of his hands. But believe me, Gil, you'd be just as frustrated if you did. Suffolk Moulding is about as big as it can get under one-man management. Oh, I don't say that the profit margin couldn't be improved a little. It could. But beyond that—" He shook his head. "It's a rough go, Gil—trying to make that big jump the slow way."

"But there has to be *some* way. After all, small companies do grow into—"

"Yes, there's a way. You take the jump in one leap—make a big one out of a bunch of little ones."

"You mean merge them?"

"Of course. Isn't that the way most companies have gotten up the ladder—at least in the last twenty years?"

"But doesn't it depend on the kind of business?" Gil countered, feeling solider ground under his feet as he remembered a study he had made last year. "It might be possible, of course, to merge several molding companies, but it's hard to see how there would be enough advantage to—"

"I like your other idea better."

"Other idea?"

"Cavalier Chemical."

Gil Clark felt himself completely in the dark, in no way enlightened when Cash McCall said approvingly, "That's exactly the kind of help I want from you, Gil. The Cavalier idea never occurred to me until you mentioned it." He had crossed the length of the room again and, leaning down, opened a drawer in the cabinet under the bookshelves. Running his hand over the jutting index tabs, he pulled out an inch-thick volume bound in a limp imitation-leather cover. "Just happens that I have a report here on Cavalier Chemical. It's one of the companies I've been watching."

Gil saw, before the drawer was closed, that it was packed with similar reports.

Cash McCall riffled pages, stopping now and then to read briefly, finally locating what seemed to be the object of his search. He slumped down on the couch again, tossing aside the heavy report. "How much do you know about Cavalier Chemical?"

"Well, not much—except that they produce plastic molding materials. I've met Christiansen several times. He's one of their top men on research. Suffolk uses a lot of their stuff—and, as I said a minute ago, Cavalier used to do development work down at Suffolk."

"Yes, that's the point I'd missed." Cash McCall stood again, pacing the length of the room. "Let's think out loud for a minute. But you need a little background that you don't have. Back in '48, I happened to pick up the Eagle Harbor Paper Company—had a mill up in Maine. That was the start of Paper Enterprises, the company that bought your uncle's publishing house. Eagle Harbor had a small subsidiary—Diviso Fiber—that owned a process for fibrating wood. The product it produced was too expensive for papermaking, but I put Aurora Laboratories on the job and they found that the fiber had some special characteristics that made it highly desirable for use in phenolic molding compounds. I eventually sold Diviso to Cavalier Chemical. That's what originally sparked my interest in the company. Since then I've followed it rather closely."

He dropped to the couch, fingering the report that lay beside him. "For the last two years, Cavalier has been contemplating a substantial expansion of their research laboratory facilities, particularly on the practical side."

Suddenly, as if the thought had been exploded in his mind by the electric impulse that radiated from Cash McCall's eyes, Gil saw the possibility far more clearly than his stumbling voice indicated as he asked, "You mean—use Suffolk Moulding as a Cavalier research center?"

"But with an added twist. Ever since that fiber deal I told you about, Cavalier has been retaining Aurora Laboratories to supplement their own research work. Cavalier is Aurora's biggest client.

169

I'd say that Aurora is carrying a good half of Cavalier's total research program. Now suppose we merge Aurora with Suffolk Moulding, give Schnader and his boys the whole Suffolk plant as a research center. Would it work?"

Habit made Gil Clark search for flaws but the only fault he could find was with his own obtuseness in having failed to recognize how perfectly Suffolk Moulding could be fitted into its new role. The heterogeneous collection of presses, assembled by Grant Austen in years past, would provide ideal pilot-plant facilities for production research. The machine shop, still manned by men who had grown up in the days when Grant Austen had concentrated on development work, was an inventor's dream come true. The Administration Building could be easily converted to a chemical laboratory.

The flame that Cash McCall touched to a cigarette flared briefly and then snapped out. "I happen to know that Schnader is worried about having nothing to leave his family. I'm sure he'd jump at the chance to pick up a couple hundred thousand that could be capital gained. And you're sure that Suffolk Moulding is for sale?"

"Absolutely," Gil said. "Unless Grant Austen changes his mind, and I don't think he will."

"So far, so good. Then the problem would be to sell the idea to Cavalier. If we could—" He cut himself off. "I'm getting in a little deep here without knowing whether you're going along or not. What about it, Gil, want to deal yourself in—or don't you?"

"Well, I—this is what it would be, working on things like this?"

"Right. But I'm not trying to push you into a fast decision. If you want a day or two to make up your mind—or if you want to talk to your wife—?"

"No, it isn't that," Gil said quickly, unable to explain that his hesitance arose, not from indecision, but from his surprise that Cash McCall didn't know that his decision had already been made. "You can count me in."

"Good," Cash McCall said simply, the easy sweep of his arm picking up the report. "Take this along and study it. It's a Lockwood report on Cavalier—give you a lot of background. If there's anything more that you want the Lockwood boys to dig up, let me know and we'll put them on the trail. I own the outfit so we might as well make use of it." He tossed the report to Gil's lap. "Don't let that get out of your hands. After you've had a chance to study it—oh, you'd better have this, too."

He found a scrap of paper and scrawled something on it. "My telephone number. It's not listed and the hotel won't connect you. Only way I can protect myself from all the Grant Austens with com-

170

panies to sell. Give me a ring when you're ready to talk—tonight, tomorrow morning, whenever it suits you."

Nudged by a tone of dismissal, Gil found himself moving toward the door. "What about Grant Austen? What shall I tell him when he calls—that you're interested and want to talk to him?"

Cash McCall jammed his hands deep in his jacket pockets. "Go back to your office and stand by until he calls. Tell him you have a buyer—but not who it is. My name isn't to be used. Get him to set his price—and warn him that there'll be no haggling. It will be a one-price deal—take it or leave it, yes or no. We'll buy or not buy, that's all there'll be to it. Understand?"

Gil nodded. "And I'll call you then, after I've talked to him?"

"Right. If I buy, take him to Winston Conway at Jamison, Conway & Slythe. He'll handle the details."

"But won't you want to at least see the plant?" Gil asked incredulously.

"No need of that. I rarely see the properties I buy—too dangerous. If I start roaming around factories I get intrigued with gadgets and lose my perspective. But look now—don't be disappointed if I turn it down. The woods are full of Grant Austens with companies to sell. We can't buy them all."

"I know," he said automatically, further response cut off by the strangely chiding smile that had settled on Cash McCall's face.

"Gil, I thought you were interested in making money?"

"I am. I—"

"You haven't even asked what your salary will be."

"Well, I—I wasn't worrying about that."

The smile faded. "I didn't tell you because I didn't want it to influence you, one way or another. But just in case your wife is interested, you can tell her that your salary will be twenty-five thousand a year."

There was a parched dryness in Gil Clark's throat that made it impossible to express the gratitude that welled up within him. His salary at Corporation Associates had been six hundred a month.

••••• 10

The luncheon at The Wharf had scarcely reached its midpoint when Will Atherson picked a hint out of Grant Austen's conversation that the president of the Suffolk Moulding Company had something on his mind other than a loan to finance the expansion that Andscott demanded. By the time they left the club, building hint upon hint, Atherson suspected that Austen was planning to sell his company. The first minutes after their return to the bank had confirmed it.

"Maybe you think I'm crazy," Austen said, "but it looks to me like the smart thing to do."

"You may well be right," Atherson said soberly, tamping his pipe. "As a matter of fact, I'm inclined to think that you are."

Grant Austen responded to the encouragement. "I know what I'm doing, Will. I've thought the whole thing through and I've made up my mind."

Will Atherson sat back, taking advantage of a quality of character that he had purposefully developed for such occasions, a pipe-smoking taciturnity that forced the man on the other side of the desk to do most of the talking.

Grant Austen endured the silence to the breaking point. "I've never done anything like this before, Will, and I know there's a right way and a wrong way to go about it. I've always worked with you before—anything financial—so that's why I came down today."

"Appreciate it," Atherson said. "Have anything in mind?"

"Well, nothing special—except I remember back about the start of the war you had someone on the string that wanted to buy me out."

"Yes, I recall."

"Always had a suspicion it was Andscott," Austen said, his tone adding a question mark.

Atherson found himself a victim of his own tactics. Now it was Austen who was forcing him to talk. "There's been a lot of water over the dam since then."

"But you're still close to Andscott, aren't you?" Austen asked accepting evasion as confirmation. "What I mean is, you'd be in a position to approach them to see whether they might be interested now, wouldn't you? From their standpoint I should think it would make a lot of sense, getting their own molding plant."

"Might," Atherson admitted, going through the slow-motion movements of lighting his pipe. It was clear now that Grant Austen had made his decision. But the next step was a puzzler. It was true that Andscott might be interested, but only at a bargain price, and then only if Suffolk Moulding could be bought for stock instead of cash. On the other hand, it would undoubtedly improve the bank's future relations with Andscott to throw the deal their way ... and it was true the biggest account in the Trust Department had heavy holdings of Andscott stock. But the bank had an obligation to Grant Austen, too. He was an old customer, one of the oldest.

One of the first loans that Will Atherson had made, after his father had given him the freedom to act entirely on his own judgment, had been to Grant Austen. He had been proved right in backing Austen and, afterwards, through all the years that had followed, loan after loan, he had found great personal satisfaction in the role that he played in the building of the Suffolk Moulding Company. It was a good example of constructive banking practice, a pleasant rebuttal against the all too common estimate of a banker as a usurious leech. Now, at the end, despite the loss of the admiration he once felt for Grant Austen's ingenuity and driving energy, there was still the debt of an old friendship. The least he could do was to make a fair final payment.

"I'll help you, Grant," he said. "Do anything I can. Gladly."

"What about Andscott?"

"Frankly, I think you'd do better in another quarter. I'll be glad to sound them out if you want me to, but I doubt if they'd be either willing or able to pay you what the business is worth. Of course, if you were interested in a merger—taking payment for your company in Andscott stock—?"

"No, that's out, Will."

"You've considered the fact that a tax-free transfer of stock might be arranged?"

Austen shook his head vigorously. "I want to get *out*, Will, all the way out. Don't you think that's the smart thing to do?"

"Yes, in your case, I think it is," Atherson said with cautious honesty. "Frankly, Andscott looks extremely shaky to me. I'm afraid General Danvers made a bad move in getting into the television business. It's been bleeding the rest of the company white and I doubt now whether it's ever going to pay off."

"Sure, I know," Austen persisted. "But even if Andscott isn't the best bet, don't you think it might still be a good idea to sound them out? What I mean is—well, if they'd make me an offer it would be something to start with, wouldn't it? Give us something to play off against another buyer? Selling a company is like selling anything else—the more prospects you've got bidding, the higher you can work up the price."

"Let's consider that for a moment," Atherson said, remembering the call that he had had from the president of Andscott the day before. "If Andscott shouldn't be interested, isn't there a possibility that they would be seriously concerned if they found out that you were planning to sell?"

"I don't get what you mean, Will."

"Might they not think that a new ownership of Suffolk Moulding would jeopardize their cabinet supply? If they did, wouldn't they be inclined to shift their business to another source in order to protect their position? If that happened—if you lost the Andscott business— wouldn't your company be harder to sell? Might it not substantially reduce the price you could get?"

Grant Austen hesitated, an oddly preoccupied expression on his face, finally saying, "Maybe you're right, Will. I guess the best thing would be to leave Andscott out of it."

For a moment, Will Atherson had the feeling that there was something that Grant Austen wasn't telling him, but quickly decided that Austen's hesitance indicated only embarrassment at not having thought his way through the Andscott situation. "Any other prospects in mind, Grant?"

"Well, Gil Clark's got someone who's interested."

"Clark?"

"He's the Corporation Associates man who handles our account. You met him in the hotel this noon."

Atherson nodded, resorting again to the saving diversion of relighting his pipe.

"Corporation Associates is Harrison Glenn, you know," Grant Austen went on. "He has a lot of contacts and—well, I didn't see any harm in having him tip me off on anything he might have on tap."

"Perhaps not," Atherson said, but feeling now the urgent necessity of taking command of the situation, motivated not by any gain to the bank that might come from participation in the sale of Suffolk Moulding Company, but rather by the loss of pride that he would experience if Grant Austen were to secure the help that he needed from another source.

Backspinning, his mind quickly sorted the possibilities. Selling the Suffolk Moulding Company shouldn't prove too difficult. It was a sound little company in a growing industry. But it would take time to find the right buyer, possibly several months. In the meantime, Andscott would be sure to hear about it and what he'd told Austen about losing the Andscott business was no empty threat. That was the way Danvers would probably react. If there were only someone who might buy in a hurry ...

His mind braked to a quick stop. Hadn't Cash McCall once said that he was interested in Suffolk? The incident came back, materializing out of wisps of discarded memory. It had been after McCall had returned from Maine, that summer he'd put through the paper-mill deal that had ended in the Paper Enterprises Corporation. Cash had walked in that day on an unprecedented visit to the bank and, masking his real purpose, had said something about having met a girl named Lory Austen who had told him that she was a friend of the Athersons. For a brief moment, he had imagined that McCall's interest in Lory was personal. But, of course, it hadn't been and, afterwards, inwardly and silently, he had laughed at himself for having allowed the thought to occur to him. He had thought himself as silly as his wife had been at that party for Lory, imagining every man that looked at the child as a matchmaking prospect.

What Cash McCall had been interested in, of course, had been Suffolk Moulding. And he must have been impressed with the story of how it had grown with the help of the Freeholders Bank & Trust Company because, afterwards, he had said, 'Keep an eye on that company, Will. If Austen ever wants to sell it, I might be interested.' But that was a long time ago now and Cash McCall's interests were even more mercurial than most men's ... and the situation had changed ... but if Cash McCall *were* still interested ...

Atherson blew a curling spiral of smoke. "I know someone who might be a prospect, Grant. If he were, he'd be an ideal buyer. He's the kind of man who has no trouble making up his mind—and when his mind's made up he moves in a hurry."

"That's what I want," Austen said impatiently. "But I want to get a decent price, too. After all I don't *have* to sell. It isn't as if I were being forced into it."

"Do you have an asking price in mind?"

"Two million."

Austen's quick reply was clinching proof that his desire to sell was sincere and Will Atherson's mind, spinning figures like a calculating machine, came up with an answer that matched Austen's. His study of the Suffolk folder yesterday morning had engraved the company's current balance sheet on his memory and two million seemed a sound asking price. It was high enough so that Austen could back down two or three hundred thousand and still get what the company was worth, yet the figure was not so high that a good prospect would be frightened away.

"Who's this buyer you're thinking about?" Austen asked.

"I've no idea whether he'll be interested or not," Atherson said. "But if you'll authorize me to contact him, I'll see what I can find out."

"How long will it take?"

"Not very long—if he's in the city. If he isn't, a few days at the most. Shall I go ahead?"

Grant Austen shifted restlessly. "Well, I guess there's no harm in

175

telling him the company is for sale. Sure, go ahead, Will. But make it as fast as you can. Now that I've decided to do it, I'm anxious to get it over with. As I was saying, Gil Clark said that he had someone who might be interested, too."

"When are you leaving Philadelphia?" Atherson asked, convinced now that Grant Austen was in a state of mind where he would snap up the first good offer.

"Well, I'd planned to leave before long. I told Lory that I'd meet her at three." He looked at his watch. "Later than I thought. Half an hour from now."

"Where are you meeting her?"

"At the Ivanhoe. In the lobby."

"Suppose we leave it this way, Grant. If I know anything by then I'll leave a message for you at the desk and you can give me a ring."

"All right," Grant Austen said, rising. "I'll call Gil Clark right away."

"I wouldn't jump *too* fast, Grant."

Austen put his arm into the topcoat that Will Atherson was holding for him. "Sure I know, but I'm not going to fool around. I know what I want to do and I'm going to do it."

Atherson surrendered his hold on the coat. "Grant, if you want to make a call there's no reason why you can't make it from here."

"Oh, I—"

"That's what our customer's room is for. Completely private. No one will disturb you."

He guided Austen to the door of the room that was reserved for the use of important bank customers and returned quickly to his own office, throwing open the door to his secretary's adjoining cubicle. "Get Mr. McCall on the line. His number isn't in the book but you have it there somewhere. If he doesn't answer, keep trying."

Unexpectedly, his buzzer sounded almost immediately, signaling that the call had been completed, and he picked up the receiver, anticipating incongruity. Cash McCall's voice always sounded strangely out of place when heard in the polished glass atmosphere of the bank. It was the voice of a man before a log fire with a mug of hot buttered rum in his hand, or astride a good hunter, or fondling a new-born pup out of his best bitch, or sitting on a rail fence in the hazy October sun.

"Will Atherson," the banker identified himself.

The tone of McCall's response was as he had expected it to be.

"You may have forgotten," Atherson said, "but several years ago you asked me to let you know if the Suffolk Moulding Company ever came on the market."

"I haven't forgotten," McCall's voice came back, loose syllabled with lounging ease.

"It's for sale. Grant Austen is here in the bank now."

"In your office?"

"He's outside at the moment, making a phone call. Are you interested?"

"Oh, I don't know, Will. Possibly."

"I believe it might be worth looking into."

"Have any idea what the price tag would be?"

"He's asking two million. I have a good file on the company with a year-end balance sheet and operating statement. If you'd want to see the file, I'll bring it over."

"Oh, I don't think that's necessary, Will. Perhaps later."

Atherson hesitated. "I doubt if it stays on the market too long. Austen is anxious to sell and there's someone else moving in. If there's any chance of your being interested, I'd suggest that you have a chat with him right away. It could be arranged quite easily. He's meeting his daughter in the lobby of the hotel at three o'clock. If you'd want me to, I could—"

"His daughter?"

"Yes—Lory. You may have forgotten, but you met her that summer up in Maine. I recall that you mentioned it to me at the time."

"He's meeting her here at three?"

"Yes. If you want to have a talk with Austen, I could bring him over and—"

"No, don't bother about that, Will. If I decide I want to talk to him, I can pick him up easily enough in the lobby."

"Yes, I suppose you could," Atherson said, masking his annoyance at this repetition of McCall's persistent tendency to play the lone wolf. "But do you think—perhaps it might not be a bad idea if I were to mention it to him—so that he'll at least know who you are?"

McCall's voice came back, smile toned after a moment of hesitation. "I'm afraid you're a little slow on this one, Will."

"Slow?"

"I knew about Suffolk being for sale. I've had it from another source."

The banker felt himself stunned into silence.

"But I know that Austen's an old friend of yours," McCall went on. "And I suppose you would like to let him know that you're in on it, too, wouldn't you? All right, Will, tell him that I might get in touch with him—but make it *might*. No promises. It all depends on—"

Atherson lost the last of the sentence, seeing that the door of his office had opened and that Grant Austen was listening. There was nothing more that he dared say except to acknowledge McCall's ending of the conversation.

"Well, I'll be on my way," Grant Austen said.

"Get your man?" Atherson asked from the surface of his mind, his thoughts still with McCall.

"No, Gil wasn't back yet and Harrison Glenn was out, too. But they're both expected in a few minutes. I'll call them from the hotel."

Atherson rose and walked to the door. "I made a telephone call too, Grant."

"This fellow you were telling me about?"

"There's a possibility that he may have you paged in the lobby of the Ivanhoe. Nothing definite about it, but he *might*—so I'd wait around for a few minutes if I were you."

"What's his name?"

"Cash McCall."

Grant Austen's expression made it obvious that he had never heard the name before.

"Grant, tell me something. You said that you'd told this man from Corporation Associates that you were thinking of selling?"

"Yes?"

"Anyone else?"

"No."

"You told no one else?"

Grant Austen shook his head. "Absolutely not. I haven't mentioned it to a soul—well, except Lory, of course. Why?"

"Didn't want to cross lines, that's all." He extended his hand. "Let me know what happens, Grant, and if I can help you in any way, give me a call."

After the door had closed, walking to the glassed front of his office, he watched Grant Austen go down the spiraling staircase and out across the banking floor, but the seeing was without impression, his mind occupied with the task of attempting to fit together the jigsaw events of the last hour. In spite of what Austen had said, it was still possible that he might have tipped off someone else, perhaps unknowingly. Grant had acquired the bad habit of talking too much. But if it *were* true that the only person that Grant had told was this fellow from Corporation Associates ... and Cash McCall had been tipped off ... damn it, why couldn't Grant have kept his mouth shut! This put him in a hell of a spot, letting someone else get ahead of him with Cash. Made him look like a fool.

Into the twenty minutes that had elapsed since she had felt it safe to leave her post at the door of the Fontainebleau Room, Maude Kennard had crowded a brusque interview with a linen salesman, a mezzanine conference to adjudicate a jurisdictional argument between the Housekeeper and the Chief Engineer, the initialing for payment of a stack of bills, and the dictation of three short letters. She was about to escape her office when Nathan, the room clerk, appeared in the doorway.

"He just came down, Mrs. Kennard," Nathan said in a conspiratorial whisper. "That Mr. Clark who had lunch with Mr. McCall?"

"Did you find out who he is?"

Nathan's saccharine smile made it plain that he had. "He's with Corporation Associates. Dear me, I knew that his face was familiar but—"

She stared past him, unseeing ... Corporation Associates ... the same firm that had made that study of the hotel's operations last year ... if Cash McCall had called in Corporation Associates again it might mean that he was getting ready to sell the hotel ...

"Thank you, Nathan," she said, dismissing him, rising to close the door, attempting to insure the few minutes of privacy that she needed.

Her instinct had warned her yesterday that she would have to work fast ... and she had been a fool last night ... new dress ... all ready to step in and handle the service of his dinner and then, at the last minute, she'd lost her nerve and called in Louis. No, she *hadn't* lost her nerve! It was only that ... whatever it was had been a mistake. The dinner party had broken up at ten. She could have gone back to see him afterwards, asked him whether everything was all right ... *Faisan à la McCall*. Of course! That would have given her the perfect excuse ... she was thinking of putting it on the Fontainebleau Room menu and ...

Was it too late now?

Cash McCall was in his suite, alone.

She started out of her office, stepped back for a quick inspection in the mirror, retouched her lipstick, and then made a second start. At the doorway, the sweep of her eyes picked up a shadowy figure on the other side of the mezzanine, a man standing beside one of the pillars in front of the elevator bank. The man was Cash McCall.

It was her first reaction that this was a stroke of luck, that she'd be able to talk to him now without invading his suite. But, second-glancing, she saw that he was watching someone down in the lobby. Her eyes followed the direction of his fixed stare. A young girl sat in one of the high-backed chairs against the far wall, reading what looked like a travel folder, looking up now toward the door, obviously waiting for someone.

The girl half stood for an instant, straightening her dress and there was something about the quickness of her movement, the supple grace of her body, the flash of her sweeping hand ... who was it?

She tried to blink away the hallucination that had plagued her for so many years—but not for a long time now—that every girl was that high school bitch in Chicago ... that little tart that Wilfred had ...

Out of the corner of her eye, she caught sight of Cash McCall starting down the steps. Stepping quickly into her office, she snatched up the phone and asked for the desk, drumming her fingers impatiently until Nathan answered. "There's a girl in the lobby. I want to know who she is. Make some kind of excuse—"

"Oh, it's perfectly all right, Mrs. Kennard. She's waiting for her father. Mr. Austen, you know—the gentleman who came in this noon with Mr. Atherson."

"Thank you."

"Quite all right, Mrs. Kennard. I do agree with you that we can't be too careful."

Nathan had guessed what she was thinking ... and Nathan wasn't wrong!

Was there any connection ... Austen with Mr. Atherson this noon ... this fellow Clark whispering to Austen ... then having lunch with Cash ... now Cash going down to talk to Austen's daughter? Could it possibly have anything to do with Cash selling the hotel?

● ● ● ● ● 12

Lory Austen's first sight of Cash McCall so perfectly matched the onset of so many other delusionary moments that her reaction was one of irritated rejection. She looked down and forced her eyes to focus on the fine print of the paragraph on PASSPORTS AND VISAS, fighting back the disappointing realization that she had not yet completely healed the mind fault that kept making him appear out of the solid blankness of a wall as he had appeared out of the darkness that night on the wharf, or seeing him walk down a flight of stairs as he had walked down the rocky path that day in Eagle Harbor ...

Involuntarily, her eyes glanced up and in the instant when there was still acknowledgable sensation, she saw Cash McCall standing in front of her. He spoke her name and there was the crashing descent to the truth of his presence ... *this was no dream!*

It was impossible to respond to his greeting. There was not the faintest stirring of breath in her lungs. Her heart, too, had stopped. But suddenly, it awakened from the deathlike suspension of its beat and burst into a flurry of mad pumping, driving toward her brain the hot flood of remembered embarrassment ... *this was the moment she had left him ... the door of his room at the Inn ... pushing her away from him ...*

There was the explosive impulse to run away now as she had run away before, but she was stopped by the raising of his hand, seeing the movement but not realizing until the sensation of touch that she had reached out to take it, experiencing the momentary indistinguishability of fire from ice. He spoke again but the words came into her mind as separate sounds without connected flow, hopelessly tangled by reverberation, and she heard them in one fantastic rearrangement after another, meaning changed and distorted with every rehearing, ending finally in the fantasy that he had said that he wanted to meet her father.

Now it was not Cash McCall who was an apparition but her father, materializing out of the spinning glass-glint of the revolving door, walking toward them in the onrush of the climactic moment of a nightmare's pseudo memory. Somehow, struggling against the clammy grip of terror, she managed the introduction.

Her father's astonishment was uninterpretable until Cash McCall said, "Lory and I met some years ago at a cocktail party—Jefferson Clark's, as I recall."

"Say, that's fine," her father said, broadly smiling, and she knew then that his surprise had not been what she had feared, but rather the prelude to some discovery of great good fortune.

"Never had any idea that you two knew each other," Grant Austen went on, glancing at her approvingly as if she had done him a highly appreciated favor, then looking back at Cash McCall again. "Will Atherson said that you might be getting in touch with me."

"Could you spare a few minutes now?" Cash McCall asked.

"Sure, you bet," Grant Austen said affably. "All right with you, Lory?"

She said something meaningless, not understanding what was happening.

"Then suppose we go up to my apartment," Cash McCall suggested.

She stepped back, withdrawing, but her father took her arm. "No, Lory, you come along. This concerns you, too." He turned to McCall. "My daughter is our second largest stockholder, so if you don't mind I'd like to have her sit in, too."

Protest died in her throat, overwhelmed by the realization that Cash McCall was considering the purchase of the Suffolk Moulding Company. In the shock-deadened interval of hesitation she was swept along into the elevator, only half hearing their conversation, struggling to capture the poise that would have to be mustered before she could manage a crossing of the threshold of Cash McCall's room.

But, strangely, it was not the entering that mattered when it finally happened, stepping into the apartment's foyer as Cash McCall held the door for her, but rather the sight of the living room that she saw through the open arch, the impact of actuality against the unreasoned expectation of finding herself in his cretonned and wicker-chaired room at the Inn. She walked ahead, seeing the living room not in detail but in totality, her overwhelming impression one of dominant masculinity—and Cash McCall, passing her as she hesitated a step beyond the arch, became the animated source of the room's endowment.

She took the chair that he offered her, not daring to look up to meet his eyes, glancing away. And then she saw it—her frontispiece drawing for *The Knight of the Hawk*, framed and hanging on his wall.

A moment before, it had seemed that she had passed the limit of surprise but this was a shock of surpassing weight. She was powerless to prevent the reflex that made her turn back to Cash McCall. His eyes met hers, not accidentally but as if he had been expectantly waiting, and in the moment of locked glances he seemed to ask for her silence, making the picture's presence on his wall an intimacy that was not to be shared with anyone, least of all with her father.

Cash McCall moved toward the opposite wall, lounging now against the window casing, and she imagined that his shift of position had been purposefully made to keep her father's eyes away from the drawing, an act as seemingly calculated as the way that he immediately launched the subject of buying the Suffolk Moulding Company.

The conversation was entirely between the two men, Cash McCall's eyes fixed on her father's face, and she felt it safe to watch him, hearing only scattered words, unconnected and meaningless, and when her father finally turned to her for confirmation of something that he had said, she flushed at the necessity of nodding blind agreement, afterwards listening with forced intensity to avoid a repetition of the embarrassment.

Her father's voice faded into her consciousness. "—be mighty glad to show you around any time you could come over to Suffolk. I'm sure you'll find the plant everything that I've represented it to be. I don't know how much Will Atherson told you about the company, or how familiar you are with the molding business, but—"

Cash McCall's lips moved when the drone of Grant Austen's voice dropped off into silence. "It happens, Mr. Austen, that I know quite a bit about your business—more, perhaps, than you suspect. I believe you've used the services of Corporation Associates for some years now?"

"Why, sure—yes, we have. Fine man, Harrison Glenn."

"Under the circumstances there's something that I want you to know, Mr. Austen. I have a substantial interest in Corporation Associates—as a matter of fact, the controlling interest."

Lory Austen expected her father to mirror her questioning surprise at Cash McCall's revelation but when she turned to look at him, there was no reflection of her own suspicion in his apparently pleased response.

"Well, I'll be darned," Grant Austen chuckled. "You've sure kept yourself a silent partner. Never knew but what it was all Harrison Glenn's. Well now, if you're that close to Corporation Associates, I guess you do know something about my company, don't you?"

Cash McCall nodded. "I'm not active in Corporation Associates' management but I do keep in touch. For example, I've seen all the studies that have been made of your operations—at least the major ones."

"Say, I'll bet this is what Gil Clark had in mind," her father said to her, then turning to speak to McCall again. "That where you found out about my wanting to sell, Mr. McCall—from Gil Clark?"

"Yes, Harrison Glenn called me last night after Gil Clark got back from your place," Cash McCall said. "And when Gil was here for lunch today we discussed the possibility of my being interested in the purchase of your company."

Grant Austen shook his head in chuckling amazement. "This is sure a surprise to me. I thought all the time that—well, you see, it was Will Atherson who mentioned you to me, so I thought—"

"That was a coincidence," Cash McCall said quickly. "I understand that he's an old friend of yours."

"Will Atherson? Sure, you bet. Will and I have worked together for a good many years now, going right back to the start of the company. Guess he must be a friend of yours, too?"

"I've been associated with his bank on a number of undertakings," Cash McCall said, his expression signaling the even more serious tone that came into his voice as he asked, "Tell me, Mr. Austen, have you authorized Mr. Atherson to act for you in this matter of selling your company?"

"Well, I just told him that it was for sale, that's all."

"Am I to take it then that it's a matter that you are handling yourself? There are no agents involved?"

"Agents? No, you see, it was only last night that I really made up my mind to sell so I haven't had time to—no, I'm handling it myself."

"Tell me something, Mr. Austen," Cash McCall said, his voice easing as he shifted his lounging position on the wide window sill. "Or perhaps you'd prefer not to tell me—which, of course, is your privilege. How interested is Andscott in buying your company?"

Lory waited through her father's hesitation, relieved when he finally said, "Well, I'd say, Mr. McCall, that's more a question of how interested I'd be in the kind of proposition Andscott could offer me. You see—well I might as well make this clear, Mr. McCall—I'm not interested in a stock deal or anything like that."

"You want cash?"

"Sure, you bet—cash."

"Then the price that Mr. Atherson mentioned—two million—means two million in cash?"

"Yes—in cash."

"That's for complete ownership, all the stock?"

"That's right."

"And I assume you're authorized to act for all the other stockholders?"

She anticipated her father's glance in her direction and was ready to meet it, lip smiling as he said, "I guess there won't be any trouble on that score, will there, Lory? You see, it's all in the family, Mr. McCall. Lory has about five thousand shares and I hold the rest."

"And there are no other stockholders?"

"No sir!" her father said proudly. "Not even a bank loan. Don't know whether you saw our year-end statement or not—I gave it to Gil last week—but that tells the whole story."

"There's been no change since that statement was drawn—except, of course, the profit you've made since the first of the year."

"Change? No, nothing important. Oh, there's been a little shifting around—raw material inventory is up a few thousand—"

184

"All right, Mr. Austen," Cash McCall interrupted, pivoting off the window seat, his hand extended.

Lory felt the blankness of her father's face as if it were a mirrored image of her own.

"I'm accepting your offer," McCall said, smiling and casual. "You offered me all the stock of the Suffolk Moulding Company for two million dollars. All you have to do to make it a deal is to shake hands."

Lory held her breath through the eternity of waiting until her father's hand, immobile at first, then moving in a fantasy of time-extended slow motion, finally met Cash McCall's.

"It's a deal," she heard her father say.

Those words alone registered sharply. The words that came afterwards were only breaks in the verbal haze ... *adjustment to the statement ... subject to verification ... attorneys ... tomorrow ... settlement April first ... no announcement ...*

She turned away, looking into the darkness of the foyer, still finding it difficult to accept the fantastic coincidence of Cash McCall turning out to be the man who had bought the Suffolk Moulding Company.

A door opened at the far end of the foyer and she saw the figure of a woman silhouetted against the lighted back hall, a silver bowl in her hand, listening, wifelike.

But before Lory could focus her eyes to discern features, the woman saw that she was being watched and the door was quickly closed. Lory looked back at Cash McCall, blinking. Something had happened to him. He was only a man now ... flesh and blood ... a man with a suite at the Hotel Ivanhoe ... rich ... buying a two-million dollar company as casually as if he were picking up some little trinket for the wife who was waiting at the back of the apartment.

She could breathe now, freely and easily. Her heart settled back to its normal beat. Testing her composure, she looked directly at Cash McCall. There was no quickening of her breath, no speeding of her heart. Her only sensation was the relieving realization that she would never again be haunted by those terrible hallucinations. She had fought for three years to free her mind of him and now, strangely, it was he himself who had released her.

Her father's voice cut into her consciousness. "—you bet, Gil's a good boy. I don't know whether he's quite up to that or not but—"

Gil? Of course! That was why Cash McCall had her drawing on his wall. Gil Clark had given it to him ... Gil had always liked her things ... Gil was with Corporation Associates and Cash McCall owned it. A present for the boss, that's all it meant. How could she have ever imagined anything else? There was nothing unusual about someone having one of her drawings. Lots of people had them. Tony had three on the wall of his office at the publishing company.

Cash McCall and her father had risen and were walking toward her. She rose quickly, keeping ahead of them as they moved out into the foyer.

"Well, I'll just say this, Mr. McCall," Grant Austen said. "You've bought yourself a good company."

"I'm satisfied," McCall said, pressing the elevator button. "And I'm sure you are, too."

"Sure, you bet, that's what it takes to make a good deal. Has to work both ways."

Cash McCall extended his hand and she took it. This was the final test. It was only a hand ... a man's hand ... any man's. He'd probably been married all the time ... of course he had ... that explained everything.

"Good to have seen you again, Lory," Cash said. "I hope this won't be the last time."

Her father broke in. "Well, I guess we'll be seeing you in Suffolk, won't we, Mr. McCall? Want you to know that if there's anything I can do—"

Lory stepped into the elevator cab, turning to face Cash McCall as the two men shook hands.

The door closed and the elevator started down. Her father's hands clamped down on the points of her shoulders. "By golly, Lory, we've done it! Thought I might get a million seven—maybe a million eight—but never the whole two million. Wasn't that something? I still can't believe—" He exhaled an enormous sigh as if the pressure of excitement had suddenly become too great to contain.

"It's wonderful," she said boldly, looking straight into his eyes. She was free ... her own money ... two hundred thousand dollars ... Italy ...

"Yes sir, Lory, if I do say it myself, I handled that just about right. When he came out with that offer, I really stepped in there and nailed him down, didn't I? Sure wasn't giving him any chance to change his mind. Nice fellow, though, isn't he? Golly, Lory, just think of it—I'm a millionaire!"

····· 13

For the third time, Miriam Austen slipped on the lime-green taffeta, now with the long skirt pinned up, and examined her image in the mirror. Maybe if she cut it off to cocktail length ... no, it just wouldn't do. Or would it? It was so ridiculous to spend a lot of money on evening clothes when you wore them so infrequently ... but Moon Beach was probably dressy ... and the convention meant so much to Grant. Maybe the thing to do was to run down to Philadelphia and ...

Again, inescapably, she thought of how silly she had been this morning, wanting to go to Philadelphia with Grant, on the point of saying it, the words on her lips, then foolishly afraid to speak, silenced by the fear that she would destroy the look of pleasure that had come to her husband's face when Lory had offered to drive him.

She stood for a long time, staring at the mirror, the dress forgotten. Then, seemingly without the preliminary of conscious thought, she said aloud, "It's your own fault, Miriam Austen. It's no one's fault but your own."

The words were spoken as both accusation and acknowledgment and, heard and accepted, she began to take off the dress. It was a shame, such a lovely fabric, but it simply wouldn't do for the convention at Moon Beach.

····· 14

Gil Clark sat in his low-partitioned office at Corporation Associates, waiting for Grant Austen's call, still reading the Lockwood report on the Cavalier Chemical Company. It was an amazing document. He had known for a long time that there were agencies that made a business of industrial investigations, and he had heard Lockwood Reports mentioned as one of the best, but he had never imagined it as being such a fabulously efficient detective organization. Out of such apparently unrelated bits and pieces as a guest list at a wedding, a real estate transfer reported in a South Carolina weekly, the questions asked of a prospective employee, an eavesdropped conversation in a Pullman club car, and a paragraph winnowed from a paper presented to a technical association, the Lockwood staff had accurately predicted, months before the announcement, that Cavalier Chemical was secretly angling its way into the sheeted-plastic business. More to the point, and with a cunning skill no less ingeniously devious, Lockwood had found out that Cavalier's Plastics Division was having trouble keeping pace with its competitors, that the fault was recognized by company officials to lie in the unavailability of adequate pilot-plant facilities for the production testing of new molding materials, and that the Director of Research had already been secretly authorized by the Board of Directors to canvas the possibility of buying a moderate-sized molding plant to be operated as an adjunct to the Research Laboratories.

Gil Clark had often read confidential reports of the kind put out by the credit-information agencies, but he had never seen anything that approached the intensity of surveillance and analysis evidenced by the document he was reading. The only possible parallel was a Navy Intelligence report that he had once been allowed to examine. Even that suffered by comparison.

Inevitably, he recalled how much Cash McCall had known about him before he had been called to the Hotel Ivanhoe, and he felt now a resentment that had been oddly unexperienced as long as he had been in McCall's presence. He, too, had probably been the subject of a Lockwood investigation.

In much the same way that the fading of intoxication causes a man to reach back for the orienting memory of what had happened before his brain had become fogged, Gil Clark recalled the feelings with which he had approached the Hotel Ivanhoe. He had anticipated that Cash McCall would turn out to be another Harry Guizinger and now, try as he would, he could not satisfactorily explain why he had changed his opinion. Cash McCall, of course, was infinitely smoother, cultured and polished, a decidedly more likable man, but was there any other essential difference? Why had he been so willing to excuse McCall for what had been inexcusable in Guizinger? Was there any less justification for the bribery and cutbacks with which Guizinger had set up the Tronic Wire & Coil deal than there was for the network of spies that Cash McCall had set up with his secret ownership of Lockwood Reports, Hildreth-Paris and Corporation Associates?

Resolutely, Gil checked the instinctive urge for self-justification, accepting no excuse for himself until it had been carefully examined. But was there really anything wrong with Cash McCall owning Lockwood Reports? What difference could there be between retaining them and owning them? All companies bought information, even if only from credit agencies. After all, there was nothing in the Lockwood report on Cavalier Chemical that anyone who was clever enough could not have ferreted out and interpreted? Was there anything morally wrong about using information that some man had been fool enough to blab out in an open Pullman club car?

But it was more difficult to justify Cash McCall's ownership of Corporation Associates. There *was* a confidential relationship between a firm of management consultants and its clients that permitted no invasion of a third party. But was there any evidence that McCall had ever taken advantage of his ownership? Wasn't he buying Suffolk Moulding in the open market? Wasn't it true that the only way he could get it was to pay Grant Austen more money than anyone else would ...

Suddenly, he had become aware of the effort that he was expending on justification. Why was he trying so hard? Because he had been bought off with that big salary? *No!* That had nothing to do with it. He'd made up his mind long before Cash had even mentioned twenty-five thousand a year ... *"in case your wife asks you ..."*

Again, as he had done a dozen times in this last hour, Gil Clark debated an attempt to call Barbara. But how could he? All he knew was what she had written in that last letter ten days ago ... *Dad and Mother have invited me to go down to Florida so I'm leaving with them in the morning—and maybe that will give me a chance to think things over* ... just that, nothing else, not even the name of the hotel where they'd be staying.

But even if it were possible to call her, what could he say ... that everything between them would be different now because he was making twenty-five thousand dollars a year?

No, that couldn't be said ... made it sound as if love were something that could be bought. But it *would* make a difference ... buy herself some clothes ... and if she had something decent to wear maybe she'd quit slopping around in that damned old housecoat! And if she could afford to get a permanent in a beauty parlor there'd be no more of that stinking stench in the bathroom ... smelling it in every towel for a month afterward ... and maybe she'd take some interest in cooking, too, if it weren't for that penny-sweating budget ... dishes stacked in the sink ... drain plugged again ... *that damned jerry-built house!* That was what had been wrong, that more than anything else ... no wonder she had gotten fed up ... take the heart out of anyone, trying to keep that dump looking like anything ... water in the basement every time it rained ... the porch cockeyed because there was no foundation under the flagstone.

They could afford a better house now ... twenty-five thousand a year ... and Barbara would know that he'd been right to stick it out with Corporation Associates and not take that job that Harry Guizinger had offered him. That would have meant more money, too, but ...

Damn it, there *was* a difference! But it wasn't something you could explain over the telephone ... yes, Cash McCall bought and sold companies, too ... and made a lot of money. But what was wrong with that? It didn't matter how much money a man made as long as he did it honestly ... and in a way that ...

The telephone rang and his hand shot out, but he waited a moment before he picked up the receiver, resurrecting the rehearsed sentences that he had prepared for Grant Austen's call.

The voice on the other end of the wire was not Austen's. "Gil, this is Cash. I've just bought Suffolk Moulding. No need to go into the details. You can get that later. We take over on April first. That gives you a week. I'd suggest you get over to Suffolk the first thing in the morning. I'm having a short meeting to set up the legal details at seven tomorrow morning with Winston Conway and his lawyers, but they ought to be in Suffolk by ten. Vincent Thompson will be there, too, with a gang of men to make a fast audit. Nothing for you to worry about except to get your feet on the ground. I've told Austen that you'll be in charge after we take over. By the way, before I closed the deal I told him about my relationship to Corporation Associates. Thought you might be worrying about your own position, so I made that perfectly clear. Now look, Gil—you may not be able to get in touch with me for a few days. I'm leaving in the morning. Just hold the fort until I call you. Right?"

"Right," Gil echoed.

Before he could say anything more the connection was broken. He dropped the telephone receiver to its cradle, easing its fall as if the muffling of sound were a way to keep anyone from knowing what a fool he had been to imagine that Cash McCall even remotely resembled Harry Guizinger.

Eight

:
.

ON THE FIRST DAY of April, Miriam Austen awakened to the consciousness of effervescent joy, a sensation immediately challenged by the threat that she was being tricked by a dream, then miraculously confirmed when she glanced at the night table between their beds. The coffee cups were there. *It had actually happened!*

Grant was asleep, hard breathing in the deep slumber of exhaustion, suggesting the composite memory of other moments, long ago, when she had lain awake beside him after the draining away of passion, finding it strange that what had been the ultimate of his aliveness could so quickly fade to inanimate torpor. But now those old memories were mismatched and inapplicable. What had happened last night was something beyond experience, something more meaningful than anything remembered from those long ago first years of marriage.

Her mind obeyed the lover's ever-practiced habit of tracing the strange antecedents of exultation, the events of this past week, the treacherous alternation of fear and hope that had finally come to this wondrous end.

She had been hurt as never before on that night last week when Grant and Lory had returned from Philadelphia and told her that the company had been sold. To have been so completely excluded, not even knowing that her husband was considering such a move, had seemed a wounding blow from which she could never recover. Yet, only a few minutes later, everything had been excused by the prospect she saw opening out ahead of her ... *Lory was going to Italy!*

That next day, Thursday, had built her anticipation of a new life with Grant, the years ahead a never-ending extension of that week in New York when he had taken her to the N.A.M. convention and bought her the Tiffany pin, the prospect verified by the change that had so obviously come over him since his decision to sell the company. He had suggested going to the Suffolk Country Club for dinner—and they had actually gone—not Lory, just the two of them, Lory insisting that she had to stay home and work on her book, and only once during the whole evening had Grant mentioned Lory. And then he had said that a month in Italy would probably do her a lot of good!

Friday had brought the crash of hope. Something had gone wrong —she didn't know what—but Grant had come home in the middle of the day and wouldn't talk to her, her anxious questions answered with only grumbled monosyllables that made her sure the trouble must be something that might prevent final consummation of the sale.

Hope had flared up again on Saturday. Grant had called her at noon—yes, called *her,* not Lory—and the weekend had been a reassuring return to hope. But by dinnertime on Monday, the situation had changed again. Grant had chomped through his meal, grimly silent, not even talking to Lory before he went back to the office again.

Yesterday, fear heightened by loneliness, she had gone out to Lory's studio again, humbling herself into asking for an explanation. But Lory had known nothing that she hadn't known, a revelation that brought incongruous satisfaction but no relief. "Maybe he'll talk to me tonight," Lory had said, and Miriam Austen had lived through the dull terror that her daughter might be right, that Grant would come home that evening and, as he had done so many times before, deny her the sharing of his confidence, talking to Lory instead of to her.

It was desperation that had driven her to do what she had finally done last night, enduring the awful incongruity of a wife being forced to beg to be left alone with her husband ... "Lory, dear, why don't you go to bed and let me wait for your father tonight." And Lory had been *oh, so wonderful!* ... saving her the embarrassment of explanation, kissing her on the cheek and then going quickly upstairs, leaving her alone to wait for Grant.

Now, remembering, Miriam Austen felt the tear-burn of her gratitude, a sensation that dissolved, mist into mist, as she recalled the boldness of what she had forced herself to do ... being in the library when he came in through the terrace door ... then the shameless mimicry of suggesting that she make coffee for him as, on other nights when she had listened from the silence of her bedroom, she had heard her daughter do.

But it had worked!

There had been only that one blank instant when Grant had stared at her with an unreadable expression on his face. Then, miracle of miracles, he had said, "I could use a cup of coffee."

Trembling, afraid that she might be pushing her luck too far, she had suggested, "Let's have it upstairs, dear," and he had answered, "Good idea," and no words of love that he had ever said, or might have said but had not said, had been so full of meaning and promise.

And the promise had been fulfilled.

She could smile now at her bride panic in the kitchen, dropping a pan and spilling coffee, saying over and over again that watched water never boiled, so afraid that he would have fallen asleep before she could reach him that she had not dared turn back when, half up the stairs, she realized that she had forgotten the sugar.

But Grant had not been asleep. He had been waiting for her in his dressing robe, sitting not on his bed but here on hers, his arms stopping her when she had said she had to go back for sugar, whispering something that brought back the giddy memory of that morning when they had been in New York for the N.A.M. convention and hadn't answered the door for the room-service waiter returning with the spoons he had forgotten to bring with their breakfast. Grant, afterwards, seemingly famished, had eaten both dishes of strawberries with his fingers.

But even that morning had been no morning like this morning!

She lifted her head from the pillow, her senses responding to the wonder of the day. The soft wind that billowed the curtains was already day-warm, fragrant with the earth musk of spring, alive with the sound of birds exulting their happiness. She raised to her elbow and glanced at the clock, astounded to find that it was only a quarter to seven. How could she possibly be so completely awake? It had been two o'clock when they had finally turned out the lights. Even after that he had gone on talking to her ... telling her everything ... *everything* ... what Mr. Conway had said, and what he had said, and what Mr. Conway had said, and what he had said ... "It's all wrapped up, Miriam. Everything will be settled in the morning."

"Then we're really going to start living, you and I," she had whispered.

And he had made it so *right* for her to have said it. Last night everything she had done had been right. Before, so many times before, everything she had said had been so wrong.

Life was strange. The years dragged by so unendurably as you lived through them, imagining that everything was so hopelessly lost. Yet all of that had been wiped away in an instant. They were young again ... in love ... yes, truly in love now.

The bed was an impossible confinement of spirit and she slipped out of it, discovering that the nightgown she was wearing was not the one that she had expected but the one that Grant had found for her in the wrong drawer, the Alençon lace that she had never worn before. Bought and tried on in privacy, it had seemed too gross a bid for something that could only come unbidden ... as it had come last night ... and now would come again and again and again.

Silently, slipping on a robe, rejecting mules because their clatter might make a sound that would awaken him, she found the clothes she would wear and tiptoed barefoot across the hall to the guest bathroom that she sometimes used as a cloistered escape, but never before this morning as the glass-glittering chrysalis out of which a new life would emerge.

She made the shower cold and needle-sharp, wanting the body shock that would clear her mind, not trusting the bubbling of free emotion to carry her through the day, realizing the necessity of a tight control if she were to avoid committing some foolish little error that might destroy everything. Grant would awaken in a few minutes and then he would talk to her again. He would expect her to remember all the things he had told her last night, as Lory would have remembered if she had been the one he had told ... all those things about what he had said and what Mr. Conway had said ... the way he had changed things so that ...

The thoughts that were closest to the surface of her mind, like leaves floating on a pool, obscured the depths of memory. Brushed aside, they swirled back, letting her recall only scattered and disconnected words. But, suddenly, from the pool's deepest depths she felt an uprising chill, colder than the shower, sharper than its needle-prick jets ... *Grant wasn't selling Lory's stock!*

Reacting to panic, she snapped off the shower, whipped a towel from the rack, drying and dressing without conscious guidance, her mind overwhelmed with sudden realization ... *oh, what a fool she had been not to realize before what Grant had meant. Not selling Lory's stock was his trick to hold her ... not to let her get away! She must not let that happen ... Lory must go ... leave them alone ... alone as they had been alone last night ...*

Her dress tangled at her throat, a hand in the wrong armhole, and she struggled impatiently against the frustration, fighting to bring her mind back to the confirming memory of what a changed person Lory had been this last week, so strong and sure of herself. It was

Lory's knowing that she was going to have her own money that made the difference ... "Mother, it isn't that I want to leave you and Dad, it's just that I want the feeling of being independent. Try to understand that it isn't because I don't love you ..."

Miriam Austen nodded to the nodding image of her own face in the mirror. Of course she understood. Who could possibly understand more clearly? Lory was almost twenty-seven, the same age that she had been when she had married Grant. She had been lucky, Grant coming along when he had, but Lory was wise enough to know that you couldn't count on that kind of luck, not at twenty-seven. Independence ... yes, that was what her own father had tried to deny her, holding her money so that she could never break away from him ... then almost destroying her marriage by refusing to let her give her money to Grant that time when he had needed it so badly ... and now Grant was trying to do the same thing to Lory, bind her with the bondage of begging dependency, ruining her life ...

She had to stop him!

But how?

She dared not argue with him, not after last night. The first thin strand of their new happiness was too fragile to be risked. But the alternative was equally bad. If Lory didn't get her own money, she wouldn't leave them alone ...

There had to be some way!

Crossing the hall, she cracked the door of their bedroom and looked in. Grant was still asleep and she tiptoed down the stairs, remembering that he had brought home the papers that had to be signed today. If she saw them, she might be able to understand what he was planning to do and perhaps, even now, find a way to prevent it.

The briefcase lay on the library sofa where he had dropped it when she had suggested making coffee. Urged on by last night's lesson that boldness was rewarded, she opened the case and, with ears alerted to any sound from the floor above, slipped out the thick packet of legal documents. Turning the pages as noiselessly as the crackling paper would permit, she began to read. Her experience in the business management of civic enterprises had given her a good layman's knowledge of legal phraseology and she read with a confidence of understanding that hurried her on from form to form.

She reached the last one—AGREEMENT OF SALE—stunned to find that she had been totally wrong. The agreement covered all the stock, every share of it. The amount that Lory was to receive was specified to the last penny—two hundred seven thousand, two hundred eleven dollars and twenty-two cents, doubly confirmed by the parenthetical reiteration ($207,211.22).

Vertigo spun the whirl of her thoughts into a black storm and the cloud shadow that fell on her heart was more chilling than fear, an ice-edged accusation of disloyalty to her husband. Her mad suspicion had caused a shocking loss of faith and she cowered before the terrifying realization that she had proved herself unworthy of her husband's love.

Fighting against the delaying palsy of terror, she managed to get the legal forms back into the briefcase but, before she could close it, she heard Lory's footsteps on the staircase. The snap of the latch was a crash in the silence of the room. There was the impulse to hide but she saw that it was too late. Lory had already made the turn at the bottom of the staircase and had seen her.

Miriam Austen stepped to the doorway to face her daughter, her thoughts so dominated by self-recrimination that she half expected Lory to lash out with an accusation that she was guilty, not only of disloyalty to her husband but also of having wanted to drive her own daughter from this house.

Amazingly, Lory seemed to sense nothing wrong, her voice gaily unsuspecting. "What are you doing up so early, Mother?"

"Well, you're up too," she answered lamely.

"But I've work to do and I was in bed early. You weren't. What did you find out from Dad last night?"

Miriam Austen felt herself making a too-vigorous attempt at nonchalance, speaking words that were mismatched with the uneasy tone that her lips gave them. "Oh, everything's all right. Your father has it all worked out with the lawyers. I was sure that he would."

Lory nodded. "I could hardly imagine Mr. McCall welching."

"Mr. McCall?" she heard herself repeat, a moment needed before she could relax the rigidity of her mind to follow the change of subject. "Oh, he's the man from the Gammer Corporation isn't he—the man you met in Philadelphia?"

"Yes, in Philadelphia," Lory said casually, opening the wide door at the back of the center hall, letting in the brightness of the day. "I won't bother with breakfast. If Anna has time, she can bring some coffee out to the studio after you and Dad have finished."

"Now, Lory—" she began, the protest stifled by her need to be alone with her guilt, then quickly reinstated by the counterpull of her persistent fear of loneliness. "Lory, you really shouldn't go without breakfast, not when you're working as hard as you are."

"All right. Call me when Dad gets down."

Before she could be stopped, Lory had gone out through the door and started down the flagstone walk to the studio. Miriam Austen stared after her, sick with the realization that her impulsive response had destroyed a chance to be alone with Grant at breakfast.

"Lory!" she called, the word launched before she realized that it was too late to change anything now.

Lory turned in silent inquiry, squinting against the sun.

Forced to say something, Miriam Austen voiced the only thought that could be summoned. "You know, don't you, that you'll have to go downtown with your father sometime today? There are papers you'll have to sign."

"Yes, I know," Lory tossed back, walking on again.

But there had been a momentary hesitation before she answered and that moment of silence seemed to Miriam Austen as the masking of something unsaid, an unspoken accusation that brought the rise of another fear, the most terrifying of all fears, not new but seldom before exposed to daylight, the nightmare horror that she was losing her sanity.

●●●●● 2

Grant Austen was awake when he heard Lory go down the stairs, aware that Miriam's bed was empty, and since he had not looked at the clock he imagined that it was later than it was. His first impulse was to rise quickly but, recognizing it as only another of the habits to which he was no longer bound, he lay back and attempted to induce a pleasant awareness of his good fortune. Never again, as long as he lived, would he have to get out of bed until he was good and ready to get out of bed ... nor do anything else that he didn't want to do!

The attempted generation of a sense of luxurious well-being was recognizably unsuccessful and he was forced to fall back upon a reiteration of what he had been telling himself all week ... it was going to take a little time to adjust himself to this new life.

Everything would have been different, he reasoned, if it all hadn't happened so quickly. The sale of the company for two million dollars had been such an astounding accomplishment, so quickly realized, that there had been no chance for planning or preparation. He had never, until it was too late, actually faced the prospect of a life divorced from the Suffolk Moulding Company.

Last Thursday, the morning after, driving to the office, he had even gone so far as to consider reneging on the deal, a possibility immediately discarded when he had thought of the necessity of facing Cash McCall, so obviously a gentleman, with the admission that he, Grant Austen, was any less a man of honor. The only thing that had sustained him had been the knowledge that Lory was pleased, and that even Miriam had been enthusiastic after she had finally realized what a good deal he had made. That support, however, had been challenged as he turned in at the factory gate, suddenly aware that he faced the necessity of offering some kind of explanation to his employees. The complete truth was plainly prohibited. It would never do to tell them that he had simply gotten out from under by snatching at a chance to grab a lot of money for himself. The ideal explanation, as he then realized, would have been an assurance that the Suffolk Moulding Company would now, under its new ownership, become an even better place to work than it had ever been before. That, too, was prohibited. In the first place, it couldn't be true. In the second place—and this realization had come to him as something of a shock—he had no idea whatsoever of Cash McCall's plans for the company.

Crossing the areaway, walking toward the back door of the Administration Building, he had decided that the best solution was to say nothing at all. There was still a week before McCall took over. In the meantime, there was no need to say anything. By the end of the week he would know what McCall planned to do. Then he could make his announcement.

Unfortunately, his decision to conceal what he had done had been almost immediately nullified by the crowd of men jammed into the little lobby outside his office, Gil Clark's the only familiar face. There he had met Winston Conway, partner in the big Philadelphia law firm of Jamison, Conway & Slythe; and Vincent Thompson of Thompson & Slater, certified public accountants. Conway and Thompson had, in turn, introduced their assistants, nine men in all, a group so large that neither their presence nor purpose could be kept secret.

The gossip had spread to the far ends of the plant with amazing speed, and then from the plant to the town. Within an hour, the *Suffolk Tribune* had called for the story. Coached by Conway, he had replied that there was nothing to be said at the moment but that a statement would be issued in due course. Conway had reminded him, after he hung up, that such a statement, when it was finally made, was not to include Cash McCall's name but only that of the Gammer Corporation, the company to which the control of Suffolk Moulding was to be transferred. That, like so many of the things

198

that came up afterwards, had made Grant Austen uncomfortably aware that the shock of Cash McCall's unexpected snapping up of his first offer had so stunned him that he had not clearly heard everything that had been said.

He had, for example, been only vaguely aware of some mention of lawyers and accountants, never anticipating any such searching investigation as Conway and Thompson proposed to direct. He had protested at first, only to be embarrassed by the lawyer's explanation that it was all for his own benefit. The Gammer Corporation, Conway had explained, was buying the Suffolk stock at a price based upon the year-end balance sheet, and that the payment would be increased to reflect any gain in assets since the first of the year. There had been no choice except to direct that the accounting section be opened to Thompson and his men, that the display room be cleared as a working area for the lawyers, and that two adjoining offices be emptied to provide private headquarters for Winston Conway and Gil Clark.

That first hour of frenzied activity had fully occupied Grant Austen's mind but by eleven o'clock he was alone in his office. The pile of mail on his desk had lost all point and purpose. No one came in to see him. There were no telephone calls. For the first time in twenty years, he sat at his desk for a completely undisturbed hour. It was, up to that point, the longest hour in his life.

When the noon whistle sounded, he had called Miss Berk and asked her to invite Winston Conway, Vincent Thompson and Gil Clark to lunch with him at the Suffolk Country Club. She came back with the message that they had already sent out for sandwiches and coffee, her tone of voice giving him the impression—perhaps without justification—that she now regarded him as an interfering old man who had been guilty of an unwarranted intrusion upon the lives of actively important men. She did not, as had been unvarying custom, ask him if there was anything he wanted before she went out to lunch.

Since lunching at the Country Club was in his mind, he had been tempted to follow through with the plan but, on second thought, had decided against it. It was one thing to take guests to the Country Club but something quite different to lunch there alone on a weekday. The only men who ever did that were old has-beens like Colonel Emil Graatz, Fred Crosby whose sons had eased him out of the feed business, and Arch Livermore who had been retired by the Pennsylvania Railroad.

The alternative had been to follow his usual practice of lunching at the big round table at the Hotel Conomissing that was always reserved—except on Tuesdays when the Rotary Club met—for an informal gathering of the town's upper-level male citizens. That, on second thought, had seemed more than ever the thing to do, promising a pleasant reassurance that selling Suffolk Moulding would not too greatly affect the normality of his life.

He had failed, however, to anticipate that the news would be there ahead of him and, unnaturally, all conversation stopped as he approached the table, evidencing that he had been the subject of discussion. The embarrassing silence was finally broken by Don Mitchum blurting out, "Grant, anybody can say what they want to, but I think you're just being smart as hell. I always have said that a man's a plain damn fool not to retire while he's still on his feet."

He had started to protest that he wasn't *retiring*, but before he could frame a reply he became aware that if he argued that he wasn't retiring they would all want to know what he *was* going to do. He couldn't tell them. There hadn't been time enough yet to think about that part of it.

The round-table conversation had then turned to *Business Week's* current prediction that the downturn in consumer buying would be short-lived and mild. Strangely, no one asked him for his opinion and, even more strangely, when he finally offered it, he could not escape the impression that somehow, overnight, everyone had gotten together and agreed that his judgment was no longer worthy of any special respect. There would have been an entirely different attitude around the table, he knew, if he had only been able to explain that he sold out for two million dollars—a good half million more than the company was worth—but that was something he was barred from doing. Even if he had been free to speak, it was doubtful whether they would have believed him. It was one of those things that sounded too good to be true.

His office, when he returned to it, had been the same purgatory of undisturbed silence. Once during the afternoon he invented an excuse to wander out through the office building but the foray proved unrewarding. He was given only the briefest of glances as he passed through the accounting department, and the lawyers clustered around the big table in the display room had not even interrupted their methodical paper turning long enough to look up. The doors of the offices that had been assigned to Winston Conway and Gil Clark were both closed.

Encountering his own employees as he walked through the office building he had sensed a startling difference in their attitude toward him. Several failed to speak. It was almost as if there had been a general acceptance of the fact that they were no longer obligated to deference and, now released, were relishing their delinquency.

When he returned to his office, Miss Berk was gone. There was a note on his desk saying that she was doing some work for Mr. Clark. It did not conclude with an invitation to call her if there was anything he needed.

A man of a different cast of mind might then have begun to question the soundness of what he had done. Grant Austen did not. The evident defection of his supposedly loyal employees became the first real proof that he had done the right thing when he had sold the company. In much the same clear-eyed way, he saw the factory for what it really was. Through the window behind his desk he examined it with a new sense of detachment, judging it now with his awakened mind, seeing all that tolerant familiarity had made him overlook before—the rust-blotched corrugated iron on the end of the tool shop, the mossy shingles on the roof of the old mill building, a broken window through which a pigeon flew as he watched, a crumbling hole in the paving of the areaway, an over-age lift truck grinding its gears as it backed away from the loading platform with a barrel of flash scrap. Oddly, everything seemed to have shrunk in scale. The whole plant, like the object of an old and long-discarded love affair, aroused only the feeling of wonder that he could ever have found it so entrancing.

In the middle of the afternoon, telling Miss Berk to send the unanswered mail on his desk to Gil Clark, he had walked out, unable to longer endure the pointlessness of his presence at the office. Halfway across town, suddenly realizing that so early an arrival at home would necessitate an explanation to Miriam, he drove out through the country, aimlessly following back roads, killing time until five o'clock.

Miriam had greeted him at the door, handing him the evening newspaper. A hasty search finally revealed a small item—on the front page, it was true, but with only a single-column headline and one short paragraph under it—and there was nothing in it beyond the report that rumors were being circulated that control of the Suffolk Moulding Company had been purchased by Philadelphia financial interests. There was no mention of his name, only the statement that company officials declined to confirm or deny the report. The whole item reflected the newspaper's ridiculous editorial policy—giving a whole column to a chicken-corn-soup dinner put on by the Farm Women's League, but less than a tenth that much space to something that was a thousand times more important to the community.

He had taken the paper into his library but the atmosphere was unpleasantly reminiscent of his office and he came out quickly, suggesting that they have dinner at the Country Club. He had half expected Miriam to protest that it was too late now to stop things in the kitchen. Instead, she seemed extraordinarily pleased. Lory's refusal to accompany them had been a disappointment, almost prompting him to change his mind but, afterwards, he had decided that it had all worked out for the best. If Lory had been along she would have wanted to talk about the company. Miriam put no such demand upon him. She had, once or twice, edged toward asking about his future plans, but she had not pressed him for a commitment and, later, when he had said that maybe a nice long trip would be something worth thinking about, she reached across the table to pat his hand and say, "Grant, I'm so happy. Now we're going to really begin to *live!*" It was the most solid support that anyone had given him and he had been surprised that it came from Miriam. All in all, it had been a quite successful evening—except for his impulsive ordering of Lobster Newburg which, as he should have known it would, kept him awake for a long time.

Despite sleeplessness, he had awakened early that next morning, getting up at once but resolving not to go to the office until late, visualizing a pleasant lingering over breakfast. But Lory had seemed strangely jumpy, anxious to get out to her studio, and when Miriam had left the table for the third time to answer another telephone call about some fool hospital meeting, he had given up and gone to the office.

An hour later he had been on his way back home. No sooner had he arrived at the office than Gil Clark had come in—Miss Berk not even bothering to announce him—bringing back all of the mail he'd been sent yesterday. He'd told Gil that he'd be on his own in a few days, anyway, and might as well start getting used to it but Gil, of course, had protested that he had no authority to take over. All that had meant was that he was beginning to get buck fever, finding out that there was a lot more to running a company like Suffolk Moulding than anyone ever realized!

Grant Austen had not, until he was outside the plant gate that morning, actually made a conscious decision to return home. But he was confronted with the fact that there was nowhere else he wanted to go—he had no taste for lunching again at the Hotel Conomissing —and, driving out Mill Street toward Orchard Hill, the prospect of a day at home had actually seemed rather appealing.

Parking his car in the drive, he had gone in the back door to be confronted with what seemed full evidence of some catastrophic explosion—a table upside down, chairs scattered about, a throw rug tossed over the balustrade, a lamp shade on the newel post, bric-à-brac on the bottom steps—and then Miriam stepping suddenly through the living-room arch, wearing some rag of a dress, a scarf binding her hair, and red rubber gloves on her hands.

"Oh, I'm sorry," she had apologized. "I had no idea you were coming back," then turning to call, "Anna, let that go for a minute and we'll straighten up here in the hall. Be as quiet as you can now—and we'd better forget about the waxing."

He had protested and gone into the library, Miriam following to explain, "It doesn't matter, dear. It's just the Friday cleaning. We can let it go until tomorrow."

He had wanted to tell her that tomorrow would be no different, that he would be home every day from now on, and that he didn't expect to be treated as if he were a special guest in his own home. But what came out was, "There's no reason why *you* have to scrub floors, Miriam. Goodness knows, we can afford—"

"But, Grant, you simply can't get anyone who'll—" And then she had looked at him, annoyingly tolerant. "I know, dear. We'll work something out."

After she had closed the door, the distant bee buzz of the vacuum cleaner had stopped. Then, after another moment, there was no longer even the muffled clatter of furniture being moved. He had sat for a long time, consciously trying to think, but the dead quiet had dulled his brain.

Then Miriam had come back, her dress changed, the scarf and red rubber gloves gone, opening the door after an anxious tapping, peeping in to ask, ridiculously, if he would be there for lunch.

How could she imagine that he *wouldn't* be there for lunch? And then, no less annoyingly, she asked if there was something wrong at the office. His reply had been a too-sharp denial, but his regret had vanished a few minutes later when the telephone had rung and, picking up the receiver, he had found that Miriam, already on the line, was saying to someone, "—but I've got Grant home now, you know, so that changes everything. From now on I won't be able to—" Flash anger had made him want to shout back that he was *not* a doddering old man who needed a senile invalid's perpetual care, but consciousness of eavesdropping had made him let the receiver slip out of his hands, anger slowly dissolving into the admission that it wasn't really Miriam's fault. She, too, was having a little trouble getting oriented. But what she had to be made to understand was that he didn't want his life *changed*—except in the way that he *wanted* it changed.

The afterthought was a reminder and he sat bolt upright now, pushing back the satin quilt, amazed that he could have been awake as long as he had without remembering what, before he had fallen off to sleep, he had been so certain would be his first thought this morning. The lapse was alarming and he wondered for a moment if this was another case of a midnight idea that wouldn't stand the cold light of day. No, it was as sound now as it had been last night . . . he knew what he wanted to do . . . and he had Winston Conway to thank for it . . . for that and a lot of other things, too.

A yawn dismissed the embarrassed realization that his initial impression of Winston Conway had been totally wrong. Seeing him that first day, meeting him there in the office lobby, Conway's too-handsome face and prematurely white hair had made him seem one of those politically destined attorneys who rely more on a sonorous voice and a photogenic profile than a good brain and a sound knowledge of the law. But there had been more than that involved in his original dislike. On Monday, Conway had asked him to stop by the office. The lawyer, it turned out, had been digging into the way stock had been transferred to Lory, and the number of irregularities that he had uncovered had been proof enough that he was no one's fool.

Fear is often the progenitor of respect and Grant Austen had been badly frightened, all the more so after Conway had started questioning the way that Alvin T. Manson's estate had been probated. But in the strange alchemy of the human mind, the relieving of fear can transmute grudging respect into openhearted gratitude, and Winston Conway had relieved all of Grant Austen's fears. "Don't worry about it, Mr. Austen. It's obvious that your legal guidance has been somewhat less than adequate, but I'm reasonably certain that there's nothing you've done that would be held to evidence a fraudulent intent." And then he had said that Mr. McCall would certainly want him to be of any possible assistance—without, of course, interfering in any way with Mr. Austen's relationships with his own legal counsel—and that he would be only too happy to help in any way he could, to advise on procedures that would reduce, to the lowest possible point, the tax for which Grant Austen would become liable as a result of the company's sale.

Gratefully, he had accepted Winston Conway's offer, telling him that there was nothing to worry about as far as his own attorney was concerned. Old Frank Brookauser did all right handling the City Council when a complaint about odor from the plant had to be quashed, but it was plain enough now that Frank didn't know much about income tax and, as Conway had said, that was the backbone of corporation practice these days. Frank would never in a million years have figured things out the way Winston Conway had. Of course, even with Conway's plan, his tax was going to be more than he'd originally figured . . . gift tax on that last block of stock he'd transferred to Lory and a corrected declaration on his own personal income for last year ... but he'd still have more than his million clear. That was all that really mattered ... that and knowing where he was really going from here on out.

After last night's final session, settling twenty thousand as the extra payment ... and that was something he had Winston Conway to thank for, too ... squelching Gil Clark's petty squabbling by telling him that Cash McCall wasn't the kind of man who would worry about a little thing like an inventory write-down on some old molding material ... Conway had invited him up to his room for a drink, just the two of them. It was then that the lawyer had given him the idea ... no, not directly, but if Conway hadn't invited him they would never have started talking about the old OPA days in Washington and, if that hadn't happened, he might never have realized that Washington was what he wanted ... no, not politics, just a chance to dig in somewhere and really do a job.

Now, lying back in bed, Grant Austen put his plan to a final test. Methodically, he rechecked his reasoning, touching fingertips as he counted the points of argument, *First,* he knew Washington ... all of the time he'd spent there during the war ... and that had been the happiest period of his life. *Second,* there could be no doubt about his ability to make a contribution ... he was a successful businessman who had proved his ability, not one of those college professors who were full of theory and not much else. *Third,* he came from Small Business and that was good politically ... too many of the men who'd gone to Washington were from Big Business. *Fourth,* he was not only a businessman but an electrical engineer ... and that tied in with electronics, and electronics was almost the biggest thing in the whole defense program. *Fifth,* he could afford it ... plenty of money to live on, no matter how small the government salary might be. *Sixth,* he had an inside track to find the kind of spot where he really could do the most good ... there wasn't a man in Washington who knew the ropes better than Harlan Bostwick, Executive Secretary of the American Association of Plastic Molders ... and Harlan was one of his best friends, always had been.

Yawning, stretching, feeling truly relaxed for the first time in weeks, he turned his head and saw the coffee cups standing on the table between the two beds. He smiled reminiscently, pleasantly puzzled, wondering if Miriam had guessed what he had in mind. He hadn't told her, of course ... be silly to get her all excited until it was definite ... but she must have guessed something. If she hadn't, she wouldn't have been so keyed up.

For a moment, he thought back over his married life. The vague and never-defined feeling of inadequacy that had sometimes troubled him was now so faded that it was almost unrecognizable. Miriam was a good girl ... maybe just a little self-centered sometimes ... but perhaps that had been partly his own fault, his mind so full of Suffolk Moulding all the time ... and Miriam never had been interested in the plastics business. But it would be different now ... Washington would be right down Miriam's alley ... she'd really get a kick out of Washington!

The only cloud in his mind was the necessity of waiting. Now that he knew what he wanted, he was anxious to get started. Unfortunately, Harlan Bostwick wasn't in Washington. The convention was starting tomorrow and Harlan was already down at the Moon Beach Club getting things set up. He wouldn't be back in Washington until Monday. That meant a loss of five days ... but maybe five days' rest before he got back in the saddle again wouldn't do him any harm.

Grant Austen closed his eyes, attempting to induce the return of sleep, but with no success. He was wide awake, more completely awake than he had been at any time in the last ten years.

After a moment, he got out of bed, found his red brocade robe, tiptoed down the stairs, retrieving his briefcase from the sofa in the library. There were sounds from the kitchen but he got back upstairs without Miriam hearing him. Sitting on the edge of the bed, he took out the legal documents that had to be signed today and started to check through them. The first page exhausted his patience. What was the point? Everything was all right ... if he couldn't trust Winston Conway and Cash McCall who could he trust? They were a couple of really high-class men ... yes sir, they sure were.

● ● ● ● ● 3

Gil Clark's awakening required more than the recapturing of consciousness. There was the physical demand of opening heavy eyelids, the forced moving of cramped muscles, the deeper breathing that brush-burned the crown of his lungs. He felt flattened to the bed as, in his reminiscent nightmare, he had again been flattened to the deck of the carrier on that day at anchor in Anowok Bay when a B-26 from the Army field, both engines smoking, had all but crash landed on the ship.

Half awake, the plane roar still in his ears, he nodded to the foggy awareness that he was in the Conomissing Hotel in Suffolk and unfolded a leaden arm toward the telephone. But the hammer pounding still thudded his brain, beating in the slow realization that it was a knocking at the door that had awakened him, not the ringing of the telephone.

He remembered that his robe was in the bathroom and stumbled toward it, stealing the moment that it took to splash his face with cold water, not feeling the cold, hardly the wetness, finger combing his hair as he went to the door, opening it.

A man lounged against the corridor wall, shadowed, straightening to full height with leonine grace, his face vaguely familiar but not recognized until he moved into the light. It was Cash McCall.

Gil Clark was thunderclapped into full awakening. He had been trying to reach McCall for four days and four nights, bribing the telephone operator to keep calling the unlisted number of the suite on the top floor of the Hotel Ivanhoe in Philadelphia. He had not talked to him since that call in Philadelphia, last Wednesday afternoon. There had been neither guidance nor authority for all the decisions he had been forced to make after Grant Austen had walked out on Friday afternoon, washing his hands of all responsibility. Worst of all, the hour-by-hour operating problems that had piled in upon him had so completely absorbed his time that there had been no opportunity to prepare the presentation that Cash McCall had asked him to make on the desirability of Suffolk Moulding property as a research center for the Cavalier Chemical Corporation. He had spent most of last night, working until four this morning, trying to get something down on paper but, at best, he had made no more than a fair start. Too much of his mind had been absorbed with the major problem he would face this morning. This was the last day of grace with Andscott Instrument. Before nightfall, Andscott had to be told whether or not Suffolk was going ahead with the new press.

He tried now to find relief in knowing that the burden of the decision could be shifted to Cash McCall, but he could not blank his mind to the bad personal impression that he himself must be making, still seeing the image of his face in the bathroom mirror, haggard and red-eyed, unshaven, the frayed collar of his old flannel bathrobe. A quick eye-sweep took in the room, seeing it as Cash McCall must be seeing it—the tangled ragheap of the bed, the scatter of clothing, a pair of soggy socks coiled blackly on the threadbare carpet.

Cash McCall came into the room. "This place is really a dump, isn't it?"

"Well, it's not the Ivanhoe," Gil said, attempting lightness to cover his embarrassed retrieving of the pair of shorts that, aimlessly tossed last night, were now hanging from the spear-headed bedpost. "There's not much choice—only hotel in town."

"Funny thing," McCall said, sniffing. "Every old hotel always has this same odor. You even catch a whiff of it now and then around the back halls of the Ivanhoe. Strange how they all manage to stew up the same smell."

Gil turned nervously to the window. "Guess I ought to get some air in here—so fagged when I turned in last night that I forgot to open—"

The sash stuck and then, suddenly releasing, sent him sprawling awkwardly across the window sill as the shade snapped to the top with a rifle shot report.

"Take it easy, Gil," Cash McCall laughed.

The suggestion had an effect opposite to its obvious intention, making him even more acutely aware of how badly he was concealing his discomfiture, how horrifyingly inadequate he must seem to Cash McCall.

"You look as if you'd had a bad night, Gil."

"Up a little late, that's all."

"Didn't get too much sleep myself." Cash McCall's eyes lifted to the top of the unshaded window. "Flew in from Chicago. Nice up there this morning. Clear as a bell all the way. Kind of morning that makes a man glad to be alive."

Gil nodded, conscious of the hypocrisy of agreement, then pointlessly diverted by recalling that there had been a B-26 in his nightmare.

Cash said casually, "I gather from what Conway told me over the phone this morning that you've been having a little difficulty."

Gil felt a constriction in his throat, something to be swallowed, "I didn't know that Mr. Conway knew how to get in touch with you. I've been trying all week, calling the Ivanhoe, but—"

A fleeting expression on Cash McCall's face made Gil wish that he had stopped to think before he had spoken, realizing now that he had lost stature by making himself sound petulantly complaining ... a man who was worth twenty-five thousand a year didn't bellycrawl.

"It was *I* who called *him*," McCall explained easily, "—when I touched down in Pittsburgh this morning for a cup of coffee. The old boy was grumpy as the devil about my waking him up at five-thirty. Said you'd had him up until after midnight."

"Yes, I—well, he had Austen in his room and I had to wait until after he left. I was working on the presentation for Cavalier and there were a couple of things that I wanted to clear."

208

"Cavalier?" McCall asked, vaguely, then nodding as if he had suddenly recalled an almost lost memory. "Forget that Cavalier idea, Gil. We can do better than that. What's this trouble you've been having with Austen?"

Cash McCall's offhand dismissal of the possibility of a Cavalier-Suffolk merger was a tangling upset of every thought in Gil Clark's mind. "Then you—you've got something else in mind—I mean if the Cavalier thing is out?"

A screeching protest came from the wicker chair as Cash McCall sat down. "No, nothing in mind. But there's plenty of time for that. What about this trouble with Austen? I gather that it had something to do with the transfer of stock to his daughter."

Gil cleared a place to sit on the edge of the bed, an excuse to flip the faded green cover over the snarl of gray sheets. "Yes—particularly the shares that were in the Manson estate."

"Manson was her grandfather?" McCall checked.

"That's right," Gil said, composure partially regained. "Alvin T. Manson—Mrs. Austen's father."

"As I got the story from Conway, there was a question about the manner in which Manson's estate was probated."

"Yes—well, as Mr. Conway probably told you, Austen had given a block of stock to his father-in-law, supposedly with an agreement that it was to come back to Lory after Manson's death. But there was nothing in writing and Manson died without a will. It did look a little shaky—the direct transfer of the stock to Lory—but Mr. Conway dug into it and he says everything is in the clear."

"The probate court accepted Austen's story of the verbal agreement?"

"Apparently—but as Mr. Conway says, it wouldn't have made too much difference, one way or the other. Mrs. Austen was her father's only heir so whether the stock went to her or her daughter was six of one and half a dozen of the other."

"Do you think Austen may have been a little fast on his feet?"

His recognized prejudice against Grant Austen made Gil hesitate. "I don't know. Possibly. But as far as Lory's legal ownership of the stock is concerned—well, there doesn't seem to be any question there."

"That isn't all the stock she owns?"

"Oh no. He's been giving her stock for a long time."

"How long?"

"Oh, it goes back quite a few years. He started with a block of five hundred shares when she was eighteen. Fortunately, there's a record of that one so—"

"Eighteen?" McCall interrupted. "How old is she now?"

"Now?" Gil puzzled, trying to determine the pertinency of the question. "Well, let's see—twenty-six or twenty-seven."

The odd flash of interest had already faded from Cash McCall's face. "Go ahead, Gil—just hit the high spots."

He felt himself fumbling, his thought stream broken by the interruption. "Yes, well—no, I don't suppose the detail is too important. The main point is that after that first five hundred shares he kept giving her more stock, several different blocks."

"Without compensating the corporation?"

"He claims that he paid for it by leaving her dividends in the company."

"Can't that be substantiated?"

"Yes and no. The difficulty is that a lot of the corporate records are in pretty bad shape. There are some credits to the capital account but Thompson has been having trouble trying to make them check out with recorded declarations of dividends. You see, there are no minutes for some of the directors' meetings. Austen admits that sometimes there actually *weren't* any meetings."

McCall shrugged. "A directors' meeting in a company like that is only a formality, anyway."

"Yes, but—"

"Wasn't it, for all practical purposes, just a sole proprietorship? Or at most, a family partnership?"

Gil held his answer to a silent nod, relieved, feeling now that he had finally achieved self-control, catching himself before he made the stupid error of trying to give Cash McCall a freshman business-law lecture on the difference between a sole proprietorship and an incorporated enterprise.

The wicker chair creaked. "Was Austen really off base?"

"Off base?"

"Did he do anything wrong, either in the transfer of this stock to his daughter or this business of settling his father-in-law's estate?"

"Well, I—"

"*Morally* wrong," McCall emphasized. "Oh, I know he made a few legal fumbles—didn't cross a few *t*'s and forgot to dot some *i*'s—but do you think he did anything *wrong?*"

Gil Clark hesitated, less from nervousness than from the difficulty he always found in drawing a clear line through the twilight area between right and wrong. "I guess it's one of those borderline cases," he said carefully. "But, as Conway says, the only real question from our standpoint is establishment of the legal ownership of Lory's stock. That's been cleared, so I guess there's nothing to worry about."

210

"There's been no change in the amount of stock that's in Lory's name?"

"No, I don't think so," Gil said, surprised by the question. "At least I haven't heard about anything like that. I do know that Mr. Conway has worked out some kind of plan for Austen—paying some extra gift tax on a block of stock he gave her last year, something like that."

Preoccupied, Cash McCall sat looking out of the window, finally turning back to ask, "Are you in agreement with Conway's proposal —the basis on which the final closing is set up? As I get it, we're paying him an extra twenty thousand to cover the increased valuation since the first of the year."

Gil weighed his words. "Actually, it's more than *I* felt was necessary, but Mr. Conway said that he was sure you'd want to settle on the generous side so I rode along—naturally."

"What about Austen? Is he satisfied?"

"Satisfied? Of course. I'm sure that it was more than he expected."

"And Lory?"

"Lory? Well, I took it for granted that her father was representing her interests, too, so—"

"She hasn't been in on any of your sessions?"

"No, but I'm sure you don't have to worry about the Austen family being satisfied. Why shouldn't they be? Two million is a lot of money for—"

The quick dart of Cash McCall's eyes was a warning and Gil reacted instantly, letting his voice die off, then bracing himself for the consequence of having foolishly talked out of turn again.

Surprisingly, Cash McCall smiled. "I know that I could have bought Suffolk Moulding for less, Gil. If I'd put the pressure on Austen, I might have squeezed the price down a couple hundred thousand dollars, perhaps more. I know that. And if it's any consolation, Conway agrees with you that I was a fool to pay as much as I did."

"Oh, I'm sure that Mr. Conway—well, I know he admires the way—"

Cash McCall had leaned forward, a strange smile playing around his deep blue eyes. "There's only one way that I can get a wallop out of a deal like this, Gil. And that's by knowing that I haven't dug money out of another man's hide. If I'd put Austen through the wringer and then turned around afterward and resold his company at a profit—" He spread his long-fingered hands in a gesture of rejection. "As it is, he's got no kick coming. He got his asking price. I didn't chisel him for a penny. No man can expect more than that. Understand?"

Gil nodded, feeling again what had drawn him to Cash McCall on that first day at the Hotel Ivanhoe, wishing that he dared attempt an expression of admiration, yet knowing that he'd botch it if he did, forced to content himself with an inadequate nod.

McCall lighted a cigarette. "What's worrying you, Gil?"

He felt himself snatched back to an awareness of danger. "Worrying me? Well, there is one thing—one situation."

"What's that?"

"I don't know how much Grant Austen told you when you bought the company," he said cautiously, attempting to avoid any implication of rancor at not having been brought into the negotiations nor, afterwards, told anything about them. "He may have explained the situation with Andscott, I don't know."

"He told me nothing," McCall said. "But don't blame him for that. I didn't give him a chance. He made the offer and I accepted it. What about Andscott?"

Gil Clark hesitated, attempting to resurrect the smooth-flowing words of explanation that he had rehearsed last night. "You probably remember that talk we had in your apartment, my mentioning that Andscott was after Austen to put in a new press to make a television cabinet for them?"

"Yes, I recall."

"Well, what I didn't know then—this is what I've been trying to get in touch with you about all week—is that Andscott had given Austen an April first deadline."

Cash McCall's poise was unbroken, but there did seem to be a sharpening of interest.

"That's today," Gil pressed on. "We have to let them know before tonight whether we're going ahead or not. If we don't, it means losing all of their business. That's a good half of the plant's volume."

"Don't blame Austen for not telling me," McCall said. "I asked no questions so I got no answers."

"I understand that but—well, it *is* a rather tough situation."

"What's your idea, Gil?"

"Well, I don't know now," he said after a momentary pause. "I've been thinking all the time about the Cavalier merger. If that were still in the wood, it would be different. But if you're going to have to go on operating the company—"

"Not having memory trouble, are you, Gil?"

"No, I—"

"I don't buy companies to operate. I buy them to sell."

He felt himself pinned down by the intense surveillance of Cash McCall's eyes, so expressive that he could almost hear the accusation

212

that he was still sheltering, deep in his heart, the hope that Cash McCall would give him a chance to take over and run the Suffolk Moulding Company. "I haven't forgotten," he said defensively, but the retort was recognizably stronger than should have been necessary if he were completely innocent.

"We'll have to go ahead until something turns up," Cash McCall acknowledged. "But we'll just hold the line—operate the company as it's been operating."

"That's the point," Gil said cautiously. "I mean, we can't run the company as it's *been* run, not without the Andscott business. That's the backbone of—"

Cash McCall ground out the stub of a half-smoked cigarette in an ash tray tottering precariously on top of the radiator. "Who handled the Andscott account—Austen himself?"

"No, not as far as calling on them. Paul Bronson did that."

"Then it was Bronson who brought back this story about Andscott's threat to pull all their business?"

"Yes—yes, I'm sure it was."

"And it was Bronson who was trying to get a job with Andscott?"

Gil took a moment to consider the implication of Cash McCall's question. "I don't think there was anything off base there. Paul was completely honest with me about trying to get that job. He talked to me about it the first day after I got back here—brought it up himself without my even mentioning it. The only reason he was looking around was because he was fed up with Austen's kind of management. I can't really blame him for that."

"Then he hasn't taken another job?"

"No—and I've had the finest kind of co-operation from him all week. Naturally, he's concerned about what's going to happen but—"

"How strong a man is he?" Cash McCall cut in. "Strong enough to take over and run the place?"

"Well, I don't know," he said slowly, stalling for time, attempting to submerge the thrusting resurgence of his own hope. "In some ways, he's a good man."

"Do you think it might be better if you stayed on the job yourself for a while—at least until we know where we're going?"

"Maybe it would," he said quickly, hoping that he had gotten the words out before they could be tainted with excitement.

"It would mean you'd have to stay on here for a few weeks. Wouldn't your wife object to that?"

"No, she—" He knew now that he was betraying his eagerness. "Well, she's down in Florida now—spending a little time with her folks—but it wouldn't make any difference, anyway."

There was a screech of relief from the wicker chair as Cash Mc-
Call stood up. "All right, we'll leave it that way. Where's Conway's
room?"

"Twenty-seven. It's the last one on—"

"Might as well get the papers and wind this thing up."

"Are you thinking of making the settlement right now?" Gil asked
anxiously.

Cash McCall, starting for the door, broke his stride and turned
back. "Of course. Why not?"

"Well, we didn't know when you were coming—when to expect
you—so Mr. Conway told Austen not to bother to come down until
after lunch. I suppose we could call and have him come—"

"No need of that. I'll pick up the papers and go out to his house."
He started again for the door.

"You'll be back?"

Cash McCall pivoted with his hand on the door frame. "Back? No,
I'll have to get away as soon as I can. But I'll be in touch with you
in a few days."

"But what about Andscott?"

"You mean whether or not we put in that press?"

"Well, if we don't—"

"—we lose their business," Cash McCall acknowledged. "All right,
let's lose it. There's nothing else to do, Gil. If we go any farther in
turning the plant into what Andscott wants it to be, it will be tailor-
made for them and no one else will want it. The only thing we could
do then would be to sell out to them. No fun in that."

"Then I'm to tell them—when they call—that we aren't going
ahead?"

"Look, Gil—" Cash McCall began and then, oddly, almost as if he
were considering a change of mind, stood staring past him. "No, don't
wait for them to call *you*. You call *them*—nine o'clock—as soon as
they're in the office. Tell them that we're washing out their business
right now."

"But do you think—?"

"I'm not thinking anything—except that I don't like the Andscott
way of doing business."

Gil watched as Cash McCall strode off down the hall toward the
door of Conway's room. There was no temptation to stop him, to call
after him, to change anything that had been done. A wonderful sense
of rightness welled up within him. Suffolk Moulding was *his* ...
maybe for only a few weeks ... but that might be long enough. If he
could prove that Cash could make more money by letting him go

on operating ... if they could just find some new business to replace the Andscott volume ...

● ● ● ● ● 4

There was no telephone extension in Lory Austen's studio. Her father had often suggested that one be installed but refusal had always seemed a necessary reiteration of her desire for inviolate privacy. She had, however, consented to a buzzer system—privately defensible since it eliminated the necessity of anyone ever entering the studio to call her to the house—and her mother, inspired by something she had seen or heard at one of her Civil Defense meetings, had arranged an elaborate code of signals and typed them neatly on a card that Lory, dutifully, had thumbtacked to the window frame.

One long buzz was the call to a meal and, when she heard it this morning, Lory wished that there was an arranged code to signal back that she wasn't coming. Her desire to keep working was far more compelling than hunger. Going in to breakfast would mean not only the loss of the time that eating would take but also the waste of at least an extra half hour while she sat and listened to her father's pointless and rambling conversation, all the more difficult to terminate now that he had stopped going to the plant. But there would be only two more weeks of it. She would be sailing on the twelfth ... yes, less than two weeks ... only twelve days!

She was seized again by the fear that she might not be able to complete the illustrations and, suddenly needing reassurance, began a hurried recheck of progress, matching drawings and tissue sketches against the dummy of the book. The black and white key drawings for the four major illustrations were completed, the color separations made and registered to cross-marked circles, all securely rubber-cemented together under their protective flaps. Three of the chapter headings were finished and there were tissues on four of the remaining five. It was only the frontispiece that concerned her.

She found the last of the half dozen sketches that she had made and spread the tissue over a sheet of illustration board, the whiteness coming through to sharpen the contrast of the lines. It still wasn't right ... dead, lifeless, frozen ... but it was Tony's fault, really ... the mental block of those crazy instructions ... "Do what you want with the rest of it, Lory, but gimme a sizzler for the opener—the boy and the girl in a big clinch. We've got to sell those teen-agers, Lory, and that means hitting 'em where they live. You know what I want— something like the one you did for the *Knight*—only maybe a little more so, huh?"

There had been no need for him to identify the drawing he meant. It was the one that had been used to face the last chapter, the Princess of Darkness in the arms of the Knight of the Hawk, intended as only a marginal sketch but blown up by Jefferson Clark into full-page size. It was only after she had seen it enlarged and in the printed book that she had realized that her too-facile pen, using memory for a model, had tricked her into giving Cash McCall's face to the Knight and her own body to the Princess in his arms. Then, burning with the embarrassment of having nakedly paraded an inviolate privacy, she had sworn never again to do anything like it. But that was silly ... of course it was! Men and women did kiss each other ... and she was an artist ... and Tony wanted it. Anyway, she was free now of those insane hallucinations. These last few days had proved that ... she had done more work than in any week in her life ... and it was good work, the best ever. If she could only make that frontispiece come. The thing to do, probably, was to get a couple of models ... stop trying to pull everything out of her own mind ...

The buzzer sounded again, insistently, and she ran for the staircase, her body buoyant and weightless as she flew down the steps and out into the cool blaze of the April sun, down the flagged path between the bordering tulip beds, past the harshly artificial blueness of the empty swimming pool, into the patchwork of liquid shadow and glass-hard sunlight, stopped suddenly by the scream of orange-yellow.

A taxi stood in the drive. Her eyes flashed to the house, to the opening door at the back of the center hall where her mother stood strangely waiting. In the open-shuttered split second when her mind groped for an explanation, she caught a glimpse of movement inside the hall, not the full-seen image of a man, only a blurred impression of partial form, but as if her brain were fed by some extrasensory perception over and above the power of seeing, she knew that it was Cash McCall.

The sound of his voice, responding to her mother's introduction, was anticlimactic, proving nothing, only disproving the momentary suspicion that this was another hallucination, induced by the fact that she had, unavoidably, thought of him when she had thought of the *Knight of the Hawk*.

"Oh, but you two have met each other, haven't you?" Miriam

Austen said, her voice admitting a minor embarrassment. "In Philadelphia. Of course. I'd forgotten."

"I've already offered my apologies to your mother for such an early call," Cash McCall said. "Will you accept them, too?"

His hand reached out and she took it, pleased that she could do it so calmly, without the anticipation of inner explosion at the instant of contact. He was, as she had discovered at the Hotel Ivanhoe, only another married man. The world was full of married men.

"Mr. McCall has brought out the papers that have to be signed," Miriam Austen said, not to her but to him. "So we won't have to be bothered with the trip downtown. We do appreciate it, Mr. McCall. Grant was so afraid that you weren't going to come yourself, just the attorneys, and I did so want a chance to meet you."

"And I you, Mrs. Austen," he said, adroitly gracious.

Miriam Austen murmured her thanks, poise restored as she regained the practiced mannerisms of the clubwoman. "I do hope that one of these days you'll be able to slip up and have dinner with us, Mr. McCall. After all, Philadelphia isn't so far, you know. And I was just saying to Grant last evening how nice it would be to have a chance to get to know you and Mrs. McCall. Now that you're going to be one of us—in a way—Suffolk folks, I mean."

Cash McCall smiled. "As for myself, I'd be delighted. As for a Mrs. McCall, I'm afraid she's nonexistent."

"Oh, dear!" Miriam Austen's fingers went to her lips in a gesture of apology. "Now where in the world did I ever get that idea? Lory, I'm sure you—but, of course, it doesn't matter, does it? Goodness, I wonder what can be keeping Grant so long." Her quick start up the staircase was too obviously an escape from embarrassment.

"Don't hurry him, Mrs. Austen, please," Cash McCall said. "There's no great rush about it." But his protest lacked validity and when he turned back to her, Lory saw from his face that he was boldly conscious of her shattered composure.

"You thought that I was married?" His face lighted with discovery. "That day in my apartment, wasn't it? You saw a woman. That was Mrs. Kennard, the assistant manager of the hotel."

The explanation only added fuel to the fire that seemed to be burning in her cheeks but, both fortunately and surprisingly, she found herself able to say, "I'm sure Mother would still be happy to have you come to dinner."

He bowed, mocking formality, "And you, Miss Austen—may I hope that you are equally unprejudiced?"

"I'm leaving very soon—for Europe."

"Paris?"

"No. Italy."

"To paint?" he asked, solidly serious.

She lifted her eyes affirmatively, encouraged by the change in his tone, so quickly made that she judged it to be purposeful.

"Or only a trial pilgrimage of the free spirit?" he added, his smile entirely in his eyes, like the play of heat lightning in a midnight blue sky.

"Perhaps a little of both," she said, surprised at her poise, starting through the door of the library. "Won't you come in and sit down, Mr. McCall?"

She led the way, not waiting for acceptance, and when she glanced back she saw that he had not followed her. Her breath caught, a heartbeat missed, and then he appeared in the doorway carrying a file of legal papers that he tossed unceremoniously on the edge of the desk. She sat down on the red leather sofa, but he walked past the chair that faced her, his eyes on the grouping of framed photographs that flanked the windows, pictures of convention banquets that her father had attended.

"How soon are you leaving?" he asked unexpectedly.

"On the twelfth, I hope."

"Sailing or flying?"

"Sailing—if I can finish the job I'm doing."

"Another book?"

"Yes."

"Where does the space ship go this time?"

The quick thrust of surprise tricked her lips. "How did you know about those?"

There was a purse-string puckering around his eyes. "Oh, I'm a member in good standing of the Lory Austen fan club—in fact, I believe, a charter member."

Charter ... that meant the beginning ... he was remembering ...

She hurled words into the breach to bolster the threatened crumbling of her composure. "No, I'm back to earth again. This new book is more like—" She stopped short at the brink of error, having barely escaped mention of the *Knight of the Hawk.*

"And you're sailing on the twelfth?" he asked, saving her with what seemed a sensitively understanding change of subject. "Rome?"

"No, the Ligurian Coast. Fiascherino. A friend of mine is teaching there. Eric Linksman. I studied with him—" She was stopped again, seemingly lost in a tortured maze that brought her back, terrifyingly, no matter what path she chose, to that summer in Maine.

Again he seemed to sense her difficulty, turning to the wall and looking at the photographs, obviously feigning interest, asking,

"Mr. Conway told me that your father was considering a trip around the world."

"I don't know," she answered, cautious now of anything said too quickly. "I wish he would—for Mother's sake, too—but I don't know."

He gestured toward the photographs. "He's been quite active in this sort of thing, hasn't he?"

"Yes, he'll probably miss that as much as anything. He was planning to leave for the convention tomorrow but now, of course—"

There was the sound of footsteps from the stairway, her mother's, and Lory grasped at the chance for diversion, rising quickly from the sofa and going to the door to greet her.

Her mother acknowledged her presence with a fingertip touch on her shoulder, but her eyes were totally for Cash McCall. "He'll be here in a moment," she said, and then in a lowered voice, "I do hope there isn't anything wrong?"

"Wrong?" Cash McCall asked.

"He was so pleased with the way things were settled last night. I hope you haven't found something that has to be changed." Her fear was clearly the relaying of her husband's, only secondarily her own.

"There's nothing I want changed, Mrs. Austen."

"Oh, that's wonderful," Miriam Austen said, plainly honest in her relief.

Lory, still standing in the doorway, looked up and saw her father at the head of the staircase, his hands on his hips, the stubby fingers pressed nervously into the out-bulge of his little belly, poised like an apprehensive pouter pigeon about to be forced from its perch. She called, "Good morning," trying to reassure him with the brightness of her voice.

His on-guard expression softened ever so slightly as he came down the steps and, passing her, he patted her hand as if he were attempting to gain courage by pretending that it was she, not he, who needed reassurance. She followed him into the room, staying behind and a little to one side.

But there was no deflection of Cash McCall's eyes in her direction. He came straight toward her father, hand extended. "Good morning, sir. My apology for barging in like this, but since everything was settled last night I saw no reason for delaying the formalities."

"Sure—sure, you bet—might as well get it over with, Mr. McCall," Grant Austen said, his voice strengthening as he gained comprehension. "I guess you met everyone?"

"We introduced ourselves," Lory heard Cash McCall say, aware that he was looking only at her mother, pointedly failing to include her.

Miriam Austen said, a little too gaily, "Grant, I was saying to Mr. McCall when he first came in—doesn't he look like someone we know? I can't for the life of me think who—but don't you see it, Grant?"

Lory felt the light brush of Cash McCall's glance, surely unnoticed by anyone else, but it was the same look he had given her after she had seen the framed drawing from the *Knight of the Hawk* in his apartment, the quick pledge of a conspiracy of silence, and she felt half-realized regret that her reaction had been too slow to permit acknowledgment.

"Maybe so," Grant Austen said without interest, and then to Cash McCall, "I guess you saw Mr. Conway this morning?"

"Yes, I saw him." He moved to the corner of the desk, his hand on the pile of stacked documents. "He tells me that you're satisfied with the agreement."

"Satisfied? You bet, Mr. McCall, more than satisfied. Matter of fact, I'm grateful to you—damned grateful. Your men have all been just fine—especially Mr. Conway."

"He's a good lawyer, isn't he?"

"I'll just say he's about the best I ever came across," Grant Austen said. "Yes sir, he set up a couple of things for me that are really going to help out on the tax situation. Did more for me than my own lawyer and that's a fact. There's really one fine man. Sure appreciate the way this whole thing has been handled." And then as an afterthought he added, "We all do—all of us."

"Delighted that it worked out so well," Cash McCall said, sorting papers. "I believe from what Mr. Conway told me that you brought home copies of everything here, so I take it that you've had a chance to check them through. But if you haven't—if you need more time—?"

"No, no," Grant Austen said impatiently. "Everything's all right. No worry about that. Say, is that a taxi you've got waiting out there? No need of that. I'll run you back downtown. Might as well let him go."

"I'm going to the airport from here so—"

"That's easy enough," Grant Austen said. "Just over the hill."

Miriam Austen broke in, "I was about to ask Mr. McCall if he wouldn't have a bite of breakfast with us. At least a cup of coffee?"

"In that case, I will let the cab go," Cash said, starting for the door.

Grant Austen stopped him, "Here, here, let me take care of that. I'll tell him—or Lory if you'd want to—"

She took the bill that he'd dug from his pocket and ran out in the sunlight, savoring the sound of the interrupted protest that had come from Cash McCall's lips, started and then suspended without end, waiting. She paid the driver and, the change clutched in her hand, stood for a moment watching with unseeing eyes as the taxi backed out of the drive and into the street. The sunlight was a glittering dazzle, alive with scintillating images and half-images, Cash McCall's face in all the bewildering complexity of its ever-changing liquidity of expression, not one smile but a thousand, not a single line of his face that could be frozen in tight-drawn portraiture ... *but that's all it was ... an artist's fascination with a face ...*

And she ran back up the flagged walk to the house.

Anna had been brought in from the kitchen to witness the signatures and stood now beside the desk, red-faced, nervously tucking the slack of her blouse under the tight band of her apron. Grant Austen dipped his pen and Lory saw that his hand trembled as the point touched paper. He made a false start, the ink sputtering, then resolutely retraced the beginning and boldly completed his signature, repeated again and again as Cash McCall placed one paper after another in front of him.

"And now Mrs. Austen," Cash McCall directed.

"Oh!" her mother said, the single word expressing both surprise and pleasure at inclusion. "I didn't know you'd need me." She signed her name, the *t* crossed positively and then a circled period for finality, moving aside so that Anna could inscribe her cautiously drawn witnessing signature again.

Lory saw that Cash McCall was offering her the pen now and the expression on his face was still another of the endless variations of his smile. Accidentally, their fingers touched in the passing of the pen, only the infinitely small and infinitely momentary contact of flesh with flesh, but the coins that she had received from the taxi driver, forgotten, spilled from her hand in a clattering cascade on the desk top. He retrieved a rolling quarter, but she dared not thank him, and when she looked down at what the pen had written she saw that it was not her name as she usually wrote it, but the signature that she used on her drawings. The only escape from further embarrassment was to make all the others the same.

Behind her, Cash McCall said, "There you are, sir," and, laying down the pen, she looked up to see her father accepting a check.

"And this, I believe, is yours."

She stared at the check Cash offered her, unprepared for this moment of climax, never having thought of her money as something she would receive from his hands. She looked at her father.

"Sure, go ahead and take it," he said with an off-key laugh. "It's yours. You bet, that's the way I wanted it."

She felt the need for some expression of gratitude to her father, if only as a correction of the error into which her mind had tricked her, but he was looking at Cash McCall and they were shaking hands. "Sure want to thank you, Mr. McCall, for the way everything's been handled. Been fine, sure has. Well now, how about a little breakfast?" He looked around and saw that Anna and his wife had disappeared. "Guess they'll be ready in a minute. Sit down, Mr. McCall, sit down."

Lory was trapped beside the desk, the way to the door blocked by the two men, her father straight-backed on a chair, Cash McCall on the sofa, and she shrank from the necessity of walking between them. Their conversation excluded her and, habit-driven, her mind picked up an imaginary sketching pencil and began to draw, searching out the key line of Cash's relaxed body, finding it in the long arc of his back, sweeping into the half-circling turn at his hip, then down the top profile of his thigh. It was a clean line, sharp as drypoint, but her fingertips felt the life-class knowledge of bone and muscle underneath, and there was the modeling of light and shade in the line she drew, the line alive with life, breathing, and she breathed to the breathing of the line, more slowly now, tension slackening, apprehension fading, finding in his body the reserve of strength and confidence that had been so lacking in her own.

"—convention?" Cash asked, his voice materializing out of thin air, the word climaxing a question that she had not heard him ask.

And her father replied, "Matter of fact, that's what held me up this morning—on the phone canceling our reservations. Just happened to think I'd forgotten to do it. We'd been planning on going down tonight on the special train—but that was before this came up."

"No reason why you shouldn't go," Cash said. "After all, you must have a lot of old friends that you'd like to see."

"Sure, you bet. Well, I was thinking of it, but—"

"Then why don't you? No reason why you shouldn't."

"Well, I'd thought that Gil Clark might be going and I didn't want to butt in after I'd—"

"Gil? No, I'm sure he isn't. Look—when does the convention begin?"

"Well, it doesn't actually start until Friday morning—but there's the Associates Reception tomorrow night."

"And you'd want to be there tomorrow, wouldn't you? Of course. Look, Mr. Austen—suppose you be out at the airport tomorrow morning—Moon Beach, isn't it? I'll pick you up in my plane and you'll be there in two hours. There is a field right there, as I recall."

"Oh, I wouldn't want you to—yes, there's an airport, all right— right near the hotel. I was over there last time I was down. Harv Bannon, you know, president of Cavalier Chemical? Has his own plane and some of us took a run over to see it. Beautiful."

"Would nine o'clock be too early?"

"No, be fine—if you're sure that it isn't going to be too much trouble?"

"Mrs. Austen will be with you?"

"You bet. I mean—well, she was planning on going—"

Lory was caught unaware as Cash asked, turning with the question, "How about you? Join us?"

"No, I'm sorry." She said it too quickly but, once said, it could not be withdrawn. "I'm afraid I can't spare the time."

She saw the look of resigned disappointment on her father's face and then, strangely, there was the suspicion that Cash seemed almost pleased.

Her mother was in the doorway. "Well, if you folks will come in the dining room—"

••••• 5

In the Coffee Shop of the Hotel Conomissing, a blue-lighted and blue-glassed cavern that represented the hotel's one faltering attempt at modernization, Gil Clark sat down to breakfast with Winston Conway. He had met the lawyer on the staircase and eagerly accepted his invitation to breakfast together, hoping that Conway might be willing to answer some of the questions that were in his mind.

Disappointingly, Winston Conway evidenced no inclination toward conversation. He sat silent as he studied the menu, his aristocratic face hidden except for the top bulge of his high forehead and the shock of white hair that surmounted it. Waiting, Gil experienced a fading of hope, realizing that there was no real reason to expect the lawyer to be any less cautious this morning than he had been all during this past week. Although he had been friendly enough, and reasonably willing to talk about anything else, he had pointedly deflected every effort to draw him into a discussion of Cash McCall.

Suddenly the menu dropped, slapping the table, a gesture out of character with Winston Conway's normally deliberate manner. The newly revealed expression on his face was something of a shock. If he had been an ordinary man, untrained in the long-practiced art of concealing his feelings, the break in Winston Conway's composure would not have been notable. As it was, Gil was immediately certain that he was deeply disturbed about something.

"You talked to him?" the lawyer asked, his tone betraying a struggle for self-control.

"Mr. McCall? Yes, he stopped by my room for a minute."

"You know that he's on his way out to Austen's?"

"Yes, I know. He said—well, that's what he told me he was going to do."

"Why?" Conway demanded. "Why is he stepping in and handling it himself? He's never done anything like this before—never—not once in all these years. Usually he won't even *meet* the seller. What's up? Something is."

Gil found his own position strengthened by the clear fact that Winston Conway knew no more about what was happening than he did. "He said that he was in a hurry to get it over with, that's all I know. I gathered that he was anxious to get away."

"That's all he told you?"

"Yes—at least as far as going out to Austen's is concerned. I thought, too, that it was a little unusual for him to step in and take over on his own." He made his words a conscious prod, hoping that it would incite Conway to some revelation, but the waitress came up then—skeleton-thin and thrusting out a bony hipbone as she slumped beside their table—and any reaction that might have come from Winston Conway was lost as he again raised the menu to shield his face.

"What'll it be, boys?" the waitress asked.

Gil waited deferentially for a moment and then ordered. Conway still sat silently studying the menu, finally ordering the three-minute eggs that he invariably ate for breakfast. When the menu dropped, his face was a re-set stage, all evidence of inner conflict safely behind the scenes, and there was what seemed a slight undertone of embarrassment in his voice when he spoke, as if he realized that he had exhibited an unseemly lack of self-control. "I regret having given you the impression, Mr. Clark—which apparently I did—that there was any standardized procedure. There isn't. The mere fact that he's never done anything like this before doesn't make it unusual. With Mr. McCall, only the unexpected is to be expected. He's a decidedly unpredictable man."

Gil saw a chance to smile and grasped at it. "I'm beginning to understand that."

"Nevertheless, there's always the temptation to attempt outguessing him—what my father used to call the fascination of futility. It was a phrase that he'd coined to explain why he spent hours playing a variety of solitaire that someone had taught him. The game was reputedly impossible to win—and he never did, yet he kept on playing it for years. It's a bit like that with this game of attempting to outguess Cash McCall."

"I know *I* don't have much chance," Gil said. "But, of course, I've known him for only a week."

"That, I should say, is less of a disadvantage than you might imagine it to be."

"But you've known him for a long time."

"Known him?" the lawyer repeated as if testing the words. "I've been associated with him for some eight years, if that's what you mean."

"Yes, I—"

"But the fact of acquaintance should not be interpreted as carrying the implication of knowing him—using *knowing*, in this instance, as a synonym for *understanding*. I dare say you *know* him as well right now, at the end of your first week, as you ever will. At least that's been true in my case. To repeat myself—he's a most unpredictable man. But that, of course, is the key reason for his success. His unpredictability is his greatest asset. No one is ever able to anticipate him—and the art of strategic surprise, I might note in passing, is no less valuable in business than it is in war."

"I know," Gil acknowledged, "but I can't see the point in keeping his own people in the dark. After all, how can we help him if we don't know what it is that he's trying to do?"

"Quite right, he's a difficult man to help," Conway acknowledged crisply. "I've been attempting it for some years now but, I fear, with only indifferent success."

Gil felt himself cued to say, "I doubt if he'd agree with that, sir."

For the first time since they had sat down at the table, Winston Conway smiled freely. "I sometimes suspect that my only real value to him is that I am occasionally able to advise him as to what a normal, intelligent, straight-thinking man would do when faced with some particular set of circumstances. Then Mr. McCall takes precisely the opposite tack and makes a great success of it."

An answering smile was indicated and Gil managed it.

Conway went on, "You'll see him go off on some kind of a tangent that appears to be the wildest sort of a fool's errand. You'll counsel him against it. And do you know what will happen? Before it's over you'll find the dunce cap on yourself, wondering how you could possibly have been so stupid as to have missed seeing something that should have been evident from the beginning. After he's done it, it always appears so damnably evident, so painfully obvious."

"But I still don't see why there's any point in keeping his own people in the dark," Gil persisted.

Conway looked at him, "There is always the possibility, of course, that we're no more in the dark than he is."

It took a moment for the implication to come clear. "Are you suggesting that he doesn't know himself what he's going to do with Suffolk Moulding?"

"I suggest nothing beyond the fact that it's possible," Conway said. "With Cash McCall, anything is possible."

"Do you mean that he might not—well, that he might not sell it?" Gil asked, guardedly hopeful.

"Not at all," Conway said. "He'll sell it, of course—but he may not have made up his mind as yet what tack he'll take in going about it. In such an event, his reluctance to discuss possibilities is quite understandable. I, myself, hate nothing worse than to be forced into talking about something that hasn't fully jelled in my mind."

The waitress served their orange juice in pinch-waisted glasses, holding much less than their appearance indicated. Conway, draining his with a single draught, scowled at the deception. Then, smiling again, he said, "In any event, Mr. Clark, you should not get the impression that Cash McCall's action in this instance evidences any lack of faith or confidence in those of us who work with him. It doesn't."

There was, at first, the suspicion that Conway was talking to convince himself, but when Gil recalled all the revelations that Cash McCall had so freely made on the day of their first meeting at the Hotel Ivanhoe, he found himself forced to nod in honest agreement. "No, I must say that he's been completely open and aboveboard as far as I'm concerned."

"As far as everyone is concerned," Conway said forcibly. "Unfortunately, those who know him only by rumor sometimes get quite a different impression. The secrecy with which most of his operations are necessarily conducted tends to make many people think of him in the wrong way."

"I'll have to admit that it took me a little while to get my own perspective. You see, I'd spent a couple of years with Simonds, Farrar & Peters, so—"

"Oh, then you do know something about *operators*, don't you. I had a bit of contact on one occasion with that fellow Peters. Hardly a savory character, I'd say."

"The place was full of them," Gil said, recalling a Christmas party where someone had put up a sign that labeled the client's conference room: VULTURE'S NEST. He recounted the incident and Conway laughed appreciatively, saying, "I hope you've learned by now that Mr. McCall is no vulture."

"If I hadn't, I wouldn't be here."

Conway seemed highly pleased. "I'm glad you feel that way, Gil."

"I do," he said, not missing the fact that Conway had used his first name, an unprecedented informality. "As a matter of fact, I don't know when I've met any man who has impressed me as being so completely—well, I guess you'd say *ethical*."

Winston Conway sighed. "Yes, the practice of law would be much more pleasant these days if there were a few more gentlemen of the Cash McCall stripe—and I use the word *gentleman* in its true meaning. They're becoming rare, you know, men who recognize the difference between a thing being *morally* right and *legally* right. Perhaps it's only an old man's viewpoint—the tendency of age to decry the deterioration of the younger generations—but it does seem to me that more and more we find the viewpoint that legality is synonymous with morality. You don't agree?"

Gil realized that his smile must have given Conway the wrong impression. "No, I do agree. I'm just surprised to hear you make the distinction."

"Between legality and morality? Of course there's a distinction. Why are you surprised?"

"I didn't suppose a member of the legal profession would acknowledge it."

Conway pressed a palm to his right temple, flattening the bulge of his bushy white hair. "I make no pretense of speaking for the bar —although I dare say you'd find less disagreement in the profession than you'd imagine. By the way, do you happen to know Clay Torrant—Judge Torrant?"

"Only by name."

"And I don't suppose you see the *Review*, do you? No, of course you wouldn't. There was a piece by Torrant in the last issue on this same point—the tendency to increasingly accept the letter of law and the regulations of the Federal Bureau of Internal Revenue as a code of conduct among businessmen. Can't say that I put too much stock in Torrant's scribblings—he's a gadfly sort of character with a vinegary outlook on life—but I must admit that in this instance he was thinking soundly." Conway had taken out his notebook. "I'll send a copy along to you. Perhaps you'll find it of interest—at least as a definition of the type of man that Mr. McCall most definitely is not."

"I'd like to read it," Gil said honestly, anxious to grasp at the chance to continue discussing Cash McCall. But the waitress arrived with their eggs and toast and there was a necessary delay before he could go on.

"To get back to what we were talking about before, Mr. Conway, I still—well, I'm perfectly willing to agree with everything you say about Mr. McCall—obviously, he's a high type man with a great deal of ability—but the whole situation still doesn't make sense to me. I just don't see what he can accomplish with the kind of a life he leads. Oh, I know he makes a lot of money—probably clears more on one deal than the total salary I'll earn in the rest of my life—but what satisfaction can he get out of it?"

"As contrasted with what?" the lawyer asked.

"Well, as contrasted with the sense of accomplishment that a man can have after he's built up a company, or started a new industry, or created—well, so that he has something to show for his life."

"In your case, yes," Winston Conway agreed, solemnly judicial. "You'd ask no more of life than a chance to take the Suffolk Moulding Company and build it into a hundred million dollar concern."

"I'd be willing to settle for a lot less than that," Gil said hurriedly, momentarily disconcerted by Conway's shrewd exposure of his inner desire.

"You're a *builder*," Conway went on. "It's your way of life. But what you must recognize, Mr. Clark, is that Cash McCall is a very different sort of man. He's a *trader*." There was a beat of hesitation and then he added with unexpectedly sharp emphasis, "And there's nothing wrong with that. It's a perfectly honorable occupation."

"I didn't mean to imply that there was, sir."

"Are you sure?" Conway probed. "You said a moment ago that he made more on one deal than the total salary you'd earn in the rest of your life. Aren't you—perhaps subconsciously—harboring a little resentment at that state of affairs?"

"No sir," Gil said positively. "All I meant to say was that—well, I can't see how just making money can mean anything to him. He can't use *two* suites at the Ivanhoe—or *two* B-26's—"

Conway broke into a free laugh.

"But isn't it true?" Gil demanded.

"If you're asking me to agree that he could be a great success as an industrialist, I'm quite willing to concede that he has the essential requirements—courage, imagination, a capacity for leadership, everything except one necessary qualification."

228

"What's that?"

"The desire. It isn't what he wants."

"But what *does* he want?"

Winston Conway poised a knife over his egg. "If you ever find out, Mr. Clark, I'd consider it a great personal favor if you'd let me know." He brought the knife down and there was a spill of yellow-orange yolk into his cup. "In the course of my lifetime I've learned a few truths. One of the least assailable is that the desires by which men shape the living of their lives are strangely varied and rarely explainable."

"I guess that's right," Gil said dully, giving up and starting to eat.

"Most of us," Conway went on, "encounter enough difficulty in attempting to explain our own desires, let alone those of our fellow men. In my own case, for example, I've not infrequently searched without result for the factors of character that attracted me to the law—yet that attraction was always there, even as a child. In consequence, I've never felt myself the thwarted man—and I've had, by my standards at least, a happy life."

"I can believe that."

Conway pounced, suddenly the cross-examiner. "You can? Then don't you see that my success, such as it is, measures up to absolutely nothing by your standards? I've *built* nothing. A law firm, yes, but there's nothing physical or tangible about that—a few desks, a library of books. I can point to no great assemblage of bricks and mortar and say—ah, there's my monument, the great company I built!" He spooned his egg. "Think about that, Gil. All men don't want what you want."

"Oh, I know that."

"And do try to accept the fact that Cash McCall is one of those who doesn't. You'll be happier if you do."

The waitress finally brought their coffee and, sugaring his, watching the circling spoon as he stirred, Winston Conway said, "Be that as it may, there are many times when I'm tempted to believe that true satisfaction is more likely to be found in *how* a man lives than what he actually accomplishes. Not exactly an original thought, I'll grant you—the basis of most religious philosophy, the old conflict between the end and the means—but it's still valid. There's something fine and good about a man with Cash McCall's standards. Time after time, I've seen him pass up extremely attractive deals, perfectly legal in every way, simply because he felt that—no, not even that there was a moral flaw—simply because he suspected that someone might think him unfair. Or, perhaps, *unsporting* is the better word."

"I know," Gil said in unthinking agreement. "When he was talking to me this morning, he seemed more concerned about whether Austen was satisfied than he was about—"

He saw the lawyer's face go suddenly cold, and hurriedly explained, "That isn't a contradiction, sir. I said I hadn't talked to him about Austen and I hadn't—only that one point, whether or not he was satisfied with the settlement. There was nothing about any reason why Mr. McCall wanted to go out there himself this morning, except that he was in a hurry to get it over with."

Winston Conway's voice was frosty. "There's no need to explain yourself to me, Mr. Clark. You're under no obligation on that score."

"But there's no reason either why I shouldn't tell you anything I can. You've been a lot of help to me this past week. I've learned a great deal and I'm extremely grateful to you."

"I've enjoyed it, too," Conway said, his tone still prompting Gil to make an attempt to restore the warmth that had been there earlier.

"There's only one point, Mr. Conway—well, I don't know whether this has any bearing or not, but do you suppose his having known Lory before might figure in this, one way or another?"

"Austen's daughter?" Conway asked. "Known her? What do you mean?"

Gil hesitated before answering, feeling the necessity of caution, recognizing how easy it would be to fall into the trap of taking what was only the vaguest of suspicions and giving it the substance of fact. There was, too, the further block of not knowing how much he could reveal without the violation of a confidence. It seemed safe to say, "When I was up in Mr. McCall's apartment last week there was one of Lory Austen's drawings on the wall—she's an artist, you know, an illustrator? It was the frontispiece for one of her books."

Conway's brow was furrowed by the effort of recollection. "Just inside the living room, to your left as you enter?"

Gil nodded. "I happen to know that drawing was made at least four years ago. I know that from the publication date of the book."

"But might not Mr. McCall have obtained the drawing at some later date?" the lawyer asked with a courtroom intonation.

"That isn't my point, sir. The drawing is a *portrait* of Cash Mc-Call."

"Oh!" The lawyer cleared his throat, absent-mindedly crumbled a bit of toast. "Yes, that does prove that she must have known him at least four years ago, doesn't it. What else do you know?"

"Nothing, except that—" He was stopped by the difficulty of expressing the feeling that he'd had this morning when Cash McCall had asked him about Lory Austen's age. A mere reiteration of what had actually been said seemed to argue that McCall was not well acquainted with Lory, yet there had been something intangible about the incident that gave it a countersignificance, a feeling supported by the memory of Cash McCall's odd reaction to the mention of Lory's name that first day he had met him. Confused, he felt it best to say no more than, "It just struck me that there might be something back of it. I only mentioned it because I thought it might have some significance to you."

Conway pursed his lips and tapped them with his forefinger, a gesture that Gil had come to recognize as an accompaniment of his deepest thought. "Possibly, possibly," he said, preoccupied. "I do know that his interest in Suffolk Moulding dates back at least several years."

"Oh, I know that too. When I first went to work on the account, Harrison Glenn told me that if the company ever came up for sale—"

Two men, seating themselves at the next table, upset a chair and Gil, wondering if perhaps he hadn't gone too far, anyway, took advantage of the interruption and left the sentence incompleted.

The lawyer sat tapping his lips, finally saying, "I still fail to see the significance of his having known the girl before. Where does it lead you?"

"As I said, I merely mentioned it because—"

"If it were anyone but Cash McCall, the *cherchez la femme* approach might be applicable. In his case—what's the girl like?"

"Lory? Oh, I don't know how to describe her."

"Attractive?"

"Yes, I'd say so—but that's a matter of taste, I guess. She's—well, the strange thing is that I've always thought of her as being so much younger than she actually is. She's small and rather reticent—and then the fact that she illustrates children's books—well, it caught me up short this morning when I figured back and realized that she's at least twenty-six, maybe twenty-seven."

"Never married?"

"No."

"You say she's an artist. Where did she study?"

"Prather."

"That's in Philadelphia?"

"Yes."

"And she was there when?"

"Well, let's see—she must have finished five or six years ago this spring. A friend of Barbara's met her up in Maine that summer—yes, it was five years ago."

"In Maine?"

"Yes, she was there studying with—"

There was an interrupting commotion near the revolving door, a feminine squeal from the cashier's cage and a burst of masculine laughter from a man who stood in front of it. Heads turned all over the Coffee Shop, people half rising from their chairs to get a better vantage point. The thin waitress, her face contorted with indignation, came up beside Winston Conway's chair. "One of them wise guys with an April Fool mouse. Some joke, huh?"

The lawyer looked up as if startled. "Yes, that's true, isn't it—it is the first of April."

"You boys going to have anything else?" the waitress asked, check pad poised. "More coffee, huh?"

Winston Conway shook his head and pushed back his chair. Gil matched the action, standing, and they went together to the cashier's cage, paying their checks. They parted at the door and, except for the meaningless words of Winston Conway's farewell, nothing more was said.

••••• 6

Maude Kennard stood near the door of the Fontainebleau Room alerted by the sound of shuffling chairs that signaled the end of the second Andscott breakfast conference. The surf roar came toward her and she took a backward step, watching through the cut-edged leaves of the giant philodendron as the released flood of men poured down the three-step spillway to the lobby level. Inhaling, squaring her shoulders, she prepared herself for the peaking of personality that would be demanded by the appearance of Park Cady, Vice-president for Merchandising of the Andscott Instrument Corporation. Mr. Cady was the man who signed the check.

The consciousness that an effort was required came to Maude Kennard as a disturbing realization. Over the years, her response to the best interest of the hotel had become so automatic that it was a rare and disconcerting experience to find herself tempted to allow the intrusion of a superior personal consideration. Unquestionably, the solid accomplishment of showing a breakfast-time profit on the operation of the Fontainebleau Room was more important than solving the mystery of Cash McCall's disappearance ... or was it? If he sold the hotel, what did anything else matter? The Luxor chain would put in their own management ... there would be no place for her after ...

Again, uncontrollably, her mind submitted to the masochistic torture of reviewing the evidence. Cash McCall had left the hotel a week ago tomorrow noon and had not since returned. At ten minutes after seven that morning, five men had gone up to his suite. Nathan knew two of them, both so well that mistaken identity was impossible. One man was Winston Conway of Jamison, Conway & Slythe, the law firm that handled the legal affairs of the Hotel Ivanhoe. The other was Vincent Thompson of Thompson & Slater, the certified public accountants who audited the hotel's books. She had known that something was up and, before noon, had managed to confirm her suspicion. On Will Atherson's desk at the bank, she had seen the letter—actually only the letterhead but, even read upside down, there was no doubt that it was the stationery of the Luxor Hotel Corporation. Luxor was buying hotels all over the country and the Ivanhoe was exactly the kind of house that Luxor would want.

"Well!" The sound was that of a bursting balloon and she knew before she turned that it was Park Cady. "Yes sir, did it again, didn't you, Mrs. Kennard! Wonderful breakfast. Yes sir, just wonderful. Want you to meet our president."

Cady stood on the top step, a rubbery caricature right out of the Mummers parade, turning back to watch the ramrod-straight figure of the man who was slowly making his way down the aisle, a general reviewing his troops, bestowing his set smile as if it were a beribboned decoration.

"Our president," Cady trumpeted wheezily as the man approached, preceding him down the steps, back-reaching a guiding hand. "General Danvers, want you to meet Mrs. Kennard. Yes sir, our honored guest today, Mrs. Kennard—president of our company. Pardon me, sir, Dick's over here on the telephone, I'll tell him you're available now."

Cady started a fast duck-waddle toward the telephone booth under the staircase to the mezzanine and Danvers watched him, waiting until he was safely out of earshot, then facing her with the expression of a sensible man embarrassed by imbecility.

"He's quite a personality," Maude Kennard cut in quickly, speaking before Danvers could clear his throat, her instinct suggesting that he would appreciate being relieved of the necessity of first comment.

"Yes, apparently that's what it takes. That and this sort of thing," Danvers said, his iron-jawed visage slackening with weary forbearance. "I've always regarded breakfast as a rite to be privately performed—and mass singing at any time of day as the most horrible manifestation of our so-called American way of life. But please don't

233

misunderstand me, Mrs. Kennard—I meant no reflection on your part of it. The food was excellent."

"Thank you, General, and I do hope it won't be so long before we see you again. It's been almost three months, that night you had dinner here with Mr. McCall?"

"You do have a memory," he said, cautiously pleased. "By the way, speaking of Mr. McCall, do you happen to know—"

Cady's return could not have been more inopportunely timed. He was accompanied by a man whose name she knew was Sweetzer because he had been paged out of the Fontainebleau Room twice during breakfast to take telephone calls. By the deference with which Cady treated him, she judged that Sweetzer was a higher ranking vice-president, a man with the look of congealed torment on his face, an expression that Cady was now trying to mimic with almost ludicrous results.

Sweetzer locked eyes with the president. "It's Cash McCall, no doubt about it."

Maude saw that her presence had been forgotten but she sidestepped to the philodendron screen and averted her eyes, pretending that she wasn't listening.

"You're sure?" Danvers' voice demanded.

"Yes, I'm sure," Sweetzer slapped back. "After Fred heard Winston Conway and this other guy talking at breakfast, he took a run out to the airport. That's where he just called me from. McCall's plane is there. It all checks. He's out at Austen's right now signing up the deal."

"That bastard!" a strange voice snarled, but strange only until Maude Kennard stole a quick glance and saw that Danvers' face had gone livid with rage, his lips moving as he confirmed the first epithet with a second.

"And I'm afraid that isn't the worst of it, sir," Sweetzer said reluctantly. "Joe Keening's had word from Suffolk Moulding. They've turned down the proposition—told us to go fly our kite."

"Damn it, damn it, *damn it!*" Danvers exploded, emphasis building with every repeated expletive. "Didn't I tell you that you were playing with fire! Didn't I? Yes, damn it, I *did* tell you! I told all of you. But no, you were so sure that Austen would knuckle under! Now you've gotten us into a hell of a mess! This is Padua Furniture all over again! Another half million dollars' ransom. How the hell did McCall find out, that's what I want to know? Somebody talked and, by God, I want to know who it was!"

Sweetzer attempted a delaying interjection, but Danvers brushed him aside and plunged toward the street door, Park Cady following in his wake like a balloon being towed into a headwind. Sweetzer stood immobilized by fury, his face drained, his eyes hard with the hatred of a man goaded beyond endurance.

But Maude Kennard had no interest in any anger other than her own, the icy contempt with which she now regarded herself for having been so stupidly deluded by that letterhead on Will Atherson's desk. She had lost her objectivity, accepted fear as a fact, permitted her imagination to control her mind. That was the sin of sins.

It was clear now that Cash had not been out of town on an expedition to sell the Ivanhoe, but she was across the lobby and starting up the stairs to the mezzanine before she allowed herself the relief that came with recognition. She should have known before ... and if it hadn't been for that stupid guess about Luxor she would have known! Cash was in Suffolk, buying that man Austen's company. How could she have been so wrong? She should have realized ... Will Atherson bringing Austen to The Wharf that day ... that young man from Corporation Associates, Clark or whatever his name was, whispering to Austen in the lobby ... then having lunch with Cash ... Austen going up to the suite afterwards. She should have known that it didn't have anything to do with the hotel. Or that meeting the next morning either. Conway was the hotel's attorney ... of course he was ... but only because Cash owned the hotel. Conway was Cash's attorney ... just as Thompson was his chief accountant ... and Will Atherson his financial man ...

She was stopped at the head of the staircase by the excitement of unfolding discovery, suddenly visualizing the enormousness of Cash McCall's secret empire ... Freeholders Bank & Trust Company ... Jamison, Conway & Slythe ... Thompson & Slater ... Corporation Associates. The Ivanhoe must be only one of hundreds of properties that he owned. There was the company that he had just bought from Austen ... the fear that she had seen in Danvers' eyes ... the Andscott Instrument Corporation ...

She had glanced over the mezzanine rail and her spinning mind had flashed the recalled image of that little bitch waiting for Cash ... Austen's daughter ... Suffolk ... *and that was where Cash had been all week!*

A deep breath filled her lungs and she forced her mind to accept the flesh-bite of her tightened brassière as the iron-banded curbing of apprehension. She wouldn't make the same mistake twice. No, it couldn't be, not when you thought it through ... Cash was no sex maniac like Wilfred, chasing every giggling piece of jailbait in

235

Chicago. Cash was too clever to let himself be fooled by a little high school slut like that ... *much, much, much too clever!*

Everett Pierce was watching her from the doorway of his office, the green-glowing MANAGER sign above his head giving a mildewed cast to the gray skin of his face, and she was sure that he would ask, as he asked twice a day all through the past week, "Anything on that report yet, Mrs. Kennard?"

But for once Everett Pierce proved unpredictable. He said nothing. Instead he gave her a rabbity smirk and handed her an envelope that she knew, even before she looked at the corner card, was from Judge Torrant. There was no stamp, only her hand-written name and an underscored *Personal and Confidential.*

"Messenger just brought it," Pierce explained, his voice high pitched with anticipatory excitement. "I saw you down there with those Andscott people and didn't think it would be smart to bother you."

She took the envelope without acknowledgment and walked toward her office, knowing that Pierce would follow her. She had decided several days ago that she would find some way to keep him from seeing the report. Now that was impossible ... oh, why had Torrant been such an addle-pated old fool as to send it to her here at the hotel!

A sudden inspiration saved her. "I'm afraid this may not be what you think it is. Judge Torrant is handling something else for me, too— a personal matter."

Everett Pierce made no move to leave the doorway of her office. She stared at him, waiting. But he stood his ground. Did he think that she would betray Cash for him? Did the little idiot imagine that she would put a knife in his hands so he could get back that precious suite of his!

She rarely used a letter opener but the search of her top desk drawer allowed her to maneuver her body into a position where, as the envelope was finally opened, its contents would be safely guarded from Pierce's eager eyes. There was only a single sheet, not a letterhead but plain paper, and there was neither salutation nor signature.

The following is from a letter received late yesterday afternoon. "We regret the delay in responding to your recent inquiry. It is quite true, as you suggest, that we did at one time supply background reports from our files on individuals. Unfortunately we are no longer in a position to do so. Since the cost involved

*in a special investigation would undoubtedly be substantially
greater than your client would feel justified by the information
produced, there is apparently no way in which we can be
of service to you."*

Without hesitation, she handed the letter to Pierce, risking a bold
smile as he started to read, watching his face collapse like a slowly
squeezed sponge.

He looked up, folding the letter. "I don't understand this, Mrs.
Kennard. It sounds to me as if they're just ducking."

"I wouldn't know," she said, turning away from him and starting
to examine the night auditor's report on her desk.

"There must be some reason."

"There probably is," she replied, still not looking at him.

He tossed the letter on her desk and it fell within the circle of
her vision but she restrained herself from reaching out to pick it up
until she heard him leave. Then she read it again, not only the typed
words but also what was written between the lines. It *must* be true
... Cash controlled Lockwood Reports, too! What other reason could
they possibly have for protecting him?

Or were they only being honest, admitting that they weren't smart
enough to solve the mystery ... that Cash was too clever for them?
Yes, that was it ... they were licked, throwing up their hands. So
was Torrant ... and Everett Pierce ... and the Andscott crowd ...
everyone!

Everyone?

She toyed with the word, whispering it aloud as she tested varying
pronunciations, baiting her mind with the annoyance of delay until
she was finally willing to acknowledge the truth, smiling then as she
would smile when she finally let Cash know that she was the one
person in the world who knew his secrets.

She closed her fingers, crumpling the letter, feeling the physical
strength that discovery had given her. There was an unbreakable
bond between them now. This was the end of fear and worry, the
end of loneliness, the end of endless nights where there had been
no voice but her own to answer questions that had never been asked
aloud before. She would help him. They would work together. Cash
would find out that she was clever, too.

To her consternation she felt the threat of weeping, so quick-rising
that an uncontrollable shudder shook loose a pair of full-made tears
before she could regain her self-control.

The telephone rang and she answered it. It was Nathan at the
desk. He had a full report now on the toilet trouble in 406 and Smitty

said that the only way to fix it was to put in a whole new flush valve. Would she get Mr. Pierce to sign a replacement order?

"There's no need of that," she said tartly. "Go ahead."

• • • • • 7

Gingerly toeing the accelerator, Grant Austen pulled away from the filling station, braking too quickly when a car leaped at him from the left, stalling the motor, restarting it, finally managing a plunging entrance into the traffic stream that roared down the Philadelphia Pike. At best, he was not a confident driver and now, preoccupied, he was content to follow the silvery bull's-eye of the tank truck ahead of him, making no effort to pass even when the truck was slowed by a long uphill grade.

There had been no prior planning of this trip to Philadelphia. As had been the case so often this past week, he had been swept along by the millrace of circumstances. At the breakfast table, Cash McCall had taken it for granted that he would be going to Philadelphia to-day to deposit the checks, giving him no choice except quick agreement. The impossible alternative would have been an admission that he failed to realize how important it was to prevent the loss of a single day in the investment of a sum as large as two million dollars, and now that he was going to the convention, four days would have been lost.

Committed to leaving the moment he had finished breakfast, there had been no ground for protest when Miriam had suggested that Lory drive Mr. McCall to the airport. He had counted on those few minutes alone with Cash McCall—meaning to ask him what his plans were for the future of Suffolk Moulding—and losing them had been a momentary disappointment. But now, the situation reviewed, he decided that he had probably taken the wiser course in getting away at once. Suffolk Moulding was water over the dam. The company was sold. The checks were in his pocket.

It was only now that he realized that he had forgotten to get Lory's check. He had meant to ask her for it, but there had been that call from the *Tribune*—they were finally doing a decent story about what Suffolk Moulding had done for the community—and then Lory had gone out for the car. But it didn't matter too much. He would make all the arrangements and she could get the check down to-morrow.

The tank truck blinked a turning signal and pulled off toward a roadside diner, opening a stretch of free road, and Grant Austen stepped down on the gas, closed the gap that separated another queue of traffic, swept past two cars following a laboring truck and then, with open road ahead of him again, began to plan his day in Philadelphia.

It was not until he was coming into Devon, stopped by a file of udder-swinging Holsteins crossing the road, that it occurred to him that this was Wednesday. The thing to do, he decided in a quick reversal of plan, was not to go directly to the bank. He would stop in first to see Harrison Glenn at Corporation Associates ... after all, Glenn might have some ideas about investments, too ... and by not going to the bank until after eleven, Will Atherson would be sure to invite him to The Wharf.

● ● ● ● ● 8

Turning into the rutted lane that connected the Suffolk Municipal Airport with the highway—the money from a federal grant, augmented by a local fund-raising campaign, had run out before the entrance road had been paved—Lory Austen noticed an unusual number of cars lined up against the fence that joined the hangar to the glass-cupolated administration building. Momentarily distracted, she failed to see a chuck-hole. The front wheel hit with a crunching thud and she glanced apologetically at Cash McCall. To her surprise, she saw that he was staring at her intently and she had the feeling that she had been watched for longer than she had realized.

He looked away as their eyes met, not quickly as if embarrassed, but slowly as if some silent question had been answered, and she saw his hand raise to the door latch as she swung the car around the end of the hangar and braked to a stop in the cindered area beyond. Ten or a dozen cars were parked and twice that many people were crowded against the high wire fence. She saw then that the object of their attention was an airplane standing at the end of the runway, giant and glittering, dwarfing the little yellow planes that peeped out like frightened birds hiding in the black depths of the hangar. As if in explanation of the crowd's presence, a car that was going down the highway slowed in obvious curiosity, hesitated, and then turned into the lane.

239

"Looks like we have a reception committee," Cash said, opening the door, starting to get out. "Come aboard for a look-see?"

"You don't mean—that plane isn't yours?"

"Of course. Why not?"

"But it's so—"

"Come on, don't deprive me of my fun," he grinned. "I'm a kid with a new toy."

He offered his hand, giving her no chance to decline, and she slid across the seat instead of getting out on her own side, suddenly aware as she swung her feet to the ground that she had been suppressing a sense of excitement that was now threatening to break out of control.

The old watchman was already opening the gate for them, a signal to the crowd, and there was a curious turning of heads all along the fence. Almost at the gate, two youngsters dashed into their path, sweatered and blue-jeaned, the older of the two boys twisting his right sleeve to display a felt medallion that proclaimed him an accredited JUNIOR PILOT, demanding in a just-cracking voice, "Hey, mister, ain't that a B-26? It is a B-26, ain't it, mister? You tell him it's a B-26." The smaller youngster, carrot-topped and freckle-faced, was thrust forward to face the degradation of proved stupidity.

Cash squatted to match eye-levels with the little redhead. "You don't think it's a B-26, huh?"

"I guess I oughta know a B-26," the first boy shouted. "I'm a Junior Pilot, see, and I passed my Aircraft Identification and everything!"

"Well, fellows, you're both right," Cash said soberly, man-to-man. "It *used* to be a B-26—"

"I told you, I told you!" the Junior Pilot crowed.

"—but now it's been converted," Cash continued with a private wink for the redhead, "so it really *isn't* a B-26 any more."

The little fellow grinned gratefully, exposing a missing front tooth.

"You going to take her off now?" the Junior Pilot demanded.

"Yup," Cash said, straightening.

Worshipful blue eyes stared up from the redhead's snub-nosed face.

The Junior Pilot kicked cinders and looked at Lory. "I bet you're going with him, ain't you?"

"She sure is," Cash said, his hand gripping her elbow as they went through the gate.

Her heart quickened to match the faster pace as she tried to keep up with his long-striding legs. She felt the stare of the crowd but did not look back, even when she stopped hesitantly in the shadow of the wing as Cash went ahead to touch a control hidden somewhere in the plane's fuselage. The door opened and a flight of aluminum steps came down. He beckoned and she went up the stairs, stopped at the threshold by the visual impact of the plane's interior. Once, that first year at Prather, she had spent a weekend with Anne Robinson's family on their sailing yacht, feeling then as she had sat in the little ship's cabin this same warming sensation of safe containment within close-sheltering walls, the comforting assurance of life compressed to manageable size, the linked memory of that little studio that her father had built for her when she was a child.

"Don't keep me waiting," Cash said, a half whisper close to her ear. "I'm a glutton for flattery."

"You'll have to wait until I catch my breath," she heard herself say, her breathlessness more than a figure of speech.

"Like it?"

"It's wonderful," she said, stepping across the threshold.

"Want the full conducted tour—lecture and all?"

"Lecture and all," she laughed, giving way to a strangely giddy gaiety that somehow relieved the unexplainable tension.

For a moment, his voice picked up the flamboyancy of a tourist guide but that quality was soon lost, his pride too genuine to be screened by mockery. Even before he had finished showing off the little stainless steel galley with its frosted refrigerator and banked thermos bottles, the mimicry was completely gone. He moved forward, passing her, bending to touch some unseen button. Magically, the wide-seated lounge unfolded into a bed, a reading light glowing on the white pillow and the shelf of books behind it.

"A person could almost live here," she said.

"A person almost does." And he opened a closet door to offer the proof of a full rack of clothing. "Impressed?"

"Oh, I am!" she said, frightened at the explosive burst of the words, relieved when she saw only the response of appreciation in his eyes.

"Come along and see the rest of it," he commanded, guiding her forward with the touch of his fingers, his shoulder brushing against her as he reached out to open the door ahead of her.

She slipped through a narrow passageway and found herself confronted by the hundred-eyed stare of the cockpit, a welter of instrument faces and controls scattered about in incredible complexity. She turned to voice her astonishment and saw that Cash had left her and was striding toward the back of the cabin. Watching, she saw the barred glint of the sun on the rising steps and then the light was cut off by the closing door. She imagined the quick explanation that he was shutting out the too-curious spectators but, back in the cockpit, his hand forced her down into one of the two seats. Before there was time for either question or protest, he slipped into the seat beside her, his hands moving over the instrument board. The intensity of his preoccupation was so great that she dared not attempt interruption. One motor burst into a roar and then the other. The plane began to move, taxiing away from the crowd-lined fence. As it turned, she caught a glimpse of the redheaded youngster, spread-eagled as he clutched the wire fence.

"Can't let the kids down," Cash shouted, barely audible over the roar of the motors.

She tried to shout back but he shook his head, touching his ear to indicate that hearing was impossible.

The line of Lombardy poplars that bordered the end of the field rose higher and higher in the glazed frame of her vision, then suddenly slid off to the right as the horizon fanned past. The full length of the runway lay ahead of them now, the hangar far away, dwarfed by distance. The roar of the motor faded slightly and she leaned toward him, trying to hear what his moving lips were shouting. He gestured an explanation, reaching across the narrow separation between the two seats to pick up the buckle-ended half of her seat belt, tossing it across her lap. The roar of the motors rose to an ear-splitting scream and the plane shook like some mad animal staked to the earth, setting up a body-shaking tremor that seemed to originate where his fingertips had brushed her body. Threading the buckle was an endlessly fumbled task but it was finally done, cinched down with tourniquet tightness in a vain attempt to contain the backsurge of emotional reaction that threatened to stop the beating of her heart.

The plane was moving down the runway now, gathering speed, blurring detail into streaming parallelism, banishing normality, opening her mind to a sensation never before experienced, a projectile rush into the unknown, the feeling of being hurtled into space, alone, disassociated from the bulk and substance of the plane. Then, suddenly, there was the realized miracle of free flight, seemingly self-accomplished until she glanced at the man beside her.

His eyes were safely averted and she studied his profile for a moment, intently, as if every line were about to be etched into copper, unchangeable after the final commitment of a first drawing. Suddenly, the wing-modeled curve at the juncture of his lips softened in a signal of impending relaxation and she looked away quickly, forcing herself to study the strangely geometric mosaic of the earth, the solid underpainting of the ocher soil, the palette-scraping grays of the dead fields and leafless trees, the overglaze of blue reflected from the sky. Her eyes lifted through the chromatic scale, the sun-greened band along the horizon, the interrupting whiteness of a cloud bank, on through the infinitely subtle blending of blue into blue that ended with the deep cobalt of the zenith. When she looked down again the earth was screened with a translucent white veil and the cloud bank was no longer ahead of them.

A spreading warmth flowed from the point of her shoulder and she turned to see that it was cupped by his hand. He was pointing to the headset that hung from a hook over her head. She took it down, put it on, guided by his gestured instructions, suddenly hearing his voice ask loudly, "Can you hear me?"

She nodded, experiencing again the dream sensation of being able to hear his voice so close to her that he should have been touchable, only to awaken to the reality of endlessly distant separation.

"Swing the mike around," he said, demonstrating.

"Like this?" she asked, fighting off the madness of unreasoning desire, the blind hope that his hand would again reach out to her.

"Can't hear a thing," his voice said in her ear. "Still speechless?"

"I'm afraid so," she said. "But it's—it's wonderful."

He frightened her with an amused smile. "What's wonderful?"

"This," she said quickly. "All of it."

They were suspended in space now, all sensation of movement gone. Below, an earth-shrouding veil of cloud was being slowly drawn away, a chiffon scarf in the gentlest of summer winds.

"Know where you are?" he asked, after a long silence, pointing.

She looked far ahead and saw that the blue of the sky had lost its horizon and was wandering aimlessly across the land. "Isn't that —it's water, isn't it?"

"Chesapeake Bay," he explained. "At three hundred miles an hour you get places in a hurry. That's Baltimore over there on the horizon. In a few minutes we should be able to see Washington."

"But I—I thought we were just—"

"Does it matter?" the voice in her ear asked, intently serious.

She whispered that it did not matter, thinking that her words were safely inaudible, but forgetting the microphone so close to her lips. He must have heard. There was no other explanation for the way he looked at her, only for an instant, not long enough to be a warning, and then so quickly that she did not see even the movement of his arm, she felt the crush of his body and the hard press of his lips, and the whispering of her name was a microphoned roar in her ears, thunder-loud but still impossibly far away, and the safety belt was a maddening restraint against erasure of the distance between them. There was the sensation of falling through space, a leaf dropped into a depthless void, but when she finally opened her eyes the horizon was still a level line and the plane was an island solidly anchored in the great blue sea of the sky.

The roar of the motors was a lost sound—she heard only the thudding pound of her heart and the sibilant microphoned rasp of her breath—and her mind seemed emptied by some strange outpouring, tremulously expectant now, waiting for the delayed surge of some surpassing sensation. But the sound of breathing faded until it fell below the threshold of audibility. She could no longer hear the pounding of her heart, and the return of conscious thought came with neither the high pitch of madness nor the clawing threat of fear, but clean and true and honest, unquestionable and inescapable. She was a woman, complete and total, wanted and wanting. For the moment that was all that mattered.

● ● ● ● ● 9

There was a new girl at the reception desk in the Corporation Associates lobby—a startlingly blond head that was bent, no less startlingly, over a copy of *Parents Magazine*—and when she looked up, Grant Austen was forced to identify himself, speaking his name and then adding, automatically, "—Suffolk Moulding," unaware until after he heard himself speak the words that they were now untrue.

The girl started to dial and he turned away, blindly surveying the lighted niches displaying the products of Corporation Associates' major clients, his mind occupied with the newly recognized strangeness of his position. It had been the habit of a lifetime to introduce himself, "Grant Austen, Suffolk Moulding," and the realization that his name would now have to stand nakedly alone, unassociated, came to him as something of a shock. He had, at odd moments during the past week, thought of some of the ways that his life would be changed but he had not faced before the disquieting problem of how to reply when, as had happened so many times, someone in the next seat in a plane or club car asked what line of business he was in. But it wouldn't be for long ... "Well, you see I'm in Washington now, heading up the ..."

"I'm sorry, Mr. Austen—"

He turned back to face the girl at the desk.

"—Mr. Glenn is in a staff meeting. If you could stop by this afternoon—?"

"It's all right," he said, automatically raising his guard against a display of disappointment. "Not important, anyway. Just tell him that I dropped in."

244

"I surely will, Mr. Austen." Her voice sounded tape recorded from Chapter III of the Corporation Associates manual on public relations.

Out on the street again, he looked at his watch. It was ten thirty-two. Too early to go to the bank. He stood for a moment, attempting to think of some way that an hour might be filled. Then, still without an idea, he walked briskly toward Broad Street in a perfect pretense of purpose. No one, seeing him, would ever guess that he was a man who didn't know where he was going.

•••••• 10

The flat disc of the earth tilted, slowly revolving, and Cash's voice in the earphones said, "Fasten your seat belt, we're landing."

His voice shattered the thin shell of reverie and she looked down to see wooded hills rapidly gaining dimension, the detail of individual trees becoming visible as the ridges swelled upward from the valley floor below. A mountainside streamed past, restoring perspective, and then it was the plane that was moving, not the earth, and she caught her breath as the wing-tip went up and up, reaching for the zenith. The plane leveled and rocketed in through a narrow gap in the sheer face of a high cliff. There was the blur of treetops and then the blue-black ribbon of a landing strip streamed out ahead of them across the flat floor of a faintly green-tinged valley. The plane settled, touched, lost the grace of flight, became a mechanical behemoth lumbering ahead to an awkward stop. The motors snuffed out and there was the vacuum of silence. She looked away from him, out across the valley, afraid that he would say now what had not been said before ... apologize for having kissed her ... and she braced herself against the need of reply.

But he only asked, "Know where you are?" and after a moment of recovery, tempted to reply again that it didn't matter, she said, "I haven't the vaguest idea."

For a suspended instant it seemed that he had heard the silent words of her thought instead of the words her lips had spoken, but the movement of his body was only the act of standing. He helped her up from the seat and the touch of his hands was no longer the firebrand of madness but was now the silent promise of eventual fulfillment, unquestioned and unanswerable, accepted.

They walked together back through the cabin and at the door, denying hope, he did not hesitate but immediately touched the control button. The sunlight flooded in as the steps went down and, momentarily blinded, she did not see, until after she heard a strange voice, the gray-stubbled face of the old man who sat grinning up at them from the front seat of a battered pickup truck.

"Whyn't you let a fellow know you was coming?" the oldster shouted in a poor pretense of anger. "Didn't have no warning at all, 'cept them guinea hens cackling as if there was a chicken hawk around. Like to broke my fool neck getting down here in time. Hadn't been downhill all the way, I'd never made it."

Cash laughed an affectionate greeting, turning back to her as she came down the steps. "Lory, this is Abe Jefferson, direct descendant of Abe Lincoln and Tom Jefferson—not to mention a little Indian blood that he picked up from the queen of the Cherokees."

Abe howled gleefully, rattling the loose steering wheel of the old truck. "Don't you go believing a word of it, miss!" He long-legged out without opening the door, extending a gnarled hand. "Warning you right now, I'm a no-good liar and ain't to be trusted. Sure pleased to welcome you, miss."

"Hello, Mr. Jefferson," she said, taking his hand, feeling the crackling texture of old parchment.

"If Cash here'd only let me know you was coming I'd a shaved— even if 'tis only Friday."

She found it astonishingly easy to laugh. "But this isn't Friday, Mr. Jefferson, it's Wednesday."

"'Tis?" He looked appealingly at Cash.

"That's right, Abe."

"Which Wednesday? Don't do no good to tell a man it's Wednesday if you don't say whether it's last Wednesday or next Wednesday. Doggone, Cash, whyn't you bring me a new calendar? One I got's so old 'tain't even got Armistice Day on it."

"Don't know when Sunday comes, do you, Abe?" Cash asked.

Abe slapped his thigh in high glee. "Cora still ain't got over that one. You see, miss, she wakes up on this morning Cash is talking about and nothing would do but she's got to have her soul saved. I argues it's Friday but she's so all fired sure it's Sunday that right then and there we gotta hitch up the mules and drive clear down to Shell Creek for services. Know what day it is when we get there? Tuesday!"

"Wait a minute, Abe," Cash interrupted. "That isn't the way you told it before."

"That so?" Abe asked, elaborately innocent. "Well, I got different ways of telling it, depending on who's listening."

Cash accused, "You told me Cora was taking you down to make you marry her."

246

"Nope, you got that wrong, Cash. This particular time there was three of the kids with us. Time we went down to get married there was only one!" He interrupted his own quick laughter. "You two figuring on fishing? No use if you are. Trouts gone plumb lazy. Can't get more'n eight or ten without moving to a different pool."

"Even have to cast for them, huh?" Cash asked.

"Ain't had one jump ashore by hisself all this week."

"Thought the fishing season didn't open until the fifteenth."

"Ain't it that yet? Doggone, boy, I told you I needed a calendar."

Cash's change of tone cut off the banter. "Abe, how about letting us use that limousine of yours?"

"Sure, take her," the old man said with a magnanimous gesture.

"We can drop you off at your place."

"No, you don't!" Abe balked in quick alarm. "Cora's got a idea of me washing windows. I ain't getting near that place till she settles down. Anyway, there's a covey of quail needs looking at. Nothing better for a man's soul than seeing a nice big covey of quail. Beats window washing all hollow."

The doors of the pickup proved unopenable. "Safer that way," Abe explained. "Can't lose nothing if one of them doors comes flapping open."

Unexpectedly, Cash swept her up in his arms and deposited her, breathless, on the front seat.

Abe grinned, tongue-in-cheek, winking. "Knowed a girl once—that's what she wanted this feller to do, carry her in the house like that when they got home from the wedding. Only thing was, this gal she weighs about two hundred pounds and the feller was a little half pint no bigger'n a squirrel, so when—"

Cash had started the motor and Abe broke off his narrative with a sudden windmilling of his arms, dashing around to the back of the truck and dragging out two sets of wheel chocks for the plane. His feet tangled in the ropes and he fell backward, landing in a sitting position, grinning, then waving them on with an expression of happy resignation.

The motors coughed and clattered, gears ground, and the truck started down the dirt lane that angled off from the runway.

"What a wonderful character," she marveled, the words less important than the need for exultation.

Cash chuckled. "He's a character, all right."

"Where in the world did he come from?"

"Oh, he was here when I got the place."

"You can't mean—this isn't all yours?"

"You haven't seen it yet," he said.

They were driving along a stream now, green-knotted fringe hanging from the bordering willows, and he made a sharp right turn, stopping on a log-railed bridge. The rush of the water was under them, its babbling rustle the only sound after the motor sputtered out.

"Look," he whispered, gesturing toward a widening pool beyond the bridge shadow. She leaned toward him, her eyes directed by his pointing finger, seeing the sunlighted gravel at the lip of the pool, then the shadowy silhouettes that moved across it.

"Trout," he whispered, his voice colored with the little-boy wonder of a youngster impressed with some fabulous phenomenon.

She tried to capture the quality of his excitement, but her mind would accept no stimulus beyond the realization of how totally different he was from anyone she had ever known. It was impossible to imagine the intonation of his voice being duplicated by another's lips, even harder to visualize another face that could even partially match his infinite variety of expressions. They were not the simple masks that ordinary men put on and took off to express pleasure or displeasure, acceptance or rejection. His was a living face, the mirror of a mind unshackled by convention, soaring its own free course without apology for freedom, regarding pleasure not as a frivolity to be grudgingly tolerated but as something organically linked to life itself, not as a weakness but as a strength, not as a contradiction of power but as the proof of its existence. He was strong. That was undeniable. No man could stand against him. If she were to touch him now ... and it would require only the slightest movement of her head to brush his cheek ... that strength would be released ... crushing ... enveloping ...

But she could not move toward him. Her body was locked in the firm grip of reason, not by the fear of another such rejection as she had experienced that night in Maine, nor even the fear of physical inadequacy that had kept her sleepless on so many brooding nights, but by the calm acceptance of normal woman's waiting role. It was a rare sensation, this feeling of maturity, this passport to womanhood that he had given her.

He turned and she turned with him, slipping away, their bodies neither near nor far. The motor started and they drove ahead, the road following the stream again, blue-grass lushly verdant in clumps sheltered under the bank, a red-winged blackbird swaying on the brown stalk of a cattail in a marshy backwater. The road wound tortuously, leaving the stream, and they tunneled into a pine forest, the sun lost as they climbed, restored again as softly filtered light

248

fell hazily through the bare branches of giant oaks. White stars flickered on the forest floor.

"Bloodroot," he said, breaking the long silence.

She nodded, her eyes following the red tracery of a cardinal's swift flight. Through a break in the trees she caught a quick glimpse of the valley, now far below them.

"Soon there," he said, shifting gears to ease the stuttering motor as the road hairpinned a jutting cliff, ending on the flat platform of a red rock, an observation point unscreened by trees.

They got out and he led her to the edge of the cliff, leaping lightly to the top of a flat boulder, giving her his hand as she climbed. She saw, after a moment of orientation, that they were standing high on the rim of a giant bowl. A circling mountain ridge enclosed the entire valley except for the single break of the notch through which they had flown in. Distance was unappreciated until she saw the plane, now the tiniest of silver insects feeding at the end of a black line ruled across the floor of the valley. The willows along the stream were faintly green vapor rising from a thread of water.

"See the river?" he asked, directing her eyes with the sweep of his hand. "I'll show you where it comes from."

He jumped down and reached up to lift her from the rock. His hands, open palmed under her arms, left an oddly lingering sensation of pressure, a strange swelling of her breasts that persisted long after the release of his hands, and she was relieved that her face was hidden from him as she went ahead down the path he indicated.

They walked without speaking, even the sound of their footsteps finally lost in the deepening cushion of pine needles, and it was in that silence that she first heard what seemed the faint rustling of wings. But as they climbed downward, the sound changed character and she finally identified it as the rush of water. Cash came up beside her, parting a screen of low-hanging hemlock boughs. Then she saw the waterfalls. It was a sight so beautiful that full comprehension came slowly. From high up on the rock-face of the cliff, a torrent of water gushed out into space and fell through an enormous rock chalice until, far below, it feathered into a plume of spray over a foaming green cauldron from which, with almost incredible placidity, the creek flowed out to the valley.

"The whole river comes right out of the rock," she finally said, awe demanding the voicing of an explanation. "Does it have a name?"

"Aurora," he said. "Aurora Falls—Aurora Valley."

"It can't possibly be real," she whispered. "It's something in a dream."

"Sometimes I don't believe it either."

"You can't mean that it's yours?"

"That's what the deed says."

"All of it?"

"The whole valley."

"But—" She stopped, lost for words.

"If it hadn't been for you, I'd never have found it. That's why I brought you here today."

"I—?"

"Do you remember that night in Maine?"

The question came as a blow without warning and her body stiffened against its impact, a wordless protest escaping her lips before it could be stopped.

Cash looked at her as if shocked by the awareness of error. "I meant that first night at Jefferson Clark's." His hands reached out, manacles on her wrists. "But I want to tell you about that other night, too."

"It doesn't matter," she tried to say, uncertain whether the words were actually spoken.

"It does matter," he said fiercely. "All that day, every minute of it, I'd been fighting against hope, telling myself that it couldn't be, that you were thinking of me as an old man, that it was insane to hope that—"

"I was the one who was insane."

"No, Lory, no! You were—"

She was in his arms, neither a moment too soon nor a moment too late, but the imp of conscience whispered that none of this could be true, that the moment of revealed reality had been dissipated and that they were back in a dream world again.

But if it had been a dream world he would have kissed her and he did not. Her tense body slackened with the slow subsiding of inner tremor, and then came the dull awareness that it was right that he did not kiss her now. That would have been the end of words. And there was a need for words. Now she hungered for them.

"After you were gone I realized what a fool I'd been," he was saying. "I followed you but it was too late. You were gone and I didn't know where. All I knew was your name. I had only one clue—that you knew the Athersons. When I got back to Philadelphia, Will Atherson was away on a vacation. It was a week before I could reach him. I finally found out who you were, your father's name, and where you lived. I drove to Suffolk."

"You did?" she asked, the words jarred loose by surprise.

"It was Labor Day. There was a dance out at your country club. You had a date. He was a fine-looking boy—young—at least young enough to have a crew cut and to know how to rumba." A smile flickered, tentative and testing. "I'm not the rumba type and I was ten years past the crew cut age."

She shook her head, not as a gesture of negation but as an attempt to free the choke in her throat. "I wore a silly pink dress and it rained."

His smile broadened as if the test had been successful. "And it was very wet rain—particularly outside, looking in."

"Why didn't you let me know? Oh, I wish you had."

"I was being very wise, and very sensible, telling myself that it was impossible."

"That what was impossible?" she asked, amazed at her boldness.

"That you could—" He paused, looking down into her eyes.

She was so certain that he was about to speak of love that the answer was already on her lips. But the words were wasted. Cash squared his shoulders as if it were an act of suddenly demanded self-control and his voice was firmly flattened as he said, "I was going to tell you how I got all this, wasn't I?"

"Yes."

"That night at Jefferson Clark's—" He hesitated as if retesting her composure, going on after she had nodded. "I came back again the next morning, trying to find you."

"I'd gone back to Eagle Harbor."

"So I found out when I talked to Clark. In the course of our conversation—mentioning Eagle Harbor brought it up—he told me about a paper company up there that was for sale. I had no idea of buying it, but it did give me an excuse to come up there and see you."

"Did you need an excuse?"

"I thought I did. You see—" There was that same shoulder-squaring again, the same determined flatness of his voice. "In any event, I did buy the paper company. Later, I merged it into Paper Enterprises. But during the time I had it, I got digging around in their old records and found a deed for eighteen thousand acres of Pennsylvania land that no one around the place had ever even seen. Old man Dufrene—that was the family that had owned the mill—had bought it thirty years before. No one knew why—maybe he'd had the idea of starting a mill here—but in any event here it was."

"You don't mean this place?"

"Yes."

"I thought you said it was in Pennsylvania?"

"Where do you think you are?"

"But we flew south—Chesapeake Bay—"

"Didn't you notice me turn back over Washington?"

"Something must have distracted me," she said, guardedly tongue-in-cheek, almost certain that the memory of his having kissed her would break his rigid self-composure. And for a split second it did seem that he was going to smile. But the hope was lost and he went on, his voice even more severely restrained than it had been before. "We're only thirty-odd miles from the Turnpike—a half hour by air to Philadelphia, maybe twenty minutes to Suffolk."

"I'm sorry I interrupted your story," she said, mocking his impersonal tone.

Again there was the fleeting hope of a smile, but he denied it with his voice. "There isn't much more to tell. Apparently the property wasn't worth much—it had been on the market for years and years with no one interested—so I thought I might as well hang on to it. In the beginning, I had the devil's own time even finding it. No road comes in except a goat's trail down through the notch that Cora and Abe use a couple times a year."

"No one else lives here?"

"Only Cora and Abe—and they sort of belong, like the trout and the deer."

"And Cash McCall?"

Still there was no smile. "I don't know whether I belong or not. But I built a cabin a couple of years ago. Want to see it?"

"Of course."

He guided her, not back up the path by which they came, but along a ledge of rock on the cliffside. He walked behind her, his arm extended as a guard when the path was narrow. Once she slipped and, instantly, his hand was on the bulge of her hip, solidly sustaining. She moved quickly ahead, escaping the touch of his fingers, charging the shortness of her breath against the fear of falling.

"There's an easier way to come," he apologized. "But this is the way I wanted you to see it first."

"You should have warned me this was going to be a mountain-climbing expedition. I'd have worn different shoes."

"I didn't know it would be today."

Today? Involuntarily, she glanced back at him.

"Watch it!" he warned.

Her eyes went ahead again, seeing a downstep and then, only two strides away, the path ended against a dead-end wall of rock.

"To your right," Cash directed.

Turning, she saw a totally incongruous door, varnished and shining

252

in the sun, that and nothing else, no visible structure, only the door against the sheer wall of natural rock, the only mark that the hand of man had left on the whole enormous landscape.

Cash stepped around her, opening the door. Ahead, there was a short tunnel through naked rock and then, framed in the opening, a sight that was even more of a visual shock than the falls had been at first seeing. It was a room that seemed less an actuality than something suddenly flashed on a motion picture screen, the imagined interior of a Park Avenue penthouse. She reached out to touch the end of a long upholstered divan, almost surprised to find that her fingertips confirmed its reality. But it was when she turned to the left, drawn by the light, that the full quality of the room burst upon her. The outer wall was largely glass, exposing the full panorama of the falls, not as if seen through the end opening of a cave but as if she were standing on a projected suspension in space, the same feeling of detachment from the earth that she had experienced in the cockpit of the plane. The room seemed unwalled and without limit but, as she watched, there was a dark side movement across the sky and the falls were gone, the room suddenly materializing as a close containment ... the cabin of the plane ... her childhood studio ...

An exclamation of wonder rose in her throat but it was silenced by an awareness of inadequacy. Cash's hand moved, a sorcerer's wand, and the curtain slipped soundlessly back across the window. They were out in space again and she moved forward, experiencing the sensation of walking in air, heightened as she came to the glass and looked almost straight down into the pool at the base of the falls, its emerald depths glimpsed through the swirling mists as, looking upward, she might have seen patches of cobalt sky between the clouds. Again, as had happened before, she was struck by the almost incredible placidity of the stream that flowed from the tortured turbulence of falling water.

"Impressed?" Cash asked behind her.

"Oh, I am. It's the most—"

Words failed her and she turned back to face the room, experiencing a slow restoration of the sense of reality that had been lost as she had stepped through the door. Then, incongruity had made everything seem the creation of a Hollywood set designer, but now it was no longer the eye-tricking product of a scenic artist. This was something solidly built by masons and carpenters, undeniably real.

"How did you ever manage to build it?" she asked, vaguely visualizing the problems that must have been involved in nesting this mountain house against the high sheer face of the cliff.

"The only difficult part was trying to convince the workmen that I really wanted it. There wasn't any way to explain *why* I did—" He smiled self-consciously. "There still isn't."

"But why wouldn't you want it? It's so—it's such a wonderful place —so perfect. When you're here, you can forget the rest of the world even exists."

"Yes, that's the temptation," he said soberly, almost as if it were a reluctant admission.

"Is it important *not* to forget?" she asked gaily.

"Isn't it?"

She shook her head, still smiling, afraid for an instant that he might be interpreting her silence as a too-personal boldness, relieved when he turned away to let his eyes run back over the room.

"In some ways, I suppose, it was a hang-over from my kid days," Cash said. "There was a mountain behind our house—actually only an old claybank back of the brickyards, but still a very fine mountain. I built myself a wonderful cabin up there—two old packing crates with a Calumet Baking Powder sign for a roof—but it was a splendid place, much finer than this."

"I know," she said quickly, caught up in the memory of her own little backyard studio. "When you were there, it could be any place in the world."

Cash laughed. "Until there was a lawn to mow or a front porch to sweep."

"Or your father came and told you that there was something wrong with you because you weren't out playing with the other little boys."

"You, too?" he asked, amazed.

She nodded. "Except that mine wasn't a cabin on a mountain top. No, wait—once it was—after I'd read *Shangri-La.*"

"Did you ever try Mount Kilimanjaro?" he asked with the pseudo-seriousness of rigid make-believe. "Wonderful place—you could sit up there and see all the animals in Africa. And very convenient, too. When you got tired of being the great white hunter you could just snap your fingers and change all the safari boys into Sherpas. Then you could spend the rest of the afternoon climbing Mount Everest."

"Oh, I was much too busy for any such waste of time as that. You see, I had all my studios. There was one in Paris—that was an attic with candles in wine bottles—and then Greenwich Village, of course. But sometimes I'd get very bored with being such a famous artist and then I'd run away to my lovely villa in the south of France. Or my house in the casbah of Algiers."

"Then you must have known an old friend of mine—Pépé le Moko?"

Cash's twinkling eyes made the mood impossible to sustain and she broke out in laughter. "At least this has the advantage of being real."

"Come along and see the rest of it," Cash said, gesturing toward a corridor along an extension of the enormous window that opened on the falls, creating the illusion of a passageway through the clouds. The view was so demanding that Lory had taken a half dozen steps before her attention was caught by the opposite wall. She saw then that it was the bare rock of the cliff, niched and shelved to hold a large collection of sculptured figures that she immediately recognized as East Indian. Breaking her stride, she stopped abruptly before a Buddha in a niche so deep that only by standing directly in front could she see the serenely contemplative face in the deep shadows.

"I was in India for a while," Cash said, a seemingly simple explanation, but his tone of voice carried the implication that what he had brought back was something beyond these tangible relics.

Her eyes left the Buddha and she saw then that the deep niche was flanked by terra cotta bas reliefs, so close in color to the stone into which they were inset that they seemed to be modeled from the living rock. "The Prince Gautauma renounces the world and flees to the forest," she whispered, explaining the pageantry of the carved figures as if it were an inscription to be read aloud.

Cash's eyes narrowed. "You surprise me."

"Why?"

"That you'd know that."

"I used the life of the Buddha for my senior mural project at Prather. One of my instructors had a great passion for Buddhism and Hinduism—well, actually not the religions as much as their arts—but he got all of us terribly interested. He used to go out there almost every summer—India or Burma."

"Dr. Borg?"

"Do you know him?" she asked, surprised.

Cash nodded. "I helped stake a couple of his expeditions."

"You did? What a wonderful thing to do."

"Oh I always got much the best of the bargain," Cash said off-handedly, almost as if embarrassed by her approval. "He always managed to bring me something or other that was worth more than I ever gave him. That's one of the Borg things up there."

Half turning, she looked up to the high niche he had indicated and saw a beautifully wrought stone figurine rising from the shell of a full-blown lotus.

"It's Lakshmi, isn't it?" she asked.

"You do know your Hinduism, don't you? Yes, I suppose Borg thought she'd be appropriate—the goddess of wealth, you know."

Lory laughed. "He was probably looking out for his own interests,

255

hoping that if Lakshmi was good to you, you'd finance another expedition."

Cash's smile was quick-fading, his voice serious as he said, "Of all the strange things about Hinduism, that's always struck me as the strangest—that they should have a goddess of wealth and prosperity and accept the fact that it's perfectly all right to worship her. As far as I know, it's the only religion that does."

"But don't we do the same thing?" she asked. "Maybe *worship* is the wrong word, but isn't that the main interest in life for most Christians—making money?"

"But we never acknowledge it—at least religiously," Cash mused. "Our whole Western civilization is based on the profit motive—and yet it's one of the key tenets of our Christian religion that the pursuit of riches is the root of all evil—that virtue is somehow associated with poverty."

"Maybe the Hindus are just more honest about it."

"There've been times when I've thought so," Cash chuckled wryly. "But of course, they have the advantage of an entirely different philosophic approach—the division of a man's life into the four stages. It's only in the second stage that the pursuit of riches is justified but, after all, that covers the full period of a man's most productive life."

"Then he renounces the world," Lory supplied, glancing toward the bas relief. "That's the third stage, isn't it?"

"Yes, then it's off to the forest."

"Or the mountain top," Lory added too quickly, regretting what had been a purposeless flippancy when she saw the sudden freezing of Cash's expression.

For a moment he seemed one of the sculptured figures that peopled the rock wall, voiceless, withdrawn and remote, as far beyond understanding as the incomprehensible Buddha, as remote from her own life as the temple gods of the Hindus.

Suddenly, surprisingly, he smiled. "That's probably my trouble—there's too much of the Christian in me to ever believe that the world is really escapable—except temporarily—now and then."

He led the way to the door at the end of the corridor, opening it to reveal a dining alcove. A second door opened on a small kitchen, gleaming metallically, copper and stainless steel.

"And, anyway, a hermit's life is much more appealing if you have all the modern conveniences," Cash added. But the lightness of his voice seemed oddly forced and he turned quickly, letting the kitchen door swing shut, moving on down the corridor.

"My bedroom," he explained, opening another door, giving her only the quickest glimpse of a room almost monastically plain except for a grouping against the white walls of what appeared to be framed pages from old illuminated manuscripts.

Beyond, he opened another door. "Guest room," he said crisply. "Want a chance to get off some of the dust?"

She nodded gratefully, stepped through the door, reaching back to close it, aware then that Cash had already done it. At first glance, the room seemed of matching plainness, starkly bare, but closer examination revealed that the bedspread was an Indian brocade, almost colorless but woven in a design of surpassing intricacy, and then that the headboard of the bed was not wood but old bronze, delicately engraved in a portrayal of the Ramayana legend. Bending close, her eyes were drawn to one of the feminine figures—no more a logical center of interest than any of the others but somehow magnetically demanding—fantastically voluptuous in form and pose, yet with a serenity of facial expression that recalled Dr. Borg's explanation of the Indian representation of ideal womanhood as the perfect blending of her two natures.

Quickly, she found the bathroom door and stood for a long moment with the open taps flooding water over her hands and wrists, cold and then hot, waiting through the subsiding of an excitement of which she had become aware only after Cash had closed the door behind her.

Finally, assured that she had attained the security of reason, she dried her hands and opened her purse, finding her comb and lipstick. This was the end ... it had to be! This day couldn't be allowed to be a repetition of that day at Eagle Harbor ... the transient excitement of his presence and then, afterwards, nothing but those endless nights. To live through that aftermath again would be totally pointless. She had been a child that night in Maine, mad with an unmanageable desire ... but now she was a woman, wise enough to know that there could be no happiness in unreasoned hunger for the unattainable. She had seen Cash McCall again ... flown in his plane ... he'd shown her his mountain hideaway and his collection of East Indian art ... all very interesting. But that was that! Now it would end. He would take her back to Suffolk and it would all be over and done with. That would be the end. And this time the end would be the ending.

She snapped shut her purse and walked quickly across the bedroom and out into the corridor. Cash was nowhere in sight. But a door stood open and she walked to it, stepping out onto the sunlighted terrace. The roar of the falls burst upon her ears again, the instant of first hearing strangely timed to the quickly caught image of Cash's figure silhouetted against the sky. He was standing on the rock parapet that surrounded the terrace, looking out at the falls, unaware of her presence.

"It's a beautiful place," she said.

He turned at her first word, leaping lightly down now to face her, his expression questioning.

"And I'm so glad you brought me," she added with a curtaining finality.

There was an instant when he seemed surprised enough to protest. Then, quickly—too quickly—she heard him say, "Yes, I wanted you to see it."

Watching, she felt the strange unreasonableness of disappointment as he stepped back to the house and started to close the door, catching her breath through the indecisive moment when his hand seemed held back by some decision yet to be made. But then he closed the door, the click of the latch incredibly loud against the thunder of the falls.

"There's no need to make the climb back," he explained, curtly businesslike. "There's a car down below. Abe can pick up the truck afterwards."

····· 11

The faceless clock on the glass wall of the Freeholders Bank & Trust Company registered only eleven-twenty as Grant Austen pushed open the front door. It was earlier than he had planned to arrive, but walking the streets had exhausted his patience as well as his strength ... and Will Atherson might be leaving early for lunch, this being a Wharf day.

He looked up to the mezzanine and saw the banker through the transparent wall of his office, sitting alone at his desk, and walked confidently toward the silvery spiral of the staircase.

Atherson's secretary met him at the top step. "Why, Mr. Austen, this is a surprise! Or was Mr. Atherson expecting you?"

"Well, nothing definite," he said. "But I guess he probably figured I'd be down."

"I hope he's free," she said, uncertainly but still smiling. "Sit down, Mr. Austen, and I'll tell him that you're here."

He drew his wallet from his inside coat pocket, taking out the check, not bothering to sit down because he was sure that Will Atherson would appear immediately—and he did, taking the pipe out of his mouth long enough to offer a quiet greeting.

"Don't want to break in on you if you're busy," Austen said, hesitantly hopeful that the banker would offer a disclaimer. But the pipe had gone back. "Had the settlement with McCall this morning, you know—well, it's a lot of money so I thought I ought to get it down here as soon as I could."

Atherson nodded, taking the check, examining it, looking up then with a silent question.

"Sure, there's Lory's check too," Grant Austen said. "I thought she'd get a kick out of banking it herself. But we can make the arrangements about investing it and all that."

Atherson turned to his hovering secretary. "Will you see if Mr. Brown is busy?"

They were standing outside the bank president's office and Grant Austen made a guardedly suggestive move toward the door. "I thought we could sort of run over the investment situation, Will. It's a lot of money and I'd like to get it working for me as soon as I can."

"Naturally," Atherson said. "That's why I sent for Brown. He's the head of our Trust Department, you know. Be a lot more help to you than I'd be. Investments are Fred's specialty. As you know, I stick pretty much to the industrial end."

Fred Brown came around the corner, his face remembered only because of its oddly tinted complexion, his skin always looking as if it had been stained by color leaching out of his sandy hair. Atherson offered a cryptic explanation and, with a maneuver too adroit to be circumvented, put Grant Austen in a position where he had no choice except to follow Brown down the hall.

Until a minute or two before twelve, Grant Austen sat in a labored pretense of listening, nettled by Brown's constant references to his *retirement*, held back from walking out only by the expectation that, at any moment, Atherson would rescue him with an invitation to lunch at The Wharf. That hope was still alive until, finally escaping with the promise that he would give some thought to Brown's investment suggestions, he came back down the hall to find Atherson's office empty and his hat and coat gone from the clothestree in the corner.

Spiraling his way down the staircase to the banking floor, Grant Austen was more stunned than angered, attempting to excuse Atherson by trying to make himself believe that the banker might have had a date to go somewhere else today. But acceptance was made difficult by the juxtaposed memory of the strange way that Harrison Glenn had treated him. Never before would the head of Corporation

Associates have passed up an opportunity to see him, particularly with such a lame excuse as a staff meeting. And now Will Atherson had treated him the same way, shoving him off on a clerk and then sneaking out. What was wrong? He was a millionaire ... he had a deposit slip to prove it ... but everyone was treating him as if he were a nobody, as if he didn't matter any more.

He hailed a taxicab, blinking his disbelief when the driver said, seemingly only a moment later, "Here you are, sir."

Austen could not recall having asked to be taken to the Hotel Ivanhoe but neither could he remember exactly what he had said, so he got out and paid the fare, tossing back the change.

Inside the lobby, he caught a glimpse of a group of men moving toward the elevator that would take them up to The Wharf. One of them was that big lawyer he had met last week ... Torrant? Yes, that was his name ... Judge Torrant.

Half consciously, he hoped that Torrant would glance back and see him but, hope denied, he strode resolutely toward the door of the Fontainebleau Room ... *damn it, he didn't need any of them ... There were clubs in Washington that were a hell of a lot more important than The Wharf ever thought of being!*

Suddenly inspired, he turned right and went to the newsstand, buying two Washington newspapers and a copy of *United States News* ... wouldn't hurt to get a little background before he talked to Harlan Bostwick at Moon Beach tomorrow.

Through the smoke haze, he saw a woman's beaming smile, bright with recognition. It was that woman who ran the place ... Atherson had introduced her ... Kennard ... Mrs. Kennard.

"Why, Mr. Austen!" she said, extending her hand. "How very, very nice. Don't tell me you're deserting The Wharf?"

"Sure, you bet. Just thought I'd have a nice quiet lunch—that is if you've got a table for me."

"For you?" she laughed. "Always!"

She led him to a table, sharing conspiracy with a wink as she lifted a RESERVED sign, signaling the head waiter but holding his chair herself.

"I've been hearing things about you," she said as she bent over him.

"What's that?"

"A little bird told me that you've sold your company—and for just millions and millions of dollars."

"Oh, not that many millions," he said modestly, smiling in spite of himself. "But I'll have to say I didn't do too badly."

"I'll just bet you didn't—not *you!* And now I suppose you'll be into something else?"

"Anyway, I'm not retiring."

"Well, I should think not!" she exclaimed. "Not a young man like you. But I hope you're not thinking of getting too far away from Philadelphia. We want to see you once in a while, you know."

"Sure, I'll be around. Don't worry about that."

She moved away toward the door but her smile stayed with him. At least there was one person with sense enough to realize that he wasn't retiring. Will Atherson had been right last week when he had said that Mrs. Kennard was one smart woman. If you wanted to get right down to the truth, she was a damned sight smarter than Will was. There was one thing that Will was missing ... and a lot of other people, too! A friend in some important spot down in Washington never did anyone any harm.

"You will order, please, sir?"

"Sure, you bet," he said, wasting a moment as he scanned the enormous menu. "I'll tell you what—just bring me a nice well-done filet mignon."

Nine

.
.
.
.
.

WILL ATHERSON'S love of Starwood, his Main Line estate, was divisible into a hundred smaller loves—the chain-draped gateposts with their festoons of ivy that his grandfather had planted, the path at the back of the house that wound up the hill through the gray rocks that were draped in early spring with the gem-tipped lace of wild columbine, the long-grassed meadow where the spaniels spent endless days in mad pursuit of some never-seen quarry, the deep pool under the catalpas at the turn of the creek where there was a lazy old carp who would occasionally rise to the lure of toast crumbs, the moss-smelling springhouse, the boxwood-hedged hideaway in the garden that Helen teasingly insisted was the scene of their first child's conception, the clearing in the woods that was always signal-fired with red sumac to herald the coming of autumn, the front hall with its parade of family portraits climbing the stair well, every room of this home that had housed four full generations of Athersons.

But of all those places, if Will Atherson had been put to the task of selecting his favorite spot on Starwood, he would not have hesitated in choosing the breakfast alcove. Here he could sit with the whole estate spread out for his survey, the creek purling pleasantly past the big bay window with its fluffy white curtains, the intimacy of the small table, the quite remarkably recurring phenomenon of Helen always managing to be her most appealing self at breakfast time.

And of all the interruptions that disturbed Will Atherson's pleasantly ordered life, nothing annoyed him more than being called away from the breakfast table to answer the telephone. Such calls were irritatingly frequent. His Main Line neighbors knew the exact time of the early commuting train that he always took to Philadelphia and calculated therefrom the best time to inflict upon him such small requests as were deemed unworthy of a call to his office. Most of the breakfast-time calls could be more or less anticipated from the calendar and he had imagined, when he heard the ring, that it would be someone asking him to donate a piece of sterling for the spring horse show.

Returning to the table, he attempted to register the same expression of annoyed dismissal that he would have exhibited if his anticipation had been correct. Rearranging his napkin, he slipped back into the interrupted routine of breakfast, silently preoccupied.

"Will, dear—" Helen said, her voice suspended, anticipatory, as it was when she was awakening him from sleep.

He looked up, startled, saw that her eyes were on his plate, looked down again, and realized that he had been absent-mindedly turning the pepper grinder. His egg was black.

"Oh, darling, I'm sorry," Helen said, characteristically assuming responsibility. "I'll ring for another egg."

"No, no, not at all." He waved back her hand as she was reaching for the bell. "Doesn't matter."

"Worries, dear?"

He picked up his knife and made an ineffectual attempt to scrape away the pepper with the blade's point. "No, not exactly."

"Cash McCall?"

He was surprised, having consciously avoided using McCall's name all through the telephone conversation.

"I thought so," she said, amused.

"Why?"

"You have a very special tone of voice for him."

"I do?" he asked blandly, picking up his fork.

"What did he want?"

"Nothing, dear," he said, not because he had any aversion to discussing business with his wife—her instinctive judgment in financial affairs was frequently more trustworthy than the considered opinion of some of the bank's directors—but rather because he recognized his disgruntled feeling as being unjustified. After all, there was no reason why Cash McCall had to confide in him.

But Helen was still waiting for an explanation and to divert her he said, "He's flying the Austens down to Moon Beach this morning," belatedly realizing that telling her that much was a mistake; she had always evinced a special interest in anything having to do with Cash McCall and now, instead of dropping the subject, would probably go on talking about it all during breakfast.

"Lory, too?" Helen asked, raising her eyebrows.

"He said the Austens. That's all I know."

"But isn't that a little strange, dear? I'm sure you told me once that he made it a rule never to have any social contact with anyone he did business with."

"I doubt if you'd call this social. Grant's attending a plastic molder's convention. And don't ask me why he's going. I don't know. He's completely out of the business now—but that's his affair, not mine."

"Well, at least you can stop worrying about him from now on," Helen said, finally agreeing to a partial shift of subject.

"Oh, Grant hasn't been too bad," he replied, using tolerance as a shield.

She wrinkled her nose in a taunting smile. "You've just loved taking him to The Wharf every Wednesday, haven't you?"

"Not every Wednesday."

"Enough Wednesdays."

"Yes, enough," he sighed, then admitting, "It was getting to the point where he was starting to be a problem. I was afraid yesterday that I was going to be stuck with him. Fortunately, I managed to turn him over to Brown."

"What's he planning to do from now on, Will?"

"I've no idea."

"I imagine he'll be lost for a while."

"Probably."

"I feel a little sorry for men like that," Helen said. "There's been nothing in their lives except their companies. When that's gone, there's so little left."

He nodded agreement, looking out over Starwood, seeing the proof of her point. He could retire tomorrow ... not that he was thinking of doing it ... but he could stay here the rest of his life, never leave, and be perfectly happy.

"Of course, he does have two million dollars," Helen said as a disclaimer. "So you can hardly say that he has nothing left."

"Oh, I don't believe I told you before—things were set up so that his daughter got about two hundred thousand."

"Lory? How nice for her! But I suppose it was a way to save tax, wasn't it?"

"I imagine so," he said, tight-lipped against another rise of annoyance, then forced to cough to clear the pepper tingle from his

264

throat. The least Grant might have done would have been to tell him what the deal had been ... made him look like a fool with Cash McCall, not even knowing what had happened.

"What did Cash want this morning?" Helen asked, the question unexpected until he realized that it shouldn't have been. Sooner or later, Helen always got back around the circle to worm out of him anything that she wanted to know.

"Oh, some information about Andscott Instrument," he said. "General Danvers."

"Goodness, Cash isn't thinking of buying Andscott Instrument, is he?"

"How should I know?" he said, irritation slipping beyond control. "Confound the fellow, anyway. I can't see why he doesn't do business like other people—all this secrecy about everything."

"But the way other people do business is so *dull*," she laughed. "And to quote a learned authority—none other than yourself, my dear—the right of privacy is an inalienable privilege of the free man."

"Excluding always the right of a banker to know what the devil his clients are up to—particularly when there's some of the bank's money involved."

"Now, darling, you're not worrying about that," Helen chided him.

"No," he admitted.

A flash of movement caught his eye and he turned to see a pair of mallards wheel through the air and pitch to the pool at the turn of the creek. It was the mating season and the creek had been full of ducks all this past week, the gaudy drakes preening themselves before the drab little hens in day after day of ardent courtship.

"Will, do they really?"

"Really what?"

"The little girl ducks—are they really under water when it happens?"

"Of course."

She burlesqued a shiver and he laughed in spite of himself, Cash McCall quickly forgotten.

He rolled his napkin, remembering as he never failed to do that the heavy silver ring had been his grandfather's.

"And I'll meet you at the bank at four?" Helen reminded him.

"Yes, four," he said, rising. "Unless it would be handier for you to—would the Ivanhoe be more convenient, dear? Then you wouldn't have to worry about the car."

"It would be better," she said gratefully.

He kissed her quickly, the barest brush of their lips, but he needed no more to remind him that he was a very fortunate man, and he was anxious to escape before Helen became suspicious that her trip into town this afternoon was not, as he had led her to think, for the purpose of inspecting John Guardine's plans for the restoration of the springhouse. The white lie that he had told her still rested uneasily in his memory. But surely, in this one instance, the end was worthy of the means.

●●●●●● 2

Grant Austen was in the library when he heard the sound, at first only a low-pitched pulsing whine but building swiftly to a thundering crescendo, roaring past, fading as fast as it had come, leaving the nervous rattle of window panes in its wake. He rushed out on the terrace and saw, in the instant before its disappearance behind Orchard Ridge, an airplane making its landing turn for the Suffolk Municipal Airport.

By the time he had reached the center hall, Miriam had come to the head of the stairs. "Grant, do you suppose that's Mr. McCall?"

"Who else would it be?" he snapped, starting to climb.

"But it's only twenty after eight."

"Hurry up now," he said, short of breath, anticipating the annoyance of waiting for her to finish packing, deflated when he saw the four pieces of their matched luggage ready and waiting in a straight-lined row at the door of their bedroom.

"Where's Lory?" he demanded.

She answered for herself, calling through the closed door of her room, appearing as he started down with the first two bags, brushing past him, telling him that she would get out the car. She wore a dress that he could not remember having seen before, and he sensed an odd excitement in her voice, strangely unaccountable until he realized that her intonation perfectly matched the expression on his wife's face. Then, carrying the two bags to the edge of the drive, the strangeness was only within himself. He knew that he, too, should be experiencing that same high-keyed anticipation—and there had been a moment of it when he had first heard the plane. But it had been as fast fading as the sound, leaving him still exposed to the same gnawing apprehension that had kept him awake in the night. It was a sensation not unlike the feeling that he sometimes had on the day when he came down with a head cold and, returning to the house, he asked Miriam if she had put in his sulphathiazine tablets.

"Of course, dear. Aren't you feeling well?"

Her concern gave him the momentary illusion of relief, but by the time he came down with the other two bags, she had forgotten. "Grant, are you sure they'll be wearing summer things? Maybe I'd better take my other coat, just in case. Do you think I should?"

"You're all right," he said gruffly, his tone urging haste, waiting for her to open the door for him. But Anna had come in from the kitchen and Miriam, of course, had to go over everything with her again ... the casserole that Lory could heat up for her dinner ... damn it, Miriam shouldn't have let Anna off for tonight! She'd known all along that they'd be going to the convention ... Lory here all alone ...

He saw that his daughter had driven up with the car and pushed awkwardly out through the door, grimacing at the sting of pain when he banged his knee, then attempting to salve his irritation with the repetitious reasoning that everything would be all right as soon as he got to Moon Beach.

Lory was out of the car, opening the trunk for him.

"You won't forget about your check?" he asked. "Just endorse it the way I said—for deposit only."

"I'll remember," she said, pulling the keys from the lifted trunk lid, not looking at him, acting almost as if she weren't listening to him, the same way she had acted last night when he had tried to talk to her about that crazy Italy business. This was no time for her to go running off ... but, of course, she didn't know yet about Washington ... and he couldn't tell her ... couldn't tell anyone until it was settled. But it would be settled by the time he got back ... well, maybe not exactly *settled*, but at least he'd have a pretty good idea of what it was going to be after he'd talked to Harlan Bostwick. Today was Thursday ... Friday, Saturday, Sunday ... yes, that was the thing to do, have a good old-fashioned talk with Lory on Monday night.

He had gone on piling in the bags, discovering now that they had to be restacked before the lid would close. Annoyed, hurrying, he barked a knuckle.

"Miriam!" he shouted toward the house.

She answered close at hand and he saw that, unnoticed, his wife had come out and was already in the back seat of the car. He had no choice and was forced to join her, leaving Lory alone in the front seat. She looked so tiny, so much a child, only her head showing over the back of the seat, that there was an automatic impulse to say something to ease her bleak prospect of a long weekend alone at home. But before he could speak, Miriam cut in and snatched his words away, saying exactly what he had planned to say, "Lory, you're sure you'll be all right?"

"Of course," she answered, glancing up at the rear-vision mirror with a smile that he saw was wholly for Miriam.

Squirming, he pulled out a handkerchief and dabbed at the ooze of blood on his knuckle.

His wife saw him. "Grant, what in the world—!"

"Nothing," he grumbled, doubling a fist over the wrapped handkerchief, stuffing his hand in his pocket.

Shifting with the car as it swung the turn off Boulevard Drive, he happened to catch Lory's eyes in the rear-vision mirror. She flashed a quick smile and now it was unmistakably for him. He settled back, reassured. Lory would get a kick out of being in Washington again ... the time she'd come over from Mount Oak and they'd seen John L. Lewis at the Carlton ... that G.E. vice-president saying that what had been General Electric's loss had been ...

Distracted by pleasant reverie, he had allowed the bar of caution to drop and there was the cutting stab of another memory that linked Washington to Lory ... *he had been in Washington that day she had come home from Maine.*

"Is it your hand, dear?" Miriam asked anxiously.

"Hand?" he asked, conscious of revealed blankness, then quickly grasping the opportunity for evasion, worming his hand out of his pocket, shucking the handkerchief. There was only a pea-sized spot of blood on the white linen.

"Let me see," she said, reaching out.

"It's nothing," he grumbled, resisting the tug of her fingers until he felt their damp warmth as they closed over his hand.

"Excited?" he asked, surprising himself, unaware of the instinctive reasoning that had made him say it. But she looked at him as if he had given her some special pleasure, her eyes brighter than he had ever seen them before, somehow prompting him to go on and ask with a teasing smile, "Still worrying about those gold slippers?"

"I'm not worrying about anything," she whispered, "—except you."

"No reason to worry about me," he said gruffly. But he returned the squeeze of her hand, sharing her glance at the rear-vision mirror to make certain that Lory was not watching them, experiencing a moment of intimacy so rare that it completely filled his mind until they crested Orchard Ridge and he saw the airport ahead of them.

Gil Clark had started for the Suffolk airport immediately after
Cash McCall had telephoned from Philadelphia but the B-26 was already over the field when he arrived and, by the time he had parked
his car, the plane was off the runway, wing-sweeping the fence as it
made a tight turn on the apron in front of the gate. He saw that Cash
McCall was at the controls but, in less time than seemed possible, the
door at the back of the cabin opened and Cash was impatiently beck-
oning him up the steps.

"This has to be fast, Gil," he said, hurriedly by-passing the preliminary of a greeting. "I'm flying the Austens to Moon Beach and they'll
be here in a few minutes."

Gil slipped into a lounge chair, limiting himself to a fast glance
around the cabin, feeling the danger of a single unperceptive moment. Whatever it was that had happened had made some undefin-
able change in Cash McCall. There was still that same ease of
manner, the lithe and leathery movement with which he turned to
sit on the arm of the chair across the aisle, but now it seemed somehow
deceptive, concealing a spring-steel tension, coiled and hair-trig-
gered.

"That call I asked you to make yesterday morning?" Cash asked as
an abrupt introduction. "The call to Andscott?"

"Yes?" Gil responded, stiffening, racking his brain to recall every
word that he had said to Keening, searching for something that might
have been an unperceived error.

"I almost called you back and told you to forget it," Cash said with
a sardonic chuckle. "Which goes to show, I suppose, that it's better
to be lucky than bright. If we'd been looking for a smart move, we
couldn't have doped out a better one. That telephone call really
pulled the rug out from under the General. Do you know him?"

"General Danvers? No. Only by reputation."

"Then you don't know him at all. By reputation, he was one of our
great generals—and he must have been—but as a corporation president—" He spread his hands in a gesture of despairing rejection.
"Pitiful spectacle to see a man like that finish out his career as a fumbling old fool."

"I know the company isn't doing too well. They passed their last
dividend."

"Danvers had been trying to get in touch with me all day yesterday. There was a collection of frantic notes and telephone messages when I got back to the hotel—very urgent, had to see me immediately —so I invited him down for dinner. I was certain that he knew about the Gammer Corporation buying Suffolk Moulding, and I suspected that he'd somehow found out that *I* was the Gammer Corporation. I imagined that he was going to put the heat on me to install the new press that he'd been trying to get Austen to buy. Instead, he came storming in, all pop-eyed and red-faced, accusing me of being all kinds of an unprincipled blackguard. I discovered from what he told me that I was out to ruin him and wreck the Andscott Instrument Corporation by refusing to let Suffolk Moulding go on supplying them with molded parts."

Gil stared, dumbfounded. "But how could he accuse *you?* They're the ones who—"

"Danvers informed me that no gentleman would stoop to such a low trick as hiring a spy and sending him down to Andscott on the pretense of looking for a job."

"He didn't mean Paul Bronson?"

"He's thoroughly convinced that Bronson is one of my—I believe he called them my *undercover operatives.*"

"But that's ridiculous."

"According to the General I have dozens of them, but it was Bronson who sneaked out the information that Heckledorf wouldn't take the Andscott business."

"Wouldn't take it? I don't understand."

"I didn't either at first, but by sitting back and letting Danvers accuse me of all the despicable things I'd supposedly done, I finally got the story." He snapped a light to a cigarette. "Did you talk to Bronson about his having been down at Andscott?"

"Yes, I—well, actually he talked to me. Paul's a decent chap and he wanted me to know that he'd—"

"Did Bronson tell you anything about Andscott's operations, anything at all?"

"He talked mostly about his interview with General Danvers—the kind of impression he'd gotten."

"What was that?"

"Very much the same as yours—that he was fumbling pretty badly. That's the main reason Paul wasn't interested in the job they offered him. He said that trading Austen for Danvers would be like jumping from the frying pan into the fire."

"Did he mention anything about patents?"

"Patents? No, sir."

"Do you know anything about a patent that Austen took out in '44—assigned to the Suffolk Moulding Company—a method of eliminating hand wiring in electrical instruments by molding a grid of connectors into a plastic base?"

Gil Clark's first impulse was to excuse himself for never having made a detailed study of all the dozens of patents that Austen had taken out, but he was suddenly struck by what seemed extreme good fortune, a clear recollection of that rainy afternoon when Grant Austen had wasted two hours with a meandering reminiscence of all the things he had invented in the good old days. Grateful now that he had forced himself to listen, Gil was able to resurrect a reasonably detailed description of the patent to which Cash McCall had referred.

"Yes, that checks out," McCall said, stamping out his half-smoked cigarette. "Sounds like the one he was talking about. Austen never did anything with the idea?"

"Well, he was talking about doing some more work on it but I doubt if he ever did. He's let things like that slide pretty badly these last few years. And then, of course, there have been some new developments that have come along since—printed circuits and that sort of thing. I'm no expert but I'd guess they'd be cheaper."

"Apparently the Andscott engineers don't agree. They've sold Danvers that the basic idea is the salvation of their business."

"This patent of Austen's?"

"At least a variation. As I pieced the story together, some engineer at Andscott had worked it out on his own, but when they made their search they found themselves in interference with this Austen patent. Does the name Gratz mean anything to you—Ray Gratz?"

"He was one of Suffolk's engineers. Quit a couple of years ago and went to work for Andscott."

"I thought so," Cash said grimly. "He's the supposed inventor of this process."

Gil Clark's amazement was no longer containable. "Did General Danvers tell you all this?"

Cash chuckled wryly. "There's nothing like anger to loosen a babbling mouth. Every time Danvers accused me of knowing something I *shouldn't* know, he told me something I *didn't* know. All I had to do was sit back and listen."

"Does this tie up in any way with the new press they wanted?"

"They had to have that big press to try out the process on a full production scale. They still weren't certain that it was going to work."

"Do you mean they were going to let Suffolk hold the bag?" Gil demanded, transferring to himself the corporate indignity of the Suffolk Moulding Company. "That if it flopped, it would be Suffolk instead of Andscott that was out the quarter million?"

"That was the general idea," Cash said. "But there was another angle too. I gather they thought that if they could get Austen deeply enough involved, he wouldn't dare kick up a fuss about patent infringement."

"But that was stupid!" Gil protested. "He would have given them a license. Do you really mean that they weren't going to use this new press for cabinets at all—that the whole thing was a phony—just like this story that Heckledorf was ready to take over all their molding business?"

"There may have been a certain legitimacy to the Heckledorf threat," Cash said. "They did go as far as to give Heckledorf samples of all the parts and ask them to figure prices. Danvers' real mistake— this sounds almost incredible but he admitted it himself—was that he got ants and jumped too fast. He pulled the bluff on Austen before he had his answer from Heckledorf."

"And I'll bet Heckledorf's prices were a lot higher than Suffolk's," Gil anticipated.

"Yes, but that wasn't the worst blow. Apparently Heckledorf has some smart boys over there. They found out that all down through the years, Austen has been taking out patents on special presses and mold constructions."

Gil was stunned by the implications of what Cash McCall had discovered. "Do you mean that a lot of Andscotts' parts are tied up by Austen's patents?"

"That's what the despicable Mr. McCall is supposed to have known," Cash smiled. "But apparently Austen didn't even know it himself."

"At least he never realized what it meant," Gil said groggily. "But how can Andscott keep on operating without molded parts?"

"They can't—at least until they work out ways to get around the Suffolk patents. That's possible, of course, but it will take a long time —just to rebuild the molds if nothing else. And a lot of cash, which Andscott doesn't have."

"General Danvers must be crazy!" Gil exclaimed. "Why would he ever let himself get into such an impossible position?"

"To quote the General himself, he finds himself *outflanked*—due, of course, to the unscrupulous tactics of a blackguard named Cash McCall."

"Unscrupulous!" Gil exploded. "What does he call what they were trying to do? It sounds like one of those stories you hear about what used to go on back in the robber baron days. Doesn't the man have any ethical standards at all? What does he think—that you can run a business nowadays the way you fight a war—that *anything* goes?"

"Maybe so," Cash said tolerantly. "But don't be too hard on the old boy. He's really in a spot. If Suffolk Moulding stops supplying molded parts, Andscott is practically out of business for at least six months, maybe longer."

"Well, he's dug his own grave, let him lie in it," Gil flashed back, then suddenly conscious that his show of anger, by contrast with Cash's equanimity, betrayed a serious lack of poise.

Cash saved him by saying, "Yes, I'll have to admit that was my own first reaction. Danvers had me a little annoyed."

"I should think so."

"But I can understand why he feels the way he does about me. You see, I sold Andscott a cabinet plant a year or so ago—the old Padua Furniture Company. It was a good property, worth every cent he paid for it. At the time, Danvers thanked me for giving them the chance to buy it, but afterwards someone discovered that the plant had been offered to Andscott a year before at about half the price they'd paid me. That made the General look like a fool—and there's nothing a man of that stripe hates worse."

"I know," Gil said, thinking of Grant Austen.

"As I said," Cash went on, "Danvers had gotten my back up with his nasty cracks and my first reaction was to make him pay for it— but there was no fun in that, kicking an old man after he was down —so I offered to keep on supplying him."

"You did!"

"Oh, I wasn't being entirely altruistic," Cash said brusquely, almost as if he had been accused of soft-heartedness. "You see, I still have the Andscott stock that I got for Padua Furniture—not that I've wanted to hold it, simply because I haven't been able to get rid of it at a fair price—but, in any event, I had a selfish motive."

"But didn't Danvers know that you were a stockholder when he accused you of trying to wreck the company?"

"It's possible that he doesn't know. I transferred my Andscott stock to the Aurora Corporation and he may not have taken the trouble to find out that I control Aurora. Anyway, I told him that Suffolk Moulding would go on supplying him." He interjected a brief smile. "But I did tell him that there'd be a ten per cent price increase right across the board. I thought that was letting him off easily enough, particularly since I knew from what he'd said that the Heckledorf bids had been even higher than that."

"Now you're talking!" Gil exclaimed, his mind already at work recasting the prospects of the Suffolk Moulding Company. With the

Andscott business restored and prices up ten per cent there was no question that the company could be made extremely profitable.

Cash McCall was shaking his head. "Danvers turned it down."

"Turned it down! But what else can he do?"

"He wants to buy Suffolk Moulding."

"Buy it? But how can—"

"It's his opinion that a fine company like Andscott Instrument dares not jeopardize its future by having vital parts produced by a source of supply controlled by an *operator* like Cash McCall."

"I don't see how you kept from socking the guy," Gil marveled.

"Oh, he's an old man," Cash tossed off. "Anyway, he wound up by offering me three hundred thousand shares of Andscott common."

Gil found his mind torn between an instinctive urge to fight back against the sale of Suffolk Moulding Company and the realization that there was an enormous profit to be made—if, as he recalled Paul Bronson having told him, Andscott stock was selling for about ten dollars a share.

As had happened so many times before, Cash McCall seemed to have read his mind. "Yes, if I could get the market price—somewhere around ten—it would be a good deal. But of course I couldn't, not as things stand now. The market for Andscott stock is thin as the devil. Has been ever since they passed their last dividend. I know because I've been trying to work off some of the stock I already have. If someone were to dump a sizable block—even ten thousand shares —the price would hit the skids."

"Then you aren't going to sell?" Gil asked, barely managing to hide a show of relief.

"I don't know," Cash mused. "The darned thing has me intrigued. If I could somehow manage to get *control—*"

"Control of Andscott?"

Cash nodded. "With the stock I'd get for Suffolk—what I already have and what I know I could pick up—I could put together about a half million shares."

"But it would take a lot more than that for control, wouldn't it?"

"Yes, there'd still be a long way to go—and if I missed I'd really be stuck, several million tied up in Andscott stock and no way to get out from under. But if I *could* pull it off—"

There had been the savoring of danger in the sound of his voice, the look of high excitement in his narrowing eyes, at last an open revelation of the tension that Gil had sensed the moment he boarded the plane.

"You'd change management, of course?" Gil prompted.

Cash nodded, but as if the response had come from some detached segment of his mind. The racing mainstream of his thought seemed uninterrupted, his voice unable to keep pace, snatching out a phrase here and there, almost as if he were making notes. "Wash out that white elephant television business—hopeless without a distribution system. Get back to the basic electronic business—beef up research—build back the development staff—concentrate on computers and automation components. Put the whole company on an economy diet—get rid of the belly-fat. A year and we could have operations in the black again. One decent dividend and there *would* be a market for the stock—get the price back to where it was—fifteen—"

Fifteen! Gil Clark's hope that Suffolk Moulding might not be sold was overwhelmed by the prospect Cash McCall opened up. If the Suffolk Moulding block could be sold for fifteen dollars a share, there would be a profit of *two and a half million dollars!* And that was only part of it. Cash had two hundred thousand more shares to sell. That would mean at least another million in profit. And it would all be a capital gain. Suffolk Moulding couldn't add that much to cash surplus if it were operated for twenty years. They would be crazy not to sell if . . .

They? For the briefest instant, barely perceived, Gil Clark was conscious of the plural pronoun. Whatever reserve he may have had before was submerged now in the excitement of participation.

"It sounds terrific," he heard himself say, conscious after he had spoken that what he had said might be out of context with Cash's last unheard words, then hurriedly adding, "But it would all hinge on being able to get control, wouldn't it?"

"Yes, that's the big *if,*" Cash said. "But there's a chance—an outside one, I'll admit—but still a chance. Have you ever heard of the Andrews Foundation?"

"Isn't it a medical-research setup?"

"Yes. It was established by Horace Andrews. He was one of the two founders of Andscott—Andrews and Scott—that's where the name came from."

"I know," Gil said, vaguely recalling something he had read or heard.

"Andrews left all of his Andscott stock to the Foundation. At that time—'49—they had a majority interest. Since then there've been other stock issues so the Foundation doesn't have a majority now, but Lockwood and his boys have been working on it all night and they're certain that if we could add a Foundation proxy to our own half million shares, it would mean control."

"Then it would all depend on lining up the Foundation's support?"

"Right," Cash said crisply. "The Foundation is dependent on Andscott dividends for its financial support and, with no dividends, they must be feeling the pinch. They *should* be interested in getting a new management into Andscott that would put the company back on a profitable basis again. But whether the pressure is strong enough yet to force Bergmann into a break with Danvers—well, that's the question."

"Bergmann is the head of the Foundation?"

"Yes, Dr. Martin Bergmann. As far as we're concerned, he *is* the Foundation. There's a board of governors, but they're all research scientists—so's Bergmann for that matter—but he's the administrative head and, according to Lockwood's information, the board invariably rides with him on financial matters."

"Then it all depends on Bergmann?"

"And getting his support may prove difficult," Cash admitted. "Bergmann was very close to Horace Andrews and putting in General Danvers as the president of Andscott was the old man's last move. There'd be a sentimental tug there—tossing out Andrews' choice—plus the fact that apparently Danvers has done a good job of buttering up Bergmann. He's put him on the Andscott board, entertained him socially, had him down in Nassau last winter—so it doesn't look as if the odds were in favor of Bergmann breaking with Danvers. Still there's a chance."

"But if he doesn't, won't the Foundation fold up—I mean, if they're dependent on Andscott dividends?"

"Eventually, yes—but it's a question of timing. I don't know how much of a businessman Bergmann is. It's possible he may not realize how bad the situation really is."

"But couldn't we make him realize it—get to him some way—make him see how hopeless it is as long as Danvers stays in control?"

Cash shook his head. "If Bergmann is still in the Danvers camp, the minute we tried to talk to him the word would get back that we were out to get control."

"I guess that's right," Gil mumbled, feeling himself chastised for stupidity.

"Our only hope is that Bergmann has already made up his mind to break," Cash supplied. "That's what we have to find out."

"But how can we?"

"And even if he has," Cash went on, brushing aside the question, "there's no assurance that he'd give *me* his support. That's question number two—Bergmann's attitude toward being tied up with Cash McCall."

"You mean that he—?" Gil found his voice choked off by the memory of how he himself would have reacted to the name of Cash Mc-Call only a few days ago.

"I've crossed Bergmann's path before," Cash went on. "At the time I got control of the Cox-Farrington Company, he was there as the head of their research laboratories."

"Cox-Farrington? That's the X-ray company, isn't it?"

Cash nodded. "The company was badly overexpanded after the war and I had to ride a little roughshod to get it down to earth again. As soon as I got rid of the old Farrington crowd and brought in a new president, Bergmann resigned. I didn't talk to him myself—in fact I've never seen the man—but I'm reasonably certain that he felt extremely resentful toward me. Possibly he's changed his mind. What's happened at Cox-Farrington since proves that the moves I made were what saved the company—but Bergmann may not know that. Even if he does, he may still be harboring a prejudice. That's what you have to find out."

"Me?" Gil asked, stunned.

"I called George Lockwood as soon as Danvers left my apartment. His boys have been digging for dope all night. They'll have a report on Bergmann ready for you at Conway's office at ten o'clock—every scrap of information that they've been able to pull together. Soak it up—get all the background on Bergmann you can—then go out and have a talk with him."

"But what if I muff the ball—"

"Then the deal's off, that's all."

"And you lose a chance to make two or three million dollars," Gil said, dry-mouthed at the enormousness of his responsibility.

Cash grinned, "This isn't worm fishing, Gil."

"I'll say not!"

"I know it's a gamble—a long one. But if we *could* pull it off—well, it would be the biggest one yet. You don't get a break like this very often."

"I shouldn't think so," Gil said weakly.

"Funny how the breaks come," Cash mused. "I'd almost convinced myself that buying Suffolk had been a mistake—and then, right out of the blue, in walks General Danvers and tosses this in my lap. I've had a lot of breaks but this tops them all."

Half listening, Gil waited for a chance to say, "Are you sure that I'm the right person to talk to Bergmann?"

Cash's face clouded. "Would you rather not?"

"No, I want to do it," Gil said hurriedly. "If you think I can handle it."

"You've got the best chance of anyone. You're managing the Suffolk plant. You have the responsibility of advising your principals as to whether or not they should sell and take Andscott stock in payment. What would be more logical than for you to go to Andscott's largest stockholder for an opinion as to the soundness of Andscott's management? You ask a lot of questions and that gives you a chance to see where Bergmann stands. If you decide that he might ride along, then you can raise the possibility of our getting together to force a reorganization."

"But won't Bergmann know that you're behind it? You say he's a director of Andscott. Danvers must have talked to his directors to get approval of the offer. Wouldn't he have told them that they were buying Suffolk from you?"

"Apparently not," Cash said. "Lockwood has a pipeline to one director and all he'd been told was that Suffolk was being bought from the Gammer Corporation—nothing beyond that."

"But Bergmann *might* know—or guess."

"Of course," Cash acknowledged. "In that case, there's only one thing to do, obviously—tell him the truth. He'll have to know in the end, anyway."

"And if he—?"

"If the old prejudice is still there, the deal's off—unless, of course, you can convince him that I'm not quite as unsavory a character as he imagines." He glanced out through the porthole, suddenly alerted. "There are the Austens. If you have any more questions, talk them over with Winston Conway."

Gil rose. "When will I see you?"

Cash was still looking out through the porthole and his answer was slow in coming, astoundingly casual when it did. "Oh, call me at the hotel about five o'clock. I should be back by then. You have my number, haven't you?"

"Yes, I have it."

There were no more instructions and Gil Clark went down the plane's steps, breaking into a run as he headed for the gate. He caught a glimpse of Lory Austen and her mother, but they were looking out toward the plane and, with no time to spare, he ran on toward his car. He was away from the fence, making the turn into the lane, when he saw Grant Austen standing at the back of the Cadillac, the half-raised trunk lid in his hands, plainly watching him. But in the moment that it took Gil to get his arm out of the window, Austen looked away and did not see him wave.

The glimpse that Grant Austen caught of Gil Clark seemed strangely irrelevant, the intrusion of something oddly misplaced, the fleeting memory of a world long lost. During those first few days after he had stopped going to the plant, he had worried about the stupid blunders that Gil was undoubtedly committing, plowing ahead on his own without even showing the good sense to telephone for advice and counsel when he found he was in over his head. But as the days had gone by that concern had melted away. All that remained now was a vague resentment that arose with the thought of Gil occupying his private office and using his private washroom. Even that reaction, weak as it was, was further dulled by the difficulty of resurrecting a sharply detailed memory of what his office had looked like. Astoundingly, the mental image had already bleached to a fuzzy blur. It was hard to believe that it was only nine days since he had first met Cash McCall ... and now here he was coming down the steps of his B-26, smiling and just as friendly as he could be! And this *was* friendship, nothing else. The company didn't have anything to do with this. Suffolk Moulding was water over the dam. This was *personal*. Cash McCall could have given him the brush-off, too ... just as Will Atherson and Harrison Glenn had done. But he hadn't. Winston Conway had been right the other night when he'd said that Cash McCall was a really *big* man ... and there was another fine man, that Winston Conway!

Out of the corner of his eye, Grant Austen watched McCall walk in from the plane, timing himself so that he would finish taking out the luggage just as Cash got to the car. Then he would walk around and greet him without making a scene of it ... casually ... the way it was done at The Wharf ... and in Washington.

But Miriam ruined everything, calling out and making Cash stop up there at the front of the car.

Grant Austen hung back, pretending an intent examination of a scratch on his two-suiter.

"Did you hear that, Grant?" Miriam called back to him. "Mr. McCall has asked Lory if she doesn't want to come along with us, just down and back for the ride?"

He had no choice now except to step around the fender and face Cash McCall.

"Isn't that nice of him, dear?" Miriam insisted.

"Sure, you bet—that is, if it isn't too much trouble," he felt himself forced to say, even before he had a chance to shake hands.

And it was easy to see that Mr. McCall, too, felt how clumsy the situation was, fumbling his explanation that it was no trouble at all, that he had to come back this way, anyway. Only after all that was out of the way could they shake hands ... and now it had come too late, awkwardly formal, pleasureless.

"That's quite a plane you've got there," Grant Austen said, finally back on a straight course.

"It's an old B-26 that I picked up and had converted," Cash said modestly ... the way a really big man always said things like that.

"Well, I'll just say that the gang down at Moon Beach is going to get a kick out of seeing something like that come in," Grant Austen said, attempting to generate the hearty warmth that he wanted the moment to have. "Harv Bannon has his own plane—Cavalier Chemical, you know? Nice plane but it can't hold a candle to yours."

Mr. McCall just smiled, signaling to the gateman who came over to pick up the bags, and Grant Austen turned to his daughter, ready to urge her to accept Mr. McCall's invitation to go along for the ride.

Lory was already snapping the buttons to lock the doors.

Surprised, he said, "Sure, the car will be all right until you get back, Lory. Just see that it's locked."

Getting out, locking the last door, she forgot that you didn't have to use the key ... excited ... but you couldn't blame her for that. It wasn't every day she had a chance to go down to Moon Beach in a private B-26.

They walked together, the four of them, out through the gate and across the black-topped apron, he and Cash stepping aside as they reached the plane, Miriam and Lory going up the steps to the cabin. He was startled to hear Lory say to her mother, even before she had looked inside, "You're going to love this, it's such a beautiful plane," surprised at her implication that she had seen it before. But then he recalled that Lory had driven Mr. McCall out here to the airport yesterday ... he'd probably invited her aboard, just to be nice to her. He was the kind of man who'd do a thing like that ... thoughtful. That was one way you could always tell a really big man ... always thoughtful. There was a good point there, something to remember in Washington.

••••• 5

Goaded by the fast-circling minute hand of his watch, Gil Clark had driven from the Suffolk airport to downtown Philadelphia in one hour flat. It was nine fifty-five when he pulled into the parking lot on Sansom Street. Cash McCall had not made it a matter of any special urgency that he be at Conway's office at precisely ten o'clock, but he had accepted that necessity as a tangible first objective, mind-filling enough to keep himself from being overwhelmed by apprehension.

Out of the car, the full weight of his assignment pressed down. Hurrying, his anxious fingers tore a page in the telephone book as he searched out the location of Conway's office, his preoccupation so complete that he was a half block away from the parking lot before he realized that the offices of Jamison, Conway & Slythe were in the same building as those of Corporation Associates.

Proximity aroused the anticipation of offices similar in character, an expectation immediately canceled as he stepped from the elevator. The reception room in which the clients of Jamison, Conway & Slythe were received was, except in minor detail, indistinguishable from the center hall of one of the finer old eighteenth century manor houses. Winston Conway's private office, to which Gil was immediately escorted, might well have been the library of that same aristocratic home and Winston Conway, rising from the beautifully inlaid table that served him as a desk, was every inch the lord of the manor, arousing in Gil's mind not only a sharp consciousness of his junior status but also the memory of Conway having said, when they had breakfasted together in Suffolk, that he had many reasons for being grateful to Cash McCall. One was undoubtedly financial.

"Lockwood called to say that he would be a few minutes late," Conway explained as he led the way to a grouping of Philadelphia stick chairs around an antique butterfly table. "You may recall, Mr. Clark, that yesterday morning I offered an observation on the futility of attempting to outguess our Mr. McCall."

"You were sure right," Gil said, grateful that Conway had opened the subject with no time-wasting preliminaries. "It looks like a terrific deal, doesn't it?"

"Terrific?" Conway asked, weighing the word. "In what sense—*tremendous* or *terrifying?* Forgive me for sounding captious, but it's a professional habit—rather deeply ingrained, I fear—and I do want to be certain of your precise meaning."

Winston Conway was playing his word game again and Gil felt a prickle of annoyance, recognized too late to keep him from reaching back to the memory of his meeting with Cash McCall for the quick retort, "Well, it's not worm fishing."

The words were no sooner out of his mouth than he realized, unhappily, that he was getting off to the worst possible start. He needed Conway's help and support and now, foolishly, he had let nervous tension destroy his poise.

Surprisingly, the lawyer's face did not harden. There was a perceptible softening, almost a crumbling, as he leaned forward, palms flat to the table. "Sorry, Gil. I deserved that. Nerves are a little on edge. Not enough sleep. Cash called me about midnight and I haven't been able to get this thing off my mind. You're quite right—it's a terrific deal."

Gil exhaled slowly, consciously giving his voice a deference that was a clear acceptance of Conway's apology. "Something worrying you, sir?"

The lawyer used a weary sigh as an affirmative acknowledgment. "But don't let that concern you too much. I've been wrong before, I can be wrong again. Actually, it's probably a good omen. It often works that way with Mr. McCall's deals—the ones that most frighten me usually come off best."

"Well, I'm a little concerned about one thing myself," Gil admitted. "This Bergmann business—"

"Then that's still the plan—for you to talk to Dr. Bergmann? I've been hoping Mr. McCall had changed his mind about that. When did you talk to him?"

"About an hour ago."

"Then he's still in town?"

"No, I saw him at the Suffolk airport. He came in there to pick up the Austens. He's flying them down to Moon Beach this morning."

"The girl too?"

Gil hesitated at the unexpected question. "At least she was out there at the airport."

"I've been thinking about what you said yesterday—the fact that they must have known each other before. I still find myself unable to give it any significance."

"I didn't mean to imply that it had any, sir," Gil said quickly. "It was just something that I mentioned because—"

"I know," Conway cut in as if suddenly aware of having wandered down a sidetrack. "So he still wants you to see Bergmann?"

"Yes, that's the plan."

Winston Conway fingered the pewter inkwell that stood on the table. "Do you have any background on Mr. McCall's prior relationship with Dr. Bergmann?"

"If you mean the Cox-Farrington story—yes, he told me that."

There was a moment of silence broken only by the metronome beat of Conway's forefinger tapping the inkstand. "I still can't bring myself to like the idea."

"But there's no alternative," Gil protested. "At least I can't see one. Cash would be crazy to sink two million dollars in Andscott if he weren't certain of getting control."

"Two million?" Conway questioned.

"Yes, I know," Gil said. "It's really more than that. There's the stock he got in the Padua Furniture deal, too."

"Do you know that he's planning to buy even more?"

Gil hesitated. "Well, yes—yes, he did say there was some more he might get his hands on."

The lawyer gestured toward his desk. "There's a twenty-four hour option over there for another big block. He's instructed me to exercise it as soon as we're certain of Bergmann's support. That's another million dollars."

Gil Clark felt the crush of added responsibility. Before, he had visualized the loss of a profit as the only penalty of failure, thinking that if the deal didn't go through, Cash McCall would still own Suffolk Moulding and be no worse off than he had been at the start. Now there was an extra million dollars at stake, committed beyond recall once the decision to move was made.

"You were right when you said this isn't worm fishing," Conway commented sardonically. "And the bait comes high. That million would be as good as lost if something went wrong."

"But what *could* go wrong?" Gil asked earnestly. "If we're certain of Dr. Bergmann's support—and we won't move, of course, until we are?"

"You do recognize, don't you, that Mr. McCall *won't* have control until the three hundred thousand shares he'll get for Suffolk Moulding have been issued and transferred? Before that can be done, there must be stockholder approval to raise the charter authorization. The law requires sixty days notice. That means two months before the deal could be consummated—two months when he won't have control—two months when anything might happen."

"You aren't suggesting that the stockholders might *not* approve."

"I suggest nothing beyond a *possibility*."

"But what else can Andscott do? They've got to have Suffolk Moulding in order to keep operating."

"Consider this, Gil—why is General Danvers so anxious to buy Suffolk Moulding?"

"Because he was fool enough to get himself in a position where it's the only way out."

Conway shook his head. "No, that isn't completely true. Didn't Mr. McCall offer to continue supplying Andscott with parts?"

"Yes, but—"

"Exactly!" the lawyer said with point-clinching emphasis. "General Danvers' real motivation is his personal prejudice against Cash McCall, the feeling that he didn't want anything controlled by him, even a source of supply."

"Far be it from me to defend Danvers," Gil countered, "but after all, there is some logic in what he's doing. Andscott *should* get its hands on those patents."

"Granted," Conway said. "But one of the axioms I've learned to trust is never to accept logic as a prime motivation when personal prejudice is obviously present."

"I'm afraid I don't see what you're getting at, sir."

"I'm assuming that Mr. McCall told you the things that Danvers accused him of doing."

"Yes, he told me," Gil said, his voice colored by the memory of anger.

"Then you must grant that Danvers has a rather violent prejudice against Mr. McCall."

"Of course."

"Very well. Now what do you think General Danvers' reaction would be if, some time during that two months period before the deal finally went through, he discovered that by letting Cash get his hands on those three hundred thousand shares he was actually handing over control of the company? Wouldn't Danvers find some way to block the deal? It wouldn't take much, you know, only enough votes to keep the new issue from being approved."

"But he'd be in an impossible situation!"

"As bad as being booted out and branded a failure? Think about that, Gil. General Danvers is a famous man—and very much aware of it. He'd fight back fang and claw, no holds barred. He's a fighter, Gil. And don't imagine that he wouldn't rally a lot of support. He would! Yes, I know—he's in trouble over there now—but he won some battles in the war that looked bad for a while. Winning lost battles is a part of the Danvers legend."

"He'll never win this one."

"I'll agree that he shouldn't," Conway said. "But suppose it came down to an open proxy fight between Danvers and Cash McCall. General Danvers is a national hero, one of the best-known men in the country."

"And Cash McCall is one of the least known," Gil reluctantly conceded.

"He's known only by the rumors about him," Conway said grimly, "and they're not in his favor. Suppose you were an Andscott stockholder, knowing no more about Cash McCall than you did before you went to work for him, only the rumors you'd heard—"

"But he *would* put a sound management into Andscott," Gil protested. "He'd have to—that's the only way he can get the company back on its feet. How else could he cash in if he didn't? That's what the stockholders want, isn't it—a profitable company?"

"You don't have to argue with me," Conway smiled. "*I* know he'd do it—and *you* know it—but I still ask if you would have given him your proxy a month ago?"

"Maybe not," Gil conceded, recalling only too vividly the thoughts that had been in his mind as late as last week. "And I suppose that's going to be the trouble in trying to line up Dr. Bergmann. He probably feels the same way about Cash McCall that so many people do."

Winston Conway started to respond but got no further than a nod of agreement when he was cut off by his secretary coming in with the Lockwood reports which she explained had just arrived. There were four volumes, all bound in the same leatherette cover that Gil recalled from the report on the Cavalier Chemical Company.

"Good," Conway said after examining the labels. "He's sent us two copies of each. This one is Andscott Instrument." He indicated the thicker of the two volumes and handed across a copy of the thinner one, "And here's our friend Bergmann."

Gil took the report and, after a hurried scanning of the fifty-odd pages, followed Winston Conway's example and settled down to read. The report was an astounding document, an incredibly detailed assemblage of biographical fact, put together with great perception of the purpose for which it was to be used. There was far more than the bare bone outline of Dr. Bergmann's professional career as a research physicist, widely honored for his contributions to the science of roentgenology and the development of electromechanical aids to diagnosis and therapy. The Lockwood report added the flesh and blood of a human being, personal detail assembled with infinite patience and quite obviously the result of some very clever detective work.

After the first ten pages, Gil could not restrain himself from comment. "This is really something, isn't it?"

Conway looked up. "Yes, they do a very competent job, don't they?"

"I thought we used to get out some pretty fair survey reports up at Corporation Associates," Gil said, "but they didn't hold a candle to what Lockwood does. In fact, I never realized there *were* reports like this. How in the world do they get all their dope?"

The question seemed to please Conway. "That's a very interesting story. You'd enjoy a day over there sometime, just going over their operations."

"I'd like to do it."

"That's one of our assignments," Conway explained. "Giving them a check-up now and then to be certain that they haven't strayed from the straight and narrow. Lockwood is a bit annoyed at times, I fear. He regards Mr. McCall as being a little too straight-laced for this day and age—he'll have nothing to do with wire-tapping or any of that sort of thing. In fact—I imagine you know this—that's the reason he bought the agency—to control it and make certain that nothing off base was done."

"But what they do get their hands on is still astounding," Gil marveled.

"Yes, it really is," Conway agreed. "But as you'll see when you get over there, it's all quite legitimate. An amazing amount of information that seems very secret to the man who thinks it is, isn't really secret at all. Take credit information, for example. I often wonder if the average businessman realizes how many of the skeletons in his closet are common knowledge to a great many people."

"I've seen some credit reports that have made me wonder the same thing."

"And I've speculated, too," Conway went on, "how many fewer conventions there would be—and how many cocktail bars would close down—if it weren't for the tongue-loosening effect of a couple of good dry Martinis. The right word, dropped in the wrong place, can be very dangerous—or extraordinarily valuable, depending upon which side of the fence you're on."

"What's the legal situation on that sort of thing?" Gil asked.

"Oh, rather vague," Conway said. "And I'd say getting progressively more so. Actually, what law there is has been largely undermined by a shift in general attitude. There was a time, of course, when the invasion of a man's privacy by eavesdropping was considered rather serious. Today, we've largely come around to the counter-view that there must be something wrong with any man who objects to having his privacy invaded—the point I was making in our talk at breakfast."

"I know," Gil acknowledged, but trying to think his way through the seeming anomaly of Cash McCall owning an agency engaged in penetrating the same sort of secrecies that he so zealously guarded in his own case.

"By the way," Conway asked, indicating the report, "where are you reading?"

"Page eleven."

"Skip back to forty-one," the lawyer said. "I always read these things backward—get the last first. Quite interesting bit here—this outline of the social relationship between the Bergmanns and the Danverses."

Gil found the page and began to read, amazed again at the Lockwood skill. With no more evidence than had been available in a file of clippings taken from the society pages of the newspapers, a fascinating fabric had been woven to reveal the personal relationship between General Danvers and Dr. Martin Bergmann. Until a year ago last January, the names of Dr. and Mrs. Bergmann had never appeared on the guest list of one of the big Danvers dinner parties. Suddenly, they had blossomed out as guests of honor. Two weeks later they were reported as house guests at the Danverses' winter home in Nassau. Both events immediately preceded the annual meeting of the stockholders of the Andscott Instrument Corporation.

"As you'll note," Conway pointed out, "that was the meeting where it was first revealed that the company was in serious difficulty. It seems a likely conjecture that General Danvers was attempting to prevent stockholder trouble by making a personal friend of Dr. Bergmann. You might note, too, that there was the further flattery of electing him to the Andscott board."

The report went on to offer continuing evidence. The Bergmanns had been in the Danverses' box at the spring horse show, together on a July trip to Maine, pictured at the Danverses' table at the Military Ball. Then, three months ago, it had all stopped as suddenly as it had begun.

"Look at that second paragraph on forty-three," Conway said, then reading, "There have been open-house receptions at the Andrews Foundation every year since its establishment. Always before, General Danvers has been on the program for a talk. This year his name did not appear even on the list of invited guests."

"This really looks encouraging," Gil said, reading on. "Don't you think so, sir?"

There was no reply and he looked up to see the lawyer's face frozen in astonishment, staring at a penciled note that had been added at the bottom of the last page of the report. Turning the page, Gil saw that the same note was in his copy:

4/2 Dr. Bergmann left his home at 8:05 A.M. and drove to 1304 Wheelwright Road, home of Mr. and Mrs. John Allenby. Left at 9:17 A.M. and drove to Andrews Foundation.

"Good lord, don't you see what this means?" Conway demanded. "If Dr. Bergmann has gone to Allenby for advice—you know who Allenby is, of course?"

Gil shook his head.

"He's president of Cox-Farrington, the man that Cash McCall put in when he reorganized the business. If there were any bad feelings on Bergmann's part, surely he wouldn't have gone to Allenby." He stopped, suddenly cautious. "But that may be wishful thinking. We ought to know for sure. I wonder if I should call Allenby?"

"Do you know him?"

"Oh, yes. Worked with him on a couple of Mr. McCall's deals before he went into Cox-Farrington—the same way I'm working with you on this one." He reached for the telephone. "He may not be in a position to tell me anything—Bergmann may have sworn him to secrecy—but it's worth the gamble."

While the call was being put through, Gil wandered off toward the windows that looked down upon the street, his mounting excitement broken only by a momentary recognition of the parallel between himself and John Allenby that Conway had suggested, a line of thought snapped at the instant he heard the lawyer start to speak over the telephone.

There was an exchange of introductory banter and then, almost as soon as Winston Conway mentioned Bergmann's name, the lawyer fell silent, listening intently. His occasional interjections were meaningless, offering no clue to what he was hearing.

"All right, John, I'll take over and see that it's followed up," Winston Conway said to conclude the conversation, only then smiling as he turned to Gil Clark. His right hand raised to an oath-taking position. "I, Winston Conway, solemnly swear that I shall never again doubt the unassailable perspicacity of Cash McCall."

"What's happened, sir?"

"I should have known," Conway said with a chuckling sigh. "While we've been sitting here worrying about whether or not you should talk to Bergmann, Allenby has been trying to reach Cash to set up that very meeting—at Bergmann's request!"

"You mean that *Bergmann* wants the meeting?" Gil asked groggily.

288

Conway nodded but did not reply, lost in silent speculation, suddenly broken when he got to his feet. "You'd better get out there, Gil. There's no time to lose. General Danvers is pressuring Bergmann for a decision as to whether or not he'll support the proposal to buy Suffolk Moulding."

"But he *has* to support it," Gil said, alarmed. "If he doesn't, we're licked before we start."

"Exactly. Driving your own car?"

"Yes."

"I'd take a cab if I were you. Give you a chance to study this report on the way out. According to Allenby, Bergmann's pretty well worked up over what's happened. He may require a little handling. In any event, it won't hurt you to have all the background you can get."

Gil had already picked up his topcoat. "Maybe I ought to call him first to make an appointment."

"I'll call him and tell him you're on your way," Conway said, reaching out to hold his coat, making it a gesture that could not have been more deferential if he had been serving Cash McCall himself. "I'm sorry to have plagued you with all my pointless worrying. I should have known better."

Gil Clark was going down in the elevator before his mind cleared enough to question the lawyer's last remark. Winston Conway's concern had been about General Danvers, not Dr. Bergmann. That situation was in no way changed. Or was it? Had Allenby told Conway something that the lawyer had not repeated?

••••• 6

A mechanical voice, barely recognizable as Cash McCall's, burst in from a loudspeaker hidden in the plane's ceiling, telling them to fasten their seat belts, that they would be landing at Moon Beach in five minutes. Lory Austen responded with the same lift of courage that an all but exhausted runner feels upon finally sighting the tape. Bad as it had been, she knew now that she could see it through to the end.

Sitting in the cabin with her parents, there had been none of the exhilaration of rapturously free flight that she had experienced yesterday at Cash's side in the cockpit. Instead, she had felt imprisonment, the onerous punishment of being forced to talk and talk, feeding her father's egocentric pleasure in being so luxuriously transported to Moon Beach, responding to his fulsome descriptions of the hotel's wonders, rationalizing her lack of sincerity as the feeling of a righteously discharged duty, excusing the white lie of her pretended interest as the final payment on the price of freedom.

But it was all her own fault. Cash had given her a chance of escape, looking at her after they had come aboard, silently asking whether she wanted to join him in the cockpit. It was yesterday's error of omission that had forced her to decline. Her mistake had been in not telling her mother about going to Aurora Valley with Cash ... not because there had been need or reason for secrecy, only because she had gone directly to her studio after she had arrived home, not seeing her mother until late afternoon ... and by then her father had gotten home from Philadelphia. But it was just as well the way it was. If she had gone up front with Cash, there would have been the silly temptation to go on hoping that yesterday hadn't been the end. It *was* the end! Cash had only asked her to come along today because he knew it was something her father had wanted ... and she had only done it because agreement was easier than refusal. They would be together on the way back, of course ... he'd probably ask her to ride up front again ... but it wouldn't matter now. She had made her decision yesterday. There would be no more little-girl fantasies from now on, no foolish hopes, no senseless daydreams that could come to no end but nightmares of terrorizing ecstasy.

Her father had been speaking to her and she had let his words beat unheard against her ears, but her mother's voice, lower and softer, broke through. "I wish I hadn't told Anna that she could go to Reading this afternoon. But you'll be all right, won't you? It's just for the night and she *is* counting on it."

"Of course I'll be all right," Lory said, responding to the hunger for intimacy that showed so plainly in her mother's eyes. Miriam had sat across the aisle from them all during the flight, somehow separated by a distance greater than the space between their chairs, taking less and less part in their conversation, peculiarly preoccupied except when her husband made some demand for a show of pleasure.

There was another demand now as he excitedly identified the Atlantic Ocean. Lory kept her eyes on her mother, seeing the attention that lighted her expression, wondering if her interest could possibly be as sincere as she made it seem, asking herself if it were possible that she failed to realize that this trip was a fool's errand.

Grant Austen's demand for the sharing of excitement was repeated now, stronger, and Lory turned to him, seeing him in cold appraisal. There was no reason for him to come to this convention ... he'd sold the company, he was out of the business ... what could he hope to gain by this silly hanging on, this pointless clinging? He was an old man whose abilities had been consumed, slipping now into the first stages of bothersome senility, his ego straw-stuffed with meaningless desires, the childishness of his silly hunger for self-importance. It was a good thing that he was rich.

Suddenly conscious of having gone beyond bounds, she flinched at the cruelty of bare thought, even attempting to feel sorry for him. But the only honest compassion she could feel was for her mother.

The plane was turning now, out over the ocean, and she looked down, seeing the blue-gray water edged with the white ruffle of breakers on the beach. There was another turn and she saw that the earth was green, reasoning the quick explanation that by flying south they had intercepted the north-moving tide of spring. The trees that streaked under them as the plane settled to the runway were in full leaf.

"There it is!" Grant Austen said excitedly, his face pressed to the porthole. "Look, Lory, look! You bet, that's old Moon Beach. See it, Miriam?" He was already struggling with his seat belt, loosening its grip on his little pot belly as the plane touched down with a soft thud and rolled along the runway.

The land was flat, the earth color that of cruelly sunburned flesh, covered with mangy patches of green-grassed hair, pockmarked by the golf course that bordered the airport. Beyond, against a file of pine trees as tattered as old scenery, was the brilliantly white and high-pillared veranda of the Moon Beach Club, the front façade an ineffectual attempt to hide the grayed purple stucco of the hotel's back wings. There was not a living soul in sight, neither on the golf course nor on the veranda of the hotel. The hangar that had come to a stop outside the porthole was lifeless, deserted.

Attention diverted, Lory almost missed Cash's quick passage down the length of the cabin and, before she could loosen her seat belt and swing her chair, her father was up and heading for the door.

She offered a hand to her mother who rose hesitantly from her seat, found her purse for her and tucked down the upturned collar of her blouse. "You'll have a wonderful time, Mother. I know you will."

Miriam Austen looked at her without direct response, her face tortured with something suppressed, and Lory yielded to impulse and kissed her on the cheek. Her mother's reaction was unexpectedly emotional, the tight squeeze of her circling arm, a tremor in her voice as she whispered, "Everything's going to be all right, Lory."

It seemed an odd remark, revealingly self-centered, until Lory became aware that her mother had been looking toward the now opened door where Cash stood against the arch-topped rectangle of brilliant sunlight. Was it possible that her mother was imagining that there could be something between her and Cash? The truth was an encouragement to boldness and she let her eyes meet her mother's, openly revealing, hiding nothing, feeling the full strength of her resolution not to be victimized by imagination, her own or anyone else's.

They walked together to the door, silent until her mother thanked Cash. "I can't tell you how grateful I am, Mr. McCall. It was a wonderful trip."

"Glad you enjoyed it," he said, his hand guiding her to the first step.

Grant Austen was already on the ground, his expression one of disabling disappointment. "Where the devil is everybody?" he grumbled aimlessly into space. "They always have those little buggies down here to take you up to the club."

"Here comes someone," Lory heard Cash say as he followed her down the steps.

A turkey-necked man ambled out of the little office in the corner of the hangar, yawning, tugging at the visor of a duck-billed cap. "Morning, folks. Guess you all going up to the hotel, huh? They'll be a coming in a minute. I called 'em when I saw you landing."

"Where is everybody?" Grant Austen demanded, looking out across the deserted golf course.

"Wasn't expecting nobody this early. You about the first I guess. Most of 'em coming this afternoon on the special." His eyes wandered. "Man, that's sure one nice airplane. Don't many like that come in here. Can't recollect even one."

Lory saw her father's face brighten. "Mr. McCall's," he said, turning to bestow a magnanimous gesture on his host. But Cash had gone back up the steps again and was handing out the luggage. She watched him, every motion a flowing line, the line drawn in liquid fire by the strong top lighting of the high sun.

"About time!" her father snorted.

She turned toward the hotel, her eyes guided by the sound of tinkling bells, distant but growing closer. A pony cart was coming down the sandy lane, the carriage gaudily yellow-fringed, the ponies cockaded with red pompons, the driver in green livery and a white turban, the whole effect one of a backstage theatricalism unwisely exposed to the light of day.

"This was what I was telling you about," her father said, proudly possessive, and Lory managed a passable smile of approval, surprised when she glanced aside and saw that her mother had outdone her.

Despite the driver's frantic show of high-pitched shouts and some mild response from the ponies, the movement of the carriage toward them was excruciatingly slow. But it finally reached them, the driver losing his turban as he jumped down.

"Sure you don't want to come up and see the place?" Grant Austen asked Cash McCall as the luggage was being piled behind the pony cart's single seat. "It's really something."

Gratefully, she heard Cash answer. "Sorry, but I'm a little pushed today."

Her father clambered into the buggy after her mother was seated, sitting heavily, frightening the ponies, and they lurched ahead, their little legs back-slanted as they strained against the now weighted carriage and the drag of the loose sand on the wheels.

Thankful that what might have been an endless leavetaking had been so fortunately terminated, Lory ran to the steps and up into the cabin of the plane. Then, mildly conscience-stricken, she bowed to duty and watched through the porthole of the plane, ready to wave. Strangely, her mother did not turn back.

"Passenger or pilot?" Cash asked behind her.

She swung around, still kneeling on the lounge, not understanding.

"Want to be back here?" he explained. "Or up front with me?"

"Whatever you want," she said quickly.

Cash's eyes were fixed on her face, strangely questioning, and she was suddenly conscious of what she had said, the tone as well as the words, the totality of her offering. The urge for a denying reservation rose within her but it was beaten down by the pounding of her heart, washed away by the driving surge of blood through her arteries. *It was happening again ... the same way it had happened so many times before ... the mad hallucination of a thousand nights ... even last night ...*

"We'll have lunch in Philadelphia," Cash said, neither as a question nor as decision but as an unalterable fact, as unopposable as the hunger of her body for the touch of his hands.

She walked up the aisle.

7

Long before his taxicab reached the gatepost of the old Main Line
estate that was now the headquarters of the Andrews Foundation,
Gil Clark was fully appreciative of the wisdom there had been in
Winston Conway's suggestion. By taking a cab he had managed to
thoroughly digest the Lockwood report on Dr. Martin Bergmann
and, with the advantage of these extra twenty-odd minutes, had
acquired the factual equivalent of what he might have learned in
twenty years of personal friendship.

Getting out of the taxi, telling the driver to wait, walking up the
front steps of the old mansion house that now served the Foundation as its administrative center, Gil Clark was struck by a fact that
he realized should not have escaped him before—the Lockwood
report could not possibly have been prepared overnight. A start on
collecting information about Dr. Bergmann must have been made
several years ago, probably at the time of Cash McCall's first interest
in Cox-Farrington. The important point was that the very existence
of the report was evidence that Cash McCall's deals, seemingly blessed
with enormous luck and executed with such spur-of-the-moment
abandon, were actually grounded in the careful assemblage of solid
fact. That awareness was as reassuring to Gil Clark as the feeling
that, having read the Lockwood report, he really *knew* the man he
was about to meet. After such a revealing exposure, no man could
be a stranger. There were even pictures to prepare him for Bergmann's odd appearance, the very tall and almost incredibly thin
figure that unfolded like a carpenter's rule as he rose from his desk,
the bare-skull Teutonic appearance of his head, the high dome with
its thin covering of close-cropped hair, deep-set eyes that blinked
at only astoundingly long intervals.

If anything, Bergmann seemed at first a too-perfect replica of
the pictures, his face as frozen in expression as a photograph, as im-
passive as the grillwork of a phonograph through which his voice was
heard saying, "There's no need to explain who you are, Mr. Clark.
I asked Mr. Conway if you were a representative of Mr. McCall's.
He told me that you were. I know now that I was right. This molding
company is really being bought from Cash McCall. That's true, isn't
it? The Gammer Corporation is Cash McCall?"

The questions were knife slashes, cutting away Gil Clark's planned approach, leaving him with a mind suddenly emptied of everything except the awareness that Allenby's prediction of a state of extreme nervous tension was more than justified.

Bergmann had already taken silence for an affirmative answer. "I thought it was Mr. McCall but General Danvers wouldn't tell me. There was no other way to find out. That's why I went to John Allenby. He told me that he didn't know anything about it, but I was sure that if I was right word would get back to Cash McCall and that he'd get in touch with me."

"Well, I'm here," Gil said, forcing a smile against trepidation, reacting to the alarming suspicion that he was in the presence of a man who was mentally ill. Bergmann's colorless voice and unblinking stare made him seem the Hollywood mad scientist, diabolically capable of touching some hidden switch that would disintegrate the world into atoms. This man across the desk was not the Dr. Martin Bergmann he had gotten to know in the pages of the Lockwood report, the dedicated scientist who had time after time rejected the big salaries that industry had offered him, sacrificing all personal reward in order that he might live the cloistered life of the Foundation, devoting himself to the gentlehearted service of all mankind. This Dr. Bergmann who faced him now was a different man, believably capable of the most devious deception. It now seemed entirely possible that his call on Allenby was only the setting of a trap, triggered by some vindictive desire to revenge the supposed harm that Cash McCall had done him at Cox-Farrington.

"My only miscalculation was that I didn't expect such an accelerated reaction," Bergmann muttered to himself, his big-knuckled hands nervously stirring the magpie-nest of papers and electrical parts on the top of his desk.

For an instant, Gil considered diverting the conversation down some directionless side road with the hope that it might have a calming effect on Bergmann, but his experience over the years with distraught executives—the head of the Andrews Foundation was by no means the first to arouse suspicions of mental derangement—argued strongly against the circuitous approach. Resorting to pointless chatter typically produced no effect other than the arousing of suspicion. The direct and unhesitating approach was usually best and, in this instance, he had the advantage of being able to attribute the initiative to the man who was now regarding him with staring silence.

"Well, Dr. Bergmann, what do you have on your mind?"

From the litter on his desk, a slide rule had found its way into the scientist's hand and the trembling rattle of the extended slide against the glass bulb of a partially dissected vacuum tube was a betrayal of rising agitation, but still with no discernible effect on Bergmann's frozen mien or the flatness of his tone. "I understand that Mr. McCall is to receive three hundred thousand shares of Andscott stock."

"I believe that's correct," Gil said as casually as he could manage.

"Would that mean that he'd take an interest in the management of the company?"

"An interest in the management?" Gil repeated. "Just what do you mean, Doctor?"

As suddenly as if the hard shell of an egg had fractured, Bergmann's expression changed, the inner man revealed, tortured by doubt and fear. "I don't know what I mean. All I know is that something has to be done. We can't go on this way!"

"I'm afraid I don't understand," Gil said honestly.

Distraught, Bergmann half rose from his chair, his body braced by rigid arms. "I'm probably going about this in entirely the wrong way—I don't know how these things should be done—but we *must* have Mr. McCall's help. It's our only hope!"

"His help?" Gil puzzled, hardly able to believe what he heard, suddenly deciding that a quick thrust was the best way to clarify the situation. "Just how did you expect to get Mr. McCall's help by threatening to block the sale of Suffolk Moulding?"

Bergmann reacted as if he had been slapped. "But I didn't! I *want* him to have that stock. Don't you understand, Mr. Clark—I had to be certain that it *was* Mr. McCall, not someone who was just out to make a lot of money for himself and ruin the Andscott Instrument Company."

Could that possibly be true? Did Bergmann really mean that he was thinking of Cash McCall as someone other than an operator out for a fast profit? The scientist seemed too uncontrollably emotional to be devious ... but there was too much at stake to gamble on an unproved assumption.

"You surprise me," Gil said, cautiously casual. "I had no idea you felt that way about Mr. McCall. I'd gotten the impression that you weren't too favorably disposed toward him."

Bergmann's face blanched, "Why would you think that?"

"Weren't you with Cox-Farrington?"

"Yes."

"And when Mr. McCall moved in, you got out."

The scientist's expression twisted torturously. "Yes, I was wrong—I believed the things that were being said about him—but I know now that none of those things were true. Mr. McCall didn't wreck Cox-Farrington. He *saved* it! And that's what I must get him to do now—help me save the Foundation. He's our only hope. There's no other chance."

Bergmann's body had straightened to full height, tall and gaunt, breaking away from the confines of his desk as if impelled by the uncontainably explosive energy of pent-up emotion. "I didn't know how to reach him. His name isn't in the telephone book. I found out that he lived at the Hotel Ivanhoe. They wouldn't connect me. That's why I went to John Allenby, trying to get in touch with him. Maybe that wasn't the right thing to do—forgive me if I was wrong—but I was desperate, Mr. Clark, desperate!"

"Just what kind of help do you want from Mr. McCall?"

"I don't know what can be done," Bergmann said miserably. "But I'm sure that Mr. McCall will know. At least he could talk to General Danvers. I've tried but he won't listen to me. Perhaps he's right—I'm not a businessman—but Mr. McCall *is*, he'd have to listen to him. And if Mr. McCall were a big stockholder it would surely be to his own interest to get things straightened out." He paused, his lips trembling in abject appeal. "He would, wouldn't he?"

"What you want is to get those dividends coming again, is that it?" Gil asked, testing the effect of a smile.

The reaction was far more pronounced than he had expected. Bergmann sighed as if some tremendous load had been lifted from his shoulders. "Yes, that's it. The Foundation has no other source of support. We can't even sell our stock—the terms of the trust prevent that—and Mr. Andrews' will also stops us from taking any government support. We could accept private contributions, I believe, but there's very little hope in that quarter. We're not concerned here with any of the attractively horrible diseases that touch the public fancy and open their pocketbooks."

"Yes, I can see your problem," Gil said sympathetically, hoping to encourage the already evident calming of Bergmann's nerves.

"Without Andscott dividends, the Foundation dies," Bergmann went on. "And all of us who are here die with it—all our hopes and dreams, everything we've wanted out of life, all that this Foundation could accomplish. And we can do some great things, Mr. Clark. We *are* doing great things. We have some brilliant men here, some of the finest minds in the world. They need what the Foundation can offer them—absolute freedom to work in their own way, equipment, facilities, enough financial support to keep body and soul together. I ask nothing for myself—I haven't taken a cent of salary in the last year, Mrs. Bergmann has a small income that's enough to keep us going—but I can't let the *Foundation* die! Do you understand, Mr. Clark."

297

"Of course."

"Thank you," Bergmann said as fervently as if simple understanding constituted some great personal favor.

"Let's talk about this Andscott situation for a minute," Gil said, his thoughts racing ahead of his words, grappling with the evident fact that Dr. Bergmann's ideas encompassed no more than a reformation of General Danvers, not his ejection as the corporation's chief executive. "Doctor, what's been the nature of your relationship with General Danvers?"

Bergmann came back to the desk, folding his body down into the chair, slumping. The tension that had been so evident in the beginning had almost totally gone. Now he was the Dr. Martin Bergmann described in the Lockwood report. "I suppose I've handled that part of it rather badly—I know I have—and I'm sure I must be wrong about General Danvers. It stands to reason that he must be an able man. He couldn't have done the things he has if he weren't."

"Don't worry about talking frankly," Gil smiled. "As for General Danvers—you're quite right in raising plenty of questions about his management of Andscott."

"Then you think so, too?" Bergmann asked, clearly surprised.

Gil shrugged. "The facts speak for themselves, don't they?"

"That's the way it seemed to me," Bergmann said, greatly relieved. "May I talk to you confidentially?"

A reservation leaped in to stop Gil Clark's automatic assent, "Well, I'm here as Mr. McCall's representative. Naturally, I'd have to talk to him."

"Oh, of course—yes, I'd expect that," Bergmann said quickly, but there was a hesitant pause before he went on. "Until a little more than a year ago—a year ago last September—I didn't concern myself at all with the Andscott Instrument Corporation. As you know, the Foundation held a great deal of stock, but still—well, this will sound naïve to you, I suppose, but I never worried about what was going on down there. Mr. Andrews had put in General Danvers as president and I hardly felt like questioning his judgment."

"And he was a famous man and apparently very able."

"Quite so," Bergmann said gratefully. "And we got our dividends regularly—that is until this case a year ago in September. It may not be important but I think you should know about it."

"I'd like the whole story."

"To be honest about it, I hadn't realized that the check hadn't come until our bookkeeper called it to my attention—two or three weeks after we should have received it. I thought there'd been a mistake so I called General Danvers. It was no mistake. But he said that it was only a temporary situation and not to worry about it."

"The dividend had been declared?"

"Oh, yes, the other stockholders had been paid—Mrs. Bergmann's brother owned some Andscott stock at the time and I knew that he'd gotten his check. He's an attorney, by the way, and when it got on into November and the Foundation still hadn't received our dividend, I talked to him about it. Frankly, I was a little worried."

"I should think you would have been. That's an extremely irregular procedure—declaring a dividend and then withholding payment."

"Yes, so Harold told me, and on the strength of that I went down to see General Danvers. He explained that something unexpected had come up in connection with the television business, that the company was a little short of cash, but that we'd get our check very shortly."

"And did you?"

"Yes, it finally came and I—well, actually, I thought no more about it." He paused and his voice took on a shade of embarrassment. "Very soon after that, Mrs. Bergmann and I started seeing a lot of the Danverses. They entertained us and we took several trips together." He paused and a shade of embarrassment came into his voice. "Perhaps I do General Danvers an injustice but—well, some things happened that convinced me that his friendship wasn't completely sincere."

"In the meantime, I believe, you'd gone on the Andscott board?"

Bergmann sighed heavily. "Yes, and I probably handled that badly, too. I'm no businessman—I realize that—but I couldn't accept the soundness of what was being done. The instrument business was making a very good profit, but all of that and more was being put into the television business. I realize, of course, that it takes time to get something like that going, but it seemed to me Andscott was losing ground rather than gaining it. Instead of the losses getting smaller, they were getting bigger."

"And you objected to the management policy that was being followed?"

"Yes, I—well, it seemed to me that the best thing to do would be to drop the television business. In research, when we find that we've started to follow some unproductive line, we get out as rapidly as we can, even if it does mean the loss of what we've put into it."

"That's an equally good rule in business," Gil agreed. "Did you have any support in the board?"

"None at all," Bergmann said, but with a hesitant reservation. "Actually, I—well, I did have the feeling that there were several who agreed with me but no one would speak up. You see, most of the directors are executives in the company and, naturally, they weren't going to risk putting themselves in a bad light with General Danvers."

"But aren't there a couple of outside directors, too?"

"Yes, Mr. Bannon and Mr. Shaughn, but they—forgive me if I sound inexperienced in these things, Mr. Clark, but I couldn't get over the impression that it was a case of *noblesse oblige*. They're presidents of companies, too, and it seemed that they didn't want to interfere with General Danvers any more than they would want some outside director to interfere with them in their own companies. I may be wrong but that's the way it impressed me."

"I don't think you are wrong," Gil said with a complimentary smile. "That's an extremely common situation. So I gather your protest didn't accomplish very much?"

"Nothing except to incur General Danvers' displeasure—and even more seriously through what happened next. That may have been a mistake, too, but I'd been talking with Harold—this brother of Mrs. Bergmann's—and he told me that the amount of stock the Foundation held entitled us to more than one member of the board."

"Did you suggest that to Danvers?"

Bergmann's pained expression described the unpleasantness of the occasion. "I probably went about it in entirely the wrong way. I didn't mean it as criticism of General Danvers. He may be entirely right in the course he's been following but—"

Gil cut in, sure now that he was on solid ground. "General Danvers is *not* right, Dr. Bergmann. The truth might as well be faced—the Andscott Instrument Corporation is rapidly approaching an extremely critical situation. It's completely obvious that there must be a new president—perhaps a number of other new top executives as well."

Bergmann looked as if he had been slapped. "I—I'd never thought of going that far."

"There's nothing else to do."

"But—is that possible?"

"Yes," Gil said quietly. "If you're willing to do what has to be done."

"I'll do anything to save the Foundation," Bergmann said slowly, a total commitment, grimly resolute and transparently honest.

Gil weighed the gamble and decided that the odds were heavily in his favor. "Dr. Bergmann, if you will give Mr. McCall a proxy to vote the Foundation's shares, he'll be able to elect a majority of the board, bring in a new president, do whatever needs to be done to put the company back on a dividend-paying basis again."

300

Bergmann got heavily to his feet, shuffling to the window, looking out. "Who would the new president be?"

"I don't know. Nor can I tell you what Mr. McCall's plans would be for reorganizing the company. It will take some time and study to work that out. But you know what Mr. McCall did at Cox-Farrington."

"Yes, if he could get a man to do what John Allenby has done."

"I'm sure he would."

Bergmann turned back from the window. "I said that I'd do anything to save the Foundation and I meant it. If that's what has to be done, I'd appreciate Mr. McCall's help in doing it."

For an instant, Gil was taken aback by Bergmann's assumption of the major responsibility. But it was actually true. The Foundation was the big stockholder, not Cash McCall.

"When can I talk to Mr. McCall?" Bergmann asked.

"Probably some time this evening."

"Not before that?" Bergmann asked, disturbed. "I promised General Danvers that I would give him word by five o'clock on whether or not I'd support this idea of buying the molding company. If I could talk to Mr. McCall before that—get a little more idea of what he had in mind—"

"Suppose I do this," Gil suggested. "I'll try to get in touch with him and set up a meeting at the earliest possible moment."

"I'll be in town after lunch," Bergmann said. "Where can I reach you?"

"At Mr. Conway's office," Gil said, adding as he saw a telephone book within arm's reach, "I'll find the number for you."

While he was looking up the telephone number, the door behind him opened and a nervously secretarial voice said, "I'm sorry, Dr. Bergmann, but if you're going to make your luncheon date with General Danvers—"

"But I haven't a luncheon date with him," Bergmann protested.

"I left a note there on your desk. He called the first thing this morning."

"Did you tell him I'd be there?"

"No sir—but I just thought you would."

Dr. Martin Bergmann shook his head and Gil heard the door behind him close. He had written the telephone number on a page from his pocket notebook. Now he ripped it and handed it across the table.

"Thank you," Bergmann said—and the words were far more than a meaningless formality.

••••• 8

Grant Austen was fully recovered from the disconcerting circumstance of his unobserved arrival at Moon Beach in a private B-26, disappointment more than offset now by the realization that arriving ahead of the crowd had given him the best of all chances for a talk with Harlan Bostwick. A call to the switchboard operator had produced the information that the association's Executive Secretary was in the Congressional Room.

Getting off the elevator at the first floor, Grant Austen crossed the lobby, holding to a dignified saunter until he was safely through the doorway to the Annex, then speeding his pace to its top limit as he walked rapidly toward the Congressional Room where, beginning tomorrow morning, the convention sessions would be staged.

"Why, Mr. Austen!" he heard a feminine voice squeal as he came to the reception area that fronted the auditorium. Miss Witham and Miss Rogers from the association's Washington office were behind the green-felted registration desk, party-dressed and newly permanented, both smiling so eagerly that he was uncertain which one had called the greeting. They were a couple of fine girls, neither of them ever forgetting that he had been on the Executive Committee back in '49 when the resolution had been passed to bring both of them to Moon Beach every year as a reward for their loyal service to A.A.P.M. And it had worked out fine ... after that first year, of course ... and even that first year hadn't really been their fault. They just hadn't realized that a Moon Beach Special Mint Julip wasn't one of the watered-down Martinis that you got at a Washington cocktail party ... and that there was a limit to what an A.A.P.M. member had a right to expect from the Washington staff.

"But we didn't think you were *coming!*" Miss Witham squealed excitedly, and Miss Rogers added in what seemed the same breath, "We mean we were *afraid* you weren't!"

"Thought you were going to get rid of me, didn't you?" he chuckled, a little out of breath.

"Why it just wouldn't *be* a convention without you, Mr. Austen," one said, and then the other, "Goodness me, you haven't been down to see us in Washington for ages and ages."

"Maybe you'll be seeing more of me from now on," he said with a

302

sly smile that neither of them saw, both of them so excited about trying to find his badge for him.

"Things are a little mixed up," Miss Witham said nervously, fingering through the big envelopes in the file box, and Miss Rogers added, "We'll have everything straightened out in just a minute or two, Mr. Austen."

"Now don't you worry about that," he said. "Just came down to see Mr. Bostwick for a minute. He in here?"

"Yes, he's in there," they both said, almost in unison. "And we'll have your badge right away."

He pushed through the door of the Congressional Room, finding himself in total darkness, pierced only by the arrowhead beam of a slide projector and a huge chart glowing red and yellow from the stage. From somewhere in the darkness, Harlan Bostwick's sonorous voice called the instructions that directed the rehearsal and, feeling his way from chair to chair, Grant Austen edged toward the voice.

The American flag was on the screen now, frozen in furious flapping, and Harlan Bostwick's shouts were close at hand. "There's your cue! Fade in *America, the Beautiful!* Bring your houselights up on the dimmer!"

There was an enormous burst of needle-scratching from a tin-throated loudspeaker and the houselights exploded like a bomb burst.

"No, no, *no!*" Bostwick screamed. "I want an *effect* here! Who in hell is on those—"

The Executive Secretary's breath seemed to suck back into his throat and Grant Austen found himself staring into a face that accused him of being a ghost.

"Grant!" Bostwick expelled the name as if it had used up the last whisper of a deep breath. "But I thought—good god, man, I had no idea you were coming. I thought that—I'll do something about your room right now."

Grant Austen stopped him as he moved toward the door, sure now that his suspicions had been justified ... it had been no accident that there had been a mix-up at the desk about his reservation, nor that the girls hadn't been able to find his badge. But there was no better way to put a man under obligation than to catch him off base and then be magnanimous about it. "Oh, that's all right, Harlan. No harm done."

"But your room?" Bostwick asked, his handsome face contorted with concern. "Did they take care of you at the desk? I never had any idea—I wouldn't have canceled—"

"Now don't you worry, Harlan. Everything's all right. Best they could do was put us in the back wing but that doesn't matter."

"Grant, listen, I'll go right out and see if I can't do something about—"

Austen blocked him with an outstretched hand. "It's only a couple of nights and I know you've got plenty on your mind without worrying about me."

Harlan Bostwick swallowed uncertainly. "I just don't know how to excuse myself, Grant. I don't know what to say."

"Don't say anything, Harlan. Just forget it. Everything's fine."

"If there's anything I can do to—anything at all—"

Grant Austen waited out a timed pause. "Well, there is one thing, Harlan—that is if you have a minute?"

"Of course, Grant, of course."

"You see I've sold Suffolk Moulding and—"

"I know. That's what threw me off. I—" He gulped a new breath and made a fresh start. "What have you got on your mind, Grant?"

"Well, the truth is, Harlan—" He saw the projector operator watching them and lowered his voice. "This is confidential, you understand, but—well, as I say, I've sold Suffolk Moulding—one of those offers that a man just couldn't turn down—"

"That's fine, Grant, fine. I figured it must have been something like that. By the way, who is this Gammer—?"

"What I'm trying to say, Harlan, is that I've got things fixed now so that I don't have to worry any more about making money. From now on—well, you know I spent a lot of time down in Washington during the war, and one of the things that really impressed me was how much good the right man could do—I mean if he's in the right spot. That's what I wanted your advice on, Harlan. I know darn well there isn't anybody around Washington that knows his way around like you do. Didn't want to make any move before I talked to you."

"I appreciate that, Grant, really do. Glad to tell you anything I can."

"I thought maybe you would know some spot where—well, I mean where a man could do some good. You see, I've got the chance now —free and not having to worry about money any more—and I figure it's something a man like me *ought* to do."

"That's a wonderful attitude, Grant, really is," Bostwick said thoughtfully. "I'll tell you what—suppose you give me a chance to turn this around in my mind. I've got this rehearsal on my hands and I have to get things set before the gang gets here on the special."

"Sure, you bet," Grant Austen said, starting to extend his hand.

But Harlan Bostwick had backed out of reach. "Be seeing you, Grant."

The lights went off before Grant Austen reached the door and the sudden darkness aroused a feeling of blind panic. Was it possible that Harlan was giving him a brush-off? No, that *couldn't* be! Harlan was one of his best friends ... but Will Atherson ... and Harrison Glenn ... no, it was only because Harlan was busy with this rehearsal.

Bostwick's shouts in the darkness were a solid confirmation. "All right, now, this time let's get on the ball. This is our last chance to rehearse this opening so let's make it good. Go back to that flag slide again!"

Grant Austen turned and, sight restored, saw the American flag on the screen.

"Ready!" Bostwick's shout rang out. "Bring in your music—fade it, fade it—easy—"

The opening strains of *America, the Beautiful* floated in from the darkness, lifting to the swell of massed voices.

A choke came into Grant Austen's throat as he listened. Yes, he was right ... Washington was what he wanted.

Groping, he pushed out through the door, momentarily blinded by the blaze of light in the anteroom.

"Here's your badge, Mr. Austen!"

Miss Witham held his lapel while Miss Rogers pinned on the square of transparent plastic. Looking down, his smile of appreciation was dimmed as he saw that the name card was not the clear white of a full-fledged Member but the watery blue of a Special Guest. His name was blankly alone, unsupported by any corporate association—just GRANT AUSTEN, that and nothing else.

• • • • • 9

The bedroom came alive as Miriam Austen unpacked. Familiar dresses in the closet and her own bottles and jars on the mirror-topped dressing table banished the barren lifelessness of the suite as effectively as opening the windows to the sea breeze had washed out the stale hotel-smelling air.

Through the open window she heard the faint sound of distant music ... *America the Beautiful*. She began to hum, actually singing the phrases she remembered. Everything was going so wonderfully, so much better than she had dared to hope! That had always

305

been her trouble ... imagining all sorts of awful things that never happened ... so frightened of running the gauntlet of eyes that would be watching her come into the hotel ... and then there hadn't been anyone at all! And then so afraid that something was wrong when Grant had talked to the man at the desk so long ... but nothing had been wrong. It was always that way. Why couldn't she learn? She *had* learned ... she wouldn't let it happen again ... never, never, *never!*

She lifted the Alençon-laced nightgown, letting it slither silkily across her fingers as it unfolded, laughing at herself for the silly way she had let herself be annoyed in the plane because Grant had talked to Lory all the time ... and he hadn't mentioned her since. Nor Cash McCall either ... but, of course, Grant didn't know about yesterday.

The tremor of her hands sent shimmering ripples down the length of the nightgown. Should she have told Grant ... Lory hadn't said a word about it but she had been gone all that time and she must have been with Cash because she hadn't come home until after the plane came back. Yes, she should have told Grant. At least it would have been something to talk about, a warm confidence to share. But not now ... no, it was too late to tell him now ... only make him think of Lory.

She tested the appearance of the nightgown draped airily across the counterpane, felt as foolish as if she had heard herself giggle, started to put it in the closet, changed her mind, went into the bathroom and hung it on the back of the door. The towels on the bar were crooked and she refolded and rehung them, pausing a moment to polish a greasy smudge from the mirror with a piece of cleansing tissue. In the mirror, reflected through the open door, she saw Grant standing at the living-room window, looking out.

"I'm sorry, dear," she said as she hurried to him. "I didn't hear you come back. Did you find whoever it was you wanted to see?"

He nodded, glancing at his watch and then up at the sky. "They ought to be there by now."

"I think the driver said the train was due at one-ten," she said.

"I didn't mean that. I meant Lory and Mr. McCall."

She muffled the little cry that threatened to escape ... she wouldn't let it happen again ... she *had* learned her lesson.

Grant was marking his watch dial with a pointing finger. "Same time to get back as we took to get down—that would put them back in Suffolk again just about now. Nice of him to do it, wasn't it —asking her to come along?"

"Very nice."

"You bet, that's the way you can always tell a really big man—thoughtful." He ended with a little nod that said that was the end of that. "Well, what do you think of Moon Beach?"

"It's wonderful, dear, it really is. Everything you said it was."

"Heck, you haven't even seen it yet. Come on, how about taking a look around. The gang ought to be getting in before long. Lot of people I want you to meet."

"Just give me a minute to change my shoes," she said, not because her shoes needed changing, but because she needed an excuse to hide her brimming eyes. Grant wasn't worrying about Lory ... he was thinking about *her!*

••••• 10

This was a good day, one of the best. It was only seven minutes after one and Maude Kennard had already surmounted the Fontainebleau Room's daily turnover crisis. The twelve o'clock crowd had been safely evicted, every one o'clock reservation had been filled, and her guess as to the number of unrejectables who would turn up without reservations had proved precisely accurate. So adroitly had she juggled people and tables that there was only one empty chair in the entire dining room. Resentfully, she turned toward it. But what could she have done? General Danvers had walked in demanding a table for two, claiming that he was expecting a guest, even telling her to watch out for a "Dr. Bergmann," a phony if she had ever heard one. Of course, he'd tried to bluff it out, waiting to order, but now he'd given up after his second double Martini and the waiter was serving his soup.

Unexpectedly the president of the Andscott Instrument Corporation glanced in her direction and their eyes met. She returned his smile with bland innocence, thinking how shocked he would be if he knew that she had been in the serving pantry of Cash's suite all during dinner last night and had heard every word that had been said. Reminiscently, she felt a resurgence of the anger that had been aroused by his accusations against Cash. Afterwards, of course, Danvers had belly-crawled and begged that everything he had said be forgotten. But she wouldn't forget ... and neither would Cash. He had paid only two million for that Suffolk company and Danvers was giving him three hundred thousand shares of Andscott common ... $10\frac{1}{2}$–$10\frac{1}{4}$ in the morning paper ... that was more than three million dollars. Before it was over, she and Cash would be paid a million dollars for that empty seat at Table 17.

General Danvers began to eat his soup—*Crème d'Epinards Florentine*—and she let her gaze drift to the gold-laced screen that hid the swinging door at the back of the dining room, visualizing the dank tunnel that connected the Fontainebleau Room to the kitchen. Only a tenth of that million dollars would do everything that needed to be done. She would rip out the back of the old building, extend the kitchen area, add another refrigerator room ...

Louis was coming toward her, the look of crisis on his drawn lips. She waited for him, counseling herself to patience with whatever petty complaint he was relaying, attempting to trace it to its origin by back-tracking the headwaiter's path across the room, smiling a blanket reassurance to the whole area beyond the center pillars.

"*Oeufs Moulés à la Nicollet,*" the headwaiter said, the identifying name spoken as a curse.

"They're not on the menu but you may order them," she ordained, her benevolent smile less for Louis than for whoever might be watching her.

"I *have* order them," he said with a Gallic hiss. "I, Louis, give the promise! Now the kitchen say they cannot make because Max is not there."

"Not in the kitchen? Where is he?"

Louis's blazing eyes raised to the ceiling. "He say he must make special dish for Mr. McCall. Cannot be cook in kitchen, must make upstairs. So he go. How you like that?"

She waited out the moment of first shock, rigid with anger, ready to start for the kitchen the instant she could be certain of self-control. The uniformed arm of a bellboy stabbed into her field of vision, his hand holding a note for her. She took it without acknowledgment, not reading it.

Inside the kitchen, her eyes hurriedly canvassed the white-clad horde, seeing cooks of every size and shape but no figure that even remotely approached Max's unmistakable proportions. This was absolutely the last straw ... if Max thought he could get away with running out right in the middle of the lunch hour when the whole Fontainebleau Room was jammed with ...

The flame of anger suddenly sputtered out, quenched with the cold-water realization of helplessness. Cash owned the hotel ... if *he* wanted Max, there was nothing she could do to ...

Her eyes caught a white flutter and she looked down. Her fingers had loosened their grip and the note had fallen. She bent to pick it up, frustrated by the clinging hold of the wet floor on the thin paper.

308

Then the dampness came through, blackening the single penciled line, and she read the message:

1:09 P.M.—He went up with Miss Austen.

For an instant she stared without comprehension. Then she remembered that she had instructed Nathan at the desk to let her know the moment Cash returned to the hotel.

She felt suddenly dizzy and straightened to full height, trying to convince herself that she was nauseated because of the steam and heat of the kitchen . . . *that little bitch . . . up in his room!*

The note was still on the floor but she dared not risk bending again to retrieve it. Instead, she ground the white paper under the sole of her shoe until the words were obliterated in a gray smear.

••••• 11

Cash opened the door and Lory was inside the foyer and turning left toward the arch of the living room before she realized that she had crossed the threshold without an interrupting recollection of that night in Maine when she had come to Cash's room at the Inn. Now, even consciously recalled, that memory was only the faint scar of a well-healed wound. She walked boldly forward, slipping out of her coat without waiting for Cash to help her, opening a door in the corner of the foyer, not tentatively as she would have done in a strange house but with the sureness of familiarity. And she was right. It was the coat closet. There was no strangeness in these rooms. She had been here before.

Nor was there strangeness in this man. Nothing of accountable importance had happened on the flight up from Moon Beach, nor as they had driven into Philadelphia from the airport. There had been only the simple fact of presence but that, in an odd reversal of anticipation, had proved a calming inducement of reasoned thought. There had been, and still was, the response of acknowledged excitement but it had rapidly become an emotion cleansed of adulterating fear or apprehension. There was nothing unusual, she told herself, in a woman having lunch with a man—thousands upon thousands of men and women were lunching together at this very minute, sensibly free from any expectation beyond the sharing of a pleasant hour.

As she entered the living room, her eye was caught by her frontispiece illustration for the *Knight of the Hawk*, white-matted and black-framed, its presence on Cash's wall another proof of the normality of her being here in his apartment.

Aware that Cash had seen her glance at the drawing, she said, "I'm very flattered."

He looked at her with an enigmatic smile. "Is it—or isn't it?"

"Isn't it what?"

"Several people have imagined a resemblance. Jefferson Clark was the first, but there have been others since."

"Resemblance?"

"They think I was your model."

"But I didn't have a model," she protested quickly, too quickly, and then was forced to go on. "It was just an imaginary face, something that came to me—"

"Out of your memory?" he added, linking his words to hers.

"Perhaps," she said, side-stepping the threat of a loss of composure by adding, "But I'm sorry if I embarrassed you. I didn't mean it to be your portrait, honestly I didn't."

His expression was a gay mockery of disappointment. "Now you've spoiled everything. I've been imagining myself as that romantic fellow, dashing around on a white charger with a falcon on my wrist, rescuing fair damsels in distress and whisking them off to my princely castle."

She amazed herself by being able to match his banter. "Oh, it's much more romantic to do your dashing around in a B-26 and bring your damsel to a lovely apartment in the Ivanhoe."

"And, anyway, it wasn't the damsel who was in distress—it was the rescuer. I was frightened that you might decide to stay at Moon Beach."

"Really frightened?" she teased.

"I'm not a very brave knight. I was even afraid to ask if you *wanted* to be rescued."

"Oh, that wouldn't have been right at all," she laughed. "Who ever heard of the knight asking the damsel's permission!"

So suddenly that there was no chance for even the split-second decision of submission, she found herself in his arms, the crush of his lips a sensation that instantly spread through her body, all pervading, without focus, sustained through the long blanking of perception until she was finally aware that somewhere in the distant outer world there was the sound of knocking. Cash had left her but there had been no consciousness of the moment of parting—and, apart, there was no diminution, no loss, no wrenching tear that left a wound to be healed, no guard of caution that needed to be raised. Passion was no longer a caged animal clawing at iron bars. There were no

310

bars. The only restraint was the knowledge that restraint was no longer necessary.

She heard the sound of Cash's voice and saw that he was whispering to someone through the half-opened door of the living room. The door closed and he turned back to her. "Lunch in ten minutes—all right?"

"Don't ask me, just tell me," she said, laughing away the tiny fear that tears might be showing in her eyes, sitting down on the edge of the great green couch, bracing her arms behind her, looking up at Cash.

His nod of understanding was barely perceptible—but all that it needed to be—and then he turned away from her and walked to the window. Intuition warned her that something was wrong and for a frantic instant she faced the fear that her brashness had been a mistake.

But he turned suddenly and said, "I'm a little concerned about your father, Lory."

"Concerned?" she asked blankly, her relief at the reprieve from blame instantly replaced by surprise that Cash would force the intrusion of something so foreign to the moment.

Cash walked back to her. "I may be wrong, Lory—you know him so much better than I do—but I couldn't escape the feeling this morning that those nerves were stretched very tight. Or didn't you notice it?"

The question startled her and the necessity of fumbling for an answer made her realize that she dared not be completely honest. A moment before it had seemed that there was nothing within her that could not be shared with Cash. Now she recognized that she dared not admit to anyone, even herself, how she had felt about her father this morning in the plane.

"Well, he *was* keyed up about going to the convention," she said guardedly. "I don't know why it meant so much to him—he's completely out of it—but I know that it did."

"Then he doesn't have any plans for going back into the plastics business?"

"No, I'm sure he doesn't have anything like that in mind."

Cash sat down beside her. "What is he planning to do?"

"Well, he was talking about a trip around the world. I'd suggested it and at first he seemed interested, but he hasn't mentioned it for several days now."

"You don't think he'll do it, do you?"

"I wish he would—for Mother's sake, too—but I just don't know what he'll do."

311

"It's my guess that he doesn't know either," Cash said soberly. "I may have done the wrong thing in suggesting that he go to that convention."

"Oh, but you didn't! You can't imagine what it meant to him—and having you take him down in your plane." She paused, waiting hopefully, but there was no lightening of his expression. "Why do you say that it might have been the wrong thing to do?"

"If he's getting out of the business, the best thing would have been a clean break. This is just dragging it out, making it all the more painful."

"Oh, I don't think so," she said positively. "It isn't as if he'd *had* to sell the company—or if it was something that he didn't *want* to do—"

"I may be wrong," he cut in stubbornly. "But I can't get over the hunch that he isn't fully awake yet to what it's really going to mean. That's a difficult transition for any man to make—spending his whole life building up a company and then suddenly discovering that he doesn't have it any more. Sometimes it works out easily enough—if a man has been thinking about it for a long time and more or less adjusted himself to a new frame of mind—but I gather that wasn't the case with your father."

"He did decide in a hurry," she admitted, feeling herself somehow criticized by the contrast of Cash's obvious sympathy for her father. "But it isn't as if it were something he hadn't considered. I talked to him about it that night before we came down here—even asked him if he was sure he could be happy without the company—and there wasn't the slightest doubt in his mind, not the slightest. You see—well, the company hasn't meant so much to him these last few years. It did in the old days—and it was exciting during the war, all the new things—but it's never been quite the same since. It's been almost as if—well, if you could have seen him this last week, I'm sure you'd realize how relieved he is that he's out of it now."

"But still he ought to have *something* to do," Cash said, not as argument but as a supplement. "And you don't really think he'll take this trip around the world, do you?"

"He might. I just don't know."

"It's my guess that he won't," Cash said crisply, standing abruptly. "And if he doesn't we ought to have something else up our sleeves."

Cash had walked to the window again but this time Lory felt no separation. They were linked by the still echoing sound of that one wonderful word ... *we* ... not *you*, not *I*, but *we!* He had spoken it without special emphasis but it was no less a commitment, and there was no doubt that he had meant it to be just that.

Never in the wildest fantasy of her dark-of-the-night dreams had Lory Austen's imagination carried her beyond transient ecstasy, an adventure somewhere outside the boundaries of reality, the moment sufficient unto itself, stolen, lived through with an awareness of imminent ending. Now there would be no ending. Her life had suddenly acquired substance and solidity. It seemed that a miracle had taken place, accomplished in the split-second voicing of a single syllable. But nothing so indisputably right could have happened without preamble and now, in the odd way that the human mind is capable of rationalizing the blindest of hopes into the most clear-eyed of truths, she fully believed that she had always known she would someday marry Cash McCall.

In the lost moment when her attention had been totally inward, she failed to notice Cash walking back from the window. He was standing in front of her and there was the realization that she had missed his first words.

"—and I have no idea whether it would interest him or not," he was saying. "But I happen to know the man in Washington who's organizing it. It's one of those good-will deals—partly window-dressing and hoopla, of course, but still more substance to it than there's been to some of the others. They're pulling together a group of men with both management and specialized technical experience to spend a couple of months down there advising some of their new industries. Venezuela and Brazil are definitely scheduled, possibly Argentina. It ought to be a nice junket—ten or twelve key men, most of them taking their wives. What would you think?"

"I couldn't imagine anything more wonderful for him," she exclaimed, grateful that she could be so honestly exuberant. "And Mother would love it, I know she would. Do you think there's any chance at all of their being included?"

He sat down beside her. "Oh, I think it might be arranged." His voice pretended a doubt that his tongue-in-cheek grin denied. "But you'll have to make one promise."

"What?"

"He's not to know that I had anything to do with it—he, nor your mother, nor anyone else."

"But that's not fair!" There was a choke in her throat. "Why won't you let me tell them what a wonderful person you are?"

The last word was almost lost as the impulse that raced her words won in the split second that still separated her lips from his. She kissed him quick and hard, momentarily embarrassed by the consciousness of her own bold strength until the crush of his arms made it seem, by contrast, such a weak thing that it needed no excusing.

313

The weight of his body carried her down into the leathery softness of the couch and they clung together for that breathless moment before she became aware that the sound she heard was not the beating of her heart but someone rapping on the dining-room door, unimportant until she felt herself suddenly released into aloneness.

Cash was standing, calling an acknowledgement, bringing her to her feet with a tug of his outstretched hands. "Lunch," he said, "And there's a very fierce giant downstairs who chops off the heads of bad little girls who insult his masterpieces by being late to the table."

She made her mockery of terror gayer than laughter. "But even a bad little girl can't have her head cut off without her nose being powdered."

"Use my room," he commanded, whisking her off with a sweep of his hand, then calling after her, "It's the far door."

But somehow she knew without being told, her hand on the knob of the right door before he called. Then she was inside, the door closed behind her, and she stood with her back pressed hard against it, her eyes drinking in the intimate wonder of his bedroom. The faint man-odor was an intoxicating vapor whirling through her brain, Cash's presence so real that when she returned to the living room there was almost the feeling of having left him behind, strengthened by momentary alarm at finding herself alone.

But the door to the dining room was open and when she stepped to the doorway she saw Cash waiting for her, holding her chair at a candlelit table for two, backgrounded by tightly drawn draperies in a semicircular window bay. The only light was from the candles, vignetting Cash's face and the table top, sparkling on crystal and silver, painting the scene with an overtone of elegance that she found vaguely disquieting until, as she sat down, Cash leaned over her and whispered, "This is Andrew's idea of the way a very sophisticated gentleman lures an innocent maiden."

She threw back her head, looking up into his face. "Are you?"

"Oh, very sophisticated. And you?"

"Very, very innocent."

He leaned over her, kissing her cheek quickly and lightly, and the sound of an elaborate throat-clearing on the other side of the pantry door seemed a ludicrous entrance cue borrowed from some old farce comedy.

Cash gained the propriety of his own chair in the moment of grace before the door opened, the candlelight dancing in his deep blue eyes as he struggled to suppress an open smile before the old waiter's entrance. "Miss Austen, this is Andrew," he introduced her.

She acknowledged the introduction and Andrew bowed silently, stealing a glance at her so fleeting that it made him seem an almost embarrassed conspirator. He served her and she looked down at a beautifully composed arrangement of what she was reasonably certain were slices of some kind of melon interleaved with a mysterious substance, tissue thin and translucently red.

"*Jambon d'Ardennes*," Cash whispered, answering the question that she had just told herself she dared not ask.

Her two years of high school French allowed her to translate *jambon* into *ham*, but nothing had prepared her for the epicure's delight that glowed on Cash's face as he tasted the first paper-thin slice, nodding an acknowledgment to Andrew who withdrew with another conspiratorial glance.

Lory Austen felt herself frightened by inadequacy. She had been aware that Cash lived in an entirely different world than she had ever known but it was not until now, seeing him in a gourmet's role, that she was alerted to the danger that her own ignorance lay between them as a separating moat, threatening the possibility of a shared life. She knew that there was an esoteric cult that practiced dining as one of the finer arts, but its members had been as remote from her own existence as the morning-coated men and poodle-leading women that she had seen on the pages of *Town and Country* in the library at Mount Oak. On several occasions her father had taken her to expensive restaurants recommended by admired top executives of big corporations. Usually they were steak houses, but one had been French—so French that the waiter pretended, at first, that he couldn't even speak English. The food on the tables near them had seemed fascinatingly different and very intriguing, but she had not had the courage to reject her father's suggestion of a nice well-done filet mignon—he explained that *filet mignon* was just as French as anything else—or if she wasn't that hungry, she could have some nice filet of sole, with tartar sauce—*filet of sole* was French, too—and the waiter assured her father that it could be had without any of that fancy gravy.

At home, her experience had been no more broadening. Her mother's interest in the affairs of the kitchen had always been confined to keeping Anna happy, and Anna's happiness depended upon noninterference. Several times over the years, her mother had seen some dish illustrated in a magazine color page interesting enough to risk the suggestion that Anna try it. On rare occasions Anna had agreed to the experiment, but pride in her Pennsylvania Dutch ancestry had always been an ingredient added to the recipe, sullenly calculated to keep the result from throwing the slightest reflection upon the superiority of good plain Berks County cooking. The only

315

victory ever scored over Anna had been Lory's—the hard-won admission that French dressing might occasionally be used on a fruit salad—but Anna never served it without a pointed reminder that her Aunt Martha's boiled dressing had been good enough to win a blue ribbon three years straight at the Farm Show. It was not difficult to imagine what Anna's reaction would be if she were told that the epicurean way to serve honeydew melon was with some kind of French ham that looked like nothing in the world but raw chipped beef.

"Of course, that's really a misnomer—*jambon d'Ardennes*," Cash explained, mildly apologetic. "Actually, it's Italian *prosciutto*—but the real Verona, not that Naples stuff—and it's casaba, too, not Spanish."

"It looks wonderful," she said weakly, hopelessly entangled in strange languages and mixed nationalities.

A furtive glance across the table finally revealed the proper technique—you cut off a bit of melon and then, with a dexterous twist of the fork, wrapped it in a flake of ham. Her first attempt was an awkward failure but, fortunately, Cash's attention was distracted by Andrew who came back now with a bottle of wine, parting its swathing of white linen to expose the label in the manner of a fond mother displaying the face of a sleeping child.

Cash looked at the label and then up at the waiter with a puzzled frown, his whisper so low that his words were more lip-read than heard. "But I'd ordered the *chablis* that I had—"

Andrew stopped him with the expression of a miserable martyr. "I know, sir, but I had no choice in the matter. You see—"

Cash's eyes followed Andrew's self-excusing glance toward the pantry door. "You mean—?"

"That's it, sir," Andrew said after sighing his relief at the smile of understanding that came to Cash's face. "May I serve, sir?"

"Of course, of course," Cash said hurriedly, waiting until the wine had been poured and Andrew had left the room before he leaned across the table to whisper, "Max has come up to do our lunch himself. You should be impressed."

"Oh, I am," she said too quickly, not realizing for an instant that her only hope was to be honest and throw herself on Cash's mercy. "—except that I don't know who Max is."

"You don't know Max? Max Nicollet, the famous Continental chef of the Hotel Ivanhoe?"

"I suppose I should, shouldn't I?"

"You will!" he promised chuckling. "And wait until you see him! He's a fabulous cook but an even more fabulous man." He raised his wine glass. "This was supposed to be a very special *chablis*—but Max disagreed so it isn't."

She followed his example and sipped, attempting a properly appreciative expression but handicapped by the dry and puckery taste on her tongue.

"It's a *hock*, of course," he said. "*Johannisberger.*"

"Of course," she replied absent-mindedly, confused by the intrusion of still another nationality.

"What do you think of it?" he asked earnestly.

"Wonderful," she said, hoping that the second sip would be easier.

It was. And she even managed a bite of ham-wrapped melon with Cash watching her. Consciously tasting for the first time, she found the blend of flavors surprisingly pleasant, wanting to say so but uncomfortably aware that she didn't know the right words. And there was no encouragement to conversation in the rapt expression that came to Cash's face with every bite and a sip of wine. Anxiously, she repeated names, trying to fix them in her memory ... *prosciutto* ... *casaba* ... *hock*, not *chablis* ... *Johannisberger* ...

Andrew came in to clear the course and the fanning pantry door wafted in a faint cooking odor, rich and buttery, and she noticed that Cash's head had come up, sniffing the air.

"Whatever that is, it isn't what I ordered—but of course it never is when Max takes over. I might as well have saved myself the effort of—" He caught himself and flashed a slightly embarrassed smile. "I'm not doing a very good job of pretending that this was all impromptu, am I?"

The need for a reply was eliminated by a rumbling sound from the pantry. The door burst open and Andrew, apparently propelled from the rear by some irresistible force, almost leaped at the table, bearing a smoking platter from which, as if his life depended upon the saving of a single second, he hastily served a low mound of something covered with a faintly golden pink-speckled sauce.

Cash breathed in the dish's aroma and she tried to follow his example, defeated by self-consciousness when she attempted to imitate the ecstatic expression on his face.

"What in the world is it?" he asked.

Given courage by the realization that she was no more mystified than he, she said, "I don't know."

"Looks like an omelette," he speculated, exploring with a fork tip. "No, it's more of a soufflé texture."

He took the first bite and she followed his example, her imitation conscious until, unmatchably, he began to roll his lips as if it were somehow possible to physically separate the subtly blended flavors.

317

"Truffles in the soufflé, of course—and little river shrimp in the sauce," he decreed, lifting a tiny specimen with a fork tine to prove his point. He tasted again. "Sherry—thyme—no, I'm wrong about the sherry. It's *marsala*, definitely marsala. Agree?"

She laughed her helplessness. "I'm afraid I don't know very much about—I'm not a *gourmet*—or whatever the feminine gender of gourmet is, if there is a feminine gender."

"Max will tell you that I'm not either," Cash said, a rueful smile breaking through, quickly erased by a look of puzzled concern. "You're not really taking me seriously, are you? Don't! I'm only trying to impress you with what a sophisticated fellow I am—and not making out very well. You're doing a much better job of being the innocent maiden."

"But I have the advantage," she laughed. "It isn't anything I have to try to be—I *am*. I don't know anything about food at all. Nor a million other things either."

There was a beat of hesitation before he said, unsmiling, "There's a lot of fun to be had in the learning."

"I'm sure you're right," she said. "If this is a sample."

"Life can't be all big adventures," he said. "There have to be some little ones, too. The big ones are too few and far between."

"In your life? I can't quite believe that."

"Why not?"

"Well—this," she groped, looking around the apartment. "Living here—Aurora—your plane. I can't imagine your life ever being short of adventures—either kind, big or small."

His reply was slow in coming. "Yes, I suppose it could look that way to someone else. The truth is that—"

Andrew could not have selected a more unpropitious time to return to the room, serving asparagus from a great silver platter and then tiny rolls from a filigreed basket. He hovered over them, endlessly delayed his exit, and Lory was acutely aware that every lost second was adding to the difficulty of bringing Cash back to whatever it was that he had been about to say to her. There had been the promise of personal revelation and she was intently anxious that it be fulfilled, realizing now that her earlier feeling of complete understanding had been a delusion. The truth was that she knew next to nothing about this man who sat across the table from her and, only by knowing his innermost thoughts, could she hope to come to a sharing of his life. Instinct told her that an opportunity had been lost, that he would talk about himself only in the moment of a rare mood, and now that mood had been broken.

Without too much hope, she attempted to restore it when Andrew finally left the room. "You were about to tell me something."

There was a half hope in the way he looked at her for a moment, but he said, "I'm sure we can find something more interesting to talk about."

"I don't agree. Tell me, please."

"What?"

"Whatever it was that you were going to say," she said, forcing gaiety as a last desperate effort.

What little hope still remained was dashed by his abrupt change of subject. "We'll have to call in Max in a minute or two. Catch him before he goes back downstairs. I want you to meet him."

"And I want to," she said, resigned to waiting for Cash to tell her more about himself until some later time when there was no separating table between them. "I'd like to thank him for such a wonderful lunch. Or isn't that the right thing to do?"

"Oh, very much the right thing to do. And don't worry about going overboard with your praise. You can't, not with Max. Modesty is not one of his virtues—nor are most of the other admired attributes of the normal man. Actually, he's mad as a March hare."

"Aren't all great chefs supposed to be a little mad? I've read that somewhere."

"Well, don't tell Max. If he thought he was supposed to be mad, he'd change. And that would be a tragedy."

"I take it he's a nonconformist."

"One of the last—and we don't dare lose what few there are left. We need to keep a few individualists—as museum pieces if nothing else."

"He does sound as if he was one."

"Oh, he is, make no mistake about that." He paused, spreading Hollandaise sauce with his fork tip. "Sometimes I think they're the only really sensible people—the off-beat characters who don't make sense at all. They create their own world and go on living in it, no matter what anyone else thinks of them. To Max, the edge of his cookstove is the rim of the universe and nothing ever concerns him but what's happening right in his own saucepan."

"And he's happy?"

Cash chuckled affectionately. "You'd never know it to see him—he looks like an ogre and acts as if he were in a perpetual rage—but, yes, I'd say he's happy. At least, I'm reasonably certain that he's never lain awake at night asking himself whether he was doing the right thing with his life—and that's about as good a test for happiness as there is."

319

The timbre of his voice had changed, coming close now to what it had been before Andrew's interruption, suggesting a return to the mood in which he had been willing to talk about himself. A dozen questions suggested themselves, any one of which might turn him in that direction, but she was kept from speaking by an intuitive awareness that what she wanted most was knowledge that could only come to her unprompted and freely given.

Cash ate in silence, so preoccupied with whatever he was thinking about that she could, with safety, watch him without his knowing that he was being observed. He was eating automatically now, no longer the epicure, no catchlights of pleasure dancing in his eyes. Once they narrowed, as if to hint the return of sight, and she quickly looked down at her plate. But he did not speak and she let her eyes drift up to his face again. It was still expressionless and the small fear grew that his thoughts were hidden for some reason more serious than she had suspected.

"Sorry," he apologized, speaking so unexpectedly that she had no chance to wash the concern from her face. "I—I was thinking about Max."

She did not believe him—nor that he expected to be believed—but the way he looked at her now, as if some decision had been met and made, told her that she had been in his thoughts. That was enough to know.

Cash tinkled the silver bell and Andrew appeared to clear the table and serve the dessert, enormous strawberries glazed until they glittered like rubies displayed in a silken puff of glistening spun sugar.

"Please ask Max to come in when he has a chance," Cash whispered to the old waiter, who nodded at the first word as if it were an anticipated request.

The anticipation must have been shared behind the pantry door because it no sooner closed than it opened again, not narrowly this time to admit Andrew's sparse figure but flung wide. And every inch of the full doorway was needed. Lory had never seen a human figure that seemed a more improbable apparition, a mountainous bulk of starched white rising to the crest of a high cap, the only color the cherubic pink of bulging cheeks, every line of both body and face drawn with a circle-making compass—except, startlingly, the pen-ruled spikes of a black mustache.

The blast of voice fitted the man. "You like?" he demanded with a guttural roar, a gesture sweeping aside Cash's attempt at introduction.

Max was looking down on her, the giant of giants, the ogre of ogres, and she saw herself in self-portraiture, the cowering child lost in the forest, and she said as a desperate bid for favor, "Please believe me, it was the most wonderful lunch I ever had in my life. It was the most delicious—delectable—oh, it was simply superlative!"

A barely perceptible nod indicated Max's acceptance of her effort as having satisfied his minimum requirement and he turned to Cash for a further contribution.

"A magnificent achievement," Cash said earnestly. "You're the master of masters, my friend, the greatest of the great."

An explosive snort of disdain fluttered the giant's lips. "You do not know even what you eat!"

"Oh, but I do," Cash protested. "Let me tell you. In the sauce there are little river shrimp and—"

Max blasted in with a thundering interruption, his body quaking as if the mountain were harboring an incipient volcano. His face became an agonized appeal for simple justice as he turned back to face Lory. "Please you will help me make our friend understand. Can he explain the Michelangelo if he says what are the colors of the paint? What they have to eat for Last Supper—is it only the yellow ocher, the burnt sienna, the lapis lazuli?" A cunning smile bulged the circles-within-circles contours of his face. "You think I do not know the lapis lazuli? Ha! I know the lapis lazuli like our friend know the little shrimp! Who does not know the little shrimp? Anyone who is not blind can see it is the little shrimps. But is the lapis lazuli the secret of the Michelangelo?" He rocked his head, stabbing a mustache in Cash's direction. "To him I am nothing but the little shrimps."

Her own laughter was uncontainable but Cash made a valiant attempt at sober concern. "Max, believe me, I would never make the mistake of thinking you were only—"

The raising of the chef's giant hand was an imperious command for silence, broken finally when he said in a sweet-sad voice, "What you eat—only once it has ever been made before—once—when it was create by the great Réchaud for the wedding breakfast of Napoleon and the beautiful Josephine."

She saw Cash gulp and then the flashing twinkle in his eyes. "My dear friend, you are a magnificent chef, but a miserable historian. It was *not* for the wedding breakfast—it was for their luncheon on the day of their betrothal."

Max took a breath that seemed to suck in half the air of the room. But in the instant when an explosion seemed inevitable, his inflated body began a slow collapse and a kewpie smile settled on his face. "You must also say, I am no better liar than you. Réchaud does not create this dish for the Napoleon and Josephine, *I* create it for you, mademoiselle."

He bowed to her, apparently a last-second inspiration, as unexpected to him as it was to her, so suddenly executed that catastrophe seemed certain. Surprisingly, he recovered his balance and then, as an even more startling feat, executed a light-footed dance step that carried him nimbly to the pantry door. Again he bowed, the backthrust of his posterior banging back the door. "You have eat the great love dish of the little pink shrimps—*Soufflé aux Petite Crevettes Roses.*" He hesitated and then added as a final fillip, "*De Héloïse et Abélard.*"

For an instant after the door closed, her mind flashed back, wondering if there had been a significance in Cash's mention of a betrothal luncheon. But if there had been it was lost now. His head was thrown back, tears in his eyes as he tried to muffle the sound of uncontrollable laughter. She was mystified. There was no doubt that Max had been amusing but was it really that hilariously funny?

••••• 12

In all the years that he had attended conventions of the American Association of Plastic Molders, Grant Austen had never found himself the center of as much attention as during the few minutes that the delegates were pouring into the Moon Beach Club after the arrival of the special train. As a not entirely coincidental happenstance, he was in the lobby waiting to go into lunch with Miriam when he heard the tinkling bells of the approaching pony cart parade. Lou and Ed Floeger of L & E Molding were the first two through the door. Naturally he had to get up to greet Lou and Ed—they were real old-timers in A.A.P.M. and a couple of grand guys—and from then on he was stuck, the whole gang pouring in and there was nothing he could do but stay there at the front door shaking hands. A couple of the fellows—Sid Murkle and Charlie Fergus—tried to kid him about being a one-man reception committee, but anyone could see that Sid and Charlie had been hitting it up pretty hard on the train coming down.

Everybody was really surprised to see him, all of them patting him on the back and telling him that he was the smartest guy in the plastic molding business, saying that they wished they could do just what he'd done. Of course, they'd all been talking about his *retiring,* and there'd been no chance to set them straight, everyone rushing to get in line to register. But one thing was certain—he'd made no mistake in coming to the convention. It took something like this to make a man appreciate how many friends he really had.

The gang was rushing back down from their rooms now, getting into the dining room before it closed, and Grant Austen was glad that he'd had the foresight to get a table near the door so that he could point out everyone to Miriam and tell her who they were.

"You'll meet 'em all later," he assured her. "That's Luke Hoover from Interstate—Frank Smith and his wife—Frank's really a card when he gets wound up. Wait until you see him at the Associates Reception tonight! What you going to have to eat?"

She looked down at the menu again. "Dear me, I just don't know, Grant. Everything looks so good. What should I have?"

"How about a nice well-done filet mignon?"

"Oh that's much too much for lunch, really it is."

"Then maybe some nice filet of sole with tartar sauce?"

"That's better," she agreed, folding the menu.

"Sure, you bet. Well, what do you think of—say, there's Harlan Bostwick."

He waved but Harlan was talking so hard to Bill Tottmeyer that he couldn't catch his eye. "That's one fellow I sure want you to meet. Harlan Bostwick. Swell personality. Executive Secretary of the Association. Handles all of our Washington contacts."

"*Our* Washington contacts?" Miriam asked, her eyes teasing him.

For a minute he didn't get what she meant. Then he did and grinned at her and she smiled back ... but, of course, she didn't get the point.

Frank Smith was up on the bandstand where the orchestra played at night, putting on one of those gold hats that the cornet player had left hanging on his music stand, and right away the gang at Charlie's table started singing *Sidewalks of New York*. In a minute there'd be *Chicago* and then the Indiana crowd would try to drown them out with *Wabash Moon*.

"They always do this," he explained to Miriam. "Everybody's got their own song to show where they're from. You know, like *St. Louis Blues—California, Here I Come!*"

Miriam was really getting such a kick out of it, laughing at the way Frank was acting the fool, that Grant Austen took a chance and added, "I guess if you were from Washington, D.C. it would have to be *America the Beautiful.*"

But she still didn't get it. She thought it was just a joke.

••••• 13

Driven by the need to talk to someone ... *anyone* ... Maude Kennard blindly pushed open the door of Everett Pierce's office. In the instant of the door's opening she knew that she had made a mistake. What could she say to him? Nothing! That little bitch was still up in Cash's suite ... but what could Pierce do about it ... or about Max ... or anything else?

The manager stared at her. "Is something wrong, Mrs. Kennard?"

The pressure within her burst through her lips. "I've found out who your Mr. McCall is," she blurted out, the words as uncalculated as the tone of anger in which they were bathed. "He owns the hotel!"

Everett Pierce started to rise from his chair but then, as if the movement was only the spastic response to a mortal wound, he sank back.

In a flash of acute perception, Maude Kennard knew what he was thinking ... *now he would never get back his tenth-floor suite!*

She looked at him with the disgust of the madly brave for the cringing coward ... he was whipped ... licked ... totally beaten. Watching, her disdain became a restorative, Everett Pierce's weakness a gauge of her own strength. She backed out of the office, closing the door, feeling that she had scored an important victory. She was clear-headed now, no longer sickened by the clinging aftermath of the nausea that had struck her in the kitchen.

••••• 14

"Will there be anything else?" Andrew asked.

Cash McCall shook his head. "Thank you, Andrew, for a very nice lunch."

The old waiter bowed his acknowledgment and left, leaving them alone in a silence broken only by the thrumming of the pantry door, fast fading as the spring hinges snubbed its pendulum swing.

"Was it?" Cash asked, edging back his chair.

"Was it what?"

"A nice lunch."

324

"More than *nice*. Much more!"

"Have I made my point—about the small adventures?"

She shook her head, laughing. "This hasn't been a small adventure. It's been a big one—for me, a very big one."

He was standing, moving behind her chair, and when she arose it was into the circle of his arms. "Not past tense," he said. "Don't say that it *has* been."

There was no need to accept his correction. She was certain that he had felt the tremor that had gone through her body, and that it had said everything that needed to be said. He knew—and she wanted him to know—that for her this was the great adventure, the adventure of adventures.

The telephone rang but it was not an annoying interruption, only the pleasant proof of reality. Telephones did not ring in dreams. She drew back her head, parting their lips, pushing him away toward the living room.

He offered her the flattery of resistance but she rejected it, slipping out of his arms, seeing then his look of puzzled inquiry as he glanced toward the bell sound, repeated now.

Moving quickly, he left her and when she followed him into the living room he was already listening to what someone was saying on the other end of the line. He glanced at her as she came into the room but it was not a diversion of attention from what he was hearing, only a reassuringly matter-of-fact acceptance of her presence.

Cash began to talk and she listened, at first only to the sound of his voice, not bothering to give meaning to his words until the consciousness dawned that he was speaking the language of another world, a second life that was something beyond the imagined sharing that, in these last few minutes, had begun to seem completely attainable.

"Yes, Gil, I understand that," Cash was saying. "But I can't possibly see him this afternoon. I'm sorry but—"

"Please!" she called out, quicker than thought. "If it's because of me—please don't let me be a nuisance!"

His hand went over the mouthpiece and his eyes searched her face. "Do you mean you'd forgive me if I left you for a half hour?"

"I wouldn't forgive you if you didn't."

The look he gave her was a glittering reward for her sacrifice. He withdrew his hand from the telephone instrument, glancing at his wrist watch. "All right, Gil, I'll see him at three-thirty. If that can't be arranged, call me back. Otherwise, I'll see you then."

325

His hand reached out after he had hung up and she moved into the inviting circle of his arm.

"That was a nice thing to do," he said.

"You have your work, I know that," she said, leaving unsaid what couldn't be said, the subconscious realization that happiness was dependent upon only her life changing, not his. He was the stability of solid earth, the immutable rock, the steadfast rallying point of unchangeable desire.

"Will you promise to be here when I get back?" he asked.

"Maybe," she said quickly, surprised that she was suddenly confident enough to risk coquetry, even more that she could resist the obvious invitation of his lips, so close now as he drew her to him. She pirouetted out of his arm, a turn and backstep carrying her to a chair, dropping to a half-sitting posture on its arm, gaily asking, "Do you have to leave right away?"

"Not for a few minutes."

"Then tell me about it."

"About what?"

"You."

"What about me?"

"Anything! Everything! Tell me what you do."

"Do?"

"Your business."

"But I did tell you—yesterday."

"Only that you bought companies."

"*And* sold them."

"Well, I know you work for the Gammer Corporation—but that's all I do know."

A quizzical smile broke. "Is that what you really thought—that I worked for the Gammer Corporation?"

"Don't you?"

He laughed and for an instant she was afraid that it was at her expense. But his face sobered. "I don't work *for* the Gammer Corporation, Lory. I *am* the Gammer Corporation—and the Aurora Corporation, and the Scotch Valley Corporation, and goodness how many others, past, present and future."

"But I—but you—"

He came to her, sitting on the other chair arm, then slipping down into the seat, his face almost level with hers. "Don't be too impressed, Lory. A corporation is only a piece of paper. Almost every time I buy and sell a company, the lawyers find some excuse for setting up another corporation."

326

"And that's all the Gammer Corporation is, just a piece of paper—but the piece of paper is really you?"

He chuckled a part denial. "That's what I get for trying to be facetious."

"I was being silly, too."

"There's more than that to the Gammer Corporation. It was an operating company when I bought it. When I sold the assets and inventory I kept the corporate shell because there was a loss carry-over that I could use. That's why I bought your company through Gammer—so I could take advantage of it. I don't suppose that makes much sense to you—"

She caught his side glance and, following it, saw that he had looked at her drawing. "What have you been imagining about me—that I've been living in some kind of fairy-tale world where there wasn't any such thing as income tax—or phenol-formaldehyde resins, or double-ram presses, or thermoplastic extruders? Would you like me to give you some hints on how you can reduce cycle time with electronic preheating? Or would you prefer my ideas on the advantages of the declining balance method of amortizing mold costs?"

He laughed his incredulity. "You can't really mean that you're interested in business?"

"Aren't *you?*" she countered, trying to make her eyes say that there was nothing about him that didn't interest her.

"Of course but—yes, I suppose I have been thinking of you as something out of a fairy-tale world."

His hand found hers, making self-denial even more difficult than it had been before, but she managed to ask, "If you're the Gammer Corporation, then you bought Suffolk Moulding for yourself?"

"But you knew that, didn't you?"

The grip of his fingers had slackened alarmingly and she hesitated, not certain now what she had known, knowing only that in her anxiety to share the small secrets of his life she had gone too far, opening doors that were best left closed. "It doesn't matter one way or the other."

Cash asked anxiously, "You didn't think I was buying it to operate?"

"No, I—well, I suppose I thought you were buying it for someone else."

"I was." An odd smile flashed. "But until last night I didn't know who it was going to be."

Watching, she saw the smile change from a kindling spark to an expression of full-blown excitement, rigidly contained but unmistakable.

"Is this one of those big adventures?" she asked.

"It could be," he said. "But still not big enough to worry about unless you'll promise to be here when I get back."

"I promise."

He rose, glancing at his watch. "It shouldn't take too long, a half hour, three quarters at the most. Sure you won't get bored here all by yourself?"

"I won't."

"Unless there's something else you want to do?"

The thought of her undeposited check popped into her mind, but she shook her head, grasping at the excuse that the bank was certain to be closed by now. "Is it all right if I just stay here?"

"All right? Of course. Why not?"

"I don't know the rules for a very innocent girl in the apartment of a very sophisticated man."

He laughed, starting for the foyer, the sweep of his arm carrying her with him. "I don't either—but I'll lock the door just in case one of those very sophisticated characters turns up."

"The door doesn't need to be locked," she said, her voice fading to a whisper before she had finished.

"I know that," he said, so intently serious that she expected the crush of his arms. Instead, his hands stopped at her shoulders and he kissed her lightly, as a husband would kiss his wife when he left the house for work in the morning. And he said, "If anything holds me up I'll call you."

He was gone then and she walked back into the living room, straightening the slip cover on the chair where they had been sitting, picking up a dropped match, seeing an ash tray that needed emptying.

••••• 15

As Winston Conway had suggested, Gil Clark intercepted Cash McCall in the law firm's reception lobby and took him to a vacant office for an account of his interview with Dr. Martin Bergmann. He had given Cash the highlight facts over the telephone and now he filled in the detail, attempting an almost verbatim report of the entire interview, driving resolutely ahead despite the discouraging suspicion that Cash McCall was no more than half listening. He seemed impenetrably preoccupied, staring silently out of the window, his only expression an oddly inscrutable smile that came to his face when, now and then, his eyes lifted to the patch of blue sky that was visible through the wedged gap between the two buildings across the street.

It was not until Gil had reached the end of his account of the Bergmann interview and had begun to search out pertinent paragraphs in the Lockwood report, that Cash suddenly loosed a volley of rapid-fire questions. Their incisiveness proved—although, to Gil, such proof was unnecessary—that Cash McCall had picked up more with half an ear than an ordinary man could possibly have heard with the full exercise of his faculties. Cash had missed nothing, even the subtle implications that Gil had felt himself unable to convey with direct description.

Cash nodded to the last answer, shucking a cigarette out of a crumpled package. "Good work, Gil. I like the way you handled Bergmann."

"Well, there wasn't much to it. Everything was all set up for me."

"It still took some handling."

"Not too much. As soon as I found out that it was Bergmann who wanted *your* help, instead of the other way around—well, that was the real break, his feeling the way he does about what's happened at Cox-Farrington."

"And you say that he mentioned John Allenby as a possible president?"

"Oh no," Gil said in hasty correction. "I'm sorry if I gave you that impression. All he said was that he hoped whoever you put in as president would do as good a job at Andscott as Mr. Allenby had done at Cox-Farrington."

Cash finally lighted his cigarette. "But it's an idea. I happen to know that Allenby is available. I talked to him a month or so ago. He's bumping his head against the ceiling over at Cox-Farrington— gone about as far as he can there—beginning to get a little bored with it. You don't know him?"

"No."

"Extremely able man," Cash said. "And what he'd have to do at Andscott would be exactly what his Cox-Farrington experience has proved he *can* do. We'd have to give him a big stock-option deal in order to interest him, I imagine, but that would be simple enough to arrange." He stumped out his just-lighted cigarette, a gesture of final decision. "And he'd be able to handle Danvers."

"Handle Danvers?" Gil asked blankly. "But he won't have to—"

"Look, Gil," Cash cut in. "I know how you feel about General Danvers—and it's my fault, telling you the things I did this morning.

I threw you and I know it. I shouldn't have done it. He's not a bad sort."

"But the things that he accused you of doing?"

"That was all in the heat of battle. You can't blame him too much. He's an old man and in a very tough spot. There'd be no fun in cutting his neck. There'd be a lot more fun in saving it."

"But how could you? I mean—well, you can't possibly let him go on managing the company, not after the mess he's gotten himself into."

"Yes, we'd have to get him away from the financial end of things. But that wouldn't be too difficult. With Allenby in there to keep him on the right track, it could be handled so that no one would know what was happening—probably not even Danvers himself."

"What would you do?"

"Kick him upstairs."

"Chairman of the board?"

"Sure."

Gil paused, finally saying, "It might not be such a bad idea at that," the admission grudging until he experienced a feeling that was closely akin to relief, then vaguely aware that General Danvers' fate had troubled his conscience more than he had realized. "It would be rough on a man like that—a general who's done what he did for the country—booting him out with a dishonorable discharge."

Cash said gruffly, "We don't have to wave any flags to justify it. He can pay his way—at least for the two years that he still has to go before retirement. Those Washington contacts of his are worth a lot. When we dump the television business, Andscott will need some new defense contracts to take up the slack."

"Yes, that's a point," Gil agreed. "And it probably wouldn't do Andscott Instrument any good in Washington to let the impression get around the Armed Forces that one of their own boys had gotten a rough shake up here."

"That's probably true," Cash acknowledged, but so offhandedly that it seemed a thought that hadn't occurred to him before. "Look, Gil, the way to get the most fun out of a deal like this is to work it so that everybody comes out a winner. If we take care of Danvers, we've just about made it. Austen sold his company for his asking price—more than it was worth—so he's a winner. Andscott Instrument gets a new management setup—which they need very badly. Bergmann gets his dividends—that saves the Andrews Foundation. General Danvers gets out from under—and it's my guess he'll welcome the chance."

"He probably will."

"So," Cash went on, "when we pick up our own chips, there's no

330

blood on them. No one got hurt. That's the way I want it to be. It's more fun."

"Well, it's a wonderful attitude—"

Cash clipped off the possibility of compliment. "Do you think Bergmann will object?"

"To what?"

"To making General Danvers chairman of the board. Or is he so prejudiced against him that he'd insist on giving him the ax?"

"Oh, I'm sure he won't care," Gil said quickly, recalling the cold-blooded intensity with which Dr. Bergmann vowed that he would do *anything* to save the Andrews Foundation. "To be honest about it, I don't think that anything you'd do at Andscott Instrument would matter in the least to Bergmann—whether General Danvers stays or goes—or anything else."

"As long as the Foundation gets its dividends?"

"That's right."

Cash nodded soberly. "That's the impression I'd gotten from what you'd said about him, but I wanted to be sure. Strange, isn't it?"

"What's that?"

"How widespread that attitude is becoming, not just in this case but so many others. Maybe this isn't a very good example—Bergmann probably hasn't any special obligation to worry about what happens to General Danvers—but there are getting to be so many men whose only standard of personal conduct is the good of some impersonal institution."

"I'm not certain that I know exactly what you mean."

"Surely you've run into a lot of it in the companies you've worked with—the man who does things as a corporation executive that he wouldn't do as a person, always justifying himself by saying that it was something that had to be done for the *good of the company*."

"Of course," Gil conceded, but his mind slipped into a groove deeply cut by his often repeated argument that the ethical standards of business, particularly big business, were so much higher than outsiders ever credited them with being. "But it works the other way around, too. Don't you think that there are a lot of corporation executives who—well, what I'm trying to say is that a corporation's ethical standards are usually higher than the personal standards of the men who manage it."

"Possibly," Cash McCall said, not with complete acceptance. "But you've made my point—that there are two sets of standards these days, one personal and another corporate. You say that Bergmann would do *anything* to get money for the Foundation. Would he do

331

anything to get money for himself? Doesn't that make the point that there's a double standard?"

Remembering the scene in Bergmann's office, Gil had no choice but agreement.

"It shows up even more clearly when you get outside business," Cash went on. "It's essentially the same thing but it hits you harder, seeing it in a different perspective. I ran into one a year or so ago—not too unlike the Bergmann situation—a college that stood to get about a half million dollars providing that the assets of a company that was being dissolved could be juggled in a certain way. The president of the college came here to Conway trying to get him to work out some way to make it legal. Conway turned the case down cold—it was nothing but a flagrant attempt to defraud the other stockholders. So the college got another law firm and went ahead. I happened to be involved in a minor way so I arranged to see the president and tried to point out how wrong he was in what he was attempting to do."

"But he couldn't see it?"

"Oh, he could see it. He admitted readily enough that the circumstances were regrettable. But how could anyone possibly criticize him? He wasn't doing it for personal gain—it was all for the good of the college."

"Did they get the money?"

"Of course. They took the case to court, followed exactly that same line of argument, and won hands down."

"And the next day, the president probably made a speech about how they had triumphed over the iniquitous forces of big business," Gil said with a twisted smile, recalling his own college experiences.

"Right on the nose," Cash agreed with a clipped laugh, looking at his watch. "We've wandered off the track here—Bergmann's probably out there by now—but this was something I wanted to try to get across, Gil. If we're going to go on working together, we have to think alike. When we make a deal it's all on our own heads. There's no umbrella. We can't justify anything we do by claiming it was for the good of the college—or the Foundation, or the company, or anything else."

"I know what you mean," Gil said, driven by some uncontrollable emotion to add, "And I just want to say—well, I'm proud as hell to be associated with you."

For an instant, Gil Clark felt that he had made the same mistake that he had made so many times before, blurting out what he felt, realizing too late that it made him sound like a naïve and unsophisticated kid.

332

But Cash's hand reached out, gripping his, and there was almost the suspicion of a choke in his voice as he said, "Thanks, Gil. I won't forget that."

Then, as if a shutter had opened and closed, the moment of exposure was over and Cash said, "All right, go out and get Bergmann. But hold him off for about five minutes. I've a couple of phone calls to make."

Gil started for the door but Cash's voice stopped him. "I'm assuming that you'd rather stay on this job than go back to Suffolk."

There was a lost moment before Gil managed to respond with a grinning nod. It was difficult to believe how far away six hours had made the Suffolk Moulding Company seem.

"After you bring in Bergmann, get together with Conway and tell him what we've talked about—Allenby and Danvers. I'm calling Allenby now. I'll leave Danvers for you."

"For me," Gil exclaimed, slapped by the same shock reaction that he had experienced when Cash had told him that he was to talk to Bergmann. That hadn't been too hard but talking to General Danvers would be a different matter.

"I'd do it myself, but I've something more important on my calendar," Cash said, the flicker of an unreadable smile crossing his face.

"Do you want me to—well, are you planning to show your whole hand?"

"Why not?" Cash shrugged. "We're holding the high cards. Don't forget that we still haven't agreed to sell Suffolk Moulding. But it's my guess you won't have any trouble with Danvers. He'll have cooled off a lot since last night—his temperature had gone down considerably before he left—and his big complaint was that he didn't have a chief of staff to lift the load from his shoulders. Unless I'm wrong, he'll welcome John Allenby with open arms."

"Of course there'd be one big advantage in having him in on it now," Gil said, recalling Conway's fear of the two-month waiting period before Cash McCall could receive the block of stock that would be the key to control. "If General Danvers is riding with us from the start, there won't be any chance of a foul-up along the way."

Cash McCall looked at him through a moment of silence, his face expressionless as he said crisply, "You're learning fast," but as he turned to pick up the telephone, Gil was almost certain that he saw the flash of a satisfied smile.

····· 16

As he crossed Rittenhouse Square, Will Atherson put the final polish on the pleasantly contrived scheme to continue the deception of his wife. She thought he had brought her downtown to see the architect's plans for restoring the springhouse on Starwood, never suspecting that this was the day when her twenty-year search of antique furniture shops would end with the discovery of a perfectly matched companion for her Randolph chest. He could, of course, have had the piece delivered to the house but that would have cost him the pleasure of seeing Helen's face when she first saw the chest in the curtained back room of Comsey's shop. That moment would be worth every cent he had spent and, as Helen would never be allowed to learn, he had spent a quite ridiculous sum. He had been forced to outbid a Du Pont representative who had wanted it for Winterthur, the final price made even more shocking by the necessity of paying, in addition to Comsey's undoubtedly handsome profit, a quite exorbitant finder's fee to this fellow Sabin who had actually located the chest in an old home in Lancaster.

If Helen ever discovered that he had spent that much money for a piece of furniture, even for something that she wanted as much as she wanted that matching chest, she would think that he had lost his mind. A very few years ago he would have shared her opinion. His father had taught him to regard any expenditure in terms of the capital required to earn a comparable sum at a reasonable rate of interest—but that had been back in the gold standard days when a man could still measure what something was worth by assigning it a value in dollars.

The proximity of the Hotel Ivanhoe brought Cash McCall to mind and Will Atherson decided that if his wife ever managed to worm out of him how much he had spent for the chest—which, unfortunately, was a distinct possibility—he would defend himself by telling her that her constant admiration of McCall had made him decide to emulate him. It was such an amusingly ridiculous idea—Will Atherson turning into a Cash McCall—that he was tempted to use it anyway.

The remnant of a fading smile was still on his face as he pushed through the revolving door into the lobby of the Hotel Ivanhoe, immediately seeing the back of a hat that was recognizably Helen's,

334

but not realizing until he was only a stride away that she was not alone. A young girl sat beside her, hidden by the high back of the davenport, popping up at the last minute to greet him by name.

Fortunately, Helen helped him by saying, "Lory's been waiting to give you a message," an assist without which he might not have recognized Lory Austen, a lapse that would have been inexcusable despite the fact that he had not seen her since that party they had given for her when she had graduated from art school. It was his immediate presumption that Grant Austen was in town again, a circumstance that called for some quickly devised side-stepping, the urgent need so occupying his mind that there was no preparation for hearing Lory say, "I have a message for you from Mr. McCall."

"Oh," he said, realizing after he had let the exclamation escape that he had been too obviously surprised which, unaccountably, seemed to strike Helen as being very amusing.

There was almost open laughter in his wife's voice as she explained, "Lory and Cash flew her folks down to a convention at Moon Beach and stopped over here for lunch on their way back."

He knew then that Helen was off on another of her matchmaking escapades and, silly as it was, that he'd be forced into submitting to whatever she had in mind. He had long since become resigned to this one imperfection in his wife's character and the futility of attempting to do anything about it. In this mood, Helen was capable of the most absurd machinations and when Lory told him that Cash McCall wanted him to call him at Jamison, Conway & Slythe, it was his unreasoned suspicion that it was all a part of some scheme of Helen's to get him out of the way.

She gave him all the proof his suspicion required by saying, "Cash probably wants to see you, dear, but don't worry about leaving me alone. Lory has invited me to go up to his suite for a cup of tea. We haven't had a talk for ages and those plans will wait until we get there. You come up when you're finished, dear."

He could not avoid noticing that Lory Austen was as embarrassed as he was—and equally helpless—so he walked off to make the call. By the time he had looked up the number and dialed it, Helen and Lory had already gone up in the elevator so, when Cash asked him to wait for the five minutes that it would take to get to the hotel, he decided to go up the mezzanine stairs and see Everett Pierce. He had nothing in particular that he wanted to talk to the hotel manager about, but dropping in on him would be a pleasanter waste of time than sitting alone in the lobby.

He pushed open the office door and, in the split second before Pierce could react, caught a glimpse of the hotel manager slumped

335

over his desk, his head burrowed into the crook of his arm. Pierce jerked upright, attempting an apologetic smile, but unable to hide the ashen pallor of his skin and the hard color-drained line of his lips.

"What's the matter, man?" Will Atherson asked anxiously. "Are you ill?"

Everett Pierce seemed about to speak but gulped as if swallowing the words. Then Will Atherson saw the trembling of his hands. Instinct, reinforced by the experience of having faced more than one businessman in a state of high-pitched emotional stress, told the banker that the hotel manager's illness was not organic but mental, that it was related to the affairs of the Hotel Ivanhoe, and Pierce's involuntary glance at the frosted glass wall that separated his office from Maude Kennard's was a clear indication of the source of his difficulty.

Atherson sat down and took out his pipe. He had been aware for some time that trouble was brewing at the Ivanhoe, but he had gone on hoping against hope that Pierce might somehow manage to resolve it. He knew now that he would have to step in himself. Maude Kennard was too clever for Pierce unaided. The poor devil needed help and, apparently, in a hurry. There was only five minutes before Cash McCall would arrive, but Atherson knew that he had to do what he could by way of emergency treatment.

In careful preparation, he lighted his pipe, tamped the bowl, then relighted it. His voice picked up the same slow tempo. "What's happened, Everett?"

Pierce stared at him, silent.

"Might as well get it off your chest," Atherson said, assuring himself by a glance to his right that there was no light in Maude Kennard's office.

Suddenly, startlingly, Everett Pierce blurted out, "The least you could have done would have been to tell me."

"Tell you what?" Atherson asked, startled by Pierce's tonal implication of resentment against him. In the long years, there had been nothing like this.

The hotel manager swallowed twice before he managed to say, "That he owns the hotel."

"What? That who owns the hotel?"

Pierce gulped as if short of breath. "Cash McCall."

"Where did you get that idea?"

"Well, I—I know it, that's all!"

Will Atherson puffed his way through a long pause. "No, Everett, you don't know that. You can't know something that isn't true."

"It—it isn't?"

336

"No."

"But—"

Everett Pierce's involuntary glance toward the glass partition had already answered Atherson's question, but there was a point in getting Pierce's open acknowledgment. "Who told you that Cash McCall owned this hotel—Mrs. Kennard?"

The hotel manager nodded, clearly relieved that he had been excused from the necessity of tattle-taling.

"There's been no change in the ownership of this hotel," Will Atherson said slowly. "But I wonder if this shouldn't be a warning to you."

"Yes, it—well, it is," Pierce said, evidencing embarrassment.

"I've sensed lately that you've been having a little difficulty with Mrs. Kennard."

The color was returning to the hotel manager's lips. "You don't know half of it, sir, not half of it. She's getting away with murder. She thinks she can do anything she wants to around here."

Atherson rubbed the bowl of his pipe. "You're still the manager of the hotel, aren't you?"

Pierce looked at him uncertainly, "Yes—if *you* say so."

"We probably should have talked about this before," Atherson said. "Perhaps it's time to start asserting yourself, Everett. If you once let her get the upper hand, it's my guess that you'll have some real trouble."

Everett Pierce stiffened his back against the chair. "All I need is to know that you're back of me."

"I'm back of you—but watch your step, Everett. She's a valuable asset to the hotel."

"I know," Pierce said as if confronted with an embarrassing mystery. "People like her."

"Yes, she's very clever," Atherson said, standing. "Sorry, Everett, but I have to run. If there are any problems, come over and talk to me."

"I'll try not to bother you any more than I have to," Pierce said, attempting a resolute manner. "It would be easier if she weren't a woman. I'm not at my best, trying to handle a woman."

"You're not unique in that," Will Atherson answered with a smile that barely survived his passage through the door.

He stopped at the mezzanine rail, looking down on the lobby, watching for Cash McCall's appearance, his mind occupied with the question of whether it might have been a wiser course to have told Everett the whole truth. After all these years, was there any point in continuing to hide his identity behind the bank's supposed trusteeship for an anonymous client?

337

As was true of so many things that affected his life, Will Atherson's ownership of the Hotel Ivanhoe stemmed from the depression—and, co-incidentally, from the creeping senility that had adversely affected his father's judgment in those last years of his life. The loan to the old Ivanhoe Hotel Company had been made on George Atherson's own responsibility, without the specific authorization of the board. Legally, he had every right to do what he had done—and it would have been unprecedented for the board to have voted down his recommendation—but after the loan had turned sour, Will Atherson had not been able to escape the conviction that his father had been motivated more by sentimental attachment to one of his old cronies than by sound business judgment. George Atherson had died that spring but his son felt that his inheritance inescapably included moral responsibility for his father's acts. That was why he had taken over the loan himself, fully reimbursing the bank. It had made a severe inroad on his personal fortune but, despite the protests of the board and the bank's legal advisers that it was by no means necessary, he could satisfy his own moral code in no other way. Everyone concerned had been sworn to secrecy because of the danger of someone misconstruing what he had done as evidence of something questionable having taken place in the management of the Freeholders Bank & Trust Company—and that, of course, would have defeated his whole purpose.

Within weeks after Will Atherson had taken over the loan, the Ivanhoe Hotel Company had come face to face with bankruptcy and, in order to salvage what he could, he had been forced to step in and assume control. Again thinking of the reputation of the bank, he had not revealed his personal ownership. Ostensibly, Freeholders began managing the property as a trustee, and that was the way he had left it all through the years.

He should, he knew, have gotten rid of the hotel a long time ago, but he had hung on and on, first because of the faintly glimmering hope that he might somehow manage to get his money back, then because he became intrigued with the possibilities of proving—for his own satisfaction if nothing else—that if heredity had not destined him for banking he would have been equally successful in general business management. The trouble now was that he had been too successful. The Hotel Ivanhoe was worth at least five times what he had invested in it and, if he were to sell it, it might possibly be construed that he had taken advantage of the bank by picking up the Ivanhoe at a bargain price. Ethics were, as he had often said, one of the most troublesome aspects of banking—and now, seeing Cash McCall come in through the revolving door, he resurrected

338

another well-worn thought, the wish that he had the advantage of Cash McCall's freedom of action.

He started down the staircase to the lobby, waving to attract McCall's attention, wondering what he had on his mind. From what Cash had said over the telephone, there seemed to be a hope that he was finally ready to tell him what was going on ... and it was about time! There was no point to all the secrecy with which McCall insisted on cloaking his deals ... no point at all! In fact it was rather ridiculous.

• • • • • 17

In her darkened office, Maude Kennard sat with the knuckled back of her hand pressed against her open mouth, fighting the screaming sob that nausea was forcing up into her throat. This was Wilfred and Chicago all over again ... that little bitch up in his room ... laying her was bad enough but this was worse ... *lying ... lying and lying and lying! He didn't own the Ivanhoe ... he never had owned the Ivanhoe ... one lie after another ... lies, lies, lies!*

• • • • • 18

When Cash had called Lory and asked her to try to catch Will Atherson in the lobby, he had told her that the banker was meeting his wife there and suggested inviting Mrs. Atherson up to the suite for tea as a way of filling in the time while he would be talking to Mr. Atherson. Lory had grasped eagerly at the chance, partially because she had always liked Mrs. Atherson and was grateful to her for her kindnesses during the years at Prather, but even more because doing something at Cash's request gave her the opportunity for helpful participation in his life. She did not stop to think, until she saw the startled expression on Helen Atherson's face, that she was exposing herself to possible censure. Too late, she uncovered the fear that Mrs. Atherson might not approve of her being in Cash's apartment, trepidation heightened by the memory of the strict chaperonage that had been enforced at the two weekend houseparties at the Athersons' during her last year at Prather. Her perturbation was not enough to incite any qualms of conscience, but it did arouse an uneasiness that persisted until Helen Atherson stood in the middle of Cash's living room and said, "My dear, I can't imagine how you can possibly be so calm about it."

Lory had just called Room Service, ordering tea as Cash had suggested, and for a moment she thought that Mrs. Atherson was complimenting her on managing to make her voice sound as if ordering tea at the Hotel Ivanhoe was something she had done every day of her life.

But then Helen Atherson asked, "How long have you known him, Lory?" her tone making it plain enough that she was not only approving but vicariously sharing her excitement.

"Oh, I met him a long time ago," Lory heard herself say, pleased by the poise she had suddenly acquired. "It was right after that wonderful party you gave for me. I went to Maine for the summer and—"

"But of course, my dear. How stupid I've been. I knew you'd met Cash there—Will told me—but I never imagined that you two had— oh, how perfectly wonderful!" Her eyes were eagerly surveying the room, darting about as if confronted with a complex of wonders all so tempting that a choice was impossible. "And the most wonderful thing about it is that it's so absolutely *right*."

Lory was again confused as to the subject of Mrs. Atherson's allusion, imagining it to be the apartment, caught unaware when she added, "You're so exactly the kind of girl that I've always imagined him falling in love with."

"Oh, but he isn't!" The illusion of poise had completely vanished. "I mean—well, I don't—"

Helen Atherson's smile was confidently derisive. "Tell me what you will, my dear, but don't try to tell me that *you're* not in love with *him*. It shows too plainly for that, much too plainly."

Lory felt herself weakening before the tempting opportunity to talk, reassured by the warmth and solidity of character that she had found in Helen Atherson since the moment of their first meeting.

But there was a countervailing embarrassment that rose when Mrs. Atherson said, "Surely you weren't imagining that it was a secret? It's about as much a secret, my dear, as that sun up there in the sky." She reached out, her fingertips touching Lory's cheek as if the length of her arm was the precisely right spacing for a perfect inspection. "Haven't you looked in the mirror lately—all that stardust sparkling in your eyes? But no, of course you haven't. You've only been looking at *him*—worrying, I suppose, whether or not *he* loves *you!*"

That wasn't true ... she hadn't really worried at all. Or was it?

Had she? Was this another of those mysterious things that went on unobserved in the secret recesses of her mind, the genesis of the little fears that sprang up now and then from nowhere? She yielded to the reassurance of Helen Atherson's knowing smile and nodded, not at anything in particular, more than anything else at the memory of what Barbara Hough had said about Mrs. Atherson after one of those weekend parties—that she was the kind of woman who should have been the mother of twelve children, all girls.

"That's one of the strangest things about falling in love," Helen Atherson went on. "The people that it happens to are usually the last to know about it. I'll never forget when Mother informed me one night that I was in love with Will. It was as plain to her as if I'd just broken out with measles. But I simply couldn't believe it. There I was, all fat and dumpy with a most horrible pimple on my chin—and he was rich, an Atherson, and such a wonderful, wonderful person! It seemed so incredible that it couldn't possibly mean anything—even if it were true. But that very next week he took me over to Starwood to get some dahlias to use at the horse show dance—I was the girl they always put on a working committee because I never had a date—and afterwards Mother invited Will to stop in for tea. He hadn't said a word to me, not a word, but somehow Mother saw the same kind of measles on his face that she had seen on mine. After Will was gone, she said that June weddings were nice but that there really wasn't any point in waiting around if a man wanted to get married sooner."

"And were you?" Lory laughed.

"April."

"Your mother must have been a very discerning person."

"At least a very wise person. I still don't know whether Will and I were in love then or not—but Mother convinced me that we were, and that's what gave me enough courage to believe that it was possible. That's about all it took. Goodness knows, I wanted him—and Will had been looking around long enough so that he knew he wasn't ever going to find the perfect wife."

"But I think he did."

"Thank you, my dear, you're very sweet. But entirely too flattering. Starwood could hardly have acquired a more poorly prepared mistress. I shall never forget that first formal dinner party. I'd been raised in a meat-and-potatoes kind of a life and Will had ordered diamondback terrapin—one of the Atherson traditions, you see. I knew, of course, that it was a stewy sort of soup, but when a whole crate of the most horrible looking *turtles* turned up in the kitchen—you've no idea what a panic I was in."

"You couldn't have been as frightened as I was at lunch," Lory said in confidential confession. "I'd never heard of *jambon* something or other—or *prosciutto,* or whatever it was."

"For which you can thank your lucky stars," Helen Atherson said with a confident toss of her head. "There's nothing that pleases a man as much as a chance to be outrageously superior—very *male,* you know—and all a wife has to do, really, is keep them that way. Husbands are so much more fun, my dear, when they're nice and male, superior and very independent. All a man really wants out of a wife is someone to help convince him that he needs neither help nor convincing."

"You make it sound a little confusing," Lory said, not knowing whether or not to smile.

She was glad she hadn't when she saw Helen Atherson's suddenly serious expression. "It *is* confusing. And all the more so in these topsy-turvy times—so many new standards, so many pressures. I remember back in the depression days—"

There was a knock at the door and Lory's heart fell, thinking that it must be Cash, returning too soon. But it was only Andrew with the tea service, responding to her greeting with the whispered explanation that, fortunately, her call had come just before he had gone off duty. He brought in a huge tray, nervously assembling china and a beautiful brass teakettle under which he lighted a spirit lamp, then opening a cloisonné caddy to indicate that the tea had not yet been brewed.

"How nice," Helen Atherson exclaimed. "Usually these days you're served one of those horrid tea bags, slopping about in a cup like a rag in a wash basin."

"It was the chef's orders, madame," Andrew explained.

"Do give him my thanks. I'm Mrs. Atherson."

"Yes, Mrs. Atherson, and thank you," Andrew said, withdrawing, leaving Lory with the task of brewing tea.

"Here, let me do that," Helen Atherson said, taking over. "Young girls in love are not to be trusted with boiling water."

Lory attempted a laughing protest but let it drop, less anxious to maintain the pretense of poise than to prompt Helen Atherson into picking up the broken thread of conversation. "You were going to tell me about the depression."

"It wasn't important," Helen Atherson said, spooning tea from the caddy. "I'm afraid I've acquired, along with my gray hair, an unfortunate tendency to gabble—plus, so Will says, a bad habit of meddling in love affairs. I'm sure you need no advice from me."

"Oh, but I do. I know so little."

"You've gotten this far on your own," Helen Atherson said with a significant glance around the apartment. "And with a man like Cash McCall I'd say that was a very considerable accomplishment. I've always thought him about as fascinating a male as I've ever known."

"Then you've—I mean, have you known him a long time?"

"Oh, ever since—well, ten years or more."

"Has he lived here a long time—in Philadelphia, I mean?"

Helen Atherson looked up, sympathetically horror-stricken. "Don't you know anything at all about him?"

Swallowing, Lory admitted, "There are so many other things to— and it's so difficult to get him to talk about himself."

A wisp of steam rose from the teakettle and Helen Atherson lifted it. "Hardly a typical male characteristic. But then he's hardly a typical male, is he? For which you can be very grateful. We're producing such a dull crop these days. Or perhaps it's only because I'm getting old. No, it can't be entirely that. I've still enough of those little hormones, or whatever they are, to appreciate Cash McCall."

"I really know so little about him," Lory said, feeling the shamelessness of the admission yet desperately anxious to learn what Helen Atherson had, a moment before, seemed willing to tell her.

The older woman continued filling the teapot. "I've not forgotten your question, Lory. I've been considering how much I could tell you, realizing how little I really do know about him. We've had him at Starwood a few times, of course, but what I actually know is only what I've been able to worm out of Will. But I did know his grandfather."

"I didn't know he even had one," Lory said, tricked by anxiety into sounding silly.

Helen Atherson laughed. "What were you imagining, my dear— that he was something dropped from heaven? He's not *that* unusual."

"I didn't mean—"

"Of course you didn't. I'm gabbling again. His grandfather was Andrew McCall. But I don't suppose that name means a thing to you, does it? No, you're much too young. He was old even when I was a girl, but still the most fascinating man. I suppose I got some of that feeling from Mother. She'd had a date with him once in her debutante year and Father, poor dear, never heard the last of it. The only times he ever had his innings were when word got around that Andy McCall had lost another fortune—which he did, of course, at regular intervals—but he'd always make another and then Mother would be in her glory again. Mr. McCall once owned an estate that was just down the Pike from us and every time he'd go by in his carriage—matched blacks with star blazes and he always drove himself—Mother would dash to the window. She always pretended, of course, that she did it to tease Father but I knew better. Oh, he *was* a handsome man, such a magnificent beard! I know, I know, you girls these days don't think a beard's romantic but that's only because you were born too late."

"And that was Cash's grandfather?"

"Yes, his grandfather—and Cash is so much like him in so many ways. That's one of Will's theories, you know—that inheritance usually jumps a generation, that a son is much more likely to resemble his grandfather than his father. I've no idea whether there's any scientific foundation for it, but it does hold true in a surprising number of cases—surely in Cash's."

"Then you knew Cash's father, too?"

"Not really—I met him only once or twice—but Will knew him quite well. John? Yes, I'm sure that's right—John McCall. He managed a wallpaper factory—Lancaster or Reading, one of those towns out there—and Will handled the firm's banking. He was a nice enough man, I suppose, but the way so many businessmen get these days— dull and stolid and all full of wallpaper. You know the type, I'm sure."

"Yes, I do know," Lory heard herself say, alarmed for an instant that her unthinking reply had been a too transparent allusion to her father.

"Well, now, let's see now how much I can tell you—goodness, I wish my memory for dates was better. Cash must have gone in with his father about '37—no it was before Susan was married—probably '36. I do remember meeting his father at Susan's wedding and he was so pleased that Cash was going to work for his company. And for a while it did seem as if it would take—oh, quite a long time really. Let's see, I can remember Will talking about what a fine businessman Cash was going to make that summer we were in Vermont. That must have been '37. Yes, that's about right, it was over a year. Then Cash just walked out, disappeared."

"Disappeared?"

Mrs. Atherson nodded. "To me it was perfectly understandable— he just wasn't the sort of person who could stand to be bored to death with the wallpaper business—but Will has always insisted that it was because of his father's death. I can't quite believe that—Cash is much too self-sufficient—but in any event he disappeared."

"Was that when he was in India?"

"Oh, then you do know this part of it?"

"No, not really," Lory said quickly, anxious not to miss anything that Helen Atherson might tell her. "I only know that he was there, that's all. I've seen some of the things he brought back."

344

"Yes, that's where he was when Will finally located him—India or Burma or somewhere out there. You see, the bank was the executor of his father's estate and there were some papers that Cash had to sign." Her expression indicated a suddenly recalled memory. "There was a little property that had been willed to Cash—a small block of stock, I believe—but he wouldn't accept it. Insisted that everything go to his mother—actually his *step*mother, his own mother had died when he was a child—which was very sweet of him, of course, but it didn't mean an earthly thing. It wasn't a year until she married some horrible old goat, really a quite impossible person—I believe Will said he'd made his money in road contracting or something of the sort. Dear me, I've let this tea oversteep, haven't I?"

As Helen Atherson poured, Lory asked, "How long was Cash in India?"

"Now let me see," Mrs. Atherson puzzled, the teapot suspended. "I really don't know, my dear. Perhaps a year or two. I do remember Will telling me that he'd come into the bank—yes, it must have been the spring of '39. I was just home from Boston—Anne's first baby. Cream, my dear?"

"No, thank you."

"Will was so worried about the boy, afraid he wasn't going to get along, and he tried to help him. There were several openings in companies that Will was interested in but Cash turned down all of them." She laughed in amused reminiscence. "I shall never forget the poor dear's face the night he came home and told me that Cash had made some enormous sum of money, buying and selling some company—and without a cent of his own capital, mind you! The thing that Will couldn't get over, of course, was that Cash had seen the opportunity and he hadn't! It had been right there under Will's nose all the time—one of his own customers." She paused, looking up from her tea cup. "You do know that's what he does—buys and sells companies?"

Lory found herself grateful for the chance to nod, but the feeling of poise that it gave her was destroyed by the consciousness of a question that demanded the marshaling of her full courage. "Do you know, Mrs. Atherson, if he's ever been married?"

Helen Atherson's tea cup clattered down to its saucer. "Oh, you poor dear child, don't you even know—"

"I know it sounds silly to ask but—"

"Of course it isn't," the older woman said, reaching out for her hand. "And I can understand perfectly how difficult it would be for you to ask him. No, Lory, he's never been married—but I'm sure you're much too sensible to imagine that there's never been another woman in his life. Of course there has."

Lory feigned the poise that it took to carry her through the slowly subsiding sting of shock.

"It's not that I actually *know* that he's ever been interested in another woman," Helen Atherson added. "But it stands to reason there've been some. Just accept that, my dear, and don't let it worry you. Some girls are so silly about this business of being the first. Believe me, it's much more important to be the last!"

"Really, Mrs. Atherson, I know you think that Cash and I are—"

She was interrupted by the sound of a key in the hall door lock and turned to see Mr. Atherson enter the foyer. Cash was immediately behind him but Lory avoided his face, only chancing a quick glance to see what had made Mrs. Atherson say, "You two look as if you'd just made a million dollars."

"Or lost it," Cash said, his smile at Atherson bringing no response.

Lory offered tea but Mrs. Atherson had already moved to the coat closet, anticipating her husband's explanation that they must leave at once.

The two men stood talking together in the foyer as Lory helped Mrs. Atherson with her coat. Eavesdropping, she almost missed the whisper in her ear. "It's much more obvious than measles, my dear —and I wouldn't wait for June either."

The door closed on the Athersons and for a moment Lory did not know what to do with her eyes. What she felt was more than the simple embarrassment that Helen Atherson's whisper had aroused. Since the instant of Cash's return there had been a consciousness of wrongdoing, the feeling that she should not have stooped to furtive gossiping, that she was guilty of listening to words that should have been heard only from Cash.

She saw the lip movement that had, always before, been the beginning of his smile but now, strangely, it was the precursor of an expression that might have been her own. It was almost as if he was thinking with her mind, as if there was a sharing of embarrassment. Was it possible that all of this had been something planned, that he had *wanted* Helen Atherson to talk to her? No, it had been too accidental for that.

Cash's eyes went to the tea tray and she asked, "May I give you some tea?"

"Scotch would be better."

"Let me get it for you."

The smile came now. "All right—if you want to."

"I want to."

346

He dropped down to the green-leather couch. "It's there in that cabinet."

Exploring, conscious that he was watching her, she found the door that opened on the racked bottles, then the trays of ice in the miniature refrigerator. There was something oddly reminiscent about what was happening but she did not realize what it was until, handing him the mixed drink, she heard herself say, "You look as if you needed it." The words excited a flash of memory and she knew then what it was that made this seem so familiar ... that night in her father's library when he had decided to sell the company, saying that he wanted scotch instead of coffee, telling him that he looked as if he needed a strong drink. Recognition destroyed the parallelism, underlining the differences, smudging the similarities ... yet ...

"Sit down, Lory," Cash said as a quiet command. "I want to talk to you."

Again there was the intruding memory of that night in the library, pushed back with difficulty because there was, unmistakably, that same expression on Cash's face, apprehension blended with expectancy, a faint overpainting of something close to embarrassment. The rescuing difference was that this wouldn't be about the Suffolk Moulding Company. Cash wouldn't talk to her about business ... this would be something else. It might even be ...

"Lory, I've just sold the Suffolk Moulding Company," Cash said abruptly, "—and I want you to know what's happening."

• • • • • 19

"Why, Will Atherson!" Helen exclaimed, gaily incredulous. "You can't possibly mean there was anything wrong about Lory having lunch in Cash's apartment. After all, dear, this *is* the twentieth century."

"You know very well that I meant nothing of the sort," he said tolerantly, but relieved that a contractor's barricade jutting out across the sidewalk forced a single-file passage and gave him an excuse to drop his hand from his wife's arm. He needed this clear moment to think through the details of handling the loan that he had promised Cash McCall the bank would make. Once everything was fixed in his mind, he could forget it until tomorrow morning.

Even though he had committed the bank, the loan would probably be endlessly discussed in the board meeting tomorrow, Peregrine insisting on remaking his shopworn speech about the highflyers always stubbing their toes ... but the old boy's face would really be something to see when he found out that the loan was being made so that Cash could buy all the Andscott Instrument stock in the Jonas Scott estate!

All the directors would, of course, be relieved to learn that Freeholders had finally completed the liquidation ... but it would mean more than that to old man Peregrine ... his daughter-in-law was a one-sixth beneficiary of the Scott estate.

A frown crossed Will Atherson's face as he realized that he was being unfair to Mr. Peregrine. It was a serious thing to suspect a bank director of self-interest. Peregrine was an upright man ... if that were not the case, he wouldn't be a director of the Freeholders Bank & Trust Company ... but, as was unfortunately true for all men, there was a shady area where the demarcation was difficult to define. It would, for example, be very hard to say just where the line fell in relation to a daughter-in-law with a one-sixth interest in the Scott estate.

Helen had passed the barricade and was waiting for him at the street corner. "It's to the right, isn't it, dear?"

"No," he said, firmly taking her arm again. "Straight down Chestnut."

"But, I'm sure—Will Atherson, have you been keeping something from me?"

"Now, Helen—"

"I knew it! You had that guilty look on your face this morning. You always do when you're trying to keep a secret from me."

"I suppose," he sighed, "I'm not as good at it as Cash McCall, am I?"

He had meant the remark to be amusing, but somehow it didn't turn out that way. Helen had missed the point. But maybe there wasn't a point. After all, Cash had been quite right in not telling him *why* he wanted the Andscott stock ... to have done so would have made Freeholders a party to whatever was going to happen and that might put the bank in an untenable position. As his father had once said, a banker's life had to be lived on the knife-edge of always knowing just enough, never too much.

"Will?"

"Yes?"

"Let's stop at Comsey's for a minute."

"Comsey's?" he repeated, swallowing a sigh of defeat ... confound it, if Cash McCall could get away with his secrets, why couldn't he at least keep Helen from finding out every blessed little thing that ever

348

entered his mind! But it was easier for Cash . . . he didn't have Helen to contend with.

"Florence said Mr. Comsey had gotten in a lot of lovely old English silver," Helen explained. "And we'll have to find something nice for a wedding present."

"All right, dear," he said, patting his pockets to find his pipe.

••••• 20

"But I don't think that at all," Lory broke in. "I think it's the most exciting thing that—do you really mean that you might make a million dollars?"

"Or lose it," Cash replied, repeating what she remembered he had said to Mrs. Atherson. "Everything depends on what we can do with Andscott Instrument. If we can get the company back on its feet again, there ought to be a good pay-off. If we can't—" He glanced around the apartment with a dismissing shrug. "The Ivanhoe will probably lose a tenant."

"You don't really mean that?"

"Oh, but I do." He hunched forward over his knees. "I'm gambling every cent I have, Lory—plus every dollar I can borrow. That's why I wanted to see Mr. Atherson—to get another loan so I could buy a block of stock that will absolutely insure having control."

"And he gave you the loan?"

"Luckily, the stock is in an estate that the bank is anxious to settle. They've been trying to dump it for months and months. But it's another million dollars on the line."

Lory blinked, swallowing hard. "Honestly, I—well, I just never knew that things like this happened!"

"That's why I wanted to tell you about it," Cash said, unaccountably serious. "I wanted you to know."

"But it will be a wonderful thing for so many people—everyone in the Andscott company—this Dr. Bergmann and his Foundation—" She let her voice fade, then added as a quick afterthought, "And for you, too, of course."

"That's the part of it that doesn't make sense."

"What part?"

"My getting into this Andscott affair. It's as senseless as all of the other crazy things I've done with my life. There's no point to it. If I lose, I've tossed away enough money to let me live like a maharajah

349

for the rest of my life. If I win, all I get out of it is some more money—and I didn't need that."

"But think of the fun you're having," Lory said, remembering the glow of excitement that she had seen in his eyes when he had been describing the way the deal had developed.

"*This* isn't fun," he said wryly. "At least I'm making an unholy mess of it."

"Of what?"

"Trying to tell you what an off-beat character I am." He raised his glass as if looking for the courage to go on. It was empty.

She reached out. "I'll get you another."

He shook his head. "Another drink might convince me that I don't have to tell you—and I do."

"That you're not an ordinary nine-to-five kind of man?"

"Worse than that."

"Because you were bored with the wallpaper business?"

He looked up sharply. "Mrs. Atherson talked to you?"

"Yes."

"I hoped she would," he said, a surprising confirmation of Lory's earlier suspicion. "What did she tell you?"

Lory hesitated, wishing that her lack of courage did not make so much of what had been said unrepeatable. "Well, she did say that the world was producing a very dull crop of men these days—but that you weren't one of them."

For an instant, she thought she had earned a smile but Cash stood abruptly and crossed to the bar cabinet. He was facing away from her when he said, "She did tell you that I've never married?"

"Yes," Lory answered quickly, the single word expelled ahead of the rise of a chilling fear.

There was the cold clatter of ice in his glass. "But she couldn't have told you *why*—and that's what I want you to know, Lory."

She waited for him to turn back to her, hoping that the expression on his face would be a denial of his words. It was not. His blue eyes were cold, the set of his jaw grimly resolute.

"No man has a right to ask any woman to marry him unless there's a reasonable chance that he can give her the kind of life she has a right to expect." His voice was as flat as if he were reading from a textbook, only slightly more expressive as he went on. "A woman wants security and solidity—what every sensible person wants. I've never been able to offer that. I'm a gambler—nothing more, nothing less, rich one day and broke the next. And there's nothing I can do to change myself into a different person. I know. I've tried. It doesn't work. I can't be something I'm not. Can you understand that, Lory?"

Her nod was meaningless, only an acknowledgment that she had heard, not that she understood. What was he trying to tell her ... that this was the end of everything ... or the beginning of something for which there would be no ending?

Cash sat down on the edge of the couch, an arm's length away from her, and she saw then that there was nothing in his glass except the bare ice cubes.

"No, Lory, you don't understand," Cash said. "I know you don't. How could you?"

"Does it matter?" she asked, the question more meaningful than she realized until she saw the reaction on Cash's face.

"Yes, it matters," he said. "At least to me. Maybe that's not reason enough to ask you to listen—but will you?"

"If you want me to."

"I do," he said positively. "At least I want to try to—maybe that's all it will be, just a *try*." He wrapped the glass in the long-fingered grip of his doubled hands. "I don't know why this should be such a tough assignment—maybe because I've never done it before—but it is. Have *you* ever tried this—telling someone *why* you're the kind of person you are?"

"I don't suppose I've ever thought about it."

Cash shook his head. "I haven't that excuse. I've thought about it enough—maybe too much. But it's been the kind of thinking that's hard to translate into words. That's one of the troubles with living alone—you do all your thinking to yourself and there's no need for words. When you do need them—"

He had made the self-conscious discovery that there was nothing but ice in his glass and Lory caught up his smile.

"Here, let me have that," she demanded, taking the glass from his hands, refilling it and handing it back to him.

"All right," she laughed, bridging the long gap of silence. "Now you can tell me all the awful things you've done in your life."

To herself, Lory's brightness seemed recognizably false, but it did appear to have eased the tension. Cash smiled as he said, "It isn't only the things I *have* done, it's the things I haven't done."

"Like not staying put in the wallpaper business?"

"What did Mrs. Atherson tell you about that?"

"Nothing much—except that you'd been in it for a while and then left."

"Did she tell you why?"

"I don't suppose she knew. She said she thought you were bored with it—but that Mr. Atherson thought it was because of your father."

The shake of his head came quickly but there was a long reflective pause before he spoke. "No, it wasn't because of my father's death —except in the sense of that being the precipitating incident. I would have left in any event. I just didn't *belong*. I suppose I should have realized that before I ever started, but somehow I hadn't—and it hit me hard when I finally woke up. You see, I'd always taken it for granted that I'd work for Conestoga Wallpaper."

"Is that what you wanted to do?"

"I thought so. But maybe I was only drifting down the path of least resistance. Looking back now, I realize that it was never any real burning desire—never anything that meant as much to me as research work means to Dr. Bergmann—or cooking to Max—or as Conestoga Wallpaper meant to my father. There was never anything that aimed my life in any particular direction. I suppose that's hard for you to understand—you were born with a *talent*—"

"Not a very big one."

"But big or little, still it gave point and purpose to your life. Isn't that true? Didn't you know from the time you were a child that you were going to be an artist?"

"Yes, I suppose I did," Lory said, remembering that first time her father had taken her to Eloise Tassman's studio at Chester Springs.

"There was never anything like that for me," Cash said. "No particular talent, not even an aptitude. I didn't have an engineering mind, or a research mind, or a legal mind, or any other special kind of a mind. I don't think I ever thought it through in exactly that way—I'm sure I didn't—but, anyway, I wound up in the college of business administration. I got there in the same way most of the other boys got there, not because we had a special talent or aptitude for business, but just because that was what was left. Oh, there were exceptions, of course—boys of the Gil Clark type—but the rest of us were the small potatoes that were left after the big ones had been picked out."

Lory laughed. "There were an awful lot of people in art school who weren't there because they had any special talent."

"But at least they *thought* they had it," Cash argued. "And I suppose I thought so, too. I left college with—well, actually, by the time I graduated I was pretty much steamed up about a business career. This was '36, the depression was still on, but I'd had a reasonable scholastic record and I got a half dozen job offers. One of them was with Conestoga, of course. Dad had been there all his working life —his sun rose and set right over the plant roof—so there's where I went."

"Your father owned the company?" Lory asked, trying to confirm a parallelism that would account for the concern for her own father that Cash had shown before lunch.

"No, he was just the plant manager—Conestoga was a division of the Columbia Furnishings—but it couldn't have been any more a part of his life if he'd owned every brick of the factory. No, that's wrong—it wasn't a *part* of his life, it was all of it. Actually, I think he was more totally absorbed in it than if he had owned it. That made it something even more *detached—inanimate*—no, that doesn't say it."

"I believe I know what you mean," Lory said, but by no means certain that she did.

"When I was in India I lived for a while in a little village in Rajputana. I asked a group of people who owned their temple. They were horror-stricken at the idea of my imagining that anyone could *own* a temple. I think that's more or less the way my father felt. I'm sure he never thought of the plant as something that anyone *owned*. It was an institution—"

"*His* temple," she suggested.

"That's it," Cash said gratefully. "Conestoga Wallpaper was his religion and the plant was his temple, his shrine, his place of worship. He'd do anything for the company—*anything!* No personal consideration could ever be superior to that."

"It sounds a little like what you were saying about Dr. Bergmann and the Foundation."

"Of course," Cash said with a wry smile. "And there are a million other men just like that. It's a popular religion, Lory—this company worship—and maybe it's the right one, I don't know."

"But not for you?"

"No, not for me. I couldn't accept the gospel. I tried—two years on my knees—but I was still an infidel, still the heathen in the temple. I didn't belong. I just couldn't generate the blind faith that you have to have. And you *do* have to have it, Lory. That's what business demands today. If the high priests lose their faith, the temple walls start to crumble."

Lory nodded, accepting her father as an example.

"And of course it has to carry down the line," Cash went on. "The low priests, the altar boys, everyone. There's no place in the temple for the non-believers. Every religion has a curse for the infidels—and this one does, too. My father shouted it at me once. I'll never forget it." Cash paused, a bitter smile quickly softening to tolerance. "He accused me of not being a *company man*—and he said it as if he'd just looked into my soul and seen all the devils of hell writhing around in there."

"I'm sure he didn't mean it that way," Lory said, but conviction was tempered by the recollection of those nights in the library when her father had talked about men at Suffolk Moulding. There was no greater compliment he could pay anyone than to say he was a *company man,* no greater fear than that someone might not turn out to be one.

"It was over such a little thing, too," Cash reminisced. "But it was typical. This was in the late thirties and there was a home-furnishings style trend that was more or less away from wallpaper—painted and textured walls were coming in—and my father had made a speech at the sales convention. He really went overboard—if this horrible trend wasn't stopped, civilization was doomed. I remember one of his lines—*imagine if you can, a whole generation growing up without their cultural heritage of artistic wallpaper!*"

"And he probably believed it," Lory said with a smile.

"Oh, he did. But when he asked me in all seriousness what I thought of what he'd said, I couldn't resist saying what *I* really believed—that I couldn't see that it would make a great deal of difference in the future of civilization, one way or another. I shouldn't have needled him but—"

"I know," Lory broke in without intention, then forced to go on as Cash waited. "It's been like that with my father, too. The plastics business was no subject for humor. I remember how terribly upset he was once when he heard the wife of one of his men say that she hated plastic dishes."

"Yes, that was disloyalty," Cash agreed. "One of my father's assistants built a new house and paneled the living room—no wallpaper. I don't think Dad ever really trusted him after that. To him, it had to be one hundred per cent or nothing. A man had to give *everything,* his whole life. And that's what he did himself—literally."

Cash sat for a moment, lost in thought, but she was certain that he would go on without prompting. And he did. "It was a horrible thing—at least it seemed so to me at the time. They were working on some wonderful new machine—all it did, actually, was put a spray-gun effect on the background before the design was printed—but, of course, right then that was the most important thing in the world. There'd been a memo from the New York office about it—and that was a stone tablet right from Mount Sinai. The machine had to be operating in time to get samples in the new line. Dad went out in the factory himself and worked on the thing. He drove himself like a madman, day and night—and then a heart attack."

"How awful," Lory whispered.

"The awful part was still to come. They took him to the hospital.

Somehow, after midnight when the nurse was out of the room for a minute, he sneaked out and went back to the plant. We found him there a couple of hours later—dead."

"Oh, no."

"Men die—I could accept that," Cash said gravely. "But what I couldn't get over was the terrifying fanaticism that would make a man offer up himself as a human sacrifice—and all for something no more consequential than a gadget to spray ink on wallpaper. Of course, I was still pretty much of a kid—I was only seeing one side of it—but I couldn't accept the philosophy that *that* should be the end-point of a man's life. It seemed horrible."

"It was," Lory whispered.

"But not to the other men. I remember the funeral—all the big brass down from the main office in New York. To them, my father had done something very noble. What more could any man want than a chance to lay down his life for a great company?"

"It really is something like a religion, isn't it?"

Cash hesitated. "Maybe I'm a little overboard in calling it that, but I've been trying to make you understand the way I felt at the time."

"And I think I do."

"Anyway, I couldn't accept the philosophy. I couldn't believe that the individual didn't matter, that it was only the company that counted—always the *group*, never the man—always the individual must submerge himself in the mass."

"And you wouldn't submerge?"

"I couldn't. You see—but there was another side of it, too. How important it was, I don't know—I can't look back now and re-create everything that was in my mind then—but I was a depression product, college during the Roosevelt years, and I suppose I'd been inoculated with the anti-business virus. That must have been true because if it hadn't been, the rest of the world wouldn't have hit me the way it did. I'd left the United States with the idea that the American businessman was a pretty awful character—cold, materialistic, nothing but a money-grubber. But when I stacked him up against what I found around the rest of the world, he looked like a fairly decent character. The longer I went, the more I began to feel that same way about the whole American idea. All right, maybe we had turned company worship into something like a national religion, but could anyone argue that it didn't work? Look at the results. Could anyone say that we hadn't created the best way of life that the world had ever known? Anyway, I came home a convert and headed right down the sawdust trail, looking for a job."

"You didn't go back to Conestoga Wallpaper?"

"No. That was the past and this was a new start. I thought I might get into aviation. I'd started flying when I was in college and liked it. All over Europe and Asia, I'd hung around airports, grubstaking myself now and then with a mechanic's job. I knew what conditions were like abroad so I thought I'd have something to offer some manufacturer in the aviation field who was interested in export. I landed on the West Coast—this was the spring of '39—and started looking for a job. I found three companies that had openings. But they all turned me down—one, two, three. No reason, just thank you very much but no go. The last company I talked to had the job that I really wanted—assistant export sales manager—so I kept going back. Finally, I got to the president. At first he wouldn't talk either, but in the end I managed to nag him into telling me what the score was. I'll never forget the look on his face when he did. He acted as if he were pronouncing a death sentence."

"But what did he say?"

"That I was one of those most displaced of all persons—an individualist."

"How silly."

"No, not silly at all. He said that he was afraid I'd never be a real *company man*. And he was right. I wouldn't have. I'd rationalized away all my instincts, but that didn't change the essential me. I was still the infidel, still the heathen in the temple, still the guy that couldn't accept the gospel of allowing myself to be completely swallowed up."

Cash sipped his drink. "I came back to Philadelphia and then something happened that—well, anyway, that was the start of the kind of a life I've led ever since. I happened to run into a man named Allen Ranson. He was a very personable character and didn't seem to have too much of a prejudice against individualists. He was out to buy a little company that made airport equipment— runway lights and that sort of thing—and he offered me a job managing the company, providing that he could close the deal to buy it. It was a family business, the old man had died and the three boys who had inherited it couldn't get together on what they wanted. I suppose I should have suspected something—why had Ranson picked me?—but I was green, trusted him completely, and plunged into the thing, head over heels. I worked twenty hours a day, reading corporation law and tax manuals, trying to work out some deal that the heirs would accept. Finally, at midnight one night, we shook hands on an agreement. When I went to Ranson the next day, he welched, claiming that he hadn't given me the authority to act. I found out later what he'd done—used me for a catspaw to keep this company I'd bought from selling out to someone else and spoiling another deal he had on the fire. You can see the spot that left me in—I'd made the deal, given my personal word, and somehow I had to go through with it. But I didn't know how. Operating the business was out of the question—I couldn't possibly have financed it—but I was positive that the company was worth more than I'd agreed to pay. Somehow, I talked Will Atherson into loaning me the option money —and then I remembered the president of this company in California."

"The one who had called you an individualist?"

"That's right. He'd mentioned something about his company wanting to diversify with supplementary lines, so I packed up a bunch of samples, bummed a ride across the country with a pilot I knew, and finally wound up selling him the company."

"This same man who wouldn't give you a job?"

Cash nodded. "In nine days, I made a profit of over a hundred thousand dollars. I was flabbergasted. It just didn't make sense. A month ago, this same man wouldn't give me five thousand a year to work for him. Now he'd handed me twenty years' salary for a month's work."

"It would have been cheaper to have hired you."

"Much! But the strange thing was that it didn't bother him. He was actually pleased. You see, I'd confirmed his judgment about me."

"No, I'm afraid I don't understand."

"I'd proved I wasn't a company man. If I had been, I'd never have done such a crazy thing as to jump in and buy a quarter million dollar business with no money to pay for it, and no idea what I was going to do with it after I'd bought it. Furthermore, I'd done it all on my own—no consultations, no committees, no group action."

Assured by Cash's ironic humor, Lory laughed. "But you made a hundred thousand dollars."

"It wasn't only the money, Lory. Oh, I don't mean to say that wasn't important—when you've been flat broke for a year or two, a hundred thousand dollars can look like a first-class miracle—but it was more than that. For the first time, I'd really gotten a wallop out of something. That experience—first buying the company and then selling it—was the most exciting thing that had ever happened to me."

"I can easily believe that."

"Probably sounds ridiculous to make the comparison, but it was something like mountain climbing—all the preparation, every detail so important, knowing that if you slip once you're done. Then you make it and you're up there on top. Once that's happened, you're never quite the same again—you never get it out of your system. I don't suppose that makes any sense but—"

"Oh, but it does! Of course it makes sense."

Cash looked at her almost as if he was finding it difficult to accept her understanding, pausing before he continued. "Afterwards, I kept trying to tell myself that it was a freak case—one lucky break—something that could never happen again. But I had enough money to live on for a while so I started looking around, prospecting for another company that could be bought and sold. Luckily—or maybe unluckily, I don't know—I did stumble into another one. In less than two years, there were five of them. By the fall of '41, I had a million dollars. Then came the war and India again—Burma—and the Hump. I'd sit there in the cockpit and tell myself that when it was over I'd buy some good company and not sell it, settle down and run it myself. But I didn't. Oh, I tried—more than once. It's just no go, Lory. There's a wallop in it for the first six months—bracing up a shaky outfit, reorganizing it, taking it apart and putting it back together again so that it runs. But then the fun's over so far as I'm concerned. For me, that's the end. From there on out, I don't belong—I'm not a company man."

There had been a curtaining quality in his last words, a tone of finality, as if this were the end of the story. Puzzled, Lory looked up at him.

"That's it," he said. "That's all I've ever done."

Lory felt herself completely bewildered. What was the point? He had started out to tell her why he had never married. Was there something she had missed, some significant meaning that slipped past her realization?

Cash was frowning as if to criticize her lack of understanding. "Don't you see what it means, Lory—the off-beat kind of life, no solidity, no security, nothing like that. Can't you understand what I'm trying to say?"

She searched his face. "No, I'm afraid I don't."

There was a ripple of muscles along his set jaw. "I wish I could promise you I'd change—it's a terrible temptation, I want you so much—but it would be a promise I couldn't keep."

A supreme effort was required to keep her voice as rigidly calm as his had been. "Why do you imagine that I'd want you to change?"

"The world doesn't think very much of my kind any more. I was born a couple of generations too late."

"Your grandfather?"

"Mrs. Atherson told you about him?"

358

"A little."

"What?"

"Nothing very much—except that he was a wonderful person—and that he had a magnificent beard. And that you were a little like him. Mr. Atherson has a theory that inheritance works that way."

"I know. He told me. And it *is* strange how close I've always felt to my grandfather. I hardly knew him myself—he died when I was a child—and my father couldn't have influenced me because he never mentioned him except as an example of everything that a good businessman shouldn't be—the robber baron, the lone-wolf gambler, the man who once made a million dollars between breakfast and lunch and then lost it before dinner. I don't know how much money he made in the course of his lifetime—millions—and he died leaving almost nothing. I think my father always thought of that as a triumph of right over wrong, a bad man coming to a bad end."

"Mr. Atherson must have felt differently about him."

Cash nodded. "Yes, I'll never forget that day. I'd told him how I felt personally obligated to go through with this deal that Ranson had welched on. He hadn't said a word all the time I'd been talking, just sat there smoking his pipe, but when I was through he said he could see how I'd feel that way, being Andrew McCall's grandson. And then he loaned me the money with no more security than my grandfather's reputation as an honorable man. I'll never forget one thing he told me—that my grandfather had once said that the only thing that ever worried him was giving another man just cause to think that he had been treated unfairly."

Her hands went up, fingertips to his cheekbones. "Yes, you'd look very nice in a beard."

"Lory, I—"

"You're perfectly safe. I've been warned. You've been an honorable man and told me all about yourself. I'll never be able to say that I've been treated unfairly."

"Lory, you can't—"

"Except that you are being a little unfair about one thing—making me wait so long to tell you that I *do* want to marry you."

"Without even being told that I love you?"

"You've told me—a thousand times—as many times as I've told you."

"Shall I say it out loud? Just once—for convention's sake?"

"It isn't necessary—unless you want to."

"I want to." He held her away from him, looking down into her face. "I love you, Lory Austen."

"And I love you, Cash McCall."

359

Their bodies came together as if drawn by the magnetic pull of the earth. But their lips were lightly touched, neither the pledge nor fulfillment of passion, but a solemn covenant consciously offered and knowingly accepted.

As they parted, Cash glanced toward the window, measuring the height of the low sun, and it seemed that it was a response to her mind rather than his. There had been, in the instant before his eyes had moved, the memory of his having said yesterday that there were no lights on the airstrip in Aurora Valley, that the plane could be brought in only during the hours before sundown.

Her eyes dropped and she saw the red rock of the cliffside above the falls, the voice of memory reminding her that she should have worn a different pair of shoes.

And Cash's mind, inside her own, must have heard because he said, "It doesn't have to be Aurora."

"I want it to be Aurora."

Cash's words had been whispered, but hers were clearly spoken, the strong words of a mature woman in that first moment of discovery, realizing at last the fulfillment of self-determination. Decision had indelibly marked the point beyond which there was no need for either question or answer. He was a man and she a woman and they were in love. Now it was as simple as that. This was the end of aloneness, the beginning of her real life.

Ten

⋮

GRANT AUSTEN was more or less responsible for the middle-of-the-road position that had been taken on the question of the Associates Reception. It was one of his accomplishments during the first year that he had served on the Program Committee. He had not argued with those who maintained that there was a need to generate a feeling of fellowship and good cheer on the evening before the start of the formal sessions, nor could he oppose the view that the Associate Members—defined in the by-laws of A.A.P.M. as *all manufacturers or distributors of materials, machinery or services to the molding industry*—could rightfully be called upon to provide the entertainment and foot the bill. On the other hand, he had seen the point of those who held that, over the years, the Associates Reception had developed into nothing but a drunken brawl that was a disgrace to one of America's great industries.

If the matter had ever been brought to a morning-after vote, the more conservative element would undoubtedly have triumphed, the opposition being largely incapacitated and not in attendance. However, the decision lay with the Program Committee which rarely began its work until last year's convention had faded into a rosy glow and, by then, indignation over past transgressions had usually given way to a balancing concern over convention attendance, the point being well made that there were, unfortunately, some members who might not turn up at all if it weren't for the Associates Reception.

Grant Austen, as his first contribution to the working of the Program Committee, had forced through a meeting in the month immediately following the convention, demanding that the question of the Associates Reception be resolved once and for all, an effort that had ended in the compromise that was now in effect. At 7:00 P.M. the Associate Members, black-tie, formed a receiving line down which the Active Members filed in decorous submission, shaking hands with a representative of each of the industry suppliers, thereby earning the reward of what few cocktails could be snatched from waiters pushing their way through the mob, and as much food as could be carried away from the famous Moon Beach buffet table. Everyone now agreed that the atmosphere of the whole affair had been substantially elevated, making the Associates Reception a true reflection of the character of the industry, and a party to which any man could bring his wife without arousing suspicions of what he might have been doing at past conventions without her.

All proprieties having thus been satisfied, the exodus began. Guided by invitations made especially intriguing by the whispering of room numbers, the delegates slipped away with a great show of secrecy and, minutes later, just as they had always done, reassembled in the upstairs suites where the manufacturers and suppliers kept open house for their customers and prospects. Since there was no delegate who could not be classified in one of those two categories, there were few who stayed behind. Additionally, since all owners of molding plants recognized the wisdom of maintaining a strongly competitive situation among their sources of supply, none stayed long in any one place. The result was a constant milling from suite to suite, slowing only as the night wore on and the merits of competition were outweighed by the difficulty of negotiating long hallways and the dangers inherent in a bad memory for room numbers. It was then, in the small hours of the morning, that there were happenings destined to become A.A.P.M. legends, either hilarious or disgusting according to the hearer's point of view.

But now it was still early in the evening and, as Grant Austen explained to his wife, there was no reason why she shouldn't accompany him on a first-round visit—unless, of course, she preferred to join the Ladies Bridge Tournament which had been announced for the West Lounge, provided that at least four women showed up.

"I'd much rather go with you," Miriam Austen said. "If you're certain it's all right and I won't be the only woman."

"Sure, it's all right," he assured her. "We won't stay long, anyway— just drop in a few places and say hello. Couple of fellows I want to see for a minute." His eyes wandered the room, looking for Harlan

Bostwick who, strangely, hadn't even come to their table to meet Miriam.

"And there's one man who said he was anxious to see you."

"Who's that?"

"Remember the gray-haired man who was talking to me when you came back to the table? I think you called him Harvey."

"Yah, Harv Bannon," he said wearily, knowing what the president of Cavalier Chemical Company was trying to find out ... the same thing all the material manufacturers wanted to talk to him about. The only thing any of them were interested in knowing was who was taking over Suffolk Moulding ... so they could jump in fast and get their hands on the business.

Miriam edged forward as the elevators, a gulp at a time, gnawed into the waiting crowd. "If you don't mind, dear, I think I'd like to go up to the room first."

He nodded, thinking that if it weren't so necessary to have a minute alone with Harlan Bostwick, he'd go up to the room and just stay there! There were a lot of fellows he hadn't talked to yet ... but what was there to talk about? Right away they all wanted to know who the Gammer Corporation was ... and when he couldn't tell them, that was about the end of it. Most of them said something about his retiring but that didn't lead anywhere ... what was the use of trying to argue that he *wasn't* retiring when he couldn't tell them what he *was* going to do? He *had* to find Harlan Bostwick.

"There's no use of you going up if you don't want to," Miriam said. "I could meet you somewhere."

"No, I'll go along." The other elevator was down now and he took Miriam's arm, guiding her toward the opening door. "I'd better try to call home again."

Miriam shot a peculiar glance at him but her eyes fell almost instantly, the strange look on her face gone so quickly that he couldn't be sure what it had meant.

"What's the matter?" he asked.

"Nothing, dear." The door closed in front of her. "I want you to have a good time, that's all."

They were pressed closely together in the crowded elevator and Miriam's hand found his, her fingers a tight band on his wrist. He guessed then what the trouble was ... Miriam was worried, too, just as worried as he was. Everybody kept saying all the time that airplanes were as safe as automobiles, but still there was always the possibility of something happening. There'd been another plane crash story in the paper tonight ... somewhere out in Arizona ... no survivors ...

The elevator door opened and they walked down the long hall, neither of them speaking. Miriam kept glancing at him but he pretended not to notice it, not wanting to add to her fears by a sharing of his own ... and maybe there *wasn't* anything to worry about. As Miriam had said, Lory might still have been out in the studio when he had called the last time. But now it was after nine ... Lory wouldn't be out in the studio now. If she didn't answer this time ...

Fear urged him toward the telephone as they entered the living room of the suite but he hung back, not wanting to alarm Miriam unnecessarily, picking up the instrument only after she went in the bathroom.

But she hadn't closed the door and he had no more than given the call to the operator when Miriam came back to the doorway and stood watching him. He closed his eyes when the ringing started, listening with growing apprehension to the unrewarded repetition of the distant sound, hope fading but still alive until the operator told him, unnecessarily, that the number didn't answer, asking if she should try again in twenty minutes.

He hung up without reply, forced now to face Miriam.

"Grant, it's nothing to be concerned about, really it isn't," she said, surprising him with how good a job he'd done in keeping her from becoming alarmed. "She's probably still out in the studio. You know how anxious she was to get that book finished. Or she may have gone out somewhere for the evening."

"Maybe that's right."

"And Anna wouldn't be there yet. She never gets back from one of those Reading trips until way after midnight. Anyway, Grant, there's no point in worrying about it. Lory's old enough to take care of herself. After all, dear, she's a grown woman."

"Sure," he said ... but if something went wrong with a plane, what difference did it make how old you were?

This time Miriam closed the bathroom door and there was no longer the necessity of preserving the innocently unconcerned look on his face. He would wait another hour. If there was no answer then, he'd call the Suffolk Municipal Airport. Someone there would know whether or not Cash McCall's plane had gotten back. But why wait? He could call the airport now ... then he'd *know*.

He reached for the telephone instrument but stopped himself before he lifted it ... Miriam would be panicked for sure if she heard him trying to check up on the plane ... no, he'd better wait. Visiting a couple of suites would be enough for Miriam. By that time, things would probably start getting a little rough and she'd be glad enough to come back here. Then he'd make some kind of excuse ...

somebody else he still had to see ... slip downstairs and call from there.

"You all ready, dear?" Miriam asked, opening the bathroom door.

"Sure, you bet."

It took him a moment to find where he had dropped the key and Miriam moved ahead of him to the door.

"Grant, if you'd have a better time alone—?"

"No, come on, you'll get a kick out of it, just seeing it. But we don't have to stay any longer than you want to. We can come back any time you feel like it."

Her eyes were very bright ... he'd done the right thing, keeping it to himself, not spoiling Miriam's fun ... but the sooner he got that call through, the better it would be.

• • • • • 2

"I'm sorry, Mrs. Kennard, but I can't refill this prescription without your doctor's permission."

"But that's ridiculous! It's nothing but a little phenobarbital, you know that as well as I do."

"If I could do it for anyone, I'd do it for you. I know it's a silly law but that's the way it is. We can't refill a prescription like this."

She fixed the pharmacist with her eyes and, finally, there was the crumbling.

"Maybe I could call your doctor for you," he said to the counter top. "Would you want me to do that?"

"Just get it for me, that's all I want."

He went behind the partition. Listening, she heard only the dialing of the telephone, no voices, but when he came back he handed her the filled box.

• • • • • 3

Lights blazed behind every door along the corridor as Gil Clark hurried toward Winston Conway's office. The entire Jamison, Conway & Slythe staff had been drawn into the all-night drive to knit up the legal loose ends that the completion of the deal required.

Vincent Thompson of Thompson & Slater came out of Conway's office as Gil approached, holding open the door for him.

"How are things going?" Gil asked.

"It's a tax man's dream," Thompson grinned. "The further we go, the better it looks. Having those Gammer losses to carry ahead is really sweet."

Thompson was off down the hall and Conway was nodding his agreement to the overheard conversation as Gil entered the office, his smile a fulsome greeting. "So it went all right with General Danvers, eh?"

"Couldn't have been better," Gil exulted. "Oh, it was a little touchy for the first few minutes, but Cash's telephone call had paved the way and—well, as I told you over the phone, he's riding with us a hundred per cent. Allenby can't get on the job too fast to suit him."

"And it's set up so that making Allenby president will look like the General's own idea?"

"Yes, and he's grateful as the devil for being allowed to handle it that way."

"He should be."

"I know but—well, you know, Danvers really isn't such a bad sort. All of this mess over there wasn't his making. He inherited a lot of it. Andrews had really gone to seed before he got out—and there were a lot of places where General Danvers' hands were tied, even after the old man was dead. What I mean is—well, there are two sides to the story."

"There usually are," Conway said philosophically. "And there are very few people in the world who aren't fundamentally decent characters—with only one proviso."

"What's that?"

"That you don't challenge their pride. There's more of the Oriental view around than we sometimes suspect. The fear of *losing face* drives more men into trouble than almost any human frailty —even sex. You can't be around the law very long without realizing that."

"That was true of General Danvers all right," Gil agreed.

"It's so often true," Conway said. "And Cash understands that— along with a great many other things, I might add."

"He's really a wonderful man," Gil said, an effervescent bubbling of the admiration that had been building up within him all day. "What I mean is—well, it looks so easy to come in and do what I've done, just pick up the ball, but you know all the time that it was Cash who set up the play for you. A lot of things look like lucky breaks—Bergmann calling Allenby, even General Danvers coming to see Cash last night—but the whole trick is in always being ready to take advantage of these breaks."

Conway looked at him steadily. "You're a very discerning young man, Mr. Clark."

"Well, it's plain enough."

"But so few people see it," Conway observed. "It's rather a shame you didn't go into the law, Gil."

It was, Gil knew, as full-bodied a compliment as Winston Conway could offer. "Thank you, sir, but—well, I'm happy enough with the spot I'm in right now."

"Getting into your blood?"

"I guess that's it."

The lawyer said with a teasing grin, "As I recall, yesterday morning you were hoping that Cash would hang on to Suffolk Moulding and let you run it."

Gil felt the warmth of a blush. "That seems a lot longer ago than yesterday morning."

"Suffolk Moulding would be a little dull after this, eh?"

"Well, I—I'll have to admit it's pretty darn exciting to be in on one like this."

Conway nodded. "Yes, it's good to have someone like Cash in your life. Makes your blood run a little faster—even if you're only hanging on to his coattails trying to keep up with him. So many clients these days are so damned dull—so unrelievedly, impossibly, never-endingly *dull!*"

Gil laughed. "That's one thing you can say about being around Cash McCall—it's never dull."

"Right you are!"

"And as you were saying at breakfast yesterday morning—you can't outguess him. I never had any idea that all of this would happen—and in less than forty-eight hours."

"Neither did I," Conway said. "Anyone else would have been fussing around with a deal like this for six months. But this is a fast one, even for Cash."

"I just hope it isn't too fast."

"So do I," Conway said, his face sobering. "But for the life of me I can't see a single hole. It's the most beautiful job of knitting a deal together that I've ever seen."

"And the best part of it is that everybody comes out a winner."

"Of course," Conway said, but as if he was surprised that Gil had missed some obvious point. "That's the essence of the McCall technique—and very clever, too. If you get everyone in the same camp, there's no one left to ambush you from the other side of the fence."

For an instant, the word *clever* reverberated in Gil's mind, flashing the suspicion that Winston Conway didn't really understand what a sound and solid man Cash McCall really was. But of course he did.

"Well, let's check up on how the boys are coming," Conway said, starting to the door. "The Andscott attorneys are breathing down our neck. They want to get those proxy forms on the press. You'll be here in the morning, won't you?"

"I'm not sure," Gil said uncertainly. "I really ought to run over to Suffolk—there are some things that will have to be done there—but I'm not certain yet. I haven't been able to reach Cash."

"I've been calling him, too," Conway acknowledged. "He must have gone out somewhere for the evening."

"Probably."

They started down the corridor. A fountain clerk from the drugstore on the first floor was going from office to office with an enormous coffeepot and a carton of paper cups.

••••• 4

The light snapped off as Grant Austen started to open the door of the telephone booth. He stopped his hand, accepting the compelling invitation of darkness, trying to think, staring at the mouthpiece of the telephone instrument. Cash McCall's plane had not returned to Suffolk.

In the ten minutes that he had spent on the telephone, first trying to get someone to answer at the airport, then putting through a call to the home of the watchman, he had imagined himself steeled against tragedy. But so long as there had been the faintest of hopes he had not fully faced the prospect. Now his brain was strangled by the clutch of terror, the flow of image stopped dead on the news picture of a crashed airplane. He saw no movement, not the slightest sign of life. But then he heard sound, the tin drum beating of fists pounding against hollow metal, and he felt himself driven toward the wreckage, fighting his way through the trees, narrowing the span of his vision until he saw only the door of the cabin. He clawed at the latch, pushing and shoving, suddenly aware that the trunks of the trees around him were marble columns rising from an underbrush of potted palms. Strangely, the plane was still ahead of him and he plunged toward the gaping hole in the fuselage.

"Floor, please?"

Why had he waited so long? It was almost midnight now and the plane had crashed at noon ... the police should have been notified hours ago ... search parties ...

"What floor, sir?"

The face of the elevator operator wavered as if seen in watery reflection ... Miriam ... yes, that's what he had to do now ... tell Miriam ... "Three."

Out of the elevator, the long hall was an uptilting tunnel, steeper and steeper as he climbed, the suite door gained only with the last gasp of effort. The living room was dark and he plunged through it, heading for the lighted door of the bedroom.

Miriam was in bed, sitting against propped pillows, her magazine dropping as he opened the door, exposing a smile that was shockingly insensitive to what had happened. He had pre-set his mind to a sympathetically slow breaking of the news, but the blandness of his wife's expression made him blurt out, "It's Lory!"

"What about Lory?" she asked, irritatingly calm.

"They never got there!"

"They never got where, Grant?"

"Good god, Miriam, can't you understand?" He started toward the bedside table. "We've got to do something—find them—call the police—"

Her arm reached out to stop him, holding his hand from raising the telephone.

"Grant, what do you know?"

"I called the airport. His plane never got there."

"What airport?"

"What airport?" he repeated, hurling the question at the irritating imperturbability of her face. "What airport do you think I'd call?"

"Grant, listen to me. All you know is that Mr. McCall's plane didn't get to the Suffolk airport. Isn't that true?"

"What more do you—" His voice was sucked out of his throat by the enigmatic smile on his wife's face.

Miriam said quietly, "If they didn't go back to Suffolk, they went somewhere else, that's all."

"Somewhere else?"

"Didn't Mr. McCall say that he was going to Philadelphia?"

"He said that *he* was but—"

"Then Lory went with him. They probably stayed over for the evening—dinner and then maybe a show."

"You mean that Mr. McCall invited her to—" There was an emptiness now where there had been terror before.

"Of course," she said gaily, almost laughing. "Didn't you see them look at each other when we got off the plane?"

"What are you talking about?" he asked blankly, a new fear rushing in to fill the vacuum. "What do you mean—when we got off the plane?"

"Oh, Grant, it was so plain. You'd have seen it yourself if you hadn't been so—"

"Miriam, you're crazy. That's impossible! Lory's only a—why, he's old enough to be her father."

"Don't be silly, dear. I don't know how old Cash is but I'm sure he isn't over—"

"Miriam! You don't know what you're talking about. Lory wouldn't —she *couldn't*—"

In the agony of attempted comprehension he looked away, missing the transition of expression on his wife's face. When he glanced back, he saw that her smile had been blended with confident determination.

"Grant, this is partly my fault. I should have told you last night. But I wasn't sure then." There was a meaningful pause before she added, "They were together all morning yesterday."

"Together? Yesterday?"

"Don't you remember, she took him out to the airport?"

"Sure, but—"

"She didn't get home until after noon. They went somewhere in his plane."

"Where?"

"I don't know."

"Didn't you ask her?"

"No."

"Miriam! How could you—"

"Why should I? She's no child. She has a right to live her own life. If she's in love with Cash McCall, it's her own—"

"*Love!*" he exploded. "She's only known him—" His plunging voice smashed against the hard barrier of memory. That day in the lobby of the Hotel Ivanhoe ... McCall had said he had met her before ... somewhere ...

The pull of his wife's hands was timed to his collapsing weakness and he let himself be guided down to the bed, sitting beside her.

Miriam's voice softened. "Grant, don't you remember when he was at the house yesterday morning, how I kept saying that he looked so familiar? When I saw him again this morning, I knew where I'd seen that face before. Grant, he's the man in that first book of Lory's—

those drawings she did after she got back from Maine. Don't you see what must have happened? She met him that summer—"

Maine! The energy of inner explosion was lost in the upward propelling of his body, the surge of outrage muffled by the still frightening memory of Miriam's outburst on that night when Lory had come home from Maine, the mysteriously maniacal fury with which Miriam had lashed out at him. What he had faced then had been not only the revelation of something unsuspected within his wife, but also a weakness within himself, a crumbling that could be denied only by an avoidance of repetition.

"You did see Mr. Bannon, didn't you?"

"Bannon?" He was caught off guard, reacting before he recalled that seeing Harvey Bannon had been the excuse he had given Miriam for going back to the second floor again.

"He telephoned just after you went down. I told him that you were going to stop at their suite."

He grasped at the chance to get away, moving quickly to the door. "I'll have to go back."

Miriam was ahead of him. "Oh, Grant, why do you have to go now? Can't it wait until morning?"

"Won't take but a minute," he said, brushing past her, out through the door and down the full length of the long hall before he had exhausted the blind energy of escape.

He was stopped by the rail of the stairwell, his senses slowly awakening, hearing the cacophony of sound that drifted up from the second floor, the thumping march of a snake dance down the corridor, the crash of a bottle, the high-pitched scream of a girl's laughter and then the echoing howl of male glee. Bannon or no Bannon, he wasn't going back into that mess again! It was Harlan Bostwick he really wanted to see ... Bannon was only an excuse to keep Miriam from knowing until it was settled ... and she *didn't* know! How could she? She was only guessing that Lory was in Philadelphia with ...

A grotesquely foreshortened couple on the floor below had come into view as he looked down. They wove a drunken path across the visible rectangle of the second floor hall, collapsing in a clumsy embrace as they came to the stair railing. A shudder of revulsion went through Grant Austen's body as he found himself looking straight down into the wanton face of the girl. She had thrown back her head, her parted lips lewdly inviting, her arms offering no resistance to the snaking exploration of the man's hand. Grant Austen started to back away, feeling himself nauseated by the stench of stale cigarette smoke and spilled whiskey that came up the flue of the stairwell. Now the man had produced a room key, dangling it mesmerically in front of the girl's face, still waving it long after she nodded, even after she had started to drag him away down the hall.

"Down?"

Blinking, he saw that the elevator door had opened in front of him. He must have pushed the button.

"Second!" the elevator operator announced.

The door opened and faces swam in from the gray-smoked sea, crushing down upon him, pinning him against the cold steel wall. And then he was alone again, alone as he had been alone in every crowded room tonight, staring back at the circling eyes of the telephone dial.

"I'm sorry, sir, but your Suffolk number doesn't answer. Shall I try again in twenty minutes?"

He exhaled a grumble of resignation and started to hang up, then suddenly struck with an inspiration so clear-minded that he felt himself completely recovered from the lethargy of shock. "Operator!"

The connection had been broken and he had to dial again. "Operator, get me the Hotel Ivanhoe in Philadelphia."

While the call went through, he tried to prepare himself for what he would say to Cash McCall, suddenly conscious that anything he said would provoke frightening complications. If McCall *was* in his apartment ...

A distant voice repeated, "Hotel Ivanhoe," for the third time before he could ask, "I wonder if you could give me some information?"

"Yes, sir?"

"What I want to know is—I wonder if you could tell me whether or not Mr. McCall got back to the hotel this afternoon?"

"I'm sorry, sir, but that's information we wouldn't have."

"What do you mean—wouldn't have?" he snapped, then quickly dropped his voice to a placating softness. "All I want to know is whether he—you see, Mr. McCall was flying back to Philadelphia this afternoon and all we want to know is whether he got there all right."

"I'm sorry, sir, but we wouldn't know that."

"Now just a minute, young lady. This is Mr. Austen—Grant Austen of the Suffolk Moulding Company—" His tongue had slipped again and the recognition momentarily blocked his recall of the name of that woman he knew at the Hotel Ivanhoe ... Kennard? ... yes, that was it. "It just happens that I'm a friend of Mrs. Kennard's."

"I'm sorry, sir, but Mrs. Kennard—" The voice wavered indecisively. "One moment, sir."

The heat of his resentment cooled as he waited through a long silence, the final chill imparted by the shock of a voice saying, "Hello, Mr. Austen. This is Maude Kennard. What can we do for you?"

Embarrassment was a voice-muffling handicap, finally surmounted. "I'm sorry, Mrs. Kennard. I didn't want anyone to bother you but—well, you see, Mr. McCall brought us down here in his plane and we didn't know—well, he started back about eleven and there was something in the paper about a plane crash—"

"And you were concerned about your daughter, weren't you, Mr. Austen? Of course, you were! But there's nothing to worry about. Everything's all right. They got in about—oh, I believe it was about one-fifteen when they went up to his suite."

The expelled sound of his wordless exclamation was a deflation that left his body unsupported. He reached out to brace himself against the booth wall. "Thanks, Mrs. Kennard, I—sorry to have bothered you, Mrs. Kennard—this time of the night."

"Now don't you worry about that, Mr. Austen. I know exactly how you feel. She is such a dear sweet child, isn't she? And do come see us whenever you're in Philadelphia, won't you, Mr. Austen?"

"Sure—sure, you bet, Mrs. Kennard."

The receiver missed the hook and fell the length of the cord, bouncing to crash against the drum-hollow wall of the booth. Groping, he made the blind moves of retrieval, no more aware of what he was doing than of the undirected wandering that carried him out across the lobby. He was only vaguely conscious of a man walking rapidly toward him, not realizing until the path ahead of him was blocked that it was Harvey Bannon.

"By golly, Grant, you're a hard man to find!" Bannon said with a double-handed shoulder slap. "Wouldn't have found you now if Ed Fisher hadn't seen you go down in the elevator a few minutes ago. Listen, fellow, you and I've got to have a little talk. How about slipping over here in the corner for a minute?"

Grant Austen's submission to the firm grip of Harvey Bannon's guiding hand was more than the blind response of his preoccupied mind. It was, partially at least, an involuntary reaction to the pleasure he had always found in being accepted as a personal friend of the President of the Cavalier Chemical Company. There were a lot of Associate Members who couldn't remember your name from one convention to another unless you were way up on the top quantity bracket, but not Harv Bannon. He was the kind of friend a man could really count on. Some of the fellows thought Harv was sort of a phony ... he did have that funny nervous laugh and there were times when maybe he tried too hard to be one of the boys ... but

373

you could say what you wanted to about Harv Bannon and he still stacked up as about as good a friend as a man could have.

"I wish I could help you, Harv," Grant Austen said as they came to the palm-sheltered divan, anticipating the same question about the future of the Suffolk Moulding Company that he had been asked by all the other manufacturers. "All I can tell you is that they've put in a young fellow named Gil Clark as a sort of general manager. As far as I know, it'll be up to him where they buy their resins. But Gil's one of my boys—all he knows is what I taught him—so I'd say you folks would have the inside track, Harv."

"That isn't exactly what I had in mind," Bannon said.

Grant Austen looked at him, puzzled by the cat-and-canary tone in Bannon's voice. "But that's all I know, Harv."

"Now come on, boy, you wouldn't try to fox an old fox, would you?"

"Harv, I don't know what you're talking about."

Bannon's oddly high-pitched laugh ran ahead of his voice. "Grant, I don't blame you for playing cagy until the thing is settled—do the same thing myself if I was in your place—"

"Settled? What do you mean? It *is* settled."

"Maybe as far as General Danvers is concerned," Bannon acknowledged. "But don't forget it still has to be approved by the board."

"I don't get you, Harv."

Bannon shook loose another strangely incongruous laugh. "Now look, Grant, I'm not bucking you. If you were smart enough to get Andscott over a barrel, more power to you. The only thing is, boy, I just want to be sure you're doing the right thing for your own sake."

"Harv, you've got this all wrong."

"Aren't you forgetting something?" Bannon asked, his smile slightly frosted now. "Maybe it's slipped your mind, Grant, but I happen to be a director of Andscott Instrument."

"Sure, Harv, I know that—but what's that got to do with my selling Suffolk Moulding?"

"It's got this to do with it, boy—I'm going to be voting on whether or not you get those three hundred thousand shares." The laugh trickled in again. "There's no use playing cagy with me, boy. I've got the whole story. The General called me to get my vote on going ahead with the deal, but before I told him yes or no, I said I wanted to talk to you. Now don't get me wrong, Grant—you and I are old friends and when the other guy's got the high cards, I'm as willing as the next man to toss in—but I just didn't want to see you doing anything foolish."

From the first, Grant Austen had suspected that his failure to comprehend was caused by the difficulty of getting Lory and Cash

McCall out of his mind, but it was plain now that the fault of understanding was not his but Harvey Bannon's. "Harv, you're off somewhere if you've got the idea that I'm selling the company to Andscott Instrument. Maybe Danvers thought he was going to get it—I guess he figured he had me in a spot where I couldn't do anything else—but you'll just have to tell him it's too late. I've sold to someone else."

"Someone else?" Bannon asked with a shocked scowl. "But you can't do that—not when you've given an option to Andscott."

"I never gave any option to Andscott. I never even talked to them."

"You didn't? But Danvers told me this morning—" An expression of startled comprehension came to Bannon's face. "You say you've already sold to someone else?"

"Sure, you bet."

"When?"

"Well, last week—that is, as far as settling the deal is concerned."

"But it isn't actually closed yet?"

"Sure—yesterday morning."

"Who did you sell to?"

"I don't know whether you've heard of them or not—Philadelphia concern—the Gammer Corporation."

"Name doesn't mean anything to me."

"I guess it's sort of—well, I suppose you might call it a holding company," Grant Austen said, using the explanation that he had evolved in his talks with other manufacturers. "They invest in different industrial properties."

"I see," Bannon said with another mirthless laugh. "Funny I wouldn't have heard about them—especially if they're interested in the plastics business. Who's behind it, Grant?"

Grant Austen hesitated, finally deciding that his pledge of secrecy had expired with the final settlement. "The man I dealt with was a Mr. McCall."

"Not *Cash* McCall!"

"Yes, he's the—"

"Good god, Grant, don't you know—Grant, how did you ever let yourself get tangled up with that bastard?"

"But what's wrong with—"

"Wrong! Don't you know that he's—well, I'll be goddamned! So that's the story, is it?" He got up from the divan, swinging around behind it, digging his clenched fingers into the upholstery. "I wondered why in hell Danvers was so close-mouthed. So he's gotten himself in McCall's clutches again."

"Harv, I still don't see—I got my price—the money's in the bank—"

375

For a moment, Bannon seemed not to have heard him. Then he inhaled sharply, exploding, "What did he pay you for it? All right, all right, I know—none of my business—but I'll bet you got a hell of a lot less from him than he's going to get out of Andscott! Do you know what Andscott is going to have to give that bastard? Three hundred thousand shares of stock."

"But, Harv, I—"

"At the market price, that's three million dollars!"

"Three—" The next word lodged in his throat, choking him.

"Am I right?" Bannon demanded. "Isn't that a lot more than he paid you? You're damned right I'm right! If McCall hadn't seen a way to take you for a ride, he'd never have been in on it in the first place. Grant, what were you thinking of? Why didn't you come to me? I could have told you plenty about that bastard. Do you know what he did to us? Got us over a barrel with this wood-fiber company in Maine. Nothing we could do but buy him out. Do you know what we had to pay that son of a bitch? Six hundred thousand dollars! And just one year before—I swear it's the truth, by god, and I've got a letter right in my files to prove it—that same company was offered to us by the owners for just exactly half that price. He took those poor bastards the same way he's taken you. Grant, why in hell didn't you come talk to me? I could have told you."

"I don't know, Harv—it just happened so fast—"

Bannon exhaled, his laugh more oddly misplaced than ever. "Well, I guess it's water over the dam now. Nothing for me to do but call Danvers. I thought maybe if it was you, I could talk sense—but if it's Cash McCall that's out. When that bastard gets you by the short hair, he never lets go. Be seeing you, Grant."

Helplessly, Grant Austen stared at the retreating figure of the president of the Cavalier Chemical Company. He wanted to cry out to stop him, to shout the words that would explain that he hadn't been the fool that Bannon thought he was, but the paralysis of total humiliation locked his throat as rigidly as it froze the muscles of his body. Only his eyes were still functioning and he watched Bannon grow smaller and smaller, seeing the unexplainable effect that the passage of so tiny a figure was having—the marble pillars falling like dominoes, the floor rising as the pillars fell, up and up, past dead center and then whirling into the blur of a spinning wheel, falling through space, the crash and then the stillness broken only by the drumbeat of Lory's fist pounding on the metal fuselage, trying to fight his way through the trees, clawing back the palms ... the swinging hotelroom key that Cash McCall was dangling in front of his eyes ... three million ...

"Watch it, fellow!"

Someone was holding his arm ... not Cash McCall ... a face that he knew but couldn't place ... more faces ...

"You're all right, Grant," one of the blurred voices said. "All you need is a little fresh air."

The shimmering fog broke and he was back in the lobby of the Moon Beach Club again, reassuringly surrounded by friends. He was the hub of their whiskey-scented breathing and, without conscious decision, he accepted the suggestion that it offered. Slurring an unintelligible mumble as a feigning of drunkenness, he broke away and stumbled toward the elevator.

As he stepped into the cab he heard someone behind him say, "For crissake, and he's one of those bluenoses that's always bitching about too many guys getting plastered."

Then there was laughter reverberating in the closed cage of the elevator ... they were laughing at *him* ... they knew ... they all knew ... Harv Bannon had told them. Cash McCall had made a fool of him ... and everyone knew it.

••••• 5

Maude Kennard threw up the lower sash to its full height and stood breathing in the cold air in great purposeful gulps. It had been a mistake to take those sleeping tablets. They always did this to her ... stuffing her brain with fuzzy wool that made it hard to think. And now she *had* to think. Angrily, she tried to repeat to herself the exact words that she had spoken to that man Austen over the telephone, but she was defeated by the trick of memory that had made him sound exactly like the father of that girl in Chicago. That time it had worked ... she had gotten even with Wilfred for everything, just by what she said to that little bitch's father ... but then she had been wide-awake, *knowing* what she was doing. She could still remember exactly what she had said ... every word, after all of these years ... but now she couldn't remember what she had said ten minutes ago.

The cold came through her nightgown and she stood close-legged, the hunch of her shoulders pressing her arms against the heart that seemed to be pounding in her tightly squeezed breasts.

Deliberately, every move consciously made, she retreated the four steps that brought her back to the bed, reached out with her right

377

hand, picked up the pillbox from the bedside table. Three longer steps retraced the path to the window. Without hesitation, she hurled the open box, and a moment later heard the faint hail-like spatter on the concrete floor of the areaway.

Eleven

●
●
●
●

WILL ATHERSON accepted the necessity of frequent directors' meetings in much the same reluctant but submissive spirit
with which he bore the burden of all the other changes that had
been imposed upon the banking profession during the years since
he had assumed the presidency of the Freeholders Bank & Trust Company. It was not entirely a matter of all the ham-stringing governmental regulations. Bad as they were, and as much as they had done
to dull a banker's life, they were less responsible than this current
notion that an individual man was no longer capable of clear thinking, sound judgment, or independent action. Nowadays you had to
go through the motions of having everything done by the board—or
if not the board, then by some committee. They called it *group
thinking*. The ridiculous part of it was that the only way group thinking ever worked was to have the right man to do the group's thinking.

Nevertheless, as he left the directors' room and walked toward his
office, Will Atherson felt an intangible satisfaction in having the
board of directors approve the sale of the Andscott stock in the Scott
trust, and the loan to Cash McCall that was financing its purchase.
The board's action had been nothing but a rubber-stamp gesture, of
course, yet there had been a rather pleasant concurrence of opinion,
and everyone had been quite complimentary about how well he had
done in finding a customer for a block of stock that a half dozen brokers had been trying to sell for the last year. Even old man Peregrine
had slapped him on the back and pumped his hand. The only ques-

tion that had arisen had been on Brown's point that the stock wasn't really worth as much as Cash McCall had paid for it, thereby reducing the equity over the amount of the loan. But what could be done about it? Since the bank had set the selling price, it was impossible to argue that the stock wasn't worth what Cash McCall had paid.

Only one thing that had happened at the directors' meeting had been in any way surprising, and that had been nothing more than Brown's gossipy observation, when Cash McCall's name had first come up, that he had seen him come out of Hotel Ivanhoe late yesterday afternoon and drive off with what Brown had described as a "very cute little number."

That would have been Lory Austen, of course—and the assurance that Will Atherson had found in the tractability of the board was augmented now by the memory of what Helen had told him about Cash and Lory. As always, Helen's reporting of romantic possibilities was subject to discounting, yet the fact could not be denied that the girl had been in Cash's apartment. He had seen her there himself, her presence as surprising as the poise with which she had carried it off.

He recalled now an incident of that night, some years ago, when they had given a party for Lory. He had remarked to Helen, after they had gone up to their room, that in spite of Lory's introverted shyness she was the sort of girl who might respond in a quite extraordinary manner if the right man ever came along. Helen, of course, had made one of her bedroom jokes out of it—her accusation of a suppressed desire had really been rather amusing—but, actually, he had meant exactly what he had said. And it was nice to know that he had been right. He had always wondered, too, why Cash had never married. Now it did look as if it were at least a possibility. Normality was comforting.

Helen had asked him last night whether there was any connection between Cash's feeling for Lory and his purchase of her father's company. At the time, he had brushed the question aside but he recalled it now, resurrecting the possibly linked memory that, on the day he had called Cash to tell him that Suffolk Moulding was for sale, Cash had said that he had already heard about it from another source. Had that been Lory? But, even if it was true, what did it mean? Nothing—except as a possible explanation of Cash having paid more than the company was worth by at least two hundred thousand dollars.

Incongruously, his mind interjected the thought that two hundred thousand dollars was exactly the amount that Lory had been given for her share of the stock—and that reminded him, by simple association, that he had forgotten to ask Brown whether Lory's check had been received for deposit this morning and, if so, whether Austen had given instructions as to its investment.

His concern over whether Brown was following through, weak to begin with, died as he saw that Everett Pierce was waiting outside his office. That, too, brought an unanswered question to mind— whether or not he had acted wisely yesterday when he had suggested that Pierce be a little stronger in his handling of Maude Kennard.

Theoretically, his position was unquestionably sound—the General Manager of the Hotel Ivanhoe could not brook the insubordination of his assistant—yet, as was so often the case, the theory of business management seemed poorly fitted to the personalities involved. It was definitely questionable whether or not Everett Pierce had the strength of character to make Maude Kennard knuckle under, a question almost answered by the look of groveling apology that he saw now in Pierce's face.

"Come in, Everett," Atherson said sympathetically, anticipating that Pierce was about to admit his defeat. Reaching for his pipe, the banker gained the moment of time that he needed to orient his thinking, wishing as he had often wished before that he had taken any one of the dozens of chances that there had been to sell the Hotel Ivanhoe. Suddenly, in an instant of time that might have been measured by the flash of flame that leaped to the end of the match he scratched, Will Atherson made his decision. He *would* sell the hotel . . . the Luxor chain wanted it and he'd let them have it!

"You told me, sir, that if there was anything I wanted to talk over with you—" Pierce began tentatively.

"Yes, of course, Everett," Atherson said, conscious of the suddenly acquired feeling of profound relief that his decision had produced . . . Cash McCall was right! The thing to do with a business was to sell it, not operate it. And Grant Austen had been sound, too . . . you just couldn't get the right people any more. That was always the trouble . . . *people* . . . no matter what business you were in, sooner or later it always turned into the *people business*. He had enough of that here in the bank . . . and, anyway, he could probably make more net money by selling the Ivanhoe to the Luxor chain and cashing in his profit as a capital gain than he could by continuing to operate the hotel for the rest of his life.

"There may not be any point in my telling you this—" Pierce began again, waiting until he had the banker's full attention.

"Go ahead, Everett," Atherson said apologetically. "What's happened?"

"Maybe I'd better start at the beginning," Everett Pierce said in-

381

decisively, stopping. "But I wonder if you'd mind telling me—you know, yesterday after you talked to me?"

Atherson tamped and relit his pipe. "Yes?"

"What you told me about Mr. McCall not owning the hotel?"

"Yes."

"Did you tell her that?"

"Mrs. Kennard? No. Why?"

Pierce stared back at him, his face gray and drained. "I just don't know how to explain it then."

"Explain what?" Atherson asked, finding it necessary to force the effort of inquiry, his mind wandering off to the letter from the Luxor Hotels Corporation that he had absent-mindedly shuffled out of his correspondence folder.

"This morning when Andrew brought my breakfast—that was a little before nine—he said that Max wanted to see me right away. Well, I just didn't know what to do. You see, Mrs. Kennard has always handled the kitchen end of things—and Max *is* a rather difficult person—but still I thought I'd better go down to see him." Pierce hesitated, swallowing. "Max was all ready to quit."

Atherson registered the demanded look of surprise. "Why?"

"Because of Mrs. Kennard. She'd been down there last night giving all sorts of orders—telling Max that he mustn't ever talk to Mr. McCall again. You see, Max had made up some special dish for a luncheon that Mr. McCall had up in his suite yesterday noon. He'd left the kitchen for a few minutes to go up and—well, on the whole I do agree, naturally, that Max shouldn't be out of the kitchen when we're serving in the Fontainebleau Room, but still—"

"What about Max?" Will Atherson asked, hoping to compress Pierce's recital of what, now that he had decided to sell the Ivanhoe, was of very little interest.

"It wasn't only Max," Pierce went on. "It was everyone else, all around the hotel. Andrew wasn't to serve Mr. McCall any more—Frank wasn't to run any more errands for him—Mrs. Schilling wasn't to give his suite any special attention."

Will Atherson's pipe came out of his mouth, his interest suddenly sharpened. Cash McCall knew that he owned the hotel and this was no time to offend him, just when he had given the bank such a fine piece of business. Alerted now, his mind went to work setting fact against fact. Pierce had told him yesterday that Mrs. Kennard thought Cash McCall owned the hotel. That had undoubtedly led her to go overboard on special service to McCall. Now, somehow, she had discovered that he *wasn't* the owner and was apparently knocking him down again to the status of an ordinary guest.

"I honestly don't know what to make of it," Pierce went on, his face contorted as if he were being tortured into saying something against his will. "It's almost as if she were *trying* to drive him out of the hotel."

The banker took a speculative puff at his pipe, now more concerned by Everett Pierce's peculiar behavior than by the unacceptable possibility that as profit-conscious a person as Maude Kennard would knowingly drive away gilt-edged business.

"But maybe I'd better tell you what happened after that," Pierce added.

"Yes, do."

"Well, I didn't say much to Max—just got him quieted down enough so that he wouldn't walk out until I could have another talk with him. Then I went up to my office. I thought I'd get Mrs. Kennard's side of the story but I waited and waited and she didn't show up until about ten o'clock. The minute I started talking to her—I just don't know how to explain it, sir, she just seemed to go crazy. She went running off down to the lobby and I saw her heading for the kitchen. I got up to try to stop her—reason with her, you know?—and I was standing there in front of her office when her telephone started to ring. Well, it rang a couple of times so I answered it. It was a man named Austen."

"Grant Austen?"

"Yes, sir. I'm sure of the name because I asked him to repeat it. Do you know who he is?"

The pipe came out of Atherson's mouth. There was something about the timbre of Pierce's voice that sent a prickle of apprehension up his spine. "What did Mr. Austen want?"

"Well, he insisted on talking to Mrs. Kennard—said something about his having talked to her before from Moon Beach."

"Yes, he's down there at a convention," the banker acknowledged.

"But this call was from Norfolk, sir."

"Norfolk?"

"Yes, sir."

"Go on."

"As I say, I'd seen Mrs. Kennard go out to the kitchen, so I had the operator switch the call there. I didn't know what it was about until—well, you see, I was worried about what might be happening between her and Max—you know what it would mean to the Ivanhoe if we lost Max—so I went down to the kitchen. She was gone by the time I got there but—I don't know, sir, maybe there isn't any point in my telling you all this, but I know that Mr. McCall is a friend of yours, so—"

"Yes, yes, go on," Atherson said impatiently, unaware until he saw the spill of ashes that his pipe had tipped in his hand.

"I guess Max wouldn't have told me this except that he's quite a friend of Mr. McCall's—and then, of course, hating Mrs. Kennard the way he does—but anyway, Max heard her telling this Mr. Austen how Mr. McCall had cheated him out of a million dollars, how he was the head of a gang that had gotten Mr. Austen's company away from him."

The banker's hand gripped down on his pipe, quieting its rattling tremor. Cautiously he asked, "Were there any other names mentioned?"

"No—well, you see, I got all this secondhand from Max—maybe there were some other people mentioned but Max didn't say anything about it. All I know is that this Mr. Austen is getting in on a plane at noon and she's arranged for him to see some lawyer."

"Lawyer!"

"That's the way Max got it, sir."

Will Atherson recovered enough to light his pipe. "I don't suppose you'd know who the lawyer is?"

Pierce hesitated. "Not for sure, sir—but there is one lawyer that I know she knows—and when I mentioned his name to Max he thought it sounded right."

"Who's that?"

"His name is Torrant, sir—Judge Torrant. But, as I say, I couldn't swear to that."

Blue smoke curled from Will Atherson's lips as he waited through the moment that allowed him to say with masking casualness, "That isn't very important anyway, I don't suppose."

"Maybe I shouldn't have wasted your time with all of this," Everett Pierce apologized. "The only thing is—well, maybe Mr. McCall *isn't* the sort of guest we ought to have at the Ivanhoe but as long as he *is* a guest—well, it just seemed to me that it wasn't right for Mrs. Kennard to involve the hotel in something like that. That's always been my attitude—the Ivanhoe has to come first."

"You did the right thing, Everett," Atherson said quickly, putting a quick end to Pierce's apologetic jitters. "Glad you came over. Suppose you do this—let this thing sit for the time being. Don't say anything to anyone about it."

"Not even to Mrs. Kennard?"

"No, definitely not. Give me a chance to think about this over the weekend. I'll give you a ring sometime Monday."

Pierce stood. "That's fine, sir. Well—"

384

"Goodbye, Everett, and thanks again. As usual, your judgment was excellent."

"Thank you, sir," Pierce said with a lighthearted laugh that Will Atherson wished he could share.

As soon as Everett Pierce was out of the office, Atherson called his secretary and told her to get Cash McCall on the telephone. After a seemingly endless wait, she reported back that there was no answer. He told her to keep trying and then, as a second thought, told her to get Winston Conway at Jamison, Conway & Slythe. The whole thing sounded so ridiculously implausible that it hardly merited repetition, yet it was probably best to get word to Conway. Cash McCall had instructed him, a long time ago, that if he ever picked up even the faintest rumor of any threatened legal action, Conway was to be advised at once.

●●●●● 2

Among its many remarkable abilities, the human brain has a marked capacity for self-protection. When the imprint of stimuli continues at a level where the resultant sensation becomes overpowering, there is a normal dulling of perception. That had happened to Miriam Austen. The fear that had struck when Grant had come back to their suite at midnight had in no way lessened, but there had been a slackening of the tension of terror. She still had no idea what would happen after they arrived at Philadelphia, but her brain refused to spin out new apprehensions—or perhaps it was only because the possibilities had been exhausted. During the long hours of the night, her mind had explored every conceivable horror to the limit of her imagination.

Now, as the plane climbed from its take-off, she saw the city of Washington falling away and, almost without emotion, accepted the inevitable. The hope that Grant would turn back was gone. There was no point in further argument. Nothing that she had been able to say had made the slightest impression upon him, even her last-ditch threat that Lory would hate him for the rest of her life if he tried to interfere. His response had been to stare at her with those glassy eyes and say again, "This doesn't have anything to do with Lory."

She did not believe him. She had seen those eyes before. They were her father's eyes on that night when her mother had told her of the mad behavior that led him to defraud the Suffolk National Bank. "It's in the family," her mother had said. "He's going the same way his father did." And that had reminded Miriam where she had seen those eyes even before that—her grandfather on that night of her early childhood when two strange men had come and taken him to what, afterwards, was always referred to as "The Home." Later, at the time of her grandfather's death, she had discovered that the place where he had spent his last years was a private sanitarium for the mentally ill.

Miriam Austen had never forgotten her mother's distraught voice saying, "It's in the family," and the fear that she herself might become the victim of hereditary insanity had always been a challenge to reason in times of emotional stress. Now there was a transfer of that fear. She suspected—almost to the point of conviction—that what she had seen in Grant's face was what she so long had feared that she might find in her own mirror.

At midnight last night when Grant had flung open the door of the suite, she had thought he was drunk. Improbable as that explanation had seemed—so far as she knew, he had never been drunk in his life —she had momentarily accepted it, reasoning that since this was her first convention, it might have happened before without her having known about it. And she remembered what he had told her about the unpredictable behavior at the Associates Reception of even some of the most respected members of A.A.P.M.

But she had been wrong about his being drunk—and wrong, too, in her earlier belief that he would be relieved to know that Cash and Lory had arrived safely in Philadelphia. Her guess had been right —Grant had told her that, but almost nothing else, lapsing then into a stony silence, turning out the light and telling her to go to sleep.

All through the night she had listened to his restless tossing, trying to talk to him when she was certain that he was awake, receiving no reply except an unexplained cursing of Cash McCall, in itself a denial of his claim that his madman's behavior had nothing to do with Lory.

Sometime in the night she had heard him talking on the telephone about plane schedules to Philadelphia and, even before dawn, he was up and starting to pack. The sun was only a fiery break on the sea horizon when they got into the car that he had ordered. She had not known until they arrived that they were driving to Norfolk, and only deduction had explained that catching the Washington plane was the fastest way to get to Philadelphia.

At Norfolk he had spent almost the entire waiting time in a telephone booth. When he came out, she had tried to talk to him but his ears had been as unhearing as his eyes were unseeing. At Washington, he had again disappeared into a telephone booth. That was when desperation had driven her to threaten Lory's hatred if he tried to interfere between her and Cash. The only result had been his maniacal repetition of the claim that what he was going to do did not concern Lory. It was then that she had given up, no longer looking at his madman's eyes, accepting the surcease of attention that her mind demanded.

But the self-protective dulling of perception is not as simply explainable as it seems. Ears that have been closed to the continued pounding of some constantly repeated noise are still oddly capable of being alerted by the interjection of a strange sound, the ticking of a watch suddenly louder than the smashing crash of some great machine. It was that phenomena that caused Miriam Austen to hear her husband's almost inaudible sigh.

"All right, I'll tell you," he said, the words spilling out as if his brain lacked the normality of self-protection and could only save itself by disclosure. "Those crooks cheated me out of my company! McCall is nothing but a gangster and they're all in his gang—Conway—Gil Clark and Harrison Glenn—even Will Atherson."

"Oh, Grant, that can't be true. Mr. Atherson is one of your oldest friends."

"That's what I thought, too," he said, madly bitter. "But I know better now. I can see the whole thing. I tried to get him to let me sell to Andscott. No, I couldn't do that! He wouldn't let me. I had to sell to this McCall. Now do you know what they've done, that rotten gang of thieves? *They've* turned right around and sold to Andscott! Three million dollars. They've cheated me. Stolen a million dollars from me. That's why I'm going to Philadelphia. I've got to see a lawyer. They can't do this. They can't make a fool out of me!"

● ● ● ● ● 3

As Miss Fitch closed her notebook, Clay Torrant said, "When this man Austen comes, send him right in."

His secretary only nodded, still as grim-visaged as she had been all during his dictation of a memorandum to record the essence of his conversation with Mrs. Kennard. As usual, Miss Fitch made no effort to hide her dislike of Maude Kennard and, as if she was not certain that her viewpoint was strongly enough registered, she gave the door a vicious little slam as she went out.

Clay Torrant knew that he had every reason to be annoyed with Miss Fitch's petulance—a man couldn't let his secretary dictate his life—but he found it difficult to disagree with an attitude that so closely paralleled what he imagined his own to be. When Maude Kennard had called him at home and announced that she was coming to see him the minute he arrived at the office, he tried to sidestep but, as had happened so many times before, he found himself powerless to resist. She had told him that she was bringing him the most important case he had ever handled. And she was right, it would be ... if this man Austen's story checked out ... and *if* he decided to represent him.

Now that Maude was gone and his notes dictated, he sat doodling multi-faceted diamonds on his note pad, imagining that what was going on in his mind was a debate over the pros and cons of taking the case. Actually, the sensation of calmly weighing considerations was a delusion. He did not—and could not—weight the scales with a recognition of his odd compulsion to do anything that Maude Kennard wanted him to do. Nor could he admit to himself that he was being egged on by a blind—and clearly unprofessional—dislike of Cash McCall and everything the man represented. Still more deeply buried, far below the level of recognition, was his relief that the affair between Maude and McCall had broken up—but, even though there had been that awareness, he could not have admitted his sharing of Maude Kennard's malicious desire for revenge.

Admittedly, Maude had been in a state of extreme nervousness and that was usually an indication of unreliable testimony. Furthermore, she had flatly refused to tell him how she had learned all of the things she claimed to know. Yet, even with due allowance for prejudice, the main outlines of her story had the ring of truth. It stood to reason that Cash McCall wasn't pulling off those big deals of his without something going on under the table ... and he was a clever devil, setting up a shakedown gang with such a perfect front ... no two men in all Philadelphia were less open to suspicion than Winston Conway and Will Atherson.

The thought of Conway brought a twisted smile to Torrant's face, an anticipation of the satisfaction there would be in giving that pompous pretty-boy his comeuppance ... it was about time somebody showed up that phony for the crook's pimp he really was! But there would be even more justice in exposing Will Atherson.

In the same manner that a wound becomes more painful after inspection, Clay Torrant now recognized how much Atherson had hurt him over the years ... never speaking to him at The Wharf unless he was forced into it, yet never forgetting that he was a member of the House Committee when there was something to complain about ... those shavings that the carpenters had left in the coat closet back in '45 ... that chipped goblet in '48 ... the fan that had rattled last summer ... those silver bowls that had been missing last week. To see Will Atherson going around The Wharf with that self-satisfied smirk on his face ... *and that stinking pipe*! ... you'd think no one else in Philadelphia even *had* a great-grandfather! The truth was that Nathaniel Torrant had been a distinguished member of the Pennsylvania Bar when Isaac Atherson had been nothing but a street-corner loan shark ... actually no more than a pawnbroker!

Was it possible that Atherson had been fool enough to lay himself open to a charge of *conspiracy?* But, of course, he'd thought he'd get away with it ... all bankers got away with plenty ... gossip was as much their stock-in-trade as money. If you wanted to get the dope on someone, just get next to his banker. In the guise of asking for "credit information" a banker could dig up more dirt than a private detective agency.

And that was another thing about Maude's story that checked out ... that Lockwood Reports was a part of the swindle gang ... they had refused to supply a report on Cash McCall. Maude didn't have to tell him that, he knew it himself.

Damn it, it did look as if there might be a case here!

But it would all depend on Austen's side of the story ... and to win the case they would have to prove *conspiracy*.

In all the years of his practice, Clay Torrant had never had a case in which conspiracy was an issue, but he was well aware that its proof was a traditionally difficult legal assignment. Getting heavily to his feet, he crossed the hall and went into the windowless room that served as his law library. Going to the long shelf of *American Jurisprudence*, he found the right volume alphabetically—COMMERCE TO CONSTITUTIONAL LAW—and turned to the outline index at the head of the CONSPIRACY section, searching for leading topics, skimming pages, now and then dropping his eyes to pick up a footnote, discouraged to find that all of the cited cases were in other jurisdictions and difficult to appraise.

Pushing his way along the narrow aisle between the center table and the book stacks, he started on *Vale*, searching for Pennsylvania cases. He accumulated a list of citations that was encouragingly long but, as he made his way through the buckram-bound volumes of the *State Reports*, the list shrank discouragingly. He found one case that seemed to be leading—*Ballantine v. Cummings 220 Pa.*

621. But one would be enough if it were the right one. A check of the tabular columns in *Shepherd's* showed that *Ballantine v. Cummings* had been frequently cited.

Assured, he began a careful word-by-word reading of the opinion but, try as he would, his eyes kept being drawn back to the discouraging cautions.

> *When conspiracy is alleged, it must be proven by full, clear and satisfactory evidence ... must be such as to clearly indicate the prior collusive combination and fraudulent purpose, not slight circumstances of suspicion.*

Taking off his glasses and burrowing the heels of his hands into his eye sockets, Clay Torrant accepted the extreme difficulty of assembling *full, clear and satisfactory evidence.* Pennsylvania procedural rules did not permit discovery in aid of a contemplated suit, only after an action was started. By then he would be in the quicksand up to his neck. There was not a judge on the bench, nor a member of the Bar, who did not know that operators of the Cash McCall ilk were trapping their victims in a web of conspiracy ... but try to prove it within the straitjacket of the law! Even if it were possible to get hold of McCall's records—and it wasn't—there would be nothing on paper. Everything would have been verbal. Courtroom interrogation would be useless. McCall was clever, he had to be ... and a man with his ethical standards wouldn't worry about an oath to tell the whole and complete truth.

It would be an enormously difficult case to prepare ... and he would be all alone, not even a law clerk to help him. Conway would have one of the biggest law offices in Philadelphia behind him ... a dozen bright youngsters to do his research ... specialists to advise him ... a million dollars to spend if he needed it ...

Miss Fitch appeared in the doorway. "Mr. Austen's here. He's waiting in your office."

If Grant Austen had been out in the vestibule, Clay Torrant might have seen him there for a minute and gotten rid of him. As it was, he had no choice except to talk to him. But he delayed as long as he could, deciding to first wash his hands. After handling all of those dirty books, they needed it. In her younger days, Miss Fitch had been very good about keeping the library clean but, of late, she had been slipping rather badly.

····· 4

An hour after Will Atherson had telephoned Winston Conway, the lawyer had called back asking if it would be possible for Atherson to stop in at the Jamison, Conway & Slythe offices during the noon hour. The banker's first inclination had been to refuse. He had the legitimate excuse of a luncheon date—the executive vice-president of the Luxor Hotel Corporation was arriving from New York on the one o'clock train—and furthermore, if Cash McCall was running into a little difficulty with Grant Austen, it only served him right for not having asked for some advice before the deal to buy Suffolk Moulding had been closed.

But that second excuse was admittedly petty, unworthy of an Atherson, and it was almost in the spirit of penance that he had finally agreed to stop at Conway's office for a few minutes. It was the first time he had ever been in the Jamison, Conway & Slythe offices—in fact, the first time he had ever engaged in a private conversation with Winston Conway. Until now, he had "known" him only in the same sense that he "knew" several hundred other Philadelphians whom he occasionally encountered and greeted at public affairs. What little special attention he had ever given Conway was accountable only to his reputation as one of the city's most able attorneys, and his status as legal counsel for one of the Freeholders Bank & Trust Company's most important customers. Winston Conway was neither a Main Liner nor a member of The Wharf.

Now, sitting across the desk from the handsomely white-haired attorney, Will Atherson found himself perceptibly annoyed by Conway's rather obvious implication that Freeholders was somehow involved in whatever it was that was going on between Cash McCall and Grant Austen.

"Let's get one thing clear, Mr. Conway," Atherson said coolly. "My only reason for calling you was that Mr. McCall once asked me to do so in the event that I happened to pick up any seriously malicious gossip. I may have been wrong in putting this rumor in that category, but I felt it better not to take the chance."

"Quite so—but am I to take it that you regard yourself as not being personally involved?" Conway asked with annoying blandness. "After all, Mr. Atherson, you do own the hotel, don't you?"

Will Atherson was startled. He had once told Cash McCall that he controlled the Ivanhoe but he had not expected Cash to pass along that information to Conway.

"Which would make Mrs. Kennard an employee of yours," the lawyer added.

The banker was taken aback by the clear implication that he was responsible for Maude Kennard's stupid gossiping, and for any harm to Cash McCall that might arise from it. Reluctantly, he admitted, "Yes, in that sense I suppose I am concerned," more than ever convinced now that he was ready to sell the Hotel Ivanhoe.

"It would seem so to me," Conway said.

Regaining his poise, Atherson said, "I wouldn't be too concerned, Mr. Conway. Apparently Mrs. Kennard is upset about something—very bad judgment for her to have talked to Grant Austen, of course, and I intend to take steps to insure having no more of it—but I feel quite certain that it was nothing that Austen would take seriously."

"Unfortunately, Mr. Atherson, that doesn't seem to be the case." Conway paused as if waiting for his words to hit with their full impact. "Fortunately—and I might say, thanks to the promptness with which you advised me—we were able to get a couple of Lockwood men to the airport in time to pick up Mr. and Mrs. Austen and trail them downtown."

"Lockwood men?" Atherson asked blankly, unable to complete a vague association.

Conway seemed surprised, as if he had assumed knowledge that did not exist. "Lockwood Reports, you know? We occasionally use them in cases of this sort."

"I see," Atherson said, his surprise quickly fading as he accepted the fact that the use of a private detective agency by a law firm was not essentially different from the bank's use of skip tracers and credit agencies, both of whom employed men who did what was essentially detective work.

"I had a progress report just before you arrived," Conway went on, turning over a sheet of notes that, until now, had been lying face down on his desk pad. "The Austens took a cab to the railroad station where Mrs. Austen got out. She went to the information desk and was told that the next train to Suffolk, Pennsylvania, would not be until two-ten. She seemed very upset, quite nervous. Went into the women's rest room and when she came out she appeared to have been crying."

"But what could that have to do with—?"

"I don't know," Conway cut in. "I'm giving you the whole story in case any of it registers as being significant. Here's the rest of it—and this, of course, *is* directly pertinent. Austen continued down into the city. He went to the Hotel Ivanhoe and met Mrs. Kennard in the lobby. They went up to her office and were there about ten minutes. Austen came down and took a cab. The address he gave to the driver was the address of Clay Torrant's office. That's where he is now."

"But I still don't see what Grant Austen could—" Will Atherson felt himself fumbling and took a moment to collect his thoughts. "What's it all about, Mr. Conway?"

"I wish I knew!" the lawyer said fervently.

"You have no idea?"

"None. Do you?"

"No. I can't for the life of me imagine what Austen could be concerned about. He got a handsome price for his company—settlement's been made—no, I'm at a complete loss. I realize that Mrs. Kennard told him that he'd been victimized in some way—but he couldn't have given much weight to that. He knows very well that he got every cent his company was worth."

Conway folded his sheet of notes. "The only thing that's occurred to me—I know this wasn't in what you picked up, but it's possible that Mrs. Kennard may have learned that Suffolk Moulding was being sold and told him about it in one of their earlier conversations. If she did tell him that Mr. McCall was getting three hundred thousand shares of Andscott Instrument stock for—"

"Andscott Instrument?" Atherson heard himself ask.

"I thought you knew," Conway said. "But I'm sure that there's no reason why you shouldn't know—now that it's all signed, sealed and delivered."

The rocketing sensations that exploded in Will Atherson's mind were totally unidentifiable. His life had provided little experience with fear, none with terror. What was happening within his brain was as mysterious as death—and no less fearsome. He seemed to have lost the power to think, his mind stopped dead on a single exposed memory, the frighteningly clear recollection that he had advised Grant Austen not to consider selling the Suffolk Moulding Company to the Andscott Instrument Corporation.

• • • • • 5

It was Clay Torrant's first impression that Grant Austen was under even more nervous tension than Maude Kennard had been—and my story at least equally open to distrust—but the longer he listened the more clear it became that what Austen was telling him checked out surprisingly well. Corroborative testimony is usually accepted as reflecting favorably upon the reliability of both witnesses, but in this instance Torrant weighted it heavily in Austen's favor. There were places, of course, where Austen's story might be slightly colored by prejudice—but having been cheated out of a million dollars was a much more acceptable justification than the female vindictiveness that had so obviously motivated Maude Kennard.

Torrant had confidence in his ability to judge a man's character and no doubts troubled his estimate of Grant Austen as a very decent sort of man, not the brightest in the world—he had been grossly negligent in not informing himself about the character of the people with whom he had done business—but even that lapse was, in a way, a reflection of essential honesty. The most commonly duped were those whose own righteousness aroused no suspicion of others.

There was still a very real question in Torrant's mind about taking the case—he was not forgetting the pitfalls of trying to prove *conspiracy*—but since he had gone this far, there was no harm in going a little farther. Pulling his note pad toward him, he asked, "Now as I understand it, Mr. Austen, you feel that you have been the victim of a conspiracy?"

"Don't you?" Austen demanded. "You talked to Mrs. Kennard, didn't you?"

"Well, at this stage I'm not in a position to *have* an opinion," Torrant said mildly, slow-pacing his voice and smiling in a way that he hoped would calm Grant Austen. "Suppose we start back at the beginning and trace this thing through, step by step."

"Sure, you bet," Austen agreed, almost eagerly.

"You say that you'd never really thought about selling your company until last week—Tuesday. That would be the twenty-fourth?"

"Yes, Tuesday."

"And on that Tuesday you were visited by this man Clark who is the representative of a firm you had retained to advise you in the management of your business."

"Corporation Associates," Austen supplied. "It's Harrison Glenn's company—or at least I *thought* it was. Now I know that it's nothing but a Cash McCall cover-up."

"Oh, yes—Harrison Glenn," Torrant said, syllabizing the name as he wrote it. Here was something he had missed . . . McCall was clever, all right . . . Glenn was another of those holier-than-thou characters that no one would ever suspect of being a front. "Now, Mr. Austen, you're quite certain that you did *not* make your decision to sell your company until *after* your talk with this man Clark?"

"Absolutely. I didn't decide until—I thought it over that night, talked to my daughter about it, and then I decided—I mean I more or less decided."

"Now what was the nature of your conversation with Clark? I believe you said before that he advised you to sell. How did he do that?"

"He said he thought I'd be smart to do it," Austen said, his tone ironic as he added, "He said I might even get as much as two million dollars—if I was lucky enough to find the right buyer—as if he didn't know all the time who the buyer was going to be!"

Torrant overlooked the outburst, going calmly on. "And it was Clark—not you—who suggested the two million price?"

"How could I suggest anything? I didn't know what Suffolk Moulding was worth. Selling a company isn't like selling a bag of flour. There isn't any standard price. A company is worth whatever somebody is willing to pay for it."

"And Clark told you that if anyone offered you two million, you'd better take it in a hurry?"

Austen hesitated and then nodded, sullenly silent.

"And since you had retained Corporation Associates as your management counsel, you felt that establishing a fair and equitable selling price for your company was a service that you had a right to expect from them?"

"I know better now."

"But at the time, Mr. Austen—were you disposed to accept this valuation of two million dollars?"

"I just didn't know. That's why I went down to see Will Atherson."

"At the Freeholders Bank?"

"That's right."

"Tell me this, Mr. Austen—did you have reason to believe that Mr. Atherson would give you a fair appraisal of your company's worth? In other words, give you advice that you could rely upon?"

"Why wouldn't I? I'd done business with him almost from the very beginning, way back to '28."

"And you thought he was a trustworthy friend of yours—at least a *business friend,* if I may call him that."

"Sure, after all these years."

"Now did you, or did you not, talk to Mr. Atherson about that two million dollar price?"

"Yes, I—"

"And what did he say about it?"

"Well, he said I'd be lucky to get it."

"In other words, the same thing that Clark had said?"

"Judge, you don't have to dig around to know they were all in cahoots," Austen said, breaking out of the straitjacket of cross-examination. "All you have to know is this—Gil Clark told me that I ought to get one buyer bidding against another—you know, so I could get the price up?"

"I understand."

"Well, I thought that's what I was doing, but the whole thing was a frame-up to pull the wool over my eyes. Gil said he had a buyer—and Will Atherson said he had another buyer—but when it got to the showdown, they both turned out to be the same man."

Torrant felt himself lost. "Did you say there was *bidding*? I thought I understood you to say before—"

"How could there be any bidding?" Austen demanded angrily. "There was only one buyer."

"But you did accept this offer of McCall's?"

Austen seemed momentarily puzzled, as if he didn't understand the question, but then mumbled, "What would you have done—everyone telling you that two million was a good price?"

"By *everyone*, you mean Clark and Atherson?"

"Sure, who else did I have to trust—or *thought* I could trust."

Torrant wrote rapidly, catching up with his notes. "Now let's get back to Atherson. You say that you *talked* to him. How much of a talk was that, Mr. Austen—a casual conversation—or did you sit down and have a real talk?"

"You remember that day, don't you?" Austen demanded. "That's the day I met you at The Wharf. Will Atherson introduced us. Well, after lunch we went back to his office and talked for—it must have been an hour. I remember I was going to meet my daughter in the Ivanhoe lobby at three and it was almost that when I left the bank."

"Now, Mr. Austen, think carefully before you answer this next question. During your talk with Mr. Atherson was any mention made—any reference at all—to the possibility of selling your company to Andscott Instrument?"

"I don't have to think about that," Austen snapped back. "That was practically all we did talk about."

Torrant felt the thrust of excitement, the sudden discovery of rich pay-dirt. "It was?"

"Sure, that was my idea from the beginning—selling to Andscott. You see, Judge, I knew all along that Andscott had been trying to get hold of my plant. They tried back during the war—and just before this happened they'd been pushing me to put in a lot of expensive equipment. It was all a part of this same deal—I know that now—nothing but a squeeze play to get me to sell out."

For a moment, Torrant found himself unable to follow Austen's reasoning. Then, suddenly, he recalled that Andscott Instrument had also bought Padua Furniture from McCall at a high price. Was that what this was going to turn into—a ring inside Andscott Instrument that was milking the company by draining off its assets with these buys from Cash McCall? There was plenty of talk around town about Andscott Instrument being in trouble and passing their last dividend. This might well be the reason. And that fight that Maude had heard between Danvers and McCall—General Danvers was a too high-type man to be involved himself, of course, but he might well have discovered that McCall and his gang were out to wreck the company.

Making a note for later reference, Torrant drew himself back to the main line of his questioning. "Now, Mr. Austen, in this discussion with Mr. Atherson about the possibility of selling your company to Andscott Instrument—am I to understand that Atherson advised you *against* it?"

"He sure did."

"Precisely what did he say?"

"He said it wasn't even worth talking to them," Austen replied angrily. "He gave me a big story about Andscott not having any money —how they couldn't afford to pay me what the company was worth."

"And he advised you to sell to Mr. McCall?"

"Sure, he said that was the thing to do."

"And you trusted him?"

"Didn't I have a right to think I could?"

"Of course, of course," Torrant murmured. "Now, let's get along to your meeting with Mr. McCall. How did that happen, Mr. Austen? What were the circumstances?"

A strange flush had come to Grant Austen's face, a dulled redness that Torrant recognized as a symptom of extreme agitation, and he decided that perhaps he had been driving the witness a little too hard. He eased his voice and supplied, "It was at the Hotel Ivanhoe?"

Austen nodded, staring past him.

"You'd never met him before?"

Austen shook his head.

"Did Atherson introduce you?"

Austen's stare had become even more distracted. "No—my daughter did."

Torrant's attention sharpened. "Your daughter introduced you?"

There was no answer.

"Then McCall had managed to meet your daughter before he got to you?"

397

"I guess so," Grant Austen mumbled, the admission obviously painful.

Torrant gave his attention to his notes again ... apparently there were no depths to which McCall would not stoop!

Suddenly, Austen's voice broke out, spilling over the dam. "They'd all told me two million was a good price. I didn't know it was a frameup. I didn't know it was all the same gang. How could I—"

"Yes, yes," Torrant slid in. "I understand your feelings perfectly, Mr. Austen—but our job now is to get the cold, unemotional facts. I'm only trying to help you."

"Sure, you bet," Austen admitted, chastized, blinking the stare out of his eyes.

"Well, now—" Torrant began, looking at his notes. "So you went up to Mr. McCall's suite and that's where the deal was closed?"

For an instant, it seemed that Austen was again going to lose his self-control, but he stiffened and nodded, tight-lipped.

"And no one else was present?"

Austen shook his head. "No, my daughter was there."

"Oh—yes, I see." Torrant made another note . . . this was a break ... a witness. "And your daughter's name, Mr. Austen?"

"Lory," Austen said, spelling it. "I'd put some of the stock in her name so that—" He hesitated and then his words were suddenly anger-driven again. "He cheated her, too! She doesn't know it yet—but he did!"

Torrant underlined his note. "This stock that you say was in your daughter's name—that was your way of providing for her future welfare?"

"She's an artist—no money in anything like that—I was trying to be sure she'd always be taken care of."

"Of course, of course," Torrant sympathized, Austen's emotional state now more easily understandable ... there was more involved here than money ... there usually was. "Your daughter is not married?"

Austen seemed not to have heard the question and the lawyer repeated it.

"No," Austen finally said.

"Did you see Mr. McCall again?"

"Not until the settlement."

"That was—?"

"Wednesday. Day before yesterday."

"But in the meantime, I believe you said a gang of McCall's henchmen had moved into your plant?"

398

"Yes—Conway and this fellow Thompson and a lot of accountants—and Gil Clark, of course."

"Was all that with your permission?"

"The deal was made on the year-end balance sheet and I was supposed to get an extra payment for anything over that."

"And did you?"

"It didn't amount to anything—twenty thousand."

"Very clever of McCall," Torrant observed. "If he hadn't found what he wanted, he could have welched on the deal. Tell me, Mr. Austen, who was your legal counsel on all of this?"

Austen's embarrassment was plainly evident. "I know now that was a mistake—but the lawyer I'd had was just one of our Suffolk men and—well, to be frank about it, Judge, that day I met you in The Wharf I was wishing I had someone like you to represent me. I'm sorry now that I didn't talk to you then."

"Yes, it might have helped," Torrant said as a side comment. "But that's water over the dam now."

"I thought about it again afterwards when all the tax questions started coming," Austen went on. "But Mr. Conway kept making suggestions—"

Torrant snapped him up. "Conway? Do you mean that Winston Conway was advising you?"

Austen nodded but as if he wasn't certain what the admission meant. "Sure, I—well, he did have some ideas on how I could cut down the tax I'd have to pay. I guess that wasn't the right thing to do, was it?"

"*Not* for Winston Conway," Torrant said, scribbling a long note. This was a break he had not expected ... catching Conway off base on a clear violation of the professional code. But there was no point in explaining that to Austen now ... he was jittery enough as it was.

The lawyer finished his note and asked, "What was Mr. Clark doing during this period between the agreement to sell and the final settlement?"

"Didn't I tell you that?" Austen asked, surprised. "He took over the plant."

"Took it over?"

"Sure. McCall made him the plant manager right away. The next morning Gil was there ready to take charge."

Torrant nodded incredulously. McCall was really brazen ... one day he had Clark set up as Austen's supposedly confidential adviser, the next day he pushed him out in the open and admitted that he was one of his gang.

Hurriedly filling the moment of silence, Torrant asked another question. "Now about this man Bronson?"

"Bronson?" Austen asked blankly.

"Perhaps I have the name wrong," Torrant said, searching out the sheet of notes he had made during his conversation with Maude Kennard. "Didn't you have a man named Bronson working for you?"

"Yes—Paul Bronson. He was my—I guess you'd call him my first assistant."

"Which would mean, I presume, that he would have access to confidential information about your business?"

"Sure—everything. Why?"

"Do you know where Mr. Bronson was on—" Torrant hesitated, running his fingers down the Kennard notes—"on this same day you made your deal with Cash McCall?"

"Well I suppose he was—" Austen stopped. "No, I remember now, he'd asked to have the day off."

"Would it surprise you to know that he spent that day at the Andscott Instrument Corporation?"

Austen seemed to be attempting to hide his reaction. "Well, he handled the Andscott account. He was down there quite a lot."

"But he wouldn't be calling on them on his day off, would he? And if he were calling on Andscott as your representative would he have been talking to General Danvers?"

The glassy stare was back in Austen's eyes and Torrant debated whether or not to follow up General Danvers' accusation that Bronson had been a McCall spy. He finally decided that the best course would be to first attempt to smoke out Bronson's status in the Suffolk Moulding organization. "Mr. Austen, let me ask you this question— how good a man was Mr. Bronson from your point of view? Did you feel that he was completely loyal and trustworthy?"

"No, I—" Austen's eyes dropped and he seemed lost in thought. "I don't know how to put it, but I never did feel—well, to be honest about it, I never felt that Paul Bronson was a real company man. I mean he always seemed to be out for himself."

"Or someone else?" Torrant cautiously suggested.

"You don't mean—?" Austen's lips went slack.

"I don't know what it means," Torrant said. "It may mean nothing. On the other hand, I do know that he has been accused by at least one man—and a rather reputable one, I'd say—of being a McCall spy."

"Good god!" Austen exclaimed. "I knew it was bad, but not this bad! And I'd trusted him all of these years." His head suddenly jerked up. "You said you didn't know whether I had a case or not. Can't you say now that I do?"

Torrant found himself stopped by professional caution. "I'll have to give all of this some careful study, Mr. Austen. If I were to undertake to represent you in this matter—"

"You've got to, Judge! Who else can I trust?"

The lawyer found himself wavering. "Conspiracy is a very difficult thing to prove. If I were to—but tell me, Mr. Austen, what is it that *you* want? That's an important consideration."

Austen seemed not to understand.

"Do you want your company back?" Torrant explained. "Do you want this extra million dollars? What would you expect me to do for you if I should take the case?"

"All I want is to *get* those crooks," Austen said, his voice cracking. "I want them to know they can't get away with it!"

"It might be a long hard fight," Torrant cautioned.

"I don't care about that!"

For an instant, Clay Torrant was tempted to say, right then and there, that he'd take the case. But that was never a wise thing to do. "How long will you be in town, Mr. Austen?"

"I don't know," Austen said, a peculiar waver in his voice. "I've got to see Lory—tell her—but if you want me to stay here in town—"

"You were planning to go back to Suffolk? Well, that isn't so far away. Suppose I give this some hard study overnight and call you the first thing in the morning."

"You aren't thinking of *not* helping me, are you, Judge?" Austen pleaded. "If it's a question of money, don't worry about that. I've got plenty."

"No, it isn't a question of money," Torrant said slowly.

"Judge, there's got to be someone a man can turn to—someone that isn't in that gang of crooks. There's no reason why you can't take the case, is there?"

Clay Torrant's mind, suddenly reacting to Austen's strangely accusing stare, remembered that it was Will Atherson who had introduced them that day at The Wharf. Was Austen suggesting that if he didn't take the case it might prove that he was an Atherson stooge ... that he, too, might be a member of the McCall gang?

"No, Mr. Austen, there's no reason why I can't represent you," Clay Torrant said, sternly calm. "I'll call you in the morning and give you my final decision."

••••• 6

Gil Clark had decided to spend the day at the Suffolk Moulding Company. Still unable to get Cash McCall on the telephone, and finding that there was nothing helpful that he could do at Jamison, Conway & Slythe, he had driven to Suffolk after leaving a note at the Ivanhoe for Cash and telling Winston Conway where he could be reached.

He had felt mildly conscience-stricken for not having called Paul Bronson yesterday to explain his sudden disappearance and, on the way to his Suffolk Moulding Company office, he had rehearsed an explanation that would be honest, plausible, and yet not too revealing.

No explanation had been necessary. Bronson immediately exploded, "Thank god, you're here, Gil," and confronted him with three situations requiring immediate action: (1) the re-use cartons in which the Y4B Andscott Recorder cabinets were shipped had come through from the boxmaker without the padding strips and production was piling up in Shipping; (2) a knock-out pin had somehow gotten loose and wrecked two of the four cavities in the Iona-Graf mold, making scheduled delivery impossible; (3) a press operator named Furgoltz, who had eighteen years of company service and a wife and six children, had been caught rifling lockers in the plant wash-up room.

The air of crisis with which Bronson endowed each situation was justified—all were important to the company—but as Gil Clark maneuvered his way toward the best handling of each problem, he was haunted by the memory of Winston Conway's prediction that, after yesterday, running the Suffolk Moulding Company would not seem such an enticing prospect. It was not. And when Andscott's purchasing department called to register a vehement complaint about a shipment of styrene dials being off-shade, it was difficult to generate an appropriate feeling of serious emergency.

By good fortune, Paul Bronson was forced to leave at twelve o'clock to attend a Chamber of Commerce committee meeting, giving Gil a free noon hour to devote to an attempt to draft an organization chart for the operation of the Suffolk Moulding Company as a division of the Andscott Instrument Corporation. His prime difficulty was that he found himself an odd piece that he didn't know how to fit into the puzzle. Cash had indicated that he wouldn't be coming back to Suffolk, but there had been nothing definite about it.

At one o'clock he left for lunch, driving downtown to eat at the hotel and then, afterwards, went up to his room to change from the rumpled suit that he had worn since yesterday morning. He was pulling out of the hotel parking lot, turning west, when he heard the roar of a plane overhead, the unmistakable pulsing whine of a B-26. With his vision blocked by the car top, he didn't actually see the plane itself but there was no question that it was Cash McCall's.

Decisively, he made a right turn to avoid the slow-moving traffic on King, crossed Jefferson and State, swung left and picked up Boulevard Drive and then Airport Road. He assumed that Cash Mc-Call wanted to see him and hoped that he could reach the airport before Cash could get a cab for the trip into town.

No taxicabs passed him on Airport Road and he felt the satisfaction of success until, turning into the lane that led to the hangar, he was aware that the B-26 was not on the apron. For a moment he feared that the plane had not landed, or had already taken off, but then he saw it far out at the end of the runway, standing where it had rolled to a stop after its landing, a whole field's length away from the hangar.

Gil parked against the fence and, noticing that the watchman's eyes were also on the plane, called out, "Anything wrong out there?"

"Don't know," the old man speculated. "Trying to figure it out myself. He's been sitting out there for quite a while now."

But the words were no more than spoken when the airplane turned and the roar of its speeded motors was heard as it taxied toward them.

Waiting with the car door open, watching the windshield of the airplane's cockpit for the first glimpse of Cash McCall, Gil was startled to see a girl's face. The motors cut off as the plane lumbered to a stop, broadside to the gate, porthole matched to porthole so that Gil could see through the cabin. As he watched, he saw the passage of two figures down the aisle, but so close together that they seemed almost one, and there was a long wait before the cabin door opened. The girl who came down the steps was Lory Austen.

Gil felt the subconscious accusation of being a Peeping Tom and shrank back into his car.

Lory's voice drifted toward him, calling up to Cash who still stood at the head of the steps, "I'll be waiting." Then she turned and came toward the gate, half running, and for an instant Gil was sure that she would see him. But she ran to the right and he saw then, as he had not noticed before, that the Austen's blue Cadillac was parked on the other side of the gate.

The big car backed and turned and Gil struggled with the decision of whether or not to reveal his presence to Cash. The weight of his own desire finally forced him to jump out and call.

Cash saw him as the steps were coming up and, as the door opened again, his smile of greeting erased any doubt as to the warmth of his welcome.

"I was just thinking about you," Cash said as Gil came to the bottom of the steps. "Wondered if you might be here in Suffolk."

"I heard you landing," Gil explained. "Thought I might give you a lift if you were coming out to the plant."

Cash shook his head. "No, but come aboard. I want to talk to you."

"I thought I'd better get out here to Suffolk and square things away," Gil felt it necessary to explain as he reached the cabin. "I don't know what you'll want to do as far as organization is concerned, but—"

"Look, Gil," Cash interrupted. "Ride along down to Philly with me. Give us a chance to talk." He saw Gil's glance toward the gate and quickly added, "You can pick up your car this afternoon. I'm coming back at six for Lory. How did everything go last night?"

Standing in the middle of the cabin, Gil offered a quick report on his successful meeting with General Danvers, then a summary of what had happened at Jamison, Conway & Slythe.

"No foul-ups anywhere?" Cash asked.

"Not a one," Gil said. "Conway says he's never seen a deal knit together so beautifully, no loose ends anywhere."

"That's the way I want it to be," Cash said. "Don't want to go off and leave you with any headaches."

"Go off?"

"I'm getting away for a month or so," Cash said, attempting a flat statement, but there was a hint of excited anticipation in his voice, more than a hint in the crinkling smile that he was only half successful in hiding. He turned up the aisle, "Come on, let's get this ship in the air. John Allenby is meeting us at the hotel. I want to get you two together."

No clairvoyance was required to know that Cash McCall's mind was on Lory Austen and, for a moment or two, Gil Clark shared his preoccupation, but his interest in someone else's love affair was quickly submerged by the exciting experience of being back in the cockpit of an airplane again. The roar of the motors uncovered a thousand memories, all closer to the surface than he had ever suspected they were, the muscles of his body still responding to the old reflexes as the plane hurtled down the runway. Seemingly, it was the pull of his own hands that lifted them into the air.

Cash motioned to the headset and Gil slipped it over his ears, hearing the code beat of a range beacon as the plane leveled off on its easterly course, then Cash's voice saying, "It's all yours, Gil."

He hesitated for only a startled instant and then his hands reached out, tentative until he rediscovered that oneness of man and machine that he had first miraculously experienced on that day at flight school when old "Pappy" White, his instructor, had said, "You either get it or you don't get it—and once you got it, you got it for good."

For a long time, Gil Clark's mind was closed by the demanded concentration of holding the airplane in level flight, a shell of abstraction finally broken by the strangely incongruous thought that he had been right about that drawing of Lory Austen's that he had seen on the wall of Cash McCall's suite.

The plane yawed off course and he said, apologetically, "I'm a little rusty."

There was no answer and he glanced left. Apparently Cash had not noticed.

••••• 7

Clay Torrant had gone to his library immediately after finishing the dictation of his notes on the interview with Grant Austen. Miss Fitch had twice tried to dislodge him, but he had successfully resisted both attempts, even ignoring the sandwich and bottle of milk that she had finally brought to him.

Driven by an energy that was like a resurgence of youth, he roamed the room and snatched books from the shelves as leading topics popped into his mind from pigeonholes so long unused that, if he had stopped to think about it, he would have been astounded at the suddenly restored efficacy of his memory. He compiled a page-long list of cited cases and heaped the table with volumes of law reports. Most of the references proved barren but that did not, as it had in the work he had done before Austen's arrival, cause discouragement. He found nothing that promised to ease the burden of proving *conspiracy*, but his reverent respect for the Law gave him the courage to drive on, sure in his belief that sooner or later his faith would be rewarded by a revelation of the path to Justice.

And then it happened, the sudden flash of light, ... *he didn't have to prove conspiracy!* There was an easier way than that ... forget conspiracy and shift the charge to *fraud ... deceit ... breach of confidential relationship!*

Suddenly, it was simple. One tight case was all he needed. But who should he move against? Obviously, one of the two conspirators with whom Austen had been in direct contact. But which one ... Atherson or Clark?

Reluctantly, he let Atherson slip through his fingers. Clark was the ideal defendant, no doubt about it. Clark was wide open. He was the one who had perpetrated the fraud ... appraising Suffolk Moulding at two million when it was worth three ... talking Austen into selling ... then leading him to McCall ... deceiving him into the belief that there were competing prospects for the purchase of the company. It was all there ... fraudulent utterance ... inducement to act ... justifiable reliance by the recipient. There was even a provable compensation ... Clark had gotten his high-salaried job as the head of Suffolk Moulding as his cut in the pay-off!

Flipping back the uncounted sheets of yellow notepaper that had piled up behind his tablet, he found the reference that he was looking for: POMEROY CITED—FRASER FUND *v.* FRASER 350 *Pa.* 553, 566

> *Fraud in equity includes all wilful or intentional acts, omissions, and concealments which involve a breach of either legal or equitable duty, trust, or confidence, and are injurious to another, or by which an undue or unconscientious advantage over another is obtained.*

Reread, he saw a significance that he had missed before. It was almost as if some supersensory guidance had forced him into copying the quotation. And it seemed to have been the same providence that had made him note NEUMAN *v.* CORN EXCHANGE NAT'L BANK & TRUST Co. 356 Pa. 442, 454 (1947)

> *... deceived party need not prove that defendant's false and fraudulent representations were the sole reason ... sufficient that they constituted material inducement to his action.*

That was important, too ... block any defense allegation that Austen might have acted from other motives. The case was against Clark. But what about Cash McCall? It was McCall who had to be hit ... *the remedy for fraudulent acquisition of stock is restoration* ... and it was McCall who held the stock. Should the action be against McCall in the first place?

He slumped forward, removing his spectacles, rubbing his tired eyes. It wouldn't be enough to strike at Clark. He had to get deeper than that ... expose the whole gang ... get all of their shabby trickery out in the open ... the bankers who hid their adverse interests behind those glass and marble fronts, the brokers who were nothing but sheep's-clothing finders for the operators, the pack-following lawyers who covered up their tracks for a juicy fee, the Bureau boys who got so fat off the income tax racket that ...

As miraculously as it had happened before, there was a sudden break of light ... that famous line from his father's argument in ALTIMYER *v.* SMITH ... *it is physiologically inescapable that when you step on the catspaw the sensation of pain is transmitted to the cat.*

Through a suit against Clark, he could get at McCall. Or would it be wiser to sue Clark and Corporation Associates as joint defendants ... or ring in Cash McCall, too? But that didn't have to be decided now ... later ... cross that bridge when he came to it.

There was no doubt that he had his case ... *his* case. This was his chance to make the Law what he had always wanted it to be, a shining sword to strike down the sneak thieves who preyed upon honest men, pulling the wool over the eyes of the Bureau of Internal Revenue, filching their dirty millions, living in suites at the Ivanhoe, apartments at the Carwick Arms, white-fenced gentlemen farms supported by income tax deductions, blue-ribboned horses and mink-coated mistresses ... the Cash McCalls ...

He had replaced his spectacles and the first thing that his restored vision saw was the last thing he had written, the underlined reminder of what would become the foundation of his case ... CONFIDENTIAL RELATION ... yes, that would be the soft spot in the defendant's armor.

Again flipping through his pages of notes, he confirmed a truth that had suddenly revealed itself. He had traced every citation under that heading. All had involved bankers, brokers, physicians or attorneys. There was not a single case, not one that even remotely touched the confidential relationship between a retained business consultant and a corporation client. He would be blazing a new path, setting a new landmark in the Law ... AUSTEN *v.* CLARK ... cited as a leading case for the next hundred years ... sustained by the Supreme Court of the United States ... Clay Torrant for the appellee.

The prospect was, if anything, too enticing. Consciously, Torrant opened his mind to caution. It would be a rough case. Cash McCall would stop at nothing. His business life would be at stake and he would fight like the cornered rat that he was ... and all the rest of the rats would come running to his help ... and the leader of the pack would be Winston Conway.

Clay Torrant closed his eyes as if impelled to shut away the image

407

of Conway's sickeningly handsome face taunting him with the sardonic disdain of a man who held all the trumps. What chance did he have against Conway ... that reputation ... even the judges showing their deference.

The old lawyer's eyes opened and he set his jaw. There *was* such a thing as Justice ... there *had* to be ... something that couldn't be bought with dollars ...

There *was* a case here ... and he could win it! Yes, even though he was all alone ... Clay Torrant *v.* Jamison, Conway & Slythe, Cash McCall, Will Atherson and the Freeholders Bank & Trust Company, Clark and Harrison Glenn and Corporation Associates, Lockwood Reports ... all the men and money in the world and, damn it, he'd still lick them! And he wouldn't take a penny for himself ... spend every cent of his fee for the help he would need to build the case ... prove to those rats that there was at least one man left in the world who was above their dirty money-grubbing!

Again there was the reflex of caution and now, finally, he listened to the question that his subconscious mind had been whispering for the last two hours. Would Austen stand his ground and go through with it? Or would he lose his guts and back out ... make him look an old fool ... a has-been lawyer desperate for a case? It happened constantly in every legal practice, the irate client who was ready to sue everyone in sight until the chips started going down ... and Austen had obviously been in a neurotic state. And there were weaknesses in his story, holes that anyone could see ... questions that still had to be answered ... yes, he should have dug a little deeper ... but he had gone as far as he could, Austen as keyed up as he'd been.

But was there any doubt that Cash McCall was guilty, any doubt at all? If this were the first time it might be different ... it wasn't ... McCall had done it again and again, millions upon millions. Everyone knew that ... every decent right-minded man in Philadelphia knew it was time someone clipped that vulture's wings!

Austen *couldn't* back down now! Damn it, why had he let him get away? There wasn't a minute to lose ... Austen had to be convinced that he *did* have a case ... and that he had to go through with it! There was a million dollars at stake here ... but more than money ... more than a company ... more than one man or one lawyer or one ...

Without conscious decision, he had gotten to his feet and plunged to the door. "Miss Fitch, put in a call—Mr. Austen at Suffolk. If he isn't there yet, keep trying."

"Yes, Mr. Torrant," she said, again as sullenly grim as she had been before lunch. "There's a message on your desk."

He suspected from Miss Fitch's manner that the message would be from Maude Kennard. It was. She wanted him to call her at once. The message was more than a half hour old. Instinctively, he hesitated —and then decided to put through the call himself without bothering Miss Fitch. It was strange about Maude ... always seemed as if she never cared about anyone but herself ... but it was Maude who had brought him the Austen case ... AUSTEN *v.* CLARK ...

"Wait a minute," Maude Kennard said when she heard his voice. He waited, hearing a door close in the background. Then, in a barely audible whisper, she said, "A man's been here trying to dig information out of me. His whole story was phony. He claimed he was with the Luxor Hotel chain but I'm sure he was a Lockwood man."

There was a click and the connection was broken. After a stunned moment, Clay Torrant stabbed at his buzzer.

When Miss Fitch appeared, he demanded, "Wasn't there someone out there with you just now?"

She shook her head. "Just a salesman for one of the office supply places."

"Which one?"

"I don't know. Some new one. There wasn't anything I wanted, anyway."

"Did he ask you any questions?"

"Yes," Miss Fitch said, her voice acidly sharp. "He asked me how long I was going to have to put up with that old wreck of a typewriter."

"Oh," Torrant said, deflated. "Yes, we'll have to do something about that, Miss Fitch. What about Mr. Austen?"

"I haven't been able to call him yet. You were on the line with Mrs. Kennard."

She closed the door without giving him a chance to reply.

Ten minutes passed before she came back to tell him that the girl who had answered at Mr. Austen's home had said that he was attending a convention and wasn't expected home until some time Monday.

● ● ● ● ● 8

"Yes sir, Mrs. Austen," the taxi driver said, relieving her of the necessity of speaking but destroying the anonymity that had been her shield in the station at Philadelphia and on the train to Suffolk, forcing her now to face the truth of arrival.

This return home had been her goal through the hours of waiting, but now she realized that her motivation had been a blindly groping hope that was impossible of fulfillment. Her guilt was as inescapable as her identity. Selfishness was her sin, blindness her curse.

All through the night, and until their plane had taken off from Washington, Miriam Austen had suspected insanity in her husband. Then, finally, Grant had told her how he had been victimized by the Cash McCall gang. That had turned the accusation of insanity upon herself and no argument had been able to dislodge it, seeing herself nakedly revealed as a horribly abnormal creature, so incorrigibly hungry for her own happiness that she had completely missed even the vaguest sensing of her husband's burden. She had failed him again as she had failed him through all of their marriage. The convention had been her chance for a new life, and she had destroyed hope with the same blindness that had always cursed her.

She had known why Grant had turned to Lory—because that was where he had found understanding—and yet, knowing, she had still failed in the opportunity he had given her to redeem herself.

Even when Grant had told her, over and over again, that what he was worried about had nothing whatsoever to do with Lory, she had been so stupidly self-centered that she hadn't believed him, her jealousy such a corrupting thing that it destroyed all understanding. Now she could see the depths of her depravity, the revolting abnormality of a mother so jealous of her own daughter that she had tried to drive her from their home, so anxious to get rid of her that she had pushed her off on the first man who had been willing to take her away. Grant was right ... she should have told him it was Cash McCall who had gone off with Lory day before yesterday ... the face in the book, the man from Maine ... but the self-seeking hope of being alone with her husband had blinded her to the truth that all Cash McCall was after was Lory's money.

"Sorry, Mrs. Austen," the cab driver called back, a remark frighteningly pertinent until, as a delayed perception, she was conscious of a jarring thump.

"They ought to do something about this street," the driver complained. "It's the frost that does it—heaving the pavement."

"I know," she said. It was the first time she had spoken aloud since she had bought her ticket in Philadelphia and the sound of her voice seemed oddly calm, strangely mismatched with the mind-spoken words of madness, and she stored the sound-image of what she had just said as something to be repeated when Anna told her that Lory hadn't been home last night.

The cab turned sharply and, before she could call out to tell the driver to bear left for the garden entrance, he had swung right and stopped at the front porch.

The opening door brushed back a pile of mail that had been dropped through the slot and she stooped immediately to gather it up, sorting out Grant's mail as she walked toward the library to put it on his desk even before she had taken off her hat, an unconscious grasping at even this minor chance to serve him. There was an inch-thick pile of letters and telegrams, the corner cards identifying a few more of the dozens of investment brokers and charitable organizations that, with equal zeal, had been writing and wiring him ever since the rumor had gotten out that he had sold Suffolk Moulding, the flow increased now that the sale had been confirmed. Momentarily, she considered destroying this pile of mail as a way to protect Grant from the painful recollection of what had happened, but then realized that she was thinking with her own mind, not her husband's ... Grant was strong enough to face the truth and not try to hide it.

She placed the mail on his desk pad, squared it to a neat pile, and then walked back to the center hall, stopping at the mirror to take off her hat. Suddenly, overhead, there was the sound of footsteps. Her flash reaction was that Anna was late in doing the upstairs work today, but the rhythm of the steps was as identifiable as a voice and she knew, even before she saw her daughter at the head of the stairs, that Lory was home.

"Mother!" Lory exclaimed, the single word as expressive as a dozen questions.

The very act of looking up was a subjection to apology and Miriam Austen climbed the stairs as a penitent striving for the expiation of a sin. There was only one way she could save herself now ... make Lory understand how much her father needed her!

"What in the world has happened?" Lory demanded.

"The most awful thing," Miriam Austen said, her voice as stiff as her body, rigidly restraining the impulse to gather her daughter in her arms, subconsciously denying herself the outlet of emotion as if its containment were a demanded part of her penance.

"It's Father, isn't it?" Lory asked.

"Yes," she acknowledged, suddenly deciding that her easiest course would be to pretend ignorance of any relationship between Lory and Cash McCall. "Your father has found out that he was cheated by this man McCall—and, even worse, that so many other men he thought were his friends were all in on it—Will Atherson and Gil Clark and Mr. Conway. They were all part of the same gang."

Lory, in her quilted challis dressing robe, her eyes wide with astonishment, looked even more childlike than usual and Miriam Austen felt herself achieving some slight command of the situation.

But what gain she had made was immediately canceled by the coldly adult tone in which Lory asked, "What have you been told?"

"Your father will tell you himself as soon as he gets home."

"It isn't true."

"Lory, listen to me—please."

"He wasn't cheated."

"Oh, he was, Lory, he was! They were all in on it together. I know how hard it is for you to believe it. I couldn't believe it myself when he first told me."

"And if you believe it now, you're believing a lie," Lory said, not raising her voice.

Her daughter's frigid calm was more devastating than a shrieked outburst, and Miriam Austen helplessly dropped her voice to a poor match of Lory's tone. "You don't know what happened. Gil Clark talked him into selling—"

"I do know what happened. Wasn't I with him when he decided to sell—that night down in the library—*alone* with him? You know I was."

Miriam Austen recoiled as if struck by a blow.

"And didn't I go to Philadelphia with him? And I was with him in Cash's apartment when he sold the company. I *know* what happened—and I'm the only one who *does* know. Cash didn't cheat him. No one cheated him. If there was anyone who did anything wrong it was Father. You say that Gil Clark talked him into selling. That isn't true. Do you want to know why he sold—and in such a hurry? I'll tell you. Because he thought he was going to lose half of the plant's business—and he thought he could trick someone into buying before they found out about it. If you want the truth, there it is."

Lory backed a step and then turned to the doorway of her bedroom, closing the door behind her.

Miriam Austen was so certain that the door would be locked against her that reaching out to the doorknob was a gesture of hopelessness. But the door was open.

●●●●● 9

During the few minutes that he had flown the plane, Gil Clark had all but forgotten that Cash McCall had said he wanted to talk to

412

him. The instant Cash had taken over the controls again, however, there was a full return of curiosity, sharpened by the memory that he had said he wanted him to "get together" with John Allenby— whatever that meant. But there had been no break in the silence. Cash had said nothing. He was lost in thought, totally preoccupied and clearly not with the handling of the airplane—he flew as "Pappy" White had flown, every move a reflex so well conditioned that there was no need for conscious thought.

It was not until they were on the ground, and after Cash had turned the airplane over to a white-jumpered mechanic with instructions that it was to be serviced for a five o'clock take-off, that he suddenly started to talk. His first crisp sentences were enough to disprove Gil's earlier guess that Cash had been thinking only of Lory Austen. It seemed then that every second of silence in the cockpit of the plane must have been used in preparation for what now developed into an astoundingly incisive analysis of the management problems that would be faced in a reorganization of the Andscott Instrument Company.

Gil had seen prior evidence of Cash McCall's amazing ability to capture and hold endless detail—his mind apparently retaining an instantly available carbon copy of every fact-filled page of the Lockwood report—but this was his first encounter with Cash's capacity for creative thinking on management problems. Many of his ideas were bold, some to the point of unorthodoxy, but everything Cash proposed was grounded upon a sure knowledge of the company's specialized problems. He drew the plan with broad strokes, wasting no time on fine shadings, yet constantly exhibiting a profound knowledge of operating detail.

Gil was so professionally intrigued that he all but lost curiosity about his own future, so occupied with the task of keeping pace with Cash's racing mind that he hardly noticed the passage of time or distance. It came as something of a shock when he saw that they were already in downtown Philadelphia, surprise compounded by Cash abruptly asking, "Where do you see yourself in the Andscott picture, Gil?"

Caught unaware, Gil hesitated and then gave himself another moment to think by saying, "That's up to you."

"No ideas?"

"I didn't know I was going to be in the picture."

"That's for you to decide—but I have been playing with one line of thought that might intrigue you." Cash twisted on the seat, half facing him now. "This may be blue-sky thinking but it seems to me that Andscott Instrument might give us a chance to learn some things

—maybe more important in the long run than the money we'll make on this one deal. We're breaking into electronics here and that's an enormous field."

"No question about that."

"I'm not worrying too much about this next year or two. It's a gold-rush business—and if you pan your way up the military creek, you can't miss pay-dirt. But sooner or later that's going to play out. When it does, finding gold will depend on how well research and development is managed."

"That's true of a lot of companies—in other fields, too," Gil said, attention alerted. Was Cash thinking of Andscott as a company that he might hold and continue to operate? That *must* be true ... he wouldn't be talking about long-range plans if he weren't.

"But particularly of an outfit like Andscott that has to live on technical development," Cash had gone on. "Andscott doesn't belong in consumer products or mass merchandising."

"The television fiasco proves that," Gil agreed hurriedly, racing his mind to catch up. "There's no question but that an Andscott-type company makes or breaks on its research and development job."

"And there's as much chance to break as make," Cash said with pointed force. "Right now, research is the shining star that a lot of company managements are following. Unless I'm wrong, plenty of them are being dazzled by the bright light and are going to wander right off to the auction block. Research is fashionable now—it's the thing to do—build a big beautiful laboratory and fill it up with Ph.D.s. Theoretically, it *has* to pay off. In a lot of cases it hasn't—and there'll be more where it doesn't. I can buy a dozen companies right now that have poured too much down the research rathole."

"I can believe that."

"The trouble usually isn't in the lab, it's up on top. As I see it, that's the most common weakness in general management today. You can walk into company after company—surely you've seen it yourself?—and find good financial management, good production management, good sales management—everything under tight control until you hit research. Then it's a wing and a prayer."

"Managing research is a tough problem," Gil acknowledged. "You're dealing with creative people—individualists—men who are often more career-minded than they are company-minded. It's particularly difficult these days—so many jobs open for research and development men—they know they can walk out any time and land on their feet. It's hard to develop company loyalty with a situation like that."

"But isn't there an answer somewhere?" Cash pressed.

414

"There might be," Gil said uncertainly. "Several years ago we made some personnel attitude studies at Corporation Associates—four different clients, all with big research laboratories or engineering development departments. Without exception, that's where we found the worst general morale and the lowest percentage of men who were putting the company's interests ahead of their own."

"Isn't that another way of saying that the company wasn't giving them what they wanted out of life?" Cash asked. "Different men want different things."

"I know that," Gil conceded, vividly recalling that Winston Conway had used almost that same phrase in his attempt to explain Cash McCall.

"Look, Gil, wouldn't it be possible to take a whole new approach to the management of research? We agree that it's the heart of a business—at least in a company of the Andscott type—and we also agree that it's usually the weakest spot in the company, morale-wise. Can't that problem be licked? Weren't you edging toward a solution a minute ago when you said that these men are individualists—that they have to have different kinds of incentives? Haven't we gone too far in our standardized personnel programs—handing every man the same package, assuming that because we put the same salary rating on a Class F_2 research chemist and a Class F_2 district sales supervisor they're both going to be satisfied? Salary isn't the only thing that counts."

"Strange you should bring that up," Gil said, his mind aroused by a reminiscent tremor. "This study I mentioned—well, I made a talk on it three or four years ago at a management conference. What you just said isn't too far from what I was trying to say."

"Not so strange," Cash said with a tongue-in-cheek smile. "I read that talk."

"You did?" Gil asked, surprised, then feeling himself forced to add, "It fell flatter than a cold pancake. The whole conference was devoted to job analysis and the necessity for the uniform treatment of all employees—and there I was saying that maybe the whole approach was wrong."

"It didn't fall flat with me," Cash said emphatically. "And that's what I'd like to have you do, Gil—go into Andscott as vice-president in charge of research and development. Find out whether your ideas will work. If they aren't the answer, then find out what the answer is."

"But I—" Gil stammered. "Well, I don't know whether I have the qualifications—the scientific or technical background—"

"That's all to the good," Cash snapped back. "That's been the trouble up to now—treating it as if it were a scientific and technical problem. It isn't. It's a management problem—a *human* problem. Don't you see the possibilities, Gil? If we can find the answer at Andscott, we can make it work in a dozen other companies."

"Sure, but—well, maybe it would be better if I didn't go barging in right away as vice-president in charge—I mean, better for the company."

Cash shot him a quick glance, an oddly quizzical smile that ended in his saying, "You *are* a company man, aren't you, Gil?"

"Well, I'd have to be on a job like that," he said blankly, not exactly certain what Cash meant.

"You're right, of course," Cash conceded, pulling out his wallet as the cab slowed to a stop in front of the Hotel Ivanhoe's entrance. "We'll talk it over with John Allenby."

Relieved, Gil followed him into the hotel, his mind spinning with the revolving door, fanning the excitement that had been sparked by the prospect that had so suddenly opened out ahead of him. As had happened so many times before, Cash had resolved everything with a snap of his fingers. Ten minutes ago, the future had been a hazy blur. Now it was crystal clear, charted and mapped, and no man could ask for a more intriguing challenge. The only strange thing was that Cash had seen that speech. How had he happened to ... ?

A man had jumped up from a seat in the lobby and was hurrying toward them. Expecting to meet John Allenby, Gil was startled by the man's familiar appearance, then suddenly realized that this wasn't Allenby but one of the young law clerks he had met last night at Jamison, Conway & Slythe.

"Mr. McCall, I'm Dick Gorham from Mr. Conway's office. He's had me camping here on the off chance that I might catch you coming in. It's extremely important that you see him right away, sir—extremely important!"

"What's it about?" Cash asked calmly, no hint of the trepidation that Gil felt within himself.

"I don't know, sir," Gorham said. "Except that it's on the Andscott situation."

Cash turned to Gil. "What do you suppose has happened?"

"I—well, I haven't the slightest idea," Gil stammered. "When I left this morning—"

"We'd better find out." Cash looked at his watch. "Allenby may not have left his office yet. I'll call and hold him off until we see what's up."

416

••••• 10

"Miss Fitch, haven't you reached Mr. Austen yet?" Clay Torrant demanded.

"No sir, but he's expected. I talked to Mrs. Austen this last time and she said that she'd have him call just as soon as he got in."

"Don't count on that—keep calling," he ordered, stumping back into his office.

••••• 11

A pall of funereal silence hung over Winston Conway's office as Gil Clark followed Cash McCall into the room. Will Atherson and Harrison Glenn rose in silent greeting, finally speaking but in voices as muffled as if the table around which they had been sitting were a coffin.

This was the first time Gil Clark had seen Harrison Glenn since he had left Corporation Associates and he made a point of selecting the chair beside him. He knew the giant man too well to expect any casual pleasantries, but the stone mask of Glenn's face seemed even more chilled than usual. Will Atherson, who sat at Gil's left, gave his presence only the barest recognition. His acquaintance with the banker was too limited to permit judgment by contrast but, even so, Atherson seemed far from his normal self, a serious lack of composure betrayed by the little stabbing glances with which he followed Cash McCall as he circled the table and took a seat beside Conway. Even the lawyer, to whom perfect poise was a professional mannerism, was clearly ill at ease.

Winston Conway had come out to meet them in the reception lobby and walking back, he and Cash had held a whispered conference. Following a pace behind, Gil had heard nothing that had been said, but Cash's seemingly offhand acceptance of what he was being told had encouraged Gil to believe that whatever had happened was not as serious as this group around the table thought it to be. That hope was sustained now by the smile on Cash's face as he looked around the table.

417

"Will someone please tell me what this is all about?" Cash asked, the question undirected.

Conway accepted the spokesman's role. "As I tried to explain outside, it seems that Grant Austen is contemplating legal action—based on the belief that he's been the victim of a fraudulent conspiracy."

Gil recoiled to the shock of the revelation but Cash was still smiling, lighting a cigarette now. "This isn't the first time I've been the subject of wild rumors."

"I'm afraid this is more than that," Conway said seriously.

"But you haven't talked to Austen himself, have you?" Cash asked.

"No, not since—"

"I *have* talked to him," Cash said. "And as late as yesterday forenoon. I'd hardly call him a dissatisfied man—quite the contrary." He tossed the dead match to the pewter ash tray. "By the way, he was extremely complimentary about the help you'd given him, Mr. Conway."

Inexplicably, the lawyer blinked as if he had been struck a blow, but his recovery was almost instantaneous. "You say you saw him yesterday?"

"I flew them down to Moon Beach. He's there at a convention."

Conway shook his head. "Not now. He's here in Philadelphia—apparently retaining a lawyer to handle his case. It's quite possible, as you say, that he was perfectly satisfied yesterday—I had that impression, too, the last time I saw him—but that was before Mrs. Kennard got on the job."

Conway's eyes had gone to Atherson and Gil followed them, seeing the banker nervously brushing a spill of pipe ash from his right trouser leg.

"Mrs. Kennard?" Cash asked. "The woman at the Ivanhoe?"

"I can't believe it either," Atherson said nervously, his manner that of a man forced to the confession of a personal sin. "I can't imagine what in the world would lead her to do a thing like this. But, I'm afraid it's true."

"What?" Cash asked.

Atherson took a deep breath. "The chef overheard her talking to Austen on the telephone this morning—telling him this horrible tale —how we'd all conspired against him and cheated him out of a million dollars."

"A million dollars?" Cash puzzled.

Conway explained, "There've been a few sales of Andscott stock at around ten. She must have noticed that. Three hundred thousand shares at ten is three million dollars. That's a million more than you paid for Suffolk Moulding."

418

The smile had completely faded from Cash McCall's face. "But how did she know about the three hundred thousand shares—or, for that matter, how much I'd paid for Suffolk?"

The lawyer studied his face. "We don't know. We thought you might."

"I don't."

Conway seemed oddly embarrassed. "There's been no occasion when you discussed your affairs with her?"

"Look, Mr. Conway—" Cash began, then suddenly looked around the group. "If any of you are suspecting that there's been any personal relationship between Mrs. Kennard and me—disabuse your minds of that right now. There hasn't been."

Winston Conway's discomfiture was evident. "Oh, I had nothing like that in mind—although it did seem a possible explanation of why she'd turn against you so viciously."

"I scarcely know the woman," Cash said coolly. "I see her around the hotel, of course, but I've rarely talked to her—nothing beyond passing the time of day."

"That makes it all the more mysterious," Conway sighed.

"It might help if I knew what she *did* tell Austen."

"Well, substantially this—that all of us are in what she called the *McCall gang*—that we'd conspired to trick him into selling his company for a lot less than it was worth—knowing all the time, of course, that Andscott Instrument was ready to buy it at a high price."

Cash squinted. "Where did you get all this?"

"Everett Pierce," Atherson supplied. "Max told him and Everett came to me." He smiled weakly. "You've Max to thank for getting the story to us. If he hadn't felt so friendly to you, he'd never have told Pierce."

"I can vouch for that," Conway added. "I talked to him, too—trying to get some additional detail—wouldn't open his mouth until I'd proved I was your attorney."

Cash nodded absent-mindedly. "But where in the devil did Mrs. Kennard get *her* information? That's as hard to understand as why she'd go out of her way to knife me."

Conway hesitated and then asked, "Is there any possibility that she might have been eavesdropping that night you talked to General Danvers?"

"Yes, I suppose she might have been," Cash said after a speculative pause. "I do recall that she *was* in the apartment that day I made the deal with Austen—doing me the special favor of personally arranging a dinner party I was having."

"It's incredible," Atherson whispered to himself. "Incredible!"

"But surely Austen isn't taking what she told him seriously?" Cash began, but then broke off to answer his own question. "But I suppose he must be or he wouldn't be in town talking to a lawyer. You're sure of that?"

"Definitely," Conway said. "We traced him to Torrant's office. He was there for over an hour."

"Torrant?"

"Judge Torrant—Clay B. Torrant."

"Some shyster?"

"No, I'd not say that," Conway said. "The Torrants are one of our old legal families. His father was on the Common Pleas bench. So was his grandfather, I believe."

"But what reputable lawyer would even entertain the idea of taking a case like this?" Cash demanded. "A man sells his company—gets his asking price—then decides after the deal is closed that he didn't ask enough. What ground for complaint could he possibly have?"

"Perhaps none," Conway said slowly. "But the fact that he got his asking price doesn't rule out the possibility of a conspiracy charge."

"Conspiracy? But that's ridiculous. What conspiracy?"

"Ridiculous, yes," Conway conceded. "We know there was no conspiracy—all of us know it—but when you take some of the things that have happened—"

"For example?" Cash curtly demanded.

The lawyer hesitated. "Well, the fact that Mr. Atherson advised Austen not to consider selling to Andscott."

Cash's head snapped around to face Atherson.

The banker's quick reaction was tensely defensive. "I've been thinking about that and we're absolutely in the clear. Yes, it's true that Austen did bring up the question of selling to Andscott—but I very definitely asked him whether he would consider taking Andscott stock for his company and he positively said he would *not*. He told me that he was interested only in a cash deal. I knew, of course, that Andscott *wouldn't* give him cash—*couldn't*—"

Conway interrupted, "You say you *knew* that, Mr. Atherson? How did you know it?"

"Simply by looking at the Andscott statement," Atherson retorted sharply. "Any fool could see it!"

"The kind of fools we might find sitting in a jury box?" Conway asked. "Could you *prove*—beyond the shadow of a doubt—that it would have been *impossible* for Andscott to have paid cash?"

Atherson swallowed. "I don't suppose you can swear that anything

420

is impossible—but I'd talked to General Danvers on several occasions and I knew they were very short of cash—"

"So you'd talked to Danvers?" Conway caught him up. "Then you had some inside information, did you? You knew, no doubt, that Andscott was ready and willing to pass out three hundred thousand shares of stock for Suffolk Moulding?"

"You know very well I didn't," Atherson retorted.

Conway pounded on. "You say that Austen wasn't interested in stock. But *might* he have been interested if you had not concealed the fact that he would get as much as three hundred thousand shares?"

"Damn it, Conway, what are you trying—?"

Cash raised his hand as a peacemaking gesture in what was rapidly developing into an angry situation, but Winston Conway jumped in to clear the air with a fulsome apology. "Forgive me, Mr. Atherson. I was only trying to make the point of how easily an innocent act can be misconstrued as evidence of guilt. Let's face the facts—doesn't it *appear* that you might have been a party to Mr. McCall's nefarious scheme to get control of Andscott—and particularly when what you told Austen might be linked to the fact that you later sold Mr. McCall a large block of Andscott stock from a trust fund you controlled?"

Atherson grudgingly admitted, "Yes, I suppose you could give it that interpretation."

"But wait a minute," Cash broke in. "My buying that block of stock at least proves that Andscott common isn't worth ten dollars a share." He looked at Atherson. "As you know, I paid you *eight* dollars a share—and I'm sure you thought you'd made a very good deal in getting rid of it at that price."

"Yes, the directors were quite pleased about it," Atherson said. "But I suppose even that could be misinterpreted to look as if Freeholders was in on the plot to get control of Andscott—if someone were to take Mr. Conway's view."

"Not *my* view," Conway corrected. "I'm only attempting to demonstrate what Torrant's view might be."

"But do you think Clay Torrant would really do a thing like that?" Atherson asked. "Oh, I know he's an old fool in a lot of ways—makes a nuisance of himself around The Wharf—but I've never thought of him as a man who would stoop to anything of this sort."

Conway paused to frame his reply. "I don't know Torrant socially —only professionally—and even there his practice is very small, apparently, and I've had little or no contact with him. My impressions are largely based upon the things he's written. He writes little poison-pen essays—clever enough, I suppose, if you care for that sort of thing—but the subject matter, I believe, is a reasonably clear revelation of character. Nothing delights him so much as to take a nasty crack at some member of the Bar who's been more successful than he's been."

Cash's eyes narrowed. "Is he the man who wrote that article you sent me—the one with the biblical quotation?"

"Proverbs—twenty-eight: twenty," Conway quoted. "—'He who maketh haste to be wealthy shall not be innocent.'"

Cash switched the subject abruptly. "Tell me this, Mr. Conway—if someone was attempting to establish the fact that there had been a conspiracy, wouldn't they have to start by proving that I'd known, before I bought Suffolk Moulding, that I could turn around and sell it to Andscott Instrument?"

"What's your point?" Conway asked. "That you had no idea what you were going to do with Suffolk Moulding until General Danvers so fortuitously walked into your apartment?"

"But it's true!" Gil heard himself whisper, the words unintentionally audible.

Conway swung around to face him. "Yes, true—but is it believable? Does it sound plausible that a man with General Danvers' reputation would actually put on such a stupid exhibition as Mr. McCall claims he did? Who would believe it—or who would believe that *you*, Mr. Clark, didn't know a thing about those patents until General Danvers let the cat out of the bag? And don't forget that you would be testifying after having had access to all of Suffolk Moulding's confidential operating information for a period of several years."

"But I *didn't* know—"

"Come, come, Mr. Clark! After all, you're a professional business analyst, aren't you? I'd hardly believe you so incompetent as to miss something as important as that—or to have failed to pass it along to Mr. McCall."

Despite the recognition that the lawyer was doing only what he'd done earlier to Atherson, Gil found it necessary to consciously restrain the rise of anger, forcing a smile as he asked, "But couldn't General Danvers himself testify as to what had happened?"

"General Danvers?" Conway asked. "Well, let's look at Danvers' status—as the prosecution might see it, of course. If we're correct in our hypothesis that Mrs. Kennard overheard him that night in the hotel, then the prosecution already knows that Danvers accused Mr. McCall of conspiracy, fraud, putting a spy in his plant—in fact, their whole case is probably based on those Danvers accusations. But then what happens? All of a sudden, Danvers meekly subsides. Why? You know the answer, don't you? We bought him off with a promise that

422

he'd be kept on as chairman of the board at a hundred thousand a year—and you, Mr. Clark, are the guilty man. You made that deal —just as you made the deal to buy off Bergmann."

The pressure of angry argument drove against Gil's lips but they were sealed by the recognition of his junior standing in the group and the realization that he knew nothing that Cash didn't know. Cash was the one to say whatever there was to be said.

"Go on, Mr. Conway," Cash said quietly. "What's the rest of their case?"

"This is all hypothetical, of course," Conway said. "And we should be able to rely on the traditional assurance that we'll be presumed innocent until proven guilty. Unfortunately, we can't. The presumption will be guilt."

"I know—Proverbs twenty-eight: twenty," Cash said flatly. "Go ahead—where else do we look bad?"

"Suppose we go back to the beginning," Conway said. "The first odd fact we encounter is the suddenness of Grant Austen's decision to sell. That's hardly normal, you know, a man making a decision like that on the spur of the moment. He'd—what's that, Mr. Atherson?"

Gil's side glance caught a fading expression of protest on the banker's face as he mumbled, "Nothing—nothing at all."

Gil felt certain he knew what Atherson was about to say and supplied it himself. "Austen was under a lot of pressure from Andscott. They were after him to—"

Conway slashed in, "Or *thought* he was under a lot of pressure. And who might have put that thought in his head? Weren't you with him the day before he sold?"

"Yes, but I—"

"And were you not an employee of Corporation Associates—an organization secretly owned by Cash McCall?"

Thoroughly in character, Harrison Glenn had sat motionless until this moment. Now his body moved, a sudden heaving as if a blast had been touched off under a rock monolith, exploding in Gil's direction. "Didn't you assure me, Clark, that you'd done nothing whatsoever to influence Austen?"

"And I didn't!" Gil retorted, flashing back to the charge, unaware until a beat later that the real purpose of Harrison Glenn's question had been to clear himself with Cash McCall, a revelation of personal weakness that Gil found shocking in a man to whom he had always attributed great strength of character.

"Suppose we follow Mr. Conway's suggestion and forget our own defense," Cash said mildly. "But since it may have some bearing, I might tell you that I made a special point of informing Mr. Austen

423

before I bought Suffolk Moulding that I did control Corporation Associates—and that I'd had access to various reports on and about his company."

Conway asked, "You told him that before he sold?"

"Definitely."

Gil felt himself prompted to add that Cash had called him immediately afterward to tell him that Austen had been told about Corporation Associates, but Conway's voice cut in ahead of him.

"Am I right, Mr. McCall, in assuming that there were no witnesses present—no one who could testify against Austen in the event that he claimed he hadn't been told?"

There was a long silence before Cash said, "No, there'd be no one to testify against him."

The dropping of Cash's voice left an ominous silence and, watching his face as everyone else was doing, Gil was horror-stricken to see an expression of resignation spread slowly across his features, an acknowledgment of defeat confirmed when he said in a coldly flat voice, "I guess this game is like all the others—sometimes you draw a bad hand—and when that happens there's nothing to do but throw it in."

A scream of objection rose in Gil's throat . . . *Cash couldn't give in now . . . it would be an admission of guilt! There had been no conspiracy. No one had done anything wrong. There were a thousand truths to hurl against the ridiculous lies of . . .*

"What do you suggest, Mr. Conway?" Cash asked.

For a moment, Gil recaptured hope. Surely Winston Conway wouldn't give ground . . . not after all the things he'd said that morning at breakfast in Suffolk . . . the way he had talked about Cash . . . how much it meant to him to have a man like Cash McCall for a client . . .

And hope was sustained as Conway said carefully, "I'm quite certain that we could defend ourselves against any charges that Austen might bring—no one has been wronged, we all know that—in fact, it's hard to imagine the case ever getting to court."

Then, in a traitorous turnabout, the lawyer added, "But you may be right, Mr. McCall, I hate saying this but—"

Cash cut in, "You think I'm licked before I start?"

"I fear that may be the case. If Austen goes only as far as to file his suit—even if the rumor gets around that he *might*—you know what will happen to this new issue that the Andscott stockholders are being asked to approve."

Gil felt himself slapped for stupidity. Until this instant he had failed to see the real crux of the situation. Unless the new Andscott

424

stock issue with which Suffolk Moulding was to be acquired received the stockholder approval, Cash would not have control of the company. A charge of fraud and conspiracy, no matter how unfounded, would arouse the stockholders to band solidly against him. Even with the support of the Andrews Foundation votes, there would be little hope of getting a majority—and it was by no means sure that Bergmann, once he heard the story, might not back water on his promise.

This was the danger that Conway had brought up yesterday. Then it had been remote and intangible. Now it was devastatingly real, a catastrophe from which there seemed no escape.

"What do you advise?" Cash asked Conway. "Try to wash the whole thing out—give Austen his company back—let him have the Andscott deal himself if he wants it?"

"I don't know what else to suggest," Conway said slowly. "It seems a terrible thing to be forced into doing—so damned unfair—but under the circumstances it might be the wisest course."

Cash turned to Atherson. "What's your opinion?"

The banker's face was blanched. "I don't know what to say. If it weren't for the bank—all the rumors that Freeholders was involved—"

"All right," Cash said abruptly, rising. "I'll see what I can do."

He strode across the office and was out through the door before Gil could break the bond that tied him to the silently staring group around the table. He ran out into the hall and when he called Cash's name he tried to make it a cry of allegiance and a vow of personal loyalty, but the single word came out as only a halting hail, and when Cash stopped and turned back to face him, Gil Clark realized the hopelessness of attempting to express what was in his mind.

"Don't worry, Gil," Cash said. "You'll be all right."

"I'm not thinking about myself!" Gil protested vehemently. "I'm thinking about you. You've done nothing wrong! No one could have been fairer than you've been. Why are you giving in? Why don't you fight it? If the stockholders realized that—"

"There are some things you can't fight, Gil."

Cash's voice was dead flat, completely devoid of expression, but in the instant before he turned away his doubled fist thumped Gil's forearm, and the faintly lingering muscle ache remained as a sensation that Gil's mind tried to translate into the words that Cash might have spoken, telling him that he knew he wasn't guilty of the same self-seeking disloyalty that Atherson had exhibited ... nothing mattering but the Freeholders Bank & Trust Company. And Harrison Glenn's silence had been a conviction of the same groveling fear ... that some whisper of gossip might besmirch his precious Corporation

425

Associates. Winston Conway was no better ... all that high-sounding talk about morality and ethics, all that praise of Cash McCall as an honorable man ... but Conway had belly-crawled like the others, all of them defending Cash only as long as it meant no sacrifice of their own selfish interests.

The frame of anger broadened and he thought of Grant Austen. Who was Austen to accuse anyone else of fraud? Hadn't he juggled the company books to transfer stock to his daughter ... that phony story about an agreement with his father-in-law!

But that was no worse than the way Austen had dumped the Suffolk Moulding Company overboard, not even waiting for the sale to be consummated ... no worry about what was going to happen to the company ... as callously selfish as any man could be ... two million for himself and not even a token bonus to men like Ed Berger and Jake Crown who had done almost as much as he had to build the business. But now two million wasn't enough ... he wanted more! And he'd do anything to get it ... *anything* ... swear that Cash hadn't told him about Corporation Associates ... even that he'd been tricked into selling ...

The cyclonic swirl of righteous anger left a strange vacuum in Gil Clark's mind and in the storm-center silence he heard the faint whisper of a question that he had never before realized his mind was sheltering. Was it true that he had done nothing to influence Grant Austen to sell ... *nothing?*

He was sure that there were no quotable words that could be used against him ... but might he still be guilty? He had *wanted* Austen to sell ... at the time not realizing why, but now he knew ... hoping that somehow he might get Suffolk Moulding for himself. That must have been obvious ... Harrison Glenn had seen it in his face ... and Cash had known, too ... and afterwards Winston Conway. Was he any less guilty of self-interest than all of the others?

No, that wasn't true! As soon as he had really gotten to know Cash he had forgotten all about Suffolk Moulding ...

The wraith of suspicion whispered again. Was it really because of Cash that he had forgotten Suffolk Moulding? Or was it because one selfishness had been displaced by another? Hadn't he been hoping that there would be a place for him in Andscott Instrument? He must have been ... Winston Conway had guessed it. Was it unrecognized jealousy that had made his heart skip a beat when Cash had told him that John Allenby would be the new Andscott president? And Cash must have known ... offering him that job today ... *You are a company man, aren't you, Gil?*

But what was wrong with that? *Different men want different things* ... Cash had said that himself. He had always known what he wanted ... his own company ... something that a man could *build* ... watch it grow ... look at it and see what he had accomplished!

Why had he ever imagined that he could find what he wanted in Cash McCall's way of life? Hadn't he known from the beginning that it wasn't there? Hadn't he said as much to Winston Conway? Then why had he done what he had done? Because he hadn't cared about the means, only the end? Would he do *anything* to get what he wanted ... Bergmann and the Foundation?

What had happened to him? He had known what he was getting into ... the jackals and vultures at S.F.&P.... the Ivanhoe gang. Had he really believed that Cash McCall was any different from the others?

But Cash *was* different! Had he hurt anyone? Had he taken the slightest unfair advantage? Had he done anything that was morally wrong?

Memory rushed to Cash McCall's support, offering the sustaining proof of what he had said that first day they had met ... *We maintain that the very foundation of our life is what we call free enterprise ... fight and die to defend it ... but now we've come to regard money-making as a secret vice indulged in by all but never mentioned in the best society.*

Cash was right! Of course he was! But wasn't there something strange about a man whose *only* interest was in making money? No, that wasn't true! Cash *was* concerned about Andscott Instrument ... getting the company back on its feet. But it was somehow different ... strange ... never getting into a company himself ... never making it *his* company ...

And even what Cash had said that noon at the Ivanhoe ... yes, it was all true, but wasn't there something peculiar about a man who talked so much about morality and ethics? And there had always been that kind of talk every time they had been together. Other men didn't do that. Was it possible that it was a sort of psychological something or other ... a cover-up to hide his own doubts ... not as sure of himself as he pretended to be? If there *weren't* something wrong, why had he given in so easily today?

"Mr. Clark?"

Gil wheeled to the sound of his name and found himself facing Will Atherson, waiting for the same elevator.

"Do you know where Mr. McCall has gone?" the banker asked.

"No, I don't."

"Perhaps to the Ivanhoe," Atherson speculated. "And if he's there

I'll see him. But if I should miss him, I wonder if you'd be kind enough to give him a message?"

Gil hesitated. "I don't know whether I'll be seeing him or not."

"If you do, please tell him that I—the bank—won't expect him to take that block of stock. Under the circumstances—well, what he's doing is for all of us." He had been looking down, grinding the bowl of his pipe into his cupped palm, but now he raised his eyes. "I only hope that this doesn't mean—"

The opening of the elevator door cut him off and whatever Atherson had been about to say was lost. Incongruously, Gil's mind flashed the thought of Lory Austen. Was it possible that what Cash had done was because of her?

Before his mind could suggest an answer the question was swept away by the explosive realization that Cash had stranded him ... his car was still standing out there at the Suffolk airport!

••••• 12

Lory Austen lay across her bed, staring at the dress that she had tossed over the back of a chair when the sounds of her mother's arrival had sent her dashing to the head of the stairs. For that first moment there had been only the blankness of surprise, then a rise of apprehension when she had imagined that something had happened to her father, finally the blast of revelation when her mother had told her what he was planning to do.

Even now, looking back with the added comprehension that this last hour had given her, Lory could not completely understand the strangeness of her reaction. She had remained astoundingly clear-headed, not even a fleeting instant when her mind had suffered the disablement of shock. It was almost as if last night had given her a new mind. But the change had not been completely for the better. Before, she could not have been as cruelly cold to her mother as she had been in these minutes at the head of the stairs.

That had all been erased after her mother had followed her into the bedroom, but Lory still felt herself guilty of a lack of initial understanding. There *was* that understanding now—she had never before known her mother as the warmly compassionate human being that this last hour had proved her to be ... but could she pay the price that her mother demanded?

Over and over, as if the words had been picked up for endless

428

repetition by the voice of her conscience, Lory heard her mother saying, "There's more than one kind of love in the world, Lory—there's the love of a father for his daughter, too. Can you forget that so easily?"

Could she?

"You mean everything to him, Lory—his whole life—and now there's so little else left. Can you brush him aside to marry a man who's done to him what Cash McCall has done?"

Had he?

Last night at Aurora nothing had seemed wrong, nothing in all the world. But this was tomorrow, and a different world, and she was thinking with a different mind. Was it possible that last night had been no more than the fulfillment of the mad desire that overwhelmed her so many times, lying here at night on this same bed, her sense of values so distorted that madness had totally displaced reason?

Had there been that same disablement of judgment when Cash had talked to her yesterday afternoon about his Andscott Instrument dream? Had she been so eager to believe in the rightness of everything that she wanted to happen, that she had blinded herself to the existence of wrong? Hadn't there been a questioning shock, too hastily brushed aside, when he had told her how much money he might make? Shouldn't she have known then that something was wrong ... making so much money ... so quickly ... so easily?

But what *was* wrong?

Money?

Because he might make a million dollars?

Was this why Cash was the infidel barred from the temples ... because he took so lightly the solemn reverence of the money-worshipers ... because he could laugh at their grim dogma that the golden coins were only for those who had grubbed them out a penny at a time ...

Lory caught herself, realizing that she was thinking with Cash's words. She had to stop this ... think for herself ... forget Cash ... free this new mind of its too automatic impulses to protect and justify him. That had been her trouble when her mother had first told her what had happened ... that flashback reflex to defend Cash.

Or had she really been defending herself?

If easy money were the measure of sin, she was more guilty than Cash. She had taken money, too ... two hundred thousand dollars ... and with no justification, none whatsoever! If it were true that there had been a conspiracy to force her father into selling the company, she had been the arch-conspirator. She was the one who had really wanted him to sell ... willed it with all her heart ... grabbing with greedy hands for what he had offered as a gift of love. If he had been cheated, she was the cheat.

She closed her eyes, telling herself that she should have been aware of all this long before now. Maybe she had been. The check was still in her purse, uncashed. Was it the subconscious recognition of guilt that had kept her from depositing it ... the knowledge that she had taken too much for too little?

This was not Lory Austen's first consciousness of her long-standing inability to respond to her father with the affection that a daughter should have held. Always before there had seemed some merit in the hiding, some blind belief that pretense constituted the discharge of her obligation. Now it appeared as a dishonesty all the more inexcusable because she had made so little effort to make it unnecessary. There was more that was fine and good in her father than she had ever bothered to discover. That *must* be true ... if it were not, her mother couldn't love him the way she did ... and she *did* love him. There was no doubt of that now, not after all the things she had said. And her mother had asked nothing for herself ... the test of love ... "I'm thinking only of what it's going to do to your father when you tell him."

Again Lory's mind countered one question with another, silently spoken now as it had been silently spoken then, but no less demanding for a lack of utterance ... *what would happen when she told Cash?*

And she was the one who would be forced to tell him. If she failed to warn him of what her father planned to do, it would be the end of Cash's love for her. And she would have no cause to blame him if it were. No love could survive the withholding of so dangerous a secret.

But if she *did* tell him ... yes, that would be the decision from which there could be no retreat. Could she face what it would mean to her father? Did she have any right to heap selfishness upon selfishness ... all these years of taking without giving ... thinking only of her own happiness, never of his?

Her eyes opened and she looked at the clock, shocked when she saw how fast the minute hand had moved ... Cash would be at the airport in half an hour!

She jumped to her feet and began to dress, still without decision, suddenly aware as she went to pull the shade that it was raining. A blue-gray veiling hung from the sky, so heavy that only the near side of the city could be translucently seen, the rest lost in invisibility.

Cash couldn't possibly fly to Suffolk now!

For a moment, she felt herself miraculously saved, even deciding

430

that there was no point in going to the airport. Then the truth struck
... not going would mean that her decision would be made by default, final and irrevocable.

Hurrying, she finished dressing and flew down the stairs, snatching up a cape from the hall closet, out into the rain before she had it over her shoulders, fearful that she might be stopped by a call from her mother.

The rain was a springtime torrent, even heavier than she had expected it to be, the car windows blanked by woven rivulets, the world reduced to the wedge of the wiped windshield. A half block away from the house there was a quick brushstroke of yellow across her vision and she guessed that it was a taxicab bringing her father home, certain when she looked in the mirror and saw the cab turn into the drive. At least there would be that much gained by going to the airport ... he would talk to her mother first ... more time to think before she would be forced to a final commitment.

The crest of Orchard Ridge was lost in a black hood that solidly bridged the gap between earth and cloud, leaving a skyless world, almost without color until she saw the soil-red water that streamed in the ruts of the airport lane. Cross-ripping freshets made her blink with uncertainty as the wheels hit them. Driving demanded such close attention that she did not realize she was holding her breath until the hangar loomed ahead of her, a two dimensional silhouette, sky tone on sky tone. The big door was closed. A single bare bulb burned mistily yellow in one of the office windows.

Only one car stood against the fence and she pulled up beside it, switching off the motor. But the windshield flooded as the wiper stopped and she started the motor again. The rain was so heavy now that she could see no more than halfway across the airport, the end of the runway lost. Cash couldn't possibly come ... but she would wait ... her father at home ... the longer, the better.

Automatically, she glanced at her wrist and saw that in her haste to dress she had forgotten her watch. But it must be almost time now. If he were coming ...

She thought she heard a sound and ran down the window beside her. The rain whipped in and she closed it quickly, sliding across the seat to try the other window. The wind was from the opposite direction and no rain came in. But the plane sound that she had imagined hearing was gone.

Looking out now, she saw the car parked beside her. It had a strangely derelict look, deserted and abandoned. A window had been left open and the upholstered back of the front seat was soggily black from the rain that had driven in.

431

Then she heard the plane sound again, positively now, a faint roar off in the west, wavering with the wind but surely coming closer and closer. She jumped out of the car. The sound passed overhead but the plane was lost to sight in the shrouding clouds.

Unmindful of the rain, she looked up at the sky, trying to follow the plane by its sound. For a moment it was lost, swallowed up by the wind, but then she heard it again. It *must* be Cash ... and he was coming back to her!

Suddenly, she saw the airplane, only a gray blur and higher than she had imagined it would be. Visibility was better than she had realized. The rain had lightened. She could see all the way across the airport now, even the farm buildings beyond. But when she looked up again, the plane was lost from sight. For an endlessly extended time the motor sound faded off, frighteningly lost in a lull of silence that made her want to cry out to the sky.

And then she saw it, breaking out of the cloud cover, swooping for the end of the runway, and she wiped the rain from her forehead as if it were the cold perspiration of a fear forgotten.

The airplane came toward her, closer and closer. Now she could see the silver fans spun out of raindrops by the whirling propellers, the misted trail of the air blast, finally Cash's face looking at her from the high perch of the cockpit.

Her arm went up in a sweeping wave, suddenly leaden as she felt the full impact of a brain-pounding realization ... this was the moment of decision, roaring down upon her, giving her no time to think ...

The plane door opened and she saw Cash—and it was as if a door had opened in her mind, letting in the clean spring wind that was bringing new life to the earth. He came down the steps and she ran to meet him, losing her rain cape as she ran, not even reaching back to catch at it.

There was a lost beat before he kissed her, the hesitation not hers but his, and she knew what had caused it when, finally out of his arms, she heard him say, "Your father's home, isn't he?"

Cash *knew*—how, she had no idea—but there was almost the feeling of disappointment in the realization that she had missed this chance to prove her love.

"I think he is now," she said. "I saw a cab come as I was leaving—but I've talked to Mother."

"I have to see him," Cash said, sharply resolute.

"See him? Why?"

"Don't you know what's happening?"

"Mother told me that—"

432

"I can't let it happen, Lory. I've got to stop it."

His pressing arm was moving her toward the car, but she resisted it. "Don't try to talk to him now—please!"

"It's all I can do—wash the whole thing out and give him the company back."

Shock collapsed her resistance and they walked toward the car, Cash's arm sweeping down to pick up her rain cape, a scarlet blotch on the black asphalt, the color crash of sudden fear. He was admitting that her father had been wronged! Yesterday ... worrying about what was going to happen after he found out ... wanting to send him on a trip ... get him far away ... keep him from knowing ...

No, that wasn't true! It *couldn't* be true. Cash didn't know what had happened that night in the library ... the real reason her father had sold the company ...

Or was this love again ... the automatic defense ... the blindness?

"Lory, let's talk this out."

She took the three silent steps that carried her up the aisle between the two parked cars. The rain squall had passed now, a distant slant-bristled brush moving off, slowly sweeping the earth, the swept path glistening green.

Cash's hands reached out, gripping her forearms. "Look, Lory, I won't do anything you don't want me to do—but what else *can* I do?"

"Why do you have to do anything?" she whispered, the question barely finished.

"I happen to be in love with you," he said, flatly factual. "I asked you to marry me because I thought I could make you happy. I can't if your father goes on feeling about me the way he does now. There'd be no happiness for you—and if I can't give you happiness there's nothing I can give you."

His hands still gripped her arms, making no move to embrace her, denying her too-sharply focused mind the edge-softening relief of sentiment.

"You're going to wash it all out?" she asked, using his words. "Give him the company back?"

"Maybe he won't listen to me—I don't know. It may have gone too far for that already. But I can try. That may mean something."

"But if you do—you'll lose—"

"The money doesn't matter. You know me well enough now to know that."

"I wasn't thinking about the money."

His hands dropped. "What were you thinking about—that it might look as if I was admitting I was wrong?"

She let silence be her answer.

"That doesn't matter either. *You* know what happened—and *I* know. If your father will listen to me, maybe *he'll* know—remember what happened. Beyond that—well, that's enough."

"But it isn't, Cash, it isn't. There are all the others—Mr. Atherson —Mr. Conway—"

"I just left them."

"They didn't ask you to do this, did they?" She waited out his silence. "Did they?"

"No, they didn't ask me to do it—but I told them I would."

"Didn't they try to stop you?"

"Why would they?"

"Don't they know that you didn't do what Father thinks you did?"

"Yes."

"But Cash, there is such a thing as right and wrong."

"Don't blame them too much, Lory," Cash said, looking away from her. "The world doesn't give them much choice. One breath of scandal and the temple is defiled. Don't you realize what it would mean to Freeholders Bank & Trust Company if your father charged Will Atherson with fraud—with being a member of the Cash McCall gang?"

"But there is no gang."

"There would be if he says there is."

"Doesn't the truth mean anything? Is it only gossip that matters— what the world thinks—whether it's right or wrong?"

"It matters to some men," Cash said slowly. "It *has* to matter—if they want to stay in the temple. The code they live by is the opinion of their fellow men. The most important thing in their lives is what the world thinks of them. It has to be."

"I'm sorry," she said quickly, afraid that he might have misinterpreted what she had said as meaning that she wanted him to be anything other than himself. "You're right, I know you are—it doesn't matter what anyone else thinks."

He looked at her intently. "You mean that, don't you?"

"I happen to be in love with you," she said, an unsuccessful attempt at mimicry, failing to catch the flatly factual tone that had been in his voice when he said those same words before.

He swept her into his arms, his hands cupping her head against the driving pressure of his lips.

"If I hadn't been in love with you before—" he whispered, "—I would be now."

"And I, too."

She reached out her hand for the door of the car, a gesture of agreement and decision, forcing herself to believe that the miracle

434

of love would somehow be matched by the miracle of her father's understanding.

Her eyes had left Cash's when she heard his exclamation of shocked surprise.

Turning, she saw that he was staring at the other car.

"This is my fault," he said. "It's Gil Clark's car. I made him leave it —told him I'd bring him back and completely forgot it." He had opened the door and was running up the window, his hand suddenly stopped as he looked at the instrument panel. "He even left his key."

"Maybe you'd better bring it into town for him," she suggested.

"Would you mind very much?" he asked, hesitant. "I feel like—"

"Of course not," she said quickly. "You can follow me."

What had been only a subconscious reaction an instant before had suddenly become a tangible plan.

And Cash implemented it by saying, "I'll get something out of the plane to throw over this wet seat."

She almost offered her rain cape but caught herself in time, quickly getting into her car, saying, "I'll be waiting for you."

For an instant she was afraid that he had guessed what she was planning to do—he looked at her as if he were about to protest—but she pretended not to have noticed and started the motor, backing the car the moment it caught, tossing a preoccupied wave as she swung the wheel but without looking at him again.

Freshets still coursed the lane and a sheet of water flooded the road where the drainage ditch had overflowed its banks, but she plowed through without cringing, intent on gaining every possible second.

The canopy of dark cloud still hung over the town but there was a break in the western horizon, an oddly sulphur-green slit through which the setting sun poured a red-orange light, the world eerily grotesque in these last minutes of the day. By the time she reached Boulevard Drive, lights were coming on in the bordering houses and, eyes straining ahead, she caught a glimpse of the multicolored glow of leaded glass windows. Her father was in the library.

Her mother met her at the terrace door, hurriedly whispering, "He's here."

Lory let a nod suffice, moving quickly to the library door, stopping for only a single deep breath before she turned the knob and pushed open the door.

Her father was sitting at the desk, staring at the scrap heap of opened mail. His eyes flashed up but dropped as quickly, settling on the hem of her skirt.

"So it's you," he said.

"Yes, it's me," she answered, putting all her courage in her voice, walking toward him, curling down into the red chair beside his desk, a conscious duplication of that night when he had decided to sell the Suffolk Moulding Company.

But he wasn't looking at her.

"Problems?" she asked.

His eyes were still fixed on the telegraph blank in his hands, his thumbnail nervously picking at the message tape that striped the yellow paper.

Softly pressing, she said, "I thought you might want to talk to me. You did once before—remember?"

Her eyes caught the muscle ripple that ran along his jaw, and she waited for his head to turn. There was no movement. It was as if the consciousness she had tried to reach was too deeply buried to be touched. His thumbnail picked away at the paper, loosening the end of a strip of tape.

"I thought you might have tried to call me last night," she said, fighting the quaver that threatened her voice, knowing the risk she was taking.

There was a tiny rip of paper, the sound incredibly loud in the silence. For an instant, his hand was rigidly tense. Then she saw a tremor, stopped as he gripped the edge of the desk.

She rose from her chair, half sitting now on the edge of the desk, looking down at him just as she had done during the moment of decision on that night she was now trying so desperately to make him recall.

"It was my fault," she said. "I shouldn't have told you that I wanted you to sell the company."

His eyes came up slowly.

"If I hadn't wanted you to do it," she went on, "you wouldn't have done it."

He blinked as if this was the first real consciousness of her presence, and his orienting glances at the walls were the gropings of a man suddenly awakened in a strange place.

"I was the one who made you sell," she repeated.

"No," he mumbled, a small cry from some very distant place, the cry and then its fading echo, "—no, no, no."

"I asked you if you could be happy without the company—and you said you could. But I shouldn't have believed you."

"It isn't that," he said in tortured whisper. "You were right—what you told your mother—I was trying to get out from under before I lost the Andscott business. If there was anyone who tried to pull

436

something crooked, I was the one. That day in his apartment—he asked me about Andscott—I lied to him, Lory, I lied to him."

"No, you didn't. All you said—"

"I don't know what happened to me," he mumbled. "I don't know how I could have done such a thing."

"Dad, you don't remember what you said to Cash—or what he said to you, either. You were so excited—we both were—and everything was happening so fast."

"I—I do remember what he said. He did tell me that he owned Corporation Associates—he told me, I know he did."

The break in his voice was the end of Lory's planning, her goal so quickly achieved that she felt herself as dazed as her father seemed.

And what happened then was not planned—it could not have been planned because it was both unprecedented and unimagined—and the impulse that drove her was too swift-running to have been guided by conscious thought. Her arms went around her father's neck and her head burrowed in his shoulder. There was something within her now that had never been there before, a warm outflow of honest affection that she had never experienced.

"I was lost, Lory—just lost," he whispered, his voice so low that she had the feeling, so close to him, that she was hearing the silent voice of his secret mind. "It all happened so fast—and there wasn't time enough to think—like I was running downhill and couldn't stop. And I didn't know where I was going—walking around Philadelphia this afternoon—walking and walking and thinking about what I'd done. He won't ever be able to forgive me—no one will—Will Atherson—"

She lifted her head, her hands still on his shoulders. "There's nothing to forgive."

His body twisted convulsively, breaking the hold of her hands as he got to his feet, turning sharply away from her, walking to the window. "You don't know the worst of it," he said explosively, an agonized admission torn from deep within him. "Even if they'd forgive me, I can't forgive myself."

He was staring into the colored glass of the leaded window, but she knew what he was seeing. She had seen him stand like this a hundred times on a hundred nights, always when he was thinking of the company, seeing the Suffolk Moulding plant as clearly as if he were hindered by neither darkness nor distance.

"Don't worry about the company," she said compassionately. "Everything's going to be all right."

"I ran out on them," he cried, the admission torn from his throat. "I was a coward—a yellow coward. I was afraid something was going to

437

happen to the company, and I ran away and left them to face it alone —Paul, Jake and Ed, George Thorson, all of them—Burke, old Tommy, Kreider. They were counting on me and I sold them out—without even knowing what was going to happen to the company. I didn't mean to do it. I just didn't realize what I was doing—everything happening so fast—"

"Dad, no harm has been done."

"You don't know, you don't know," he mumbled, still staring at what he was seeing in the window. "I've just been down at the plant —across the street—watching the men come out of the gate. I didn't dare let them see me—I knew what they were thinking—"

She had walked up behind him and knew that it was awareness of her presence that had caused the fading off of his voice. But he did not turn to face her.

"None of those men have been hurt," she said to the back of his head. "And they won't be. The company will go on—just the way you always planned that it would. Don't you remember the things we used to talk about—the Post-War Plan—"

She caught herself, warned by the tremor that ran up the cords of his neck, suddenly fearful that what she had intended as a kindly reassurance had been taken as a cruel reminder of lost dreams. There seemed only one hope now. "Dad, if you can't be happy without the company—are you listening?"

There was no response but she could almost feel the tensing of his body. She waited, finally saying, "It isn't too late to change your mind."

He uttered a wordless sound of denial.

"Cash will let you have the company back."

For a moment there was silence, her father's body frozen, rigidly stock-still. Then, suddenly, he wheeled to face her.

"That would be a fine thing to do, wouldn't it!" he exploded, the crackle of righteous anger in his voice. "Do you think I'd do that— make an honest deal and then back out on it? What would people think of me?"

And now she was staring at him as, a few minutes before, he had been staring at her. Now she was the one who had awakened to a strange presence. The man who stood in front of her was not the man who had been there a moment ago. This was Grant Austen, her father, himself again . . . as brashly righteous as always. But she would never forget the bewildered little man who, for one revealing moment, had taken Grant Austen's place . . . nor would she forget that on so many of those nights here in this library she had looked at one man but talked to another.

438

Cash had been right. Her father was one of those many men who found their guiding stars in other men's eyes. It was the judgment of the world that mattered, not the dictates of a personal conscience. He was weak where Cash was strong, too unsure of his own sense of right and wrong to stand against the censure of his fellow men ... and yet, strangely, it was that very weakness that had given him the strength to acknowledge the enormity of his error.

Or was there more to it than that? Was he really afraid of what the men at the plant were thinking about him because he had sold the company ... or was his fear a belated recognition that he had failed them in a way they knew nothing about? Wasn't it what Cash had said yesterday ... "If the high priests lose their faith, the temple walls start to crumble." Hadn't the inner man, now so completely hidden behind Grant Austen's world-facing mask, seen that the walls were beginning to crack? Wasn't that the real reason he had sold Suffolk Moulding ... running away from an acknowledgment of his loss of faith ... blaming the world in order to shield the forsaken inner man from the loss of everything that faith had once given him?

Had there been the chance, she would have thrown her arms around that lonely little man, showing him the compassion that understanding had brought her. But he was gone now. The man who stepped to the ringing telephone was the father she had known through all the years of her life.

"Grant Austen," he said, gruffly curt, acknowledging his identity, then hesitating, obviously waiting for her to leave the room.

She heard the faint murmur of voices in the hall outside and said quickly, "That must be Cash. He's taking me to Philadelphia for dinner."

Her father's nod was a meaningful acceptance.

As she went out through the door she heard him say only, "Well, I'll tell you, Mr. Torrant—" but there was no need to hear more. The tone of his voice told her everything she needed to know.

Cash was standing with her mother at the far end of the hall, their faces matched in taut expectancy.

"It's all right," Lory said, speaking to both of them. Then, catching her mother's inquiring glance at the library door, she added, "Yes, I think he wants to see you."

Their eyes met for a moment, not as mother and daughter but as two women, mature and knowing.

Miriam Austen walked back to the door of the library and opened it, not hesitantly as she had always done before, and Lory heard her father's voice say, "Come in, dear—something here that I want to talk

439

to you—" Again, the closing door cut off his voice but again she had heard enough.

Cash broke the silence. "You shouldn't have done that, Lory. It was my job to talk to him, not yours."

"I needed to do it," she said slowly, "I needed it very much."

He watched her in silent inquiry.

"He was a little lost," she said, her eyes drawn back to the closed library door. "But don't blame him for that—I was a little lost, too." She turned back to him, "But everything's all right now."

"Everything?"

"Everything."

"Did you tell him that he could have his company back?"

"Yes."

"Good."

"He wouldn't take it."

Cash's eyes narrowed in quick reaction, but it seemed an expression more of disappointment than surprise.

"Did you really think he would?" she asked.

"I don't know what I thought," he said, looking past her. "Maybe I wasn't thinking—except about the possibility of losing you. That's all that ever mattered. The company never did."

She reached out to him. "Cash, that isn't true. It mattered yesterday, you know it did—all your plans."

"That was yesterday."

"But nothing has changed. There's no reason why you can't go ahead just as you'd planned. He knows now that he was wrong about you."

"Maybe he wasn't," Cash said slowly. "Maybe I've been the one who was wrong—the things I've done—the way I've done them."

"No, Cash, no."

"Maybe the world is right—the pursuit of money—the root of all evil—"

"But it hasn't been the pursuit of money," she protested. "And what would be wrong, even if it were? Don't you remember what you said yesterday—that if there's something wrong with making money, there's something wrong with our whole way of life?"

"That's what I've tried to make myself believe."

"It's true, Cash, it's true."

"I've tried to convince myself that it was wrong only when it was done in the wrong way. But what *is* the wrong way? And what's the right? How do you know? Where are the rules? In the law books? Is it right if it's legal—and only wrong if it isn't?"

He had broken the hold of her hands, turning away from her,

440

vividly re-creating the memory of what had happened in the library only a few minutes ago. Now it was Cash who had been displaced by a stranger, an alter ego, a second self that lived in his shadow, carrying the fear and indecision too foreign to be tolerated in his own mind.

"I've kept on telling myself that I was just playing a game," he said. "But it isn't a game. It can't be. How can you play a game if you don't know the rules—if there aren't any rules? And what's the point of the game if you can't win—if you have to keep on telling yourself that it isn't the winning that matters?"

"But it does matter!" she said, more sharply than she had intended, her tone raised by the subconscious desire to release him from the trancelike hold of doubt.

"Why?" he asked dully, still looking away from her.

"Cash, you can't stop now," she exclaimed, reaching up to turn his shoulders. "There are so many people dependent upon you—so many hundreds of them—all the men out here at the plant—all the people down at Andscott—"

Her voice faded off as she saw his eyes, stunned and staring, the deep blue storm clouded. "I thought you understood," he said. "This is what I tried to tell you yesterday. I'm not a company man, Lory. I never have been."

"Oh, I know you're not," she said, her words hurried by the fear of error. "But there are so many of them and so few of you—and they need you so much. Oh, Cash, they do! Don't you see how much they need you—all the men out at the plant—and down at Andscott, too? And Gil Clark and John Allenby—and Dr. Bergmann and the Foundation—"

And she would have added her father's name if, out of the corner of her eye, she had not seen the library door open. For a breath-held instant she watched him poised in the doorway. And then he came toward them, his smile brashly bold.

Astoundingly, Cash's hand was the quickest, reaching out as he said, "How are you, sir?"

"Fine—sure, you bet—just fine!" her father said, pumping Cash's hand, then offering him the telegram that she had seen on his desk. "I was hoping I'd catch you before you got away—want your opinion on this. Been talking it over with Miriam and it sounds pretty good to us—interesting trip, South America. Bunch of top men like that, we'd really have a chance to make a contribution. The only thing is— well, I don't want to stick out my neck unless I'm sure it's all right."

Lory felt herself trapped as her father turned to her unexpectedly, saying quickly, "Haven't had a chance to tell you about this, Lory—

they've asked me to serve on a big economic mission that's going down to South America."

"That's wonderful," she said, the vague consciousness of deceit banished by the radiant glow on her mother's face, then sharply revived as she looked away and saw Cash's troubled expression.

Her father had seen it, too. "Anything wrong?" he asked anxiously.

"I want to tell you something about this," Cash said slowly. "It might make a difference. It just happens that I know the man who's heading up this mission. I was the one who suggested your name. I want you to know that."

"You did?" Grant Austen exclaimed. "Well, that *does* make a difference. Sets it right up as far as I'm concerned. If it's something you're tied up with, Cash, I know it's all right. Just puts me that much more in your debt—yes sir, you bet—for everything, I mean."

Cash handed the telegram back and they were shaking hands again, her father saying, "Sure wish you two could come out to the Country Club with us—Friday night buffet, you know—but I guess you've got other plans?"

"I'm afraid we do," Cash said. "But there'll be another time."

"Sure, you bet," Grant Austen said, his set smile broken for one fleeting instant as he was about to turn away. "I've been wanting to say something about—well, the men at the plant—but I know you'll take care of them."

Lory saw that her mother's hand had reached out, as if to tell him that it was unnecessary to wait for a reply. And then they went up the staircase, still hand in hand, and Lory was aware that there was no matching memory anywhere in her mind.

Tears were flooding her eyes but the impulse to hide them was overridden by the need to look up into Cash's face and attempt to express her gratitude.

He denied her the opportunity, his eyes still on the staircase, solemnly preoccupied with a thought unshared until he said, "Is that what it's been—worrying about what was going to happen to his men at the plant?"

She nodded, choked with the wonder of Cash's quick perception, finally managing to say, "It makes him seem such a different person."

"Yes, it does, doesn't it?" Cash said in a throaty whisper, and there was a long pause before he went on. "Maybe he's right, Lory. I've been so sure that it was enough to be absolutely honest and fair with every man I dealt with—but maybe they aren't the ones that really count in the end. Maybe it's the others—the ones I never see, the ones that never see me. That's what you were trying to tell me a few minutes ago, wasn't it?"

442

"All I was trying to say was—oh, Cash, I want you to be happy—and do the things that make you happy. But you can't be happy if you feel there's no point in it—that you can't win."

"I know," he acknowledged. "I've been trying to believe that winning wasn't important—that it was all a game—not just the pursuit of money—"

"And it hasn't been. It isn't!"

"But it hasn't been the pursuit of anything else either—and that has been the trouble. I know it now. There's always been something missing. I guess I've been so wrapped up in playing the game that I never took time enough to figure out where the goal line was—what it meant to win—or even *how* you won."

"Or who it is who really wins," she added, her hands climbing his arms. "Even if it doesn't mean much to you—oh, Cash, it means so much to so many other people. When you win, they win. And sometimes even when you don't. Do you remember yesterday when we were going to Aurora—that enormous factory we passed on the way to the airport? You said that your grandfather had gambled a fortune to start it—and lost every cent of it."

"He did."

"But is that what you were thinking? Oh, Cash, it isn't! I saw what you were watching—all those men coming out of that factory gate. And I saw your eyes when you looked back. You weren't thinking about the money your grandfather had lost. You weren't even thinking that he *had* lost. You were thinking that he had *won*."

His puzzled frown faded into an equally puzzled smile. "How did you know what I was thinking?"

She saw his face through a blur of new tears. "Do you suppose it could be because I'm so much in love with you? They say it happens that way—when you really are."

"Then I should have known sooner," he whispered, the words a hurried filling of the moment before their lips met.

There was a timeless lapse, blanked to wordlessness, and then a voice that sounded strangely like Helen Atherson's saying, "There's really no point in waiting until June."

He held her away from him, looking down at her with a plainly shocked expression . . . Cash of all people, worrying because it wasn't going to be a nice conventional June wedding!

"But that *is* what you were thinking!" she defended herself. "Maybe I should have waited for you to say it but—"

"What about Italy?" he asked unexpectedly. "You're leaving next week, aren't you?"

Leaving . . . Italy . . . what was he talking about? Oh . . . yes, she had

443

had a vague idea that she might go to Italy ... sometime. But she'd forgotten all about that ages and ages ago. Cash should know that. Why didn't he?

He did!

A smile had broken on his face. "Hurry," he demanded. "Don't you remember the ogre who chops off the heads of bad little girls who are late to dinner?"

"But I'm not a little girl any more," she protested, laughing as she ran to the door ahead of him, opening it and then turning back, catching Cash's soberly concerned upward glance as he passed the foot of the staircase.

There was no need to ask what he was thinking. She knew. When you were really in love you always knew.